DEAN KOONTZ OMNIBUS

Also by Dean Koontz

Mr Murder
Dragon Tears
Cold Fire
The Bad Place
Midnight
Lightning
Watchers
Shadowfires
The Servants of Twilight
The Door to December
The Eyes of Darkness
The Key to Midnight
The House of Thunder
The Face of Fear
The Funhouse
The Mask
Phantoms
Shattered
Chase
Twilight Eyes
The Voice of the Night
Strangers
Whispers
Darkness Comes
Night Chills

DEAN KOONTZ OMNIBUS

Comprising

Hideaway
The Vision

Dean Koontz

HEADLINE

First published in this omnibus edition in 1994
by HEADLINE BOOK PUBLISHING

This omnibus was originally published in two separate volumes. *Hideaway* was published in hardcover in 1992 and in paperback in 1992 by
HEADLINE BOOK PUBLISHING PLC; *The Vision* was published
in paperback in 1980 by Corgi, reissued in 1986 by Star and reissued in
1990 by HEADLINE BOOK PUBLISHING PLC (also in hardcover).

10 9 8 7 6 5 4 3 2 1

British Library Cataloguing in Publication Data

Koontz, Dean R.
Dean Koontz Omnibus.
I. Title
813.54 [F]

ISBN 0-7472-1031-4

Phototypeset by Intype, London

Printed and bound in Great Britain by
Mackays of Chatham PLC, Chatham, Kent.

HEADLINE BOOK PUBLISHING
A division of Hodder Headline PLC
338 Euston Rd, London NW1 3BH

CONTENTS

Hideaway

To Gerda.
Forever.

O, what may man within him hide
Though angel on the outward side!

– William Shakespeare

Part One

JUST SECONDS FROM A CLEAN GETAWAY

Life is a gift that must be given back,
and joy should arise from its possession.
It's too damned short, and that's a fact.
Hard to accept, this earthly procession
to final darkness is a journey done,
circle completed, work of art sublime,
a sweet melodic rhyme, a battle won.

– The Book of Counted Sorrows

ONE

·1·

An entire world hummed and bustled beyond the dark ramparts of the mountains, yet to Lindsey Harrison the night seemed empty, as hollow as the vacant chambers of a cold, dead heart. Shivering, she slumped deeper in the passenger seat of the Honda.

Serried ranks of ancient evergreens receded up the slopes that flanked the highway, parting occasionally to accommodate sparse stands of winter-stripped maples and birches that poked at the sky with jagged black branches. However, that vast forest and the formidable rock formations to which it clung did not reduce the emptiness of the bitter March night. As the Honda descended the winding blacktop, the trees and stony out-croppings seemed to float past as if they were only dream images without real substance.

Harried by fierce wind, fine dry snow slanted through the head-light beams. But the storm could not fill the void, either.

The emptiness that Lindsey perceived was internal, not external. The night was brimming, as ever, with the chaos of creation. Her own soul was the only hollow thing.

She glanced at Hatch. He was leaning forward, hunched slightly over the steering wheel, peering ahead with an expression which might be flat and inscrutable to anyone else but which, after twelve years of marriage, Lindsey could easily read. An excellent driver, Hatch was not daunted by poor road conditions. His thoughts, like hers, were no doubt on the long weekend they had just spent at Big Bear Lake.

Yet again they had tried to recapture the easiness with each other that they had once known. And again they had failed.

The chains of the past still bound them.

7

The death of a five-year-old son had incalculable emotional weight. It pressed on the mind, quickly deflating every moment of buoyancy, crushing each new blossom of joy. Jimmy had been dead for more than four and a half years, nearly as long as he had lived, yet his death weighed as heavily on them now as on the day they had lost him, like some colossal moon looming in a low orbit overhead.

Squinting through the smeared windshield, past snow-caked wiper blades that stuttered across the glass, Hatch sighed softly. He glanced at Lindsey and smiled. It was a pale smile, just a ghost of the real thing, barren of amusement, tired and melancholy. He seemed about to say something, changed his mind, and returned his attention to the highway.

The three lanes of blacktop – one descending, two ascending – were disappearing under a shifting shroud of snow. The road slipped to the bottom of the slope and entered a short straightaway leading into a wide, blind curve. In spite of that flat stretch of pavement, they were not out of the San Bernardino Mountains yet. The state route eventually would turn steeply downward once more.

As they followed the curve, the land changed around them: the slope to their right angled upward more sharply than before, while on the far side of the road, a black ravine yawned. White metal guardrails marked that precipice, but they were barely visible in the sheeting snow.

A second or two before they came out of the curve, Lindsey had a premonition of danger. She said, 'Hatch . . . '

Perhaps Hatch sensed trouble, too, for even as Lindsey spoke, he gently applied the brakes, cutting their speed slightly.

A downgrade straightaway lay beyond the bend, and a beer distributor's large truck was halted at an angle across two lanes, just fifty or sixty feet in front of them.

Lindsey tried to say, *Oh God*, but her voice was locked within her.

While making a delivery to one of the area ski resorts, the trucker evidently had been surprised by the blizzard, which had set in only a short while ago but half a day ahead of the forecasters' predictions. Without benefit of snow chains, the big truck tires churned ineffectively on the icy pavement as the driver struggled desperately to bring his rig around and get it moving again.

8

Cursing under his breath but otherwise as controlled as ever, Hatch eased his foot down on the brake pedal. He dared not jam it to the floor and risk sending the Honda into a deadly spin.

In response to the glare of the car headlights, the trucker looked through his side window. Across the rapidly closing gap of night and snow, Lindsey saw nothing of the man's face but a pallid oval and twin charry holes where the eyes should have been, a ghostly countenance, as if some malign spirit was at the wheel of that vehicle. Or Death himself.

Hatch was heading for the outermost of the two ascending lanes, the only part of the highway not blocked.

Lindsey wondered if other traffic was coming uphill, hidden from them by the truck. Even at reduced speed, if they collided head-on, they would not survive.

In spite of Hatch's best efforts, the Honda began to slide. The tail end came around to the left, and Lindsey found herself swinging away from the stranded truck. The smooth, greasy, out-of-control motion was like the transition between scenes in a bad dream. Her stomach twisted with nausea, and although she was restrained by a safety harness, she instinctively pressed her right hand against the door and her left against the dashboard, bracing herself.

'Hang on,' Hatch said, turning the wheel where the car wanted to go, which was his only hope of regaining control.

But the slide became a sickening spin, and the Honda rotated three hundred and sixty degrees, as if it were a carousel without calliope: around . . . around . . . until the truck began to come into view again. For an instant, as they glided downhill, still turning, Lindsey was certain the car would slip safely past the other vehicle. She could see beyond the big rig now, and the road below was free of traffic.

Then the front bumper on Hatch's side caught the back of the truck. Tortured metal shrieked.

The Honda shuddered and seemed to *explode* away from the point of collision, slamming backward into the guardrail. Lindsey's teeth clacked together hard enough to ignite sparks of pain in her jaws, all the way into her temples, and the hand braced against the dashboard bent painfully at the wrist. Simultaneously, the strap of the shoulder harness, which stretched diagonally across her chest from right shoulder to left hip, abruptly cinched so tight that her breath burst from her.

The car rebounded from the guardrail, not with sufficient momentum to reconnect with the truck but with so much torque that it pivoted three hundred and sixty degrees again. As they spun-glided past the truck, Hatch fought for control, but the steering wheel jerked erratically back and forth, tearing through his hands so violently that he cried out as his palms were abraded.

Suddenly the moderate gradient appeared precipitously steep, like the water-greased spillway of an amusement-park flume ride. Lindsey would have screamed if she could have drawn breath. But although the safety strap had loosened, a diagonal line of pain still cut across her chest, making it impossible to inhale. Then she was rattled by a vision of the Honda skating in a long glissade to the next bend in the road, crashing through the guardrail, tumbling out into the void – and the image was so horrifying that it was like a blow, knocking breath back *into* her.

As the Honda came out of the second rotation, the entire driver's side slammed into the guardrail, and they slid thirty or forty feet without losing contact. To the accompaniment of a grinding-screeching-scraping of metal against metal, showers of yellow sparks plumed up, mingling with the falling snow, like swarms of summer fireflies that had flown through a time warp into the wrong season.

The car shuddered to a halt, canted up slightly at the front left corner, evidently hooked on a guard post. For an instant the resultant silence was so deep that Lindsey was half stunned by it; she shattered it with an explosive exhalation.

She had never before experienced such an overwhelming sense of relief.

Then the car moved again.

It began to tilt to the left. The guardrail was giving way, perhaps weakened by corrosion or by the erosion of the highway shoulder beneath it.

'Out!' Hatch shouted, frantically fumbling with the release on his safety harness.

Lindsey didn't even have time to pop loose of her own harness or grab the door handle before the railing cracked apart and the Honda slipped into the ravine. Even as it was happening, she couldn't believe it. The brain acknowledged the approach of death, while the heart stubbornly insisted on immortality. In almost five years she had not adjusted to Jimmy's death, so she was not easily going to accept the imminence of her own demise.

In a jangle of detached posts and railings, the Honda slid sideways along the ice-crusted slope, then flipped over as the embankment grew steeper. Gasping for breath, heart pounding, wrenched painfully from side to side in her harness, Lindsey hoped for a tree, a rock outcropping, anything that would halt their fall, but the embankment seemed clear. She was not sure how often the car rolled – maybe only twice – because up and down and left and right lost all meaning. Her head banged into the ceiling almost hard enough to knock her out. She didn't know if she'd been thrown upward or if the roof had caved in to meet her, so she tried to slump in her seat, afraid the roof might crumple further on the next roll and crush her skull. The headlights slashed at the night, and from the wounds spouted torrents of snow. Then the windshield burst, showering her with minutely fragmented safety glass, and abruptly she was plunged into total darkness. Apparently the headlights blinked off, and the dashboard lights, reflected in Hatch's sweat-slicked face. The car rolled onto its roof again and stayed there. In that inverted posture it sledded farther into the seemingly bottomless ravine, with the thunderous noise of a thousand tons of coal pouring down a steel chute.

The gloom was utterly tenebrous, seamless, as if she and Hatch were not outdoors but in some windowless funhouse, rocketing down a roller-coaster track. Even the snow, which usually had a natural phosphorescence, was suddenly invisible. Cold flakes stung her face as the freezing wind drove them through the empty windshield frame, but she could not see them even as they frosted her lashes. Struggling to quell a rising panic, she wondered if she had been blinded by the imploding glass.

Blindness.

That was her special fear. She was an artist. Her talent took inspiration from what her eyes observed, and her wonderfully dexterous hands rendered inspiration into art with the critical judgment of those eyes to guide them. What did a blind painter paint? What could she hope to create if suddenly deprived of the sense that she relied upon the most?

Just as she started to scream, the car hit bottom and rolled back onto its wheels, landing upright with less impact than she had anticipated. It came to a halt almost gently, as if on an immense pillow.

'Hatch?' Her voice was hoarse.

11

After the cacophonous roar of their plunge down the ravine wall, she felt half deaf, not sure if the preternatural silence around her was real or only perceived.

'Hatch?'

She looked to her left, where he ought to have been, but she could not see him – or anything else.

She *was* blind.

'Oh, God, no. Please.'

She was dizzy, too. The car seemed to be turning, wallowing like an airborne kite dipping and rising in the thermal currents of a summer sky.

'Hatch!'

No response.

Her lightheadedness increased. The car rocked and wallowed worse than ever. Lindsey was afraid she would faint. If Hatch was injured, he might bleed to death while she was unconscious and unable to help him.

She reached out blindly and found him crumpled in the driver's seat. His head was bent toward her, resting against his own shoulder. She touched his face, and he did not move. Something warm and sticky covered his right cheek and temple. Blood. From a head injury. With trembling fingers, she touched his mouth and sobbed with relief when she felt the hot exhalation of his breath between his slightly parted lips.

He was unconscious, not dead.

Fumbling in frustration with the release mechanism on her safety harness, Lindsey heard new sounds that she could not identify. A soft slapping. Hungry licking. An eerie, liquid chuckling. For a moment she froze, straining to identify the source of those unnerving noises.

Without warning the Honda tipped forward, admitting a cascade of icy water through the broken windshield onto Lindsey's lap. She gasped in surprise as the arctic bath chilled her to the marrow, and realized she was not lightheaded after all. The car *was* moving. It was afloat. They had landed in a lake or river. Probably a river. The placid surface of a lake would not have been so active.

The shock of the cold water briefly paralyzed her and made her wince with pain, but when she opened her eyes, she could see again. The Honda's headlights were, indeed, extinguished, but the dials and gauges in the dashboard still glowed. She must have been suffering from hysterical blindness rather than genuine physical damage.

She couldn't see much, but there was not much to see at the bottom of the night-draped ravine. Splinters of dimly glimmering glass rimmed the broken-out windshield. Outside, the oily water was revealed only by a sinuous, silvery phosphorescence that high-lighted its purling surface and imparted a dark obsidian sparkle to the jewels of ice that floated in tangled necklaces atop it. The riverbanks would have been lost in absolute blackness but for the ghostly raiments of snow that cloaked the otherwise naked rocks, earth, and brush. The Honda appeared to be motoring through the river: water poured halfway up its hood before parting in a 'V' and streaming away to either side as it might from the prow of a ship, lapping at the sills of the side windows. They were being swept downstream, where eventually the currents were certain to turn more turbulent, bringing them to rapids or rocks or worse. At a glance, Lindsey grasped the extremity of their situation, but she was still so relieved by the remission of her blindness that she was grateful for the sight of anything, even of trouble this serious.

Shivering, she freed herself from the entangling straps of the safety harness, and touched Hatch again. His face was ghastly in the queer backsplash of the instrument lights: sunken eyes, waxen skin, colorless lips, blood oozing – but, thank God, not spurting – from the gash on the right side of his head. She shook him gently, then a little harder, calling his name.

They wouldn't be able to get out of the car easily, if at all, while it was being borne down the river – especially as it now began to move faster. But at least they had to be prepared to scramble out if it came up against a rock or caught for a moment against one of the banks. The opportunity to escape might be short-lived.

Hatch could not be awakened.

Without warning the car dipped sharply forward. Again icy water gushed in through the shattered windshield, so cold that it had some of the effect of an electrical shock, halting Lindsey's heart for a beat or two and locking the breath in her lungs.

The front of the car did not rise in the currents, as it had done previously. It was settling deeper than before, so there was less river under it to provide lift. The water continued to pour in, quickly rising past Lindsey's ankles to mid-calf. They were sinking.

'Hatch!' She was shouting now, shaking him hard, heedless of his injuries.

The river gushed inside, rising to seat level, churning up foam that refracted the amber light from the instrument panel and looked like garlands of golden Christmas tinsel.

Lindsey pulled her feet out of the water, knelt on her seat, and splashed Hatch's face, desperately hoping to bring him around. But he was sunk in deeper levels of unconsciousness than mere concussive sleep, perhaps in a coma as plumbless as a mid-ocean trench.

Swirling water rose to the bottom of the steering wheel.

Frantically Lindsey ripped at Hatch's safety harness, trying to strip it away from him, only half aware of the hot flashes of pain when she tore a couple of fingernails.

'Hatch, damn it!'

The water was halfway up the steering wheel, and the Honda all but ceased its forward movement. It was too heavy now to be budged by the persistent pressure of the river behind it.

Hatch was five feet ten, a hundred and sixty pounds, only average in size, but he might as well have been a giant. As dead weight, resistant to her every effort, he was virtually immovable. Tugging, shoving, wrenching, clawing, Lindsey struggled to free him, and by the time she finally managed to disentangle him from the straps, the water had risen over the top of the dashboard, more than halfway up her chest. It was even higher on Hatch, just under his chin, because he was slumped in his seat.

The river was unbelievably icy, and Lindsey felt the warmth pumping out of her body as if it were blood gushing from a severed artery. As body heat bled from her, the cold bled in, and her muscles began to ache.

Nevertheless, she welcomed the rising flood because it would make Hatch buoyant and therefore easier to maneuver out from under the wheel and through the shattered windshield. That was her theory, anyway, but when she tugged on him, he seemed heavier than ever, and now the water was at his lips.

'Come on, come on,' she said furiously, 'you're gonna drown, damn it!'

14

Finally pulling his beer truck off the road, Bill Cooper broadcast a Mayday on his CB radio. Another trucker responded and, equipped with a cellular telephone as well as a CB, promised to call the authorities in nearby Big Bear.

Bill hung up the citizen's-band handset, took a long-handled six-battery flashlight from under the driver's seat, and stepped out into the storm. The frigid wind cut through even his fleece-lined denim jacket, but the bitterness of the winter night was not half as icy as his stomach, which had turned sour and cold as he had watched the Honda spin its luckless occupants down the highway and over the brink of the chasm.

He hurried across the slippery pavement and along the shoulder to the missing section of guardrail. He hoped to see the Honda close below, caught up against the trunk of a tree. But there were no trees on that slope – just a smooth mantle of snow from previous storms, scarred by the passage of the car, disappearing beyond the reach of his flashlight beam.

An almost disabling pang of guilt stabbed through him. He'd been drinking again. Not much. A few shots out of the flask he carried. He had been certain he was sober when he'd started up the mountain. Now he wasn't so sure. He felt . . . fuzzy. And suddenly it seemed stupid to have tried to make a delivery with the weather turning ugly so fast.

Below him, the abyss appeared supernaturally bottomless, and the apparent extreme depth engendered in Bill the feeling that he was gazing into the damnation to which he'd be delivered when his own life ended. He was paralyzed by that sense of futility that sometimes overcomes even the best of men – though usually when they are alone in a bedroom, staring at the meaningless patterns of shadows on the ceiling at three o'clock in the morning.

Then the curtains of snow parted for a moment, and he saw the floor of the ravine about a hundred or a hundred and fifty feet below, not as deep as he had feared. He stepped through the gap in the guardrail, intending to crab down the treacherous hillside and assist the survivors if there were any. Instead he hesitated on the narrow shelf of flat earth at the brink of the slope, because he was whiskey-dizzy but also because he could not see where the car had come to rest.

A serpentine black band, like satin ribbon, curved through the snow down there, intersecting the tracks the car had made. Bill blinked at it uncomprehendingly, as if staring at an abstract painting, until he remembered that a river lay below.

The car had gone into that ebony ribbon of water.

Following a winter of freakishly heavy snow, the weather had turned warmer a couple of weeks ago, triggering a premature spring melt. The runoff continued, for winter had returned too recently to have locked the river in ice again. The temperature of the water would be only a few degrees above freezing. Any occupant of the car, having survived both the wreck and death by drowning, would perish swiftly from exposure.

If I'd been sober, he thought, I would've turned back in this weather. I'm a pathetic joke, a tanked-up beer deliveryman who didn't even have enough loyalty to get plastered on beer. Christ.

A joke, but people were dying because of him. He tasted vomit in the back of his throat, choked it down.

Frantically he surveyed the murky ravine until he spotted an eerie radiance, like an otherworldly presence, drifting spectrally with the river to the right of him. Soft amber, it faded in and out through the falling snow. He figured it must be the interior lights of the Honda, which was being borne downriver.

Hunched for protection against the biting wind, holding on to the guardrail in case he slipped and fell over the edge, Bill scuttled along the top of the slope, in the same direction as the waterswept car below, trying to keep it in sight. The Honda drifted swiftly at first, then slower, slower. Finally it came to a complete halt, perhaps stopped by rocks in the watercourse or by a projection of the riverbank.

The light was slowly fading, as if the car's battery was running out of juice.

·3·

Though Hatch was freed from the safety harness, Lindsey could not budge him, maybe because his clothes were caught on something she could not see, maybe because his foot was wedged under the brake pedal or bent back and trapped under his own seat.

The water rose over Hatch's nose. Lindsey could not hold his

16

head any higher. He was breathing the river now.

She let go of him because she hoped that the loss of his air supply would finally bring him around, coughing and spluttering and splashing up from his seat, but also because she did not have the energy to continue struggling with him. The intense cold of the water sapped her strength. With frightening rapidity, her extremities were growing numb. Her exhaled breath seemed just as cold as every inhalation, as if her body had no heat left to impart to the used air.

The car had stopped moving. It was resting on the bottom of the river, completely filled and weighed down with water, except for a bubble of air under the shallow dome of the roof. Into that space she pressed her face, gasping for breath.

She was making horrid little sounds of terror, like the bleats of an animal. She tried to silence herself but could not.

The queer, water-filtered light from the instrument panel began to fade from amber to muddy yellow.

A dark part of her wanted to give up, let go of this world, and move on to someplace better. It had a small quiet voice of its own: *Don't fight, there's nothing left to live for anyway, Jimmy has been dead for so long, so very long, now Hatch is dead or dying, just let go, surrender, maybe you'll wake up in Heaven with them . . .* The voice possessed a lulling, hypnotic appeal.

The remaining air could last only a few minutes, if that long, and she would die in the car if she did not escape immediately.

Hatch is dead, lungs full of water, only waiting to be fish food, so let go, surrender, what's the point, Hatch is dead . . .

She gulped air that was swiftly acquiring a tart, metallic taste. She was able to draw only small breaths, as if her lungs had shriveled.

If any body heat was left in her, she was not aware of it. In reaction to the cold, her stomach knotted with nausea, and even the vomit that kept rising into her throat was icy; each time she choked it down, she felt as if she had swallowed a vile slush of dirty snow.

Hatch is dead, Hatch is dead . . .

'No,' she said in a harsh, angry whisper. 'No. No.'

Denial raged through her with the fury of a storm: Hatch could not be dead. Unthinkable. Not Hatch, who never forgot a birthday or an anniversary, who bought her flowers for no reason at all,

17

who never lost his temper and rarely raised his voice. Not Hatch, who always had time to listen to the troubles of others and sympathize with them, who never failed to have an open wallet for a friend in need, whose greatest fault was that he was too damn much of a soft touch. He could not be, must not be, *would* not be dead. He ran five miles a day, ate a low-fat diet with plenty of fruits and vegetables, avoided caffeine *and* decaffeinated beverages. Didn't that count for something, damn it? He lathered on sunscreen in the summer, did not smoke, never drank more than two beers or two glasses of wine in a single evening, and was too easy-going ever to develop heart disease due to stress. Didn't self-denial and self-control count for anything? Was creation so screwed up that there was no justice any more? Okay, all right, they said the good died young, which sure had been true of Jimmy, and Hatch was not yet forty, young by any standard, okay, agreed, but they also said that virtue was its own reward, and there was plenty of virtue here, damn it, a whole shitload of virtue, which ought to count for something, unless God wasn't listening, unless He didn't care, unless the world was an even crueler place than she had believed.

She refused to accept it.

Hatch. Was. Not. Dead.

She drew as deep a breath as she could manage. Just as the last of the light faded, plunging her into blindness again, she sank into the water, pushed across the dashboard, and went through the missing windshield onto the hood of the car.

Now she was not merely blind but deprived of virtually all five senses. She could hear nothing but the wild thumping of her own heart, for the water effectively muffled sound. She could smell and speak only at the penalty of death by drowning. The anesthetizing effect of the glacial river left her with a fraction of her sense of touch, so she felt as if she were a disembodied spirit suspended in whatever medium composed Purgatory, awaiting final judgment.

Assuming that the river was not much deeper than the car and that she would not need to hold her breath long before she reached the surface, she made another attempt to free Hatch. Lying on the hood of the car, holding fast to the edge of the windshield frame with one numb hand, straining against her body's natural buoyancy, she reached back inside, groped in the blackness until she located the steering wheel and then her husband.

18

Heat rose in her again, at last, but it was not a sustaining warmth. Her lungs were beginning to burn with the need for air.

Gripping a fistful of Hatch's jacket, she pulled with all her might – and to her surprise he floated out of his seat, no longer immovable, suddenly buoyant and unfettered. He caught on the steering wheel, but only briefly, then bobbled out through the windshield as Lindsey slid backward across the hood to make way for him.

A hot, pulsing pain filled her chest. The urge to breathe grew overpowering, but she resisted it.

When Hatch was out of the car, Lindsey embraced him and kicked for the surface. He was surely drowned, and she was clinging to a corpse, but she was not repulsed by that macabre thought. If she could get him ashore, she would be able to administer artificial respiration. Although the chance of reviving him was slim, at least some hope remained. He was not truly dead, not really a corpse, until all hope had been exhausted.

She burst through the surface into a howling wind that made the marrow-freezing water seem almost warm by comparison. When that air hit her burning lungs, her heart stuttered, her chest clenched with pain, and the second breath was harder to draw than the first.

Treading water, holding tight to Hatch, Lindsey swallowed mouthfuls of the river as it splashed her face. Cursing, she spat it out. Nature seemed alive, like a great hostile beast, and she found herself irrationally angry with the river and the storm, as if they were conscious entities willfully aligned against her.

She tried to orient herself, but it was not easy in the darkness and shrieking wind, without solid ground beneath her. When she saw the riverbank, vaguely luminous in its coat of snow, she attempted a one-arm sidestroke toward it with Hatch in tow, but the current was too strong to be resisted, even if she'd been able to swim with both arms. She and Hatch were swept downstream, repeatedly dragged beneath the surface by an undertow, repeatedly thrust back into the wintry air, battered by fragments of tree branches and chunks of ice that were also caught up in the current, moving helplessly and inexorably toward whatever sudden fall or deadly phalanx of rapids marked the river's descent from the mountains.

He had started drinking when Myra left him. He never could handle being womanless. Yeah, and wouldn't God Almighty treat that excuse with contempt when it came time for judgment?

Still holding the guardrail, Bill Cooper crouched indecisively on the brink of the slope and stared intently down at the river. Beyond the screen of falling snow, the lights of the Honda had gone out.

He didn't dare take his eyes off the obscured scene below to check the highway for the ambulance. He was afraid that when he looked back into the ravine again, he would misremember the exact spot where the light had disappeared and would send the rescuers to the wrong point along the riverbank. The dim black-and-white world below offered few prominent landmarks.

'Come on, hurry up,' he muttered.

The wind – which stung his face, made his eyes water, and pasted snow in his mustache – was keening so loudly that it masked the approaching sirens of the emergency vehicles until they rounded the bend uphill, enlivening the night with their headlights and red flashers. Bill rose, waving his arms to draw their attention, but he still did not look away from the river.

Behind him, they pulled to the side of the road. Because one of their sirens wound down to silence faster than the other, he knew there were two vehicles, probably an ambulance and a police cruiser.

They would smell the whiskey on his breath. No, maybe not in all that wind and cold. He felt that he deserved to die for what he'd done – but if he wasn't going to die, then he didn't think he deserved to lose his job. These were hard times. A recession. Good jobs weren't easy to find.

Reflections of the revolving emergency beacons lent a strobo-scopic quality to the night. Real life had become a choppy and technically inept piece of stop-motion animation, with the scarlet snow like a spray of blood falling haltingly from the wounded sky.

Sooner than Lindsey could have hoped, the surging river shoved her and Hatch against a formation of water-smoothed rocks that rose like a series of worn teeth in the middle of its course, wedging them into a gap sufficiently narrow to prevent them from being swept farther downstream. Water foamed and gurgled around them, but with the rocks behind her, she was able to stop struggling against the deadly undertow.

She felt limp, every muscle soft and unresponsive. She could barely manage to keep Hatch's head from tipping forward into the water, though doing so should have been a simple task now that she no longer needed to fight the river.

Though she was incapable of letting go of him, keeping his head above water was a pointless task: he had drowned. She could not kid herself that he was still alive. And, minute by minute, he was less likely to be revived with artificial respiration. But she would not give up. Would not. She was astonished by her fierce refusal to relinquish hope, though just before the accident she had thought she was devoid of hope forever.

The chill of the water had thoroughly penetrated Lindsey, numbing mind as well as flesh. When she tried to concentrate on forming a plan that would get her from the middle of the river to the shore, she could not bring her thoughts into focus. She felt drugged. She knew that drowsiness was a symptom of hypothermia, that dozing off would invite deeper unconsciousness and ultimately death. She was determined to keep awake and alert at all costs – but suddenly she realized that she had closed her eyes, giving in to the temptation of sleep.

Fear twisted through her. Renewed strength coiled in her muscles.

Blinking feverishly, eyelashes frosted with snow that no longer melted from her body heat, she peered around Hatch and along the line of water-polished boulders. The safety of the bank was only fifteen feet away. If the rocks were close to one another, she might be able to tow Hatch to shore without being sucked through a gap and carried downriver.

Her vision had adapted sufficiently to the gloom, however, for her to see that centuries of patient currents had carved a five-foot-wide hole in the middle of the granite span against which she was wedged. It was halfway between her and the river's edge. Dimly glistening under a lacework shawl of ice, the ebony water quickened as it was funneled toward the gap; no doubt it exploded out the other side with tremendous force.

Lindsey knew she was too weak to propel herself across that powerful affluxion. She and Hatch would be swept through the breach and, at last, to certain death.

Just when surrender to an endless sleep began, again, to look more appealing than continued pointless struggle against nature's hostile power, she saw strange lights at the top of the ravine, a couple of hundred yards upriver. She was so disoriented and her mind so anesthetized by the cold that for a while the pulsing crimson glow seemed eerie, mysterious, supernatural, as if she were staring upward at the wondrous radiance of a hovering, divine presence.

Gradually she realized that she was seeing the throb of police or ambulance beacons on the highway far above, and then she spotted the flashlight beams nearer at hand, like silver swords slashing the darkness. Rescuers had descended the ravine wall. They were maybe a hundred yards upriver, where the car had sunk.

She called to them. Her shout issued as a whisper. She tried again, with greater success, but they must not have heard her above the keening wind, for the flashlights continued to sweep back and forth over the same section of riverbank and turbulent water.

Suddenly she realized that Hatch was slipping out of her grasp again. His face was underwater.

With the abruptness of a switch being thrown, Lindsey's terror became anger again. She was angry with the truck driver for being caught in the mountains during a snowstorm, angry with herself for being so weak, angry with Hatch for reasons she could not define, angry with the cold and insistent river, and *enraged* at God for the violence and injustice of His universe.

Lindsey found greater strength in anger than in terror. She flexed her half-frozen hands, got a better grip on Hatch, pulled his head out of the water again, and let out a cry for help that was louder than the banshee voice of the wind. Upstream, the flashlight beams, as one, swung searchingly in her direction.

The stranded couple looked dead already. Targeted by the flash-lights, their faces floated on the dark water, as white as apparitions – translucent, unreal, lost.

Lee Reedman, a San Bernardino County Deputy Sheriff with emergency rescue training, waded into the water to haul them ashore, bracing himself against a rampart of boulders that extended out to midstream. He was on a half-inch, hawser-laid nylon line with a breaking strength of four thousand pounds, secured to the trunk of a sturdy pine and belayed by two other deputies.

He had taken off his parka but not his uniform or boots. In those fierce currents, swimming was impossible anyway, so he did not have to worry about being hampered by clothes. And even sodden garments would protect him from the worst bite of the frigid water, reducing the rate at which body heat was sucked out of him.

Within a minute of entering the river, however, when he was only halfway toward the stranded couple, Lee felt as if a refriger-ant had been injected into his bloodstream. He couldn't believe that he would have been any colder had he dived naked into those icy currents.

He would have preferred to wait for the Winter Rescue Team that was on its way, men who had experience pulling skiers out of avalanches and retrieving careless skaters who had fallen through thin ice. They would have insulated wetsuits and all the necessary gear. But the situation was too desperate to delay; the people in the river would not last until the specialists arrived.

He came to a five-foot-wide gap in the rocks, where the river gushed through as if being drawn forward by a huge suction pump. He was knocked off his feet, but the men on the bank kept the line taut, paying it out precisely at the rate he was moving, so he was not swept into the breach. He flailed forward through the surging river, swallowing a mouthful of water so bitterly cold that it made his teeth ache, but he got a grip on the rock at the far side of the gap and pulled himself across.

A minute later, gasping for breath and shivering violently, Lee reached the couple. The man was unconscious, but the woman was alert. Their faces bobbed in and out of the overlapping flashlight beams directed from shore, and they both looked in terrible shape. The woman's flesh seemed both to have shriveled and blanched of all color, so the natural phosphorescence of bone shone like a light within, revealing the skull beneath her skin. Her lips were as white as her teeth; other than her sodden black hair, only her eyes were dark, as sunken as the eyes of a corpse and bleak with the pain of dying. Under the circumstances he could not guess her age within fifteen years and could not tell if she was ugly or attractive, but he could see, at once, that she was at the limit of her resources, holding on to life by willpower alone.

'Take my husband first,' she said, pushing the unconscious man into Lee's arms. Her shrill voice cracked repeatedly. 'He's got a head injury, needs help, hurry up, go on, go on, damn you!'

Her anger didn't offend Lee. He knew it was not directed against him, really, and that it gave her the strength to endure.

'Hold on, and we'll all go together.' He raised his voice above the roar of the wind and the racing river. 'Don't fight it, don't try to grab on to the rocks or keep your feet on the bottom. They'll have an easier time reeling us in if we let the water buoy us.'

She seemed to understand.

Lee glanced back toward shore. A light focused on his face, and he shouted, 'Ready! Now!'

The team on the riverbank began to reel him in, with the unconscious man and the exhausted woman in tow.

·7·

After Lindsey was hauled out of the water, she drifted in and out of consciousness. For a while life seemed to be a videotape being fast-forwarded from one randomly chosen scene to another, with gray-white static in between.

As she lay gasping on the ground at the river's edge, a young paramedic with a snow-caked beard knelt at her side and directed a penlight at her eyes, checking her pupils for uneven dilation. He said, 'Can you hear me?'

'Of course. Where's Hatch?'

'Do you know your name?'

'Where's my husband? He needs . . . CPR.'

'We're taking care of him. Now do you know your name?'

24

'Lindsey.'

'Good. Are you cold?'

That seemed like a stupid question, but then she realized she was no longer freezing. In fact, a mildly unpleasant heat had arisen in her extremities. It was not the sharp, painful heat of flames. Instead, she felt as if her feet and hands had been dipped in a caustic fluid that was gradually dissolving her skin and leaving raw nerve ends exposed. She knew, without having to be told, that her inability to feel the bitter night air was an indication of physical deterioration.

Fast forward . . .

She was being moved on a stretcher. They were heading along the riverbank. With her head toward the front of the litter, she could look back at the man who was carrying the rear of it. The snow-covered ground reflected the flashlight beams, but that soft eerie glow was only bright enough to reveal the basic contours of the stranger's face and add a disquieting glimmer to his iron-hard eyes.

As colorless as a charcoal drawing, strangely silent, full of dreamlike motion and mystery, that place and moment had the quality of a nightmare. She felt her heartbeat accelerate as she squinted back and up at the almost faceless man. The illogic of a dream shaped her fear, and suddenly she was certain that she was dead and that the shadowy men carrying her stretcher were not men at all but carrion-bearers delivering her to the boat that would convey her across the Styx to the land of the dead and damned.

Fast forward . . .

Lashed to the stretcher now, tilted almost into a standing position, she was being pulled along the snow-covered slope of the ravine wall by unseen men reeling in a pair of ropes from above. Two other men accompanied her, one on each side of the stretcher, struggling up through the knee-deep drifts, guiding her and making sure she didn't flip over.

She was ascending into the red glow of the emergency beacons. As that crimson radiance completely surrounded her, she began to hear the urgent voices of the rescuers above and the crackle of police-band radios. When she could smell the pungent exhaust fumes of their vehicles, she knew that she was going to survive.

Just seconds from a clean getaway, she thought.

Though in the grip of a delirium born of exhaustion, confused and fuzzy-minded, Lindsey was alert enough to be unnerved by that thought and the subconscious longing it represented. Just seconds from a clean getaway? The only thing she had been seconds away from was death. Was she still so depressed from the loss of Jimmy that, even after five years, her own death was an acceptable release from the burden of her grief?

Then why didn't I surrender to the river? she wondered. Why not just let go?

Hatch, of course. Hatch had needed her. She'd been ready to step out of this world in hope of setting foot into a better one. But she had not been able to make that decision for Hatch, and to surrender her own life under those circumstances would have meant forfeiting his as well.

With a clatter and a jolt, the stretcher was pulled over the brink of the ravine and lowered flat onto the shoulder of the mountain highway beside an ambulance. Red snow swirled into her face.

A paramedic with a weather-beaten face and beautiful blue eyes leaned over her. 'You're going to be all right.'

'I didn't want to die,' she said.

She was not really speaking to the man. She was arguing with herself, trying to deny that her despair over the loss of her son had become such a chronic emotional infection that she had been secretly longing to join him in death. Her self-image did not include the word 'suicidal,' and she was shocked and repulsed to discover, under extreme stress, that such an impulse might be a part of her.

Just seconds from a clean getaway . . .

She said, 'Did I want to die?'

'You aren't going to die,' the paramedic assured her as he and another man untied the ropes from the handles of the litter, preparatory to loading her into the ambulance. 'The worst is over now. The worst is over.'

TWO

·1·

Half a dozen police and emergency vehicles were parked across two lanes of the mountain highway. Uphill and downhill traffic shared the third lane, regulated by uniformed deputies. Lindsey was aware of people gawking at her from a Jeep Wagoneer, but they vanished beyond shatters of snow and heavy plumes of crystallized exhaust fumes.

The ambulance van could accommodate two patients. They loaded Lindsey onto a wheeled gurney that was fixed to the left wall by two spring clamps to prevent it from rolling while the vehicle was in motion. They put Hatch on another identical gurney along the right wall.

Two paramedics crowded into the rear of the ambulance and pulled the wide door shut behind them. As they moved, their white, insulated nylon pants and jackets produced continuous frictional sounds, a series of soft whistles that seemed to be electronically amplified in those close quarters.

With a short burst of its siren, the ambulance started to move. The paramedics swayed easily with the rocking motion. Experience had made them surefooted.

Side by side in the narrow aisle between the gurneys, both men turned to Lindsey. Their names were stitched on the breast pockets of their jackets: David O'Malley and Jerry Epstein. With a curious combination of professional detachment and concerned attentiveness, they began to work on her, exchanging medical information with each other in crisp emotionless voices but speaking to her in soft, sympathetic, encouraging tones.

That dichotomy in their behavior alarmed rather than soothed Lindsey, but she was too weak and disoriented to express her

27

fear. She felt infuriatingly delicate. Shaky. She was reminded of a surrealistic painting titled 'This World and the Next,' which she had done last year, because the central figure in that piece had been a wire-walking circus acrobat plagued by uncertainty. Right now consciousness was a high wire on which she was precariously perched. Any effort to speak to the paramedics, if sustained for more than a word or two, might unbalance her and send her into a long, dark fall.

Although her mind was too clouded to find any sense in most of what the two men were saying, she understood enough to know that she was suffering from hypothermia, possibly frostbite, and that they were worried about her. Blood pressure too low. Heartbeat slow and irregular. Slow and shallow respiration.

Maybe that clean getaway was still possible.

If she really wanted it.

She was ambivalent. If she actually had hungered for death on a subconscious level since Jimmy's funeral, she had no special appetite for it now – though neither did she find it particularly unappealing. Whatever happened to her would happen, and in her current condition, with her emotions as numb as her five senses, she did not much care about her fate. Hypothermia switched off the survival instinct with a narcotizing pall as effective as that produced by an alcoholic binge.

Then, between the two muttering paramedics, she caught a glimpse of Hatch lying on the other gurney, and abruptly she was jolted out of her half-trance by her concern for him. He looked so pale. But not just white. Another, less healthy shade of pale with a lot of gray in it. His face – turned toward her, eyes closed, mouth open slightly – looked as if a flash fire had swept through it, leaving nothing between bone and skin except the ashes of flesh consumed.

'Please,' she said, 'my husband.' She was surprised that her voice was just a low, rough croak.

'You first,' O'Malley said.

'No. Hatch. Hatch . . . needs . . . help.'

'You first,' O'Malley repeated.

His insistence reassured her somewhat. As bad as Hatch looked, he must be all right, must have responded to CPR, must be in better shape than she was, or otherwise they would have tended to him first. Wouldn't they?

28

Her thoughts grew fuzzy again. The sense of urgency that had gripped her now abated. She closed her eyes.

·2·

Later . . .

In Lindsey's hypothermic torpor, the murmuring voices above her seemed as rhythmic, if not as melodic, as a lullaby. But she was kept awake by the increasingly painful stinging sensation in her extremities and by the rough handling of the medics, who were packing small pillowlike objects against her sides. Whatever the things were – electric or chemical heating pads, she supposed – they radiated a soothing warmth far different from the fire burning within her feet and hands.

'Hatch needs warming up, too,' she said thickly.

'He's fine, don't you worry about him,' Epstein said. His breath puffed out in small white clouds as he spoke.

'But he's cold.'

'That's what he needs to be. That's just how we want him.'

O'Malley said, 'But not too cold, Jerry. Nyebern doesn't want a Popsicle. Ice crystals form in the tissue, there'll be brain damage.'

Epstein turned to the small half-open window that separated the rear of the ambulance from the forward compartment. He called loudly to the driver: 'Mike, turn on a little heat maybe.'

Lindsey wondered who Nyebern might be, and she was alarmed by the words 'brain damage.' But she was too weary to concentrate and make sense of what they said.

Her mind drifted to recollections from childhood, but they were so distorted and strange that she must have slipped across the border of consciousness into a half-sleep where her subconscious could work nightmarish tricks on her memories.

. . . *she saw herself, five years of age, at play in a meadow behind her house. The sloped field was familiar in its contours, but some hateful influence had crept into her mind and meddled with the details, wickedly recoloring the grass a spider-belly black. The petals of all the flowers were blacker still, with crimson stamens that glistened like fat drops of blood . . .*

. . . *she saw herself, at seven, on the school playground at twilight, but alone as she had never been in real life. Around her stood the usual*

29

array of swings and seesaws and jungle gyms and slides, casting crisp
shadows in the peculiar orange light of day's end. These machines of joy
seemed curiously ominous now. They loomed malevolently, as if they
might begin to move at any second, with much creaking and clanking,
blue St Elmo's fire glowing on their flanks and limbs, seeking blood for
a lubricant, robotic vampires of aluminum and steel . . .

·3·

Periodically Lindsey heard a strange and distant cry, the mournful
bleat of some great, mysterious beast. Eventually, even in her
semi-delirious condition, she realized that the sound did not orig-
inate either in her imagination or in the distance but directly
overhead. It was no beast, just the ambulance siren which was
needed only in short bursts to clear what little traffic had ventured
onto the snowswept highways.

The ambulance came to a stop sooner than she had expected,
but that might be only because her sense of time was as out of
whack as her other perceptions. Epstein threw the rear door open
while O'Malley released the spring clamps that fixed Lindsey's
gurney in place.

When they lifted her out of the van, she was surprised to see
that she was not at a hospital in San Bernardino, as she expected
to be, but in a parking lot in front of a small shopping center. At
that late hour the lot was deserted except for the ambulance
and, astonishingly, a large helicopter on the side of which was
emblazoned a red cross in a white circle and the words 'Air Ambulance Service.'

The night was still cold, and wind hooted across the blacktop.
They were now below the snow line, although just at the base of
the mountains and still far from San Bernardino. The ground was
bare, and the wheels of the gurney creaked as Epstein and O'Malley rushed Lindsey into the care of the two men waiting beside
the chopper.

The engine of the air ambulance was idling. The rotors turned
sluggishly.

The mere presence of the craft – and the sense of extreme
urgency that it represented – was like a flare of sunlight that
burned off some of the dense fog in Lindsey's mind. She realized

30

that either she or Hatch was in worse shape than she had thought, for only a critical case could justify such an unconventional and expensive method of conveyance. And they obviously were going farther than to a hospital in San Bernardino, perhaps to a treatment center specializing in state-of-the-art trauma medicine of one kind or another. Even as that light of understanding came to her, she wished that it could be extinguished, and she despairingly sought the comfort of that mental fog again.

As the chopper medics took charge of her and lifted her into the aircraft, one of them shouted above the engine noise, 'But she's alive.'

'She's in bad shape,' Epstein said.

'Yeah, okay, she looks like shit,' the chopper medic said, 'but she's still alive. Nyebern's expecting a stiff.'

O'Malley said, 'It's the other one.'

'The husband,' Epstein said.

'We'll bring him over,' O'Malley said.

Lindsey was aware that a monumental piece of information had been revealed in those few brief exchanges, but she was not clear-headed enough to understand what it was. Or maybe she simply did not want to understand.

As they moved her into the spacious rear compartment of the helicopter, transferred her onto one of their own litters, and strapped her to the vinyl-covered mattress, she sank back into frighteningly corrupted memories of childhood.

. . . she was nine years old, playing fetch with her dog Boo, but when the frisky labrador brought the red rubber ball back to her and dropped it at her feet, it was not a ball any longer. It was a throbbing heart, trailing torn arteries and veins. It was pulsing not because it was alive but because a mass of worms and sarcophagus beetles churned within its rotting chambers . . .

·4·

The helicopter was airborne. Its movement, perhaps because of the winter wind, was less reminiscent of an aircraft than of a boat tumbling in a bad tide. Nausea uncoiled in Lindsey's stomach.

A medic bent over her, his face masked in shadows, applying a stethoscope to her breast.

31

Across the cabin, another medic was shouting into a radio head-set as he bent over Hatch, talking not to the pilot in the forward compartment but perhaps to a receiving physician at whatever hospital awaited them. His words were sliced into a series of thin sounds by the air-carving rotors overhead, so his voice fluttered like that of a nervous adolescent.

' . . . minor head injury . . . no mortal wounds . . . apparent cause of death . . . seems to be . . . drowning . . . '

On the far side of the chopper, near the foot of Hatch's litter, the sliding door was open a few inches, and Lindsey realized the door on her side was not fully closed, either, creating an arctic cross-draught. That also explained why the roar of the wind outside and the clatter of the rotors was so deafening.

Why did they want it so cold?

The medic attending to Hatch was still shouting into his head-set: ' . . . mouth-to-mouth . . . mechanical resuscitator . . . 0-2 and CO-2 without results . . . epinephrine was ineffective . . . '

The real world had become too real, even viewed through her delirium. She didn't like it. Her twisted dreamscapes, in all their mutant horror, were more appealing than the inside of the air ambulance, perhaps because on a subconscious level she was able to exert at least *some* control on her nightmares but none at all on real events.

. . . she was at her senior prom, dancing in the arms of Joey Delvecchio, the boy with whom she had been going steady in those days. They were under a vast canopy of crepe-paper streamers. She was speckled with sequins of blue and white and yellow light cast off by the revolving crystal-and-mirror chandelier above the dance floor. It was the music of a better age, before rock-'n'-roll started to lose its soul, before disco and New Age and hip-hop, back when Elton John and the Eagles were at their peak, when the Isley Brothers were still recording, the Doobie Brothers, Stevie Wonder, Neil Sedaka making a major comeback, the music still alive, everything and everyone so alive, the world filled with hope and possibilities now long since lost. They were slow-dancing to a Freddy Fender tune reasonably well rendered by a local band, and she was suffused with happiness and a sense of well-being – until she lifted her head from Joey's shoulder and looked up and saw not Joey's face but the rotting countenance of a cadaver, yellow teeth exposed between shriveled black lips, flesh pocked and blistered and oozing, bloodshot eyes bulging and weeping vile fluid from lesions of decay. She tried to

32

scream and pull away from him, but she could only continue to dance, listening to the overly sweet romantic strains of 'Before the Next Tear-drop Falls,' aware that she was seeing Joey as he would be in a few years, after he had died in the Marine-barracks explosion in Lebanon. She felt death leeching from his cold flesh into hers. She knew she had to tear herself from his embrace before that mortal tide filled her. But when she looked desperately around for someone who might help her, she saw that Joey was not the only dead dancer. Sally Ontkeen, who in eight years would succumb to cocaine poisoning, glided by in an advanced stage of decomposition, in the arms of her boyfriend who smiled down on her as if unaware of the corruption of her flesh. Jack Winslow, the school football star who would be killed in a drunken driving accident in less than a year, spun his date past them; his face was swollen, purple tinged with green, and his skull was crushed along the left side as it would be after the wreck. He spoke to Lindsey and Joey in a raspy voice that didn't belong to Jack Winslow but to a creature on holiday from a graveyard, vocal cords withered into dry strings: 'What a night! Man, what a night!'

Lindsey shuddered, but not solely because of the frigid wind that howled through the partly open chopper doors.

The medic, his face still in shadows, was taking her blood pressure. Her left arm was no longer under the blanket. The sleeves of her sweater and blouse had been cut away, exposing her bare skin. The cuff of the sphygmomanometer was wound tightly around her biceps and secured by Velcro strips.

Her shudders were so pronounced that they evidently looked to the paramedic as if they might be the muscle spasms that accompanied convulsions. He plucked a small rubber wedge from a nearby supply tray and started to insert it in her mouth to prevent her from biting or swallowing her tongue.

She pushed his hand away. 'I'm going to die.'

Relieved that she was not having convulsions, he said, 'No, you're not that bad, you're okay, you're going to be fine.'

He didn't understand what she meant. Impatiently, she said, 'We're *all* going to die.'

That was the meaning of her dream-distorted memories. Death had been with her from the day she'd been born, always at her side, constant companion, which she had not understood until Jimmy's death five years ago, and which she had not *accepted* until tonight when death took Hatch from her.

33

Her heart seemed to clutch up like a fist within her breast. A new pain filled her, separate from all the other agonies and more profound. In spite of terror and delirium and exhaustion, all of which she had used as shields against the awful insistence of reality, truth came to her at last, and she was helpless to do anything but accept it.

Hatch had drowned.

Hatch was dead. CPR had not worked.

Hatch was gone forever.

. . . she was twenty-five years old, propped against bed pillows in the maternity ward at St Joseph's Hospital. The nurse was bringing her a small blanket-wrapped bundle, her baby, her son, James Eugene Harrison, whom she had carried for nine months but had not met, whom she loved with all her heart but had not seen. The smiling nurse gently conveyed the bundle into Lindsey's arms, and Lindsey tenderly lifted aside the satin-trimmed edge of the blue cotton blanket. She saw that she cradled a tiny skeleton with hollow eye sockets, the small bones of its fingers curled in the wanting-needing gesture of an infant. Jimmy had been born with death in him, as everyone was, and in less than five years cancer would claim him. The small, bony mouth of the skeleton-child eased open in a long, slow, silent cry . . .

·5·

Lindsey could hear the chopper blades carving the night air, but she was no longer inside the craft. She was being wheeled across a parking lot toward a large building with many lighted windows. She thought she ought to know what it was, but she couldn't think clearly, and in fact she didn't care what it was or where she was going or why.

Ahead, a pair of double doors flew open, revealing a space warmed by yellow light, peopled by several silhouettes of men and women. Then Lindsey was rushed into the light and among the silhouettes . . . a long hallway . . . a room that smelled of alcohol and other disinfectants . . . the silhouettes becoming people with faces, then more faces appearing . . . soft but urgent voices . . . hands gripping her, lifting . . . off the gurney, onto a bed . . . tipped back a little, her head below the level of her body . . .

34

rhythmic beeps and clicks issuing from electronic equipment of some kind . . .

She wished they would just all go away and leave her alone, in peace. Just go away. Turn off the lights as they went. Leave her in darkness. She longed for silence, stillness, peace.

A vile odor with an edge of ammonia assaulted her. It burned her nasal passages, made her eyes pop open and water.

A man in a white coat was holding something under her nose and peering intently into her eyes. As she began to choke and gag on the stench, he took the object away and handed it to a brunette in a white uniform. The pungent odor quickly faded.

Lindsey was aware of movement around her, faces coming and going. She knew that she was the center of attention, an object of urgent inquiry, but she did not – could not manage to – care. It was all more like a dream than her actual dreams had been. A soft tide of voices rose and fell around her, swelling rhythmically like gentle breakers whispering on a sandy shore:

'. . . marked paleness of the skin . . . cyanosis of lips, nails, fingertips, lobes of the ears . . . '

'. . . weak pulse, very rapid . . . respiration quick and shallow . . . '

'. . . blood pressure's so damned low I can't get a reading . . .'

'Didn't those assholes treat her for shock?'

'Sure, all the way in.'

'Oxygen, CO-2 mix. And make it fast!'

'Epinephrine?'

'Yeah, prepare it.'

'Epinephrine? But what if she has internal injuries? You can't see a hemorrhage if one's there.'

'Hell, I gotta take a chance.'

Someone put a hand over her face, as if trying to smother her. Lindsey felt something plugging up her nostrils, and for a moment she could not breathe. The curious thing was that she didn't care. Then cool dry air hissed into her nose and seemed to force an expansion of her lungs.

A young blonde, dressed all in white, leaned close, adjusted the inhalator, and smiled winningly. 'There you go, honey. Are you getting that?'

The woman was beautiful, ethereal, with a singularly musical voice, backlit by a golden glow.

35

A heavenly apparition. An angel.

Wheezing, Lindsey said, 'My husband is dead.'

'It'll be okay, honey. Just relax, breathe as deeply as you can, everything will be all right.'

'No, he's dead,' Lindsey said. 'Dead and gone, gone forever. Don't you lie to me, angels aren't allowed to lie.'

On the other side of the bed, a man in white was swabbing the inside of Lindsey's left elbow with an alcohol-soaked pad. It was icy cold.

To the angel, Lindsey said, 'Dead and gone.'

Sadly, the angel nodded. Her blue eyes were filled with love, as an angel's eyes should be. 'He's gone, honey. But maybe this time that isn't the end of it.'

Death was always the end. How could death not be the end?

A needle stung Lindsey's left arm.

'This time,' the angel said softly, 'there's still a chance. We've got a special program here, a real—'

Another woman burst into the room and interrupted excitedly: 'Nyebern's in the hospital!'

A communal sigh of relief, almost a quiet cheer, swept those gathered in the room.

'He was at dinner in Marina del Rey when they reached him. He must've driven like a bat out of Hell to get back here this fast.'

'You see, dear?' the angel said to Lindsey. 'There's a chance. There's still a chance. We'll be praying.'

So what? Lindsey thought bitterly. Praying never works for me. Expect no miracles. The dead stay dead, and the living only wait to join them.

THREE

·1·

Guided by procedures outlined by Dr Jonas Nyebern and kept on file in the Resuscitation Medicine Project office, the Orange County General Hospital emergency staff had prepared an operating room to receive the body of Hatchford Benjamin Harrison. They had gone into action the moment the on-site paramedics in the San Bernardino Mountains had reported, by police-band radio, that the victim had drowned in near-freezing water but had suffered only minor injuries in the accident itself, which made him a perfect subject for Nyebern. By the time the air ambulance was touching down in the hospital parking lot, the usual array of operating-room instruments and devices had been augmented with a bypass machine and other equipment required by the resuscitation team.

Treatment would not take place in the regular emergency room. Those facilities offered insufficient space to deal with Harrison in addition to the usual influx of patients. Though Jonas Nyebern was a cardiovascular surgeon and the project team was rich with surgical skills, resuscitation procedures seldom involved surgery. Only the discovery of a severe internal injury would require them to cut Harrison, and their use of an operating room was more a matter of convenience than necessity.

When Jonas entered from the surgical hallway after preparing himself at the scrub sinks, his project team was waiting for him. Because fate had deprived him of his wife, daughter, and son, leaving him without family, and because an innate shyness had always inhibited him from making friends beyond the boundaries of his profession, these were not merely his colleagues but the only people in the world with whom he felt entirely comfortable and about whom he cared deeply.

37

Helga Dorner stood by the instrument cabinets to Jonas's left, in the penumbra of the light that fell from the array of halogen bulbs over the operating table. She was a superb circulating nurse with a broad face and sturdy body reminiscent of any of countless steroid-saturated female Soviet track stars, but her eyes and hands were those of the gentlest Raphaelite Madonna. Patients initially feared her, soon respected her, eventually adored her.

With the solemnity that was characteristic of her in moments like this, Helga did not smile but gave Jonas a thumbs-up sign.

Near the bypass machine stood Gina Delilo, a thirty-year-old RN and surgical technician who chose, for whatever reasons, to conceal her extraordinary competence and sense of responsibility behind a pert, cute, ponytailed exterior that made her seem to be an escapee from one of those old Gidget or beach-party movies that had been popular decades ago. Like the others, Gina was dressed in hospital greens and a string-tied cotton cap that concealed her blond hair, but bright pink ankle socks sprouted above the elastic-edged cloth boots that covered her shoes.

Flanking the operating table were Dr Ken Nakamura and Dr Kari Dovell, two hospital-staff physicians with successful local private practices. Ken was a rare double threat, holding advanced degrees in internal medicine and neurology. Daily experience with the fragility of human physiology drove some doctors to drink and caused others to harden their hearts until they were emotionally isolated from their patients; Ken's healthier defense was a sense of humor that was sometimes twisted but always psychologically healing. Kari, a first-rate specialist in pediatric medicine, was four inches taller than Ken's five-feet-seven, reed-thin where he was slightly pudgy, but she was as quick to laugh as the internist. Sometimes, though, a profound sadness in her eyes troubled Jonas and led him to believe that a cyst of loneliness lay so deep within her that friendship could never provide a scalpel long or sharp enough to excise it.

Jonas looked at each of his four colleagues in turn, but none of them spoke. The windowless room was eerily quiet.

For the most part the team had a curiously passive air, as if disinterested in what was about to happen. But their eyes gave them away, for they were the eyes of astronauts who were standing in the exit bay of an orbiting shuttle on the brink of a space walk:

38

aglow with excitement, wonder, a sense of adventure – and a little fear.

Other hospitals had emergency-room staffs skilled enough at resuscitation medicine to give a patient a fighting chance at recovery, but Orange County General was one of only three centers in all of southern California that could boast a separately funded, cutting-edge project aimed at maximizing the success of reanimation procedures. Harrison was the project's forty-fifth patient in the fourteen months since it had been established, but the manner of his death made him the most interesting: drowning, followed by rapidly induced hypothermia. Drowning meant relatively little physical damage, and the chill factor dramatically slowed the rate at which postmortem cell deterioration took place.

More often than not, Jonas and his team had treated victims of catastrophic stroke, cardiac arrest, asphyxiation due to tracheal obstruction, or drug overdose. Those patients usually had suffered at least some irreversible brain damage prior to or at the moment of death, before coming under the care of the Resuscitation Project, compromising their chances of being brought back in perfect condition. And of those who had died from violent trauma of one kind or another, some had been too severely injured to be saved even after being resuscitated. Others had been resuscitated and stabilized, only to succumb to secondary infections that swiftly developed into toxic shock. Three had been dead so long that, once resuscitated, brain damage was either too severe to allow them to regain consciousness or, if they were conscious, too extensive to allow them to lead anything like a normal life.

With sudden anguish and a twinge of guilt, Jonas thought of his failures, of life incompletely restored, of patients in whose eyes he had seen the tortured awareness of their own pathetic condition . . .

'This time will be different.' Kari Dovell's voice was soft, only a whisper, but it shattered his reverie.

Jonas nodded. He felt considerable affection for these people. For their sake more than his own, he wanted the team to have a major, unqualified success.

'Let's do it,' he said.

Even as he spoke, the double doors to the operating room crashed open, and two surgical orderlies rushed in with the dead man on a gurney. Swiftly and skillfully, they transferred the body onto the slightly tilted operating table, treating it with more care and respect than they might have shown a corpse in other circumstances, and then exited.

The team went to work even as the orderlies were heading out of the room. With speed and economy of movement, they scissored the remaining clothes off the dead man, leaving him naked on his back, and attached to him the leads of an electrocardiograph, an electroencephalograph, and a skin-patch digital-readout thermometer.

Seconds were golden. Minutes were beyond price. The longer the man remained dead, the less chance they had of bringing him back with any degree of success whatsoever.

Kari Dovell adjusted the controls of the EKG, sharpening the contrast. For the benefit of the tape recording that was being made of the entire procedure, she repeated what all of them could see: 'Flat line. No heartbeat.'

'No alpha, no beta,' Ken Nakamura added, confirming the absence of all electrical activity in the patient's brain.

Having wrapped the pressure cuff of a sphygmomanometer around the patient's right arm, Helga reported the reading they expected: 'No measurable blood pressure.'

Gina stood beside Jonas, monitoring the digital-readout thermometer. 'Body temperature's forty-six degrees.'

'So low!' Kari said, her green eyes widening with surprise as she stared down at the cadaver. 'And he must've warmed up at least ten degrees since they pulled him out of that stream. We keep it cool in here, but not *that* cool.'

The thermostat was set at sixty-four degrees to balance the comfort of the resuscitation team against the need to prevent the victim from warming too fast.

Looking up from the dead man to Jonas, Kari said, 'Cold is good, okay, we want him cold, but not too damned cold. What if his tissues froze and he sustained massive cerebral-cell damage?'

Examining the dead man's toes and then his fingers, Jonas was almost embarrassed to hear himself say, 'There's no indication of vesicles—'

'That doesn't prove anything,' Kari said.

Jonas knew that what she said was true. They all knew it. There would not have been time for vesicles to form in the dead flesh of frost-bitten fingertips and toes before the man, himself, had died.

But, damn it, Jonas did not want to give up before they had even started.

He said, 'Still, there's no sign of necrotic tissue—'

'Because the entire patient is necrotic,' Kari said, unwilling to let go of it. Sometimes she seemed as ungainly as a spindly-legged bird that, although a master of the air, was out of its element on the land. But at other times, like now, she used her height to advantage, casting an intimidating shadow, looking down at an adversary with a hard gaze that seemed to say better-listen-to-me-or-I-might-peck-your-eyes-out-mister. Jonas was two inches taller than Kari, so she couldn't actually look down at him, but few women were that close to being able to give him even a level-eyed stare, and the effect was the same as if he had been five-feet-two.

Jonas looked at Ken, seeking support.

The neurologist was having none of it. 'In fact the body temperature could have fallen below freezing *after* death, then warmed up on the trip here, and there'd be no way for us to tell. You know that, Jonas. The only thing we can say for sure about this guy is that he's deader than Elvis has ever been.'

'If he's only forty-six degrees *now* . . . ' Kari said.

Every cell in the human body is composed primarily of water. The percentage of water differs from blood cells to bone cells, from skin cells to liver cells, but there is always more water than anything else. And when water freezes, it expands. Put a bottle of soda in the freezer to quick-chill it, leave it too long, and you're left with just the exploded contents bristling with shattered glass. Frozen water bursts the walls of brain cells – all body cells – in a similar fashion.

No one on the team wanted to revive Harrison from death if they were assured of bringing back something dramatically less than a whole person. No good physician, regardless of his passion to heal, wanted to battle and defeat death only to wind up with a conscious patient suffering from massive brain damage or one who could be sustained 'alive' only in a deep coma with the aid of machines.

Jonas knew that his own greatest weakness as a physician was the extremity of his hatred for death. It was an anger he carried at all times. At moments like this the anger could swell into a quiet fury that affected his judgment. Every patient's death was a personal affront to him. He tended to err on the side of optimism, proceeding with a resuscitation that could have more tragic consequences if it succeeded than if it failed.

The other four members of the team understood his weakness, too. They watched him expectantly.

If the operating room had been tomb-still before, it was now as silent as the vacuum of any lonely place between the stars where God, if He existed, passed judgment on His helpless creations.

Jonas was acutely aware of the precious seconds ticking past.

The patient had been in the operating room less than two minutes. But two minutes could make all the difference.

On the table, Harrison was as dead as any man had ever been. His skin was an unhealthy shade of gray, lips and fingernails and toenails a cyanotic blue, lips slightly parted in an eternal exhalation. His flesh was utterly devoid of the tension of life.

However, aside from the two-inch-long shallow gash on the right side of his forehead, an abrasion on his left jaw, and abrasions on the palms of his hands, he was apparently uninjured. He had been in excellent physical condition for a man of thirty-eight, carrying no more than five extra pounds, with straight bones and well-defined musculature. No matter what might have happened to his brain cells, he *looked* like a perfect candidate for resuscitation.

A decade ago, a physician in Jonas's position would have been guided by the Five-Minute Limit, which then had been acknowledged as the maximum length of time the human brain could go without blood-borne oxygen and suffer no diminution of mental faculties. During the past decade, however, as resuscitation medicine had become an exciting new field, the Five-Minute Limit had been exceeded so often that it was eventually disregarded. With new drugs that acted as free-radical scavengers, machines that could cool and heat blood, massive doses of epinephrine, and other tools, doctors could step well past the Five-Minute Limit and snatch some patients back from deeper regions of death. And hypothermia – extreme cooling of the brain which blocked the swift and ruinous chemical changes in cells following death – could extend the length of time a patient might lie dead yet be successfully revived. Twenty minutes was common. Thirty was not hopeless. Cases of triumphant resuscitation at forty and fifty minutes were on record. In 1988, a two-year-old girl in Utah, plucked from an icy river, was brought back to life without any apparent brain damage after being dead at least sixty-six minutes, and only last year a twenty-year-old woman in Pennsylvania had been revived with all faculties intact seventy minutes after death.

The other four members of the team were still staring at Jonas.

Death, he told himself, is just another pathological state.

Most pathological states could be reversed with treatment.

Dead was one thing. But *cold* and dead was another.

To Gina, he said, 'How long's he been dead?'

Part of Gina's job was to serve as liaison, by radio, with the on-site paramedics and make a record of the information most vital to the resuscitation team at this moment of decision. She looked at her watch – a Rolex on an incongruous pink leather band to match her socks – and did not even have to pause to calculate: 'Sixty minutes, but they're only guessing how long he was dead in the water before they found him. Could be longer.'

'Or shorter,' Jonas said.

While Jonas made his decision, Helga rounded the table to Gina's side and, together, they began to study the flesh on the cadaver's left arm, searching for the major vein, just in case Jonas decided to resuscitate. Locating blood vessels in the slack flesh of a corpse was not always easy, since applying a rubber tourniquet would not increase systemic pressure. There *was* no pressure in the system.

'Okay, I'm going to call it,' Jonas said.

He looked around at Ken, Kari, Helga, and Gina, giving them one last chance to challenge him. Then he checked his own Timex wristwatch and said, 'It's nine-twelve pm, Monday night, March fourth. The patient, Hatchford Benjamin Harrison, is dead . . . but retrievable.'

To their credit, whatever their doubts might be, no one on the team hesitated once the call had been made. They had the right – and the duty – to advise Jonas as he was making the decision, but once it was made, they put all of their knowledge, skill, and training to work to insure that the 'retrievable' part of his call proved correct.

Dear God, Jonas thought, I hope I've done the right thing.

Already Gina had inserted an exsanguination needle into the vein that she and Helga had located. Together they switched on and adjusted the bypass machine, which would draw the blood out of Harrison's body and gradually warm it to one hundred

43

degrees. Once warmed, the blood would be pumped back into the still-blue patient through another tube feeding a needle inserted in a thigh vein.

With the process begun, more urgent work awaited than time to do it. Harrison's vital signs, currently non-existent, had to be monitored for the first indications of response to therapy. The treatment already provided by the paramedics needed to be reviewed to determine if a previously administered dose of epinephrine – a heart-stimulating hormone – was so large as to rule out giving more of it to Harrison at this time. Meanwhile Jonas pulled up a wheeled cart of medications, prepared by Helga before the body had arrived, and began to calculate the variety and quantity of ingredients for a chemical cocktail of free-radical scavengers designed to retard tissue damage.

'Sixty-one minutes,' Gina said, updating them on the estimated length of time that the patient had been dead. 'Wow! That's a long time talking to the angels. Getting this one back isn't going to be a weenie roast, boys and girls.'

'Forty-eight degrees,' Helga reported solemnly, noting the cadaver's body temperature as it slowly rose toward the temperature of the room around it.

Death is just an ordinary pathological state, Jonas reminded himself. Pathological states can usually be reversed.

With her incongruously slender, long-fingered hands, Helga folded a cotton surgical towel over the patient's genitals, and Jonas recognized that she was not merely making a concession to modesty but was performing an act of kindness that expressed an important new attitude toward Harrison. A dead man had no interest in modesty. A dead man did not require kindness. Helga's consideration was a way of saying that she believed this man would once more be one of the living, welcomed back to the brotherhood and sisterhood of humanity, and that he should be treated henceforth with tenderness and compassion and not just as an interesting and challenging prospect for reanimation.

·2·

The weeds and grass were as high as his knees, lush from an unusually rainy winter. A cool breeze whispered through the

44

meadow. Occasionally bats and night birds passed overhead or swooped low off to one side, briefly drawn to him as if they recognized a fellow predator but immediately repelled when they sensed the terrible difference between him and them.

He stood defiantly, gazing up at the stars shining between the steadily thickening clouds that moved eastward across the late-winter sky. He believed that the universe was a kingdom of death, where life was so rare as to be freakish, a place filled with countless barren planets, a testament not to the creative powers of God but to the sterility of His imagination and the triumph of the forces of darkness aligned against Him. Of the two realities that coexisted in this universe – life and death – life was the smaller and less consequential. As a citizen in the land of the living, your existence was limited to years, months, weeks, days, hours. But as a citizen in the kingdom of the dead, you were immortal.

He lived in the borderland.

He hated the world of the living, into which he had been born. He loathed the pretense to meaning and manners and morals and virtue that the living embraced. The hypocrisy of human interaction, wherein selflessness was publicly championed and selfishness privately pursued, both amused and disgusted him. Every act of kindness seemed, to him, to be performed only with an eye to the payback that might one day be extracted from the recipient.

His greatest scorn – and sometimes fury – was reserved for those who spoke of love and made claims to feeling such a thing. Love, he knew, was like all the other high-minded virtues that family, teachers, and priests blathered about. It didn't exist. It was a sham, a way to control others, a con.

He cherished, instead, the darkness and strange anti-life of the world of the dead in which he belonged but to which he could not yet return. His rightful place was with the damned. He felt at home among those who despised love, who knew that the pursuit of pleasure was the sole purpose of existence. Self was primary. There were no such things as 'wrong' and 'sin.'

The longer he stared at the stars between the clouds, the brighter they appeared, until each pinpoint of light in the void seemed to prick his eyes. Tears of discomfort blurred his vision, and he lowered his gaze to the earth at his feet. Even at night, the land of the living was too bright for the likes of him. He didn't

45

need light to see. His vision had adapted to the perfect blackness of death, to the catacombs of Hell. Light was not merely superfluous to eyes like his; it was a nuisance and, at times, an abomination.

Ignoring the heavens, he walked out of the field, returning to the cracked pavement. His footsteps echoed hollowly through this place that had once been filled with the voices and laughter of multitudes. If he had wanted, he could have moved with the silence of a stalking cat.

The clouds parted and the lunar lamp beamed down, making him wince. On all sides, the decaying structures of his hideaway cast stark and jagged shadows in moonlight that would have seemed wan to anyone else but that, to him, shimmered on the pavement as if it were luminous paint.

He took a pair of sunglasses from an inside pocket of his leather jacket and put them on. That was better.

For a moment he hesitated, not sure what he wanted to do with the rest of the night. He had two basic choices, really: spend the remaining pre-dawn hours with the living or with the dead. This time it was even an easier choice than usual, for in his current mood, he much preferred the dead.

He stepped out of a moon-shadow that resembled a giant, canted, broken wheel, and he headed toward the moldering structure where he kept the dead. His collection.

·3·

'Sixty-four minutes,' Gina said, consulting her Rolex with the pink leather band. 'This one could get messy.'

Jonas couldn't believe how fast time was passing, just speeding by, surely faster than usual, as if there had been some freak acceleration of the continuum. But it was always the same in situations like this, when the difference between life and death was measured in minutes and seconds.

He glanced at the blood, more blue than red, moving through the clear-plastic exsanguination tube into the purring bypass machine. The average human body contained five liters of blood. Before the resuscitation team was done with Harrison, his five liters would have been repeatedly recycled, heated, and filtered.

46

Ken Nakamura was at a light board, studying head and chest X-rays and body-sonograms that had been taken in the air ambulance during its hundred-eighty-mile-per-hour journey from the base of the San Bernardinos to the hospital in Newport Beach. Kari was bent close to the patient's face, examining his eyes through an ophthalmoscope, checking for indications of dangerous cranial pressure from a buildup of fluid on the brain.

With Helga's assistance, Jonas had filled a series of syringes with large doses of various free-radical neutralizers. Vitamins E and C were effective scavengers and had the advantage of being natural substances, but he also intended to administer a lazeroid – tirilazad mesylate – and phenyl tertiary butyl nitrone.

Free radicals were fast-moving, unstable molecules that ricocheted through the body, causing chemical reactions that damaged most cells with which they came into contact. Current theory held that they were the primary cause of human aging, which explained why natural scavengers like vitamins E and C boosted the immune system and, in long-term users, promoted a more youthful appearance and higher energy levels. Free radicals were a by-product of ordinary metabolic processes and were always present in the system. But when the body was deprived of oxygenated blood for an extended period, even with the protection of hypothermia, huge pools of free radicals were created in excess of anything the body had to deal with normally. When the heart was started again, renewed circulation swept those destructive molecules through the brain, where their impact was devastating.

The vitamin and chemical scavengers would deal with the free radicals before they could cause any irreversible damage. At least that was the hope.

Jonas inserted the three syringes in different ports that fed the main intravenous line in the patient's thigh, but he did not yet inject the contents.

'Sixty-five minutes,' Gina said.

A long time dead, Jonas thought.

It was very near the record for a successful reanimation.

In spite of the cool air, Jonas felt sweat breaking out on his scalp, under his thinning hair. He always got too involved, emotional. Some of his colleagues disapproved of his excessive empathy; they believed a judicious perspective was insured by the maintenance of a professional distance between the doctor and those he treated. But no patient was *just* a patient. Every one of them was loved and needed by someone. Jonas was acutely aware that if he failed a patient, he was failing more than one person, bringing pain and suffering to a wide network of relatives and friends. Even when he was treating someone like Harrison, of whom Jonas knew virtually nothing, he began to *imagine* the lives interlinking with that of the patient, and he felt responsible to them as much as he would have if he had known them intimately.

'The guy looks clean,' Ken said, turning away from the X-rays and sonograms. 'No broken bones. No internal injuries.'

'But those sonograms were taken after he was dead,' Jonas noted, 'so they don't show *functioning* organs.'

'Right. We'll snap some pictures again when he's reanimated, make sure nothing's ruptured, but it looks good so far.'

Straightening up from her examination of the dead man's eyes, Kari Dovell said, 'There might be concussion to deal with. Hard to say from what I can see.'

'Sixty-six minutes.'

'Seconds count here. Be ready, people,' Jonas said, although he knew they were ready.

The cool air couldn't reach his head because of his surgical cap, but the sweat on his scalp felt icy. Shivers cascaded through him.

Blood, heated to one hundred degrees, began to move through the clear plastic IV line and into the body through a thigh vein, surging rhythmically to the artificial pulse of the bypass machine.

Jonas depressed the plungers halfway on each of the three syringes, introducing heavy doses of the free-radical scavengers into the first blood passing through the line. He waited less than a minute, then swiftly depressed the plungers all the way.

Helga had already prepared three more syringes according to his instructions. He removed the depleted ones from the IV ports and introduced the full syringes without injecting any of their contents.

Ken had moved the portable defibrillation machine next to the patient. Subsequent to reanimation, if Harrison's heart began to beat erratically or chaotically – fibrillation – it might be coerced into a normal rhythm by the application of an electric shock. That was a last-hope strategy, however, for violent defibrillation could also have a serious adverse effect on a patient who, having been

48

recently brought back from the dead, was in an exceptionally fragile state.

Consulting the digital thermometer, Kari said, 'His body temperature's up to only fifty-six degrees.'

'Sixty-seven minutes,' Gina said.

'Too slow,' Jonas said.

'External heat?'

Jonas hesitated.

'Let's go for it,' Ken advised.

'Fifty-seven degrees,' Kari said.

'At this rate,' Helga said worriedly, 'we're going to be past eighty minutes before he's anywhere near warm enough for the heart to kick in.'

Heating pads had been placed under the operating-table sheet before the patient had been brought into the room. They extended the length of his spine.

'Okay,' Jonas said.

Kari clicked the switch on the heating pads.

'But easy,' Jonas advised.

Kari adjusted the temperature controls.

They needed to warm the body, but potential problems could arise from a too-rapid reheating. Every resuscitation was a tightrope walk.

Jonas tended to the syringes in the IV ports, administering additional doses of vitamins E and C, tirilazad mesylate, and phenyl tertiary butyl nitrone.

The patient was motionless, pale. He reminded Jonas of a figure in a life-size tableau in some old cathedral: the supine body of Christ sculpted from white marble, rendered by the artist in the position of entombment as He would have rested just prior to the most successful resurrection of all time.

Because Kari Dovell had peeled back Harrison's eyelids for the ophthalmoscopic examination, his eyes were open, staring sightlessly at the ceiling, and Gina was putting artificial tears in them with a dropper to insure that the lenses did not dry out. She hummed 'Little Surfer Girl' as she worked. She was a Beach Boys fan.

No shock or fear was visible in the cadaver's eyes, as one might have expected. Instead, they held an expression that was almost peaceful, almost touched by wonder. Harrison looked as if he had seen something, in the moment of death, to lift his heart.

Finishing with the eyedrops, Gina checked her watch. 'Sixty-eight minutes.'

Jonas had the crazy urge to tell her to shut up, as though time would halt as long as she was not calling it out, minute by minute.

Blood pumped in and out of the bypass machine.

'Sixty-two degrees.' Helga spoke so sternly that she might have been chastising the dead man for the laggardly pace of his reheating.

Flat lines on the EKG.

Flat lines on the EEG.

'Come on,' Jonas urged. 'Come on, come on.'

·4·

He entered the museum of the dead not through one of its upper doors but through the waterless lagoon. In that shallow depression, three gondolas still lay on the cracked concrete. They were ten-passenger models that had long ago been tipped off the heavy chain-drive track along which they'd once carried their happy passengers. Even at night, wearing sunglasses, he could see they did not have the swan-neck prows of real gondolas in Venice, but sported leering gargoyles as figureheads, hand-carved from wood, garishly painted, perhaps fearsome at one time but now cracked, weathered, and peeling. The lagoon doors, which in better days had swung smoothly out of the way at the approach of each gondola, were no longer motorized. One of them was frozen open; the other was closed, but it was hanging from only two of its four corroded hinges. He walked through the open door into a passageway that was far blacker than the night behind him.

He took off the sunglasses. He didn't need them in that gloom.

Neither did he require a flashlight. Where an ordinary man would have been blind, he could see.

The concrete sluiceway, along which the gondolas had once moved, was three feet deep and eight feet wide. A much narrower channel in the sluiceway floor contained the rusted chain-drive mechanism – a long series of blunt, curved, six-inch-high hooks that had pulled the boats forward by engaging the steel loops on the bottoms of their hulls. When the ride had been in operation, those hooks had been concealed by water, contributing to the illusion that the gondolas were actually adrift. Now, dwindling into the dreary realm ahead, they looked like a row of stubby spines on the back of an immense prehistoric reptile.

The world of the living, he thought, is always fraught with deception. Beneath the placid surface, ugly mechanisms grind away at secret tasks.

He walked deeper into the building. The gradual downward slope of the sluiceway was at first barely perceptible, but he was aware of it because he had passed that way many times before.

Above him, to either side of the channel, were concrete service walks, about four feet wide. Beyond them were the tunnel walls, which had been painted black to serve as a non-reflective back-drop for the moments of half-baked theater performed in front of them.

The walkways widened occasionally to form niches, in some places even whole rooms. When the ride had been in operation, the niches had been filled with tableaus meant to amuse or horrify or both: ghosts and goblins, ghouls and monsters, ax-wielding madmen standing over the prostrate bodies of their beheaded victims. In one of the room-sized areas, there had been an elabor-ate graveyard filled with stalking zombies; in another, a large and convincing flying saucer had disgorged bloodthirsty aliens with a shark's profusion of teeth in their huge heads. The robotic figures had moved, grimaced, reared up, and threatened all passersby with tape-recorded voices, eternally repeating the same brief pro-grammed dramas with the same menacing words and snarls.

No, not eternally. They were gone now, carted away by the official salvagers, by agents of the creditors, or by scavengers.

Nothing was eternal.

Except death.

A hundred feet beyond the entrance doors, he reached the end of the first section of the chain-drive. The tunnel floor, which had been sloping imperceptibly, now tilted down sharply, at about a thirty-five-degree angle, falling away into flawless blackness. Here, the gondolas had slipped free of the blunt hooks in the channel floor and, with a stomach-wrenching lurch, sailed down a hundred-and-fifty-foot incline, knifing into the pool below with a colossal splash that drenched the passengers up front, much to the delight of those fortunate – or smart – enough to get a seat in the back.

Because he was not like ordinary men and possessed certain

special powers, he could see part of the way down the incline, even in that utterly lightless environment, although his perception did not extend to the very bottom. His catlike night vision was limited: within a radius of ten or fifteen feet, he could see as clearly as if he stood in daylight; thereafter, objects grew blurry, steadily less distinct, shadowy, until darkness swallowed everything at a distance of perhaps forty or fifty feet.

Leaning backward to retain his balance on the steep slope, he headed down into the bowels of the abandoned funhouse. He was not afraid of what might wait below. Nothing could frighten him any more. After all, he was deadlier and more savage than anything with which this world could threaten him.

Before he descended half the distance to the lower chamber, he detected the odor of death. It rose to him on currents of cool dry air. The stench excited him. No perfume, regardless of how exquisite, even if applied to the tender throat of a lovely woman, could ever thrill him as profoundly as the singular, sweet fragrance of corrupted flesh.

·5·

Under the halogen lamps, the stainless-steel and white-enameled surfaces of the operating room were a little hard on the eyes, like the geometric configurations of an arctic landscape polished by the glare of a winter sun. The room seemed to have gotten chillier, as if the heat flowing into the dead man was pushing the cold out of him, thereby lowering the air temperature. Jonas Nyebern shivered.

Helga checked the digital thermometer that was patched to Harrison. 'Body temperature's up to seventy degrees.'

'Seventy-two minutes,' Gina said.

'We're going for the brass ring now,' Ken said. 'Medical history, the *Guinness Book of World Records*, TV appearances, books, movies, T-shirts with our faces on 'em, novelty hats, plastic lawn ornaments in our images.'

'Some dogs have been brought back after ninety minutes,' Kari reminded him.

'Yeah,' Ken said, 'but they were *dogs*. Besides, they were so screwed up, they chased bones and buried cars.'

Gina and Kari laughed softly, and the joke seemed to break the tension for everyone except Jonas. He could never relax for a moment in the process of a resuscitation, although he knew that it was possible for a physician to get so tightly wound that he was no longer performing at his peak. Ken's ability to vent a little nervous energy was admirable, and in the service of the patient; however, Jonas was incapable of doing likewise in the midst of a battle.

'Seventy-two degrees, seventy-three.'

It *was* a battle. Death was the adversary: clever, mighty, and relentless. To Jonas, death was not *just* a pathological state, not merely the inevitable fate of all living things, but actually an entity that walked the world, perhaps not always the robed figure of myth with its skeletal face hidden in the shadows of a cowl, but a very real presence nonetheless, Death with a capital D.

'Seventy-four degrees,' Helga said.

Gina said, 'Seventy-three minutes.'

Jonas introduced more free-radical scavengers into the blood that surged through the IV line.

He supposed that his belief in Death as a supernatural force with a will and consciousness of its own, his certainty that it sometimes walked the earth in an embodied form, his awareness of its presence right now in this room in a cloak of invisibility, would seem like silly superstition to his colleagues. It might even be regarded as a sign of mental imbalance or incipient madness. But Jonas was confident of his sanity. After all, his belief in Death was based on empirical evidence. He had *seen* the hated enemy when he was only seven years old, had heard it speak, had looked into its eyes and smelled its fetid breath and felt its icy touch upon his face.

'Seventy-five degrees.'

'Get ready,' Jonas said.

The patient's body temperature was nearing a threshold beyond which reanimation might begin at any moment. Kari finished filling a hypodermic syringe with epinephrine, and Ken activated the defibrillation machine to let it build up a charge. Gina opened the flow valve on a tank containing an oxygen-carbon dioxide mixture that had been formulated to the special considerations of resuscitation procedures, and picked up the mask of the pulmonary machine to make sure it was functioning.

'Seventy-six degrees,' Helga said, 'seventy-seven.'

Gina checked her watch. 'Coming up on ... seventy-four minutes.'

·6·

At the bottom of the long incline, he entered a cavernous room as large as an airplane hangar. Hell had once been re-created there, according to the unimaginative vision of an amusement-park designer, complete with gas-jet fires lapping at formed-concrete rocks around the perimeter.

The gas had been turned off long ago. Hell was tar-black now. But not to him, of course.

He moved slowly across the concrete floor, which was bisected by a serpentine channel housing another chain-drive. There, the gondolas had moved through a lake of water made to look like a lake of fire by clever lighting and bubbling air hoses that simulated boiling oil. As he walked, he savored the stench of decay, which grew more exquisitely pungent by the second.

A dozen mechanical demons had once stood on higher formations, spreading immense bat wings, peering down with glowing eyes that periodically raked the passing gondolas with harmless crimson laser beams. Eleven of the demons had been hauled away, peddled to some competing park or sold for scrap. For unknown reasons, one devil remained – a silent and unmoving agglomeration of rusted metal, moth-eaten fabric, torn plastic, and grease-caked hydraulic mechanisms. It was still perched on a rocky spire two-thirds of the way toward the high ceiling, pathetic rather than frightening.

As he passed beneath that sorry funhouse figure, he thought, *I am the only real demon this place has ever known or ever will*, and that pleased him.

Months ago he stopped thinking of himself by his Christian name. He adopted the name of a fiend that he had read about in a book on Satanism: Vassago. One of the three most powerful demon princes of Hell, who answered only to His Satanic Majesty. Vassago. He liked the sound of it. When he said it aloud, the name rolled from his tongue so easily that it seemed as if he'd never answered to anything else.

'Vassago.'

54

In the heavy subterranean silence, it echoed back to him from the concrete rocks: '*Vassago.*'

·7·

'Eighty degrees.'

'It should be happening,' Ken said.

Surveying the monitors, Kari said, 'Flat lines, just flat lines.'

Her long, swanlike neck was so slender that Jonas could see her pulse pounding rapidly in her carotid artery.

He looked down at the dead man's neck. No pulse there.

'Seventy-five minutes,' Gina announced.

'If he comes around, it's officially a record now,' Ken said. 'We'll be obligated to celebrate, get drunk, puke on our shoes, and make fools of ourselves.'

'Eighty-one degrees.'

Jonas was so frustrated that he could not speak – for fear of uttering an obscenity or a low, savage snarl of anger. They had made all the right moves, but they were losing. He hated losing. He hated Death. He hated the limitations of modern medicine, all circumscriptions of human knowledge, and his own inadequacies.

'Eighty-two degrees.'

Suddenly the dead man gasped.

Jonas twitched and looked at the monitors.

The EKG showed spastic movement in the patient's heart.

'Here we go,' Kari said.

·8·

The robotic figures of the damned, more than a hundred in Hell's heyday, were gone with eleven of the twelve demons; gone as well were the wails of agony and the lamentations that had been broadcast through their speaker-grille mouths. The desolate chamber, however, was not without lost souls. But now it housed something more appropriate than robots, more like the real thing: Vassago's collection.

At the center of the room, Satan waited in all his majesty, fierce and colossal. A circular pit in the floor, sixteen to eighteen feet in

diameter, housed a massive statue of the Prince of Darkness himself. He was not shown from the waist down; but from his navel
to the tips of his segmented horns, he measured thirty feet. When
the funhouse had been in operation, the monstrous sculpture
waited in a thirty-five-foot pit, hidden beneath the lake, then
periodically surged up out of its lair, water cascading from it, huge
eyes afire, monstrous jaws working, sharp teeth gnashing, forked
tongue flickering, thundering a warning – 'Abandon hope all ye
who enter here!' – and then laughing malevolently.

Vassago had ridden the gondolas several times as a boy, when
he had been one of the wholly alive, before he had become a
citizen of the borderland, and in those days he had been spooked
by the handcrafted devil, affected especially by its hideous laugh.
If the machinery had overcome years of corrosion and suddenly
brought the cackling monster to life again, Vassago would not
have been impressed, for he was now old enough and sufficiently
experienced to know that Satan was incapable of laughter.

He halted near the base of the towering Lucifer and studied it
with a mixture of scorn and admiration. It was corny, yes, a
funhouse fake meant to test the bladders of small children and
give teenage girls a reason to squeal and cuddle for protection in
the arms of their smirking boyfriends. But he had to admit that it
was also an inspired creation, because the designer had not opted
for the traditional image of Satan as a lean-faced, sharp-nosed,
thin-lipped Lothario of troubled souls, hair slicked back from a
widow's peak, goatee sprouting absurdly from a pointed chin.
Instead, this was a Beast worthy of the title: part reptile, part
insect, part humanoid, repulsive enough to command respect,
just familiar enough to seem real, alien enough to be awesome.
Several years of dust, moisture, and mold had contributed a
patina that softened the garish carnival colors and lent it the
authority of one of those gigantic stone statues of Egyptian gods
found in ancient sand-covered temples, far beneath the desert
dunes.

Although he didn't know what Lucifer actually looked like, and
though he assumed that the Father of Lies would be far more
heart-chilling and formidable than this funhouse version, Vassago
found the plastic and polyfoam behemoth sufficiently impressive
to make it the center of the secret existence that he led within his
hideaway. At the base of it, on the dry concrete floor of the

56

drained lake, he had arranged his collection partly for his own pleasure and amusement but also as an offering to the god of terror and pain.

The naked and decaying bodies of seven women and three men were displayed to their best advantage, as if they were ten exquisite sculptures by some perverse Michelangelo in a museum of death.

·9·

A single shallow gasp, one brief spasm of the heart muscles, and an involuntary nerve reaction that made his right arm twitch and his fingers open and close like the curling legs of a dying spider – those were the only signs of life the patient exhibited before settling once more into the still and silent posture of the dead.

'Eighty-three degrees,' Helga said.

Ken Nakamura wondered: 'Defibrillation?'

Jonas shook his head. 'His heart's not in fibrillation. It's not beating at all. Just wait.'

Kari was holding a syringe. 'More epinephrine?'

Jonas stared intently at the monitors. 'Wait. We don't want to bring him back only to overmedicate him and precipitate a heart attack.'

'Seventy-six minutes,' Gina said, her voice as youthful and breathless and perkily excited as if she were announcing the score in a game of beach volleyball.

'Eighty-four degrees.'

Harrison gasped again. His heart stuttered, sending a series of spikes across the screen of the electrocardiograph. His whole body shuddered. Then he went flatline again.

Grabbing the handles on the positive and negative pads of the defibrillation machine, Ken looked expectantly at Jonas.

'Eighty-five degrees,' Helga announced. 'He's in the right thermal territory, and he wants to come back.'

Jonas felt a bead of sweat trickle with centipede swiftness down his right temple and along his jaw line. The hardest part was waiting, giving the patient a chance to kick-start himself before risking more punishing techniques of forced reanimation.

A third spasm of heart activity registered as a shorter burst of spikes than the previous one, and it was not accompanied by a pulmonary response as before. No muscle contractions were visible, either. Harrison lay slack and cold.

'He's not able to make the leap,' Kari Dovell said.

Ken agreed. 'We're gonna lose him.'

'Seventy-seven minutes,' Gina said.

Not four days in the tomb, like Lazarus, before Jesus had called him forth, Jonas thought, but a long time dead nevertheless.

'Epinephrine,' Jonas said.

Kari handed the hypodermic syringe to Jonas, and he quickly administered the dosage through one of the same IV ports that he had used earlier to inject free-radical scavengers into the patient's blood.

Ken lifted the negative and positive pads of the defibrillation machine, and positioned himself over the patient, ready to give him a jolt if it came to that.

Then the massive charge of epinephrine, a powerful hormone extracted from the adrenal glands of sheep and cattle and referred to by some resuscitation specialists as 'reanimator juice,' hit Harrison as hard as any electrical shock that Ken Nakamura was prepared to give him. The stale breath of the grave exploded from him, he gasped air as if he were still drowning in that icy river, he shuddered violently, and his heart began to beat like that of a rabbit with a fox close on its tail.

·10·

Vassago had arranged each piece in his macabre collection with more than casual contemplation. They were not simply ten corpses dumped unceremoniously on the concrete. He not only respected death but loved it with an ardor akin to Beethoven's passion for music or Rembrandt's fervent devotion to art. Death, after all, was the gift that Satan had brought to the inhabitants of the Garden, a gift disguised as something prettier; he was the Giver of Death, and his was the kingdom of death everlasting. Any flesh that death had touched was to be regarded with all the reverence that a devout Catholic might reserve for the Eucharist. Just as their god was said to live within that thin wafer of unleavened bread, so the face of Vassago's unforgiving god could be seen everywhere in the patterns of decay and dissolution.

The first body at the base of the thirty-foot Satan was that of Jenny Purcell, a twenty-two-year-old waitress who had worked the evening shift in a re-creation of a 1950s diner, where the jukebox played Elvis Presley and Chuck Berry, Lloyd Price and the Platters, Buddy Holly and Connie Francis and the Everly Brothers. When Vassago had gone in for a burger and a beer, Jenny thought he looked cool in his black clothes, wearing sunglasses indoors at night and making no move to take them off. With his baby-faced good looks given interest by a contrastingly firm set to his jaw and a slight cruel twist to his mouth, and with thick black hair falling across his forehead, he looked a little like a young Elvis. *What's your name?* she asked, and he said *Vassago*, and she said, *What's your first name?* so he said, *That's it, the whole thing, first and last*, which must have intrigued her, got her imagination going, because she said, *What, you mean like Cher only has one name, or Madonna or Sting?* He stared hard at her from behind his heavily tinted sunglasses and said, *Yeah – you have a problem with that?* She didn't have a problem. In fact she was attracted to him. She said he was 'different,' but only later did she discover just *how* different he really was.

Everything about Jenny marked her as a slut in his eyes, so after killing her with an eight-inch stiletto that he drove under her ribcage and into her heart, he arranged her in a posture suitable for a sexually profligate woman. Once he had stripped her naked, he braced her in a sitting position with her thighs spread wide and knees drawn up. He bound her slender wrists to her shins to keep her upright. Then he used strong lengths of cord to pull her head forward and down farther than she could have managed to do while alive, brutally compressing her midriff; he anchored the cords around her thighs, so she was left eternally looking up the cleft between her legs, contemplating her sins.

Jenny had been the first piece in his collection. Dead for about nine months, trussed up like a ham in a curing barn, she was withered now, a mummified husk, no longer of interest to worms or other agents of decomposition. She did not stink as she had once stunk.

Indeed, in her peculiar posture, having contracted into a ball as she had decayed and dried out, she resembled a human being so little that it was difficult to think of her as ever having been a living person, therefore equally difficult to think of her as a dead person. Consequently, death seemed no longer to reside in her remains. To Vassago, she had ceased to be a corpse and had become merely a curious object, an impersonal thing that might always have been inanimate. As a result, although she was the start of his collection, she was now of minimal interest to him.

He was fascinated solely with death and the dead. The living were of interest to him only insofar as they carried the ripe promise of death within them.

·11·

The patient's heart oscillated between mild and severe tachycardia, from a hundred and twenty to over two hundred and thirty beats per minute, a transient condition resulting from the epinephrine and hypothermia. Except it wasn't acting like a transient condition. Each time the pulse rate declined, it did not subside as far as it had previously, and with each new acceleration, the EKG showed escalating arrhythmia that could lead only to cardiac arrest.

No longer sweating, calmer now that the decision to fight Death had been made and was being acted upon, Jonas said, 'Better hit him with it.'

No one doubted to whom he was speaking, and Ken Nakamura pressed the cold pads of the defibrillation machine to Harrison's chest, bracketing his heart. The electrical discharge caused the patient to bounce violently against the table, and a sound like an iron mallet striking a leather sofa – *wham!* – slammed through the room.

Jonas looked at the electrocardiograph just as Kari read the meaning of the spikes of light moving across the display: 'Still two hundred a minute but the rhythm's there now ... steady ... steady.'

Similarly, the electroencephalograph showed alpha and beta brain waves within normal parameters for an unconscious man.

'There's self-sustained pulmonary activity,' Ken said.

'Okay,' Jonas decided, 'let's respirate him and make sure he's getting enough oxygen in those brain cells.'

Gina immediately put the oxygen mask on Harrison's face.

60

'Body temperature's at ninety degrees,' Helga reported.

The patient's lips were still somewhat blue, but that same deathly hue had faded from under his fingernails.

Likewise, his muscle tone was partially restored. His flesh no longer had the flaccidity of the dead. As feeling returned to Harrison's deep-chilled extremities, his punished nerve endings excited a host of tics and twitches.

His eyes rolled and jiggled under his closed lids, a sure sign of REM sleep. He was dreaming.

'One hundred and twenty beats a minute,' Kari said, 'and declining . . . completely rhythmic now . . . very steady.'

Gina consulted her watch and let her breath out in a *whoosh* of amazement. 'Eighty minutes.'

'Sonofabitch,' Ken said wonderingly, 'that beats the record by ten.'

Jonas hesitated only a brief moment before checking the wall clock and making the formal announcement for the benefit of the tape recorder: 'Patient successfully resuscitated as of nine-thirty-two Monday evening, March fourth.'

A murmur of mutual congratulations accompanied by smiles of relief was as close as they would get to a triumphant cheer of the sort that might have been heard on a real battleground. They were not restrained by modesty but by a keen awareness of Harrison's tenuous condition. They had won the battle with Death, but their patient had not yet regained consciousness. Until he was awake and his mental performance could be tested and evaluated, there was a chance that he had been reanimated only to live out a life of anguish and frustration, his potential tragically circumscribed by irreparable brain damage.

·12·

Enraptured by the spicy perfume of death, at home in the subterranean bleakness, Vassago walked admiringly past his collection. It encircled one-third of the colossal Lucifer.

Of the male specimens, one had been taken while changing a flat tire on a lonely section of the Ortega Highway at night. Another had been asleep in his car in a public-beach parking lot. The third had tried to pick up Vassago at a bar in Dana Point. The dive hadn't even been a gay hangout; the guy had just been drunk, desperate, lonely – and careless.

Nothing enraged Vassago more than the sexual needs and excitement of others. He had no interest in sex any more, and he never raped any of the women he killed. But his disgust and anger, engendered by the mere perception of sexuality in others, was not a result of jealousy, and it did not spring from any sense that his impotency was a curse or even an unfair burden. No, he was glad to be free of lust and longing. Since becoming a citizen of the borderland and accepting the promise of the grave, he did not regret the loss of desire. Though he was not entirely sure *why* the very thought of sex could sometimes throw him into a rage, why a flirtatious wink or a short skirt or a sweater stretched across a full bosom could incite him to torture and homicide, he suspected that it was because sex and life were inextricably entwined. Next to self-preservation, the sex drive was, they said, the most powerful human motivator. Through sex, life was created. Because he hated life in all its gaudy variety, hated it with such intensity, it was only natural that he would hate sex as well.

He preferred to kill women because society encouraged them, more than men, to flaunt their sexuality, which they did with the assistance of makeup, lipstick, alluring scents, revealing clothes, and coquettish behavior. Besides, from a woman's womb came new life, and Vassago was sworn to destroy life wherever he could. From women came the very thing he loathed in himself: the spark of life that still sputtered in him and prevented him from moving on to the land of the dead, where he belonged.

Of the remaining six female specimens in his collection, two had been housewives, one a young attorney, one a medical secretary, and two college students. Though he had arranged each corpse in a manner fitting the personality, spirit, and weaknesses of the person who had once inhabited it, and though he had considerable talent for cadaver art, making especially clever use of a variety of props, he was far more pleased by the effect he had achieved with one of the students than with all of the others combined.

He stopped walking when he reached her.

He regarded her in the darkness, pleased by his work . . .

Margaret . . .

He first saw her during one of his restless late-night rambles, in a dimly lighted bar near the university campus, where she was sipping diet cola, either because she was not old enough to be served beer along with her friends or because she was not a drinker. He suspected the latter.

She looked singularly wholesome and uncomfortable in the smoke and din of the tavern. Even from halfway across the room, judging by her reactions to her friends and her body language, Vassago could see that she was a shy girl struggling hard to fit in with the crowd, even though in her heart she knew that she would never entirely belong. The roar of liquor-amplified conversation, the clink and clatter of glasses, the thunderous jukebox music of Madonna and Michael Jackson and Michael Bolton, the stink of cigarettes and stale beer, the moist heat of college boys on the make – none of that touched her. She sat in the bar but existed apart from it, unstained by it, filled with more secret energy than that entire roomful of young men and women combined.

She was so vital, she seemed to glow. Vassago found it hard to believe that the ordinary, sluggish blood of humanity moved through her veins. Surely, instead, her heart pumped the distilled essence of life itself.

Her vitality drew him. It would be enormously satisfying to snuff such a brightly burning flame of life.

To learn where she lived, he followed her home from the bar. For the next two days, he stalked the campus, gathering information about her as diligently as a real student might have researched a term paper.

Her name was Margaret Ann Campion. She was a senior, twenty years old, majoring in music. She could play the piano, flute, clarinet, guitar, and almost any other instrument she took a fancy to learn. Perhaps the best-known and most-admired student in the music program, she was also widely considered to possess an exceptional talent for composition. An essentially shy person, she made a point of forcing herself out of her shell, so music was not her only interest. She was on the track team, the second-fastest woman in their lineup, a spirited competitor; she wrote about music and movies for the student paper; and she was active in the Baptist church.

Her astonishing vitality was evident not merely in the joy with which she wrote and played music, not just in the almost spiritual aura that Vassago had seen in the bar, but also in her physical appearance. She was incomparably beautiful, with the body of a silver-screen sex goddess and the face of a saint. Clear skin. Perfect cheekbones. Full lips, a generous mouth, a beatific smile. Limpid blue eyes. She dressed modestly in an attempt to conceal the sweet fullness of her breasts, the contrasting narrowness of her waist, the firmness of her buttocks, and the long supple lines of her legs. But he was certain that when he stripped her, she would be revealed for what he had known her to be when he had first glimpsed her: a prodigious breeder, a hot furnace of life in which eventually other life of unparalleled brightness would be conceived and shaped.

He wanted her dead.

He wanted to stop her heart and then hold her for hours, feeling the heat of life radiate out of her, until she was cold.

This one murder, it seemed to him, might at last earn him passage out of the borderland in which he lived and into the land of the dead and damned, where he belonged, where he longed to be.

Margaret made the mistake of going alone to a laundry room in her apartment complex at eleven o'clock at night. Many of the units were leased to financially comfortable senior citizens and, because they were near the University of California at Irvine, to pairs and trios of students who shared the rent. Maybe the tenant mix, the fact that it was a safe and friendly neighborhood, and the abundance of landscape and walkway lighting all combined to give her a false sense of security.

When Vassago entered the laundry room, Margaret had just begun to put her dirty clothes into one of the washing machines. She looked at him with a smile of surprise but with no apparent concern, though he was dressed all in black and wearing sunglasses at night.

She probably thought he was just another university student who favored an eccentric look as a way of proclaiming his rebellious spirit and intellectual superiority. Every campus had a slew of the type, since it was easier to *dress* as a rebellious intellectual than *be* one.

'Oh, I'm sorry, Miss,' he said, 'I didn't realize anyone was in here.'

'That's okay. I'm only using just one washer,' she said. 'There're two others.'

64

'No, I already did my laundry, then back at the apartment when I took it out of the basket, I was missing one sock, so I figure it's got to be in one of the washers or dryers. But I didn't mean to get in your way. Sorry about that.'

She smiled a little broader, maybe because she thought it funny that a would-be James Dean, black-clad rebel without a cause, would choose to be so polite – or would do his own laundry and chase down lost socks.

By then he was beside her. He hit her in the face – two hard, sharp punches that knocked her unconscious. She crumpled onto the vinyl-tile floor as if she were a pile of laundry.

Later, in the dismantled Hell under the moldering funhouse, when she regained consciousness and found herself naked on the concrete floor and effectively blind in those lightless confines, tied hand and foot, she did not attempt to bargain for her life as some of the others had done. She didn't offer her body to him, didn't pretend to be turned on by his savagery or the power that he wielded over her. She didn't offer him money, or claim to understand and sympathize with him in a pathetic attempt to convert him from nemesis to friend. Neither did she scream nor weep nor wail nor curse. She was different from the others, for she found hope and comfort in a quiet, dignified, unending chain of whispered prayers. But she never prayed to be delivered from her tormentor and returned to the world out of which she had been torn – as if she knew that death was inevitable. Instead, she prayed that her family would be given the strength to cope with the loss of her, that God would take care of her two younger sisters, and even that her murderer would receive divine grace and mercy.

Vassago swiftly came to loathe her. He knew that love and mercy were nonexistent, just empty words. *He* had never felt love, neither during his time in the borderland nor when he had been one of the living. Often, however, he had pretended to love someone – father, mother, girl – to get what he wanted, and they had always been deceived. Being deceived into believing that love existed in others, when it didn't exist in you, was a sign of fatal weakness. Human interaction was nothing but a game, after all, and the ability to see through deception was what separated the good players from the inept.

To show her that he could not be deceived and that her god was powerless, Vassago rewarded her quiet prayers with a long and painful death. At last she *did* scream. But her screams were not satisfying, for they were only the sounds of physical agony; they did not reverberate with terror, rage, or despair.

He thought he would like her better when she was dead, but even then he still hated her. For a few minutes he held her body against him, feeling the heat drain from it. But the chilly advance of death through her flesh was not as thrilling as it should have been. Because she had died with an unbroken faith in life everlasting, she had cheated Vassago of the satisfaction of seeing the awareness of death in her eyes. He pushed her limp body aside in disgust.

Now, two weeks after Vassago had finished with her, Margaret Campion knelt in perpetual prayer on the floor of that dismantled Hell, the most recent addition to his collection. She remained upright because she was lashed to a length of steel rebar which he had inserted into a hole he had drilled in the concrete. Naked, she faced away from the giant, funhouse devil. Though she had been Baptist, a crucifix was clasped in her dead hands because Vassago liked the image of the crucifix better than a simple cross; it was turned upsidedown, with Christ's thorn-prickled head toward the floor. Margaret's own head had been cut off then resewn to her neck with obsessive care. Even though her body was turned away from Satan, she faced toward him in denial of the crucifix held irreverently in her hands. Her posture was symbolic of hypocrisy, mocking her pretense to faith, love, and life everlasting.

Although Vassago hadn't received nearly as much pleasure from murdering Margaret as from what he had done to her after she was dead, he was still pleased to have made her acquaintance. Her stubbornness, stupidity, and self-deception had made her death less satisfying for him than it should have been, but at least the aura he had seen around her in the bar was quenched. Her irritating vitality was drained away. The only energy her body harbored was that of the multitudinous carrion-eaters that teemed within her, consuming her flesh and bent on reducing her to a dry husk like Jenny, the waitress, who rested at the other end of the collection.

As he studied Margaret, a familiar need arose in him. Finally the need became a compulsion. He turned away from his collection, retracing his path across the huge room, heading for the ramp that led up to the entrance tunnel. Ordinarily, selecting another acquisition, killing it, and arranging it in the most aesthetically satisfying pose would have left him quiescent and sated for as much as a month. But after less than two weeks, he was compelled to find another worthy sacrifice.

Regretfully, he ascended the ramp, out of the purifying scent of death, into air tainted with the odors of life, like a vampire driven to hunt the living though preferring the company of the dead.

·13·

At ten-thirty, almost an hour after Harrison was resuscitated, he remained unconscious. His body temperature was normal. His vital signs were good. And though the patterns of alpha and beta brain waves were those of a man in a profound sleep, they were not obviously indicative of anything as deep as a coma.

When Jonas finally declared the patient out of immediate danger and ordered him moved to a private room on the fifth floor, Ken Nakamura and Kari Dovell elected to go home. Leaving Helga and Gina with the patient, Jonas accompanied the neurologist and the pediatrician to the scrub sinks, and eventually as far as the door to the staff parking lot. They discussed Harrison and what procedures might have to be performed on him in the morning, but for the most part they shared inconsequential small talk about hospital politics and gossip involving mutual acquaintances, as if they had not just participated in a miracle that should have made such banalities impossible.

Beyond the glass door, the night looked cold and inhospitable. Rain had begun to fall. Puddles were filling every depression in the pavement, and in the reflected glow of the parking-lot lamps, they looked like shattered mirrors, collections of sharp silvery shards.

Kari leaned against Jonas, kissed his cheek, clung to him for a moment. She seemed to want to say something but was unable to find the words. Then she pulled back, turned up the collar of her coat, and went out into the wind-driven rain.

Lingering after Kari's departure, Ken Nakamura said, 'I hope you realize she's a perfect match for you.'

Through the rain-streaked glass door, Jonas watched the woman as she hurried toward her car. He would have been lying if he had said that he never looked at Kari as a woman. Though tall, rangy, and a formidable presence, she was also feminine. Sometimes he marveled at the delicacy of her wrists, at her swan-like neck that seemed too gracefully thin to support her head. Intellectually and emotionally she was stronger than she looked. Otherwise she couldn't have dealt with the obstacles and challenges that surely had blocked her advance in the medical profession, which was still dominated by men for whom – in some cases – chauvinism was less a character trait than an article of faith.

Ken said, 'All you'd have to do is ask her, Jonas.'

'I'm not free to do that,' Jonas said.

'You can't mourn Marion forever.'

'It's only been two years.'

'Yeah, but you have to step back into life sometime.'

'Not yet.'

'Ever?'

'I don't know.'

Outside, halfway across the parking lot, Kari Dovell had gotten into her car.

'She won't wait forever,' Ken said.

'Goodnight, Ken.'

'I can take a hint.'

'Good,' Jonas said.

Smiling ruefully, Ken pulled open the door, letting in a gust of wind that spat jewel-clear drops of rain on the gray tile floor. He hurried out into the night.

Jonas turned away from the door and followed a series of hallways to the elevators. He went up to the fifth floor.

He hadn't needed to tell Ken and Kari that he would spend the night in the hospital. They knew he always stayed after an apparently successful reanimation. To them, resuscitation medicine was a fascinating new field, an interesting sideline to their primary work, a way to expand their professional knowledge and keep their minds flexible; every success was deeply satisfying, a reminder of why they had become physicians in the first place – to heal. But it was more than that to Jonas. Each reanimation was a battle won in an endless war with Death, not just a healing act but an act of defiance, an angry fist raised in the face of fate. Resuscitation medicine was his love, his passion, his definition of himself, his only reason for arising in the morning and getting on with life in a world that had otherwise become too colorless and purposeless to endure.

He had submitted applications and proposals to half a dozen universities, seeking to teach in their medical schools in return for the establishment of a resuscitation-medicine research facility under his supervision, for which he felt able to raise a sizable part of the financing. He was well known and widely respected both as a cardiovascular surgeon and a reanimation specialist, and he was confident that he would soon obtain the position he wanted. But he was impatient. He was no longer satisfied with supervising reanimations. He wanted to study the effects of short-term death on human cells, explore the mechanisms of free-radicals and free-radical scavengers, test his own theories, and find new ways to evict Death from those in whom it had already taken up tenancy.

On the fifth floor, at the nurses' station, he learned that Harrison had been taken to 518. It was a semi-private room, but an abundance of empty beds in the hospital insured that it would be effectively maintained as a private unit as long as Harrison was likely to need it.

When Jonas entered 518, Helga and Gina were finishing with the patient, who was in the bed farthest from the door and nearest the rain-spotted window. They had gotten him into a hospital gown and hooked him to another electrocardiograph with a telemetry function that would reproduce his heart rhythms on a monitor at the nurses' station. A bottle of clear fluid hung from a rack beside the bed, feeding an IV line into the patient's left arm, which was already beginning to bruise from other intravenous injections administered by the paramedics earlier in the evening; the clear fluid was glucose enriched with an antibiotic to prevent dehydration and to guard against one of the many infections that could undo everything that had been achieved in the resuscitation room. Helga had smoothed Harrison's hair with a comb that she was now tucking away in the nightstand drawer. Gina was delicately applying a lubricant to his eyelids to prevent them from sticking together, a danger with comatose patients who spent long periods of time without opening their eyes or even blinking and who sometimes suffered from diminished lachrymal-gland secretion.

'Heart's still steady as a metronome,' Gina said when she saw

69

Jonas. 'I have a hunch, before the end of the week, this one's going to be out playing golf, dancing, doing whatever he wants.' She brushed at her bangs, which were an inch too long and hanging in her eyes. 'He's a lucky man.'

'One hour at a time,' Jonas cautioned, knowing too well how Death liked to tease them by pretending to retreat, then returning in a rush to snatch away their victory.

When Gina and Helga left for the night, Jonas turned off all the lights. Illuminated only by the faint fluorescent wash from the corridor and the green glow of the cardiac monitor, room 518 was replete with shadows.

It was silent, too. The audio signal on the EKG had been turned off, leaving only the rhythmically bouncing light endlessly making its way across the screen. The only sounds were the soft moans of the wind at the window and the occasional faint tapping of rain against the glass.

Jonas stood at the foot of the bed, looking at Harrison for a moment. Though he had saved the man's life, he knew little about him. Thirty-eight years old. Five-ten, a hundred and sixty pounds. Brown hair, brown eyes. Excellent physical condition.

But what of the inner person? Was Hatchford Benjamin Harrison a good man? Honest? Trustworthy? Faithful to his wife? Was he reasonably free of envy and greed, capable of mercy, aware of the difference between right and wrong?

Did he have a kind heart?

Did he love?

In the heat of a resuscitation procedure, when seconds counted and there was too much to be done in too short a time, Jonas never dared to think about the central ethical dilemma facing any doctor who assumed the role of reanimator, for to think of it then might have inhibited him to the patient's disadvantage. Afterward, there was time to doubt, to wonder . . . Although a physician was morally committed and professionally obligated to saving lives wherever he could, were all lives worth saving? When Death took an evil man, wasn't it wiser – and more ethically correct – to let him stay dead?

If Harrison was a bad man, the evil that he committed upon resuming his life after leaving the hospital would in part be the responsibility of Jonas Nyebern. The pain Harrison caused others would to some extent stain Jonas's soul, as well.

Fortunately, this time the dilemma seemed moot. Harrison appeared to be an upstanding citizen – a respected antique dealer, they said – married to an artist of some reputation, whose name Jonas recognized. A good artist had to be sensitive, perceptive, able to see the world more clearly than most people saw it, didn't she? If she was married to a bad man, she would know it, and she wouldn't remain married to him. This time there was every reason to believe that a life had been saved that *should* have been saved.

Jonas only wished his actions had always been so correct.

He turned away from the bed and took two steps to the window. Five stories below, the nearly deserted parking lot lay under hooded pole lamps. The falling rain churned the puddles, so they appeared to be boiling, as if a subterranean fire consumed the blacktop from underneath.

He could pick out the spot where Kari Dovell's car had been parked, and he stared at it for a long time. He admired Kari enormously. He also found her attractive. Sometimes he dreamed of being with her, and it was a surprisingly comforting dream. He could admit to wanting her at times, as well, and to being pleased by the thought that she might also want him. But he did not *need* her. He needed nothing but his work, the satisfaction of occasionally beating Death, and the—

'*Something's . . . out . . . there . . .*'

The first word interrupted Jonas's thoughts, but the voice was so thin and soft that he didn't immediately perceive the source of it. He turned around, looking toward the open door, assuming the voice had come from the corridor, and only by the third word did he realize that the speaker was Harrison.

The patient's head was turned toward Jonas, but his eyes were focused on the window.

Moving quickly to the side of the bed, Jonas glanced at the electrocardiograph and saw that Harrison's heart was beating fast but, thank God, rhythmically.

'Something's . . . out there,' Harrison repeated.

His eyes were not, after all, focused on the window itself, on nothing so close as that, but on some distant point in the stormy night.

'Just rain,' Jonas assured him.

'No.'

'Just a little winter rain.'

71

'Something bad,' Harrison whispered.

Hurried footsteps echoed in the corridor, and a young nurse burst through the open door, into the nearly dark room. Her name was Ramona Perez, and Jonas knew her to be competent and concerned.

'Oh, Doctor Nyebern, good, you're here. The telemetry unit, his heartbeat—'

'Accelerated, yes, I know. He just woke up.'

Ramona came to the bed and switched on the lamp above it, revealing the patient more clearly.

Harrison was still staring beyond the rain-spotted window, as if oblivious of Jonas and the nurse. In a voice even softer than before, heavy with weariness, he repeated: 'Something's out there.' Then his eyes fluttered sleepily, and fell shut.

'Mr Harrison, can you hear me?' Jonas asked.

The patient did not answer.

The EKG showed a quickly decelerating heartbeat: from one-forty to one-twenty to one hundred beats a minute.

'Mr Harrison?'

Ninety per minute. Eighty.

'He's asleep again,' Ramona said.

'Appears to be.'

'Just sleeping, though,' she said. 'No question of it being a coma now.'

'Not a coma,' Jonas agreed.

'And he was speaking. Did he make sense?'

'Sort of. But hard to tell,' Jonas said, leaning over the bed railing to study the man's eyelids, which fluttered with the rapid movement of the eyes under them. REM sleep. Harrison was dreaming again.

Outside, the rain suddenly began to fall harder than before. The wind picked up, too, and keened at the window.

Ramona said, 'The words I heard were clear, not slurred.'

'No. Not slurred. And he spoke some complete sentences.'

'Then he's not aphasic,' she said. 'That's terrific.'

Aphasia, the complete inability to speak or understand spoken or written language, is one of the most devastating forms of brain damage resulting from disease or injury. Thus affected, a patient is reduced to using gestures to communicate, and the inadequacy of pantomime soon casts him into deep depression, from which there is sometimes no coming back.

72

Harrison was evidently free from that curse. If he was also free from paralysis, and if there were not *too* many holes in his memory, he had a good chance of eventually getting out of bed and leading a normal life.

'Let's not jump to conclusions,' Jonas said. 'Let's not build up any false hopes. He still has a long way to go. But you can enter on his record that he regained consciousness for the first time at eleven-thirty, two hours after resuscitation.'

Harrison was murmuring in his sleep.

Jonas leaned over the bed and put his ear close to the patient's lips, which were barely moving. The words were faint, carried on his shallow exhalations. It was like a spectral voice heard on an open radio channel, broadcast from a station halfway around the world, bounced off a freak inversion layer high in the atmosphere and filtered through so much space and bad weather that it sounded mysterious and prophetic in spite of being less than half-intelligible.

'What's he saying?' Ramona asked.

With the howl of the storm rising outside, Jonas was unable to catch enough of Harrison's words to be sure, but he thought the man was repeating what he'd said before: 'Something's . . . out there.'

Abruptly the wind shrieked, and rain drummed against the window so hard that it seemed certain to shatter the glass.

·14·

Vassago liked the rain. The storm clouds had plated over the sky, leaving no holes through which the too-bright moon could gaze. The downpour also veiled the glow of streetlamps and the headlights of oncoming cars, moderated the dazzle of neon signs, and in general softened the Orange County night, making it possible for him to drive with more comfort than could be provided by his sunglasses alone.

He had traveled west from his hideaway, then north along the coast, in search of a bar where the lights might be low and a woman or two available for consideration. A lot of places were closed Mondays, and others didn't appear too active that late at night, between the half-hour and the witching hour.

At last he found a lounge in Newport Beach, along the Pacific

Coast Highway. It was a tony joint with a canopy to the street, rows of miniature white lights defining the roof line, and a sign advertising 'Dancing Wed Thru Sat/Johnny Wilton's Big Band.' Newport was the most affluent city in the county, with the world's largest private yacht harbor, so almost any establishment that pretended to a monied clientele most likely had one. Beginning mid-week, valet parking was probably provided, which would not have been good for his purposes, since a valet was a potential witness, but on a rainy Monday no valet was in sight.

He parked in the lot beside the club, and as he switched off the engine, the seizure hit him. He felt as if he'd received a mild but sustained electrical shock. His eyes rolled back in his head, and for a moment he thought he was having convulsions, because he was unable to breathe or swallow. An involuntary moan escaped him. The attack lasted only ten or fifteen seconds, and ended with three words that seemed to have been spoken *inside* his head: *Something's . . . out . . . there . . .* It was not just a random thought sparked by some short-circuiting synapse in his brain, for it came to him in a distinct *voice*, with the timbre and inflection of spoken words as distinguished from thoughts. Not his own voice, either, but that of a stranger. He had an overpowering sense of another presence in the car, as well, as if a spirit had passed through some curtain between worlds to visit with him, an alien presence that was real in spite of being invisible. Then the episode ended as abruptly as it had begun.

He sat for a while, waiting for a reoccurrence.

Rain hammered on the roof.

The car ticked and pinged as the engine cooled down.

Whatever had happened, it was over now.

He tried to understand the experience. Had those words – *Something's out there* – been a warning, a psychic premonition? A threat? To what did it refer?

Beyond the car, there seemed to be nothing special about the night. Just rain. Blessed darkness. The distorted reflections of electric lights and signs shimmered on the wet pavement, in puddles, and in the torrents pouring along the overflowing gutters. Sparse traffic passed on Pacific Coast Highway, but as far as he could see, no one was on foot – and he could see as well as any cat.

After a while he decided that he would understand the episode

74

when he was *meant* to understand it. Nothing was to be gained by brooding over it. If it was a threat, from whatever source, it did not trouble him. He was incapable of fear. That was the best thing about having left the world of the living, even if he was temporarily stuck in the borderland this side of death: nothing in existence held any terror for him.

Nevertheless, that inner voice had been one of the strangest things he had ever experienced. And he was not exactly without a store of strange experiences with which to compare it.

He got out of his silver Camaro, slammed the door, and walked to the club entrance. The rain was cold. In the blustering wind, the fronds of the palm trees rattled like old bones.

·15·

Lindsey Harrison was also on the fifth floor, at the end of the main corridor farthest from her husband. Little of the room was revealed when Jonas entered and approached the side of the bed, for there was not even the green light from a cardiac monitor. The woman was barely visible.

He wondered if he should try to wake her, and was surprised when she spoke.

'Who're you?'

He said, 'I thought you were asleep.'

'Can't sleep.'

'Didn't they give you something?'

'It didn't help.'

As in her husband's room, the rain drove against the window with sullen fury. Jonas could hear torrents cascading through the confines of a nearby aluminum downspout.

'How do you feel?' he asked.

'How the hell do you think I feel?' She tried to infuse the words with anger, but she was too exhausted and too depressed to manage it.

He put down the bed railing, sat on the edge of the mattress, and held out one hand, assuming that her eyes were better adapted to the gloom than his were. 'Give me your hand.'

'Why?'

'I'm Jonas Nyebern. I'm a doctor. I want to tell you about your husband, and somehow I think it'll be better if you'll just let me hold your hand.'

She was silent.

'Humor me,' he said.

Although the woman believed her husband to be dead, Jonas did not mean to torment her by withholding his report of the resuscitation. From experience, he knew that good news of this sort could be as shocking to the recipient as bad news; it had to be delivered with care and sensitivity. She had been mildly delirious upon admission to the hospital, largely as a result of exposure and shock, but that condition had been swiftly remedied with the administration of heat and medication. She had been in possession of all her faculties for a few hours now, long enough to absorb her husband's death and to begin to find her way toward a tentative accommodation of her loss. Though deep in grief and far from adjusted to her widowhood, she had by now found a ledge on the emotional cliff down which she had plunged, a narrow perch, a precarious stability – from which he was about to knock her loose.

Still, he might have been more direct with her if he'd been able to bring her unalloyed good news. Unfortunately, he could not promise that her husband was going to be entirely his former self, unmarked by his experience, able to reenter his old life without a hitch. They would need hours, perhaps days, in which to examine and evaluate Harrison before they could hazard a prediction as to the likelihood of a full recovery. Thereafter, weeks or months of physical and occupational therapy might lie ahead for him, with no guarantee of effectiveness.

Jonas was still waiting for her hand. At last she offered it diffidently.

In his best bedside manner, he quickly outlined the basics of resuscitation medicine. When she began to realize why he thought she needed to know about such an esoteric subject, her grip on his hand suddenly grew tight.

·16·

In room 518, Hatch foundered in a sea of bad dreams that were nothing but disassociated images melding into one another without even the illogical narrative flow that usually shaped nightmares. Wind-whipped snow. A huge Ferris wheel sometimes bedecked with festive lights, sometimes dark and broken and ominous in a night seething with rain. Groves of scarecrow trees, gnarled and coaly, stripped leafless by winter. A beer truck angled across a snow-swept highway. A tunnel with a concrete floor that sloped down into perfect blackness, into something unknown that filled him with heartbursting dread. His lost son, Jimmy, lying sallow-skinned against hospital sheets, dying of cancer. Water, cold and deep, impenetrable as ink, stretching to all horizons, with no possible escape. A naked woman, her head on backwards, hands clasping a crucifix . . .

Frequently he was aware of a faceless and mysterious figure at the perimeter of the dreamscapes, dressed in black like some grim reaper, moving in such fluid harmony with the shadows that he might have been only a shadow himself. At other times, the reaper was not part of the scene but seemed to be the viewpoint through which it was observed, as if Hatch was looking out through the eyes of another – eyes that beheld the world with all the compassionless, hungry, calculating practicality of a graveyard rat.

For a time, the dream took on more of a narrative quality, wherein Hatch found himself running along a train-station platform, trying to catch up with a passenger car that was slowly pulling away on the outbound track. Through one of the train windows, he saw Jimmy, gaunt and hollow-eyed in the grip of his disease, dressed only in a hospital gown, peering sadly at Hatch, one small hand raised as he waved goodbye, goodbye, goodbye. Hatch reached desperately for the vertical railing beside the boarding steps at the end of Jimmy's car, but the train picked up speed; Hatch lost ground; the steps slipped away. Jimmy's pale, small face lost definition and finally vanished as the speeding passenger car dwindled into the terrible nothingness beyond the station platform, a lightless void of which Hatch only now became aware. Then another passenger car began to glide past him (*clackety-clack, clackety-clack*), and he was startled to see Lindsey seated at one of the windows, looking out at the platform, a lost expression on her face. Hatch called to her – 'Lindsey!' – but she did not hear or see him, she seemed to be in a trance, so he began to run again, trying to board her car (*clackety-clack, clackety-clack*), which drew away from him as Jimmy's had done. 'Lindsey!' His hand was inches from the railing beside the boarding stairs . . .

77

Suddenly the railing and stairs vanished, and the train was not a train any more. With the eerie fluidity of all changes in all dreams, it became a roller coaster in an amusement park, heading out on the start of a thrill ride. (*Clackety-clack.*) Hatch came to the end of the platform without being able to board Lindsey's car, and she rocketed away from him, up the first steep hill of the long and undulant track. Then the last car in the caravan passed him, close behind Lindsey's. It held a single passenger. The figure in black – around whom shadows clustered like ravens on a cemetery fence – sat in front of the car, head bowed, his face concealed by thick hair that fell forward in the fashion of a monk's hood. (*Clackety-clack!*) Hatch shouted at Lindsey, warning her to look back and be aware of what rode in the car behind her, pleading with her to be careful and hold on tight, for God's sake, *hold on tight*! The caterpillar procession of linked cars reached the crest of the hill, hung there for a moment as if time had been suspended, then disappeared in a scream-filled plummet down the far side.

* ★ *

Ramona Perez, the night nurse assigned to the fifth-floor wing that included room 518, stood beside the bed, watching her patient. She was worried about him, but she was not sure that she should go looking for Dr Nyebern yet.

According to the heart monitor, Harrison's pulse was in a highly fluctuant state. Generally it ranged between a reassuring seventy to eighty beats per minute. Periodically, however, it raced as high as a hundred and forty. On the positive side, she observed no indications of serious arrhythmia.

His blood pressure was affected by his accelerated heartbeat, but he was in no apparent danger of stroke or cerebral hemorrhage related to spiking hypertension, because his systolic reading was never dangerously high.

He was sweating profusely, and the circles around his eyes were so dark, they appeared to have been applied with actors' grease-paint. He was shivering in spite of the blankets piled on him. The fingers of his left hand – exposed because of the intravenous feed – spasmed occasionally, though not forcefully enough to disturb the needle inserted just below the crook of his elbow.

In a whisper he repeated his wife's name, sometimes with considerable urgency: 'Lindsey . . . Lindsey . . . *Lindsey, no!*'

Harrison was dreaming, obviously, and events in a nightmare could elicit physiological responses every bit as much as waking experiences.

Finally Ramona decided that the accelerated heartbeat was solely the result of the poor man's bad dreams, not an indication of genuine cardiovascular destabilization. He was in no danger. Nevertheless, she remained at his bedside, watching over him.

·17·

Vassago sat at a window table overlooking the harbor. He had been in the lounge only five minutes, and already he suspected it was not a good hunting ground. The atmosphere was all wrong. He wished he had not ordered a drink.

No dance music was provided on Monday nights, but a pianist was at work in one corner. He played neither gutless renditions of '30s and '40s songs nor the studiedly bland arrangements of easy-listening rock-'n'-roll that rotted the brains of regular lounge patrons. But he spun out the equally noxious repetitive melodies of New Age numbers composed for those who found elevator music too complex and intellectually taxing.

Vassago preferred music with a hard beat, fast and driving, something that put his teeth on edge. Since becoming a citizen of the borderland, he could not take pleasure in most music, for its orderly structures irritated him. He could tolerate only music that was atonal, harsh, unmelodious. He responded to jarring key changes, thunderously crashing chords, and squealing guitar riffs that abraded the nerves. He enjoyed discord and broken patterns of rhythm. He was excited by music that filled his mind with images of blood and violence.

To Vassago, the scene beyond the big windows, because of its beauty, was as displeasing as the lounge music. Sailboats and motor yachts crowded one another at the private docks along the harbor. They were tied up, sails furled, engines silent, wallowing only slightly because the harbor was well protected and the storm was not particularly ferocious. Few of the wealthy owners actually lived aboard, regardless of the size of the craft or amenities, so lights glowed at only a few of the portholes. Rain, here and there transmuted into quicksilver by the dock lights, hammered the boats, beaded on their brightwork, drizzled like molten metal down their masts and across their decks and out of their scuppers. He had no tolerance for prettiness, for postcard scenes of harmonious composition, because they seemed false, a lie about what the world was really like. He was drawn, instead, to visual discord, jagged shapes, malignant and festering forms.

With its plush chairs and low amber lighting, the lounge was too soft for a hunter like him. It dulled his killing instincts.

He surveyed the patrons, hoping to spot an object of the quality suitable for his collection. If he saw something truly superb that excited his acquisitional fever, even the stultifying atmosphere would not be able to sap his energy.

A few men sat at the bar, but they were of no interest to him. The three men in his collection had been his second, fourth, and fifth acquisitions, taken because they had been vulnerable and in lonely circumstances that allowed him to overpower them and take them away without being seen. He had no aversion to killing men, but preferred women. Young women. He liked to get them before they could breed more life.

The only really young people among the customers were four women in their twenties who were seated by the windows, three tables away from him. They were tipsy and a little giddy, hunched over as if sharing gossip, talking intently, periodically bursting into gales of laughter.

One of them was lovely enough to engage Vassago's hatred of beautiful things. She had enormous chocolate-brown eyes, and an animal grace that reminded him of a doe. He dubbed her 'Bambi.' Her raven hair was cut into short wings, exposing the lower halves of her ears.

They were exceptional ears, large but delicately formed. He thought he might be able to do something interesting with them, and he continued to watch her, trying to decide if she was up to his standards.

Bambi talked more than her friends, and she was the loudest of the group. Her laugh was the loudest as well, a jackass braying. She *was* exceptionally attractive, but her incessant chatter and annoying laughter spoiled the package. Clearly, she loved the sound of her own voice.

She'd be vastly improved, he thought, if she were to be stricken deaf and mute.

80

Inspiration seized him, and he sat up straighter in his chair. By removing her ears, tucking them into her dead mouth, and sewing her lips shut, he would be neatly symbolizing the fatal flaw in her beauty. It was a vision of such simplicity, yet such power, that –

'One rum and Coke,' the waitress said, putting a glass and paper cocktail napkin on the table in front of Vassago. 'You want to run a tab?'

He looked up at her, blinking in confusion. She was a stout middle-aged woman with auburn hair. He could see her quite clearly through his sunglasses, but in his fever of creative excitement, he had difficulty placing her.

Finally he said, 'Tab? Uh, no. Cash, thank you, ma'am.'

When he took out his wallet, it didn't feel like a wallet at all but like one of Bambi's ears might feel. When he slid his thumb back and forth across the smooth leather, he felt not what was there but what might soon be available for his caress: delicately shaped ridges of cartilage forming the auricula and pinna, the graceful curves of the channels that focused sound waves inward toward the tympanic membrane . . .

He realized the waitress had spoken to him again, stating the price of his drink, and then he realized that it was the second time she had done so. He had been fingering his wallet for long, delicious seconds, daydreaming of death and disfigurement.

He fished out a crisp bill without looking at it, and handed it to her.

'This is a hundred,' she said. 'Don't you have anything smaller?'

'No, ma'am, sorry,' he said, impatient now to be rid of her, 'that's it.'

'I'll have to go back to the bar to get this much change.'

'Okay, yeah, whatever. Thank you, ma'am.'

As she started away from his table, he returned his attention to the four young women – only to discover that they were leaving. They were nearing the door, pulling on their coats as they went.

He started to rise, intending to follow them, but he froze when he heard himself say, 'Lindsey.'

He didn't call out the name. No one in the bar heard him say it. He was the only one who reacted, and his reaction was one of total surprise.

For a moment he hesitated with one hand on the table, one on the arm of his chair, halfway to his feet. While he was paralyzed in that posture of indecisiveness, the four young women left the lounge. Bambi became of less interest to him than the mysterious name – 'Lindsey' – so he sat down.

He did not know anyone named Lindsey.

He had *never* known anyone named Lindsey.

It made no sense that he would suddenly speak the name aloud.

He looked out the window at the harbor. Hundreds of millions of dollars of ego-gratification rose and fell and wallowed side to side on the rolling water. The sunless sky was another sea above, as cold and merciless as the one below. The air was full of rain like millions of gray and silver threads, as if nature was trying to sew the ocean to the heavens and thereby obliterate the narrow space between, where life was possible. Having been one of the living, one of the dead, and now one of the living dead, he had seen himself as the ultimate sophisticate, as experienced as any man born of woman could ever hope to be. He had assumed that the world held nothing new for him, had nothing to teach him. Now this. First the seizure in the car: *Something's out there!* And now Lindsey. The two experiences were different, because he heard no voice in his head the second time, and when he spoke it was with his own familiar voice and not that of a stranger. But both events were so peculiar that he knew they were linked. As he gazed at the moored boats, the harbor, and the dark world beyond, it began to seem more mysterious to him than it had in ages.

He picked up his rum and Coke. He took a long swallow of it.

As he was putting the drink down, he said, 'Lindsey.'

The glass rattled against the table, and he almost knocked it over, because the name surprised him again. He hadn't spoken it aloud to ponder the meaning of it. Rather, it had burst from him as before, a bit more breathlessly this time and somewhat louder.

Interesting.

The lounge seemed to be a magical place for him.

He decided to settle down for a while and wait to see what might happen next.

When the waitress arrived with his change, he said, 'I'd like another drink, ma'am.' He handed her a twenty. 'This'll take care of it, and please keep the change.'

Happy with the tip, she hurried back to the bar.

Vassago turned to the window again, but this time he looked at his own reflection in the glass instead of at the harbor beyond. The dim lights of the lounge threw insufficient glare on the pane to provide him with a detailed image. In that murky mirror, his sunglasses did not register well. His face appeared to have two gaping eye sockets like those of a fleshless skull. The illusion pleased him.

In a husky whisper not loud enough to draw the attention of anyone else in the lounge, but with more urgency than before, he said, 'Lindsey, no!'

He had not anticipated that outburst any more than the previous two, but it did not rattle him. He had quickly adapted to the fact of these mysterious events, and had begun to try to understand them. Nothing could surprise him for long. After all, he had been to Hell and back, both to the real Hell and the one beneath the funhouse, so the intrusion of the fantastic into real life did not frighten or awe him.

He drank a third rum and Coke. When more than an hour passed without further developments, and when the bartender announced the last round of the night, Vassago left.

The need was still with him, the need to murder and create. It was a fierce heat in his gut that had nothing to do with the rum, such a steely tension in his chest that his heart might have been a clockwork mechanism with its spring wound to the breaking point. He wished that he had gone after the doe-eyed woman whom he had named Bambi.

Would he have removed her ears when she was dead at last – or while she was still alive?

Would she have been capable of understanding the artistic statement he was making as he sewed her lips shut over her full mouth? Probably not. None of the others had the wit or insight to appreciate his singular talent.

In the nearly deserted parking lot, he stood in the rain for a while, letting it soak him and extinguish some of the fire of his obsession. It was nearly two in the morning. Not enough time remained, before dawn, to do any hunting. He would have to return to his hideaway without an addition to his collection. If he were to get any sleep during the coming day and be prepared to hunt with the next nightfall, he had to dampen his blazing creative drive.

Eventually he began to shiver. The heat within him gave way to a relentless chill. He raised one hand, touched his cheek. His face felt cold, but his fingers were colder, like the marble hand of a statue of David that he'd admired in a memorial garden at Forest Lawn Cemetery when he had still been one of the living.

That was better.

As he opened the car door, he looked around once more at the rain-riven night. This time of his own volition, he said, 'Lindsey?'

No answer.

Whoever she might be, she was not yet destined to cross his path.

He would have to be patient. He was mystified, therefore fascinated and curious. But whatever was happening would happen at its own pace. One of the virtues of the dead was patience, and though he was still half alive, he knew he could find within himself the strength to match the forbearance of the deceased.

·18·

Early Tuesday morning, an hour after dawn, Lindsey could sleep no more. She ached in every muscle and joint, and what sleep she'd gotten had not lessened her exhaustion by any noticeable degree. She did not want sedatives. Unable to bear any further delay, she insisted they take her to Hatch's room. The charge nurse cleared it with Jonas Nyebern, who was still in the hospital, then wheeled Lindsey down the hall to 518.

Nyebern was there, red-eyed and rumpled. The sheets on the bed nearest the door were not turned back, but they were wrinkled, as if the doctor had stretched out to rest at least once during the night.

By now Lindsey had learned enough about Nyebern – some of it from him, much of it from the nurses – to know that he was a local legend. He had been a busy cardiovascular surgeon, but over the past two years, after losing his wife and two children in some kind of horrible accident, he had devoted steadily less time to surgery and more to resuscitation medicine. His commitment to his work was too strong to be called mere dedication. It was more of an obsession. In a society that was struggling to emerge from three decades of self-indulgence and me-firstism, it was easy to admire a man as selflessly committed as Nyebern, and everyone did seem to admire him.

Lindsey, for one, admired the hell out of him. After all, he had saved Hatch's life.

His weariness betrayed only by his bloodshot eyes and the rumpled condition of his clothes, Nyebern moved swiftly to pull back the privacy curtain that surrounded the bed nearest the window. He took the handles of Lindsey's wheelchair and rolled her to her husband's bedside.

The storm had passed during the night. Morning sun slanted through the slats of the Levolor blinds, striping the sheets and blankets with shadow and golden light.

Hatch lay beneath that faux tiger skin, only one arm and his face exposed. Although his skin was painted with the same jungle-cat camouflage as the bedding, his extreme pallor was evident. Seated in the wheelchair, regarding Hatch at an odd angle through the bed railing, Lindsey grew queasy at the sight of an ugly bruise that spread from the stitched gash on his forehead. But for the proof of the cardiac monitor and the barely perceptible rise-and-fall of Hatch's chest as he breathed, she would have assumed he was dead.

But he was alive, *alive*, and she felt a tightness in her chest and throat that presaged tears as surely as lightning was a sign of oncoming thunder. The prospect of tears surprised her, quickening her breath.

From the moment their Honda had gone over the brink and into the ravine, through the entire physical and emotional ordeal of the night just passed, Lindsey had never cried. She didn't pride herself on stoicism; it was just the way she was.

No, strike that.

It was just the way she had had to become during Jimmy's bout with cancer. From the day of diagnosis until the end, her boy had taken nine months to die, as long as she had taken to lovingly shape him within her womb. Every day of that dying, Lindsey had wanted nothing more than to curl up in bed with the covers over her head and cry, just let the tears pour forth until all the moisture in her body was gone, until she dried up and crumbled into dust and ceased to exist. She *had* wept, at first. But her tears frightened Jimmy, and she realized that any expression of her inner turmoil was an unconscionable self-indulgence. Even when she cried in private, Jimmy knew it later; he had always been perceptive and sensitive beyond his years, and his disease seemed to make him more acutely aware of everything. Current theory of immunology gave considerable weight to the importance of a positive attitude, laughter and confidence as weapons in the battle against life-threatening illness. So she had learned to suppress her terror at the prospect of losing him. She had given him laughter, love, confidence, courage – and never a reason to doubt her conviction that he would beat the malignancy.

By the time Jimmy died, Lindsey had become so successful at repressing her tears that she could not simply turn them on again. Denied the release that easy tears might have given her, she spiraled down into a lost time of despair. She dropped weight – ten pounds, fifteen, twenty – until she was emaciated. She could not be bothered to wash her hair or look after her complexion or press her clothes. Convinced that she had failed Jimmy, that she had encouraged him to rely on her but then had not been special enough to help him reject his disease, she did not believe she deserved to take pleasure from food, from her appearance, a book, a movie, music, from anything. Eventually, with much patience and kindness, Hatch helped her see that her insistence on taking responsibility for an act of blind fate was, in its way, as much a disease as Jimmy's cancer had been.

Though she had still not been able to cry, she had climbed out of the psychological hole she'd dug for herself. Ever since, however, she had lived on the rim of it, her balance precarious.

Now, her first tears in a long, long time were surprising, unsettling. Her eyes stung, became hot. Her vision blurred. Disbelieving, she raised one shaky hand to touch the warm tracks on her cheeks.

Nyebern plucked a Kleenex from a box on the nightstand and gave it to her.

That small kindness affected her far out of proportion to the consideration behind it, and a soft sob escaped her.

'Lindsey . . . '

Because his throat was raw from his ordeal, his voice was hoarse, barely more than a whisper. But she knew at once who had spoken to her, and that it was not Nyebern.

She wiped hastily at her eyes with the Kleenex and leaned forward in the wheelchair until her forehead touched the cold bed railing. Hatch's head was turned toward her. His eyes were open, and they looked clear, alert.

'Lindsey . . . '

He had found the strength to push his right hand out from under the blankets, stretching it toward her.

She reached between the railings. She took his hand in hers.

His skin was dry. A thin bandage was taped over his abraded palm. He was too weak to give her hand more than the faintest squeeze, but he was warm, blessedly warm, and alive.

'You're crying,' Hatch said.

She was, too, harder than ever, a storm of tears, but she was smiling through them. Grief had not been able to free her first tears in five terrible years but joy *had* at last unleashed them. She was crying for joy, which seemed right, seemed healing. She felt a loosening of long-sustained tensions in her heart, as if the knotted adhesions of old wounds were dissolving, all because Hatch was alive, had been dead but was now alive.

If a miracle couldn't lift the heart, what could?

Hatch said, 'I love you.'

The storm of tears became a flood, oh God, an ocean, and she heard herself blubber, 'I love you' back at him, then she felt Nyebern put a hand on her shoulder comfortingly, another small kindness that seemed huge, which only made her cry harder. But she was laughing even as she was weeping, and she saw that Hatch was smiling, too.

'It's okay,' Hatch said hoarsely. 'The worst . . . is over. The worst is . . . behind us now.'

·19·

During the daylight hours, when he stayed beyond the reach of the sun, Vassago parked the Camaro in an underground garage that had once been filled with electric trams, carts, and lorries used by the park-maintenance crew. All of those vehicles were long gone, reclaimed by creditors. The Camaro stood alone in the center of that dank, windowless space.

From the garage, he descended wide stairs – the elevators had not operated in years – to an even deeper subterranean level. The entire park was built on a basement that had once contained the security headquarters with scores of video monitors able to reveal every niche of the grounds, a ride-control center that had been an even more complex high-tech nest of computers and monitors, carpentry and electrical shops, a staff cafeteria, lockers and changing rooms for the hundreds of costumed employees working each

87

shift, an emergency infirmary, business offices, and much more.

Vassago passed the door to that level without hesitating and continued down to the sub-basement at the very bottom of the complex. Even in the dry sands of southern California, the concrete walls exuded a damp lime smell at that depth.

No rats fled before him, as he had expected during his first descent into those realms many months ago. He had seen no rats at all, anywhere, in all the weeks he had roamed the tenebrous corridors and silent rooms of that vast structure, though he would not have been averse to sharing space with them. He liked rats. They were carrion-eaters, revelers in decay, scurrying janitors that cleaned up in the wake of death. Maybe they had never invaded the cellars of the park because, after its closure, the place had been pretty much stripped bare. It was all concrete, plastic, and metal, nothing biodegradable for rats to feed on, a little dusty, yes, with some crumpled paper here and there, but otherwise as sterile as an orbiting space station and of no interest to rodents.

Eventually rats might find his collection in Hell at the bottom of the funhouse and, having fed, spread out from there. Then he would have some suitable company in the bright hours when he could not venture out in comfort.

At the bottom of the fourth and last flight of stairs, two levels below the underground garage, Vassago passed through a doorway. The door was missing, as were virtually all the doors in the complex, hauled off by the salvagers and resold for a few bucks apiece.

Beyond was an eighteen-foot-wide tunnel. The floor was flat with a yellow stripe painted down the center, as if it were a highway – which it had been, of sorts. Concrete walls curved up to meet and form the ceiling.

Part of that lowest level was comprised of storerooms that had once held huge quantities of supplies. Styrofoam cups and burger packages, cardboard popcorn boxes and french-fry holders, paper napkins and little foil packets of ketchup and mustard for the many snack stands scattered over the grounds. Business forms for the offices. Packages of fertilizer and cans of insecticide for the landscape crew. All of that – and everything else a small city might need – had been removed long ago. The rooms were empty.

A network of tunnels connected the storage chambers to elevators that led upward into all the main attractions and restaurants.

Goods could be delivered or repairmen conveyed throughout the park without disturbing the paying customers and shattering the fantasy they had paid to experience. Numbers were painted on the walls every hundred feet, to mark routes, and at intersections there were even signs with arrows to provide better directions:

< HAUNTED HOUSE
< ALPINE CHALET RESTAURANT
COSMIC WHEEL >
BIG FOOT MOUNTAIN >

Vassago turned right at the next intersection, left at the one after that, then right again. Even if his extraordinary vision had not permitted him to see in those obscure byways, he would have been able to follow the route he desired, for by now he knew the desiccated arteries of the dead park as well as he knew the contours of his own body.

Eventually he came to a sign – FUNHOUSE MACHINERY – beside an elevator. The doors of the elevator were gone, as were the cab and the lift mechanism, sold for reuse or for scrap. But the shaft remained, dropping about four feet below the floor of the tunnel, and leading up through five stories of darkness to the level that housed security and ride-control and park offices, on to the lowest level of the funhouse where he kept his collection, then to the second and third floors of that attraction.

He slipped over the edge, into the bottom of the elevator shaft. He sat on the old mattress he had brought in to make his hideaway more comfortable.

When he tilted his head back, he could see only a couple of floors into the unlighted shaft. The rusted steel bars of a service ladder dwindled up into the gloom.

If he climbed the ladder to the lowest level of the funhouse, he would come out in a service room behind the walls of Hell, from which the machinery operating the gondola chain-drive had been accessed and repaired – before it had been carted away forever. A door from that chamber, disguised on the far side as a concrete boulder, opened into the now-dry lake of Hades, from which Lucifer towered.

He was at the deepest point of his hideaway, four feet more than two stories below Hell. There, he felt at home as much as it was possible for him to feel at home anywhere. Out in the world of the living, he moved with the confidence of a secret master of the universe, but he never felt as if he belonged there. Though he was not actually afraid of anything any more, a trace current of anxiety buzzed through him every minute that he spent beyond the stark, black corridors and sepulchral chambers of his hideaway.

After a while he opened the lid of a sturdy plastic cooler with a Styrofoam lining, in which he kept cans of root beer. He had always liked root beer. It was too much trouble to keep ice in the cooler, so he just drank the soda warm. He didn't mind.

He also kept snack foods in the cooler: Mars Bars, Reese's peanut butter cups, Clark Bars, a bag of potato chips, packages of peanut-butter-and-cheese crackers, Mallomars, and Oreo cookies. When he had crossed into the borderland, something had happened to his metabolism; he seemed to be able to eat anything he wanted and burn it off without gaining weight or turning soft. And what he wanted to eat, for some reason he didn't understand, was what he had liked when he'd been a kid.

He opened a root beer and took a long, warm swallow.

He withdrew a single cookie from the bag of Oreos. He carefully separated the two chocolate wafers without damaging them. The circle of white icing stuck entirely to the wafer in his left hand. That meant he was going to be rich and famous when he grew up. If it had stuck to the one in his right hand, it would have meant that he was going to be famous but not necessarily rich, which could mean just about anything from being a rock-'n'-roll star to an assassin who would take out the President of the United States. If some of the icing stuck to both wafers, that meant you had to eat another cookie or risk having no future at all.

As he licked the sweet icing, letting it dissolve slowly on his tongue, he stared up the empty elevator shaft, thinking about how interesting it was that he had chosen the abandoned amusement park for his hideaway when the world offered so many dark and lonely places from which to choose. He had been there a few times as a boy, when the park was still in operation, most recently eight years ago, when he had been twelve, little more than a year before the operation closed down. On that most special evening of his childhood, he had committed his first murder there, beginning his long romance with death. Now he was back.

He licked away the last of the icing.

He ate the first chocolate wafer. He ate the second.

He took another cookie out of the bag.

He sipped the warm root beer.

He wished he were dead. Fully dead. It was the only way to begin his existence on the Other Side.

'If wishes were cows,' he said, 'we'd eat steak every day, wouldn't we?'

He ate the second cookie, finished the root beer, then stretched out on his back to sleep.

Sleeping, he dreamed. They were peculiar dreams of people he had never seen, places he had never been, events that he had never witnessed. Water all around him, chunks of floating ice, snow sheeting through a hard wind. A woman in a wheelchair, laughing and weeping at the same time. A hospital bed, banded by shadows and stripes of golden sunlight. The woman in the wheelchair, laughing and weeping. The woman in the wheelchair, laughing. The woman in the wheelchair. The woman.

Part Two

ALIVE AGAIN

In the fields of life, a harvest
sometimes comes far out of season,
when we thought the earth was old
and could see no earthly reason
to rise for work at break of dawn,
and put our muscles to the test.
With winter here and autumn gone,
it just seems best to rest, to rest.
But under winter fields so cold,
wait the dormant seeds of seasons
unborn, and so the heart does hold
hope that heals all bitter lesions.
In the fields of life, a harvest.

– The Book of Counted Sorrows

FOUR

·1·

Hatch felt as if time had slipped backward to the fourteenth century, as if he were an accused infidel on trial for his life during the Inquisition.

Two priests were present in the attorney's office. Although only of average height, Father Jiminez was as imposing as any man a foot taller, with jet-black hair and eyes even darker, in a black clerical suit with a Roman collar. He stood with his back to the windows. The gently swaying palm trees and blue skies of Newport Beach behind him did not lighten the atmosphere in the mahogany-paneled, antique-filled office where they were gathered, and in silhouette Jiminez was an ominous figure. Father Duran, still in his twenties and perhaps twenty-five years younger than Father Jiminez, was thin, with ascetic features and a pallid complexion. The young priest appeared to be enthralled by a collection of Meiji Period Satsuma vases, incensors, and bowls in a large display case at the far end of the office, but Hatch could not escape the feeling that Duran was faking interest in the Japanese porcelains and was actually furtively observing him and Lindsey where they sat side by side on a Louis XVI sofa.

Two nuns were present, as well, and they seemed, to Hatch, more threatening than the priests. They were of an order that favored the voluminous, old-fashioned habits not seen so often these days. They wore starched wimples, their faces framed in ovals of white linen that made them look especially severe. Sister Immaculata, who was in charge of St Thomas's Home for Children, looked like a great black bird of prey perched on the armchair to the right of the sofa, and Hatch would not have been surprised if she had suddenly let out a screeching cry, leapt into flight with a great flap of her robes, swooped around the room, and dive-bombed him with the intention of pecking off his nose. Her executive assistant was a somewhat younger, intense nun who paced ceaselessly and had a stare more penetrating than a steel-cutting laser beam. Hatch had temporarily forgotten her name and thought of her as The Nun with No Name, because she reminded him of Clint Eastwood playing The Man with No Name in those old spaghetti Westerns.

He was being unfair, more than unfair, a little irrational due to a world-class case of nerves. Everyone in the attorney's office was there to help him and Lindsey. Father Jiminez, the rector of St Thomas's Church, who raised much of the annual budget of the orphanage headed by Sister Immaculata, was really no more ominous than the priest in *Going My Way*, a Latino Bing Crosby, and Father Duran seemed sweet-tempered and shy. In reality, Sister Immaculata looked no more like a bird of prey than she did a stripper, and The Nun with No Name had a genuine and almost constant smile that more than compensated for whatever negative emotions one might choose to read into her piercing stare. The priests and nuns tried to keep a light conversation going; Hatch and Lindsey were, in fact, the ones who were too tense to be as sociable as the situation required.

So much was at stake. That was what made Hatch jumpy, which was unusual, because he was ordinarily the most mellow man to be found outside of the third hour of a beer-drinking contest. He wanted the meeting to go well because his and Lindsey's happiness, their future, the success of their new life, depended on it.

Well, that was not true, either. That was overstating the case again.

He couldn't help it.

Since he had been resuscitated more than seven weeks ago, he and Lindsey had undergone an emotional sea change together. The long, smothering tide of despair, which had rolled over them upon Jimmy's death, abruptly abated. They realized they were still together only by virtue of a medical miracle. Not to be thankful for that reprieve, not to fully enjoy the borrowed time they had been given, would have made them ungrateful to both God and their physicians. More than that – it would have been stupid. They had been right to mourn Jimmy, but somewhere along the way they had allowed grief to degenerate into self-pity and chronic depression, which had not been right at all.

They had needed Hatch's death, reanimation, and Lindsey's near-death to jolt them out of their deplorable habit of gloom, which told him that they were more stubborn than he had thought. The important thing was that they *had* been jolted and were determined to get on with their lives at last.

To both of them, getting on with life meant having a child in the house again. The desire for a child was not a sentimental attempt to recapture the mood of the past, and it wasn't a neurotic need to replace Jimmy in order to finish getting over his death. They were just good with kids; they liked kids; and giving of themselves to a child was enormously satisfying.

They had to adopt. That was the hitch. Lindsey's pregnancy had been troubled, and her labor had been unusually long and painful. Jimmy's birth was a near thing, and when at last he made it into the world, the doctors informed Lindsey that she would not be capable of having any more children.

The Nun with No Name stopped pacing, pulled up the voluminous sleeve of her habit, and looked at her wristwatch. 'Maybe I should go see what's keeping her.'

'Give the child a little more time,' Sister Immaculata said quietly. With one plump white hand, she smoothed the folds of her habit. 'If you go to check on her, she'll feel you don't trust her to be able to take care of herself. There's nothing in the ladies' restroom that she can't deal with herself. I doubt she even had the need to use it. She probably just wanted to be alone a few minutes before the meeting, to settle her nerves.'

To Lindsey and Hatch, Father Jiminez said, 'Sorry about the delay.'

'That's okay,' Hatch said, fidgeting on the sofa. 'We understand. We're a little nervous ourselves.'

Initial inquiries made it clear that a lot – a veritable *army* – of couples were waiting for children to become available for adoption. Some had been kept in suspense for two years. After being childless for five years already, Hatch and Lindsey didn't have the patience to go on the bottom of anyone's waiting list.

They were left with only two options, the first of which was to attempt to adopt a child of another race, black or Asian or Hispanic. Most would-be adoptive parents were white and were waiting for a white baby that might conceivably pass for their own, while countless orphans of various minority groups were destined for institutions and unfulfilled dreams of being part of a family. Skin color meant nothing to either Hatch or Lindsey. They would have been happy with any child regardless of its heritage. But in recent years, misguided do-goodism in the name of civil rights had led to the imposition of an array of new rules and regulations designed to inhibit interracial adoption, and vast government bureaucracies enforced them with mind-numbing exactitude. The theory was that no child could be truly happy if raised outside of its ethnic group, which was the kind of elitist nonsense – and reverse racism – that sociologists and academics formulated without consulting the lonely kids they purported to protect.

The second option was to adopt a disabled child. There were far fewer disabled than minority orphans – even including technical orphans whose parents were alive somewhere but who'd been abandoned to the care of the church or state because of their differentness. On the other hand, though fewer in number, they were in even less demand than minority kids. They had the tremendous advantage of being currently beyond the interest of any pressure group eager to apply politically correct standards to their care and handling. Sooner or later, no doubt, a marching moron army would secure the passage of laws forbidding adoption of a green-eyed, blond, deaf child by anyone but green-eyed, blond, deaf parents, but Hatch and Lindsey had the good fortune to have submitted an application before the forces of chaos had descended.

Sometimes, when he thought about the troublesome bureaucrats they had dealt with six weeks ago, when they had first decided to adopt, he wanted to go back to those agencies and throttle the social workers who had thwarted them, just choke a little common sense into them. And wouldn't the expression of *that* desire make the good nuns and priests of St Thomas's Home eager to commend one of their charges to his care!

'You're still feeling well, no lasting effects from your ordeal, eating well, sleeping well?' Father Jiminez inquired, obviously just to pass the time while they waited for the subject of the meeting to arrive, not meaning to impugn Hatch's claim to a full recovery and good health.

Lindsey – by nature more nervous than Hatch, and usually

more prone to overreaction than he was – leaned forward on the sofa. Just a touch sharply, she said, 'Hatch is at the top of the recovery curve for people who've been resuscitated. Dr Nyebern's ecstatic about him, given him a clean bill of health, totally clean. It was all in our application.'

Trying to soften Lindsey's reaction lest the priests and nuns start to wonder if she was protesting too much, Hatch said, 'I'm terrific, really. I'd recommend a brief death to everyone. It relaxes you, gives you a calmer perspective on life.'

Everyone laughed politely.

In truth, Hatch *was* in excellent health. During the four days following reanimation, he had suffered weakness, dizziness, nausea, lethargy, and some memory lapses. But his strength, memory, and intellectual functions returned one hundred percent. He had been back to normal for almost seven weeks.

Jiminez's casual reference to sleeping habits had rattled Hatch a little, which was probably what had also put Lindsey on edge. He had not been fully honest when he had implied he was sleeping well, but his strange dreams and the curious emotional effects they had on him were not serious, hardly worth mentioning, so he did not feel that he had actually lied to the priest.

They were so close to getting their new life started that he did not want to say the wrong thing and cause any delays. Though Catholic adoption services took considerable care in the placement of children, they were not pointlessly slow and obstructive, as were public agencies, especially when the would-be adopters were solid members of the community like Hatch and Lindsey, and when the adoptee was a disabled child with no option except continued institutionalization. The future could begin for them this week, as long as they gave the folks from St Thomas's, who were already on their side, no reason to reconsider.

Hatch was a little surprised by the piquancy of his desire to be a father again. He felt as if he had been only half-alive, at best, during the past five years. Now suddenly all the unused energies of that half-decade flooded into him, overcharging him, making colors more vibrant and sounds more melodious and feelings more intense, filling him with a passion to go, do, see, *live*. And be somebody's dad again.

'I was wondering if I could ask you something,' Father Duran said to Hatch, turning away from the Satsuma collection. His wan complexion and sharp features were enlivened by owlish eyes, full of warmth and intelligence, enlarged by thick glasses. 'It's a little personal, which is why I hesitate.'

'Oh, sure, anything,' Hatch said.

The young priest said, 'Some people who've been clinically dead for short periods of time, a minute or two, report . . . well . . . a certain similar experience.'

'A sense of rushing through a tunnel with an awesome light at the far end,' Hatch said, 'a feeling of great peace, of going home at last?'

'Yes,' Duran said, his pale face brightening. 'That's what I meant exactly.'

Father Jiminez and the nuns were looking at Hatch with new interest, and he wished he could tell them what they wanted to hear. He glanced at Lindsey on the sofa beside him, then around at the assemblage, and said, 'I'm sorry, but I didn't have the experience so many people have reported.'

Father Duran's thin shoulders sagged a little. 'Then what *did* you experience?'

Hatch shook his head. 'Nothing. I wish I had. It would be . . . comforting, wouldn't it? But in that sense, I guess I had a boring death. I don't remember anything whatsoever from the time I was knocked out when the car rolled over until I woke up hours later in a hospital bed, looking at rain beating on a windowpane—'

He was interrupted by the arrival of Salvatore Gujilio in whose office they were waiting. Gujilio, a huge man, heavy and tall, swung the door wide and entered as he always did – taking big strides instead of ordinary steps, closing the door behind him in a grand sweeping gesture. With the unstoppable determination of a force of nature – rather like a disciplined tornado – he swept around the room, greeting them one by one. Hatch would not have been surprised to see furniture spun aloft and artwork flung off walls as the attorney passed, for he seemed to radiate enough energy to levitate anything within his immediate sphere of influence.

Keeping up a continuous line of patter, Gujilio gave Jiminez a bear hug, shook hands vigorously with Duran, and bowed to each of the nuns with the sincerity of a passionate monarchist greeting members of the royal family. Gujilio bonded with people as quickly as one piece of pottery to another under the influence of

Super Glue, and by their second meeting he'd greeted and said goodbye to Lindsey with a hug. She liked the man and didn't mind the hugging, but as she had told Hatch, she felt like a very small child embracing a sumo wrestler. 'He lifts me off my feet, for God's sake,' she'd said. Now she stayed on the sofa instead of rising, and merely shook hands with the attorney.

Hatch rose and extended his right hand, prepared to see it engulfed as if it were a speck of food in a culture dish filled with hungry amoebas, which is exactly what happened. Gujilio, as always, took Hatch's hand in both of his, and since each of his mitts was half-again the size of any ordinary man's, it wasn't so much a matter of shaking as being shaken.

'What a wonderful day,' Gujilio said, 'a special day. I hope for everyone's sake it goes as smooth as glass.'

The attorney donated a certain number of hours a week to St Thomas's Church and the orphanage. He appeared to take great satisfaction in connecting adoptive parents with disabled kids.

'Regina's on her way from the ladies,' Gujilio told them. 'She stopped to chat a moment with my receptionist, that's all. She's nervous, I think, trying to delay a little longer until she has her courage screwed up as far as it'll go. She'll be here in a moment.'

Hatch looked at Lindsey. She smiled nervously and took his hand.

'Now, you understand,' Salvatore Gujilio said, looming over them like one of those giant balloons in a Macy's Thanksgiving Day parade, 'that the point of this meeting is for you to get to know Regina and for her to get to know you. Nobody makes a decision right here, today. You go away, think about it, and let us know tomorrow or the day after whether this is the one. The same goes for Regina. She has a day to think about it.'

'It's a big step,' Father Jiminez said.

'An enormous step,' Sister Immaculata concurred.

Squeezing Hatch's hand, Lindsey said, 'We understand.'

The Nun with No Name went to the door, opened it, and peered down the hallway. Evidently Regina was not in sight.

Rounding his desk, Gujilio said, 'She's coming, I'm sure.'

The attorney settled his considerable bulk into the executive office chair beside his desk, but because he was six feet five, he seemed almost as tall seated as standing. The office was furnished entirely with antiques, and the desk was actually a Napoleon III table so fine that Hatch wished he had something like it in the front window of his shop. Banded by ormolu, the exotic woods of the marquetry top depicted a central cartouche with a detailed musical trophy over a conforming frieze of stylized foliage. The whole was raised on circular legs with acanthus-leaf ormolu joined by a voluted X stretcher centered with an ormolu urn finial, on toupie feet. At every meeting, Gujilio's size and dangerous levels of kinetic energy initially made the desk – and all the antiques – seem fragile, in imminent jeopardy of being knocked over or to smithereens. But after a few minutes, he and the room seemed in such perfect harmony, you had the eerie feeling that he had re-created a decor he had lived with in another – thinner – life.

A soft, distant, but peculiar *thud* drew Hatch's attention away from the attorney and the desk.

The Nun with No Name turned from the door and hurried back into the room, saying, 'Here she comes,' as if she didn't want Regina to think she had been looking for her.

The sound came again. Then again. And again.

It was rhythmic and getting louder.

Thud. Thud.

Lindsey's hand tightened on Hatch's.

Thud. Thud!

Someone seemed to be keeping time to an unheard tune by rapping a lead pipe against the hardwood floor of the hallway beyond the door.

Puzzled, Hatch looked at Father Jiminez, who was staring at the floor, shaking his head, his state of mind not easy to read. As the sound grew louder and closer, Father Duran stared at the half-open hall door with astonishment, as did The Nun with No Name. Salvatore Gujilio rose from his chair, looking alarmed. Sister Immaculata's pleasantly ruddy cheeks were now as white as the linen band that framed her face.

Hatch became aware of a softer scraping between each of the hard sounds.

Thud! Sccccuuuurrrr . . . Thud! Sccccuuuurrrr . . .

As the sounds grew nearer, their effect rapidly increased, until Hatch's mind was filled with images from a hundred old horror films: the-thing-from-out-of-the-lagoon hitching crablike toward its prey; the-thing-from-out-of-the-crypt shuffling along a grave-yard path under a gibbous moon; the-thing-from-another-world

102

propelling itself on God-knows-what sort of arachnoid-reptilian-horned feet.

THUD!

The windows seemed to rattle.

Or was that his imagination?

Sccccuuuurrrr . . .

A shiver went up his spine.

THUD!

He looked around at the alarmed attorney, the head-shaking priest, the wide-eyed younger priest, the two pale nuns, then quickly back at the half-open door, wondering just exactly what sort of disability this child had been born with, half expecting a startlingly tall and twisted figure to appear with a surprising resemblance to Charles Laughton in *The Hunchback of Notre Dame* and a grin full of fangs, whereupon Sister Immaculata would turn to him and say, *You see, Mr Harrison, Regina came under the care of the good sisters at Saint Thomas's not from ordinary parents but from a laboratory where the scientists are doing some really interesting genetic research* . . .

A shadow tilted across the threshold.

Hatch realized that Lindsey's grip on his hand had become downright painful. And his palm was damp with sweat.

The weird sounds stopped. A hush of expectation had fallen over the room.

Slowly the door to the hall was pushed all the way open.

Regina took a single step inside. She dragged her right leg as if it were a dead weight: *Sccccuuuurrrr.* Then she slammed it down: *THUD!*

She stopped to look around at everyone. Challengingly.

Hatch found it difficult to believe that she had been the source of all that ominous noise. She was small for a ten-year-old girl, a bit shorter and more slender than the average kid her age. Her freckles, pert nose, and beautiful deep auburn hair thoroughly disqualified her for the role of the-thing-from-the-lagoon or any other shudder-making creature, although there was something in her solemn gray eyes that Hatch did not expect to see in the eyes of a child. An adult awareness. A heightened perceptiveness. But for those eyes and an aura of iron determination, the girl seemed fragile, almost frighteningly delicate and vulnerable.

Hatch was reminded of an exquisite eighteenth-century

Mandarin-pattern Chinese export porcelain bowl currently for sale in his Laguna Beach shop. It rang as sweetly as any bell when pinged with one finger, raising the expectation that it would shatter into thousands of pieces if struck hard or dropped. But when you studied the bowl as it stood on an acrylic display base, the hand-painted temple and garden scenes portrayed on its sides and the floral designs on its inner rim were of such high quality and possessed such power that you became acutely aware of the piece's age, the weight of the history behind it. And you were soon convinced, in spite of its appearance, that it would bounce when dropped, cracking whatever surface it struck but sustaining not even a small chip itself.

Aware that the moment was hers and hers alone, Regina hitched toward the sofa where Hatch and Lindsey waited, making less noise as she limped off the hardwood floor onto the antique Persian carpet. She was wearing a white blouse, a Kelly-green skirt that fell two inches above her knees, green kneesocks, black shoes – and on her right leg a metal brace that extended from the ankle to above the knee and looked like a medieval torture device. Her limp was so pronounced that she rocked from side to side at the hips with each step, as if in danger of toppling over.

Sister Immaculata rose from her armchair, scowling at Regina in disapproval. 'Exactly what is the reason for these theatrics, young lady?'

Ignoring the true meaning of the nun's question, the girl said, 'I'm sorry I'm so late, Sister. But some days it's harder for me than others.' Before the nun could respond, the girl turned to Hatch and Lindsey, who had stopped holding hands and had risen from the sofa. 'Hi, I'm Regina. I'm a cripple.'

She reached out in greeting. Hatch reached out, too, before he realized that her right arm and hand were not well formed. The arm was almost normal, just a little thinner than her left, until it got to the wrist, where the bones took an odd twist. Instead of a full hand, she possessed just two fingers and the stub of a thumb that all seemed to have limited flexibility. Shaking hands with the girl felt strange – distinctly strange – but not unpleasant.

Her gray eyes were fixed intently on his, trying to read his reaction. He knew at once that it would be impossible ever to conceal true feelings from her, and he was relieved that he had not been in the least repelled by her deformity.

'I'm so happy to meet you, Regina,' he said. 'I'm Hatch Harrison, and this is my wife Lindsey.'

The girl turned to Lindsey and shook hands with her as well, saying, 'Well, I know I'm a disappointment. You child-starved women usually prefer babies young enough to cuddle—'

The Nun with No Name gasped in shock. 'Regina, really!'

Sister Immaculata looked too apoplectic to speak, like a penguin that had frozen solid, mouth agape and eyes bulging in protest, hit by a chill too cold even for arctic birds to survive.

Approaching from the windows, Father Jiminez said, 'Mr and Mrs Harrison, I apologize for—'

'No need to apologize for anything,' Lindsey said quickly, evidently sensing, as Hatch did, that the girl was testing them and that to have any hope of passing the test, they must not let themselves be co-opted into an adults-against-the-kid division of sympathies.

Regina hopped-squirmed-wriggled into the second armchair, and Hatch was fairly certain she was making herself appear a lot more awkward than she really was.

The Nun with No Name gently touched Sister Immaculata on the shoulder, and the older nun eased back into her chair, still with the frozen-penguin look. The two priests brought the client chairs from in front of the attorney's desk, and the younger nun pulled up a side chair from a corner, so they could all join the group. Hatch realized he was the only one still standing. He sat on the sofa beside Lindsey again.

Now that everyone had arrived, Salvatore Gujilio insisted on serving refreshments – Pepsi, ginger ale, or Perrier – which he did without calling for the assistance of his secretary, fetching everything from a wet bar discreetly tucked into one mahogany-paneled corner of the genteel office. As the attorney bustled about, quiet and quick in spite of his bulk, never crashing into a piece of furniture or knocking over a vase, never coming even close to obliterating one of the two Tiffany lamps with handblown trumpet-flower shades, Hatch realized that the big man was no longer an overpowering figure, no longer the inevitable center of attention: he could not compete with the girl, who was probably less than one-fourth his size.

'Well,' Regina said to Hatch and Lindsey, as she accepted a

glass of Pepsi from Gujilio, holding it in her left hand, the good one, 'you came here to learn all about me, so I guess I should tell you about myself. First thing, of course, is that I'm a cripple.' She tilted her head and looked at them quizzically. 'Did you know I was a cripple?'

'We do now,' Lindsey said.

'But I mean, before you came.'

'We knew you had – some sort of problem,' Hatch said.

'Mutant genes,' Regina said.

Father Jiminez let out a heavy sigh.

Sister Immaculata seemed about to say something, glanced at Hatch and Lindsey, then decided to remain silent.

'My parents were dope fiends,' the girl said.

'Regina!' The Nun with No Name protested. 'You don't know that for sure, you don't know any such a thing.'

'Well, it figures,' the girl said. 'For at least twenty years now, illegal drugs have been the cause of most birth defects. Did you know that? I read it in a book. I read a lot. I'm book crazy. I don't want to say I'm a bookworm. That sounds icky – don't you think? But if I were a worm, I'd rather be curled up in a book than in any apple. It's good for a crippled kid to like books, because *they* won't let you do the things ordinary people do, even if you're pretty sure you can do them, so books are like having a whole other life. I like adventure stories where they go to the North Pole or Mars or New York or somewhere. I like good mysteries, too, most anything by Agatha Christie, but I especially like stories about animals, and most especially about talking animals like in *The Wind in the Willows*. I had a talking animal once. It was just a goldfish, and of course it was really me not the fish who talked, because I read this book on ventriloquism and learned to throw my voice, which is neat. So I'd sit across the room and throw my voice into the goldfish bowl.' She began to talk squeakily, without moving her lips, and the voice seemed to come out of The Nun with No Name: '*Hi, my name's Binky the Fish, and if you try to put me in a sandwich and eat me, I'll shit on the mayonnaise.*' She returned to her normal voice and talked right over the flurry of reactions from the religiosities around her. 'There you have another problem with cripples like me. We tend to be smart-mouthed sometimes because we know nobody has the guts to whack us on the ass.'

106

Sister Immaculata looked as if *she* might have the guts, but in fact all she did was mumble something about no TV privileges for a week.

Hatch, who had found the nun as frightening as a pterodactyl when he'd first met her, was not impressed by her glower now, even though it was so intense that he registered it with his peripheral vision. He could not take his eyes off the girl.

Regina went blithely on without pause: 'Besides being smart-mouthed sometimes, what you should know about me is, I'm so clumsy, hitching around like Long John Silver – now *there* was a good book – that I'll probably break everything of value in your house. Never meaning to, of course. It'll be a regular destruction derby. Do you have the patience for that? I'd hate to be beaten senseless and locked in the attic just because I'm a poor crippled girl who can't always control herself. This leg doesn't look so bad, really, and if I keep exercising it, I think it's going to turn out pretty enough, but I don't really have much strength in it, and I don't feel too damned much in it, either.' She balled up her deformed right hand and smacked it so hard against the thigh of her right leg that she startled Gujilio, who was trying to convey a ginger ale into the hand of the younger priest, who was staring at the girl as if mesmerized. She smacked herself again, so hard that Hatch winced. She said, 'You see? Dead meat. Speaking of meat, I'm also a fussy eater. I simply can't stomach dead meat. Oh, I don't mean I eat live animals. What I am is, I'm a vegetarian, which makes things harder for you, even supposing you didn't mind that I'm not a cuddly baby you can dress up cute. My only virtue is that I'm very bright, practically a genius. But even that's a drawback as far as some people are concerned. I'm smart beyond my years, so I don't act much like a child—'

'You're certainly acting like one now,' Sister Immaculata said, and seemed pleased at getting in that zinger.

But Regina ignored it: '—and what you want, after all, is a child, a precious and ignorant blob, so you can show her the world, have the fun of watching her learn and blossom, whereas I have already done a lot of my blossoming. Intellectual blossoming, that is. I still don't have boobs. I'm also bored by TV, which means I wouldn't be able to join in a jolly family evening around the tube, and I'm allergic to cats in case you've got one, and I'm opinionated, which some people find infuriating in a ten-year-old

107

girl.' She paused, sipped her Pepsi, and smiled at them. 'There. I think that pretty much covers it.'

'She's never like this,' Father Jiminez mumbled, more to himself or to God than to Hatch and Lindsey. He tossed back half of his Perrier as if chugging hard liquor.

Hatch turned to Lindsey. Her eyes were a little glazed. She didn't seem to know what to say, so he returned his attention to the girl. 'I suppose it's only fair if I tell you something about us.'

Putting aside her drink and starting to get up, Sister Immaculata said, 'Really, Mr Harrison, you don't have to put yourself through—'

Politely waving the nun back into her seat, Hatch said, 'No, no. It's all right. Regina's a little nervous – '

'Not particularly,' she said.

'Of course, you are,' Hatch said.

'No, I'm not.'

'A little nervous,' Hatch insisted, 'just as Lindsey and I are. It's okay.' He smiled at the girl as winningly as he could. 'Well, let's see . . . I've had a lifelong interest in antiques, an affection for things that endure and have real character about them, and I have my own antique shop with two employees. That's how I earn my living. I don't like television much myself or – '

'What kind of a name is Hatch?' the girl interrupted. She giggled as if to imply that it was too funny to be the name of anyone except, perhaps, a talking goldfish.

'My full first name is Hatchford.'

'It's still funny.'

'Blame my mother,' Hatch said. 'She always thought my dad was going to make a lot of money and move us up in society, and she thought Hatchford sounded like a really upper-crust name: Hatchford Benjamin Harrison. The only thing that would've made it a better name in her mind was if it was Hatchford Benjamin Rockefeller.'

'Did he?' the girl asked.

'Who he, did what?'

'Did your father make a lot of money?'

Hatch winked broadly at Lindsey and said, 'Looks like we have a golddigger on our hands.'

'If you were rich,' the girl said, 'of course, that would be a consideration.'

Sister Immaculata let a hiss of air escape between her teeth, and The Nun with No Name leaned back in her chair and closed her eyes with an expression of resignation. Father Jiminez got up and, waving Gujilio away, went to the wet bar to get something stronger than Perrier, Pepsi, or ginger ale. Because neither Hatch nor Lindsey seemed obviously offended by the girl's behavior, none of the others felt authorized to terminate the interview or even further reprimand the child.

'I'm afraid we're not rich,' Hatch told her. 'Comfortable, yes. We don't want for anything. But we don't drive a Rolls-Royce, and we don't wear caviar pajamas.'

A flicker of genuine amusement crossed the girl's face, but she quickly suppressed it. She looked at Lindsey and said, 'What about you?'

Lindsey blinked. She cleared her throat. 'Uh, well, I'm an artist. A painter.'

'Like Picasso?'

'Not that style, no, but an artist like him, yes.'

'I saw a picture once of a bunch of dogs playing poker,' the girl said. 'Did you paint that?'

Lindsey said, 'No, I'm afraid I didn't.'

'Good. It was stupid. I saw a picture once of a bull and a bullfighter, it was on velvet, very bright colors. Do you paint in very bright colors on velvet?'

'No,' Lindsey said. 'But if you like that sort of thing, I could paint any scene you wanted on velvet for your room.'

Regina crinkled up her face. 'Puh-leeese. I'd rather put a dead cat on the wall.'

Nothing surprised the folks from St Thomas's any more. The younger priest actually smiled, and Sister Immaculata murmured 'dead cat,' not in exasperation but as if agreeing that such a bit of macabre decoration would, indeed, be preferable to a painting on velvet.

'My style,' Lindsey said, eager to rescue her reputation after offering to paint something so tacky, 'is generally described as a blending of neoclassicism and surrealism. I know that's quite a big mouthful—'

'Well, it's not my favorite sort of thing,' Regina said, as if she had a hoot-owl's idea in hell what those styles were like and what a blend of them might resemble. 'If I came to live with you, and if

I had a room of my own, you wouldn't make me hang a lot of *your* paintings on my walls, would you?' The 'your' was emphasized in such a way as to imply that she still preferred a dead cat even if velvet was not involved.

'Not a one,' Lindsey assured her.

'Good.'

'Do you think you might like living with us?' Lindsey asked, and Hatch wondered whether that prospect excited or terrified her.

Abruptly the girl struggled up from the chair, wobbling as she reached her feet, as if she might topple headfirst into the coffee table. Hatch rose, ready to grab her, even though he suspected it was all part of the act.

When she regained her balance, she put down her glass, from which she'd drunk all the Pepsi, and she said, 'I've got to go pee, I've got a weak bladder. Part of my mutant genes. I can never hold myself. Half the time I feel like I'm going to burst in the most embarrassing places, like right here in Mr Gujilio's office, which is another thing you should probably consider before taking me into your home. You probably have a lot of nice things, being in the antiques and art business, nice things you wouldn't want messed up, and here I am lurching into everything and breaking it or, worse, I get a bursting bladder attack all over something price-less. Then you'd ship me back to the orphanage, and I'd be so emotional about it, I'd clump up to the roof and throw myself off, a most tragic suicide, which none of us really would want to see happen. Nice meeting you.'

She turned and wrenched herself across the Persian carpet and out of the room in that most unlikely gait – *Sccccuuuurrr . . . THUD!* – which no doubt sprang from the same well of talent out of which she had drawn her goldfish ventriloquism. Her deep-auburn hair swayed and glinted like fire.

They all stood in silence, listening to the girl's slowly fading footsteps. At one point, she bumped against the wall with a solid *thunk!* that must have hurt, then bravely scrape-thudded onward.

'She does *not* have a weak bladder,' Father Jiminez said, taking a swallow from a glassful of amber liquid. He seemed to be drinking bourbon now. 'That is *not* part of her disability.'

'She's not really like that,' Father Duran said, blinking his owlish eyes as if smoke had gotten in them. 'She's a delightful child. I know that's hard for you to believe right now—'

110

'And she can walk much better than that, immeasurably better,' said The Nun with No Name. 'I don't know what's gotten into her.'

'I do,' Sister Immaculata said. She wiped one hand wearily down her face. Her eyes were sad. 'Two years ago, when she was eight, we managed to place her with adoptive parents. A couple in their thirties who were told they could never have children of their own. They convinced themselves that a disabled child would be a special blessing. Then, two weeks after Regina went to live with them, while they were in the pre-adoption trial phase, the woman became pregnant. Suddenly they were going to have their own child, after all, and the adoption didn't seem so wise.'

'And they just brought Regina back?' Lindsey asked. 'Just dumped her at the orphanage? How terrible.'

'I can't judge them,' Sister Immaculata said. 'They may have felt they didn't have enough love for a child of their own and poor Regina, too, in which case they did the right thing. Regina doesn't deserve to be raised in a home where every minute of every day she knows she's second best, second in love, something of an outsider. Anyway, she was broken up by the rejection. She took a long time to get her self-confidence back. And now I think she doesn't want to take another risk.'

They stood in silence.

The sun was very bright beyond the windows. The palm trees swayed lazily. Between the trees lay glimpses of Fashion Island, the Newport Beach shopping center and business complex at the perimeter of which Gujilio's office was located.

'Sometimes, with the sensitive ones, a bad experience ruins any chance for them. They refuse to try again. I'm afraid our Regina is one of those. She came in here determined to alienate you and wreck the interview, and she succeeded in singular style.'

'It's like somebody who's been in prison all his life,' said Father Jiminez, 'gets paroled, is all excited at first, then finds he can't make it on the outside. So he commits a crime just to get back in. The institution might be limiting, unsatisfying – but it's known, it's safe.'

Salvatore Gujilio bustled around, relieving people of their empty glasses. He was still an enormous man by any standard, but even with Regina gone from the room, Gujilio no longer dominated it as he had done before. He had been forever diminished by that single comparison with the delicate, pert-nosed, gray-eyed child.

'I'm so sorry,' Sister Immaculata said, putting a consoling hand on Lindsey's shoulder. 'We'll try again, my dear. We'll go back to square one and match you up with another child, the perfect child this time.'

·2·

Lindsey and Hatch left Salvatore Gujilio's office at ten past three that Thursday afternoon. They had agreed not to talk about the interview until dinner, giving themselves time to contemplate the encounter and examine their reactions to it. Neither wanted to make a decision based on emotion, or influence the other to act on initial impressions – then live to regret it.

Of course, they had never expected the meeting to progress remotely along the lines it had gone. Lindsey was eager to talk about it. She assumed that their decision was already made, had been made for them by the girl, and that there was no point in further contemplation. But they had agreed to wait, and Hatch did not seem disposed to violate that agreement, so she kept her mouth shut as well.

She drove their new sporty-red Mitsubishi. Hatch sat in the passenger seat with his shades on, one arm out his open window, tapping time against the side of the car as he listened to golden oldie rock-'n'-roll on the radio: 'Please Mister Postman' by the Marvelettes.

She passed the last of the giant date palms along Newport Center Drive and turned left onto Pacific Coast Highway, past vine-covered walls, and headed south. The late-April day was warm but not hot, with one of those intensely blue skies that, toward sunset, would acquire an electric luminescence remi-niscent of skies in Maxfield Parrish paintings. Traffic was light on the Coast Highway, and the ocean glimmered like a great swatch of silver- and gold-sequined cloth.

A quiet exuberance flowed through Lindsey, as it had done for seven weeks. It was exhilaration over just being alive, which was in every child but which most adults lost during the process of grow-ing up. She'd lost it, too, without realizing. A close encounter with death was just the thing to give you back the *joie de vivre* of extreme youth.

★ ★ ★

More than two floors below Hell, naked beneath a blanket on his stained and sagging mattress, Vassago passed the daylight hours in sleep. His slumber was usually filled with dreams of violated flesh and shattered bone, blood and bile, vistas of human skulls. Sometimes he dreamed of dying multitudes writhing in agony on barren ground beneath a black sky, and he walked among them as a prince of Hell among the common rabble of the damned.

The dreams that occupied him on that day, however, were strange and remarkable for their ordinariness. A dark-haired, dark-eyed woman in a cherry-red car, viewed from the perspective of an unseen man in the passenger seat beside her. Palm trees. Red bougainvillea. The ocean spangled with light.

★ ★ ★

Harrison's Antiques was at the south end of Laguna Beach, on Pacific Coast Highway. It was in a stylish two-story Art Deco building that contrasted interestingly with the eighteenth- and nineteenth-century merchandise in the big display windows.

Glenda Dockridge, Hatch's assistant and the store manager, was helping Lew Booner, their general handyman, with the dusting. In a large antique store, dusting was akin to the painting of the Golden Gate Bridge: once you reached the far end, it was time to come back to the beginning and start all over again. Glenda was in a great mood because she had sold a Napoleon III ormolu-mounted black-lacquered cabinet with Japanned panels *and*, to the same customer, a nineteenth-century Italian polygonal, tilt-top table with elaborate marquetry inlay. They were excellent sales – especially considering that she worked on salary against a commission.

While Hatch looked through the day's mail, attended to some correspondence, and examined a pair of eighteenth-century rose-wood palace pedestals with inlaid jade dragons that had arrived from a scout in Hong Kong, Lindsey helped Glenda and Lew with the dusting. In her new frame of mind, even that chore was a pleasure. It gave her a chance to appreciate the details of the antiques – the turn of a finial on a bronze lamp, the carving on a table leg, the delicately pierced and hand-finished rims on a set of eighteenth-century English porcelains. Contemplating the history and cultural meaning of each piece as she happily dusted it, she realized that her new attitude had a distinctly Zen quality.

★　★　★

At twilight, sensing the approach of night, Vassago woke and sat up in the approximation of a grave that was his home. He was filled with a hunger for death and a need to kill.

The last image he remembered from his dream was of the woman from the red car. She was not in the car any more, but in a chamber he could not quite see, standing in front of a Chinese screen, wiping it with a white cloth. She turned, as if he had spoken to her, and she smiled.

Her smile was so radiant, so full of life, that Vassago wanted to smash her face in with a hammer, break out her teeth, shatter her jaw bones, make it impossible for her to smile ever again.

He had dreamed of her two or three times over the past several weeks. The first time she had been in a wheelchair, weeping and laughing simultaneously.

Again, he searched his memory, but he could not recall her face among those he had ever seen outside of dreams. He wondered who she was and why she visited him when he slept.

Outside, night fell. He sensed it coming down. A great black drape that gave the world a preview of death at the end of every bright and shining day.

He dressed and left his hideaway.

★　★　★

By seven o'clock that early-spring night, Lindsey and Hatch were at Zov's, a small but busy restaurant in Tustin. The decor was mainly black and white, with lots of big windows and mirrors. The staff, unfailingly friendly and efficient, were dressed in black and white to complement the long room. The food they served was such a perfect sensual experience that the monochromatic bistro seemed ablaze with color.

114

The noise level was congenial rather than annoying. They did not have to raise their voices to hear each other, and felt as if the background buzz provided a screen of privacy from nearby tables. Through the first two courses – calamari; black-bean soup – they spoke of trivial things. But when the main course was served – swordfish for both of them – Lindsey could no longer contain herself.

She said, 'Okay, all right, we've had all day to brood about it. We haven't colored each other's opinions. So what do you think of Regina?'

'What do *you* think of Regina?'

'You first.'

'Why me?'

Lindsey said, 'Why not?'

He took a deep breath, hesitated. 'I'm crazy about the kid.'

Lindsey felt like leaping up and doing a little dance, the way a cartoon character might express uncontainable delight, because her joy and excitement were brighter and bolder than things were supposed to be in real life. She had hoped for just that reaction from him, but she hadn't known what he would say, really hadn't had a clue, because the meeting had been . . . well, one apt word would be 'daunting.'

'Oh, God, I love her,' Lindsey said. 'She's so sweet.'

'She's a tough cookie.'

'That's an act.'

'She was putting on an act for us, yeah, but she's tough just the same. She's had to be tough. Life didn't give her a choice.'

'But it's a good tough.'

'It's a great tough,' he agreed. 'I'm not saying it put me off. I admired it, I loved her.'

'She's so bright.'

'Struggling so hard to make herself unappealing,' Hatch said, 'and that only made her *more* appealing.'

'The poor kid. Afraid of being rejected again, so she took the offensive.'

'When I heard her coming down the hall, I thought it was—'

'Godzilla!' Lindsey said.

'At least. And how'd you like Binky the talking goldfish?'

'Shit on the mayonnaise!' Lindsey said.

They both laughed, and people around them turned to look,

115

either because of their laughter or because some of what Lindsey said was overheard, which only made them laugh harder.

'She's going to be a handful,' Hatch said.

'She'll be a dream.'

'Nothing's that easy.'

'*She* will be.'

'One problem.'

'What's that?'

He hesitated. 'What if she doesn't want to come with us?'

Lindsey's smile froze. 'She will. She'll come.'

'Maybe not.'

'Don't be negative.'

'I'm only saying we've got to be prepared for disappointment.'

Lindsey shook her head adamantly. 'No. It's going to work out. It has to. We've had more than our share of bad luck, bad times. We deserve better. The wheel has turned. We're going to put a family together again. Life is going to be good, it's going to be so fine. The worst is behind us now.'

·3·

That Thursday night, Vassago enjoyed the conveniences of a motel room.

Usually he used one of the fields behind the abandoned amusement park as a toilet. He also washed each evening with bottled water and liquid soap. He shaved with a straight razor, an aerosol can of lather, and a piece of a broken mirror that he had found in a corner of the park.

When rain fell at night, he liked to bathe in the open, letting the downpour sluice over him. If lightning accompanied the storm, he sought the highest point on the paved midway, hoping that he was about to receive the grace of Satan and be recalled to the land of the dead by one scintillant bolt of electricity. But the rainy season in southern California was over now, and most likely would not come around again until December. If he earned his way back into the fold of the dead and damned before then, the means of his deliverance from the hateful world of the living would be some other force than lightning.

Once a week, sometimes twice, he rented a motel room to use

the shower and make a better job of grooming than he could in the primitive conditions of his hideaway, though not because hygiene was important to him. Filth had its powerful attractions. The air and water of Hades, to which he longed to return, were filth of infinite variety. But if he was to move among the living and prey upon them, building the collection that might win him readmission to the realm of the damned, there were certain conventions that had to be followed in order not to draw undue attention to himself. Among them was a certain degree of cleanliness.

Vassago always used the same motel, the Blue Skies, a seedy hole toward the southern end of Santa Ana, where the unshaven desk clerk accepted only cash, asked for no identification, and never looked guests in the eyes, as if afraid of what he might see in theirs or they in his. The area was a swamp of drug dealers and streetwalkers. Vassago was one of the few men who did not check in with a whore in tow. He stayed only an hour or two, however, which was in keeping with the duration of the average customer's use of the accommodations, and he was allowed the same anonymity as those who, grunting and sweating, noisily rocked the headboards of their beds against the walls in rooms adjoining his.

He could not have lived there full time, if only because his awareness of the frenzied coupling of the sluts and their johns filled him with anger, anxiety, and nausea at the urgent needs and frenetic rhythms of the living. The atmosphere made it difficult to think clearly and impossible to rest, even though the perversion and dementia of the place was the very thing in which he had reveled when he had been one of the fully alive.

No other motel or boarding house would have been safe. They would have wanted identification. Besides, he could pass among the living as one of them only as long as their contact with him was casual. Any motel clerk or landlord who took a deeper interest in his character and encountered him repeatedly would soon realize that he was different from them in some indefinable yet deeply disturbing way.

Anyway, to avoid drawing attention to himself, he preferred the amusement park as primary quarters. The authorities looking for him would be less likely to find him there than anywhere else. Most important, the park offered solitude, graveyard stillness, and regions of perfect darkness to which he could escape during

117

daylight hours when his sensitive eyes could not tolerate the insistent brightness of the sun.

Motels were tolerable only between dusk and dawn.

That pleasantly warm Thursday night, when he came out of the Blue Skies Motel office with his room key, he noticed a familiar Pontiac parked in shadows at the back of the lot, beyond the end unit, not nose-in to the motel but facing the office. The car had been there on Sunday, the last time Vassago had used the Blue Skies. A man was slumped behind the wheel, as if sleeping or just passing time while he waited for someone to meet him. He had been there Sunday night, features veiled by the night and the haze of reflected light on his windshield.

Vassago drove the Camaro to unit six, about in the middle of the long arm of the L-shaped structure, parked in front, and let himself into his room. He carried only a change of clothes – all black like the clothes he was wearing.

Inside the room, he did not turn on the light. He never did.

For a while he stood with his back against the door, thinking about the Pontiac and the man behind the steering wheel. He might have been just a drug dealer working out of his car. The number of dealers crawling the neighborhood was even greater than the number of cockroaches swarming inside the walls of that decaying motel. But where were his customers with their quick nervous eyes and greasy wads of money?

Vassago dropped his clothes on the bed, put his sunglasses in his jacket pocket, and went into the small bathroom. It smelled of hastily sloshed disinfectant that could not mask a melange of vile biological odors.

A rectangle of pale light marked a window above the back wall of the shower. Sliding open the glass door, which made a scraping noise as it moved along the corroded track, he stepped into the stall. If the window had been fixed, or if it had been divided vertically into two panes, he would have been foiled. But it swung outward from the top on rusted hinges. He gripped the sill above his head, pulled himself through the window, and wriggled out into the service alley behind the motel.

He paused to put on his sunglasses again. A nearby sodium-vapor streetlamp cast a urine-yellow glare that scratched like windblown sand at his eyes. The glasses mellowed it to a muddy amber and clarified his vision.

He went right, all the way to the end of the block, turned right on the side street, then right again at the next corner, circling the motel. He slipped around the end of the short wing of the L-shaped building and moved along the covered walkway in front of the last units until he was behind the Pontiac.

At the moment that end of the motel was quiet. No one was coming or going from any of the rooms.

The man behind the wheel was sitting with one arm out of the open car window. If he had glanced at the side mirror, he might have seen Vassago coming up on him, but his attention was focused on room six in the other wing of the L.

Vassago jerked open the door, and the guy actually started to fall out because he'd been leaning against it. Vassago hit him hard in the face, using his elbow like a battering ram, which was better than a fist, except he didn't hit him squarely enough. The guy was rocked but not finished, so he pushed up and out of the Pontiac, trying to grapple with Vassago. He was overweight and slow. A knee driven hard into his crotch slowed him even more. The guy went into a prayer posture, gagging, and Vassago stepped back far enough to kick him. The stranger fell over onto his side, so Vassago kicked him again, in the head this time. The guy was out cold, as still as the pavement on which he was sprawled.

Hearing a startled intake of breath, Vassago turned and saw a frizzy-haired blond hooker in a miniskirt and a middle-aged guy in a cheap suit and a bad toupee. They were coming out of the nearest room. They gaped at the man on the ground. At Vassago. He stared back at them until they reentered their room and quietly pulled the door shut behind them.

The unconscious man was heavy, maybe two hundred pounds, but Vassago was more than strong enough to lift him. He carried the guy around to the passenger side and loaded him into the other front seat. Then he got behind the wheel, started the Pontiac, and departed the Blue Skies.

Several blocks away, he turned onto a street of tract homes built thirty years ago and aging badly. Ancient Indian laurels and coral trees flanked the canted sidewalks and lent a note of grace in spite of the neighborhood's decline. He pulled the Pontiac to the curb. He switched off the engine and the lights.

As no streetlamps were nearby, he removed his sunglasses to search the unconscious man. He found a loaded revolver in a shoulder holster under the guy's jacket. He took it for himself.

The stranger was carrying two wallets. The first, and thicker, contained three hundred dollars in cash, which Vassago confiscated. It also held credit cards, photographs of people he didn't know, a receipt from a dry cleaner, a buy-ten-get-one-free punch card from a frozen-yogurt shop, a driver's license that identified the man as Morton Redlow of Anaheim, and insignificant odds and ends. The second wallet was quite thin, and it proved to be not a real wallet at all but a leather ID holder. In it were Redlow's license to operate as a private investigator and another license to carry a concealed weapon.

In the glove compartment, Vassago found only candy bars and a paperback detective novel. In the console between the seats, he found chewing gum, breath mints, another candy bar, and a bent Thomas Brothers map book of Orange County.

He studied the map book for a while, then started the car and pulled away from the curb. He headed for Anaheim and the address on Redlow's driver's license.

When they were more than halfway there, Redlow began to groan and twitch, as if he might come to his senses. Driving with one hand, Vassago picked up the revolver he had taken off the man and clubbed him alongside the head with it. Redlow was quiet again.

·4·

One of the five other kids who shared Regina's table in the dining hall was Carl Cavanaugh, who was eight years old and acted every bit of it. He was a paraplegic, confined to a wheelchair, which you would have thought was enough of a handicap, but he made his lot in life worse by being a complete nerd. Their plates had no sooner been put on the table than Carl said, 'I really like Friday afternoons, and you know why?' He didn't give anyone a chance to express a lack of interest. 'Because Thursday night we always have beans *and* pea soup, so by Friday afternoon you can really cut some ripe farts.'

The other kids groaned in disgust. Regina just ignored him.

Nerd or not, Carl was right: Thursday dinner at St Thomas's Home for Children was always split-pea soup, ham, green beans, potatoes in herb butter sauce, and a square of fruited Jell-O with a blob of fake whipped cream for dessert. Sometimes the nuns got into the sherry or just went wild from too many years in their suffocating habits, and if they lost control on a Thursday, you might get corn instead of green beans or, if they were really over the top, maybe a pair of vanilla cookies with the Jell-O.

That Thursday the menu held no surprises, but Regina would not have cared – and might not have noticed – if the fare had included filet mignon or, conversely, cow pies. Well, she probably would have noticed a cow pie on her plate, though she wouldn't have cared if it was substituted for the green beans because she didn't like green beans. She liked ham. She had lied when she'd told the Harrisons she was a vegetarian, figuring they would find dietary fussiness one more reason to reject her flat-out, at the start, instead of later when it would hurt more. But even as she ate, her attention was not on her food and not on the conversation of the other kids at her table, but on the meeting in Mr Gujilio's office that afternoon.

She had screwed up.

They were going to have to build a Museum of Famous Screwups just to have a place for a statue of her, so people could come from all over the world, from France and Japan and Chile, just to see it. Schoolkids would come, whole classes at a time with their teachers, to study her so they could learn what *not* to do and how *not* to act. Parents would point at her statue and ominously warn their children, 'Anytime you think you're so smart, just remember her and think how you might wind up like *that*, a figure of pity and ridicule, laughed at and reviled.'

Two-thirds of the way through the interview, she had realized the Harrisons were special people. They probably would never treat her as badly as she had been treated by the Infamous Dotterfields, the couple who accepted her and took her home and then rejected her in two weeks when they discovered they were going to have a child of their own, Satan's child, no doubt, who would one day destroy the world and turn against even the Dotterfields, burning them alive with a flash of fire from his demonic little pig eyes. (Uh-oh. Wishing harm to another. The thought is as bad as the deed. Remember that for confession, Reg.) Anyway, the Harrisons were different, which she began to realize slowly – such a screwup – and which she knew for sure when Mr Harrison made

121

the crack about caviar pajamas and showed he had a sense of humor. But by then she was so *into* her act that somehow she couldn't stop being obnoxious – screwup that she was – couldn't find a way to retreat and start over. Now the Harrisons were probably getting drunk, celebrating their narrow escape, or maybe down on their knees in a church, weeping with relief and fervently saying the Rosary, thanking the Holy Mother for interceding to spare them the mistake of adopting that awful girl sight-unseen. Shit! (Oops. Vulgarity. But not as bad as taking the Lord's name in vain. Even worth mentioning in the confessional?)

In spite of having no appetite, and in spite of Carl Cavanaugh and his crude humor, she ate all of her dinner, but only because God's policemen, the nuns, would not let her leave the table until she cleaned her plate. The fruit in the lime Jell-O was peaches, which made dessert an ordeal. She couldn't understand how anyone could think that lime and peaches went together. Okay, so nuns were not very worldly, but she wasn't asking them to learn which rare wine to serve with roast tenderloin of platypus, for God's sake. (Sorry, God.) Pineapple and lime Jell-O, certainly. Pears and lime Jell-O, okay. Even bananas and lime Jell-O. But putting peaches in lime Jell-O was, to her way of thinking, like leaving the raisins out of rice pudding and replacing them with chunks of watermelon, for God's sake. (Sorry, God.) She managed to eat the dessert by telling herself that it could have been worse; the nuns could have served dead mice dipped in chocolate – though why nuns, of all people, would want to do that, she had no idea. Still, imagining something worse than what she had to face was a trick that worked, a technique of self-persuasion that she had used many times before. Soon the hated Jell-O was gone, and she was free to leave the dining hall.

After dinner most kids went to the recreation room to play Monopoly and other games, or to the TV room to watch whatever slop was on the boob tube, but as usual she returned to her room. She spent most evenings reading. Not tonight, though. She planned to spend this evening feeling sorry for herself and contemplating her status as a world-class screwup (good thing stupidity wasn't a sin), so she would never forget how dumb she had been and would remember never to make such a jackass of herself again.

Moving along the tile-floored hallways nearly as fast as a kid with two good legs, she remembered how she had clumped into the attorney's office, and she began to blush. In her room, which she shared with a blind girl named Winnie, as she jumped into bed and flopped on her back, she recalled the calculated clumsiness with which she had levered herself into the chair in front of Mr and Mrs Harrison. Her blush deepened, and she put both hands over her face.

'Reg,' she said softly against the palms of her own hands, 'you are the biggest asshole in the world.' (One more item on the list for the next confession, besides lying and deceiving and taking God's name in vain: the repeated use of a vulgarity.) 'Shit, shit, shit!' (Going to be a long confession.)

·5·

When Redlow regained consciousness, his assorted pains were so bad, they took one hundred percent of his attention. He had a violent headache to which he could have testified with such feeling in a television commercial that they would have been forced to open new aspirin factories to meet the consumer response. One eye was puffed half shut. His lips were split and swollen; they were numb and felt huge. His neck hurt, and his stomach was sore, and his testicles throbbed so fiercely from the knee he had taken in the crotch that the idea of getting up and walking sent a paroxysm of nausea through him.

Gradually he remembered what had happened to him, that the bastard had taken him by surprise. Then he realized he was not lying on the motel parking lot but sitting in a chair, and for the first time he was afraid.

He was not merely sitting in the chair. He was tied in it. Ropes bound him at chest and waist, and more ropes wound across his thighs, securing him to the seat. His arms were fixed to the arms of the chair just below his elbows and again at the wrists.

Pain had muddied his thought processes. Now fear clarified them.

Simultaneously squinting his good right eye and trying to widen his swollen left eye, he studied the darkness. For a moment he assumed he was in a room at the Blue Skies Motel, outside of which he had been running a surveillance in hope of spotting the kid. Then he recognized his own living room. He couldn't see much. No lights were on. But having lived in that house for eighteen years, he could identify the patterns of ambient night-glow at the windows, the dim shapes of the furniture, shadows among shadows of differing intensity, and the subtle but singular smell of home, which was as special and instantly identifiable to him as the odor of any particular lair to any particular wolf in the wild.

He did not feel much like a wolf tonight. He felt like a rabbit, shivering in recognition of its status as prey.

For a few seconds he thought he was alone, and he began to strain at the ropes. Then a shadow rose from other shadows and approached him.

He could see nothing more of his adversary than a silhouette. Even that seemed to melt into the silhouettes of inanimate objects, or to change as if the kid were a polymorphous creature that could assume a variety of forms. But he knew it was the kid because he sensed that difference, that *alienness* he had perceived the first time he had laid eyes on the bastard on Sunday, just four nights ago, at the Blue Skies.

'Comfortable, Mr Redlow?'

Over the past three months, as he had searched for the creep, Redlow had developed a deep curiosity about him, trying to puzzle out what he wanted, what he needed, how he thought. After showing countless people the various photographs of the kid, and after spending more than a little of his own time in contemplation of them, he had been especially curious about what the voice would be like that went with that remarkably handsome yet forbidding face. It sounded nothing like he had imagined it would be, neither cold and steely like the voice of a machine designed to pass for human nor the guttural and savage snarling of a beast. Rather, it was soothing, honey-toned, with an appealing reverberant timbre.

'Mr Redlow, sir, can you hear me?'

More than anything else, the kid's politeness and the natural formality of his speech disconcerted Redlow.

'I apologize for having been so rough with you, sir, but you really didn't give me much choice.'

Nothing in the voice indicated that the kid was being snide or mocking. He was just a boy who had been raised to address his elders with consideration and respect, a habit he could not cast off even under circumstances such as these. The detective was gripped by a primitive, superstitious feeling that he was in the presence of an entity that could imitate humanity but had nothing whatsoever in common with the human species.

Speaking through split lips, his words somewhat slurred, Morton Redlow said, 'Who are you, what the hell do you want?'

'You know who I am.'

'I haven't a fucking clue. You blindsided me. I haven't seen your face. What are you, a bat or something? Why don't you turn on a light?'

Still only a black form, the kid moved closer, to within a few feet of the chair. 'You were hired to find me.'

'I was hired to run surveillance on a guy named Kirkaby. Leonard Kirkaby. Wife thinks he's cheating on her. And he is. Brings his secretary to the Blue Skies every Thursday for some in-and-out.'

'Well, sir, that's a little hard for me to believe, you know? The Blue Skies is for low-life guys and cheap whores, not business executives and their secretaries.'

'Maybe he gets off on the sleaziness of it, treating the girl like a whore. Who the hell knows, huh? Anyway, you sure aren't Kirk-aby. I know his voice. He doesn't sound anything like you. Not as young as you, either. Besides, he's a piece of puff pastry. He couldn't have handled me the way you did.'

The kid was quiet for a while. Just staring down at Redlow. Then he began to pace. In the dark. Unhesitating, never bumping into furniture. Like a restless cat, except his eyes didn't glow.

Finally he said, 'So what're you saying, sir? That this is all just a big mistake?'

Redlow knew his only chance of staying alive was to convince the kid of the lie – that a guy named Kirkaby had a letch for his secretary, and a bitter wife seeking evidence for a divorce. He just didn't know what tone to take to sell the story. With most people, Redlow had an unerring sense of which approach would beguile them and make them accept even the wildest proposition as the truth. But the kid was different; he didn't think or react like ordinary people.

Redlow decided to play it tough. 'Listen, asshole, I wish I did know who you are or at least what the hell you look like, 'cause once this was finished, I'd come after you and bash your fuckin' head in.'

The kid was silent for a while, mulling it over.

Then he said, 'All right, I believe you.'

Redlow sagged with relief, but sagging made all of his pains worse, so he tensed his muscles and sat up straight again.

'Too bad, but you just aren't right for my collection,' the kid said.

'Collection?'

'Not enough life in you.'

'What're you talking about?' Redlow asked.

'Burnt out.'

The conversation was taking a turn Redlow didn't understand, which made him uneasy.

'Excuse me, sir, no offense meant, but you're getting too old for this kind of work.'

Don't I know it, Redlow thought. He realized that, aside from one initial tug, he had not again tested the ropes that bound him. Only a few years ago, he would have quietly but steadily strained against them, trying to stretch the knots. Now he was passive.

'You're a muscular man, but you've gone a little soft, you've got a gut on you, and you're slow. From your driver's license, I see you're fifty-four, you're getting up there. Why do you still do it, keep hanging in there?'

'It's all I've got,' Redlow said, and he was alert enough to be surprised by his own answer. He had meant to say, *It's all I know.*

'Well, yessir, I can see that,' the kid said, looming over him in the darkness. 'You've been divorced twice, no kids, and no woman lives with you right now. Probably hasn't been one living with you for years. Sorry, but I was snooping around the house while you were out cold, even though I knew it wasn't really right of me. Sorry. But I just wanted to get a handle on you, try to understand what you get out of this.'

Redlow said nothing because he couldn't understand where all of this was leading. He was afraid of saying the wrong thing, and setting the kid off like a bottle rocket. The son of a bitch was insane. You never knew what might light the fuse on a nutcase like him. The kid had been through some analysis of his own over the years, and now he seemed to want to analyze Redlow, for reasons even he probably could not have explained. Maybe it was best to

126

just let him rattle on, get it out of his system.

'Is it money, Mr Redlow?'

'You mean, do I make any?'

'That's what I mean, sir.'

'I do okay.'

'You don't drive a great car or wear expensive clothes.'

'I'm not into flash,' Redlow said.

'No offense, sir, but this house isn't much.'

'Maybe not, but there's no mortgage on it.'

The kid was right over him, slowly leaning farther in with each question, as if he could see Redlow in the lightless room and was intently studying facial tics and twitches as he questioned him. Weird. Even in the dark, Redlow could sense the kid bending closer, closer, closer.

'No mortgage on it,' the kid said thoughtfully. 'Is that your reason for working, for living? To be able to say you paid off a mortgage on a dump like this?'

Redlow wanted to tell him to go fuck himself, but suddenly he was not so sure that playing tough was a good idea, after all.

'Is that what life's all about, sir? Is that all it's about? Is that why you find it so precious, why you're so eager to hold onto it? Is that why you life-lovers struggle to go on living – just to acquire a pitiful pile of belongings, so you can go out of the game a winner? I'm sorry, sir, but I just don't understand that. I don't understand at all.'

The detective's heart was pounding too hard. It slammed painfully against his bruised ribs. He hadn't treated his heart well over the years, too many hamburgers, too many cigarettes, too much beer and bourbon. What was the crazy kid trying to do – talk him to death, scare him to death?

'I'd imagine you have some clients who don't want it on record that they ever hired you, they pay in cash. Would that be a valid assumption, sir?'

Redlow cleared his throat and tried not to sound frightened. 'Yeah. Sure. Some of them.'

'And part of winning the game would be to keep as much of that money as you could, avoiding taxes on it, which would mean never putting it in a bank.'

The kid was so close now that the detective could smell his breath. For some reason he had expected it to be sour, vile. But it

127

smelled sweet, like chocolate, as if the kid had been eating candy in the dark.

'So I'd imagine you have a nice little stash here in the house somewhere. Is that right, sir?'

A warm quiver of hope caused a diminution of the cold chills that had been chattering through Redlow for the past few minutes. If it was about money, he could deal with that. It made sense. He could understand the kid's motivation, and could see a way to get through the evening alive.

'Yeah,' the detective said. 'There's money. Take it. Take it and go. In the kitchen, there's a waste can with a plastic bag for a liner. Lift out the bag of trash, there's a brown paper bag full of cash under it, in the bottom of the can.'

Something cold and rough touched the detective's right cheek, and he flinched from it.

'Pliers,' the kid said, and the detective felt the jaws take a grip on his flesh.

'What're you doing?'

The kid twisted the pliers.

Redlow cried out in pain. 'Wait, wait, stop it, shit, please, stop it, no!'

The kid stopped. He took the pliers away. He said, 'I'm sorry, sir, but I just want you to understand that if there isn't any cash in the trash can, I won't be happy. I'll figure if you lied to me about this, you lied to me about everything.'

'It's there,' Redlow assured him hastily.

'It's not nice to lie, sir. It's not good. Good people don't lie. That's what they teach you, isn't it, sir?'

'Go, look, you'll see it's there,' Redlow said desperately.

The kid went out of the living room, through the dining room archway. Soft footsteps echoed through the house from the tile floor of the kitchen. A clatter and rustle arose as the garbage bag was pulled out of the waste can.

Already damp with perspiration, Redlow began to gush sweat as he listened to the kid return through the pitch-black house. He appeared in the living room again, partly silhouetted against the pale-gray rectangle of a window.

'How can you see?' the detective asked, dismayed to hear a faint note of hysteria in his voice when he was struggling so hard to maintain control of himself. He *was* getting old. 'What – are you wearing night-vision glasses or something, some military hardware? How in the hell would you get your hands on anything like that?'

Ignoring him, the kid said, 'There isn't much I want or need, just food and changes of clothes. The only money I get is when I make an addition to my collection, whatever she happens to be carrying. Sometimes it's not much, only a few dollars. This is really a help. It really is. This much should last me as long as it takes for me to get back to where I belong. Do you know where I belong, Mr Redlow?'

The detective did not answer. The kid had dropped down below the windows, out of sight. Redlow was squinting into the gloom, trying to detect movement and figure where he had gone.

'You know where I belong, Mr Redlow?' the kid repeated.

Redlow heard a piece of furniture being shoved aside. Maybe an end table beside the sofa.

'I belong in Hell,' the kid said. 'I was there for a while. I want to go back. What kind of life have you led, Mr Redlow? Do you think, when I go back to Hell, that maybe I'll see you over there?'

'What're you doing?' Redlow asked.

'Looking for an electrical outlet,' the kid said as he shoved aside another piece of furniture. 'Ah, here we go.'

'Electrical outlet?' Redlow asked agitatedly. 'Why?'

A frightening noise cut through the darkness: *zzzzrrrrrrrrrrr*.

'What was that?' Redlow demanded.

'Just testing, sir.'

'Testing what?'

'You've got all sorts of pots and pans and gourmet utensils out there in the kitchen, sir. I guess you're really into cooking, are you?' The kid rose up again, appearing against the backdrop of the dim ash-gray glow in the window glass. 'The cooking – was that an interest before the second divorce, or more recent?'

'What were you testing?' Redlow asked again.

The kid approached the chair.

'There's more money,' Redlow said frantically. He was soaked in sweat now. It was running down him in rivulets. 'In the master bedroom.' The kid loomed over him again, a mysterious and inhuman form. He seemed to be darker than anything around him, a black hole in the shape of a man, blacker than black. 'In the c-closet. There's a w-w-wooden floor.' The detective's bladder

129

was suddenly full. It had blown up like a balloon all in an instant. Bursting. 'Take out the shoes and crap. Lift up the back f-f-floorboards.' He was going to piss himself. 'There's a cash box. Thirty thousand dollars. Take it. Please. Take it and go.'

'Thank you, sir, but I really don't need it. I've got enough, more than enough.'

'Oh, Jesus, help me,' Redlow said, and he was despairingly aware that this was the first time he had spoken to God – or even thought of Him – in decades.

'Let's talk about who you're *really* working for, sir.'

'I told you—'

'But I lied when I said I believed you.'

Zzzzrrrrrrrrrrrr.

'What *is* that?' Redlow asked.

'Testing.'

'Testing what, damn it?'

'It works real nice.'

'*What, what is it, what've you got?*'

'An electric carving knife,' the kid said.

·6·

Hatch and Lindsey drove home from dinner without getting on a freeway, taking their time, using the coast road from Newport Beach south, listening to K-Earth 101.1 FM, and singing along with golden oldies like 'New Orleans,' 'Whispering Bells,' and 'California Dreamin'.' She couldn't remember when they had last harmonized with the radio, though in the old days they had done it all the time. When he'd been three, Jimmy had known all the words to 'Pretty Woman.' When he was four he could sing 'Fifty Ways to Leave Your Lover' without missing a line. For the first time in five years, she could think of Jimmy and still feel like singing.

They lived in Laguna Niguel, south of Laguna Beach, on the eastern side of the coastal hills, without an ocean view but with the benefit of sea breezes that moderated summer heat and winter chill. Their neighborhood, like most south-county developments, was so meticulously laid out that at times it seemed as if the planners had come to community design with a military back-

130

ground. But the gracefully curving streets, iron streetlamps with an artificial green patina, just-so arrangements of palms and jacarandas and ficus benjaminas, and well-maintained greenbelts with beds of colorful flowers were so soothing to the eye and soul that the subliminal sense of regimentation was not stifling.

As an artist, Lindsey believed that the hands of men and women were as capable of creating great beauty as nature was, and that discipline was fundamental to the creation of real art because art was meant to reveal meaning in the chaos of life. Therefore, she understood the impulse of the planners who had labored countless hours to coordinate the design of the community all the way down to the configuration of the steel grilles in the street drains that were set in the gutters.

Their two-story house, where they had lived only since Jimmy's death, was an Italian-Mediterranean model – the whole community was Italian Mediterranean – with four bedrooms and den, in cream-colored stucco with a Mexican tile roof. Two large ficus trees flanked the front walk. Malibu lights revealed beds of impatiens and petunias in front of red-flowering azalea bushes. As they pulled into the garage, they finished the last bars of 'You Send Me.'

Between taking turns in the bathroom, Hatch started a gas-log fire in the family-room fireplace, and Lindsey poured Baileys Irish Cream on the rocks for both of them. They sat on the sofa in front of the fire, their feet on a large, matching ottoman.

All the upholstered furniture in the house was modern with soft lines and in light natural tones. It made a pleasing contrast with – and good backdrop for – the many antique pieces and Lindsey's paintings.

The sofa was also hugely comfortable, good for conversation and, as she discovered for the first time, a great spot to snuggle. To her surprise, snuggling turned into necking, and their necking escalated into petting, as if they were a couple of teenagers, for God's sake. Passion overwhelmed her as it had not done in years.

Their clothes came off slowly, as in a series of dissolves in a motion picture, until they were naked without quite knowing how they had gotten that way. Then they were just as mysteriously coupled, moving together in a silken rhythm, bathed in flickering firelight. The joyful naturalness of it, escalating from a dreamy motion to breathless urgency, was a radical departure from the stilted and dutiful lovemaking they had known during the past five years, and Lindsey could almost believe it really was a dream patterned on some remembered scrap of Hollywood eroticism. But as she slid her hands over the muscles of his arms and shoulders and back, as she rose to meet each of his thrusts, as she climaxed, then again, and as she felt him loose himself within her and dissolve from iron to molten flow, she was wonderfully, acutely aware that it was not a dream. In fact, she had opened her eyes at last from a long twilight sleep and was, with this release, only now fully awake for the first time in years. The true dream was real life during the past half decade, a nightmare that had finally drawn to an end.

Leaving their clothes scattered on the floor and hearth behind them, they went upstairs to make love again, this time in the huge Chinese sleigh bed, with less urgency than before, more tenderness, to the accompaniment of murmured endearments that seemed almost to comprise the lyrics and melody of a quiet song. The less insistent rhythm allowed a keener awareness of the exquisite textures of skin, the marvelous flexibility of muscle, the firmness of bone, the pliancy of lips, and the syncopated beating of their hearts. When the tide of ecstasy crested and ebbed, in the stillness that followed, the words 'I love you' were superfluous but nonetheless musical to the ear, and cherished.

That April day, from first awareness of the morning light until surrender to sleep, had been one of the best of their lives. Ironically, the night that followed was one of Hatch's worst, so frightening and so strange.

* * *

By eleven o'clock Vassago had finished with Redlow and disposed of the body in a most satisfying fashion. He returned to the Blue Skies Motel in the detective's Pontiac, took the long hot shower that he had intended to take earlier in the night, changed into clean clothes, and left with the intention of never going there again. If Redlow had made the place, it was not safe any longer.

He drove the Camaro a few blocks and abandoned it on a street of decrepit industrial buildings where it might sit undisturbed for weeks before it was either stolen or hauled off by the police. He had been using it for a month, after taking it from one of the women whom he had added to his collection. He had changed license plates on it a few times, always stealing the replacements from parked cars in the early hours before dawn.

After walking back to the motel, he drove away in Redlow's Pontiac. It was not as sexy as the silver Camaro, but he figured it would serve him well enough for a couple of weeks.

He went to a neo-punk nightclub named Rip It, in Huntington Beach, where he parked at the darkest end of the lot. He found a pouch of tools in the trunk and used a screwdriver and pliers to remove the plates, which he swapped with those on a battered gray Ford parked beside him. Then he drove to the other end of the lot and reparked.

Fog, with the clammy feel of something dead, moved in from the sea. Palm trees and telephone poles disappeared as if dissolved by the acidity of the mist, and the streetlamps became ghost lights adrift in the murk.

Inside, the club was everything he liked. Loud, dirty, and dark. Reeking of smoke, spilled liquor, and sweat. The band hit the chords harder than any musicians he'd ever heard, rammed pure rage into each tune, twisting the melody into a squealing mutant voice, banging the numbingly repetitious rhythms home with savage fury, playing each number so loud that, with the help of huge amplifiers, they rattled the filthy windows and almost made his eyes bleed.

The crowd was energetic, high on drugs of every variety, some of them drunk, many of them dangerous. In clothing, the preferred color was black, so Vassago fit right in. And he was not the only one wearing sunglasses. Some of them, both men and women, were skinheads, and some wore their hair in short spikes, but none of them favored the frivolous flamboyancy of huge spikes and cocks' combs and colorful dye jobs that had been a part of early punk. On the jammed dance floor, people seemed to be shoving each other and roughing each other up, maybe feeling each other up in some cases, but no one there had ever taken lessons at an Arthur Murray studio or watched 'Soul Train.'

At the scarred, stained, greasy bar, Vassago pointed to the Corona, one of six brands of beer lined up on a shelf. He paid and took the bottle from the bartender without the need to exchange a word. He stood there, drinking and scanning the crowd.

Only a few of the customers at the bar and tables, or those

standing along the walls, were talking to one another. Most were sullen and silent, not because the pounding music made conversation difficult but because they were the new wave of alienated youth, estranged not only from society but from one another. They were convinced that nothing mattered except self-gratification, that nothing was worth talking about, that they were the last generation on a world headed for destruction, with no future.

He knew of other neo-punk bars, but this was one of only two in Orange and Los Angeles counties – the area that so many chamber of commerce types liked to call the Southland – that were the real thing. Many of the others catered to people who wanted to play at the lifestyle the same way some dentists and accountants liked to put on hand-tooled boots, faded jeans, checkered shirts, and ten-gallon hats to go to a country-and-western bar and pretend they were cowboys. At Rip It, there was no pretense in anyone's eyes, and everyone you encountered met you with a challenging stare, trying to decide whether they wanted sex or violence from you and whether you were likely to give them either. If it was an either-or situation, many of them would have chosen violence over sex.

A few were looking for something that transcended violence and sex, without a clear idea of what it might be. Vassago could have shown them precisely that for which they were searching.

The problem was, he did not at first see anyone who appealed to him sufficiently to consider an addition to his collection. He was not a crude killer, piling up bodies for the sake of piling them up. Quantity had no appeal to him; he was more interested in quality. A connoisseur of death. If he could earn his way back into Hell, he would have to do so with an exceptional offering, a collection that was superior in both its overall composition and in the character of each of its components.

He had made a previous acquisition at Rip It three months ago, a girl who insisted her name was Neon. In his car, when he tried to knock her unconscious, one blow didn't do the job, and she fought back with a ferocity that was exhilarating. Even later, in the bottom floor of the funhouse, when she regained consciousness, she resisted fiercely, though bound at wrists and ankles. She squirmed and thrashed, biting him until he repeatedly bashed her skull against the concrete floor.

Now, just as he finished his beer, he saw another woman who

134

reminded him of Neon. Physically they were far different, but spiritually they were the same: hard cases, angry for reasons they didn't always understand themselves, worldly beyond their years, with all the potential violence of tigresses. Neon had been five-four, brunette, with a dusky complexion. This one was a blonde in her early twenties, about five-seven. Lean and rangy. Riveting eyes the same shade of blue as a pure gas flame, yet icy. She was wearing a ragged black denim jacket over a tight black sweater, a short black skirt, and boots.

In an age when attitude was admired more than intelligence, she knew how to carry herself for the maximum impact. She moved with her shoulders back and her head lifted almost haughtily. Her self-possession was as intimidating as spiked armor. Although every man in the room looked at her in a way that said he wanted her, none of them dared to come on to her, for she appeared to be able to emasculate with a single word or look.

Her powerful sexuality, however, was what made her of interest to Vassago. Men would always be drawn to her – he noticed that those flanking him at the bar were watching her even now – and some would not be intimidated. She possessed a savage vitality that made even Neon seem timid. When her defenses were penetrated, she would be lubricious and disgustingly fertile, soon fat with new life, a wild but fruitful brood mare.

He decided that she had two great weaknesses. The first was her clear conviction that she was superior to everyone she met and was, therefore, untouchable and safe, the same conviction that had made it possible for royalty, in more innocent times, to walk among commoners in complete confidence that everyone they passed would draw back respectfully or drop to their knees in awe. The second weakness was her extreme anger, which she stored in such quantity that Vassago seemed to be able to see it crackling off her smooth pale skin, like an overcharge of electricity.

He wondered how he might arrange her death to best symbolize her flaws. Soon he had a couple of good ideas.

She was with a group of about six men and four women, though she did not seem to be attached to any one of them. Vassago was trying to decide on an approach to her when, not entirely to his surprise, *she* approached *him*. He supposed their encounter was inevitable. They were, after all, the two most dangerous people at the dance.

135

Just as the band took a break and the decibel level fell to a point at which the interior of the club would no longer have been lethal to cats, the blonde came to the bar. She pushed between Vassago and another man, ordered and paid for a beer. She took the bottle from the bartender, turned sideways to face Vassago, and looked at him across the top of the open bottle, from which wisps of cold vapor rose like smoke.

She said, 'You blind?'

'To some things, Miss.'

She looked incredulous. 'Miss?'

He shrugged.

'Why the sunglasses?' she asked.

'I've been to Hell.'

'What's that supposed to mean?'

'Hell is cold, dark.'

'That so? I still don't get the sunglasses.'

'Over there, you learn to see in total darkness.'

'This is an interesting line of bullshit.'

'So now I'm sensitive to light.'

'A real *different* line of bullshit.'

He said nothing.

She drank some beer, but her eyes never left him.

He liked the way her throat muscles worked when she swallowed.

After a moment she said, 'This your usual line of crap, or do you just make it up as you go?'

He shrugged again.

'You were watching me,' she said.

'So?'

'You're right. Every asshole in here is watching me most of the time.'

He was studying her intensely blue eyes. What he thought he might do was cut them out, then reinsert them backward, so she was looking into her own skull. A comment on her self-absorption.

★ ★ ★

In the dream Hatch was talking to a beautiful but incredibly cold-looking blonde. Her flawless skin was as white as porcelain, and

136

her eyes were like polished ice reflecting a clear winter sky. They were standing at a bar in a strange establishment he had never seen before. She was looking at him across the top of a beer bottle that she held – and brought to her mouth – as she might have held a phallus. But the taunting way she drank from it and licked the glass rim seemed to be as much a threat as it was an erotic invitation. He could not hear a thing she said, and he could hear only a few words that he spoke himself: ' . . . been to Hell . . . cold, dark . . . sensitive to light . . . ' The blonde was looking at him, and it was surely he who was speaking to her, yet the words were not in his own voice. Suddenly he found himself focusing more intently on her arctic eyes, and before he knew what he was doing, he produced a switchblade knife and flicked it open. As if she felt no pain, as if in fact she was dead already, the blonde did not react when, with a swift whip of the knife, he took her left eye from its socket. He rolled it over on his fingertips, and replaced it with the blind end outward and the blue lens gazing inward—

Hatch sat up. Unable to breathe. Heart hammering. He swung his legs out of bed and stood, feeling as if he had to run away from something. But he just gasped for breath, not sure where to run to find shelter, safety.

They had fallen asleep with a bedside lamp on, a towel draped over the shade to soften the light while they made love. The room was well enough lit for him to see Lindsey lying on her side of the bed in a tangle of covers.

She was so still, he thought she was dead. He had the crazy feeling that he'd killed her. With a switchblade.

Then she stirred and mumbled in her sleep.

He shuddered. He looked at his hands. They were shaking.

* * *

Vassago was so enamored of his artistic vision that he had the impulsive desire to reverse her eyes right there, in the bar, with everyone watching. He restrained himself.

'So what do you want?' she asked, after taking another swallow of beer.

He said, 'Out of what – life?'

'Out of me.'

'What do you think?'

'A few thrills,' she said.

'More than that.'

'Home and family?' she asked sarcastically.

He didn't answer right away. He wanted time to think. This one was not easy to play, a different sort of fish. He did not want to risk saying the wrong thing and letting her slip the hook. He got another beer, drank some of it.

Four members of a backup band approached the stage. They were going to play during the other musicians' break. Soon conversation would be impossible again. More important, when the crashing music began, the energy level of the club would rise, and it might exceed the energy level between him and the blonde. She might not be as susceptible to the suggestion that they leave together.

He finally answered her question, told her a lie about what he wanted to do with her: 'You know anybody you wish was dead?'

'Who doesn't?'

'Who is it?'

'Half the people I've ever met.'

'I mean, one person in particular.'

She began to realize what he was suggesting. She took another sip of beer and lingered with her mouth and tongue against the rim of the bottle. 'What – is this a game or something?'

'Only if you want it to be, Miss.'

'You're weird.'

'Isn't that what you like?'

'Maybe you're a cop.'

'You really think so?'

She stared intently at his sunglasses, though she wouldn't have been able to see more than a dim suggestion of his eyes beyond the heavily tinted lenses. 'No. Not a cop.'

'Sex isn't a good way to start,' he said.

'It isn't, huh?'

'Death is a better opener. Make a little death together, then make a little sex. You won't believe how intense it can get.'

She said nothing.

The backup band was picking up the instruments on the stage.

He said, 'This one in particular you'd like dead – it's a guy?'

'Yeah.'

'He live within driving distance?'

'Twenty minutes from here.'

138

'So let's do it.'

The musicians began to tune up, though it seemed a pointless exercise, considering the type of music they were going to play. They had better play the right stuff, and they had better be good at it, because it was the kind of club where the customers wouldn't hesitate to trash the band if they didn't like it.

At last the blonde said, 'I've got a little PCP. Want to do some with me?'

'Angel dust? It runs in my veins.'

'You got a car?'

'Let's go.'

On the way out he opened the door for her.

She laughed. 'You're one weird son of a bitch.'

★ ★ ★

According to the digital clock on the nightstand, it was 1:28 in the morning. Although Hatch had been asleep only a couple of hours, he was wide awake and unwilling to lie down again.

Besides, his mouth was dry. He felt as if he had been eating sand. He needed a drink.

The towel-draped lamp provided enough light for him to make his way to the dresser and quietly open the correct drawer without waking Lindsey. Shivering, he took a sweatshirt from the drawer and pulled it on. He was wearing only pajama bottoms, but he knew that the addition of a thin pajama top would not quell his chills.

He opened the bedroom door and stepped into the upstairs hall. He glanced back at his slumbering wife. She looked beautiful there in the soft amber light, dark hair against the white pillow, her face relaxed, lips slightly parted, one hand tucked under her chin. The sight of her, more than the sweatshirt, warmed him. Then he thought about the years they had lost in their surrender to grief, and the residual fear from the nightmare was further diluted by a flood of regret. He pulled the door shut soundlessly behind him.

The second-floor hall was hung with shadows, but wan light rose along the stairwell from the foyer below. On their way from the family-room sofa to the sleigh bed, they had not paused to switch off lamps.

Like a couple of horny teenagers. He smiled at the thought.

139

On his way down the stairs, he remembered the nightmare, and his smile slipped away.

The blonde. The knife. The eye.

It had seemed so *real*.

At the foot of the stairs he stopped, listening. The silence in the house was unnatural. He rapped one knuckle against the newel post, just to hear a sound. The tap seemed softer than it should have been. The silence following it was deeper than before.

'Jesus, that dream really spooked you,' he said aloud, and the sound of his own voice was reassuring.

His bare feet made an amusing slapping sound on the oak floor of the downstairs hall, and even more noise on the tile floor of the kitchen. His thirst growing more acute by the second, he took a can of Pepsi from the refrigerator, popped it open, tilted his head back, closed his eyes, and had a long drink.

It didn't taste like cola. It tasted like beer.

Frowning, he opened his eyes and looked at the can. It was not a can any more. It was a bottle of beer, the same brand as in the dream: Corona. Neither he nor Lindsey drank Corona. When they had a beer, which was rarely, it was a Heineken.

Fear went through him like vibrations through a wire.

Then he noticed that the tile floor of the kitchen was gone. He was standing barefoot on gravel. The stones cut into the balls of his feet.

As his heart began to race, he looked around the kitchen with a desperate need to reaffirm that he was in his own house, that the world had not just tilted into some bizarre new dimension. He let his gaze travel over the familiar white-washed birch cabinets, the dark granite countertops, the dishwasher, the gleaming face of the built-in microwave, and he willed the nightmare to recede. But the gravel floor remained. He was still holding a Corona in his right hand. He turned toward the sink, intent on splashing cold water in his face, but the sink was no longer there. One half of the kitchen had vanished, replaced by a roadside bar along which cars were parked in a row, and then—

—he was not in his kitchen at all. It was entirely gone. He was in the open air of the April night, where thick fog glowed with the reflection of red neon from a sign somewhere behind him. He was walking along a graveled parking lot, past the row of parked cars.

He was not barefoot any more but wearing rubber-soled black Rockports.

He heard a woman say, 'My name's Lisa. What's yours?'

He turned his head and saw the blonde. She was at his side, keeping pace with him across the parking lot.

Instead of answering her right away, he tipped the Corona to his mouth, sucked down the last couple of ounces, and dropped the empty bottle on the gravel. 'My name—'

—he gasped as cold Pepsi foamed from the dropped can, and puddled around his bare feet. The gravel had disappeared. A spreading pool of cola glistened on the peach-colored Santa Fe tiles of his kitchen floor.

* * *

In Redlow's Pontiac, Lisa told Vassago to take the San Diego Freeway south. By the time he traveled eastward on fog-filled surface streets and eventually found a freeway entrance, she had extracted capsules of what she said was PCP from the pharmacopoeia in her purse, and they had washed them down with the rest of her beer.

PCP is an animal tranquilizer that often has the opposite of a tranquilizing effect on human beings, exciting them into destructive frenzies. It would be interesting to watch the impact of the drug on Lisa, who seemed to have the conscience of a snake, to whom the concept of morality was utterly alien, who viewed the world with unrelenting hatred and contempt, whose sense of personal power and superiority did not preclude a self-destructive streak, and who was already so full of tightly contained psychotic energy that she always seemed about to explode. He suspected that, with the aid of PCP, she'd be capable of highly entertaining extremes of violence, fierce storms of bloody destruction that he would find exhilarating to watch.

'Where are we going?' he asked as they cruised south on the freeway. The headlights drilled into a white mist that hid the world and made it seem as if they could invent any landscape and future they wished. Whatever they imagined might take substance from the fog and appear around them.

'El Toro,' she said.

'That's where he lives?'

'Yeah.'

'Who is he?'

'You need a name?'

'No, ma'am. Why do you want him dead?'

She studied him for a while. Gradually a smile spread across her face, as if it were a wound being carved by a slow-moving and invisible knife. Her small white teeth looked pointy. Piranha teeth. 'You'll really do it, won't you?' she asked. 'You'll just go in there and kill the guy to prove I oughta want you.'

'To prove nothing,' he said. 'Just because it might be fun. Like I told you – '

'First make some death together, then make some sex,' she finished for him.

Just to keep her talking and make her feel increasingly at ease with him, he said, 'Does he live in an apartment or a house?'

'Why's it matter?'

'Lots more ways to get into a house, and neighbors aren't as close.'

'It's a house,' she said.

'Why do you want him dead?'

'He wanted me, I didn't want him, and he felt he could take what he wanted anyway.'

'Couldn't have been easy taking anything from you.'

Her eyes were colder than ever. 'The bastard had to have stitches in his face when it was over.'

'But he still got what he wanted?'

'He was bigger than me.'

She turned away from him and gazed at the road ahead.

A breeze had risen from the west, and the fog no longer eddied lazily through the night. It churned across the highway like smoke billowing off a vast fire, as if the entire coastline was ablaze, whole cities incinerated and the ruins smouldering.

Vassago kept glancing at her profile, wishing that he could go with her to El Toro and see how deep in blood she would wade for vengeance. Then he would have liked to convince her to come with him to his hideaway and give herself, of her own free will, to his collection. Whether she knew it or not, she wanted death. She would be grateful for the sweet pain that would be her ticket to damnation. Pale skin almost luminescent against her black clothes, filled with hatred so intense that it made her darkly radiant, she would be an incomparable vision as she walked to her destiny among Vassago's collection and accepted the killing blow, a willing sacrifice for his repatriation to Hell.

He knew, however, that she would not accede to his fantasy and die for him, even if death was what she wanted. She would die only for herself, when she eventually concluded that termination was her deepest desire.

The moment she began to realize what he really wanted from her, she would lash out at him. She would be harder to control – and would do more damage – than Neon. He preferred to take each new acquisition to his museum of death while she was still alive, extracting the life from her beneath the malevolent gaze of the funhouse Lucifer. But he knew that he did not have that luxury with Lisa. She would not be easy to subdue, even with a sudden unexpected blow. And once he had lost the advantage of surprise, she would be a fierce adversary.

He was not concerned about being hurt. Nothing, including the prospect of pain, could frighten him. Indeed, each blow she landed, each cut she opened in him, would be an exquisite thrill, pure pleasure.

The problem was, she might be strong enough to get away from him, and he could not risk her escape. He wasn't worried that she would report him to the cops. She existed in a subculture that was suspicious and scornful of the police, seething with hatred for them. If she slipped out of his grasp, however, he would lose the chance to add her to his collection. And he was convinced that her tremendous perverse energy would be the final offering that would win him readmission to Hell.

'You feeling anything yet?' she asked, still looking ahead at the fog, into which they barrelled at a dangerous speed.

'A little,' he said.

'I don't feel anything.' She opened her purse again and began rummaging through it, taking stock of what other pills and capsules she possessed. 'We need some kind of booster to help the crap kick in good.'

While Lisa was distracted by her search for the right chemical to enhance the PCP, Vassago drove with his left hand and reached under his seat with his right to get the revolver that he had taken off Morton Redlow. She looked up just as he thrust the muzzle against her left side. If she knew what was happening, she showed no surprise. He fired two shots, killing her instantly.

★　★　★

Hatch cleaned up the spilled Pepsi with paper towels. By the time he stepped to the kitchen sink to wash his hands, he was still shaking but not as badly as he had been.

Terror, which had been briefly all-consuming, made some room for curiosity. He hesitantly touched the rim of the stainless-steel sink and then the faucet, as if they might dissolve beneath his hand. He struggled to understand how a dream could continue after he had awakened. The only explanation, which he could not accept, was insanity.

He turned on the water, adjusted hot and cold, pumped some liquid soap out of the container, began to lather his hands, and looked up at the window above the sink, which faced onto the rear yard. The yard was gone. A highway lay in its place. The kitchen window had become a windshield. Swaddled in fog and only partially revealed by two headlight beams, the pavement rolled toward him as if the house was racing over it at sixty miles an hour. He sensed a presence beside him where there should have been nothing but the double ovens. When he turned his head he saw the blonde clawing in her purse. He realized that something was in his hand, firmer than mere lather, and he looked down at a revolver—

—the kitchen snapped completely out of existence. He was in a car, rocketing along a foggy highway, pushing the muzzle of the revolver into the blonde's side. With horror, as she looked up at him, he felt his finger squeeze the trigger once, twice. She was punched sideways by the dual impact as the ear-shattering crash of the shots slammed through the car.

★　★　★

Vassago could not have anticipated what happened next.

The gun must have been loaded with magnum cartridges, for the two shots ripped through the blonde more violently than he expected and slammed her into the passenger door. Either her door was not properly shut or one of the rounds punched all the way through her, damaging the latch, because the door flew open.

144

Wind rushed into the Pontiac, shrieking like a living beast, and Lisa was snatched out into the night.

He jammed on the brakes and looked at the rearview mirror. As the car began to fishtail, he saw the blonde's body tumbling along the pavement behind him.

He intended to stop, throw the car into reverse, and go back for her, but even at that dead hour of the morning, other traffic shared the freeway. He saw two sets of headlights maybe half a mile behind him, bright smudges in the mist but clarifying by the second. Those drivers would encounter the body before he could reach it and scoop it into the Pontiac.

Taking his foot off the brake and accelerating, he swung the car hard to the left, across two lanes, then whipped it back to the right, forcing the door to slam shut. It rattled in its frame but didn't pop open again. The latch must be at least partially effective.

Although visibility had declined to about a hundred feet, he put the Pontiac up to eighty, bulleting blindly into the churning fog. Two exits later, he left the freeway and rapidly slowed down. On surface streets he made his way out of the area as swiftly as possible, obeying speed limits because any cop who stopped him would surely notice the blood splashed across the upholstery and glass of the passenger door.

*　★　*

In the rearview mirror, Hatch saw the body tumbling along the pavement, vanishing into the fog. Then for a brief moment he saw his own reflection from the bridge of his nose to his eyebrows. He was wearing sunglasses even though driving at night. No. *He* wasn't wearing them. The driver of the car was wearing them, and the reflection at which he stared was not his own. Although he seemed to be the driver, he realized that he was not, because even the dim glimpse he got of the eyes behind the tinted lenses was sufficient to convince him that they were peculiar, troubled, and utterly different from his own eyes. Then—

—he was standing at the kitchen sink again, breathing hard and making choking sounds of revulsion. Beyond the window lay only the back yard, blanketed by night and fog.

'Hatch?'

145

Startled, he turned.

Lindsey was standing in the doorway, in her bathrobe. 'Is something wrong?'

Wiping his soapy hands on his sweatshirt, he tried to speak, but terror had rendered him mute.

She hurried to him. 'Hatch?'

He held her tightly and was glad for her embrace, which at last squeezed the words from him. 'I shot her, she flew out of the car, Jesus God Almighty, bounced along the highway like a rag doll!'

·7·

At Hatch's request, Lindsey brewed a pot of coffee. The familiarity of the delicious aroma was an antidote to the strangeness of the night. More than anything else, that smell restored a sense of normalcy that helped settle Hatch's nerves. They drank the coffee at the breakfast table at one end of the kitchen.

Hatch insisted on closing the Levolor blind over the nearby window. He said, 'I have the feeling . . . something's out there . . . and I don't want it looking in at us.' He could not explain what he meant by 'something.'

When Hatch had recounted everything that had happened to him since waking from the nightmare of the icy blonde, the switchblade, and the mutilated eye, Lindsey had only one explanation to offer. 'No matter how it seemed at the time, you must not have been fully awake when you got out of bed. You were sleep-walking. You didn't really wake up until I stepped into the kitchen and called your name.'

'I've never been a sleepwalker,' he said.

She tried to make light of his objection. 'Never too late to take up a new affliction.'

'I don't buy it.'

'Then what's your explanation?'

'I don't have one.'

'So sleepwalking,' she said.

He stared down into the white porcelain cup that he clasped in both hands, as if he were a gypsy trying to foresee the future in the

146

patterns of light on the surface of the black brew. 'Have you ever dreamed you were someone else?'

'I suppose so,' she said.

He looked hard at her. 'No supposing. Have you ever seen a dream through the eyes of a stranger? A specific dream you can tell me about?'

'Well . . . no. But I'm sure I must've, at one time. I just don't remember. Dreams are smoke, after all. They fade so fast. Who remembers them for long?'

'I'll remember this one for the rest of my life,' he said.

★ ★ ★

Although they returned to bed, neither of them could get to sleep again. Maybe it was partly the coffee. She thought he had wanted the coffee precisely because he hoped that it would prevent sleep, sparing him a return to the nightmare. Well, it had worked.

They both were lying on their backs, staring at the ceiling.

At first he had been unwilling to turn off the bedside lamp, though he had revealed his reluctance only in the hesitancy with which he clicked the switch. He was almost like a child who was old enough to know real fears from false ones but not quite old enough to escape all of the latter, certain that some monster lurked under the bed but ashamed to say as much.

Now, with the lamp off and with only the indirect glow of distant streetlamps piercing the windows between the halves of the drapes, his anxiety had infected her. She found it easy to imagine that some shadows on the ceiling moved, bat-lizard-spider forms of singular stealth and malevolent purpose.

They talked softly, on and off, about nothing special. They both knew what they wanted to talk about, but they were afraid of it. Unlike the creepy-crawlies on the ceiling and things that lived under children's beds, it was a real fear. Brain damage.

Since waking up in the hospital, reanimated, Hatch had been having bad dreams of unnerving power. He didn't have them every night. His sleep might even be undisturbed for as long as three or four nights in a row. But he was having them more frequently, week by week, and the intensity was increasing.

They were not always the same dreams, as he described them, but they contained similar elements. Violence. Horrific images of

147

naked, rotting bodies contorted into peculiar positions. Always, the dreams unfolded from the point of view of a stranger, the same mysterious figure, as if Hatch were a spirit in possession of the man but unable to control him, along for the ride. Routinely the nightmares began or ended – or began *and* ended – in the same setting: an assemblage of unusual buildings and other queer structures that resisted identification, all of it unlighted and seen most often as a series of baffling silhouettes against a night sky. He also saw cavernous rooms and mazes of concrete corridors that were somehow revealed in spite of having no windows or artificial lighting. The location was, he said, familiar to him, but recognition remained elusive, for he never saw enough to be able to identify it.

Until tonight, they had tried to convince themselves that his affliction would be short-lived. Hatch was full of positive thoughts, as usual. Bad dreams were not remarkable. Everyone had them. They were often caused by stress. Alleviate the stress, and the nightmares went away.

But they were not fading. And now they had taken a new and deeply disturbing turn: sleepwalking.

Or perhaps he was beginning, while awake, to hallucinate the same images that troubled his sleep.

Shortly before dawn, Hatch reached out for her beneath the sheets and took her hand, held it tight. 'I'll be all right. It's nothing, really. Just a dream.'

'First thing in the morning, you should call Nyebern,' she said, her heart sinking like a stone in a pond. 'We haven't been straight with him. He told you to let him know immediately if there were any symptoms—'

'This isn't really a symptom,' he said, trying to put the best face on it.

'Physical *or* mental symptoms,' she said, afraid for him – and for herself if something *was* wrong with him.

'I had all the tests, most of them twice. They gave me a clean bill of health. No brain damage.'

'Then you've nothing to worry about, do you? No reason to delay seeing Nyebern.'

'If there'd been brain damage, it would've showed up right away. It's not a residual thing, doesn't kick in on a delay.'

They were silent for a while.

She could no longer imagine that creepy-crawlies moved through the shadows on the ceiling. False fears had evaporated the moment he had spoken the name of the biggest real fear that they faced.

At last she said, 'What about Regina?'

He considered her question for a while. Then: 'I think we should go ahead with it, fill out the papers – assuming she wants to come with us, of course.'

'And if . . . you've got a problem? And it gets worse?'

'It'll take a few days to make the arrangements and be able to bring her home. By then we'll have the results of the physical, the tests. I'm sure I'll be fine.'

'You're too relaxed about this.'

'Stress kills.'

'If Nyebern finds something seriously wrong . . .?'

'Then we'll ask the orphanage for a postponement if we have to. The thing is, if we tell them I'm having problems that don't allow me to go ahead with the papers tomorrow, they might have second thoughts about our suitability. We might be rejected and never have a chance with Regina.'

The day had been so perfect, from their meeting in Salvatore Gujilio's office to their lovemaking before the fire and again in the massive old Chinese sleigh bed. The future had looked so bright, the worst behind them. She was stunned at how suddenly they had taken another nasty plunge.

She said, 'God, Hatch, I love you.'

In the darkness he moved close to her and took her in his arms. Until long after dawn, they just held each other, saying nothing because, for the moment, everything had been said.

* * *

Later, after they showered and dressed, they went downstairs and had more coffee at the breakfast table. Mornings, they always listened to the radio, an all-news station. That was how they heard about Lisa Blaine, the blonde who had been shot twice and thrown from a moving car on the San Diego Freeway the previous night – at precisely the time that Hatch, standing in the kitchen, had a vision of the trigger being pulled and the body tumbling along the pavement in the wake of the car.

149

·8·

For reasons he could not understand, Hatch was compelled to see the section of the freeway where the dead woman had been found. 'Maybe something will click,' was all the explanation he could offer.

He drove their new red Mitsubishi. They went north on the coast highway, then east on a series of surface streets to the South Coast Plaza shopping mall, where they entered the San Diego Freeway heading south. He wanted to come upon the site of the murder from the same direction in which the killer had been traveling the previous night.

By nine-fifteen, rush-hour traffic should have abated, but all of the lanes were still clogged. They made halting progress southward in a haze of exhaust fumes, from which the car air-conditioning spared them.

The marine layer that surged in from the Pacific during the night had burned off. Trees stirred in a spring breeze, and birds swooped in giddy arcs across the cloudless, piercingly blue sky. The day did not seem like one in which anyone would have reason to think of death.

They passed the MacArthur Boulevard exit, then Jamboree, and with every turn of the wheels, Hatch felt the muscles growing tenser in his neck and shoulders. He was overcome by the uncanny feeling that he actually had followed this route last night, when fog had obscured the airport, hotels, office buildings, and the brown hills in the distance, though in fact he had been at home.

'They were going to El Toro,' he said, which was a detail he had not remembered until now. Or perhaps he had only now perceived it by the grace of some sixth sense.

'Maybe that's where she lived – or where he lives.'

Frowning, Hatch said, 'I don't think so.'

As they crept forward through the snarled traffic, he began to recall not just details of the dream but the *feeling* of it, the edgy atmosphere of pending violence.

His hands slipped on the steering wheel. They were clammy. He blotted them on his shirt.

'I think in some ways,' he said, 'the blonde was almost as dangerous as I . . . as he was . . .'

150

'What do you mean?'

'I don't know. It's just the feeling I had then.'

Sunshine glimmered on – and glinted off – the multitude of vehicles that churned both north and south in two great rivers of steel and chrome and glass. Outside, the temperature was hovering around eighty degrees. But Hatch was cold.

As a sign notified them of the upcoming Culver Boulevard exit, Hatch leaned forward slightly. He let go of the steering wheel with his right hand and reached under his seat. 'It was here that he went for the gun . . . pulled it out . . . she was looking in her purse for something.'

He would not have been too surprised if he had found a gun under his seat, for he still had a frighteningly clear recollection of how fluidly the dream and reality had mingled, separated, and mingled again last night. Why not now, even in daylight? He let out a hiss of relief when he found that the space beneath his seat was empty.

'Cops,' Lindsey said.

Hatch was so caught up in the re-creation of the events in the nightmare, that he didn't immediately realize what Lindsey was talking about. Then he saw black-and-whites and other police vehicles parked along the interstate.

Bent forward, intently studying the dusty ground before them, uniformed officers were walking the shoulder of the highway and picking through the dry grass beyond it. They were evidently conducting an expanded search for evidence to discover anything else that might have fallen out of the killer's car before, with, or after the blonde.

He noticed that every one of the cops was wearing sunglasses, as were he and Lindsey. The day was eye-stingingly bright.

But the killer had been wearing sunglasses, too, when he had looked in the rearview mirror. Why would he have been wearing them in the dark in dense fog, for God's sake?

Shades at night in bad weather was more than just affectation or eccentricity. It was weird.

Hatch still had the imaginary gun in his hand, withdrawn from under the seat. But because they were moving so much slower than the killer had been driving, they had not yet reached the spot at which the revolver had been fired.

Traffic was creeping bumper-to-bumper not because the rush

151

hour was heavier than usual but because motorists were slowing to stare at the police. It was what the radio traffic reporters called 'gawkers' block.'

'He was really barreling along,' Hatch said.

'In heavy fog.'

'And sunglasses.'

'Stupid,' Lindsey said.

'No. This guy's smart.'

'Sounds stupid to me.'

'Fearless.' Hatch tried to settle back into the skin of the man with whom he had shared a body in the nightmare. It wasn't easy. Something about the killer was totally alien and firmly resisted analysis. 'He's extremely cold . . . cold and dark inside . . . he doesn't think like you or me.' Hatch struggled to find words to convey what the killer had felt like. 'Dirty.' He shook his head. 'I don't mean he was unwashed, nothing like that. It's more as if . . . well, as if he was contaminated.' He sighed and gave up. 'Anyway, he's utterly fearless. Nothing scares him. He believes that nothing can hurt him. But in his case that's not the same as recklessness. Because . . . somehow he's right.'

'What're you saying – that he's invulnerable?'

'No. Not exactly. But nothing you could do to him . . . would matter to him.'

Lindsey hugged herself. 'You make him sound . . . inhuman.'

At the moment the police search for evidence was concentrated in the quarter of a mile just south of the Culver Boulevard exit. When Hatch got past that activity, traffic began to move faster.

The imaginary gun in his right hand seemed to take on greater substance. He could almost feel the cold steel against his palm.

When he pointed the phantom revolver at Lindsey and glanced at her, she winced. He saw her clearly, but he could also see, in memory, the face of the blonde as she had looked up from her purse with too little reaction time even to show surprise.

'Here, right here, two shots, fast as I . . . as he could pull the trigger,' Hatch said, shuddering because the memory of violence was far easier to recapture than were the mood and malign spirit of the gunman. 'Big holes in her.' He could see it so clearly. 'Jesus, it was awful.' He was really into it. 'The way she tore open. And the sound like thunder, the end of the world.' The bitter taste of stomach acid rose in his throat. 'She was thrown back by the impact, against the door, instantly dead, but the door flew open. He wasn't expecting it to fly open. He wanted her, she was part of his collection now, but then she was gone, out into the night, gone, rolling like a piece of litter along the blacktop.'

Caught up in the dream memory, he rammed his foot down on the brake pedal, as the killer had done.

'Hatch, no!'

A car, then another, then a third, swerved around them in flashes of chrome and sun-silvered glass, horns blaring, narrowly avoiding a collision.

Shaking himself out of the memory, Hatch accelerated again, back into the traffic flow. He was aware of people staring at him from other cars.

He didn't care about their scrutiny, for he had picked up the trail as if he were a bloodhound. It was not actually a scent that he followed. It was an indefinable something that led him on; maybe psychic vibrations, a disturbance in the ether made by the killer's passage just as a shark's fin would carve a trough in the surface of the sea, although the ether had not repaired itself with the alacrity of water.

'He considered going back for her, knew it was hopeless, so he drove on,' Hatch said, aware that his voice had become low and slightly raspy, as if he were recounting secrets that were painful to reveal.

'Then I walked into the kitchen, and you were making an odd choking-gasping sound,' Lindsey said. 'Gripping the edge of the counter tight enough to crack the granite. I thought you were having a heart attack.'

'Drove very fast,' Hatch said, accelerating only slightly himself, 'seventy, eighty, even faster, anxious to get away before the traffic behind him encountered the body.'

Realizing that he was not merely speculating on what the killer had done, Lindsey said, 'You're remembering more than you dreamed, past the point when I came into the kitchen and woke you.'

'Not remembering,' he said huskily.

'Then what?'

'Sensing.'

'Now?'

'Yes.'

153

'How?'

'Somehow.' He simply could not explain it better than that. 'Somehow,' he whispered, and he followed the ribbon of pavement across that largely flat expanse of land, which seemed to darken in spite of the bright morning sun, as if the killer cast a shadow vastly larger than himself, a shadow that lingered behind him even hours after he had gone. 'Eighty . . . eighty-five . . . almost ninety miles an hour . . . able to see only a hundred feet ahead.' If any traffic had been there in the fog, the killer would have crashed into it with cataclysmic force. 'He didn't take the first exit, wanted to get farther away than that . . . kept going . . . going . . . '

He almost didn't slow down in time to make the exit for State Route 133, which became the canyon road into Laguna Beach. At the last moment he hit the brakes too hard and whipped the wheel to the right. The Mitsubishi slid as they departed the interstate, but he decreased speed and immediately regained full control.

'He got off here?' Lindsey asked.

'Yes.'

Hatch followed the new road to the right.

'Did he go into Laguna?'

'I . . . don't think so.'

He braked to a complete halt at a crossroads marked by a stop sign. He pulled onto the shoulder. Open country lay ahead, hills dressed in crisp brown grass. If he went straight through the crossroads, he'd be heading into Laguna Canyon, where developers had not yet managed to raze the wilderness and erect more tract homes. Miles of brush land and scattered oaks flanked the canyon route all the way into Laguna Beach. The killer also might have turned left or right. Hatch looked in each direction, searching for whatever invisible signs had guided him that far.

After a moment, Lindsey said, 'You don't know where he went from here?'

'Hideaway.'

'Huh?'

Hatch blinked, not sure why he had chosen that word. 'He went back to his hideaway . . . into the ground.'

'Ground?' Lindsey asked. With puzzlement she surveyed the sere hills.

' . . . into the darkness . . . '

'You mean he went underground somewhere?'

' . . . cool, cool silence . . . '

Hatch sat for a while, staring at the crossroads as a few cars came and went. He had reached the end of the trail. The killer was not there; he knew that much, but he did not know where the man had gone. Nothing more came to him – except, strangely, the sweet chocolate taste of Oreo cookies, as intense as if he had just bitten into one.

·9·

At The Cottage in Laguna Beach, they had a late breakfast of homefries, eggs, bacon, and buttered toast. Since he had died and been resuscitated, Hatch didn't worry about things like his cholesterol count or the long-term effects of passive inhalation of other people's cigarette smoke. He supposed the day would come when little risks would seem big again, whereupon he would return to a diet high in fruits and vegetables, scowl at smokers who blew their filth his way, and open a bottle of fine wine with a mixture of delight and a grim awareness of the health consequences of consuming alcohol. At the moment he was appreciating life too much to worry unduly about losing it again – which was why he was determined not to let the dreams and the death of the blonde push him off the deep end.

Food had a natural tranquilizing effect. Each bite of egg yolk soothed his nerves.

'Okay,' Lindsey said, going at her breakfast somewhat less heartily than Hatch did, 'let's suppose there was brain damage of some sort, after all. But minor. So minor it never showed up on any of the tests. Not bad enough to cause paralysis or speech problems or anything like that. In fact, by an incredible stroke of luck, a one in a billion chance, this brain damage had a freak effect that was actually beneficial. It could've made a few new connections in the cerebral tissues, and left you psychic.'

'Bull.'

'Why?'

'I'm not psychic.'

'Then what do you call it?'

155

'Even if I was psychic, I wouldn't say it was beneficial.'

Because the breakfast rush had passed, the restaurant was not too busy. The nearest tables to theirs were vacant. They could discuss the morning's events without fear of being overheard, but Hatch kept glancing around self-consciously anyway.

Immediately following his reanimation, the media had swarmed to Orange County General Hospital, and in the days after Hatch's release, reporters had virtually camped on his doorstep at home. After all, he had been dead longer than any man alive, which made him eligible for considerably more than the fifteen minutes of fame that Andy Warhol had said would eventually be every person's fate in celebrity-obsessed America. He'd done nothing to earn his fame. He didn't want it. He hadn't fought his way out of death; Lindsey, Nyebern, and the resuscitation team had dragged him back. He was a private person, content with just the quiet respect of the better antique dealers who knew his shop and traded with him sometimes. In fact, if the only respect he had was Lindsey's, if he was famous only in her eyes and only for being a good husband, that would be enough for him. By steadfastly refusing to talk to the press, he had finally convinced them to leave him alone and chase after whatever newly born two-headed goat – or its equivalent – was available to fill newspaper space or a minute of the airwaves between deodorant commercials.

Now, if he revealed that he had come back from the dead with some strange power to connect with the mind of a psycho killer, swarms of newspeople would descend on him again. He could not tolerate even the prospect of it. He would find it easier to endure a plague of killer bees or a hive of Hare Krishna solicitors with collection cups and eyes glazed by spiritual transcendence.

'If it's not some psychic ability,' Lindsey persisted, 'then what *is* it?'

'I don't know.'

'That's not good enough.'

'It could pass, never happen again. It could be a fluke.'

'You don't believe that.'

'Well . . . I want to believe it.'

'We have to deal with this.'

'Why?'

'We have to try to understand it.'

'Why?'

156

'Don't "why" me like a five-year-old child.'

'Why?'

'Be serious, Hatch. A woman's dead. She may not be the first. She may not be the last.'

He put his fork on his half-empty plate, and swallowed some orange juice to wash down the homefries. 'Okay, all right, it's like a psychic vision, yeah, just the way they show it in the movies. But it's more than that. Creepier.'

He closed his eyes, trying to think of an analogy. When he had it, he opened his eyes and looked around the restaurant again to be sure no new diners had entered and sat near them.

He looked regretfully at his plate. His eggs were getting cold. He sighed.

'You know,' he said, 'how they say identical twins, separated at birth and raised a thousand miles apart by utterly different adopted families, will still grow up to live similar lives?'

'Sure, I've heard of that. So?'

'Even raised apart, with totally different backgrounds, they'll choose similar careers, achieve the same income levels, marry women who resemble each other, even give their kids the same names. It's uncanny. And even if they don't know they're twins, even if each of them was told he was an only child when he was adopted, they'll sense each other out there, across the miles, even if they don't know who or what they're sensing. They have a bond that no one can explain, not even geneticists.'

'So how does this apply to you?'

He hesitated, then picked up his fork. He wanted to eat instead of talk. Eating was safe. But she wouldn't let him get away with that. His eggs were congealing. His tranquilizers. He put the fork down again.

'Sometimes,' he said, 'I see through this guy's eyes when I'm sleeping, and now sometimes I can even feel him out there when I'm awake, and it's like the psychic crap in movies, yeah. But I also feel this . . . this bond with him that I really *can't* explain or describe to you, no matter how much you prod me about it.'

'You're not saying you think he's your twin or something?'

'No, not at all. I think he's a lot younger than me, maybe only twenty or twenty-one. And no blood relation. But it's that kind of bond, that mystical twin crap, as if this guy and I share something, have some fundamental quality in common.'

157

'Like what?'

'I don't know. I wish I did.' He paused. He decided to be entirely truthful. 'Or maybe I don't.'

* * *

Later, after the waitress had cleared away their empty dishes and brought them strong black coffee, Hatch said, 'There's no way I'm going to go to the cops and offer to help them, if that's what you're thinking.'

'There is a duty here—'

'I don't know anything that could help them anyway.'

She blew on her hot coffee. 'You know he was driving a Pontiac.'

'I don't even think it was his.'

'Whose then?'

'Stolen, maybe.'

'That was something else you sensed?'

'Yeah. But I don't know what he looks like, his name, where he lives, anything useful.'

'What if something like that comes to you? What if you see something that could help the cops?'

'Then I'll call it in anonymously.'

'They'll take the information more seriously if you give it to them in person.'

He felt violated by the intrusion of this psychotic stranger into his life. That violation made him angry, and he feared his anger more than he feared the stranger, or the supernatural aspect of the situation, or the prospect of brain damage. He dreaded being driven by some extremity to discover that his father's hot temper was within him, too, waiting to be tapped.

'It's a homicide case,' he said. 'They take *every* tip seriously in a murder investigation, even if it's anonymous. I'm not going to let them make headlines out of me again.'

* * *

From the restaurant they went across town to Harrison's Antiques, where Lindsey had an art studio on part of the top floor in addition to the one at home. When she painted, a regular change of environment contributed to fresher work.

In the car, with the sun-spangled ocean visible between some of the buildings to their right, Lindsey pressed the point that she had nagged him about over breakfast, because she knew that Hatch's only serious character flaw was a tendency to be too easy-going. Jimmy's death was the only bad thing in his life that he had never been able to rationalize, minimalize, and put out of mind. And even with that, he had tried to suppress it rather than face up to his grief, which was why his grief had had a chance to grow. Given time, and not much of it, he'd begin to downplay the importance of what had just happened to him.

She said, 'You've still got to see Nyebern.'

'I suppose so.'

'Definitely.'

'If there's brain damage, if that's where this psychic stuff comes from, you said yourself it was *benevolent* brain damage.'

'But maybe it's degenerative, maybe it'll get worse.'

'I really don't think so,' he said. 'I feel fine otherwise.'

'You're no doctor.'

'All right,' he said. He braked for the traffic light at the crossing to the public beach in the heart of town. 'I'll call him. But we have to see Gujilio later this afternoon.'

'You can still squeeze in Nyebern if he has time for you.'

Hatch's father had been a tyrant, quick-tempered, sharp-tongued, with a penchant for subduing his wife and disciplining his son by the application of regular doses of verbal abuse in the form of nasty mockery, cutting sarcasm, or just plain threats. Anything at all could set Hatch's father off, or nothing at all, because secretly he cherished irritation and actively sought new sources of it. He was a man who believed he was not destined to be happy – and he insured that his destiny was fulfilled by making himself and everyone around him miserable.

Perhaps afraid that the potential for a murderously bad temper was within him, too, or only because he'd had enough tumult in his life, Hatch had consciously striven to make himself as mellow as his father was high-strung, as sweetly tolerant as his father was narrow-minded, as greathearted as his father was unforgiving, as determined to roll with all of life's punches as his father was determined to punch back at even imaginary blows. As a result, he was the nicest man Lindsey had ever known, the nicest by light years

159

or by whatever measure niceness was calculated: bunches, buck-etsful, gobs. Sometimes, however, he would turn away from an unpleasantness that had to be dealt with, rather than risk getting in touch with any negative emotion that was remotely reminiscent of his old man's paranoia and anger.

The light changed from red to green, but three young women in bikinis were in the crosswalk, laden with beach gear and heading for the ocean. Hatch didn't just wait for them. He watched them with a smile of appreciation for the way they filled out their suits.

'I take it back,' Lindsey said.

'What?'

'I was just thinking what a nice guy you are, too nice, but obviously you're a piece of lecherous scum.'

'Nice scum, though.'

'*I'll* call Nyebern as soon as we get to the shop,' Lindsey said.

He drove up the hill through the main part of town, past the old Laguna Hotel. 'Okay. But I'm sure as hell not going to tell him I'm suddenly psychic. He's a good man, but he won't be able to sit on that kind of news. The next thing I know, my face'll be all over the cover of the *National Enquirer*. Besides, I'm not psychic, not exactly. I don't know what the hell I am – aside from lecherous scum.'

'So what'll you tell him?'

'Just enough about the dreams so he'll realize how troubling they are and how strange, so he'll order whatever tests I ought to have. Good enough?'

'I guess it'll have to be.'

* * *

In the tomb-deep blackness of his hideaway, curled naked upon the stained and lumpy mattress, fast asleep, Vassago saw sunlight, sand, the sea, and three bikinied girls beyond the windshield of a red car.

He was dreaming and knew he dreamed, which was a peculiar sensation. He rolled with it.

He saw, as well, the dark-haired and dark-eyed woman about whom he had dreamed yesterday, when she had been behind the wheel of that same car. She had appeared in other dreams, once in a wheelchair, when she had been laughing and weeping at the same time.

160

He found her more interesting than the scantily clad beach bunnies because she was unusually vital. Radiant. Through the unknown man driving the car, Vassago somehow knew that the woman had once considered embracing death, had hesitated on the edge of either active or passive self-destruction, and had rejected an early grave—

. . . *water, he sensed a watery vault, cold and suffocating, narrowly escaped . . .*

—whereafter she had been more full of life, energetic, and vivid than ever before. She had cheated death. Denied the devil. Vassago hated her for that, because it was in the service of death that he had found meaning to his own existence.

He tried to reach out and touch her through the body of the man driving the car. Failed. It was only a dream. Dreams could not be controlled. If he could have touched her, he would have made her regret that she had turned away from the comparatively painless death by drowning that could have been hers.

FIVE

·1·

When she moved in with the Harrisons, Regina almost thought she had died and gone to Heaven, except she had her own bathroom, and she didn't believe anyone had his own bathroom up in Heaven because in Heaven no one needed a bathroom. They were not all permanently constipated in Heaven or anything like that, and they certainly didn't just do their business out in public, for God's sake (sorry, God), because no one in his right mind would want to go to Heaven if it was the kind of place where you had to watch where you stepped. It was just that in Heaven all the concerns of earthly existence passed away. You didn't even have a body in Heaven; you were probably just a sphere of mental energy, sort of like a balloon full of golden glowing gas, drifting around among the angels, singing the praises of God – which was pretty weird when you thought about it, all those glowing and singing balloons, but the most you'd ever have to do in the way of waste elimination was maybe vent a little gas now and then, which wouldn't even smell bad, probably like the sweet incense in church, or perfume.

That first day in the Harrisons' house, late Monday afternoon, the twenty-ninth of April, she would remember forever, because they were so nice. They didn't even mention the real reason why they gave her a choice between a bedroom on the second floor and a den on the first floor that could be converted into a bedroom.

'One thing in its favor,' Mr Harrison said about the den, 'is the view. Better than the view from the upstairs room.'

He led Regina to the big windows that looked out on a rose garden ringed by a border of huge ferns. The view *was* pretty.

Mrs Harrison said, 'And you'd have all these bookshelves,

162

which you might want to fill up gradually with your own collection, since you're a book lover.'

Actually, without ever hinting at it, their concern was that she might find the stairs troublesome. But she didn't mind stairs so much. In fact she liked stairs, she loved stairs, she ate stairs for breakfast. In the orphanage, they had put her on the first floor, until she was eight years old and realized she'd been given ground-level accommodations because of her clunky leg brace and deformed right hand, whereupon she immediately demanded to be moved to the third floor. The nuns would not hear of it, so she threw a tantrum, but the nuns knew how to deal with that, so she tried withering scorn, but the nuns could not be withered, so she went on a hunger strike, and finally the nuns surrendered to her demand on a trial basis. She'd lived on the third floor for more than two years, and she had never used the elevator. When she chose the second-floor bedroom in the Harrisons' house, without having seen it, neither of them tried to talk her out of it, or wondered aloud if she were 'up to it,' or even blinked. She loved them for that.

The house was gorgeous – cream walls, white woodwork, modern furniture mixed with antiques, Chinese bowls and vases, everything just so. When they took her on a tour, Regina actually felt as dangerously clumsy as she had claimed to be in the meeting in Mr Gujilio's office. She moved with exaggerated care, afraid that she would knock over one precious item and kick off a chain-reaction that would spread across the entire room, then through a doorway into the next room and from there throughout the house, one beautiful treasure tipping into the next like dominoes in a world-championship toppling contest, two-hundred-year-old porcelain exploding, antique furniture reduced to match sticks, until they were left standing in mounds of worthless rubble, coated with the dust of what had been a *fortune* in interior design.

She was so absolutely certain it was going to happen that she wracked her mind urgently, room by room, for something winning to say when catastrophe struck, after the last exquisite crystal candy dish had crashed off the last disintegrating table that had once been the property of the First King of France. 'Oops,' did not seem appropriate, and neither did, 'Jesus Christ!' because they thought they had adopted a good Catholic girl not a foul-mouthed heathen (sorry, God), and neither did 'somebody

163

pushed me,' because that was a lie, and lying bought you a ticket to Hell, though she suspected she was going to wind up in Hell anyway, considering how she couldn't stop thinking the Lord's name in vain and using vulgarities. No balloon full of glowing golden gas for her.

Throughout the house, the walls were adorned with art, and Regina noted that the most wonderful pieces all had the same signature at the bottom right corner: Lindsey Sparling. Even as much of a screwup as she was, she was smart enough to figure that the name Lindsey was no coincidence and that Sparling must be Mrs Harrison's maiden name. They were the strangest and most beautiful paintings Regina had ever seen, some of them so bright and full of good feeling that you had to smile, some of them dark and brooding. She wanted to spend a long time in front of each of them, sort of soaking them up, but she was afraid Mr and Mrs Harrison would think she was a brownnosing phony, pretending interest as a way of apologizing for the wisecracks she had made in Mr Gujilio's office about paintings on velvet.

Somehow she got through the entire house without destroying anything, and the last room was hers. It was bigger than any room at the orphanage, and she didn't have to share it with anyone. The windows were covered with white plantation shutters. Furnishings included a corner desk and chair, a bookcase, an armchair with footstool, nightstands with matching lamps – and an amazing bed.

'It's from about 1850,' Mrs Harrison said, as Regina let her hand glide slowly over the beautiful bed.

'English,' Mr Harrison said. 'Mahogany with hand-painted decoration under several coats of lacquer.'

On the footboard, side rails, and headboard, the dark-red and dark-yellow roses and emerald-green leaves seemed alive, not bright against the deeply colored wood but so lustrous and dewy-looking that she was sure she would be able to smell them if she put her nose to their petals.

Mrs Harrison said, 'It might seem a little *old* for a young girl, a little stuffy – '

'Yes, of course,' Mr Harrison said, 'we can send it over to the store, sell it, let you choose something you'd like, something modern. This was just furnished as a guest room.'

'No,' Regina said hastily. 'I like it, I really do. Could I keep it? I mean, even though it's so expensive?'

164

'It's not that expensive,' Mr Harrison said, 'and of course you can keep anything you want.'

'Or get rid of anything you want,' Mrs Harrison said.

'Except us, of course,' Mr Harrison said.

'That's right,' Mrs Harrison said, 'I'm afraid we come with the house.'

Regina's heart was pounding so hard she could barely get her breath. Happiness. And fear. Everything was so wonderful – but surely it couldn't last. Nothing so good could last very long.

Sliding, mirrored doors covered one wall of the bedroom, and Mrs Harrison showed Regina a closet behind the mirrors. The hugest closet in the world. Maybe you needed a closet that size if you were a movie star, or if you were one of those men she had read about, who liked to dress up in women's clothes sometimes, 'cause then you'd need both a girl's and boy's wardrobe. But it was much bigger than she needed; it would hold ten times the clothes that she possessed.

With some embarrassment, she looked at the two cardboard suitcases she had brought with her from St Thomas's. They held everything she owned in the world. For the first time in her life, she realized she was poor. Which was peculiar, really, not to have understood her poverty before, since she was an orphan who had inherited nothing. Well, nothing other than a bum leg and a twisted right hand with two fingers missing.

As if reading Regina's mind, Mrs Harrison said, 'Let's go shopping.'

They went to South Coast Plaza mall. They bought her too many clothes, books, anything she wanted. Regina worried that they were overspending and would have to eat beans for a year to balance their budget – she didn't like beans – but they failed to pick up on her hints about the virtues of frugality. Finally she had to stop them by pretending that her weak leg was bothering her.

From the mall they went to dinner at an Italian restaurant. She had eaten out twice before, but only at a fast-food place, where the owner treated all the kids at the orphanage to burgers and fries. This was a *real* restaurant, and there was so much to absorb that she could hardly eat, keep up her end of the table conversation, *and* enjoy the place all at the same time. The chairs weren't made out of hard plastic, and neither were the knives and forks.

165

The plates weren't either paper or Styrofoam, and drinks came in actual glasses, which must mean that the customers in real restaurants were not as clumsy as those in fast-food places and could be trusted with breakable things. The waitresses weren't teenagers, and they brought your food to you instead of handing it across a counter by the cash register. And they didn't make you pay for it until *after* you'd eaten it!

Later, back at the Harrison house, after Regina unpacked her things, brushed her teeth, put on pajamas, took off her leg brace, and got into bed, both the Harrisons came in to say goodnight. Mr Harrison sat on the edge of her bed and told her that everything might seem strange at first, even unsettling, but that soon enough she would feel at home, then he kissed her on the forehead and said, 'Sweet dreams, princess.' Mrs Harrison was next, and she sat on the edge of the bed, too. She talked for a while about all the things they would do together in the days ahead. Then she kissed Regina on the cheek, said, 'Good night, honey,' and turned off the overhead light as she went out the door into the hall.

Regina had never before been kissed goodnight, so she had not known how to respond. Some of the nuns were huggers; they liked to give you an affectionate squeeze now and then, but none of them was a smoocher. For as far back as Regina could remember, a flicker of the dorm lights was the signal to be in bed within fifteen minutes, and when the lights went out, each kid was responsible for getting tucked in himself. Now she had been tucked in twice and kissed goodnight twice, all in the same evening, and she had been too surprised to kiss either of them in return, which she now realized she should have done.

'You're such a screwup, Reg,' she said aloud.

Lying in her magnificent bed, with the painted roses twining around her in the darkness, Regina could imagine the conversation they were having, right that minute, in their own bedroom:

Did she kiss you goodnight?

No, did she kiss you?

No. Maybe she's a cold fish.

Maybe she's a psycho demon child.

Yeah, like that kid in The Omen.

You know what I'm worried about?

She'll stab us to death in our sleep.

Let's hide all the kitchen knives.

166

Better hide the power tools, too.
You still have the gun in the nightstand?
Yeah, but a gun will never stop her.
Thank God, we have a crucifix.
We'll sleep in shifts.
Send her back to the orphanage tomorrow.

'Such a screwup,' Regina said. 'Shit.' She sighed. 'Sorry, God.' Then she folded her hands in prayer and said softly, 'Dear God, if you'll convince the Harrisons to give me one more chance, I'll never say shit again, and I'll be a better person.' That didn't seem like a good enough bargain from God's point of view, so she threw in other inducements: 'I'll continue to keep an A average in school, I'll never again put Jell-O in the holy water font, and I'll give serious thought to becoming a nun.' Still not good enough. 'And I'll eat beans.' That ought to do it. God was probably proud of beans. After all, He'd made all kinds of them. Her refusal to eat green or wax or Lima or navy or any other kind of beans had no doubt been noted in Heaven, where they had her down in the Big Book of Insults to God: *Regina, currently age 10, thinks God pulled a real boner when He created beans.* She yawned. She felt better now about her chances with the Harrisons and about her relationship with God, though she didn't feel better about the change in her diet. Anyway, she slept.

·2·

While Lindsey was washing her face, scrubbing her teeth, and brushing her hair in the master bathroom, Hatch sat in bed with the newspaper. He read the science page first, because it contained the real news these days. Then he skimmed the entertainment section and read his favorite comic strips before turning, at last, to the A section where the latest exploits of politicians were as terrifying and darkly amusing as usual. On page three he saw the story about Bill Cooper, the beer deliveryman whose truck they had found crosswise on the mountain road that fateful, snowy night in March.

Within a couple of days of being resuscitated, Hatch had heard that the trucker had been charged with driving under the influence and that the percentage of alcohol in his blood had been more than twice that required for a conviction under the law. George Glover, Hatch's personal attorney, had asked him if he wanted to press a civil suit against Cooper or the company for which he worked, but Hatch was not by nature litigious. Besides, he dreaded becoming bogged down in the dull and thorny world of lawyers and courtrooms. He was alive. That was all that mattered. A drunk-driving charge would be brought against the trucker without Hatch's involvement, and he was satisfied to let the system handle it.

He had received two pieces of correspondence from William Cooper, the first just four days after his reanimation. It was an apparently sincere, if long-winded and obsequious, apology seeking personal absolution, which was delivered to the hospital where Hatch was undergoing physical therapy. 'Sue me if you want,' Cooper wrote, 'I deserve it. I'd give you everything if you wanted it, though I don't got much, I'm no rich man. But no matter whether you sue me or if not, I most sincerely hope you'll find it in your generous heart to forgive me one ways or another. Except for the genius of Dr Nyebern and his wonderful people, you'd be dead for sure, and I'd carry it on my conscience all the rest of my days.' He rambled on in that fashion for four pages of tightly spaced, cramped, and at times inscrutable handwriting.

Hatch had responded with a short note, assuring Cooper that he did not intend to sue him and that he harbored no animosity toward him. He also had urged the man to seek counseling for alcohol abuse if he had not already done so.

A few weeks later, when Hatch was living at home again and back at work, after the media storm had swept over him, a second letter had arrived from Cooper. Incredibly, he was seeking Hatch's help to get his truck-driving job back, from which he had been fired subsequent to the charges that the police had filed against him. 'I been chased down for driving drunk twice before, it's true,' Cooper wrote, 'but both them times, I was in my car, not the truck, on my own time, not during work hours. Now my job is gone, plus they're fixing to take away my license, which'll make life hard. I mean, for one thing, how am I going to get a new job without a license? Now what I figure is, from your kind answer to my first letter, you proved yourself a fine Christian gentleman, so if you was to speak up on my behalf, it would be a big help. After all, you didn't wind up dead, and in fact you got a lot of publicity out of the whole thing, which must've helped your antique business a considerable amount.'

Astonished and uncharacteristically furious, Hatch had filed the letter without answering it. In fact he quickly put it out of his mind, because he was scared by how angry he grew whenever he contemplated it.

Now, according to the brief story on page three of the paper, based on a single technical error in police procedures, Cooper's attorney had won a dismissal of all charges against him. The article included a three-sentence summary of the accident and a silly reference to Hatch as 'holding the current record for being dead the longest time prior to a successful resuscitation,' as if he had arranged the entire ordeal with the hope of winning a place in the next edition of the *Guinness Book of World Records*.

Other revelations in the piece made Hatch curse out loud and sit up straight in bed, culminating with the news that Cooper was going to sue his employer for wrongful termination and expected to get his old job back or, failing that, a substantial financial settlement. 'I have suffered considerable humiliation at the hands of my former employer, subsequent to which I developed a serious stress-related health condition,' Cooper had told reporters, obviously disgorging an attorney-written statement that he had memorized. 'Yet even Mr Harrison has written to tell me that he holds me blameless for the events of that night.'

Anger propelled Hatch off the bed and onto his feet. His face felt flushed, and he was shaking uncontrollably.

Ludicrous. The drunken bastard was trying to get his job back by using Hatch's compassionate note as an endorsement, which required a complete misrepresentation of what Hatch had actually written. It was deceptive. It was unconscionable.

'Of all the fucking nerve!' Hatch said fiercely between clenched teeth.

Dropping most of the newspaper at his feet, crumpling the page with the story in his right hand, he hurried out of the bedroom and descended the stairs two at a time. In the den, he threw the paper on the desk, banged open a sliding closet door, and jerked out the top drawer of a three-drawer filing cabinet.

He had saved Cooper's handwritten letters, and although they were not on printed stationery, he knew the trucker had included not only a return address but a phone number on both pieces of correspondence. He was so disturbed, he flicked past the correct file folder – labeled MISCELLANEOUS BUSINESS – cursed softly but fluently when he couldn't find it, then searched backward and pulled it out. As he pawed through the contents, other letters slipped out of the folder and clattered to the floor at his feet.

Cooper's second letter had a telephone number carefully hand-printed at the top. Hatch put the disarranged file folder on the cabinet and hurried to the phone on the desk. His hand was shaking so badly that he couldn't read the number, so he put the letter on the blotter, in the cone of light from the brass desk lamp.

He punched William Cooper's number, intent on telling him off. The line was busy.

He jammed his thumb down on the disconnect button, got the dial tone, and tried again. Still busy.

'Sonofabitch!' He slammed down the receiver, but snatched it up again because there was nothing else he could do to let off steam. He tried the number a third time, using the redial button. It was still busy, of course, because no more than half a minute had passed since the first time he had tried it. He smashed the handset into the cradle so hard he might have broken the phone.

On one level he was startled by the savagery of the act, the childishness of it. But that part of him was not in control, and the mere awareness that he was over the top did not help him regain a grip on himself.

'Hatch?'

He looked up in surprise at the sound of his name and saw Lindsey, in her bathrobe, standing in the doorway between the den and the foyer.

Frowning, she said, 'What's wrong?'

'What's wrong?' he asked, his fury growing irrationally, as if she were somehow in league with Cooper, as if she were only pretending to be unaware of this latest turn of events. 'I'll tell you what's wrong. They let this Cooper bastard off the hook! The son of a bitch kills me, runs me off the goddamned road and *kills* me, then slips off the hook and has the nerve to try to use the letter I wrote him to get his job back!' He snatched up the crumpled newspaper and shook it at her, almost accusingly, as if she knew what was in it. 'Get his job back – so he can run someone else off the fucking road and kill *them*!'

Looking worried and confused, Lindsey stepped into the den. 'They let him off the hook? How?'

170

'A technicality. Isn't that cute? A cop misspells a word on the citation or something, and the guy walks!'

'Honey, calm down – '

'Calm down? Calm *down*?' He shook the crumpled newspaper again. 'You know what else it says here? The jerk sold his story to that sleazy tabloid, the one that kept chasing after me, and I wouldn't have anything to do with them. So now this drunken son of a bitch sells them the story about' – he was spraying spittle he was so angry; he flattened out the newspaper, found the article, read from it – 'about "his emotional ordeal and his role in the rescue that saved Mr Harrison's life." What role did he have in my rescue? Except he used his CB to call for help after we went off the road, which we wouldn't have done if he hadn't been there in the first place! He's not only keeping his driver's license and probably going to get his job back, but he's making money off the whole damn thing! If I could get my hands on the bastard, I'd kill him, I swear I would!'

'You don't mean that,' she said, looking shocked.

'You better believe I do! The irresponsible, greedy bastard. I'd like to kick him in the head a few times to knock some sense into him, pitch *him* into that freezing river – '

'Honey, lower your voice—'

'Why the hell should I lower my voice in my own—'

'You'll wake Regina.'

It was not the mention of the girl that jolted him out of his blind rage, but the sight of himself in the mirrored closet door beside Lindsey. Actually, he didn't see himself at all. For an instant he saw a young man with thick black hair falling across his forehead, wearing sunglasses, dressed all in black. He knew he was looking at the killer, but the killer seemed to be *him*. At that moment they were one and the same. That aberrant thought – and the young man's image – passed in a second or two, leaving Hatch staring at his familiar reflection.

Stunned less by the hallucination than by that momentary confusion of identity, Hatch gazed into the mirror and was appalled as much by what he saw now as by the brief glimpse of the killer. He looked apoplectic. His hair was disarranged. His face was red and contorted with rage, and his eyes were . . . wild. He reminded himself of his father, which was unthinkable, intolerable.

He could not remember the last time he had been that angry. In fact he had *never* been in a comparable rage. Until now, he'd

171

thought he was incapable of that kind of outburst or of the intense anger that could lead to it.

'I . . . I don't know what happened.'

He dropped the crumpled page of the newspaper. It struck his desk and fell to the floor with a crisp rustling noise that wrought an inexplicably vivid picture in his mind—

dry brown leaves tumbling in a breeze along the cracked pavement in a crumbling, abandoned amusement park

– and for just a moment he was *there*, with weeds sprouting up around him from cracks in the blacktop, dead leaves whirling past, the moon glaring down through the elaborate open-beam supports of a roller-coaster track. Then he was in his office again, leaning weakly against his desk.

'Hatch?'

He blinked at her, unable to speak.

'What's wrong?' she asked, moving quickly to him. She touched his arm tentatively, as if she thought he might shatter from the contact – or perhaps as if she expected him to respond to her touch with a blow struck in anger.

He put his arms around her and hugged her tightly. 'Lindsey, I'm sorry. I don't know what happened, what got into me.'

'It's all right.'

'No, it isn't. I was so . . . so *furious*.'

'You were just angry, that's all.'

'I'm sorry,' he repeated miserably.

Even if it had appeared to her to be nothing but anger, he knew that it had been more than that, something strange, a terrible rage. White hot. Psychotic. He had felt an edge beneath him, as if he were teetering on the brink of a precipice, with only his heels planted on solid ground.

★ ★ ★

To Vassago's eyes, the monument of Lucifer cast a shadow even in absolute darkness, but he could still see and enjoy the cadavers in their postures of degradation. He was enraptured by the organic collage that he had created, by the sight of the humbled forms and the stench that arose from them. His hearing was not remotely as acute as his night vision, but he did not believe that he was entirely imagining the soft, wet sounds of decomposition to which he

172

swayed as a music lover might sway to strains of Beethoven.

When he was suddenly overcome by anger, he was not sure why. It was a quiet sort of rage at first, curiously unfocused. He opened himself to it, enjoyed it, fed it to make it grow.

A vision of a newspaper flashed through his mind. He could not see it clearly, but something on the page was the cause of his anger. He squinted as if narrowing his eyes would help him see the words.

The vision passed, but the anger remained. He nurtured it the way a happy man might consciously force a laugh beyond its natural span just because the sound of laughter buoyed him. Words blurted from him: 'Of all the fucking nerve!'

He had no idea where the exclamation had come from, just as he had no idea why he had said the name 'Lindsey' out loud in that lounge in Newport Beach, several weeks ago, when these weird experiences had begun.

He was so abruptly energized by anger that he turned away from his collection and stalked across the enormous chamber, up the ramp down which the gargoyle gondolas had once plunged, and out into the night, where the moon forced him to put on his sunglasses again. He could not stand still. He had to move, move. He walked the abandoned midway, not sure who or what he was looking for, curious about what would happen next.

Disjointed images flashed through his mind, none remaining long enough to allow contemplation: the newspaper, a book-lined den, a filing cabinet, a hand-written letter, a telephone . . . He walked faster and faster, pivoting suddenly onto new avenues or into narrower passageways between the decaying buildings, in a fruitless search for a connection that would link him more clearly with the source of the pictures that appeared and swiftly faded from his mind.

As he passed the roller coaster, cold moonlight fell through the maze of supporting crossbeams and glinted off the track in such a way as to make those twin ribbons of steel look like rails of ice. When he lifted his gaze to stare at the monolithic and suddenly mysterious structure, an angry exclamation burst from him: 'Pitch *him* into that freezing river!'

A woman said, *Honey, lower your voice.*

Though he knew that her voice had arisen from within him, as an auditory adjunct to the fragmented visions, Vassago turned in

173

search of her anyway. She was *there*. In a bathrobe. Standing just this side of a doorway that had no right to be where it was, with no walls surrounding it. To the left of the doorway, to the right of it, and above it, there was only the night. The silent amusement park. But beyond the doorway, past the woman who stood in it, was what appeared to be the entrance foyer of a house, a small table with a vase of flowers, a staircase curving up to a second floor.

She was the woman he had thus far seen only in his dreams, first in a wheelchair and most recently in a red automobile on a sun-splashed highway. As he took a step toward her, she said, *You'll wake Regina.*

He halted, not because he was afraid of waking Regina, whoever the hell she was, and not because he still didn't want to get his hands on the woman, which he did – she was so *vital* – but because he became aware of a full-length mirror to the left of the Twilight-Zone door, a mirror floating impossibly in the night air. It was filled with his reflection, except that it was not him but a man he had never seen before, his size but maybe twice his age, lean and fit, his face contorted in rage.

The look of rage gave way to one of shock and disgust, and both Vassago and the man in the vision turned from the mirror to the woman in the doorway. 'Lindsey, I'm sorry,' Vassago said.

Lindsey. The name he had spoken three times at that lounge in Newport Beach.

Until now, he had not linked it to this woman who, nameless, had appeared so often in his recent dreams.

'Lindsey,' Vassago repeated.

He was speaking of his own volition this time, not repeating what the man in the mirror was saying, and that seemed to shatter the vision. The mirror and the reflection in it flew apart in a billion shards, as did the doorway and the dark-eyed woman.

As the hushed and moon-washed park reclaimed the night, Vassago reached out with one hand toward the spot where the woman had stood. 'Lindsey.' He longed to touch her. So alive, she was. 'Lindsey.' He wanted to cut her open and enfold her beating heart in both hands, until its metronomic pumping slowed . . . slowed . . . slowed to a full stop. He wanted to be holding her heart when life retreated from it and death took possession.

★ ★ ★

174

As swiftly as the flood of rage had poured into Hatch, it drained out of him. He balled up the pages of the newspaper and threw them in the waste can beside the desk, without glancing again at the story about the truck driver. Cooper was pathetic, a self-destructive loser who would bring his own punishment down upon himself sooner or later; and it would be worse than anything that Hatch would have done to him.

Lindsey gathered the letters that were scattered on the floor in front of the filing cabinet. She returned them to the file folder labeled MISCELLANEOUS BUSINESS.

The letter from Cooper was on the desk beside the telephone. When Hatch picked it up, he looked at the hand-written address at the top, above the telephone number, and a ghost of his anger returned. But it was a pale spirit of the real thing, and in a moment it vanished like a revenant. He took the letter to Lindsey and put it in the file folder, which she reinserted into the cabinet.

★ ★ ★

Standing in moonglare and night breeze, in the shadow of the roller coaster, Vassago waited for additional visions.

He was intrigued by what had transpired, though not surprised. He had traveled Beyond. He knew another world existed, separated from this one by the flimsiest of curtains. Therefore, events of a supernatural nature did not astonish him.

Just when he began to think that the enigmatic episode had reached a conclusion, one more vision flickered through his mind. He saw a single page of a hand-written letter. White, lined paper. Blue ink. At the top was a name: William X Cooper. And an address in the city of Tustin.

'Pitch *him* into that freezing river,' Vassago muttered, and knew somehow that William Cooper was the object of the unfocused anger that had overcome him when he was with his collection in the funhouse, and which later seemed to link him with the man he had seen in the mirror. It was an anger he had embraced and amplified because he wanted to understand whose anger it was and why he could feel it, but also because anger was the yeast in the bread of violence, and violence was the staple of his diet.

From the roller coaster he went directly to the subterranean garage. Two cars waited there.

Morton Redlow's Pontiac was parked in the farthest corner, in the deepest shadows. Vassago had not used it since last Thursday night, when he had killed Redlow and later the blonde. Though he believed the fog had provided adequate cover, he was concerned that the Pontiac might have been glimpsed by witnesses who had seen the woman tumble from it on the freeway.

He longed to return to the land of endless night and eternal damnation, to be once more among his own kind, but he did not want to be gunned down by police until his collection was finished. If his offering was incomplete when he died, he believed that he would be deemed as yet unfit for Hell and would be pulled back into the world of the living to start another collection.

The second car was a pearl-gray Honda that had belonged to a woman named Renata Desseux, whom he had clubbed on the back of the head in a shopping-mall parking lot on Saturday night, two nights after the fiasco with the blonde. She, instead of the neo-punker named Lisa, had become the latest addition to his collection.

He had removed the license plates from the Honda, tossed them in the trunk, and later replaced them with plates stolen off an old Ford on the outskirts of Santa Ana. Besides, Hondas were so ubiquitous that he felt safe and anonymous in this one. He drove off the park grounds and out of the county's largely unpopulated eastern hills toward the panorama of golden light that filled the lowlands as far south and as far north as he could see, from the hills to the ocean.

Urban sprawl.

Civilization.

Hunting grounds.

The very immensity of southern California – thousands of square miles, tens of millions of people, even excluding Ventura County to the north and San Diego County to the south – was Vassago's ally in his determination to acquire the pieces of his collection without arousing the interest of the police. Three of his victims had been taken from different communities in Los Angeles County, two from Riverside, the rest from Orange County, spread over many months. Among the hundreds of missing persons reported during that time, his few acquisitions would not affect the statistics enough to alarm the public or alert the authorities.

He was also abetted by the fact that these last years of the

176

century and the millennium were an age of inconstancy. Many people changed jobs, neighbors, friends, and marriages with little or no concern for continuity in life. As a result, there were fewer people to notice or care when any one person vanished, fewer to harass authorities into a meaningful response. And more often than not, those who disappeared were later discovered in changed circumstances of their own invention. A young executive might trade the grind of corporate life for a job as a blackjack dealer in Vegas or Reno, and a young mother – disillusioned with the demands of an infant and an infantile husband – might end up dealing cards or serving drinks or dancing topless in those same cities, leaving on the spur of the moment, blowing off their past lives as if a standard middle-class existence was as much a cause for shame as a criminal background. Others were found deep in the arms of various addictions, living in cheap rat-infested hotels that rented rooms by the week to the glassy-eyed legions of the counterculture. Because it was California, many missing persons eventually turned up in religious communes in Marin County or in Oregon, worshipping some new god or new manifestation of an old god or even just some shrewd-eyed man who said he *was* God.

It was a new age, disdaining tradition. It provided for whatever lifestyle one wished to pursue. Even one like Vassago's.

If he had left bodies behind, similarities in the victims and methods of murder would have linked them. The police would have realized that one perpetrator of unique strength and cunning was on the prowl, and they would have established a special task force to find him.

But the only bodies he had not taken to the Hell below the funhouse were those of the blonde and the private detective. No pattern would be deduced from just those two corpses, for they had died in radically different ways. Besides, Morton Redlow might not be found for weeks yet.

The only links between Redlow and the neo-punker were the detective's revolver, with which the woman had been shot, and his car, out of which she had fallen. The car was safely hidden in the farthest corner of the long-abandoned park garage. The gun was in the Styrofoam cooler with the Oreo cookies and other snacks, at the bottom of the elevator shaft more than two floors below the funhouse. He did not intend to use it again.

He was unarmed when, after driving far north into the county,

177

he arrived at the address he had seen on the hand-written letter in the vision. William X Cooper, whoever the hell he was and if he actually existed, lived in an attractive garden-apartment complex called Palm Court. The name of the place and the street number were carved in a decorative wooden sign, floodlit from the front and backed by the promised palms.

Vassago drove past Palm Court, turned right at the corner, and parked two blocks away. He didn't want anyone to remember the Honda sitting in front of the building. He didn't flat-out intend to kill this Cooper, just talk to him, ask him some questions, especially about the dark-haired, dark-eyed bitch named Lindsey. But he was walking into a situation he did not understand, and he needed to take every precaution. Besides, the truth was, these days he killed most of the people to whom he bothered to talk any length of time.

★　★　★

After closing the file drawer and turning off the lamp in the den, Hatch and Lindsey stopped at Regina's room to make sure she was all right, moving quietly to the side of her bed. The hall light, falling through her door, revealed that the girl was sound asleep. The small knuckles of one clenched hand were against her chin. She was breathing evenly through slightly parted lips. If she dreamed, her dreams must have been pleasant.

Hatch felt his heart pinch as he looked at her, for she seemed so desperately young. He found it hard to believe that he had ever been as young as Regina was just then, for youth was innocence. Having been raised under the hateful and oppressive hand of his father, he had surrendered innocence at an early age in return for an intuitive grasp of aberrant psychology that had permitted him to survive in a home where anger and brutal 'discipline' were the rewards for innocent mistakes and misunderstandings. He knew that Regina could not be as tender as she looked, for life had given her reasons of her own to develop thick skin and an armored heart.

Tough as they might be, however, they were both vulnerable, child and man. In fact, at that moment Hatch felt more vulnerable than the girl. If given a choice between her infirmities – the game leg, the twisted and incomplete hand – and whatever

178

damage had been done to some deep region of his brain, he would have opted for her physical impairments without hesitation. After recent experiences, including the inexplicable escalation of his anger into blind rage, Hatch did not feel entirely in control of himself. And from the time he had been a small boy, with the terrifying example of his father to shape his fears, he had feared nothing half as much as being out of control.

I will not fail you, he promised the sleeping child.

He looked at Lindsey, to whom he owed his lives, both of them, before and after dying. Silently he made her the same promise: I will not fail you.

He wondered if they were promises he could keep.

Later, in their own room, with the lights out, as they lay on their separate halves of the bed, Lindsey said, 'The rest of the test results should be back to Dr Nyebern tomorrow.'

Hatch had spent most of Saturday at the hospital, giving blood and urine samples, submitting to the prying of X-ray and sonogram machines. At one point he had been hooked up to more electrodes than the creature that Dr Frankenstein, in those old movies, had energized from kites sent aloft in a lightning storm.

He said, 'When I spoke to him today, he told me everything was looking good. I'm sure the rest of the tests will all come in negative, too. Whatever's happening to me, it has nothing to do with any mental or physical damage from the accident or from being . . . dead. I'm healthy, I'm okay.'

'Oh, God, I hope so.'

'I'm just fine.'

'Do you really think so?'

'Yes, I really think so, I really do.' He wondered how he could lie to her so smoothly. Maybe because the lie was not meant to hurt or harm, merely to soothe her so she could get some sleep.

'I love you,' she said.

'I love you, too.'

In a couple of minutes – shortly before midnight, according to the digital clock at the bedside – she was asleep, snoring softly.

Hatch was unable to sleep, worrying about what he might learn of his future – or lack of it – tomorrow. He suspected that Dr Nyebern would be gray-faced and grim, bearing somber news of some meaningful shadow detected in one lobe of Hatch's brain or another, a patch of dead cells, lesion, cyst, or tumor. Something

179

deadly. Inoperable. And certain to get worse.

His confidence had been increasing slowly ever since he had gotten past the events of Thursday night and Friday morning, when he had dreamed of the blonde's murder and, later, had actually followed the trail of the killer to the Route 133 off-ramp from the San Diego Freeway. The weekend had been uneventful. The day just past, enlivened and uplifted by Regina's arrival, had been delightful. Then he had seen the newspaper piece about Cooper, and had lost control.

He hadn't told Lindsey about the stranger's reflection that he had seen in the den mirror. This time he was unable to pretend that he might have been sleepwalking, half awake, half dreaming. He had been wide awake, which meant the image in the mirror was an hallucination of one kind or another. A healthy, undamaged brain didn't hallucinate. He hadn't shared that terror with her because he knew, with the receipt of the test results tomorrow, there would be fear enough to go around.

Unable to sleep, he began to think about the newspaper story again, even though he didn't want to chew on it any more. He tried to direct his thoughts away from William Cooper, but he returned to the subject the way he might have obsessively probed at a sore tooth with his tongue. It almost seemed as if he were being *forced* to think about the truck driver, as if a giant mental magnet was pulling his attention inexorably in that direction. Soon, to his dismay, anger rose in him again. Worse, almost at once, the anger exploded into fury and a hunger for violence so intense that he had to fist his hands at his sides and clench his teeth and struggle to keep from letting loose a primal cry of rage.

* * *

From the banks of mailboxes in the breezeway at the main entrance to the garden apartments, Vassago learned that William Cooper was in apartment twenty-eight. He followed the breezeway into the courtyard, which was filled with palms and ficuses and ferns and too many landscape lights to please him, and he climbed an exterior staircase to the covered balcony that served the second-floor units of the two-story complex.

No one was in sight. Palm Court was silent, peaceful.

Though it was a few minutes past midnight, lights were on in the Cooper apartment. Vassago could hear a television turned low.

The window to the right of the door was covered with Levolor blinds. The slats were not tightly closed. Vassago could see a kitchen illuminated only by the low-wattage bulb in the range hood.

To the left of the door a larger window looked onto the balcony and courtyard from the apartment living room. The drapes were not drawn all the way shut. Through the gap, a man could be seen slumped in a big recliner with his feet up in front of the television. His head was tilted to one side, his face toward the window, and he appeared to be asleep. A glass containing an inch of golden liquid stood beside a half-empty bottle of Jack Daniel's on a small table next to the recliner. A bag of cheese puffs had been knocked off the table, and some of the bright orange contents had scattered across the bile-green carpet.

Vassago scanned the balcony to the left, right, and on the other side of the courtyard. Still deserted.

He tried to slide open Cooper's living-room window, but it was either corroded or locked. He moved to the right again, toward the kitchen window, but he stopped at the door on the way and, without any real hope, tried it. The door was unlocked. He pushed it open, went inside – and locked it behind him.

The man in the recliner, probably Cooper, did not stir as Vassago quietly pulled the drapes all the way shut across the big living-room window. No one else, passing on the balcony, would be able to look inside.

Already assured that the kitchen, dining area, and living room were deserted, Vassago moved catlike through the bathroom and two bedrooms (one without furniture, used primarily for storage) that comprised the rest of the apartment. The man in the recliner was alone.

On the dresser in the bedroom, Vassago spotted a wallet and a ring of keys. In the wallet he found fifty-eight dollars, which he took, and a driver's license in the name of William X Cooper. The photograph on the license was of the man in the living room, a few years younger and, of course, not in a drunken stupor.

He returned to the living room with the intention of waking Cooper and having an informative little chat with him. Who is Lindsey? Where does she live?

But as he approached the recliner, a current of anger shot

through him, too sudden and motiveless to be his own, as if he were a human radio that received other people's emotions. And what he was receiving was the same anger that had suddenly struck him while he had been with his collection in the funhouse hardly an hour ago. As before, he opened himself to it, amplified the current with his own singular rage, wondering if he would receive visions, as he had on that previous occasion. But this time, as he stood looking down on William Cooper, the anger flared too abruptly into insensate fury, and he lost control. From the table beside the recliner, he grabbed the Jack Daniel's by the neck of the bottle.

★   ★   ★

Lying rigid in his bed, hands fisted so tightly that even his blunt fingernails were gouging painfully into his palms, Hatch had the crazy feeling that his mind had been invaded. His flicker of anger had been like opening a door just a hairline crack but wide enough for something on the other side to get a grip and tear it off its hinges. He felt something unnameable storming into him, a force without form or features, defined only by its hatred and rage. Its fury was that of the hurricane, the typhoon, beyond mere human dimensions, and he knew that he was too small a vessel to contain all of the anger that was pumping into him. He felt as if he would explode, shatter as if he were not a man but a crystal figurine.

★   ★   ★

The half-full bottle of Jack Daniel's whacked the side of the sleeping man's head with such impact that it was almost as loud as a shotgun blast. Whiskey and sharp fragments of glass showered up, rained down, splattered and clinked against the television set, the other furniture, and the walls. The air was filled with the velvety aroma of corn-mash bourbon, but underlying it was the scent of blood, for the gashed and battered side of Cooper's face was bleeding copiously.

The man was no longer merely sleeping. He had been hammered into a deeper level of unconsciousness.

Vassago was left with just the neck of the bottle in his hand. It terminated in three sharp spikes of glass that dripped bourbon

182

and made him think of snake fangs glistening with venom. Shifting his grip, he raised the weapon above his head and brought it down, letting out a fierce hiss of rage, and the glass serpent bit deep into William Cooper's face.

★ ★ ★

The volcanic wrath that erupted into Hatch was unlike anything he had ever experienced before, far beyond any rage that his father had ever achieved. Indeed, it was nothing he could have generated within himself for the same reason that one could not manufacture sulfuric acid in a paper cauldron: the vessel would be dissolved by the substance it was required to contain. A high-pressure lava flow of anger gushed into him, so hot that he wanted to scream, so white-hot that he had no time to scream. Consciousness was burned away, and he fell into a mercifully dreamless darkness where there was neither anger nor terror.

★ ★ ★

Vassago realized that he was shouting with wordless, savage glee. After a dozen or twenty blows, the glass weapon had utterly disintegrated. He finally, reluctantly, dropped the short fragment of the bottle neck still in his white-knuckled grip. Snarling, he threw himself against the Naugahyde recliner, tipping it over and rolling the dead man onto the bile-green carpet. He picked up the end table and pitched it into the television set, where Humphrey Bogart was sitting in a military courtroom, rolling a couple of ball bearings in his leathery hand, talking about strawberries. The screen imploded, and Bogart was transformed into a shower of yellow sparks, the sight of which ignited new fires of destructive frenzy in Vassago. He kicked over a coffee table, tore two K-Mart prints off the walls and smashed the glass out of the frames, swept a collection of cheap ceramic knicknacks off the mantel. He would have liked nothing better than to have continued from one end of the apartment to the other, pulling all the dishes out of the kitchen cabinets and smashing them, reducing all the glassware to bright shards, seizing the food in the refrigerator and heaving it against the walls, hammering one piece of furniture against another until everything was broken and splintered, but he was halted by the sound of a siren, distant now, rapidly drawing nearer, the meaning of it penetrating even through the mist of blood frenzy that clouded his thoughts. He headed for the door, then swung away from it, realizing that people might have come out into the courtyard or might be watching from their windows. He ran out of the living room, back along the short hall, to the window in the master bedroom, where he pulled aside the drapes and looked onto the roof over the building-long carport. An alleyway, bordered by a block wall, lay beyond. He twisted open the latch on the double-hung window, shoved up the bottom half, squeezed through, dropped onto the roof of the long carport, rolled to the edge, fell to the pavement, and landed on his feet as if he were a cat. He lost his sunglasses, scooped them up, put them on again. He sprinted left, toward the back of the property, with the siren louder now, much louder, very close. When he came to the next flank of the eight-foot-high concrete-block wall that ringed the property, he swiftly clambered over it with the agility of a spider skittering up any porous surface, and then he was over, into another alleyway serving carports along the back of another apartment complex, and so he ran from serviceway to serviceway, picking a route through the maze by sheer instinct, and came out on the street where he had parked, half a block from the pearl-gray Honda. He got in the car, started the engine, and drove away from there as sedately as he could manage, sweating and breathing so hard that he steamed up the windows. Reveling in the fragrant melange of bourbon, blood, and perspiration, he was tremendously excited, so profoundly *satisfied* by the violence he had unleashed, that he pounded the steering wheel and let out peals of laughter that had a shrieky edge.

For a while he drove randomly from one street to another with no idea where he was headed. After his laughter faded, when his heart stopped racing, he gradually oriented himself and struck out south and east, in the general direction of his hideaway.

If William Cooper could have provided any connection to the woman named Lindsey, that lead was now closed to Vassago forever. He wasn't worried. He didn't know what was happening to him, why Cooper or Lindsey or the man in the mirror had been brought to his attention by these supernatural means. But he knew that if he only trusted in his dark god, everything would eventually be made clear to him.

184

He was beginning to wonder if Hell had let him go willingly, returning him to the land of the living in order to use him to deal with certain people whom the god of darkness wanted dead. Perhaps he'd not been stolen from Hell, after all, but had been *sent* back to life on a mission of destruction that was only slowly becoming comprehensible. If that were the case, he was pleased to make himself the instrument of the dark and powerful divinity whose company he longed to rejoin, and he anxiously awaited whatever task he might be assigned next.

★ ★ ★

Toward dawn, after several hours in a deep slumber of almost deathlike perfection, Hatch woke and did not know where he was. For a moment he drifted in confusion, then washed up on the shore of memory: the bedroom, Lindsey breathing softly in her sleep beside him, the ash-gray first light of morning like a fine silver dust on the windowpanes.

When he recalled the inexplicable and inhuman fit of rage that had slammed through him with paralytic force, Hatch stiffened with fear. He tried to remember where that spiraling anger had led, in what act of violence it had culminated, but his mind was blank. It seemed to him that he had simply passed out, as if that unnaturally intense fury had overloaded the circuits in his brain and blown a fuse or two.

Passed out – or blacked out? There was a fateful difference between the two. Passed out, he might have been in bed all night, exhausted, as still as a stone on the floor of the sea. But if he *blacked* out, remaining conscious but unaware of what he was doing, in a psychotic fugue, God alone knew what he might have done.

Suddenly he sensed that Lindsey was in grave danger.

Heart hammering against the cage of his ribs, he sat up in bed and looked at her. The dawn light at the window was too soft to reveal her clearly. She was only a shadowy shape against the sheets.

He reached for the switch on the bedside lamp, but then hesitated. He was afraid of what he might see.

I would never hurt Lindsey, never, he thought desperately.

But he remembered all too well that, for a moment last night,

185

he had not been entirely himself. His anger at Cooper had seemed to open a door within him, letting in a monster from some vast darkness beyond.

Trembling, he finally clicked the switch. In the lamplight he saw that Lindsey was untouched, as fair as ever, sleeping with a peaceful smile.

Greatly relieved, he switched off the lamp – and thought of Regina. The engine of anxiety revved up again.

Ridiculous. He would no sooner harm Regina than Lindsey. She was a defenseless child.

He could not stop shaking, wondering.

He slipped out of bed without disturbing his wife. He picked up his bathrobe from the back of the armchair, pulled it on, and quietly left the room.

Barefoot, he entered the hall, where a pair of skylights admitted large pieces of the morning, and followed it to Regina's room. He moved swiftly at first, then more slowly, weighed down by dread as heavy as a pair of iron boots.

He had a mental image of the flower-painted mahogany bed splashed with blood, the sheets sodden and red. For some reason, he had the crazy notion that he would find the child with fragments of glass in her ravaged face. The weird specificity of that image convinced him that he had, indeed, done something unthinkable after he had blacked out.

When he eased open the door and looked into the girl's room, she was sleeping as peacefully as Lindsey, in the same posture he had seen her in last night, when he and Lindsey had checked on her before going to bed. No blood. No broken glass.

Swallowing hard, he pulled the door shut and returned along the hall as far as the first skylight. He stood in the fall of dim morning light, looking up through the tinted glass at a sky of indeterminate hue, as if an explanation would suddenly be writ large across the heavens.

No explanation came to him. He remained confused and .anxious.

At least Lindsey and Regina were fine, untouched by whatever presence he had connected with last night.

He was reminded of an old vampire movie he had once seen, in which a wizened priest had warned a young woman that the undead could enter her house only if she invited them – but that they were cunning and persuasive, capable of inducing even the wary to issue that mortal invitation.

Somehow a bond existed between Hatch and the psychotic who had killed the young blond punker named Lisa. By failing to repress his anger at William Cooper, he had strengthened that bond. His anger was the key that opened the door. When he indulged in anger, he was issuing an invitation just like the one against which the priest in that movie had warned the young woman. He could not explain how he knew this to be true, but he *did* know it, all right, knew it in his bones. He just wished to God he *understood* it.

He felt lost.

Small and powerless and afraid.

And although Lindsey and Regina had come through the night unharmed, he sensed more strongly than ever that they were in great danger. Growing greater by the day. By the hour.

·3·

Before dawn, the thirtieth of April, Vassago bathed outdoors with bottled water and liquid soap. By the first light of day, he was safely ensconced in the deepest part of his hideaway. Lying on his mattress, staring up the elevator shaft, he treated himself to Oreos and warm root beer, then to a couple of snack-size bags of Reese's Pieces.

Murder was always enormously satisfying. Tremendous internal pressures were released with the strike of a killing blow. More important, each murder was an act of rebellion against all things holy, against commandments and laws and rules and the irritatingly prissy systems of manners employed by human beings to support the fiction that life was precious and endowed with meaning. Life was cheap and pointless. Nothing mattered but sensation and the swift gratification of all desires, which only the strong and free really understood. After every killing, Vassago felt as liberated as the wind and mightier than any steel machine.

Until one special, glorious night in his twelfth year, he had been one of the enslaved masses, dumbly plodding through life according to the rules of so-called civilization, though they made no sense to him. He pretended to love his mother, father, sister, and a host of relatives, though he felt nothing more for them than he did for strangers encountered on the street. As a child, when he was old enough to begin thinking about such things, he wondered if something was wrong with him, a crucial element missing from his makeup. As he listened to himself playing the game of love, employing strategies of false affection and shameless flattery, he was amazed at how convincing others found him, for he could hear the insincerity in his voice, could feel the fraudulence in every gesture, and was acutely aware of the deceit behind his every loving smile. Then one day he suddenly heard the deception in their voices and saw it in their faces, and he realized that none of *them* had ever experienced love, either, or any of the nobler sentiments toward which a civilized person was supposed to aspire – selflessness, courage, piety, humility, and all the rest of that dreary catechism. *They* were all playing the game, too. Later he came to the conclusion that most of them, even the adults, had never enjoyed his degree of insight, and remained unaware that other people were exactly like them. Each person thought he was unique, that something was missing in him, and that he must play the game well or be uncovered and ostracized as something less than human. God had tried to create a world of love, had failed, and had commanded His creations to pretend to the perfection with which He had been unable to imbue them. Perceiving that stunning truth, Vassago had taken his first step toward freedom. Then one summer night when he was twelve, he finally understood that in order to be really free, totally free, he had to act upon his understanding, begin to live differently from the herd of humanity, with his own pleasure as the only consideration. He had to be willing to exercise the power over others which he possessed by virtue of his insight into the true nature of the world. That night he learned that the ability to kill without compunction was the purest form of power, and that the exercise of power was the greatest pleasure of them all . . .

★ ★ ★

In those days, before he died and came back from the dead and chose the name of the demon prince Vassago, the name to which he had answered and under which he had lived was Jeremy. His

188

best friend had been Tod Ledderbeck, the son of Dr Sam Ledderbeck, a gynecologist whom Jeremy called the 'crack quack' when
he wanted to rag Tod.

In the morning of that early June day, Mrs Ledderbeck had
taken Jeremy and Tod to Fantasy World, the lavish amusement
park that, against all expectations, had begun to give Disneyland
a run for its money. It was in the hills, a few miles east of San Juan
Capistrano, somewhat out of the way – just as Magic Mountain
had been a bit isolated before the suburbs north of Los Angeles
had spread around it, and just as Disneyland had seemed to be in
the middle of nowhere when first constructed on farmland near
the obscure town of Anaheim. It was built with Japanese money,
which worried some people who believed the Japanese were going
to own the whole country some day, and there were rumors of
Mafia money being involved, which only made it more mysterious
and appealing. But finally what mattered was that the atmosphere
of the place was cool, the rides radical, and the junk food almost
deliriously junky. Fantasy World was where Tod wanted to spend
his twelfth birthday, in the company of his best friend, free of
parental control from morning until ten o'clock at night, and Tod
usually got what he wanted because he was a good kid; everyone
liked him; he knew exactly how to play the game.

Mrs Ledderbeck left them off at the front gate and shouted
after them as they raced away from the car: 'I'll pick you up right
here at ten o'clock! Right here at ten o'clock sharp!'

After paying for their tickets and getting onto the grounds of
the park, Tod said, 'What do you wanna do first?'

'I don't know. What do you wanna do first?'

'Ride the Scorpion?'

'Yeah!'

'Yeah!'

Bang, they were off, hurrying toward the north end of the park
where the track for the Scorpion – 'The Roller Coaster with a
Sting!' the TV ads all proclaimed – rose in sweet undulant terror
against the clear blue sky. The park was not crowded yet, and they
didn't need to snake between cow-slow herds of people. Their
tennis shoes pounded noisily on the blacktop, and each slap of
rubber against pavement was a shout of freedom. They rode the
Scorpion, yelling and screaming as it plummeted and whipped
and turned upside down and plummeted again, and when the

189

ride ended, they ran directly to the boarding ramp and did it once more.

Then, as now, Jeremy had loved speed. The stomach-flopping sharp turns and plunges of amusement-park rides had been a childish substitute for the violence he had unknowingly craved. After two rides on the Scorpion, with so many speeding-swooping-looping-twisting delights ahead, Jeremy was in a terrific mood.

But Tod tainted the day as they were coming down the exit ramp from their second trip on the roller coaster. He threw one arm around Jeremy's shoulders and said, 'Man, this is gonna be for sure the greatest birthday anybody's ever had, just you and me.'

The camaraderie, like all camaraderie, was totally fake. Deception. Fraud. Jeremy hated all that phoney-baloney crap, but Tod was full of it. Best friends. Blood brothers. You and me against the world.

Jeremy wasn't sure what rubbed him the rawest: that Tod jived him all the time about being good buddies and seemed to think that Jeremy was taken in by the con – or that sometimes Tod seemed dumb enough to be suckered by his *own* con. Recently, Jeremy had begun to suspect that some people played the game of life so well, they didn't realize it was a game. They deceived even themselves with all their talk of friendship, love, and compassion. Tod was looking more and more like one of *those* hopeless jerks.

Being best friends was just a way to get a guy to do things for you that he wouldn't do for anyone else in a thousand years. Friendship was also a mutual defense arrangement, a way of joining forces against the mobs of your fellow citizens who would just as soon smash your face and take whatever they wanted from you. Everyone knew that's all friendship was, but no one ever talked truthfully about it, least of all Tod.

Later, on their way from the Haunted House to an attraction called Swamp Creature, they stopped at a stand selling blocks of ice cream dipped in chocolate and rolled in crushed nuts. They sat on plastic chairs at a plastic table, under a red umbrella, against a backdrop of acacias and manmade waterfalls, chomping down, and everything was fine at first, but then Tod had to spoil it.

'It's great coming to the park without grownups, isn't it?' Tod said with his mouth full. 'You can eat ice cream before lunch, like this. Hell, you can eat it for lunch, too, if you want, and after lunch, and nobody's there to whine at you about spoiling your appetite or getting sick.'

'It's great,' Jeremy agreed.

'Let's sit here and eat ice cream till we puke.'

'Sounds good to me. But let's not waste it.'

'Huh?'

Jeremy said, 'Let's be sure, when we puke, we just don't spew on the ground. Let's be sure we puke *on* somebody.'

'Yeah!' Tod said, getting the drift right away, 'on somebody who deserves it, who's really pukeworthy.'

'Like those girls,' Jeremy said, indicating a pair of pretty teenagers who were passing by. They wore white shorts and bright summery blouses, and they were so sure that they were cute, you wanted to puke on them even if you hadn't eaten anything and all you could manage was the dry heaves.

'Or those old farts,' Tod said, pointing to an elderly couple buying ice cream nearby.

'No, not them,' Jeremy said. 'They already *look* like they've been puked on.'

Tod thought that was so hilarious, he choked on his ice cream. In some ways Tod was all right.

'Funny about this ice cream,' he said when he stopped choking.

Jeremy bit: 'What's funny about it?'

'I know the ice cream is made from milk, which comes from cows. And they make chocolate out of cocoa beans. But whose nuts do they crush to sprinkle over it all?'

Yeah, for sure, old Tod was all right in some ways.

But just when they were laughing the loudest, feeling good, he leaned across the table, swatted Jeremy lightly alongside the head, and said, 'You and me, Jer, we're gonna be *tight* forever, friends till they feed us to the worms. Right?'

He really believed it. He had conned himself. He was so stupidly sincere that he made Jeremy want to puke on *him*.

Instead, Jeremy said, 'What're you gonna do next, try to kiss me on the lips?'

Grinning, not picking up on the impatience and hostility aimed at him, Tod said, 'Up your grandma's ass.'

'Up *your* grandma's ass.'

'My grandma doesn't have an ass.'

'Yeah? Then what's she sit on?'

'Your face.'

They kept ragging each other all the way to Swamp Creature. The attraction was hokey, not well done, but good for a lot of jokes because of that. For a while, Tod was just wild and fun to be around.

Later, however, after they came out of Space Battle, Tod started referring to them as 'the two best rocket jockeys in the universe,' which half embarrassed Jeremy because it was so stupid and juvenile. It also irritated him because it was just another way of saying 'we're buddies, blood brothers, pals.' They'd get on the Scorpion, and just as it pulled out of the station, Tod would say, 'This is nothing, this is just a Sunday drive to the two best rocket jockeys in the universe.' Or they'd be on their way into World of the Giants, and Tod would throw his arm around Jeremy's shoulder and say, 'The two best rocket jockeys in the universe can handle a fucking giant, can't we, bro?'

Jeremy wanted to say, *Look, you jerk, the only reason we're friends is because your old man and mine are sort of in the same kind of work, so we got thrown together. I hate this arm-around-the-shoulders shit, so just knock it off, let's have some laughs and be happy with that. Okay?*

But he did not say anything of the sort because, of course, good players in life never admitted that they knew it was all just a game. If you let the other players see you didn't care about the rules and regulations, they wouldn't let you play. Go to Jail. Go directly to Jail. Don't pass Go. Don't have any fun.

By seven o'clock that evening, after they had eaten enough junk food to produce radically interesting vomit if they really did decide to puke on anyone, Jeremy was so tired of the rocket jockey crap and so irritated by Tod's friendship rap, that he couldn't wait for ten o'clock to roll around and Mrs Ledderbeck to pull up to the gate in her station wagon.

They were on the Millipede, blasting through one of the pitch-black sections of the ride, when Tod made one too many references to the two best rocket jockeys in the universe, and Jeremy decided to kill him. The instant the thought flashed through his mind, he knew he had to murder his 'best friend.' It felt so *right*. If life was a game with a zillion-page book of rules, it wasn't going to be a whole hell of a lot of fun – unless you found ways to break the rules and still be allowed to play. *Any* game was a bore if you played by the rules – Monopoly, 500 rummy, baseball. But if you stole bases, filched cards without getting caught, or changed the numbers on the dice when the other guy was distracted, a dull game could be a kick. And in the game of life, getting away with murder was the biggest kick of all.

When the Millipede shrieked to a halt at the debarkation platform, Jeremy said, 'Let's do it again.'

'Sure,' Tod said.

They hurried along the exit corridor, in a rush to get outside and into line again. The park had filled up during the day, and the wait to board any ride was now at least twenty minutes.

When they came out of the Millipede pavilion, the sky was black in the east, deep blue overhead, and orange in the west. Twilight came sooner and lasted longer at Fantasy World than in the western part of the county, because between the park and the distant sea rose ranks of high, sun-swallowing hills. Those ridges were now black silhouettes against the orange heavens, like Halloween decorations out of season.

Fantasy World had taken on a new, manic quality with the approach of night. Christmas-style lights outlined the rides and buildings. White twinkle lights lent a festive sparkle to all the trees, while a pair of unsynchronized spotlights swooped back and forth across the snow-covered peak of the manmade Big Foot Mountain. On every side neon glowed in all the hues that neon offered, and out on Mars Island, bursts of brightly colored laser beams shot randomly into the darkening sky as if fending off a spaceship attack. Scented with popcorn and roasted peanuts, a warm breeze snapped garlands of pennants overhead. Music of every period and type leaked out of the pavilions, and rock-and-roll boomed from the open-air dance floor at the south end of the park, and from somewhere else came the bouncy strains of Big Band swing. People laughed and chattered excitedly, and on the thrill rides they were screaming, screaming.

'Daredevil this time,' Jeremy said as he and Tod sprinted to the end of the Millipede boarding line.

'Yeah,' Tod said, 'daredevil!'

The Millipede was essentially an indoor roller coaster, like Space Mountain at Disneyland, except instead of shooting up and down and around one huge room, it whipped through a long series of tunnels, some lit and some not. The lap bar, meant to restrain the riders, was tight enough to be safe, but if a kid was slim and agile, he could contort himself in such a way as to squeeze out from under it, scramble over it, and stand in the leg well. Then he could lean against the lap bar and grip it behind his back – or hook his arms around it – riding daredevil.

It was a stupid and dangerous thing to do, which Jeremy and Tod realized. But they had done it a couple of times anyway, not only on the Millipede but on other rides in other parks. Riding daredevil pumped up the excitement level at least a thousand percent, especially in pitch-dark tunnels where it was impossible to see what was coming next.

'Rocket jockeys!' Tod said when they were halfway through the line. He insisted on giving Jeremy a low five and then a high five, though they looked like a couple of asshole kids. 'No rocket jockey is afraid of daredeviling the Millipede, right?'

'Right,' Jeremy said as they inched through the main doors and entered the pavilion. Shrill screams echoed to them from the riders on the cars that shot away into the tunnel ahead.

According to legend (as kid-created legends went at every amusement park with a similar ride), a boy had been killed riding daredevil on the Millipede because he'd been too tall. The ceiling of the tunnel was high in all lighted stretches, but they said it dropped low at one spot in a darkened passage – maybe because air-conditioning pipes passed through at that point, maybe because the engineers made the contractor put in another support that hadn't been planned for, maybe because the architect was a no-brain. Anyway, this tall kid, standing up, smacked his head into the low part of the ceiling, never even saw it coming. It instantly pulverized his face, decapitated him. All the unsuspecting bozos riding behind him were splattered with blood and brains and broken teeth.

Jeremy didn't believe it for a minute. Fantasy World hadn't been built by guys with horse turds for brains. They had to have figured kids would find a way to get out from under the lap bars, because nothing was entirely kid-proof, and they would have kept the ceiling high all the way through. Legend also had it that the low overhang was still somewhere in one of the dark sections of the tunnel, with bloodstains and flecks of dried brains on it, which was total cow flop.

For anybody riding daredevil, standing up, the real danger was that he would fall out of the car when it whipped around a sharp turn or accelerated unexpectedly. Jeremy figured there were six or eight particularly radical curves on the Millipede course where Tod Ledderbeck might easily topple out of the car with only minimal assistance.

The line moved slowly forward.

Jeremy was not impatient or afraid. As they drew closer to the boarding gates, he became more excited but also more confident. His hands were not trembling. He had no butterflies in his belly. He just wanted to *do* it.

The boarding chamber for the ride was constructed to resemble a cavern with immense stalactites and stalagmites. Strange bright-eyed creatures swam in the murky depths of eerie pools, and albino mutant crabs prowled the shores, reaching up with huge wicked claws toward the people on the boarding platform, snapping at them but not quite long-armed enough to snare any dinner.

Each train had six cars, and each car carried two people. The cars were painted like segments of a millipede; the first had a big insect head with moving jaws and multifaceted black eyes, not a cartoon but a really fierce monster face; the one at the back boasted a curved stinger that looked more like part of a scorpion than the ass-end of a millipede. Two trains were boarding at any one time, the second behind the first, and they shot off into the tunnel with only a few seconds between them because the whole operation was computer-controlled, eliminating any danger that one train would crash into the back of another.

Jeremy and Tod were among the twelve customers that the attendant sent to the first train.

Tod wanted the front car, but they didn't get it. That was the best position from which to ride daredevil because everything would happen to them first: every plunge into darkness, every squirt of cold steam from the wall vents, every explosion through swinging doors into whirling lights. Besides, part of the fun of riding daredevil was showing off, and the front car provided a perfect platform for exhibitionism, with the occupants of the last five cars as a captive audience in the lighted stretches.

With the first car claimed, they raced for the sixth. Being the last to experience every plunge and twist of the track was next-best to being first, because the squeals of the riders ahead of you raised your adrenaline level and expectations. Something about

195

being securely in the middle of the train just didn't go with dare-devil riding.

The lap bars descended automatically when all twelve people were aboard. An attendant came along the platform, inspecting to be sure all of the restraints had locked into place.

Jeremy was relieved they had not gotten the front car, where they would have had ten witnesses behind them. In the tomb-dark confines of the unlighted sections of tunnel, he wouldn't be able to see his own hand an inch in front of his face, so it wasn't likely that anyone would be able to see him push Tod out of the car. But this was a big-time violation of the rules, and he didn't want to take any chances. Now, potential witnesses were all safely in front of them, staring straight ahead; in fact they could not easily glance back, since every seat had a high back to prevent whiplash.

When the attendant finished checking the lap bars, he turned and signaled the operator, who was seated at an instrument panel on a rock formation to the right of the tunnel entrance.

'Here we go,' Tod said.

'Here we go,' Jeremy agreed.

'Rocket jockeys!' Tod shouted.

Jeremy gritted his teeth.

'Rocket jockeys!' Tod repeated.

What the hell. One more time wouldn't hurt. Jeremy yelled: 'Rocket jockeys!'

The train did not pull away from the boarding station with the jerky uncertainty of most roller coasters. A tremendous blast of compressed air shot it forward at high speed, like a bullet out of a barrel, with a *whoosh!* that almost hurt the ears. They were pinned against their seats as they flashed past the operator and into the black mouth of the tunnel.

Total darkness.

He was only twelve then. He had not died. He had not been to Hell. He had not come back. He was as blind in darkness as anyone else, as Tod.

Then they slammed through swinging doors and up a long incline of well-lighted track, moving fast at first but gradually slowing to a crawl. On both sides they were menaced by pale white slugs as big as men, which reared up and shrieked at them through round mouths full of teeth that whirled like the blades in a garbage disposal. The ascent was six or seven stories, at a steep

196

angle, and other mechanical monsters gibbered, hooted, snarled, and squealed at the train; all of them were pale and slimy, with either glowing eyes or blind black eyes, the kind of critters you might think would live miles below the surface of the earth – if you didn't know *any* science at all.

That initial slope was where daredevils had to take their stand. Though a couple of other inclines marked the course of the Milli-pede, no other section of the track provided a sufficiently extended period of calm in which to execute a safe escape from the lap bar.

Jeremy contorted himself, wriggling up against the back of the seat, inching over the lap bar, but at first Tod did not move. 'Come on, dickhead, you've gotta be in position before we get to the top.'

Tod looked troubled. 'If they catch us, they'll kick us out of the park.'

'They won't catch us.'

At the far end of the ride, the train would coast along a final stretch of dark tunnel, giving riders a chance to calm down. In those last few seconds, before they returned to the fake cavern from which they had started, it was just possible for a kid to scramble back over the lap bar and shoehorn himself into his seat. Jeremy knew he could do it; he was not worried about getting caught. Tod didn't have to worry about getting under the lap bar again, either, because by then Tod would be dead; he wouldn't have to worry about anything ever.

'I don't want to be kicked out for daredeviling,' Tod said as the train approached the halfway point on the long, long initial incline. 'It's been a neat day, and we still have a couple hours before Mom comes for us.'

Mutant albino rats chattered at them from the fake rock ledges on both sides as Jeremy said, 'Okay, so be a dorkless wonder.' He continued to extricate himself from the lap bar.

'I'm no dorkless wonder,' Tod said defensively.

'Sure, sure.'

'I'm not.'

'Maybe when school starts again in September, you'll be able to get into the Young Homemakers Club, learn how to cook, knit nice little doilies, do flower arranging.'

'You're a jerkoff, you know that?'

197

'Ooooooooooo, you've broken my heart now,' Jeremy said as he extracted both of his legs from the well under the lap bar and crouched on the seat. 'You girls sure know how to hurt a guy's feelings.'

'Creepazoid.'

The train strained up the slope with the hard clicking and clattering so specific to roller coasters that the sound alone could make the heart pump faster and the stomach flutter.

Jeremy scrambled over the lap bar and stood in the well in front of it, facing forward. He looked over his shoulder at Tod, who sat scowling behind the restraint. He didn't care that much if Tod joined him or not. He had already decided to kill the boy, and if he didn't have a chance to do it at Fantasy World on Tod's twelfth birthday, he would do it somewhere else, sooner or later. Just thinking about doing it was a lot of fun. Like that song said in the television commercial where the Heinz ketchup was so thick it took what seemed like hours coming out of the bottle: *An-tic-i-paaa-aa-tion*. Having to wait a few days or even weeks to get another good chance to kill Tod would only make the killing that much more fun. So he didn't rag Tod any more, just looked at him scornfully. *An-tic-i-paaa-aa-tion*.

'I'm not afraid,' Tod insisted.

'Yeah.'

'I just don't want to spoil the day.'

'Sure.'

'Creepazoid,' Tod said again.

Jeremy said, 'Rocket jockey, my ass.'

That insult had a powerful effect. Tod was so sold on his own friendship con that he could actually be stung by the implication that he didn't know how a real friend was supposed to behave. The expression on his broad and open face revealed not only a world of hurt but a surprising desperation that startled Jeremy. Maybe Tod *did* understand what life was all about, that it was nothing but a brutal game with every player concentrated on the purely selfish goal of coming out a winner, and maybe old Tod was rattled by that, scared by it, and was holding on to one last hope, to the idea of friendship. If the game could be played with a partner or two, if it was really everyone else in the world against your own little team, that was tolerable, better than everyone in the world against just *you*. Tod Ledderbeck and his good buddy

198

Jeremy against the rest of humanity was even sort of romantic and adventurous, but Tod Ledderbeck alone obviously made his bowels quiver.

Sitting behind the lap bar, Tod first looked stricken, then resolute. Indecision gave way to action, and Tod moved fast, wriggling furiously against the restraint.

'Come on, come on,' Jeremy urged. 'We're almost to the top.'

Tod eeled over the lap bar, into the leg well where Jeremy stood. He caught his foot in the restraining mechanism, and almost fell out of the car.

Jeremy grabbed him, hauled him back. *This* was not the place for Tod to take a fall. They weren't moving fast enough. At most he'd suffer a couple of bruises.

Then they were side by side, their feet planted wide on the floor of the car, leaning back against the restraint from under which they had escaped, arms behind them, hands locked on the lap bar, grinning at each other, as the train reached the top of the incline. It slammed through swinging doors into the next stretch of lightless tunnel. The track remained flat just long enough to crank up the riders' tension a couple of notches. *An-tic-i-paaa-aa-tion.* When Jeremy could not hold his breath any longer, the front car tipped over the brink, and the people up there screamed in the darkness. Then in rapid succession the second and third and fourth and fifth cars –

'Rocket jockeys!' Jeremy and Tod shouted in unison.

— and the final car of the train followed the others into a steep plunge, building speed by the second. Wind whooshed past them and whipped their hair out behind their heads. Then came a swooping turn to the right when it was least expected, a little upgrade to toss the stomach, another turn to the right, the track tilting so the cars were tipped onto their sides, faster, faster, then a straightaway and another incline, using their speed to go higher than ever, slowing toward the top, slowing, slowing. *An-tic-i-paaa-aa-tion.* They went over the edge and down, down, down, waaaaaaaaaay down so hard and fast that Jeremy felt as if his stomach had fallen out of him, leaving a hole in the middle of his body. He knew what was coming, but he was left breathless by it nonetheless. The train did a loop-de-loop, turning upside down. He pressed his feet tight to the floor and gripped the lap bar behind him as if he were trying to fuse his flesh with the steel,

199

because it felt as if he would fall out, straight down onto the section of the track that had led them into the loop, to crack his skull open on the rails below. He knew centripetal force would hold him in place even though he was standing up where he didn't belong, but what he knew was of no consequence: what you *felt* always carried a lot more weight than what you *knew*, emotion mattered more than intellect. Then they were out of the loop, banging through another pair of swinging doors onto a second lighted incline, using their tremendous speed to build height for the next series of plunges and sharp turns.

Jeremy looked at Tod.

The old rocket jockey was a little green.

'No more loops,' Tod shouted above the clatter of the train wheels. 'The worst is behind us.'

Jeremy exploded with laughter. He thought: *The worst is still ahead for you, dickhead. And for me the best is yet to come. An-tic-i-paaa-aa-tion.*

Tod laughed, too, but certainly for different reasons.

At the top of the second incline, the rattling cars pushed through a third set of swinging doors, returning to a grave-dark world that thrilled Jeremy because he knew Tod Ledderbeck had just seen the last light of his life. The train snapped left and right, swooped up and plummeted down, rolled onto its side in a series of corkscrew turns.

Through it all Jeremy could feel Tod beside him. Their bare arms brushed together, and their shoulders bumped as they swayed with the movement of the train. Every contact sent a current of intense pleasure through Jeremy, made the hairs stand up on his arms and on the back of his neck, pebbled his skin with gooseflesh. He knew that he possessed the ultimate power over the other boy, the power of life and death, and he was different from the other gutless wonders of the world because he wasn't afraid to *use* the power.

He waited for a section of track near the end of the ride, where he knew the undulant motion would provide the greatest degree of instability for daredevil riders. By then Tod would be feeling confident – *the worst is behind us* – and be easier to catch by surprise. The approach to the killing ground was announced by one of the most unusual tricks in the ride, a 360-degree turn at high speed, with the cars on their sides all the way around. When

200

they finished that circle and leveled out once more, they would immediately enter a series of six hills, all low but packed close together, so the train would move like an inchworm on drugs, pulling itself up-down-up-down-up-down-up-down toward the last set of swinging doors, which would admit them to the cavernous boarding and disembarkation chamber where they had begun.

The train began to tilt.

They entered the 360-degree turn.

The train was on its side.

Tod tried to remain rigid, but he sagged a little against Jeremy, who was on the inside of the car when it curved to the right. The old rocket jockey was whooping like an air-raid siren, doing his best to hype himself and get the most out of the ride, now that the worst was behind them.

An-tic-i-paa-aa-tion.

Jeremy estimated they were a third of the way around the circle . . . halfway around . . . two thirds . . .

The track leveled out. The train stopped fighting gravity.

With a suddenness that almost took Jeremy's breath away, the train hit the first of the six hills and shot upward.

He let go of the lap bar with his right hand, the one farthest from Tod.

The train swooped down.

He made a fist of his right hand.

And almost as soon as the train dropped, it swooped upward again toward the crown of the second hill.

Jeremy swung his fist in a roundhouse blow, trusting instinct to find Tod's face.

The train dropped.

His fist hit home, smashing Tod hard in the face, and he felt the boy's nose split.

The train shot upward again, with Tod screaming, though no one would hear anything special about it among the screams of all the other passengers.

Just for a split second, Tod would probably think he'd smacked into the overhang where, in legend, a boy had been decapitated. He would let go of the lap bar in panic. At least that was what Jeremy hoped, so as soon as he hit the old rocket jockey, when the train started to drop down the third hill, Jeremy let go of the lap bar, too, and threw himself against his best friend, grabbing him,

201

lifting and shoving, hard as he could. He felt Tod trying to get a fistful of his hair, but he shook his head furiously and shoved harder, took a kick on the hip –

— the train shot up the fourth hill —

— Tod went over the edge, out into the darkness, away from the car, as if he had dropped into deep space. Jeremy started to topple with him, grabbed frantically for the lap bar in the seamless blackness, found it, held on —

— down, the train swooped down the fourth hill —

— Jeremy thought he heard one last scream from Tod and then a solid *thunk!* as he hit the tunnel wall and bounced back onto the tracks in the wake of the train, although it might have been imagination —

— up, the train shot up the fifth hill with a rollicking motion that made Jeremy want to whoop his cookies —

— Tod was either dead back there in the darkness or stunned, half-conscious, trying to get to his feet —

— down the fifth hill, and Jeremy was whipped back and forth, almost lost his grip on the bar, then was soaring again, up the sixth and final hill —

— and if he wasn't dead back there, Tod was maybe just beginning to realize that another train was coming —

— down, down the sixth hill and onto the last straightaway.

As soon as he knew he was on stable ground, Jeremy scrambled back across the restraint bar and wriggled under it, first his left leg, then his right leg.

The last set of doors was rushing toward them in the dark. Beyond would be light, the main cavern, and attendants who would see that he had been daredevil riding.

He squirmed frantically to pass his hips through the gap between the back of the seat and the lap bar. Not too difficult, really. It was easier to slip under the bar than it had been to get out from beneath its protective grip.

They hit the swinging doors – *wham!* – and coasted at a steadily declining speed toward the disembarkation platform, a hundred feet this side of the gates through which they had entered the roller coaster. People were jammed on the boarding platform, and a lot of them were looking back at the train as it came out of the tunnel mouth. For a moment Jeremy expected them to point at him and cry, 'Murderer!'

Just as the train coasted up to the disembarkation gates and came to a full stop, red emergency lights blinked on all over the cavern, showing the way to the exits. A computerized alarm voice echoed through speakers set high in the fake rock formations: '*The Millipede has been brought to an emergency stop. All riders please remain in your seats—*'

As the lap bar released automatically at the end of the ride, Jeremy stood on the seat, grabbed a handrail, and pulled himself onto the disembarkation platform.

'*—all riders please remain in your seats until attendants arrive to lead you out of the tunnels—*'

The uniformed attendants on the platforms were looking to one another for guidance, wondering what had happened.

'*—all riders remain in your seats —*'

From the platform, Jeremy looked back toward the tunnel out of which his own train had just entered the cavern. He saw another train pushing through the swinging doors.

'*—all other guests please proceed in an orderly fashion to the nearest exit—*'

The oncoming train was no longer moving fast or smoothly. It shuddered and tried to jump the track.

With a jolt, Jeremy saw what was jamming the foremost wheels and forcing the front car to rise off the rails. Other people on the platform must have seen it, too, because suddenly they started to scream, not the we-sure-are-having-a-damned-fine-time screams that could be heard all over the carnival, but screams of horror and revulsion.

'*—all riders remain in your seats —*'

The train rocked and spasmed to a complete stop far short of the disembarkation platform. Something was dangling from the fierce mouth of the insect head that protruded from the front of the first car, snared in the jagged mandibles. It was the rest of the old rocket jockey, a nice bite-size piece for a monster bug the size of that one.

'*—all other guests please proceed in an orderly fashion to the nearest exit—*'

'Don't look, son,' an attendant said compassionately, turning Jeremy away from the gruesome spectacle. 'For God's sake, get out of here.'

The shocked attendants had recovered enough to begin to

direct the waiting crowd toward exit doors marked with glowing red signs. Realizing that he was bursting with excitement, grinning like a fool, and too overcome with joy to successfully play the bereaved best friend of the deceased, Jeremy joined the exodus, which was conducted in a panicky rush, with some pushing and shoving.

In the night air, where Christmasy lights continued to twinkle and the laser beams shot into the black sky and rainbows of neon rippled on every side, where thousands of customers continued their pursuit of pleasure without the slightest awareness that Death walked among them, Jeremy sprinted away from the Millipede. Dodging through the crowds, narrowly avoiding one collision after another, he had no idea where he was going. He just kept on the move until he was far from the torn body of Tod Ledderbeck.

He finally stopped at the manmade lake, across which a few Hovercraft buzzed with travelers bound to and from Mars Island. He felt as if he were on Mars himself, or some other alien planet where the gravity was less than that on earth. He was buoyant, ready to float up, up, and away.

He sat on a concrete bench to anchor himself, with his back to the lake, facing a flower-bordered promenade along which passed an endless parade of people, and he surrendered to the giddy laughter that insistently bubbled in him like Pepsi in a shaken bottle. It gushed out, such effervescent giggles in such long spouts that he had to hug himself and lean back on the bench to avoid falling off. People glanced at him, and one couple stopped to ask if he was lost. His laughter was so intense that he was choking with it, tears streaming down his face. They thought he was crying, a twelve-year-old ninny who had gotten separated from his family and was too much of a pussy to handle it. Their incomprehension only made him laugh harder.

When the laughter passed, he sat forward on the bench, staring at his sneakered feet, working on the line of crap he would give Mrs Ledderbeck when she came to collect him and Tod at ten o'clock – assuming park officials didn't identify the body and get in touch with her before that. It was eight o'clock. 'He wanted to ride daredevil,' Jeremy mumbled to his sneakers, 'and I tried to talk him out of it, but he wouldn't listen, he called me a dickhead when I wouldn't go with him. I'm sorry, Mrs Ledderbeck, Doctor Ledderbeck, but he talked that way sometimes. He thought it made him sound cool.' Good enough so far, but he needed more of a tremor in his voice: 'I wouldn't ride daredevil, so he went on the Millipede by himself. I waited at the exit, and when all those people came running out, talking about a body all torn and bloody, I knew who it had to be and I . . . and I . . . just sort of, you know, snapped. I just snapped.' The boarding attendants wouldn't remember whether Tod had gotten on the ride by himself or with another boy; they dealt with thousands of passengers a day, so they weren't going to recall who was alone or who was with whom. 'I'm so sorry, Mrs Ledderbeck, I should've been able to talk him out of it. I should've stayed with him and stopped him somehow. I feel so stupid, so . . . so helpless. How could I let him get on the Millipede? What kind of best friend am I?'

Not bad. It needed a little work, and he would have to be careful not to overdramatize it. Tears, a breaking voice. But no wild sobs, no thrashing around.

He was sure he could pull it off.

He was a Master of the Game now.

As soon as he felt confident about his story, he realized he was hungry. Starving. He was literally shaking with hunger. He went to a refreshment stand and bought a hot dog with the works – onions, relish, chili, mustard, ketchup – and wolfed it down. He chased it with Orange Crush. Still shaking. He had an ice cream sandwich made with chocolate-chip oatmeal cookies for the 'bread.'

His visible shaking stopped, but he still trembled inside. Not with fear. It was a delicious shiver, like the flutter in the belly that he'd experienced during the past year whenever he looked at a girl and thought of being with her, but indescribably better than that. And it was a little like the thrilling shiver that caressed his spine when he slipped past the safety railing and stood on the very edge of a sandy cliff in Laguna Beach Park, looking down at the waves crashing on the rocks and feeling the earth crumble slowly under the toes of his shoes, working its way back to mid-sole . . . waiting, waiting, wondering if the treacherous ground would abruptly give way and drop him to the rocks far below before he would have time to leap backward and grab the safety railing, but still waiting . . . waiting.

But this thrill was better than all of those combined. It was growing by the minute rather than diminishing, a sensuous inner heat which the murder of Tod had not quenched but fueled.

His dark desire became an urgent need.

He prowled the park, seeking satisfaction.

He was a little surprised that Fantasy World continued to turn as if nothing had happened in the Millipede. He had expected the whole operation to close down, not just that one ride. Now he realized money was more important than mourning one dead customer. And if those who'd seen Tod's battered body had spread the story to others, it was probably discounted as a rehash of the legend. The level of frivolity in the park had not noticeably declined.

Once he dared to pass the Millipede, although he stayed at a distance because he still did not trust himself to be able to conceal his excitement over his achievement and his delight in the new status that he had attained. Master of the Game. Chains were looped from stanchion to stanchion in front of the pavilion, to block anyone attempting to gain access. A CLOSED FOR REPAIRS sign was on the entrance door. Not for repairs to old Tod. The rocket jockey was beyond repair. No ambulance was in sight, which they might have *thought* they needed, and no hearse was anywhere to be seen. No police, either. Weird.

Then he remembered a TV story about the world under Fantasy World: catacombs of service tunnels, storage rooms, security and ride-computer control centers, just like at Disneyland. To avoid disturbing the paying customers and drawing the attention of the morbidly curious, they were probably using the tunnels now to bring in the cops and corpse-pokers from the coroner's office.

The shivers within Jeremy increased. The desire. The need.

He was a Master of the Game. No one could touch him.

Might as well give the cops and corpse-pokers more to do, keep them entertained.

He kept moving, seeking, alert for opportunity. He found it where he least expected, when he stopped at a men's restroom to take a leak.

A guy, about thirty, was at one of the sinks, checking himself out in the mirror, combing his thick blond hair, which glistened with Vitalis. He had arranged an array of personal objects on the ledge under the mirror: wallet, car keys, a tiny aerosol bottle of

Binaca breath freshener, a half-empty pack of Dentyne (this guy had a bad-breath fixation), and a cigarette lighter.

The lighter was what immediately caught Jeremy's attention. It was not just a plastic Bic butane disposable, but one of those steel models, shaped like a miniature slice of bread, with a hinged top that flipped back to reveal a striker wheel and a wick. The way the overhead fluorescent gleamed on the smooth curves of that lighter, it seemed to be a supernatural object, full of its own eerie radiance, a beacon for Jeremy's eyes alone.

He hesitated a moment, then went to one of the urinals. When he finished and zipped up, the blond guy was still at the sink, primping himself.

Jeremy always washed his hands after using a bathroom because that was what polite people did. It was one of the rules that a good player followed.

He went to the sink beside the primper. As he lathered his hands with liquid soap from the pump dispenser, he could not take his eyes off the lighter on the shelf inches away. He told himself he should avert his gaze. The guy would realize he was thinking about snatching the damn thing. But its sleek silvery contours held him rapt. Staring at it as he rinsed the lather from his hands, he imagined that he could hear the crisp crackle of all-consuming flames.

Returning his wallet to his hip pocket but leaving the other objects on the ledge, the guy turned away from the sink and went to one of the urinals. As Jeremy was about to reach for the lighter, a father and his teenage son entered. They could have screwed everything up, but they went into two of the stalls and closed the doors. Jeremy knew that was a sign. Do it, the sign said. Take it, go, do it, do it. Jeremy glanced at the man at the urinal, plucked the lighter off the shelf, turned and walked out without drying his hands. No one ran after him.

Clutching the lighter tightly in his right hand, he prowled the park, searching for the perfect kindling. The desire in him was so intense that his shivers spread outward from his crotch and belly and spine, appearing once more in his hands, and in his legs, too, which sometimes were rubbery with excitement.

Need . . .

★ ★ ★

Finishing the last of the Reese's Pieces, Vassago neatly rolled the empty bag into a tight tube, tied the tube in a knot to make the smallest possible object of it, and dropped it into a plastic garbage bag that was just to the left of the iceless Styrofoam cooler. Neatness was one of the rules in the world of the living.

He enjoyed losing himself in the memory of that special night, eight years ago, when he had been twelve and had changed forever, but he was tired now and wanted to sleep. Maybe he would dream of the woman named Lindsey. Maybe he would have another vision that would lead him to someone connected with her, for somehow she seemed to be part of his destiny; he was being drawn toward her by forces he could not entirely understand but which he respected. Next time, he would not make the mistake he had made with Cooper. He would not let the need overwhelm him. He would ask questions first. When he had received all the answers, and only then, he would free the beautiful blood and, with it, another soul to join the infinite throngs beyond this hateful world.

·4·

Tuesday morning, Lindsey stayed home to get some work done in her studio while Hatch took Regina to school on his way to a meeting with an executor of an estate in North Tustin who was seeking bids on a collection of antique Wedgwood urns and vases. After lunch he had an appointment with Dr Nyebern to learn the results of the tests he had undergone on Saturday. By the time he picked up Regina and returned home late in the afternoon, Lindsey figured to have finished the canvas she had been working on for the past month.

That was the plan, anyway, but all the fates and evil elves – and her own psychology – conspired to prevent the fulfillment of it. First of all the coffee maker went on the fritz. Lindsey had to tinker with the machine for an hour to find and fix the problem. She was a good tinkerer, and fortunately the brewer was fixable. She could not face the day without a blast of caffeine to jump-start her heart. She knew coffee was bad for her, but so was battery acid and cyanide, and she didn't drink either one of those, which showed she had more than her share of self-control when it came to destructive dietary habits; hell, she was an absolute rock!

By the time she got up to her second-floor studio with a mug and a full thermos besides, the light coming through the north-facing windows was perfect for her purposes. She had everything she needed. She had her paints, brushes, and palette knives. She had her supply cabinet. She had her adjustable stool and her easel and her stereo system with stacks of Garth Brooks, Glenn Miller, and Van Halen CDs, which somehow seemed the right mix of background music for a painter whose style was a combination of neoclassicism and surrealism. The only things she didn't have were an interest in the work at hand and the ability to concentrate.

She was repeatedly diverted by a glossy black spider that was exploring the upper right-hand corner of the window nearest to her. She didn't like spiders, but she was loath to kill them anyway. Later, she would have to capture it in a jar to release it outside. It crept upside-down across the window header to the left-hand corner, immediately lost interest in that territory, and returned to the right-hand corner, where it quivered and flexed its long legs and seemed to be taking pleasure from some quality of that particular niche that was apprehensible only to spiders.

Lindsey turned to her painting again. Nearly complete, it was one of her best, lacking only a few refining touches.

But she hesitated to open paints and pick up a brush because she was every bit as devoted a worrier as she was an artist. She was anxious about Hatch's health, of course – both his physical and mental health. She was apprehensive, too, about the strange man who had killed the blonde, and about the eerie connection between that savage predator and her Hatch.

The spider crept down the side of the window frame to the right-hand corner of the sill. After using whatever arachnid senses it possessed, it rejected that nook, as well, and returned once more to the *upper* right-hand corner.

Like most people Lindsey considered psychics to be good subjects for spooky movies but charlatans in real life. Yet she had been quick to suggest clairvoyance as an explanation for what had been happening to Hatch. She had pressed the theory more insistently when he had declared that he was not psychic.

Now, turning away from the spider and staring frustratedly at the unfinished canvas before her, she realized why she had become such an earnest advocate of the reality of psychic power in the car on Friday, when they had followed the killer's trail to the head of Laguna Canyon Road. If Hatch had become psychic, eventually he would begin to receive impressions from all sorts of people, and his link to this murderer would not be unique. But if he was *not* psychic, if the bond between him and this monster was more profound and infinitely stranger than random clairvoyant reception, as he insisted that it was, then they were hip-deep into the unknown. And the unknown was a hell of a lot scarier than something you could describe and define.

Besides, if the link between them was more mysterious and intimate than psychic reception, the consequences for Hatch might be psychologically disastrous. What mental trauma might result from being even briefly inside the mind of a ruthless killer? Was the link between them a source of contamination, as any such intimate *biological* link would have been? If so, perhaps the virus of madness could creep across the ether and infect Hatch.

No. Ridiculous. Not her husband. He was reliable, level-headed, mellow, as sane a human being as any who walked the earth.

The spider had taken possession of the upper right-hand corner of the window. It began to spin a web.

Lindsey remembered Hatch's anger last night when he had seen the story about Cooper in the newspaper. The implacable rage in his face. The unsettling fevered look in his eyes. She had never seen Hatch like that. His father, yes, but never him. Though she knew he worried that he might have some of his father in him, she had never seen evidence of it before. And maybe she had not seen evidence of it last night, either. What she had seen might be some of the rage of the killer leaking back into Hatch along the link that existed between them—

No. She had nothing to fear from Hatch. He was a good man, the best she had ever met. He was such a deep well of goodness that all the madness of the blond girl's killer could be dropped into him and he would dilute it until it was without effect.

A glistening, silky filament spewed from the spider's abdomen as the arachnid industriously claimed the corner of the window for its lair. Lindsey opened a drawer in her equipment cabinet and took out a small magnifying glass, which she used to observe the spinner more closely. Its spindly legs were prickled with hundreds of fine hairs that could not be seen without the assistance of the

210

lens. Its horrid, multifaceted eyes looked everywhere at once, and its ragged maw worked continuously as if in anticipation of the first living fly to become stuck in the trap that it was weaving.

Although she understood that it was a part of nature as surely as she was, and therefore not evil, the thing nevertheless revolted Lindsey. It was a part of nature that she preferred not to dwell upon: the part that had to do with hunting and killing, with things that fed eagerly on the living. She put the magnifying glass on the windowsill and went downstairs to get a jar from the kitchen pantry. She wanted to capture the spider and get it out of her house before it was any more securely settled.

Reaching the foot of the stairs, she glanced at the window beside the front door and saw the postman's car. She collected the mail from the box at the curb: a few bills, the usual minimum of two mail-order catalogues, and the latest issue of *Arts American*.

She was in the mood to seize any excuse not to work, which was unusual for her, because she loved her work. Quite forgetting that she had come downstairs in the first place for a jar in which to transport the spider, she took the mail back up to her studio and settled down in the old armchair in the corner with a fresh mug of coffee and *Arts American*.

She spotted the article about herself as soon as she glanced at the table of contents. She was surprised. The magazine had covered her work before, but she had always known in advance that articles were forthcoming. Usually the writer had at least a few questions for her, even if he was not doing a straight interview.

Then she saw the byline and winced. S. Steven Honell. She knew before reading the first word that she was the target of a hatchet job.

Honell was a well-reviewed writer of fiction who, from time to time, also wrote about art. He was in his sixties and had never married. A phlegmatic fellow, he had decided as a young man to forego the comforts of a wife and family in the interest of his writing. To write well, he said, one ought to possess a monk's preference for solitude. In isolation, one was forced to confront oneself more directly and honestly than possible in the hustle-bustle of the peopled world, and through oneself also confront the nature of every human heart. He had lived in splendid isolation first in northern California, then in New Mexico. Most recently he had settled at the eastern edge of the developed part of Orange

County at the end of Silverado Canyon, which was part of a series of brush-covered hills and ravines spotted with numerous California live oaks and less numerous rustic cabins.

In September of the previous year, Lindsey and Hatch had gone to a restaurant at the civilized end of Silverado Canyon, which served strong drinks and good steaks. They had eaten at one of the tables in the taproom, which was paneled in knotty pine with limestone columns supporting the roof. An inebriated white-haired man, sitting at the bar, was holding forth on literature, art, and politics. His opinions were strongly held and expressed in caustic language. From the affectionate tolerance the cur-mudgeon received from the bartender and patrons on the other bar stools, Lindsey guessed he was a regular customer and a local character who told only half as many tales as were told about him.

Then Lindsey recognized him. S. Steven Honell. She had read and liked some of his writing. She'd admired his selfless devotion to his art; for she could not have sacrificed love, marriage, and children for her painting, even though the exploration of her creative talent was as important to her as having enough food to eat and water to drink. Listening to Honell, she wished that she and Hatch had gone somewhere else for dinner because she would never again be able to read the author's work without remember-ing some of the vicious statements he made about the writings and personalities of his contemporaries in letters. With each drink, he grew more bitter, more scathing, more indulgent of his own dark-est instincts, and markedly more garrulous. Liquor revealed the gabby fool hidden inside the legend of taciturnity; anyone wanting to shut him up would have needed a horse veterinarian's hypoder-mic full of Demerol or a .357 Magnum. Lindsey ate faster, decid-ing to skip dessert and depart Honell's company as swiftly as possible.

Then he recognized her. He kept glancing over his shoulder at her, blinking his rheumy eyes. Finally he unsteadily approached their table. 'Excuse me, are you Lindsey Sparling, the artist?' She had known that he sometimes wrote about American art, but she had not imagined he would know her work or her face. 'Yes, I am,' she said, hoping he would not say that he liked her work and that he would not tell her who he was. 'I like your work very much,' he said, 'I won't bother you to say more.' But just as she relaxed and thanked him, he told her his name, and she was

212

obligated to say that she liked his work, too, which she did, though now she saw it in a light different from that in which it had previously appeared to her. He seemed less like a man who had sacrificed family love for his art than like a man incapable of giving that love. In isolation he might have found a greater power to create; but he had also found more time to admire himself and contemplate the infinite number of ways in which he was superior to the ruck of his fellow men. She tried not to let her distaste show, spoke only glowingly of his novels, but he seemed to sense her disapproval. He quickly terminated the encounter and returned to the bar.

He never looked her way again during the night. And he no longer held forth to the assembled drinkers about anything, his attention directed largely at the contents of his glass.

Now, sitting in the armchair in her studio, holding the copy of *Arts American*, and staring at Honell's byline, she felt her stomach curdle. She had seen the great man in his cups, when he had uncloaked more of his true self than it was his nature to reveal. Worse, she was a person of some accomplishment, who moved in circles that might bring her into contact with people Honell also knew. He saw her as a threat. One way of neutralizing her was to undertake a well-written, if unfair, article criticizing her body of work; thereafter, he could claim that any tales she told about him were motivated by spite, of questionable truthfulness. She knew what to expect from him in the *Arts American* piece, and Honell did not surprise her. Never before had she read criticism so vicious yet so cunningly crafted to spare the critic accusations of personal animosity.

When she finished, she closed the magazine and put it down gently on the small table beside her chair. She didn't want to pitch it across the room because she knew that reaction would have pleased Honell if he had been present to see it.

Then she said, 'To hell with it,' picked up the magazine, and threw it across the room with all the force she could muster. It slapped hard against the wall and clattered to the floor.

Her work was important to her. Intellect, emotion, talent, and craft went into it, and even on those occasions when a painting did not turn out as well as she had hoped, no creation ever came easily. Anguish always was a part of it. And more self-revelation than seemed prudent. Exhilaration and despair in equal measure.

213

A critic had every right to dislike an artist if his judgment was based on thoughtful consideration and an understanding of what the artist was trying to achieve. But *this* was not genuine criticism. This was sick invective. Bile. Her work was important to her, and he had shit on it.

Filled with the energy of anger, she got up and paced. She knew that by surrendering to anger she was letting Honell win; this was the response he had hoped to extract from her with his dental-pliers criticism. But she couldn't help it.

She wished Hatch was there, so she could share her fury with him. He had a calming effect greater than a fifth of bourbon.

Her angry pacing brought her eventually to the window where by now the fat black spider had constructed an elaborate web in the upper right-hand corner. Realizing that she had forgotten to get a jar from the pantry, Lindsey picked up the magnifying glass and examined the silken filigree of the eight-legged fisherman's net, which glimmered with a pastel mother-of-pearl iridescence. The trap was so delicate, so alluring. But the living loom that spun it was the very essence of all predators, strong for its size and sleek and quick. Its bulbous body glistened like a drop of thick black blood, and its rending mandibles worked the air in anticipation of the flesh of prey not yet snared.

The spider and Steven Honell were of a kind, utterly alien to her and beyond understanding regardless of how long she observed them. Both spun their webs in silence and isolation. Both had brought their viciousness into her house uninvited, one through words in a magazine and the other through a tiny crack in a window frame or door jamb. Both were poisonous, vile.

She put down the magnifying glass. She could do nothing about Honell, but at least she could deal with the spider. She snatched two Kleenex from a box atop her supply cabinet, and in one swift movement she swept up the spinner and its web, crushing both.

She threw the wad of tissues in the waste can.

Though she usually captured a spider when possible and kindly returned it to the outdoors, she had no compunction about the way she had dealt with this one. Indeed, if Honell had been present at that moment, when his hateful attack was still so fresh in her mind, she might have been tempted to deal with him in some manner as quick and violent as the treatment she had accorded the spider.

She returned to her stool, regarded the unfinished canvas, and was suddenly certain what refinements it required. She opened tubes of paint and set out her brushes. That wasn't the first time she had been motivated by an unjust blow or a puerile insult, and she wondered how many artists of all kinds had produced their best work with the determination to rub it in the faces of the naysayers who had tried to undercut or belittle them.

When Lindsey had been at work on the painting for ten or fifteen minutes, she was stricken by an unsettling thought which brought her back to the worries that had preoccupied her before the arrival of the mail and *Arts American*. Honell and the spider were not the only creatures who had invaded her home uninvited. The unknown killer in sunglasses also had invaded it, in a way, by feedback through the mysterious link between him and Hatch. And what if he was as aware of Hatch as Hatch was of him? He might find a way to track Hatch down and invade their home for real, with the intention of doing far more harm than either the spider or Honell could ever accomplish.

·5·

Previously, Hatch had visited Jonas Nyebern in his office at Orange County General, but that Tuesday his appointment was at the medical building off Jamboree Road, where the physician operated his private practice.

The waiting room was remarkable, not for its short-nap gray carpet and standard-issue furniture, but for the artwork on its walls. Hatch was surprised and impressed by a collection of high-quality antique oil paintings portraying religious scenes of a Catholic nature: the passion of St Jude, the Crucifixion, the Holy Mother, the Annunciation, the Resurrection, and much more.

The most curious thing was not that the collection was worth considerable money. After all, Nyebern was an extremely successful cardiovascular surgeon who came from a family of more than average resources. But it was odd that a member of the medical profession, which had taken an increasingly agnostic public posture throughout the last few decades, should choose religious art of any kind for his office walls, let alone such obvious denominational art that might offend non-Catholics or non-believers.

215

When the nurse escorted Hatch out of the waiting room, he discovered the collection continued along the hallways serving the entire suite. He found it peculiar to see a fine oil of Jesus's agony in Gethsemane hung to the left of a stainless-steel and white-enamel scale, and beside a chart listing ideal weight according to height, age, and sex.

After weighing in and having his blood pressure and pulse taken, he waited for Nyebern in a small private room, sitting on the end of an examination table that was covered by a continuous roll of sanitary paper. On one wall hung an eye chart and an exquisite depiction of the Ascension in which the artist's skill with light was so great that the scene became three-dimensional and the figures therein seemed almost alive.

Nyebern kept him waiting only a minute or two, and entered with a broad smile. As they shook hands, the physician said, 'I won't draw out the suspense, Hatch. The tests all came in negative. You've got a clean bill of health.'

Those words were not as welcome as they ought to have been. Hatch had been hoping for some finding that would point the way to an understanding of his nightmares and his mystical connection with the man who had killed the blond punker. But the verdict did not in the least surprise him. He had suspected that the answers he sought were not going to be that easy to find.

'So your nightmares are only that,' Nyebern said, 'and nothing more – just nightmares.'

Hatch had not told him about the vision of the gunshot blonde who had later been found dead, for real, on the freeway. As he had made clear to Lindsey, he was not going to set himself up to become a headline again, at least not unless he saw enough of the killer to identify him to the police, more than he'd glimpsed in the mirror last night, in which case he would have no choice but to face the media spotlight.

'No cranial pressure,' Nyebern said, 'no chemicoelectrical imbalance, no sign of a shift in the location of the pineal gland – which can sometimes lead to severe nightmares and even waking hallucinations . . . ' He went over the tests one by one, methodical as usual.

As he listened, Hatch realized that he always remembered the physician as being older than he actually was. Jonas Nyebern had a grayness about him, and a gravity, that left the impression of

216

advanced age. Tall and lanky, he hunched his shoulders and stooped slightly to de-emphasize his height, resulting in a posture more like that of an elderly man than of someone his true age, which was fifty. At times there was about him, as well, an air of sadness, as if he had known great tragedy.

When he finished going over the tests, Nyebern looked up and smiled again. It was a warm smile, but that air of sadness clung to him in spite of it. 'The problem isn't physical, Hatch.'

'Is it possible you could have missed something?'

'Possible, I suppose, but very unlikely. We—'

'An extremely minor piece of brain damage, a few hundred cells, might not show up on your tests yet have a serious effect.'

'As I said, very unlikely. I think we can safely assume that this is strictly an emotional problem, a perfectly understandable consequence of the trauma you've been through. Let's try a little standard therapy.'

'Psychotherapy?'

'Do you have a problem with that?'

'No.'

Except, Hatch thought, it won't work. This isn't an emotional problem. This is real.

'I know a good man, first-rate, you'll like him,' Nyebern said, taking a pen from the breast pocket of his white smock and writing the name of the psychotherapist on the blank top sheet of a prescription pad. 'I'll discuss your case with him and tell him you'll be calling. Is that all right?'

'Yeah. Sure. That's fine.'

He wished he could tell Nyebern the whole story. But then he would *definitely* sound as if he needed therapy. Reluctantly he faced the realization that neither a medical doctor nor a psychotherapist could help him. His ailment was too strange to respond to standard treatments of any kind. Maybe what he needed was a witch doctor. Or an exorcist. He *did* almost feel as if the black-clad killer in sunglasses was a demon testing his defenses to determine whether to attempt possessing him.

They chatted a couple of minutes about things non-medical.

Then as Hatch was getting up to go, he pointed to the painting of the Ascension. 'Beautiful piece.'

'Thank you. It is exceptional, isn't it?'

'Italian.'

'That's right.'

'Early eighteenth century?'

'Right again,' Nyebern said. 'You know religious art?'

'Not all that well. But I think the whole collection is Italian from the same period.'

'That it is. Another piece, maybe two, and I'll call it complete.'

'Odd to see it here,' Hatch said, stepping closer to the painting beside the eye chart.

'Yes, I know what you mean,' Nyebern said, 'but I don't have enough wall space for all this at home. There, I'm putting together a collection of *modern* religious art.'

'Is there any?'

'Not much. Religious subject matter isn't fashionable these days among the really talented artists. The bulk of it is done by hacks. But here and there . . . someone with genuine talent is seeking enlightenment along the old paths, painting these subjects with a contemporary eye. I'll move the modern collection here when I finish this one and dispose of it.'

Hatch turned away from the painting and regarded the doctor with professional interest. 'You're planning to sell?'

'Oh, no,' the physician said, returning his pen to his breast pocket. His hand, with the long elegant fingers that one expected of a surgeon, lingered at the pocket, as if he were pledging the truth of what he was saying. 'I'll donate it. This will be the sixth collection of religious art I've put together over the past twenty years, then given away.'

Because he could roughly estimate the value of the artwork he had seen on the walls of the medical suite, Hatch was astonished by the degree of philanthropy indicated by Nyebern's simple statement. 'Who's the fortunate recipient?'

'Well, usually a Catholic university, but on two occasions another Church institution,' Nyebern said.

The surgeon was staring at the depiction of the Ascension, a distant gaze in his eyes, as if he were seeing something beyond the painting, beyond the wall on which it hung, and beyond the farthest horizon. His hand still lingered over his breast pocket.

'Very generous of you,' Hatch said.

'It's not an act of generosity.' Nyebern's faraway voice now matched the look in his eyes. 'It's an act of atonement.'

That statement begged a question in response, although Hatch

218

felt that asking it was an intrusion of the physician's privacy. 'Atonement for what?'

Still staring at the painting, Nyebern said, 'I never talk about it.'

'I don't mean to pry. I just thought – '

'Maybe it would do me good to talk about it. Do you think it might?'

Hatch did not answer – partly because he didn't believe the doctor was actually listening to him anyway.

'Atonement,' Nyebern said again. 'At first . . . atonement for being the son of my father. Later . . . for being the father of my son.'

Hatch didn't see how either thing could be a sin, but he waited, certain that the physician would explain. He was beginning to feel like that party-goer in the old Coleridge poem, waylaid by the distraught Ancient Mariner who had a tale of terror that he was driven to impart to others lest, by keeping it to himself, he lose what little sanity he still retained.

Gazing unblinking at the painting, Nyebern said, 'When I was only seven, my father suffered a psychotic breakdown. He shot and killed my mother and my brother. He wounded my sister and me, left us for dead, then killed himself.'

'Jesus, I'm sorry,' Hatch said, and he thought of his own father's bottomless well of anger. 'I'm very sorry, doctor.' But he still did not understand the failure or sin for which Nyebern felt the need to atone.

'Certain psychoses may sometimes have a genetic cause. When I saw signs of sociopathic behavior in my son, even at an early age, I should have known what was coming, should've prevented it somehow. But I couldn't face the truth. Too painful. Then two years ago, when he was eighteen, he stabbed his sister to death—'

Hatch shuddered.

'—then his mother,' Nyebern said.

Hatch started to put a hand on the doctor's arm, then pulled back when he sensed that Nyebern's pain could never be eased and that his wound was beyond healing by any medication as simple as consolation. Although he was speaking of an intensely personal tragedy, the physician plainly was not seeking sympathy or the intimacy of friendship from Hatch. Suddenly he seemed almost frighteningly self-contained. He was talking about the tragedy because the time had come to take it out of his personal

219

darkness to examine it again, and he would have spoken of it to anyone who had been in that place at that time instead of Hatch – or perhaps to the empty air itself if no one at all had been present.

'And when they were dead,' Nyebern said, 'Jeremy took the same knife into the garage, a butcher knife, secured it by the handle in the vise on my workbench, stood on a stool, and fell forward, impaling himself on the blade. He bled to death.'

The physician's right hand was still at his breast pocket, but he no longer seemed like a man pledging the truth of what he said. Instead, he reminded Hatch of a painting of Christ with the Sacred Heart revealed, the slender hand of divine grace pointing to that symbol of sacrifice and promise of eternity.

At last Nyebern looked away from the Ascension and met Hatch's eyes. 'Some say evil is just the consequences of our actions, no more than a result of our will. But I believe it's that – and much more. I believe evil is a very real force, an energy quite apart from us, a presence in the world. Is that what you believe, Hatch?'

'Yes,' Hatch said at once, and somewhat to his surprise.

Nyebern looked down at the prescription pad in his left hand. He took his right hand away from his breast pocket, tore the top sheet off the pad, and gave it to Hatch. 'His name's Foster. Doctor Gabriel Foster. I'm sure he'll be able to help you.'

'Thanks,' Hatch said numbly.

Nyebern opened the door of the examination room and gestured for Hatch to precede him.

In the hallway, the physician said, 'Hatch?'

Hatch stopped and looked back at him.

'Sorry,' Nyebern said.

'For what?'

'For explaining why I donate the paintings.'

Hatch nodded. 'Well, I asked, didn't I?'

'But I could have been much briefer.'

'Oh?'

'I could have just said – maybe I think the only way for me to get into Heaven is to buy my way.'

Outside, in the sun-splashed parking lot, Hatch sat in his car for a long time, watching a wasp that hovered over the red hood as if it thought it had found an enormous rose.

The conversation in Nyebern's office had seemed strangely like a dream, and Hatch felt as if he were still rising out of sleep. He sensed that the tragedy of Jonas Nyebern's death-haunted life had a direct bearing on his own current problems, but although he reached for the connection, he could not grasp it.

The wasp swayed to the left, to the right, but faced steadily toward the windshield as though it could see him in the car and was mysteriously drawn to him. Repeatedly, it darted at the glass, bounced off, and resumed its hovering. Tap, hover, tap, hover, tap-tap, hover. It was a very determined wasp. He wondered if it was one of those species that possessed a single stinger that broke off in the target, resulting in the subsequent death of the wasp. Tap, hover, tap, hover, tap-tap-tap. If it was one of those species, did it fully understand what reward it would earn by its persistence? Tap, hover, tap-tap-tap.

★ ★ ★

After seeing the last patient of the day, a follow-up visit with an engaging thirty-year-old woman on whom he had performed an aortal graft last March, Jonas Nyebern entered his private office at the back of the medical suite and closed the door. He went behind the desk, sat down, and looked in his wallet for a slip of paper on which was written a telephone number that he chose not to include on his Rolodex. He found it, pulled the phone close, and punched in the seven numbers.

Following the third ring, an answering machine picked up as it had on his previous calls yesterday and earlier that morning: 'This is Morton Redlow. I'm not in the office right now. After the beep, please leave a message and a number where you can be reached, and I will get back to you as soon as possible.'

Jonas waited for the signal, then spoke softly. 'Mr Redlow, this is Dr Nyebern. I know I've left other messages, but I was under the impression that I would receive a report from you last Friday. Certainly by the weekend at the latest. Please call me as soon as possible. Thank you.'

He hung up.

He wondered if he had reason to worry.

He wondered if he had any reason *not* to worry.

221

Regina sat at her desk in Sister Mary Margaret's French class, weary of the smell of chalk dust and annoyed by the hardness of the plastic seat under her butt, learning how to say, *Hello, I am an American. Can you direct me to the nearest church where I might attend Sunday Mass?*

Très boring.

She was still a fifth-grade student at St Thomas's Elementary School, because continued attendance was a strict condition of her adoption. (Trial adoption. Nothing final yet. Could blow up. The Harrisons could decide they preferred raising parakeets to children, give her back, get a bird. Please, God, make sure they realize that in Your divine wisdom You designed birds so they poop a lot. Make sure they know what a mess it'll be keeping the cage clean.) When she graduated from St Thomas's Elementary, she would move on to St Thomas's High School, because St Thomas's had its fingers in everything. In addition to the children's care home and the two schools, it had a day-care center and a thrift shop. The parish was like a conglomerate, and Father Jiminez was sort of a big executive like Donald Trump, except Father Jiminez didn't run around with bimbos or own gambling casinos. The bingo parlor hardly counted. (Dear God, that stuff about birds pooping a lot – that was in no way meant as a criticism. I'm sure You had Your reasons for making birds poop a lot, all over everything, and like the mystery of the Holy Trinity, it's just one of those things we ordinary humans can't ever quite understand. No offense meant.) Anyway, she didn't mind going to St Thomas's School, because both the nuns and the lay teachers pushed you hard, and you ended up learning a lot, and she loved to learn.

By the last class on that Tuesday afternoon, however, she was full up with learning, and if Sister Mary Margaret called on her to say anything in French, she would probably confuse the word for church with the word for sewer, which she had done once before, much to the delight of the other kids and to her own mortification. (Dear God, please remember that I made myself say the Rosary as penance for that boner, just to prove I didn't mean anything by it, it was only a mistake.) When the dismissal bell rang, she was the first out of her seat and the first out of the classroom door, even though most of the kids at St Thomas's School did not come from St Thomas's Home and were not disabled in any way.

All the way to her locker and all the way from her locker to the front exit, she wondered if Mr Harrison would really be waiting for her, as he had promised. She imagined herself standing on the sidewalk with kids swarming around her, unable to spot his car, the crowd gradually diminishing until she stood alone, and still no sign of his car, and her waiting as the sun set and the moon rose and her wristwatch ticked toward midnight, and in the morning when the kids returned for another day of school, she'd just go back inside with them and not tell anyone the Harrisons didn't want her any more.

He was there. In the red car. In a line of cars driven by other kids' parents. He leaned across the seat to open the door for her as she approached.

When she got in with her book bag and closed the door, he said, 'Hard day?'

'Yeah,' she said, suddenly shy when shyness had never been one of her major problems. She was having trouble getting the hang of this family thing. She was afraid maybe she'd never get it.

He said, 'Those nuns.'

'Yeah,' she agreed.

'They're tough.'

'Tough.'

'Tough as nails, those nuns.'

'Nails,' she said, nodding agreement, wondering if she would ever be able to speak more than one-word sentences again.

As he pulled away from the curb, he said, 'I'll bet you could put any nun in the ring with any heavyweight champion in the whole history of boxing – I don't care if it was even Muhammad Ali – and she'd knock him out in the first round.'

Regina couldn't help grinning at him.

'Sure,' he said. 'Only Superman could survive a fight with a real hardcase nun. Batman? Fooie! Even your *average* nun could mop up the floor with Batman – or make soup out of the whole gang of Teenage Mutant Ninja Turtles.'

'They mean well,' she said, which was three words, at least, but sounded goofy. She might be better off not talking at all; she just didn't have any experience of this father–kid stuff.

'Nuns?' he said. 'Well, of course, they mean well. If they didn't

223

mean well, they wouldn't be nuns. They'd be maybe Mafia hitmen, international terrorists, United States Congressmen.'

He did not speed home like a busy man with lots to do, but like somebody out for a leisurely drive. She had not been in a car with him enough to know if that was how he always drove, but she suspected maybe he was loafing along a little slower than he usually did, so they could have more time together, just the two of them. That was sweet. It made her throat a little tight and her eyes watery. Oh, terrific. A pile of cow flop could've carried on a better conversation than she was managing, so now she was going to burst into tears, which would really cement the relationship. Surely every adoptive parent desperately hoped to receive a mute, emotionally unstable girl with physical problems – right? It was all the rage, don't you know. Well, if she did cry, her treacherous sinuses would kick in, and the old snot-faucet would start gushing, which would surely make her even *more* appealing. He'd give up the idea of a leisurely drive, and head for home at such tremendous speed that he'd have to stand on the brakes a mile from the house to avoid shooting straight through the back of the garage. (Please, God, help me here. You'll notice I thought 'cow flop' not 'cow shit,' so I deserve a little mercy.)

They chatted about this and that. Actually, for a while he chatted and she pretty much just grunted like she was a subhuman out on a pass from the zoo. But eventually she realized, to her surprise, that she was talking in complete sentences, had been doing so for a couple of miles, and was at ease with him.

He asked her what she wanted to be when she grew up, and she just about bent his ear clear off explaining that some people actually made a living writing the kinds of books she liked to read and that she had been composing her own stories for a year or two. Lame stuff, she admitted, but she would get better at it. She was very bright for ten, older than her years, but she couldn't expect actually to have a career going until she was eighteen, maybe sixteen if she was lucky. When had Mr Christopher Pike started publishing? Seventeen? Eighteen? Maybe he'd been as old as twenty, but certainly no older, so that's what she would shoot for – being the next Mr Christopher Pike by the time she was twenty. She had an entire notebook full of story ideas. Quite a few of those ideas were good when you crossed out the embarrassingly childish ones like the story about the intelligent pig from space

224

that she had been so hot about for a while but now saw was hopelessly dumb. She was still talking about writing books when they pulled into the driveway of the house in Laguna Niguel, and he actually seemed interested.

She figured she might get the hang of this family thing yet.

★ ★ ★

Vassago dreamed of fire. The click of the cigarette-lighter cover being flipped open in the dark. The dry rasp of the striker wheel scraping against the flint. A spark. A young girl's white summer dress flowering into flames. The Haunted House ablaze. Screams as the calculatedly spooky darkness dissolved under licking tongues of orange light. Tod Ledderbeck was dead in the cavern of the Millipede, and now the house of plastic skeletons and rubber ghouls was abruptly filled with real terror and pungent death.

He had dreamed of that fire previously, countless times since the night of Tod's twelfth birthday. It always provided the most beautiful of all the chimeras and phantasms that passed behind his eyes in sleep.

But on this occasion, strange faces and images appeared in the flames. The red car again. A solemnly beautiful, auburn-haired child with large gray eyes that seemed too old for her face. A small hand, cruelly bent, with fingers missing. A name, which had come to him once before, echoed through the leaping flames and melting shadows in the Haunted House. *Regina . . . Regina . . . Regina.*

★ ★ ★

The visit to Dr Nyebern's office had depressed Hatch, both because the tests had revealed nothing that shed any light on his strange experiences and because of the glimpse he had gotten into the physician's own troubled life. But Regina was a medicine for melancholy if ever there had been one. She had all the enthusiasm of a child her age; life had not beaten her down one inch.

On the way from the car to the front door of the house, she moved more swiftly and easily than when she had entered Salvatore Gujilio's office, but the leg brace did give her a measured and solemn gait. A bright yellow and blue butterfly accompanied her

225

every step, fluttering gaily a few inches from her head, as if it knew that her spirit was very like itself, beautiful and buoyant.

She said solemnly, 'Thank you for picking me up, Mr Harrison.'

'You're welcome, I'm sure,' he said with equal gravity.

They would have to do something about this 'Mr Harrison' business before the day was out. He sensed that her formality was partly a fear of getting too close and then being rejected as she had been during the trial phase of her first adoption. But it was also a fear of saying or doing the wrong thing and unwittingly destroying her own prospects for happiness.

At the front door, he said, 'Either Lindsey or I will be at the school for you every day – unless you've got a driver's license and would just rather come and go on your own.'

She looked up at Hatch. The butterfly was describing circles in the air above her head, as if it were a living crown or halo. She said, 'You're teasing me, aren't you?'

'Well, yes, I'm afraid I am.'

She blushed and looked away from him, as if she was not sure if being teased was a good or bad thing. He could almost hear her inner thoughts: *Is he teasing me because he thinks I'm cute or because he thinks I'm hopelessly stupid?* Or something pretty close to that.

Throughout the drive home from school, Hatch had seen that Regina suffered from her share of self-doubt, which she thought she concealed but which, when it struck, was evident in her lovely, wonderfully expressive face. Each time he sensed a crack in the kid's self-confidence, he wanted to put his arms around her, hug her tight, and reassure her – which would be exactly the wrong thing to do because she would be appalled to realize that her moments of inner turmoil were so obvious to him. She prided herself on being tough, resilient, and self-sufficient. She projected that image as armor against the world.

'I hope you don't mind some teasing,' he said as he inserted the key in the door. 'That's the way I am. I could check myself into a Teasers Anonymous program, shake the habit, but it's a tough outfit. They beat you with rubber hoses and make you eat Lima beans.'

When enough time passed, when she felt she was loved and part of a family, her self-confidence would be as unshakeable as she wanted it to be now. In the meantime, the best thing he could do for her was pretend that he saw her exactly as she wished to be

226

seen – and quietly, patiently, help her finish becoming the poised and assured person she hoped to be.

As he opened the door and they went inside, Regina said, 'I used to hate Lima beans, all kinds of beans, but I made a deal with God. If He gives me . . . something I 'specially want, I'll eat every kind of bean there is for the rest of my life without ever complaining.'

In the foyer, closing the door behind them, Hatch said, 'That's quite an offer. God ought to be impressed.'

'I sure hope so,' she said.

* * *

And in Vassago's dream, Regina moved in sunlight, one leg braced in steel, a butterfly attending her as it might a flower. A house flanked by palm trees. A door. She looked up at Vassago, and her eyes revealed a soul of tremendous vitality and a heart so vulnerable that the beat of his own was quickened even in sleep.

* * *

They found Lindsey upstairs, in the extra bedroom that served as her at-home studio. The easel was angled away from the door, so Hatch couldn't see the painting. Lindsey's blouse was half in and half out of her jeans, her hair was in disarray, a smear of rust-red paint marked her left cheek, and she had a look that Hatch knew from experience meant she was in the final fever of work on a piece that was turning out to be everything she had hoped.

'Hi, honey,' Lindsey said to Regina. 'How was school?'

Regina was flustered, as she always seemed to be, by any term of endearment. 'Well, school is school, you know.'

'Well, you must like it. I know you get good grades.'

Regina shrugged off the compliment and looked embarrassed.

Repressing the urge to hug the kid, Hatch said to Lindsey, 'She's going to be a writer when she grows up.'

'Really?' Lindsey said. 'That's exciting. I knew you loved books, but I didn't realize you wanted to write them.'

'Neither did I,' the girl said, and suddenly she was in gear and off, her initial awkwardness with Lindsey past, words pouring out of her as she crossed the room and went behind the easel to have

227

a look at the work in progress, 'until just last Christmas, when my gift under the tree at the home was six paperbacks. Not books for a ten year old, either, but the real stuff, because I read at a tenth-grade level, which is *fifteen* years old. I'm what they call precocious. Anyway, those books made the best gift ever, and I thought it'd be neat if someday a girl like me at the home got *my* books under the tree and felt the way I felt, not that I'll ever be as good a writer as Mr Daniel Pinkwater or Mr Christopher Pike. Jeez, I mean, they're right up there with Shakespeare and Judy Blume. But I've got good stories to tell, and they're not all that intelligent-pig-from-space crap. Sorry. I mean poop. I mean junk. Intelligent-pig-from-space junk. They're not all like that.'

Lindsey never showed Hatch – or anyone else – a canvas in progress, withholding even a glimpse of it until the final brush stroke had been applied. Though she was evidently near completion of the current painting, she was still working on it, and Hatch was surprised that she didn't even twitch when Regina went around to the front of the easel to have a look. He decided that no kid, just because she had a cute nose and some freckles, was going to be accorded a privilege he was denied, so he also walked boldly around the easel to take a peek.

It was a stunning piece of work. The background was a field of stars, and superimposed over it was the transparent face of an ethereally beautiful young boy. Not just any boy. Their Jimmy. When he was alive she had painted him a few times, but never since his death – until now. It was an idealized Jimmy of such perfection that his face might have been that of an angel. His loving eyes were turned upward, toward a warm light that rained down upon him from beyond the top of the canvas, and his expression was more profound than joy. Rapture. In the foreground, as the focus of the work, floated a black rose, not transparent like the face, rendered in such sensuous detail that Hatch could almost feel the velvety texture of each plush petal. The green skin of the stem was moist with a cool dew, and the thorns were portrayed with such piercingly sharp points that he half believed they would prick like real thorns if touched. A single drop of blood glistened on one of the black petals. Somehow Lindsey had imbued the floating rose with an aura of preternatural power, so it drew the eye, demanded attention, almost mesmeric in its effect. Yet the boy did not look down at the rose; he gazed up at the radiant object only he could see, the implication being that, as powerful as the rose might be, it was of no interest whatsoever when compared to the source of the light above.

From the day of Jimmy's death until Hatch's resuscitation, Lindsey had refused to take solace from any god who would create a world with death in it. He recalled a priest suggesting prayer as a route to acceptance and psychological healing, and Lindsey's response had been cold and dismissive: *Prayer never works. Expect no miracles, Father. The dead stay dead, and the living only wait to join them.* Something had changed in her now. The black rose in the painting was death. Yet it had no power over Jimmy. He had gone beyond death, and it meant nothing to him. He was rising above it. And by being able to conceive of the painting and bring it off so flawlessly, Lindsey had found a way to say goodbye to the boy at last, goodbye without regrets, goodbye without bitterness, goodbye with love and with a startling new acceptance of the need for belief in something more than a life that ended always in a cold, black hole in the ground.

'It's so beautiful,' Regina said with genuine awe. 'Scary in a way, I don't know why . . . scary . . . but so beautiful.'

Hatch looked up from the painting, met Lindsey's eyes, tried to say something, but could not speak. Since his resuscitation, there had been a rebirth of Lindsey's heart as well as his own, and they had confronted the mistake they had made by losing five years to grief. But on some fundamental level, they had not accepted that life could ever be as sweet as it had been before that one small death; they had not really let Jimmy go. Now, meeting Lindsey's eyes, he knew that she had finally embraced hope again without reservation. The full weight of his little boy's death fell upon Hatch as it had not in years, because if Lindsey could make peace with God, he must do so as well. He tried to speak again, could not, looked again at the painting, realized he was going to cry, and left the room.

He didn't know where he was going. Without quite remembering taking any step along the route, he went downstairs, into the den that they had offered to Regina as a bedroom, opened the French doors, and stepped into the rose garden at the side of the house.

In the warm, late-afternoon sun, the roses were red, white, yellow, pink, and the shade of peach skins, some only buds and some as big as saucers, but not one of them black. The air was full of their enchanting fragrance.

With the taste of salt in the corners of his mouth, he reached out with both hands toward the nearest rose-laden bush, intending to touch the flowers, but his hands stopped short of them. With his arms thus forming a cradle, he suddenly could feel a weight draped across them. In reality, nothing was in his arms, but the burden he felt was no mystery; he remembered, as if it had been an hour ago, how the body of his cancer-wasted son had felt.

In the final moments before death's hateful visitation, he had pulled the wires and tubes from Jim, had lifted him off the sweat-soaked hospital bed, and had sat in a chair by the window, holding him close and murmuring to him until the pale, parted lips drew no more breath. Until his own death, Hatch would remember precisely the weight of the wasted boy in his arms, the sharpness of bones with so little flesh left to pad them, the awful dry heat pouring off skin translucent with sickness, the heart-rending fragility.

He felt all that now, in his empty arms, there in the rose garden. When he looked up at the summer sky, he said, 'Why?' as if there were someone to answer. 'He was so small,' Hatch said. 'He was so damned small.'

As he spoke, the burden was heavier than it had ever been in that hospital room, a thousand tons in his empty arms, maybe because he still didn't want to free himself of it as much as he thought he did. But then a strange thing happened – the weight in his arms slowly diminished, and the invisible body of his son seemed to float out of his embrace, as if the flesh had been trans-muted entirely to spirit at long last, as if Jim had no need of comforting or consolation any more.

Hatch lowered his arms.

Maybe from now on the bittersweet memory of a child lost would be only the sweet memory of a child loved. And maybe, henceforth, it would not be a memory so heavy that it oppressed the heart.

He stood among the roses.

The day was warm. The late-afternoon light was golden.

The sky was perfectly clear – and utterly mysterious.

★ ★ ★

230

Regina asked if she could have some of Lindsey's paintings in her room, and she sounded sincere. They chose three. Together they hammered in picture hooks and hung the paintings where she wanted them – along with a foot-tall crucifix she had brought from her room at the orphanage.

As they worked, Lindsey said, 'How about dinner at a really super pizza parlor I know?'

'Yeah!' the girl said enthusiastically. 'I love pizza.'

'They make it with a nice thick crust, lots of cheese.'

'Pepperoni?'

'Cut thin, but lots of it.'

'Sausage?'

'Sure, why not. Though you're sure this isn't getting to be a pretty revolting pizza for a vegetarian like you?'

Regina blushed. 'Oh, that. I was such a little shit that day. Oh, Jeez, sorry. I mean, such a smartass. I mean, such a jerk.'

'That's okay,' Lindsey said. 'We all behave like jerks now and then.'

'You don't. Mr Harrison doesn't.'

'Oh, just wait.' Standing on a stepstool in front of the wall opposite the bed, Lindsey pounded in a nail for a picture hook. Regina was holding the painting for her. As she took it from the girl to hang it, Lindsey said, 'Listen, will you do me a favor at dinner tonight?'

'Favor? Sure?'

'I know it's still awkward for you, this new arrangement. You don't really feel at home and probably won't for a long time—'

'Oh, it's very nice here,' the girl protested.

Lindsey slipped the wire over the picture hook and adjusted the painting until it hung straight. Then she sat down on the step-stool, which just about brought her and the girl eye to eye. She took hold of both of Regina's hands, the normal one and the different one. 'You're right – it's very nice here. But you and I both know that's not the same as *home*. I wasn't going to push you on this. I was going to let you take your time, but . . . Even if it seems a little premature to you, do you think tonight at dinner you could stop calling us Mr and Mrs Harrison? Especially Hatch. It would be very important to him, just now, if you could at least call him Hatch.'

The girl lowered her eyes to their interlocked hands. 'Well, I guess . . . sure . . . that would be okay.'

'And you know what? I realize this is asking more than it's fair to ask yet, before you really know him that well, but do you know what would be the best thing in the world for him right now?'

The girl was still staring at their hands. 'What?'

'If somehow you could find it in your heart to call him Dad. Don't say yes or no just now. Think about it. But it would be a wonderful thing for you to do for him, for reasons I don't have time to explain right here. And I promise you this, Regina – he is a good man. He will do anything for you, put his life on the line for you if it ever came to that, and never ask for anything. He'd be upset if he knew I was even asking you for this. But all I'm asking, really, is for you to think about it.'

After a long silence, the girl looked up from their linked hands and nodded. 'Okay. I'll think about it.'

'Thank you, Regina.' She got up from the stepstool. 'Now let's hang that last painting.'

Lindsey measured, penciled a spot on the wall, and nailed in a picture hook.

When Regina handed over the painting, she said, 'It's just that all my life . . . there's never been anyone I called Mom or Dad. It's a very new thing.'

Lindsey smiled. 'I understand, honey. I really do. And so will Hatch if it takes time.'

* * *

In the blazing Haunted House, as the cries for help and the screams of agony swelled louder, a strange object appeared in the firelight. A single rose. A black rose. It floated as if an unseen magician was levitating it. Vassago had never encountered anything more beautiful in the world of the living, in the world of the dead, or in the realm of dreams. It shimmered before him, its petals so smooth and soft that they seemed to have been cut from swatches of the night sky unspoiled by stars. The thorns were exquisitely sharp, needles of glass. The green stem had the oiled sheen of a serpent's skin. One petal held a single drop of blood.

The rose faded from his dream, but later it returned – and with it the woman named Lindsey and the auburn-haired girl with the soft gray eyes. Vassago yearned to possess all three: the black rose, the woman, and the girl with the gray eyes.

★   ★   ★

After Hatch freshened up for dinner, while Lindsey finished getting ready in the bathroom, he sat alone on the edge of their bed and read the article by S. Steven Honell in *Arts American*. He could shrug off virtually any insult to himself, but if someone slammed Lindsey, he always reacted with anger. He couldn't even deal well with reviews of her work that *she* thought had made valid criticisms. Reading Honell's vicious, snide, and ultimately stupid diatribe dismissing her entire career as 'wasted energy,' Hatch grew angrier by the sentence.

As had happened the previous night, his anger erupted into fiery rage with volcanic abruptness. The muscles in his jaws clenched so hard, his teeth ached. The magazine began to shake because his hands were trembling with fury. His vision blurred slightly, as if he were looking at everything through shimmering waves of heat, and he had to blink and squint to make the fuzzy-edged words on the page resolve into readable print.

As when he had been lying in bed last night, he felt as if his anger opened a door and as if something entered him through it, a foul spirit that knew only rage and hate. Or maybe it had been with him all along but sleeping, and his anger had roused it. He was not alone inside his own head. He was aware of another presence, like a spider crawling through the narrow space between the inside of his skull and the surface of his brain.

He tried to put the magazine aside and calm down. But he kept reading because he was not in full possession of himself.

★   ★   ★

Vassago moved through the Haunted House, untroubled by the hungry fire, because he had planned an escape route. Sometimes he was twelve years old, and sometimes he was twenty. But always his path was lit by human torches, some of whom had collapsed into silent melting heaps upon the smoking floor, some of whom exploded into flames even as he passed them.

In the dream he was carrying a magazine, folded open to an article that angered him and seemed imperative he read. The

233

edges of the pages curled in the heat and threatened to catch fire. Names leaped at him from the pages. Lindsey. Lindsey Sparling. Now he had a last name for her. He felt an urge to toss the magazine aside, slow his breathing, calm down. Instead he stoked his anger, let a sweet flood of rage overwhelm him, and told himself that he must know more. The edges of the magazine pages curled in the heat. Honell. Another name. Steven Honell. Bits of burning debris fell on the article. Steven S. Honell. No. The S first. S. Steven Honell. The paper caught fire. Honell. A writer. A barroom. Silverado Canyon. In his hands, the magazine burst into flames that flashed into his face —

He shed sleep like a fired bullet shedding its brass jacket, and sat up in his dark hideaway. Wide awake. Excited. He knew enough now to find the woman.

★ ★ ★

One moment rage like a fire swept through Hatch, and the next moment it was extinguished. His jaws relaxed, his tense shoulders sagged, and his hands unclenched so suddenly that he dropped the magazine on the floor between his feet.

He continued to sit on the edge of the bed for a while, stunned and confused. He looked toward the bathroom door, relieved that Lindsey had not walked in on him while he had been . . . Been what? In his trance? Possessed?

He smelled something peculiar, out of place. Smoke.

He looked at the issue of *Arts American* on the floor between his feet. Hesitantly, he picked it up. It was still folded open to Honell's article about Lindsey. Although no visible vapors rose from the magazine, the paper exuded the heavy smell of smoke. The odors of burning wood, paper, tar, plastics . . . and something worse. The edges of the paper were yellow-brown and crisp, as if they had been exposed to almost enough heat to induce spontaneous combustion.

·7·

When the knock came at the door, Honell was sitting in a rocking chair by the fireplace. He was drinking Chivas Regal and reading one of his own novels, *Miss Culvert*, which he had written twenty-

234

five years ago when he was only thirty.

He re-read each of his nine books once a year because he was in perpetual competition with himself, striving to improve as he grew old instead of settling quietly into senescence the way most writers did. Constant betterment was a formidable challenge because he had been *awfully* good at an early age. Every time he re-read himself, he was surprised to discover that his body of work was considerably more impressive than he remembered it.

Miss Culvert was a fictional treatment of his mother's self-absorbed life in the respectable upper-middle-class society of a down-state Illinois town, an indictment of the self-satisfied and stiflingly bland 'culture' of the Midwest. He had really captured the essence of the bitch. Oh, how he had captured her. Reading *Miss Culvert*, he was reminded of the hurt and horror with which his mother had received the novel on first publication, and he decided that as soon as he had finished the book, he would take down the sequel, *Mrs Towers*, which dealt with her marriage to his father, her widowhood, and her second marriage. He remained convinced that the sequel was what had killed her. Officially, it was a heart attack. But cardiac infarction had to be triggered by something, and the timing was satisfyingly concurrent with the release of *Mrs Towers* and the media attention it received.

When the unexpected caller knocked, a pang of resentment shot through Honell. His face puckered sourly. He preferred the company of his own characters to that of anyone who might conceivably come visiting, uninvited. Or invited, for that matter. All of the people in his books were carefully refined, clarified, whereas people in real life were unfailingly . . . well, fuzzy, murky, pointlessly complex.

He glanced at the clock on the mantel. Ten past nine o'clock.

The knock sounded again. More insistent this time. It was probably a neighbor, which was a dismaying thought because his neighbors were all fools.

He considered not answering. But in these rural canyons, the locals thought of themselves as 'neighborly,' never as the pests they actually were, and if he didn't respond to the knocking, they would circle the house, peeping in windows, out of a country-folk concern for his welfare. God, he hated them. He tolerated them only because he hated the people in the cities even more, and *loathed* suburbanites.

He put down his Chivas and the book, pushed up from the

rocking chair, and went to the door with the intention of giving a fierce dressing down to whomever was out there on the porch. With his command of language, he could mortify anyone in about one minute flat, and have them running for cover in two. The pleasure of meting out humiliation would almost compensate for the interruption.

When he pulled the curtain back from the glass panes in the front door, he was surprised to see that his visitor was not one of the neighbors – in fact, not anyone he recognized. The boy was no more than twenty, pale as the wings of the snowflake moths that batted against the porch light. He was dressed entirely in black and wore sunglasses.

Honell was unconcerned about the caller's intentions. The canyon was less than an hour from the most heavily populated parts of Orange County, but it was nonetheless remote by virtue of its forbidding geography and the poor condition of the roads. Crime was no problem, because criminals were generally attracted to more populous areas where the pickings were more plentiful. Besides, most of the people living in the cabins thereabouts had nothing worth stealing.

He found the pale young man intriguing.

'What do you want?' he asked without opening the door.

'Mr Honell?'

'That's right.'

'S. Steven Honell?'

'Are you going to make a torture of this?'

'Sir, excuse me, but are you the writer?'

College student. That's what he had to be.

A decade ago – well, nearly two – Honell had been besieged by college English majors who wanted to apprentice under him or just worship at his feet. They were an inconstant crowd, however, on the lookout for the latest trend, with no genuine appreciation for high literary art.

Hell, these days, most of them couldn't even read; they were college students in name only. The institutions through which they matriculated were little more than day-care centers for the terminally immature, and they were no more likely to study than to fly to Mars by flapping their arms.

'Yes, I'm the writer. What of it?'

'Sir, I'm a great admirer of your books.'

236

'Listened to them on audiotape, have you?'

'Sir? No, I've read them, all of them.'

The audiotapes, licensed by his publisher without his consent, were abridged by two-thirds. Travesties.

'Ah. Read them in comic-book format, have you?' Honell said sourly, though to the best of his knowledge the sacrilege of comic-book adaptation had not yet been perpetrated.

'Sir, I'm sorry to intrude like this. It really took a lot of time for me to work up the courage to come see you. Tonight I finally had the guts, and I knew if I delayed I'd never get up the nerve again. I am in awe of your writing, sir, and if you could spare me the time, just a little time, to answer a few questions, I'd be most grateful.'

A little conversation with an intelligent young man might, in fact, have more charm than re-reading *Miss Culvert*. A long time had passed since the last such visitor, who had come to the eyrie in which Honell had then been living above Santa Fe. After only a brief hesitation, he opened the door.

'Come in, then, and we'll see if you really understand the complexities of what you've read.'

The young man stepped across the threshold, and Honell turned away, heading back toward the rocking chair and the Chivas.

'This is very kind of you, sir,' the visitor said as he closed the door.

'Kindness is a quality of the weak and stupid, young man. I've other motivations.' As he reached his chair, he turned and said, 'Take off those sunglasses. Sunglasses at night is the worst kind of Hollywood affectation, not the sign of a serious person.'

'I'm sorry, sir, but they're not an affectation. It's just that this world is so much more painfully bright than Hell – which I'm sure you'll eventually discover.'

★　★　★

Hatch had no appetite for dinner. He only wanted to sit alone with the inexplicably heat-curled issue of *Arts American* and stare at it until, by God, he *forced* himself to understand exactly what was happening to him. He was a man of reason. He could not easily embrace supernatural explanations. He was not in the antiques business by accident; he had a need to surround himself with things that contributed to an atmosphere of order and stability.

But kids also hungered for stability, which included regular mealtimes, so they went to dinner at a pizza parlor, after which they caught a movie at the theater complex next door. It was a comedy. Though the film couldn't make Hatch forget the strange problems plaguing him, the frequent sound of Regina's musical giggle did somewhat soothe his abraded nerves.

Later, at home, after he had tucked the girl in bed, kissed her forehead, wished her sweet dreams, and turned off the light, she said, 'Goodnight . . . Dad.'

He was in her doorway, stepping into the hall, when the word 'Dad' stopped him. He turned and looked back at her.

'Goodnight,' he said, deciding to receive her gift as casually as she had given it, for fear that if he made a big deal about it, she would call him Mr Harrison forever. But his heart soared.

In the bedroom, where Lindsey was undressing, he said, 'She called me Dad.'

'Who did?'

'Be serious, who do you think?'

'How much did you pay her?'

'You're just jealous 'cause she hasn't called you Mom yet.'

'She will. She's not so afraid any more.'

'Of you?'

'Of taking a chance.'

Before getting undressed for bed, Hatch went downstairs to check the telephone answering machine in the kitchen. Funny, after all that had happened to him and considering the problems he still had to sort out, the mere fact that the girl had called him Dad was enough to quicken his step and lift his spirits. He descended the stairs two at a time.

The answering machine was on the counter to the left of the refrigerator, below the cork memo board. He was hoping to have a response from the estate executor to whom he had given a bid for the Wedgwood collection that morning. The window on the machine showed three messages. The first was from Glenda Dockridge, his right hand at the antique shop. The second was from Simpson Smith, a friend and antique dealer on Melrose Place in Los Angeles. The third was from Janice Dimes, a friend of Lindsey's. All three were reporting the same news: *Hatch, Lind-*

sey, Hatch and Lindsey, have you seen the paper, have you read the paper, have you heard the news about Cooper, about that guy who ran you off the road, about Bill Cooper, he's dead, he was killed, he was killed last night.

Hatch felt as if a refrigerant, instead of blood, pumped through his veins.

Last evening he had raged about Cooper getting off scot free, and had wished him dead. No, wait. He'd said he wanted to hurt him, make him pay, pitch *him* in that icy river, but he hadn't actually wanted Cooper dead. And so what if he *had* wanted him dead? He had not actually killed the man. He was not at fault for what had happened.

Punching the button to erase the messages, he thought: The cops will want to talk to me sooner or later.

Then he wondered why he was worried about the police. Maybe the murderer was already in custody, in which case no suspicion would fall upon him. But why should he come under suspicion anyway? He had done nothing. *Nothing*. Why was guilt creeping through him like the Millipede inching up a long tunnel?

Millipede?

The utterly enigmatic nature of that image chilled him. He couldn't reference the source of it. As if it wasn't his own thought but something he had . . . *received*.

He hurried upstairs.

Lindsey was lying on her back in bed, adjusting the covers around her.

The newspaper was on his nightstand, where she always put it. He snatched it up and quickly scanned the front page.

'Hatch?' she said. 'What's wrong?'

'Cooper's dead.'

'What?'

'The guy driving the beer truck. William Cooper. Murdered.'

She threw back the covers and sat on the edge of the bed.

He found the story on page three. He sat beside Lindsey, and they read the article together.

According to the newspaper, police were interested in talking to a young man in his early twenties, with pale skin and dark hair. A neighbor had glimpsed him fleeing down the alleyway behind the Palm Court apartments. He might have been wearing sunglasses. At night.

'He's the same damned one who killed the blonde,' Hatch said fearfully. 'The sunglasses in the rearview mirror. And now he's picking up on my thoughts. He's acting out *my* anger, murdering people that I'd like to see punished.'

'That doesn't make sense. It can't be.'

'It is.' He felt sick. He looked at his hands, as if he might actually find the truck driver's blood on them. 'My God, I sent him after Cooper.'

He was so appalled, so psychologically oppressed by a sense of responsibility for what had happened, that he wanted desperately to wash his hands, scrub them until they were raw. When he tried to get up, his legs were too weak to support him, and he had to sit right down again.

Lindsey was baffled and horrified, but she did not react to the news story as strongly as Hatch did.

Then he told her about the reflection of the black-clad young man in sunglasses, which he had seen in the mirrored door in place of his own image, last night in the den when he had been ranting about Cooper. He told her, as well, how he lay in bed after she was asleep, brooding about Cooper, and how his anger suddenly exploded into artery-popping rage. He spoke of the sense he'd had of being invaded and overwhelmed, ending in the blackout. And for a kicker, he recounted how his anger had escalated unreasonably as he had read the piece in *Arts American* earlier this evening, and he took the magazine out of his night-stand to show her the inexplicably scorched pages.

By the time Hatch finished, Lindsey's anxiety matched his, but dismay at his secretiveness seemed greater than anything else she was feeling. 'Why'd you hide all of this from me?'

'I didn't want to worry you,' he said, knowing how feeble it sounded.

'We've never hidden anything from each other before. We've always shared everything. Everything.'

'I'm sorry, Lindsey. I just . . . it's just that . . . these last couple months . . . the nightmares of rotting bodies, violence, fire . . . and the last few days, all this *weirdness* . . . '

'From now on,' she said, 'there'll be no secrets.'

'I only wanted to spare you—'

'No secrets,' she insisted.

'Okay. No secrets.'

'And you're not responsible for what happened to Cooper. Even if there is some kind of link between you and this killer, and even if that's why Cooper became a target, it's not your fault. You didn't *know* that being angry at Cooper was equivalent to a death sentence. You couldn't have done anything to prevent it.'

Hatch looked at the heat-seared magazine in her hands, and a shudder of dread passed through him. 'But it'll be my fault if I don't try to save Honell.'

Frowning, she said, 'What do you mean?'

'If my anger somehow focused this guy on Cooper, why wouldn't it also focus him on Honell?'

★ ★ ★

Honell woke to a world of pain. The difference was, this time he was on the receiving end of it – and it was physical rather than emotional pain. His crotch ached from the kick he'd taken. A blow to his throat had left his esophagus feeling like broken glass. His headache was excruciating. His wrists and ankles burned, and at first he could not understand why; then he realized he was tied to the four posts of something, probably his bed, and the ropes were chafing his skin.

He could not see much, partly because his vision was blurred by tears but also because his contact lenses had been knocked out in the attack. He knew he had been assaulted, but for a moment he could not recall the identity of his assailant.

Then the young man's face loomed over him, blurred at first like the surface of the moon through an unadjusted telescope. The boy bent closer, closer, and his face came into focus, handsome and pale, framed by thick black hair. He was not smiling in the tradition of movie psychotics, as Honell expected he would be. He was not scowling, either, or even frowning. He was expressionless – except, perhaps, for a subtle hint of that solemn professional curiosity with which an entomologist might study some new mutant variation of a familiar species of insect.

'I'm sorry for this discourteous treatment, sir, after you were kind enough to welcome me into your home. But I'm rather in a hurry and couldn't take the time to discover what I need to know through ordinary conversation.'

'Whatever you want,' Honell said placatingly. He was shocked to hear how drastically his mellifluous voice, always a reliable tool for seduction and an expressive instrument of scorn, had changed. It was raspy, marked by a wet gurgle, thoroughly disgusting.

'I would like to know who Lindsey Sparling is,' the young man said dispassionately, 'and where I can find her.'

* * *

Hatch was surprised to find Honell's number in the telephone book. Of course, the author's name was not as familiar to the average citizen as it had been during his brief glory years, when he had published *Miss Culvert* and *Mrs Towers*. Honell didn't need to be worried about privacy these days; evidently the public gave him more of it than he desired.

While Hatch called the number, Lindsey paced the length of the bedroom and back. She had made her position clear: she didn't think Honell would interpret Hatch's warning as anything other than a cheap threat.

Hatch agreed with her. But he had to try.

He was spared the humiliation and frustration of listening to Honell's reaction, however, because no one answered the phone out there in the far canyons of the desert night. He let it ring twenty times.

He was about to hang up, when a series of images snapped through his mind with a sound like short-circuiting electrical wires: a disarranged bed quilt; a bleeding, rope-encircled wrist; a pair of frightened, bloodshot, myopic eyes . . . and in the eyes, the twin reflections of a dark face looming close, distinguished only by a pair of sunglasses.

Hatch slammed down the phone and backed away from it as if the receiver had turned into a rattlesnake in his hand. 'It's happening now.'

* * *

The ringing phone fell silent.

Vassago stared at it, but the ringing did not resume.

He returned his attention to the man who was tied spread-eagle to the brass posts of the bed. 'So Lindsey Harrison is the married name?'

'Yes,' the old guy croaked.

'Now what I most urgently need, sir, is an address.'

242

The public telephone was outside of a convenience store in a shopping center just two miles from the Harrison house. It was protected from the elements by a Plexiglas hood and surrounded by a curved sound shield. Hatch would have preferred the greater privacy of a real booth, but those were hard to find these days, a luxury of less cost-conscious times.

He parked at the end of the center, at too great a distance for anyone in the glass-fronted convenience store to notice – and perhaps recall – his license number.

He walked through a cool, blustery wind to the telephone. The center's Indian laurels were infested with thrips, and drifts of dead, tightly curled leaves blew along the pavement at Hatch's feet. They made a dry, scuttling sound. In the urine-yellow glow of the parking-lot lights, they almost looked like hordes of insects, queerly mutated locusts perhaps, swarming toward their subterranean hive.

The convenience store was not busy, and everything else in the shopping center was closed. He hunched his shoulders and head into the pay phone sound shield, convinced he wouldn't be overheard.

He did not want to call the police from home, because he knew they had equipment that printed out every caller's number at their end. If they found Honell dead, Hatch didn't want to become their prime suspect. And if his concern for Honell's safety proved to be unfounded, he didn't want to be on record with the police as some kind of nutcase or hysteric.

Even as he punched in the number with one bent knuckle and held the handset with a Kleenex to avoid leaving prints, he was uncertain what to say. He knew what he could *not* say: *Hi, I was dead eighty minutes, then brought back to life, and now I have this crude but at times effective telepathic connection to a psychotic killer, and I think I should warn you he's about to strike again.* He could not imagine the authorities taking him any more seriously than they would take a guy who wore a pyramid-shaped aluminum-foil hat to protect his brain from sinister radiation and who bothered them with complaints about evil, mind-warping extraterrestrials next door.

He had decided to call the Orange County Sheriff's Department rather than any particular city's police agency, because the

243

crimes committed by the man in sunglasses fell in several jurisdictions. When the sheriff's operator answered, Hatch talked fast, talked over her when she began to interrupt, because he knew they could trace him to a pay phone given enough time. 'The man who killed the blonde and dumped her on the freeway last week is the same guy who killed William Cooper last night, and tonight he's going to murder Steven Honell, the writer, if you don't give him protection quick, and I mean right now. Honell lives in Silverado Canyon, I don't know the address, but he's probably in your jurisdiction, and he's a dead man if you don't move now.'

He hung up, turned away from the phone, and headed for his car, jamming the Kleenex into his pants pocket. He felt less relieved than he had expected to, and more of a fool than seemed reasonable.

On his way back to the car, he was walking into the wind. All the laurel leaves, sucked dry by thrips, were now blown toward him instead of with him. They hissed against the blacktop and crunched under his shoes.

He knew that the trip had been a waste and that his effort to help Honell had been ineffective. The sheriff's department would probably treat it like just another crank call.

When he got home, he parked in the driveway, afraid that the clatter of the garage door would wake Regina. His scalp prickled when he got out of the car. He stood for a minute, surveying the shadows along the house, around the shrubbery, under the trees. Nothing.

Lindsey was pouring a cup of coffee for him when he walked into the kitchen.

He took it, sipped gratefully at the hot brew. Suddenly he was colder than he had been while standing out in the night chill.

'What do you think?' she asked worriedly. 'Did they take you seriously?'

'Pissing in the wind,' he said.

★ ★ ★

Vassago was still driving the pearl-gray Honda belonging to Renata Desseux, the woman he had overpowered in the mall parking lot on Saturday night and later added to his collection. It was a fine car and handled well on the twisting roads as he drove

244

down the canyon from Honell's place, heading for more populated areas of Orange County.

As he rounded a particularly sharp curve, a patrol car from the sheriff's department swept past him, heading up the canyon. Its siren was not blaring, but its emergency beacons splashed red and blue light on the shale banks and on the gnarled branches of the overhanging trees.

He divided his attention between the winding road ahead and the dwindling taillights of the patrol car in his rearview mirror, until it rounded another bend upslope and vanished. He was sure the cop was speeding to Honell's. The unanswered, interminably ringing telephone, which had interrupted his interrogation of the author, was the trigger that had set the sheriff's department in motion, but he could not figure how or why.

Vassago did not drive faster. At the end of Silverado Canyon, he turned south on Santiago Canyon Road and maintained the legal speed limit as any good citizen was expected to do.

·8·

In bed in the dark, Hatch felt his world crumbling around him. He was going to be left with dust.

Happiness with Lindsey and Regina was within his grasp. Or was that an illusion? Were they infinitely beyond his reach?

He wished for an insight that would give him a new perspective on these apparently supernatural events. Until he could understand the nature of the evil that had entered his life, he could not fight it.

Dr Nyebern's voice spoke softly in his mind: *I believe evil is a very real force, an energy quite apart from us, a presence in the world.*

He thought he could smell a lingering trace of smoke from the heat-browned pages of *Arts American*. He had put the magazine in the desk in the den downstairs, in the drawer with a lock. He had added the small key to the ring he carried.

He had never locked anything in the desk before. He was not sure why he had done so this time. Protecting evidence, he'd told himself. But evidence of what? The singed pages of the magazine proved nothing to anyone about anything.

No. That was not precisely true. The existence of the magazine

245

proved, to him if to no one else, that he wasn't merely imagining and hallucinating everything that was happening to him. What he had locked away, for his own peace of mind, was indeed evidence. Evidence of his sanity.

Beside him, Lindsey was also awake, either uninterested in sleep or unable to find a way into it. She said, 'What if this killer . . . '

Hatch waited. He didn't need to ask her to finish the thought, for he knew what she was going to say. After a moment she said just what he expected:

'What if this killer is aware of you as much as you're aware of him? What if he comes after you . . . us . . . Regina?'

'Tomorrow we're going to start taking precautions.'

'What precautions?'

'Guns, for one thing.'

'Maybe this isn't something we can handle ourselves.'

'We don't have any choice.'

'Maybe we need police protection.'

'Somehow I don't think they'll commit a lot of manpower to protect a guy just because he claims to have a supernatural bond with a psychotic killer.'

The wind that had harried laurel leaves across the shopping-center parking lot now found a loose brace on a section of rain gutter and worried it. Metal creaked softly against metal.

Hatch said, 'I went somewhere when I died, right?'

'What do you mean?'

'Purgatory, Heaven, Hell – those are the basic possibilities for a Catholic, if what we say we believe turns out to be true.'

'Well . . . you've always said you had no near-death experience.'

'I didn't. I can't remember anything from . . . the Other Side. But that doesn't mean I wasn't there.'

'What's your point?'

'Maybe this killer isn't an ordinary man.'

'You're losing me, Hatch.'

'Maybe I brought something back with me.'

'Back with you?'

'From wherever I was while I was dead.'

'Something?'

Darkness had its advantages. The superstitious primitive within could speak of things that would seem too foolish to voice in a well-lighted place.

246

He said, 'A spirit. An entity.'

She said nothing.

'My passage in and out of death might have opened a door somehow,' he said, 'and let something through.'

'Something,' she said again, but with no note of inquiry in her voice, as there had been before. He sensed that she knew what he meant – and did not like the theory.

'And now it's loose in the world. Which explains its link to me – and why it might kill people who anger me.'

She was silent a while. Then: 'If something was brought back, it's evidently pure evil. What – are you saying that when you died, you went to Hell and this killer piggy-backed with you from there?'

'Maybe. I'm no saint, no matter what you think. After all, I've got at least Cooper's blood on my hands.'

'That happened after you died and were brought back. Besides, you don't share in the guilt for that.'

'It was my anger that targeted him, my anger – '

'Bullshit,' Lindsey said sharply. 'You're the best man I've ever known. If housing in the afterlife includes a Heaven and a Hell, you've earned the apartment with a better view.'

His thoughts were so dark, he was surprised that he could smile. He reached under the sheets, found her hand, and held it gratefully. 'I love you, too.'

'Think up another theory if you want to keep me awake and interested.'

'Let's just make a little adjustment to the theory we already have. What if there's an afterlife, but it isn't ordered like anything theologians have ever described? It wouldn't have to be *either* Heaven or Hell that I came back from. Just another place, stranger than here, different, with unknown dangers.'

'I don't like that much better.'

'If I'm going to deal with this thing, I have to find a way to explain it. I can't fight back if I don't even know where to throw my punches.'

'There's got to be a more logical explanation,' she said.

'That's what I tell myself. But when I try to find it, I keep coming back to the illogical.'

The rain gutter creaked. The wind soughed under the eaves and called down the flue of the master-bedroom fireplace.

He wondered if Honell was able to hear the wind wherever he

was – and whether it was the wind of this world or the next.

★ ★ ★

Vassago parked directly in front of Harrison's Antiques at the
south end of Laguna Beach. The shop occupied an entire Art
Deco building. The big display windows were unlighted as Tuesday passed through midnight, becoming Wednesday.

Steven Honell had been unable to tell him where the Harrisons
lived, and a quick check of the telephone book turned up no listed
number for them. The writer had known only the name of their
business and its approximate location on Pacific Coast Highway.

Their home address was sure to be on file somewhere in the
store's office. Getting it might be difficult. A decal on each of
the big Plexiglass windows and another on the front door warned
that the premises were fitted with a burglar alarm and protected
by a security company.

He had come back from Hell with the ability to see in the dark,
animal-quick reflexes, a lack of inhibitions that left him capable of
any act or atrocity, and a fearlessness that made him every bit as
formidable an adversary as a robot might have been. But he could
not walk through walls, or transform himself from flesh into vapor
into flesh again, or fly, or perform any of the other feats that were
within the powers of a true demon. Until he had earned his
way back into Hell either by acquiring a perfect collection in his
museum of the dead or by killing those he had been sent here
to destroy, he possessed only the minor powers of the demon
demimonde, which were insufficient to defeat a burglar alarm.

He drove away from the store.

In the heart of town, he found a telephone booth beside a
service station. Despite the hour, the station was still pumping
gasoline, and the outdoor lighting was so bright that Vassago was
forced to squint behind his sunglasses.

Swooping around the lamps, moths with inch-long wings cast
shadows as large as ravens on the pavement.

The floor of the telephone booth was littered with cigarette
butts. Ants teemed over the corpse of a beetle.

Someone had taped a hand-lettered OUT OF ORDER notice to
the coin box, but Vassago didn't care because he didn't intend
to call anyone. He was only interested in the phone book, which

was secured to the frame of the booth by a sturdy chain.

He checked 'Antiques' in the Yellow Pages. Laguna Beach had a lot of businesses under that heading; it was a regular shoppers' paradise. He studied their space ads. Some had institutional names like International Antiques, but others were named after their owners, as was Harrison's Antiques.

A few used both first *and* last names, and some of the space ads also included the full names of the proprietors because, in that business, personal reputation could be a drawing card. Robert O. Loffman Antiques in the Yellow Pages cross-referenced neatly with a Robert O. Loffman in the white pages, providing Vassago with a street address, which he committed to memory.

On his way back to the Honda, he saw a bat swoop out of the night. It arced down through the blue-white glare from the service-station lights, snatching a fat moth from the air in mid-flight, then vanished back up into the darkness from which it had come. Neither predator nor prey made a sound.

★ ★ ★

Loffman was seventy years old, but in his best dreams he was eighteen again, spry and limber, strong and happy. They were never sex dreams, no bosomy young women parting their smooth thighs in welcome. They weren't power dreams, either, no running or jumping or leaping off cliffs into wild adventures. The action was always mundane: a leisurely walk along a beach at twilight, barefoot, the feel of damp sand between his toes, the froth on the incoming waves sparkling with reflections of the dazzling purple-red sunset; or just sitting on the grass in the shadow of a date palm on a summer afternoon, watching a hummingbird sip nectar from the bright blooms in a bed of flowers. The mere fact that he was young again seemed miracle enough to sustain a dream and keep it interesting.

At the moment he was eighteen, lying on a big bench swing on the front porch of the Santa Ana house in which he had been born and raised. He was just swinging gently and peeling an apple that he intended to eat, nothing more, but it was a wonderful dream, rich with scents and textures, more erotic than if he had imagined himself in a harem of undressed beauties.

'Wake up, Mr Loffman.'

249

He tried to ignore the voice because he wanted to be alone on that porch. He kept his eyes on the curled length of peel that he was paring from the apple.

'Come on, you old sleepyhead.'

He was trying to strip the apple in one continuous ribbon of peel.

'Did you take a sleeping pill or what?'

To Loffman's regret, the front porch, the swing, the apple and paring knife dissolved into darkness. His bedroom.

He struggled awake and realized an intruder was present. A barely visible, spectral figure stood beside the bed.

Although he'd never been the victim of a crime and lived in as safe a neighborhood as existed these days, age had saddled Loffman with feelings of vulnerability. He had started keeping a loaded pistol next to the lamp at his bedside. He reached for it now, his heart pounding hard as he groped along the cool marble surface of the eighteenth-century French ormolu chest that served as his nightstand. The gun was gone.

'I'm sorry, sir,' the intruder said. 'I didn't mean to scare you. Please calm down. If it's the pistol you're after, I saw it as soon as I came in. I have it now.'

The stranger could not have seen the gun without turning on the light, and the light would have awakened Loffman sooner. He was sure of that, so he kept groping for the weapon.

From out of the darkness, something cold and blunt probed against his throat. He twitched away from it, but the coldness followed him, pressing insistently, as if the specter tormenting him could see him clearly in the gloom. He froze when he realized what the coldness was. The muzzle of the pistol. Against his Adam's apple. It slid slowly upward, under his chin.

'If I pulled the trigger, sir, your brains would be all over the headboard. But I do not need to hurt you, sir. Pain is quite unnecessary as long as you cooperate. I only want you to answer one important question for me.'

If Robert Loffman actually had been eighteen, as in his best dreams, he could not have valued the remainder of his time on earth more highly than he did at seventy, in spite of having far less of it to lose now. He was prepared to hold onto life with all the tenacity of a burrowing tick. He would answer any question, perform any deed to save himself, regardless of the cost to his pride and dignity. He tried to convey all of that to the phantom who held the pistol under his chin, but it seemed to him that he produced a gabble of words and sounds that, in sum, had no meaning whatsoever.

'Yes, sir,' the intruder said, 'I understand, and I appreciate your attitude. Now correct me if I am wrong, but I suppose the antique business, being relatively small when compared to others, is a tight community here in Laguna. You all know each other, see each other socially, you're friends.'

Antique business? Loffman was tempted to believe that he was still asleep and that his dream had become an absurd nightmare. Why would anyone break into his house in the dead of night to talk about the antique business at gunpoint?

'We know each other, some of us are good friends, of course, but some bastards in this business are thieves,' Loffman said. He was babbling, unable to stop, hopeful that his obvious fear would testify to his truthfulness, whether this was nightmare or reality. 'They're nothing more than crooks with cash registers, and you aren't friends with that kind if you have any self-respect at all.'

'Do you know Mr Harrison of Harrison's Antiques?'

'Oh, yes, very well, I know him quite well, he's a reputable dealer, totally trustworthy, a nice man.'

'Have you been to his house?'

'His house? Yes, certainly, on three or four occasions, and he's been here to mine.'

'Then you must have the answer to that important question I mentioned, sir. Can you give me Mr Harrison's address and clear directions to it?'

Loffman sagged with relief upon realizing that he would be able to provide the intruder with the desired information. Only fleetingly, he considered that he might be putting Harrison in great jeopardy. But maybe it was a nightmare, after all, and revelation of the information would not matter. He repeated the address and directions several times, at the intruder's request.

'Thank you, sir. You've been most helpful. Like I said, causing you any pain is quite unnecessary. But I'm going to hurt you anyway, because I enjoy it so much.'

So it *was* a nightmare after all.

★ ★ ★

Vassago drove past the Harrison house in Laguna Niguel. Then he circled the block and drove past it again.

The house was a powerful attractant, similar in style to all of the other houses on the street but so different from them in some indescribable but fundamental way that it might as well have been an isolated structure rising out of a featureless plain. Its windows were dark, and the landscape lighting had evidently been turned off by a timer, but it could not have been more of a beacon to Vassago if light had blazed from every window.

As he drove slowly past the house a second time, he felt its immense gravity pulling him. His immutable destiny involved this place and the vital woman who lived within.

Nothing he saw suggested a trap. A red car was parked in the driveway instead of in the garage, but he couldn't see anything ominous about that. Nevertheless, he decided to circle the block a third time to give the house another thorough looking-over.

As he turned the corner, a lone silvery moth darted through his headlight beams, refracting them and briefly glowing like an ember from a great fire. He remembered the bat that had swooped into the service-station lights to snatch the hapless moth out of the air, eating it alive.

*   *   *

Long after midnight, Hatch had finally dozed off. His sleep was a deep mine, where veins of dreams flowed like bright ribbons of minerals through the otherwise dark walls. None of the dreams was pleasant, but none of them was grotesque enough to wake him.

Currently he saw himself standing at the bottom of a ravine with ramparts so steep they could not be climbed. Even if the slopes had risen at an angle that allowed ascent, they would not have been scaleable because they were composed of a curious, loose white shale that crumbled and shifted treacherously. The shale radiated a soft calcimine glow, which was the only light, for the sky far above was black and moonless, deep but starless. Hatch moved restlessly from one end of the long narrow ravine to the other, then back again, filled with apprehension but unsure of the cause of it.

Then he realized two things that made the fine hairs tingle on

252

the back of his neck. The white shale was not composed of rock and the shells of millions of ancient sea creatures; it was made of human skeletons, splintered and compacted but recognizable here and there, where the articulated bones of two fingers survived compression or where what seemed a small animal's burrow proved to be the empty eye socket in a skull. He became aware, as well, that the sky was not empty, that something circled in it, so black that it blended with the heavens, its leathery wings working silently. He could not see it, but he could feel its gaze, and he sensed a hunger in it that could never be satisfied.

In his troubled sleep, Hatch turned and murmured anxious, wordless sounds into his pillow.

★   ★   ★

Vassago checked the car clock. Even without its confirming numbers, he knew instinctively that dawn was less than an hour away.

He no longer could be sure he had enough time to get into the house, kill the husband, and take the woman back to his hideaway before sunrise. He could not risk getting caught in the open in daylight. Though he would not shrivel up and turn to dust like the living dead in the movies, nothing as dramatic as that, his eyes were so sensitive that his glasses would not provide adequate protection from full sunlight. Dawn would render him nearly blind, dramatically affecting his ability to drive and bringing him to the attention of any policeman who happened to spot his weaving, halting progress. In that debilitated condition, he might have difficulty dealing with the cop.

More important, he might lose the woman. After appearing so often in his dreams, she had become an object of intense desire. Before, he had seen acquisitions of such quality that he had been convinced they would complete his collection and earn him immediate readmission to the savage world of eternal darkness and hatred to which he belonged – and he had been wrong. But none of those others had appeared to him in dreams. *This* woman was the true jewel in the crown for which he had been seeking. He must avoid taking possession of her prematurely, only to lose her before he could draw the life from her at the base of the giant Lucifer and wrench her cooling corpse into whatever configuration seemed most symbolic of her sins and weaknesses.

As he cruised past the house for the third time, he considered leaving immediately for his hideaway and returning here as soon as the sun had set the following evening. But that plan had no appeal. Being so close to her excited him, and he was loath to be separated from her again. He felt the tidal pull of her in his blood.

He needed a place to hide that was near her. Perhaps a secret corner in her own house. A niche in which she was unlikely to look during the long, bright, hostile hours of the day.

He parked the Honda two blocks from their house and returned on foot along the tree-flanked sidewalk. The tall, green-patinated streetlamps had angled arms at the top that directed their light onto the roadway, and only a ghost of their glow reached past the sidewalk onto the front lawns of the silent houses. Confident that neighbors were still sleeping and unlikely to see him prowling through shadow-hung shrubbery around the perimeter of the house, he searched quietly for an unlocked door, an unlatched window. He had no luck until he came to the window on the back wall of the garage.

*　*　*

Regina was awakened by a scraping noise, a dull *thump-thump* and a soft protracted squeak. Still unaccustomed to her new home, she always woke in confusion, not sure where she was, certain only that she was not in her room at the orphanage. She fumbled for the bedside lamp, clicked it on, and squinted at the glare for a second before orienting herself and realizing the noises that had bumped her out of sleep had been *sneaky* sounds. They had stopped when she had snapped on the light. Which seemed even sneakier.

She clicked the light off and listened in the darkness, which was now filled with aureoles of color because the lamp had worked like a camera flashbulb on her eyes, temporarily stealing her night vision. Though the sounds did not resume, she believed they had come from the backyard.

Her bed was comfortable. The room almost seemed to be scented with the perfume of the painted flowers. Encircled by those roses, she felt safer than she had ever felt before.

Although she didn't want to get up, she was also aware that the Harrisons were having problems of some kind, and she wondered if these sneaky sounds in the middle of the night somehow might be related to that. Yesterday during the drive from school, as well as last night during dinner and after the movie, she had sensed a tension in them that they were trying to conceal from her. Even though she knew herself to be a screwup around whom anyone would have a right to feel nervous, she was sure that she was not the cause of their edginess. Before going to sleep, she had prayed that their troubles, if they had any, would prove to be minor and would be dealt with soon, and she had reminded God of her selfless pledge to eat beans of all varieties.

If there was any possibility the sneaky noises were related to the Harrisons' uneasy state of mind, Regina supposed she had an obligation to check it out. She looked up and back at the crucifix above her bed, and sighed. You couldn't rely on Jesus and Mary for everything. They were busy people. They had a universe to run. God helped those who helped themselves.

She slipped out from under the covers, stood, and made her way to the window, leaning against furniture and then the wall. She was not wearing her leg brace, and she needed the support.

The window looked onto the small backyard behind the garage, the area from which the suspicious noises had seemed to come. Night-shadows from the house, trees, and shrubs were unrelieved by moonlight. The longer Regina stared, the less she could make out, as if the darkness were a sponge soaking up her ability to see. It became easy to believe that *every* impenetrable pocket of gloom was alive and watchful.

★　★　★

The garage window had been unlocked but difficult to open. The hinges at the top were corroded, and the frame was paint-sealed to the jamb in places. Vassago made more noise than he intended, but he didn't think he had been loud enough to draw the attention of anyone in the house. Then just as the paint cracked and the hinges moved to grant him access, a light had appeared in another window on the second floor.

He had backed away from the garage at once, even though the light went off again even as he moved. He had taken cover in a stand of six-foot eugenia bushes near the property fence.

From there he saw her appear at the obsidian window, more

255

visible to him, perhaps, than she would have been if she had left the lamp on. It was the girl he had seen in dreams a couple of times, most recently with Lindsey Harrison. They had faced each other across a levitated black rose with one drop of blood glistening on a velvet petal.

Regina.

He stared at her in disbelief, then with growing excitement. Earlier in the night, he had asked Steven Honell if the Harrisons had a daughter, but the author had told him that he knew only of a son who had died years ago.

Separated from Vassago by nothing but the night air and one pane of glass, the girl seemed to float above him as if she were a vision. In reality she was, if anything, lovelier than she had been in his dreams. She was so exceptionally vital, so full of life, that he would not have been surprised if she could walk the night as confidently as he did, though for a reason different from his; she seemed to have within her all the light she needed to illuminate her path through any darkness. He drew back farther into the eugenias, convinced that she possessed the power to see him as clearly as he saw her.

A trellis covered the wall immediately below her window. A lush trumpet vine with purple flowers grew up the sturdy lattice to the windowsill, and then around one side almost to the eaves. She was like some princess locked in a tower, pining for a prince to climb up the vine and rescue her. The tower that served as her prison was life itself, and the prince for whom she waited was Death, and that from which she longed to be rescued was the curse of existence.

Vassago said softly, 'I am here for you,' but he did not move from his hiding place.

After a couple of minutes, she turned away from the window. Vanished. A void lay behind the glass where she had stood.

He ached for her return, one more brief look at her.

Regina.

He waited five minutes, then another five. But she did not come to the window again.

At last, aware that dawn was closer than ever, he crept to the back of the garage once more. Because he had already freed it, the window swung out silently this time. The opening was tight, but he eeled through with only the softest scrape of clothes against wood.

256

Lindsey dozed in half-hour and hour naps throughout the night, but her sleep was not restful. Each time she woke, she was sticky with perspiration, even though the house was cool. Beside her, Hatch issued murmured protests in his sleep.

Toward dawn she heard noise in the hall and rose up from her pillows to listen. After a moment she identified the sound of the toilet flushing in the guest bedroom. Regina.

She settled back on her pillows, oddly soothed by the fading sound of the toilet. It seemed like such a mundane – not to say ridiculous – thing from which to take solace. But a long time had passed without a child under her roof. It felt good and right to hear the girl engaged in ordinary domestic business; it made the night seem less hostile. In spite of their current problems, the promise of happiness might be more real than it had been in years.

* * *

In bed again, Regina wondered why God had given people bowels and bladders. Was that really the best possible design, or was He a little bit of a comedian?

She remembered getting up at three o'clock in the morning at the orphanage, needing to pee, encountering a nun on the way to the bathroom down the hall, and asking the good sister that very question. The nun, Sister Sarafina, had not been startled at all. Regina had been too young then to know how to startle a nun; that took years of thinking and practice. Sister Sarafina had responded without pause, suggesting that perhaps God wanted to give people a reason to get up in the middle of the night so they would have another opportunity to think of Him and be grateful for the life He had granted them. Regina had smiled and nodded, but she had figured Sister Sarafina was either too tired to think straight or a little dim-witted. God had too much class to want His children thinking about Him all the time while they were sitting on the pot.

Satisfied from her visit to the bathroom, she snuggled down in the covers of her painted mahogany bed and tried to think of an explanation better than the one the nun had given her years ago. No more curious noises arose from the backyard, and even before the vague light of dawn touched the window panes, she was asleep again.

★ ★ ★

High, decorative windows were set in the sectional garage doors, admitting just enough light from the streetlamps out front to reveal to Vassago, without his sunglasses, that only one car, a black Chevy, was parked in the three-car garage. A quick inspection of that space did not reveal any hiding place where he might conceal himself from the Harrisons and be beyond the reach of sunlight until the next nightfall.

Then he saw the cord dangling from the ceiling over one of the empty parking stalls. He slipped his hand through the loop and pulled downward gently, less gently, then less gently still, but always steadily and smoothly, until the trapdoor swung open. It was well oiled and soundless.

When the door was all the way open, Vassago slowly unfolded the three sections of the wooden ladder that were fixed to the back of it. He took plenty of time, more concerned with silence than with speed.

He climbed into the garage attic. No doubt there were vents in the eaves, but at the moment the place appeared to be sealed tight.

With his sensitive eyes, he could see a finished floor, lots of cardboard boxes, and a few small items of furniture stored under dropcloths. No windows. Above him, the underside of rough roofing boards were visible between open rafters. At two points in the long rectangular chamber, light fixtures dangled from the peaked ceiling; he did not turn on either of them.

Cautiously, quietly, as if he were an actor in a slow-motion film, he stretched out on his belly on the attic floor, reached down through the hole, and pulled up the folding ladder, section by section. Slowly, silently, he secured it to the back of the trapdoor. He eased the door into place again with no sound but the soft *spang* of the big spring that held it shut, closing himself off from the three-car garage below.

He pulled a few of the dropcloths off the furniture. They were relatively dust free. He folded them to make a nest among the boxes and then settled down to await the passage of the day.

Regina. Lindsey. I am with you.

258

SIX

·1·

Lindsey drove Regina to school Wednesday morning. When she got back to the house in Laguna Niguel, Hatch was at the kitchen table, cleaning and oiling the pair of Browning 9mm pistols that he had acquired for home security.

He had purchased the guns five years ago, shortly after Jimmy's cancer had been diagnosed as terminal. He had professed a sudden concern about the crime rate, though it never had been – and was not then – particularly high in their part of Orange County. Lindsey had known, but had never said, that he was not afraid of burglars but of the disease that was stealing his son from him; and because he was helpless to fight off the cancer, he secretly longed for an enemy who *could* be dispatched with a pistol.

The Brownings had never been used anywhere but on a firing range. He had insisted that Lindsey learn to shoot alongside him. But neither of them had even taken target practice in a year or two.

'Do you really think that's wise?' she asked, indicating the pistols.

He was tight-lipped. 'Yes.'

'Maybe we should call the police.'

'We've already discussed why we can't.'

'Still, it might be worth a try.'

'They won't help us. Can't.'

She knew he was right. They had no proof that they were in danger.

'Besides,' he said, keeping his eyes on the pistol as he worked a tubular brush in and out of the barrel, 'when I first started cleaning these, I turned on the TV to have some company. Morning news.'

259

The small set, on a pull-out swivel shelf in the endmost of the kitchen cabinets, was off now.

Lindsey didn't ask him what had been on the news. She was afraid that she would be sorry to hear it – and was convinced that she already knew what he would tell her.

Finally looking up from the pistol, Hatch said, 'They found Steven Honell last night. Tied to the four corners of his bed and beaten to death with a fireplace poker.'

At first Lindsey was too shocked to move. Then she was too weak to continue standing. She pulled a chair out from the table and settled into it.

For a while yesterday, she had hated Steven Honell as much as she had ever hated anyone in her life. More. Now she felt no animosity for him whatsoever. Just pity. He had been an insecure man, concealing his insecurity from himself behind a pretense of contemptuous superiority. He had been petty and vicious, perhaps worse, but now he was dead; and death was too great a punishment for his faults.

She folded her arms on the table and put her head down on them. She could not cry for Honell, for she had liked nothing about him – except his talent. If the extinguishing of his talent was not enough to bring tears, it did at least cast a pall of despair over her.

'Sooner or later,' Hatch said, 'the son of a bitch is going to come after me.'

Lindsey lifted her head even though it felt as if it weighed a thousand pounds. 'But why?'

'I don't know. Maybe we'll never know why, never understand it. But somehow he and I are linked, and eventually he'll come.'

'Let the cops handle him,' she said, painfully aware that there was no help for them from the authorities but stubbornly unwilling to let go of that hope.

'Cops can't find him,' Hatch said grimly. 'He's smoke.'

'He won't come,' she said, willing it to be true.

'Maybe not tomorrow. Maybe not next week or even next month. But as sure as the sun rises every morning, he'll come. And we'll be ready for him.'

'Will we?' she wondered.

'Very ready.'

'Remember what you said last night.'

He looked up from the pistol again and met her eyes. 'What?'

'That maybe he's not just an ordinary man, that he might have hitchhiked back with you from . . . somewhere else.'

'I thought you dismissed that theory.'

'I did. I can't believe it. But do you? Really?'

Instead of answering, he resumed cleaning the Browning.

She said, 'If you believe it, even half believe it, put any credence in it at all – then what good is a gun?'

He didn't reply.

'How can bullets stop an evil spirit?' she pressed, feeling as if her memory of waking up and taking Regina to school was just part of a continuing dream, as if she was not caught in a real-life dilemma but in a nightmare. 'How can something from beyond the grave be stopped with just a gun?'

'It's all I have,' he said.

* * *

Like many doctors, Jonas Nyebern did not maintain office hours or perform surgery on Wednesday. However, he never spent the afternoon golfing, sailing, or playing cards at the country club. He used Wednesdays to catch up on paperwork, or to write research papers and case studies related to the Resuscitation Medicine Project at Orange County General.

That first Wednesday in May, he planned to spend eight or ten busy hours in the study of his house on Spyglass Hill, where he had lived for almost two years, since the loss of his family. He hoped to finish writing a paper that he was going to deliver at a conference in San Francisco on the eighth of May.

The big windows in the teak-paneled room looked out on Corona del Mar and Newport Beach below. Across twenty-six miles of gray water veined with green and blue, the dark palisades of Santa Catalina Island rose against the sky, but they were unable to make the vast Pacific Ocean seem any less immense or less humbling than if they had not been there.

He did not bother to draw the drapes because the panorama never distracted him. He had bought the property because he had hoped that the luxuries of the house and the magnificence of the view would make life seem beautiful and worth living in spite of great tragedy. But only his work had managed to do that for him, and so he always went directly to it with no more than a glance out of the windows.

That morning, he could not concentrate on the white words against the blue background on his computer screen. His thoughts were not pulled toward Pacific vistas, however, but toward his son Jeremy.

On that overcast spring day two years ago, when he had come home to find Marion and Stephanie stabbed so often and so brutally that they were beyond revival, when he had found an unconscious Jeremy impaled on the vise-held knife in the garage and rapidly bleeding to death, Jonas had not blamed an unknown madman or burglars caught by surprise in the act. He had known at once that the murderer was the teenage boy slumped against the workbench with his life drizzling onto the concrete floor. Something had been wrong with Jeremy – *missing* in him – all his life, a difference that had become more marked and frightening as the years passed, though Jonas had tried for so long to convince himself the boy's attitudes and actions were manifestations of ordinary rebelliousness. But the madness of Jonas's father, having skipped one generation, had appeared again in Jeremy's corrupted genes.

The boy survived the extraction of the knife and the frantic ambulance ride to Orange County General, which was only minutes away. But he died on the stretcher as they were wheeling him along a hospital corridor.

Jonas had recently convinced the hospital to establish a special resuscitation team. Instead of using the bypass machine to warm the dead boy's blood, they employed it to recirculate *cooled* blood into his body, hastening to lower his body temperature drastically to delay cell deterioration and brain damage until surgery could be performed. The airconditioner was set all the way down at fifty, bags of crushed ice were packed along the sides of the patient, and Jonas personally opened the knife wound to search for – and repair – the damage that would foil reanimation.

He might have known at the time why he wanted so desperately to save Jeremy, but afterward he was never able to fully, clearly understand his motivations.

Because he was my son, Jonas sometimes thought, and was therefore my responsibility.

262

But what parental responsibility did he owe to the slaughterer of his daughter and wife?

I saved him to ask him *why*, to pry from him an explanation, Jonas told himself at other times.

But he knew there was no answer that would make sense. Neither philosophers nor psychologists – not even the murderers themselves – had ever, in all of history, been able to provide an adequate explanation for a single act of monstrous sociopathic violence.

The only cogent answer, really, was that the human species was imperfect, stained, and carried within itself the seeds of its own destruction. The Church would call it the legacy of the Serpent, dating back to the Garden and the Fall. Scientists would refer to the mysteries of genetics, biochemistry, the fundamental actions of nucleotides. Maybe they were both talking about the same stain, merely describing it in different terms. To Jonas it seemed that this answer, whether provided by scientists or theologians, was always unsatisfying in precisely the same way and to the same degree, for it suggested no solution, prescribed no preventative. Except faith in God or in the potential of science.

Regardless of his reasons for taking the action he did, Jonas had saved Jeremy. The boy had been dead for thirty-one minutes, not an absolute record even in those days, because the young girl in Utah had already been reanimated after being in the arms of Death for sixty-six minutes. But she'd been severely hypothermic, while Jeremy had died warm, which made the feat a record of one kind, anyway. Actually, revival after thirty-one minutes of warm death was as miraculous as revival after eighty minutes of cold death. His own son and Hatch Harrison were Jonas's most amazing successes to date – if the first one qualified as a success.

For ten months Jeremy lay in a coma, feeding intravenously but able to breathe on his own and otherwise in need of no life-support machines. Early in that period, he was moved from the hospital to a high-quality nursing home.

During those months, Jonas could have petitioned a court to have the boy removed from the intravenous feed. But Jeremy would have perished from starvation or dehydration, and sometimes even a comatose patient might suffer pain from such a cruel death, depending on the depth of his stupor. Jonas was not prepared to be the cause of that pain. More insidiously, on a level

263

so deep that even he did not realize it until much later, he suffered from the egotistic notion that he still might extract from the boy – supposing Jeremy ever woke – an explanation of sociopathic behavior that had eluded all other seekers in the history of mankind. Perhaps he thought he would have greater insight owing to his unique experience with the madness of his father and his son, orphaned and wounded by the first, widowed by the second. In any event he paid the nursing-home bills. And every Sunday afternoon, he sat at his son's bedside, staring at the pale, placid face in which he could see so much of himself.

After ten months, Jeremy regained consciousness. Brain damage had left him aphasic, without the power to speak or read. He had not known his name or how he had gotten to be where he was. He reacted to his face in the mirror as if it were that of a stranger, and he did not recognize his father. When the police came to question him, he exhibited neither guilt nor comprehension. He had awakened as a dullard, his intellectual capacity severely reduced from what it had been, his attention span short, easily confused.

With gestures, he complained vigorously of severe eye pain and sensitivity to bright light. An ophthalmological examination revealed a curious – indeed, inexplicable – degeneration of the irises. The contractile membrane seemed to have been partially eaten away. The sphincter pupillae – the muscle causing the iris to contract, thereby shrinking the pupil and admitting less light to the eye – had all but atrophied. Also, the dilator pupillae had shrunk, pulling the iris wide open. And the connection between the dilator muscle and oculomotor nerve was fused, leaving the eye virtually no ability to reduce the amount of incoming light. The condition was without precedent and degenerative in nature, making surgical correction impossible. The boy was provided with heavily tinted, wraparound sunglasses. Even then he preferred to pass daylight hours only in rooms where metal blinds or heavy drapes could close off the windows.

Incredibly, Jeremy became a favorite of the staff at the rehabilitation hospital to which he was transferred a few days after awakening at the nursing home. They were inclined to feel sorry for him because of his eye affliction, and because he was such a good-looking boy who had fallen so low. In addition, he now had the sweet temperament of a shy child, a result of his IQ loss, and there was no sign whatsoever of his former arrogance, cool calculation, and smoldering hostility.

For over four months he walked the halls, helped the nurses with simple tasks, struggled with a speech therapist to little effect, stared out the windows at the night for hours at a time, ate well enough to put flesh on his bones, and exercised in the gym during the evening with most of the lights off. His wasted body was rebuilt, and his straw-dry hair regained its luster.

Almost ten months ago, when Jonas was beginning to wonder where Jeremy could be placed when he was no longer able to benefit from physical or occupational therapy, the boy had disappeared. Although he had shown no previous inclination to roam beyond the grounds of the rehabilitation hospital, he walked out unnoticed one night, and never came back.

Jonas had assumed the police would be quick to track the boy. But they had been interested in him only as a missing person, not as a suspected murderer. If he had regained all of his faculties, they would have considered him both a threat and a fugitive from justice, but his continued – and apparently permanent – mental disabilities were a kind of immunity. Jeremy was no longer the same person that he had been when the crimes were committed; with his diminished intellectual capacity, inability to speak, and beguilingly simple personality, no jury would ever convict.

A missing-person investigation was no investigation at all. Police manpower had to be directed against immediate and serious crimes.

Though the cops believed that the boy had probably wandered away, fallen into the hands of the wrong people, and already been exploited and killed, Jonas knew his son was alive. And in his heart he knew that what was loose in the world was not a smiling dullard but a cunning, dangerous, and exceedingly sick young man.

They had all been deceived.

He could not prove that Jeremy's retardation was an act, but in his heart he knew that he had allowed himself to be fooled. He had accepted the new Jeremy because, when it came right down to it, he could not bear the anguish of having to confront the Jeremy who had killed Marion and Stephanie. The most damning proof of his own complicity in Jeremy's fraud was the fact that he had not requested a CAT scan to determine the precise nature of

265

the brain damage. At the time he told himself the fact of the damage was the only thing that mattered, not its precise etiology, an incredible reaction for any physician but not so incredible for a father who was unwilling to come face-to-face with the monster inside his son.

And now the monster was set free. He had no proof, but he knew. Jeremy was out there somewhere. The old Jeremy.

For ten months, through a series of three detective agencies, he had sought his son, because he shared in the moral, though not the legal, responsibility for any crimes the boy committed. The first two agencies had gotten nowhere, eventually concluding that their inability to pick up a trail meant no trail existed. The boy, they reported, was most likely dead.

The third, Morton Redlow, was a one-man shop. Though not as glitzy as the bigger agencies, Redlow possessed a bulldog determination that encouraged Jonas to believe progress would be made. And last week, Redlow had hinted that he was onto something, that he would have concrete news by the weekend.

The detective had not been heard from since. He had failed to respond to messages left on his phone machine.

Now, turning away from his computer and the conference paper he was unable to work on, Jonas picked up the telephone and tried the detective again. He got the recording. But he could no longer leave his name and number, because the incoming tape on Redlow's machine was already full of messages. It cut him off.

Jonas had a bad feeling about the detective.

He put down the phone, got up from the desk, and went to the window. His spirits were so low, he doubted they could be lifted any more by anything as simple as a magnificent view, but he was willing to try. Each new day was filled with so much more dread than the day before it, he needed all the help he could get just to be able to sleep at night and rise in the morning.

Reflections of the morning sun rippled in silver filaments through the incoming waves, as if the sea were a great piece of rippling blue-gray fabric with interwoven metallic threads.

He told himself that Redlow was only a few days late with his report, less than a week, nothing to be worried about. The failure to return answering-machine messages might only mean the detective was ill or preoccupied with a personal crisis.

But he knew. Redlow had found Jeremy and, in spite of every

266

warning from Jonas, had underestimated the boy.

A yacht with white sails was making its way south along the coast. Large white birds kited in the sky behind the ship, diving into the sea and out again, no doubt snaring fish with each plunge. Graceful and free, the birds were a beautiful sight, though not to the fish, of course. Not to the fish.

★ ★ ★

Lindsey went to her studio between the master bedroom and the room beside Regina's. She moved her high stool from the easel to the drawing board, opened her sketch pad, and started to plan her next painting.

She felt that it was important to focus on her work, not only because the making of art could soothe the soul as surely as the appreciation of it, but because sticking to everyday routine was the only way she could try to push back the forces of irrationality that seemed to be surging like black floodwaters into their lives. Nothing could really go too far wrong – could it? – if she just kept painting, drinking her usual black coffee, eating three meals a day, washing dishes when they needed to be washed, brushing her teeth at night, showering and rolling on her deodorant in the morning. How could some homicidal creature from Beyond intrude into an *orderly* life? Surely ghouls and ghosts, goblins and monsters, had no power over those who were properly groomed, deodorized, fluoridated, dressed, fed, employed, and motivated.

That was what she wanted to believe. But when she tried to sketch, she couldn't still the tremors in her hands.

Honell was dead.

Cooper was dead.

She kept looking at the window, expecting to see that the spider had returned. But there was no scurrying black form or the lace-work of a new web. Just glass. Treetops and blue sky beyond.

After a while Hatch stopped in. He hugged her from behind, and kissed her cheek.

But he was in a solemn rather than romantic mood. He had one of the Brownings with him. He put the pistol on the top of her supply cabinet. 'Keep this with you if you leave the room. He's not going to come around during the day. I know that. I feel it. Like he's a vampire or something, for God's sake. But it still

267

doesn't hurt to be careful, especially when you're here alone.'

She was dubious, but she said, 'All right.'

'I'm going out for a while. Do a little shopping.'

'For what?' She turned on her stool, facing him more directly.

'We don't have enough ammunition for the guns.'

'Both have full clips.'

'Besides, I want to get a shotgun.'

'Hatch! Even if he comes, and he probably won't, it's not going to be a war. A man breaks into your house, it's a matter of a shot or two, not a pitched battle.'

Standing before her, he was stone-faced and adamant. 'The right shotgun is the best of all home-defensive weapons. You don't have to be a good shot. The spread gets him. I know just which one I want. It's a short-barreled, pistol-grip with—'

She put one hand flat against his chest in a 'stop' gesture. 'You're scaring the crap out of me.'

'Good. If we're scared, we're likely to be more alert, less careless.'

'If you really think there's danger, then we shouldn't have Regina here.'

'We can't send her back to St Thomas's,' he said at once, as if he had already considered that.

'Only until this is resolved.'

'No.' He shook his head. 'Regina's too sensitive, you know that, too fragile, too quick to interpret everything as rejection. We might not be able to make her understand – and then she might not give us a second chance.'

'I'm sure she—'

'Besides, we'd have to tell the orphanage something. If we concocted some lie – and I can't imagine what it would be – they'd know we were flimflamming them. They'd wonder why. Pretty soon they'd start second-guessing their approval of us. And if we told them the truth, started jabbering about psychic visions and telepathic bonds with psycho killers, they'd write us off as a couple of nuts, never give her back to us.'

He *had* thought it out.

Lindsey knew what he said was true.

He kissed her lightly again. 'I'll be back in an hour. Two at most.'

When he had gone, she stared at the gun for a while.

Then she turned angrily away from it and picked up her pencil. She tore off a page from the big drawing tablet. The new page was blank. White and clean. It stayed that way.

Nervously chewing her lip, she looked at the window. No web. No spider. Just the glass pane. Treetops and blue skies beyond.

She had never realized until now that a pristine blue sky could be ominous.

* * *

The two screened vents in the garage attic were provided for ventilation. The overhanging roof and the density of the screen mesh did not allow much penetration by the sun, but some wan light entered with the vague currents of cool morning air.

Vassago was untroubled by the light, in part because his nest was formed by piles of boxes and furniture that spared him a direct view of the vents. The air smelled of dry wood, aging cardboard.

He was having difficulty getting to sleep, so he tried to relax by imagining what a fine fire might be fueled by the contents of the garage attic. His rich imagination made it easy to envision sheets of red flames, spirals of orange and yellow, and the sharp pop of sap bubbles exploding in burning rafters. Cardboard and packing paper and combustible memorabilia disappeared in silent rising curtains of smoke, with a papery crackling like the manic applause of millions in some dark and distant theater. Though the conflagration was in his mind, he had to squint his eyes against the phantom light.

Yet the fantasy of fire did not entertain him – perhaps because the attic would be filled merely with burning *things*, mere lifeless objects. Where was the fun in that?

Eighteen had burned to death – or been trampled – in the Haunted House on the night Tod Ledderbeck had perished in the cavern of the Millipede. *There* had been a fire.

He had escaped all suspicion in the rocket jockey's death and the disaster at the Haunted House, but he'd been shaken by the repercussions of his night of games. The deaths at Fantasy World were at the top of the news for at least two weeks, and were the primary topic of conversation around school for maybe a month. The park closed temporarily, reopened to poor business, closed

269

again for refurbishing, reopened to continued low attendance, and eventually succumbed two years later to all of the bad publicity and to a welter of lawsuits. A few thousand people lost their jobs. And Mrs Ledderbeck had a nervous breakdown, though Jeremy figured it was part of her act, pretending she had actually loved Tod, the same crappy hypocrisy he saw in everyone.

But other, more personal repercussions were what shook Jeremy. In the immediate aftermath, toward morning of the long sleepless night that followed his adventures at Fantasy World, he realized he had been out of control. Not when he killed Tod. He knew that was right and good, a Master of the Game proving his mastery. But from the moment he had tipped Tod out of the Millipede, he had been drunk on power, banging around the park in a state of mind similar to what he imagined he'd have been like after chugging a six-pack or two. He had been swacked, plastered, crocked, totally wasted, polluted, stinko with power, for he had taken unto himself the role of Death and become the one whom all men feared. The experience was not only inebriating, it was addictive; he wanted to repeat it the next day, and the day after that, and every day for the rest of his life. He wanted to set someone afire again, and he wanted to know what it felt like to take a life with a sharp blade, with a gun, with a hammer, with his bare hands. That night he had achieved an early puberty, erect with fantasies of death, orgasmic at the contemplation of murders yet to be committed. Shocked by that first sexual spasm and the fluid that escaped him, he finally understood, toward dawn, that a Master of the Game not only had to be able to kill without fear but had to *control* the powerful desire to kill again that was generated by killing once.

Getting away with murder proved his superiority to all the other players, but he could not continue to get away with it if he were out of control, berserk, like one of those guys you saw on the news who opened up with a semiautomatic weapon on a crowd at a shopping mall. That was not a Master. That was a fool and a loser. A Master must pick and choose, select his targets with great care, and eliminate them with style.

Now, lying in the garage attic on a pile of folded dropcloths, he thought that a Master must be like a spider. Choose his killing ground. Weave his web. Settle down, pull in his long legs, make a small and insignificant thing of himself . . . and wait.

270

Plenty of spiders shared the attic with him. Even in the gloom they were visible to his exquisitely sensitive eyes. Some of them were admirably industrious. Others were alive but as cunningly still as death. He felt an affinity for them. His little brothers.

★ ★ ★

The gun shop was a fortress. A sign near the front door warned that the premises were guarded by multi-system silent alarms and also, at night, by attack dogs. Steel bars were welded over the windows. Hatch noticed the door was at least three inches thick, wood but probably with a steel core, and that the three hinges on the inside appeared to have been designed for use on a bathysphere to withstand thousands of tons of pressure deep under the sea. Though much weapons-associated merchandise was on open shelves, the rifles, shotguns, and handguns were in locked glass cases or securely chained in open wall racks. Video cameras had been installed near the ceiling in each of the four corners of the long main room, all behind thick sheets of bulletproof glass.

The shop was better protected than a bank. Hatch wondered if he was living in a time when weaponry had more appeal to thieves than did money itself.

The four clerks were pleasant men with easy camaraderie among themselves and a folksy manner with customers. They wore straight-hemmed shirts outside their pants. Maybe they prized comfort. Or maybe each was carrying a handgun in a holster underneath his shirt, tucked into the small of his back.

Hatch bought a Mossberg, short-barreled, pistol-grip, pump-action 12-gauge shotgun.

'The perfect weapon for home-defense,' the clerk told him. 'You have this, you don't really need anything else.'

Hatch supposed that he should be grateful he was living in an age when the government promised to protect and defend its citizens from threats even so small as radon in the cellar and the ultimate environmental consequences of the extinction of the one-eyed, blue-tailed gnat. In a less civilized era – say the turn of the century – he no doubt would have required an armory containing hundreds of weapons, a ton of explosives, and a chain-mail vest to wear when answering the door.

He decided irony was a bitter form of humor and not to his

271

taste. At least not in his current mood.

He filled out the requisite federal and state forms, paid with a credit card, and left with the Mossberg, a cleaning kit, and boxes of ammunition for the Brownings as well as the shotgun. Behind him, the shop door fell shut with a heavy thud, as if he were exiting a vault.

After putting his purchases in the trunk of the Mitsubishi, he got behind the wheel, started the engine – and froze with his hand on the gearshift. Beyond the windshield, the small parking lot had vanished. The gun shop was no longer there.

As if a mighty sorcerer had cast an evil spell, the sunny day had disappeared. Hatch was in a long, eerily lighted tunnel. He glanced out the side windows, turned to check the back, but the illusion or hallucination – whatever the hell it might be – enwrapped him, as realistic in its detail as the parking lot had been.

When he faced forward, he was confronted by a long slope in the center of which was a narrow-gauge railroad track. Suddenly the car began to move as if it were a train pulling up that hill.

Hatch jammed his foot down on the brake pedal. No effect.

He closed his eyes, counted to ten, listening to his heart pound harder by the second and unsuccessfully willing himself to relax. When he opened his eyes, the tunnel was still there.

He switched the car engine off. He heard it die. The car continued to move.

The silence that followed the cessation of the engine noise was brief. A new sound arose: *clackety-clack, clackety-clack, clackety-clack.*

An inhuman shriek erupted to the left, and from the corner of his eye, Hatch detected threatening movement. He snapped his head toward it. To his astonishment he saw an utterly alien figure, a pale white slug as big as a man. It reared up and shrieked at him through a round mouth full of teeth that whirled like the sharp blades in a garbage disposal. An identical beast shrieked from a niche in the tunnel wall to his right, and more of them ahead, and beyond them other monsters of other forms, gibbering, hooting, snarling, squealing as he passed them.

In spite of his disorientation and terror, he realized that the grotesqueries along the tunnel walls were mechanical beasts, not real. And as that understanding sank in, he finally recognized the familiar sound. *Clackety-clack, clackety-clack.* He was on an indoor

272

roller coaster, yet in his car, moving with decreasing speed toward the high point, with a precipitous fall ahead.

He did not argue with himself that this couldn't be happening, did not try to shake himself awake or back to his senses. He was past denial. He understood that he did not have to *believe* in this experience to insure its continuation; it would progress whether he believed in it or not, so he might as well grit his teeth and get through it.

Being past denial didn't mean, however, that he was past fear. He was scared shitless.

Briefly he considered opening the car door and getting out. Maybe that would break the spell. But he didn't try it because he was afraid that when he stepped out he would not be in the parking lot in front of the gun shop but in the tunnel, and that the car would continue uphill without him. Losing contact with his little red Mitsubishi might be like slamming a door on reality, consigning himself forever to the vision, with no way out, no way back.

The car passed the last mechanical monster. It reached the crest of the inclined track. Pushed through a pair of swinging doors. Into darkness. The doors fell shut behind. The car crept forward. Forward. Forward. Abruptly it dropped as if into a bottomless pit.

Hatch cried out, and with his cry the darkness vanished. The sunny spring day made a welcome reappearance. The parking lot. The gun shop.

His hands were locked so tightly around the steering wheel that they ached.

* * *

Throughout the morning, Vassago was awake more than asleep. But when he dozed, he was back in the Millipede again, on that night of glory.

In the days and weeks following the deaths at Fantasy World, he had without doubt proved himself a Master by exerting iron control over his compulsive desire to kill. Merely the memory of having killed was sufficient to release the periodic pressure that built in him. Hundreds of times, he relived the sensuous details of each death, temporarily quenching his hot need. And the knowledge that he would kill again, any time he could do so without

273

arousing suspicion, was an additional restraint on self-indulgence.

He did not kill anyone else for two years. Then, when he was fourteen, he drowned another boy at summer camp. The kid was smaller and weaker, but he put up a good fight. When he was found floating facedown in the pond, it was the talk of the camp for the rest of that month. Water could be as thrilling as fire.

When he was sixteen and had a driver's license, he wasted two transients, both hitchhikers, one in October, the other a couple of days before Thanksgiving. The guy in November was just a college kid going home for the holiday. But the other one was something else, a predator who thought he had stumbled across a foolish and naive high-school boy who would provide him with some thrills of his own. Jeremy had used knives on both of them.

At seventeen, when he discovered Satanism, he couldn't read enough about it, surprised to find that his secret philosophy had been codified and embraced by clandestine cults. Oh, there were relatively benign forms, propagated by gutless wimps who were just looking for a way to play at wickedness, an excuse for hedonism. But real believers existed, as well, committed to the truth that God had failed to create people in His image, that the bulk of humanity was equivalent to a herd of cattle, that selfishness was admirable, that pleasure was the only worthwhile goal, and that the greatest pleasure was the brutal exercise of power over others.

The ultimate expression of power, one privately published volume had assured him, was to destroy those who had spawned you, thereby breaking the bonds of family 'love.' The book said that one must as violently as possible reject the whole hypocrisy of rules, laws, and noble sentiments by which other men pretended to live. Taking that advice to heart was what had earned him a place in Hell – from which his father had pulled him back.

But he would soon be there again. A few more deaths, two in particular, would earn him repatriation to the land of darkness and the damned.

The attic grew warmer as the day progressed.

A few fat flies buzzed back and forth through his shadowy retreat, and some of them settled down forever on one or another of the alluring but sticky webs that spanned the junctions of the rafters. *Then* the spiders moved.

In the warm, closed space, Vassago's dozing became a deeper sleep with more intense dreams. Fire and water, blade and bullet.

274

Crouching at the corner of the garage, Hatch reached between two azaleas and flipped open the cover on the landscape-lighting control box. He adjusted the timer to prevent the pathway and shrubbery lights from blinking off at midnight. Now they would stay on until sunrise.

He closed the metal box, stood, and looked around at the quiet, well-groomed street. All was harmony. Every house had a tile roof in shades of tan and sand and peach, not the more stark orange-red tiles of many older California homes. The stucco walls were cream-colored or within a narrow range of coordinated pastels specified by the 'Covenants, Conventions & Restrictions' that came with the grant deed and mortgage. Lawns were green and recently mown, flower beds were well tended, and trees were neatly trimmed. It was difficult to believe that unspeakable violence could ever intrude from the outer world into such an orderly, upwardly mobile community, and *inconceivable* that anything supernatural could stalk those streets. The neighborhood's normalcy was so solid that it seemed like encircling stone ramparts crowned with battlements.

Not for the first time, he thought that Lindsey and Regina might be perfectly safe there – but for him. If madness had invaded this fortress of normalcy, he had opened the door to it. Maybe he was mad himself; maybe his weird experiences were nothing as grand as psychic visions, merely the hallucinations of an insane mind. He would bet everything he owned on his sanity – though he also could not dismiss the slim possibility that he would lose the bet. In any event, whether or not he was insane, he was the conduit for whatever violence might rain down on them, and perhaps they would be better off if they went away for the duration, put some distance between themselves and him until this crazy business was settled.

Sending them away seemed wise and responsible – except that a small voice deep inside him spoke against that option. He had a terrible hunch – or was it more than a hunch? – that the killer would not be coming after him but after Lindsey and Regina. If they went away somewhere, just Lindsey and the girl, that homicidal monster would follow them, leaving Hatch to wait alone for a showdown that never happened.

All right, then they had to stick together. Like a family. Rise or fall as one.

Before leaving to pick Regina up at school, he slowly circled the house, looking for lapses in their defenses. The only one he found was an unlocked window at the back of the garage. The latch had been loose for a long time, and he had been meaning to fix it. He got some tools from one of the garage cabinets and worked on the mechanism until the bolt seated securely in the catch.

As he'd told Lindsey earlier, he didn't think the man in his visions would come as soon as tonight, probably not even this week, maybe not for a month or longer, but he *would* come eventually. Even if that unwelcome visit was days or weeks away, it felt good to be prepared.

·2·

Vassago woke.

Without opening his eyes, he knew that night was coming. He could feel the oppressive sun rolling off the world and slipping over the edge of the horizon. When he did open his eyes, the last fading light coming through the attic vents confirmed that the waters of the night were on the rise.

* * *

Hatch found that it was not exactly easy to conduct a normal domestic life while waiting to be stricken by a terrifying, maybe even bloody, vision so powerful it would blank out reality for its duration. It was hard to sit in your pleasant dining room, smile, enjoy the pasta and Parmesan bread, make with the light banter, and tease a giggle from the young lady with the solemn gray eyes – when you kept thinking of the loaded shotgun secreted in the corner behind the Coromandel screen or the handgun in the adjacent kitchen atop the refrigerator, above the line of sight of a small girl's eyes.

He wondered how the man in black would enter when he came. At night, for one thing. He only came out at night. They didn't have to worry about him going after Regina at school. But would he boldly ring the bell or knock smartly on the door, while they

276

were still up and around with all the lights on, hoping to catch them off-guard at a civilized hour when they might assume it was a neighbor come to call? Or would he wait until they were asleep, lights off, and try to slip through their defenses to take them unaware?

Hatch wished they had an alarm system, as they did at the store. When they sold the old house and moved into the new place following Jimmy's death, they should have called Brinks right away. Valuable antiques graced every room. But for the longest time after Jimmy had been taken from them, it hadn't seemed to matter if anything – or everything – else was taken as well.

Throughout dinner, Lindsey was a trooper. She ate a mound of rigatoni as if she had an appetite, which was something Hatch could not manage, and she filled his frequent worried silences with natural-sounding patter, doing her best to preserve the feeling of an ordinary night at home.

Regina was sufficiently observant to know something was wrong. And though she was tough enough to handle nearly anything, she was also infected with seemingly chronic self-doubt that would probably lead her to interpret their uneasiness as dissatisfaction with her.

Earlier Hatch and Lindsey had discussed what they might be able to tell the girl about the situation they faced, without alarming her more than was necessary. The answer seemed to be: nothing. She had been with them only two days. She didn't know them well enough to have this crazy stuff thrown at her. She'd hear about Hatch's bad dreams, his waking hallucinations, the heat-browned magazine, the murders, all of it, and figure she had been entrusted to a couple of lunatics.

Anyway the kid didn't really need to be warned at this stage. They could look out for her; it was what they were sworn to do.

Hatch found it difficult to believe that just three days ago the problem of his repetitive nightmares had not seemed significant enough to delay a trial adoption. But Honell and Cooper had not been dead then, and supernatural forces seemed only the material of popcorn movies and *National Enquirer* stories.

Halfway through dinner he heard a noise in the kitchen. A click and scrape. Lindsey and Regina were engaged in an intense conversation about whether Nancy Drew, girl detective of countless books, was a 'dorkette,' which was Regina's view, or whether she was a smart and savvy girl for her times but just old-fashioned when you looked at her from a more modern viewpoint. Either they were too engrossed in their debate to hear the noise in the kitchen – or there had been no noise, and he had imagined it.

'Excuse me,' he said, getting up from the table, 'I'll be right back.'

He pushed through the swinging door into the large kitchen and looked around suspiciously. The only movement in the deserted room was a faint ribbon of steam still unraveling from the crack between the tilted lid and the pot of hot spaghetti sauce that stood on a ceramic pad on the counter beside the stove.

Something thumped softly in the L-shaped family room, which opened off the kitchen. He could see part of that room from where he stood but not all of it. He stepped silently across the kitchen and through the archway, taking the Browning 9mm off the top of the refrigerator as he went.

The family room was also deserted. But he was sure that he had not imagined that second noise. He stood for a moment, looking around in bafflement.

His skin prickled, and he whirled toward the short hallway that led from the family room to the foyer inside the front door. Nothing. He was alone. So why did he feel as if someone was holding an ice cube against the back of his neck?

He moved cautiously into the hallway until he came to the coat closet. The door was closed. Directly across the hall was the powder room. That door was also shut. He felt drawn toward the foyer, and his inclination was to trust his hunch and move on, but he didn't want to put either of those closed doors at his back.

When he jerked open the closet door, he saw at once that no one was in there. He felt stupid with the gun thrust out in front of him and pointing at nothing but a couple of coats on hangers, playing a movie cop or something. Better hope it wasn't the final reel. Sometimes, when the story required it, they killed off the good guy in the end.

He checked the powder room, found it also empty, and continued into the foyer. The uncanny feeling was still with him but not as strong as before. The foyer was deserted. He glanced at the stairs, but no one was on them.

He looked in the living room. No one. He could see a corner of

278

the dining-room table through the archway at the end of the living room. Although he could hear Lindsey and Regina still discussing Nancy Drew, he couldn't see them.

He checked the den, which was also off the entrance foyer. And the closet in the den. And the kneehole space under the desk.

Back in the foyer, he tried the front door. It was locked, as it should have been.

No good. If he was this jumpy already, what in the name of God was he going to be like in another day or week? Lindsey would have to pry him off the ceiling just to give him his morning coffee each day.

Nevertheless, reversing the route he had just taken through the house, he stopped in the family room to try the sliding glass doors that served the patio and backyard. They were locked, with the burglar-foiling bar inserted properly in the floor track.

In the kitchen once more, he tried the door to the garage. It was unlocked, and again he felt as if spiders were crawling on his scalp.

He eased the door open. The garage was dark. He fumbled for the switch, clicked the lights on. Banks of big fluorescent tubes dropped a flood of harsh light straight down the width and breadth of the room, virtually eliminating shadows, revealing nothing out of the ordinary.

Stepping over the threshold, he let the door ease shut behind him. He cautiously walked the length of the room with the large roll-up sectional doors on his right, the backs of the two cars on his left. The middle stall was empty.

His rubber-souled Rockports made no sound. He expected to surprise someone crouched along the far side of one of the cars, but no one was sheltering behind either of them.

At the end of the garage, when he was past the Chevy, he abruptly dropped to the floor and looked under the car. He could see all the way across the room, beneath the Mitsubishi, as well. No one was hiding under either vehicle. As best as he could tell, considering that the tires provided blind spots, no one appeared to be circling the cars to keep out of his sight.

He got up and turned to a regular door in the end wall. It served the side yard and had a thumb-turn dead-bolt lock, which was engaged. No one could get in that way.

Returning to the kitchen door, he stayed to the back of the garage. He tried only the two storage cabinets that had tall doors and were large enough to provide a hiding place for a grown man. Neither was occupied.

He checked the window latch he had repaired earlier in the day. It was secure, the bolt seated snugly in the vertically mounted hasp.

Again, he felt foolish. Like a grown man engaged in a boy's game, fancying himself a movie hero.

How fast would he have reacted if someone *had* been hiding in one of those tall cabinets and had flung himself outward when the door opened? Or what if he had dropped to the floor to look under the Chevy, and *right there* had been the man in black, face-to-face with him, inches away?

He was glad he hadn't been required to learn the answer to either of those unnerving questions. But at least, having asked them, he no longer felt foolish, because indeed the man in black might have been there.

Sooner or later the bastard *would* be there. Hatch was no less certain than ever about the inevitability of a confrontation. Call it a hunch, call it a premonition, call it Christmas turkey if you liked, but he knew that he could trust the small warning voice within him.

As he was passing the front of the Mitsubishi, he saw what appeared to be a dent on the hood. He stopped, sure that it must be a trick of light, the shadow of the pull-cord that hung from the ceiling trap. It was directly over the hood. He swatted the dangling cord, but the mark on the car didn't leap and dance as it would have done if it had been just the cord shadow.

Leaning over the grille, he touched the smooth sheet metal and felt the depression, shallow but as big as his hand. He sighed heavily. The car was still new, and already it needed a session in the body shop. Take a brand new car to the mall, and an hour after it's out of the showroom, some damn fool will park beside it and slam open his door into yours. It never fails.

He hadn't noticed the dent either when he had come home this afternoon from the gun shop or when he'd brought Regina back from school. Maybe it wasn't as visible from inside the car, behind the steering wheel; maybe you had to be out in front, looking at it from the right angle. It sure seemed big enough to be seen from anywhere.

He was trying to figure how it could have happened – somebody

280

must have been passing by and dropped something on the car –
when he saw the footprint. It was in a gossamer coating of beige
dust on the red paint, the sole and part of the heel of a walking
shoe probably not much different from the ones he was wearing.
Someone had stood on or walked across the hood of the
Mitsubishi.

It must have happened outside St Thomas's School, because it
was the kind of thing a kid might do, showing off to friends.
Having allowed too much time for bad traffic, Hatch had arrived
at St Tom's twenty minutes before classes let out. Rather than
wait in the car, he'd gone for a walk to work off some excess
nervous energy. Probably, some wiseass and his buddies from the
adjacent high school – the footprint was too big to belong to a
smaller kid – sneaked out a little ahead of the final bell, and were
showing off for each other as they raced away from the school,
maybe leaping and clambering over obstacles instead of going
around them, as if they'd escaped from a prison with the blood-
hounds close on their—

'Hatch?'

Startled out of his train of thought just when it seemed to be
leading somewhere, he spun around toward the voice as if it did
not sound familiar to him, which of course it did.

Lindsey stood in the doorway between the garage and kitchen.
She looked at the gun in his hand, met his eyes. 'What's wrong?'

'Thought I heard something.'

'And?'

'Nothing.' She had startled him so much that he had forgotten
the footprint and dent on the car hood. As he followed her into the
kitchen, he said, 'This door was open. I locked it earlier.'

'Oh, Regina left one of her books in the car when she came
home from school. She went out just before dinner to get it.'

'You should have made sure she locked up.'

'It's only the door to the garage,' Lindsey said, heading toward
the dining room.

He put a hand on her shoulder to stop her, turned her around.
'It's a point of vulnerability,' he said with perhaps more anxiety
than such a minor breach of security warranted.

'Aren't the outer garage doors locked?'

'Yes, and this one should be locked, too.'

'But as many times as we go back and forth from the kitchen' –

281

they had a second refrigerator in the garage – 'it's just convenient to leave the door unlocked. We've always left it unlocked.'

'We don't any more,' he said firmly.

They were face-to-face, and she studied him worriedly. He knew she thought he was walking a fine line between prudent precautions and a sort of quiet hysteria, even treading the wrong way over that line sometimes. On the other hand, *she* hadn't had the benefit of his nightmares and visions.

Perhaps the same thought crossed Lindsey's mind, for she nodded and said, 'Okay. I'm sorry. You're right.'

He leaned back into the garage and turned off the lights. He closed the door, engaged the dead-bolt – and felt no safer, really.

She had started toward the dining room again. She glanced back as he followed her, indicating the pistol in his hand. 'Going to bring that to the table?'

Deciding he had come down a little heavy on her, he shook his head and bugged his eyes out, trying to make a Christopher Lloyd face and lighten the moment: 'I think some of my rigatoni are still alive. I don't like to eat them till they're dead.'

'Well, you've got the shotgun behind the Coromandel screen for that,' she reminded him.

'You're right!' He put the pistol on top of the refrigerator again. 'And if that doesn't work, I can always take them out in the driveway and run them over with the car!'

She pushed open the swinging door, and Hatch followed her into the dining room.

Regina looked up and said, 'Your food's getting cold.'

Still making like Christopher Lloyd, Hatch said, 'Then we'll get some sweaters and mittens for them!'

Regina giggled. Hatch *adored* the way she giggled.

* * *

After the dinner dishes were done, Regina went to her room to study. 'Big history test tomorrow,' she said.

Lindsey returned to her studio to try to get some work done. When she sat down at her drawing board, she saw the second Browning 9mm. It was still atop the low art-supply cabinet, where Hatch had put it earlier in the day.

She scowled at it. She didn't necessarily disapprove of guns

282

themselves, but this one was more than merely a handgun. It was a symbol of their powerlessness in the face of the amorphous threat that hung over them. Keeping a gun ever within reach seemed an admission that they were desperate and couldn't control their own destiny. The sight of a snake coiled on the cabinet could not have carved a deeper scowl on her face.

She didn't want Regina walking in and seeing it.

She pulled open the first drawer of the cabinet and shoved aside some gum erasers and pencils to make room for the weapon. The Browning barely fit in that shallow space. Closing the drawer, she felt better.

During the long morning and afternoon, she had accomplished nothing. She had made lots of false starts with sketches that went nowhere. She was not even close to being ready to prepare a canvas.

Masonite, actually. She worked on Masonite, as did most artists these days, but she still thought of each rectangle as a canvas, as though she were the reincarnation of an artist from another age and could not shake her old way of thinking. Also, she painted in acrylics rather than oils. Masonite did not deteriorate over time the way canvas did, and acrylics retained their true colors far better than oil-based paints.

Of course if she didn't *do* something soon, it wouldn't matter if she used acrylics or cat's piss. She couldn't call herself an artist in the first place if she couldn't come up with an idea that excited her and a composition that did the idea justice. Picking up a thick charcoal pencil, she leaned over the sketch pad that was open on the drawing board in front of her. She tried to knock inspiration off its perch and get its lazy butt flying again.

After no more than a minute, her gaze floated off the page, up and up, until she was staring at the window. No interesting sight waited to distract her tonight, no treetops gracefully swaying in a breeze or even a patch of cerulean sky. The night beyond the pane was featureless.

The black backdrop transformed the window glass into a mirror in which she saw herself looking over the top of the drawing board. Because it was not a true mirror, her reflection was transparent, ghostly, as if she had died and come back to haunt the last place she had ever known on earth.

That was an unsettling thought, so she returned her attention to the blank page of the drawing tablet in front of her.

★ ★ ★

After Lindsey and Regina went upstairs, Hatch walked from room to room on the ground floor, checking windows and doors to be sure they were secured. He had inspected the locks before. Doing it again was pointless. He did it anyway.

When he reached the pair of sliding glass doors in the family room, he switched on the outdoor patio lights to augment the low landscape lighting. The backyard was now bright enough for him to see most of it – although someone could have been crouched among the shrubs along the rear fence. He stood at the doors, waiting for one of the shadows along the perimeter of the property to shift.

Maybe he was wrong. Maybe the guy would never come after them. In which case, in a month or two or three, Hatch would almost likely be certifiably mad from the tension of waiting. He almost thought it would be better if the creep came now and got it over with.

He moved on to the breakfast nook and examined those windows. They were still locked.

★ ★ ★

Regina returned to her bedroom and prepared her corner desk for homework. She put her books to one side of the blotter, pens and felt-tip Hi-Liter to the other side, and her notebook in the middle, everything squared-up and neat.

As she got her desk set up, she worried about the Harrisons. Something was wrong with them.

Well, not wrong in the sense that they were thieves or enemy spies or counterfeiters or murderers or child-eating cannibals. For a while she'd had an idea for a novel in which this absolute screwup girl is adopted by a couple who *are* child-eating cannibals, and she finds a pile of child bones in the basement, and a recipe file in the kitchen with cards that say things like 'Little Girl Kabob' and 'Girl Soup,' with instructions like 'Ingredients: one tender young girl, unsalted; one onion, chopped; one pound carrots, diced . . . ' In the story the girl goes to the authorities, but

284

they will not believe her because she's widely known as a screwup and a teller of tall tales. Well, that was fiction, and this was real life, and the Harrisons seemed perfectly happy eating pizza and pasta and hamburgers.

She clicked on the fluorescent desk lamp.

Though there was nothing wrong with the Harrisons themselves, they definitely had problems, because they were tense and trying hard to hide it. Maybe they weren't able to make their mortgage payments, and the bank was going to take the house, and all three of them would have to move back into her old room at the orphanage. Maybe they had discovered that Mrs Harrison had a sister she'd never heard about before, an evil twin like all those people on television shows were always discovering they had. Or maybe they owed money to the Mafia and couldn't pay it and were going to get their legs broken.

Regina withdrew a dictionary from the bookshelves and put it on the desk.

If they had a bad problem, Regina hoped it was the Mafia thing, because she could handle that pretty well. The Harrisons' legs would get better eventually, and they'd learn an important lesson about not borrowing money from loansharks. Meanwhile, she could take care of them, make sure they got their medicine, check their temperatures now and then, bring them dishes of ice cream with a little animal cookie stuck in the top of each one, and even empty their bedpans (Gross!) if it came to that. She knew a lot about nursing, having been on the receiving end of so much of it at various times over the years. (Dear God, if their big problem is *me*, could I have a miracle here and get the problem changed to the Mafia, so they'll keep me and we'll be happy? In exchange for the miracle, I'd even be willing to have my legs broken, too. At least talk it over with the guys at the Mafia and see what they say.)

When the desk was fully prepared for homework, Regina decided that she needed to be dressed more comfortably in order to study. Having changed out of her parochial-school uniform when she had gotten home, she was wearing gray corduroy pants and a lime-green, long-sleeve cotton sweater. Pajamas and a robe were much better for studying. Besides, her leg brace was making her itch in a couple of places, and she wanted to take it off for the day.

When she slid open the mirrored closet door, she was face-to-face with a crouching man dressed all in black and wearing sunglasses.

·3·

On yet one more tour of the downstairs, Hatch decided to turn off the lamps and chandeliers as he went. With the landscape and exterior house lights all ablaze but the interior dark, he would be able to see a prowler without being seen himself.

He concluded the patrol in the unlighted den, which he had decided to make his primary guard station. Sitting at the big desk in the gloom, he could look through the double doors into the front foyer and cover the foot of the stairs to the second floor. If anyone tried to enter through a den window or the French doors to the rose garden, he would know at once. If the intruder breached their security in another room, Hatch would nail the guy when he tried to go upstairs, because the spill of second-floor hall light illuminated the steps. He couldn't be everywhere at once, and the den seemed to be the most strategic position.

He put both the shotgun and the handgun on top of the desk, within easy reach. He couldn't see them well without the lights on, but he could grab either of them in an instant if anything happened. He practiced a few times, sitting in his swivel chair and facing the foyer, then abruptly reaching out to grab the Browning, this time the Mossberg 12-gauge, Browning, Browning, Mossberg, Browning, Mossberg, Mossberg. Every time, maybe because his reactions were heightened by adrenaline, his right hand swooped through darkness and with precise accuracy came to rest upon the handgrip of the Browning or the stock of the Mossberg, whichever was wanted.

He took no satisfaction in his preparedness, because he knew he could not remain vigilant twenty-four hours a day, seven days a week. He had to sleep and eat. He had not gone to the shop today, and he could take off a few days more, but he couldn't leave everything to Glenda and Lew indefinitely; sooner or later he would have to go to work.

Realistically, even with breaks to eat and sleep, he would cease to be an effective watchman long before he needed to return to work. Sustaining a high degree of mental and physical alertness was a draining enterprise. In time he'd have to consider hiring a guard or two from a private security firm, and he didn't know how much that would cost. More important, he didn't know how reliable a hired guard would be.

He doubted he would ever have to make that decision, because the bastard was going to come soon, maybe tonight. On a primitive level, a vague impression of the man's intentions flowed to Hatch along whatever mystical bond they shared. It was like a child's words spoken into a tin can and conveyed along a string to another tin can, where they were reproduced as dim fuzzy sounds, most of the coherency lost due to the poor quality of the conductive material but the essential tone still perceptible. The current message on the psychic string could not be heard in any detail, but the primary meaning was clear: *Coming . . . I'm coming . . . I'm coming . . .*

Probably after midnight. Hatch sensed that their encounter would take place between that dead hour and dawn. It was now exactly 7:46 by his watch.

He withdrew his ring of car and house keys from his pocket, found the desk key that he had added earlier, opened the locked drawer, and took out the heat-darkened, smoke-scented issue of *Arts American,* letting the keys dangle in the lock. He held the magazine in both hands in the dark, hoping the feel of it would, like a talisman, amplify his magical vision and allow him to see precisely when, where, and how the killer would arrive.

Mingled odors of fire and destruction – some so bitterly pungent that they were nauseating, others merely ashy – rose from the crisp pages.

* * *

Vassago clicked off the fluorescent desk lamp. He crossed the girl's room to the door, where he also switched off the ceiling light.

He put his hand on the doorknob but hesitated, reluctant to leave the child behind him. She was so exquisite, so vital. He *knew* the moment he had pulled her into his arms that she was the caliber of acquisition that would complete his collection and win him the eternal reward he sought.

Stifling her cry and cutting off her breathing with one gloved hand, he had swept her into the closet and crushed her against him with his strong arms. He had held her so fiercely that she could barely squirm and couldn't kick against anything to draw attention to her plight.

When she had passed out in his arms, he had been almost in a swoon and had been overcome by the urge to kill her right there. In her closet. Among the soft piles of clothes that had fallen off the hangers above them. The scent of freshly laundered cotton and spray starch. The warm fragrance of wool. And girl. He wanted to wring her neck and feel her life energy pass through his powerful hands, into him, and through him to the land of the dead.

He had taken so long to shake off that overpowering desire that he almost *had* killed her. She fell silent and still. By the time he unclamped his hand from her nose and mouth, he thought he had smothered her. But when he put his ear to her parted lips, he could hear and feel faint exhalations. A hand against her chest rewarded him with the solid thud of her slow, strong heartbeat.

Now, looking back at the child, Vassago repressed the need to kill by promising himself that he would have satisfaction long before dawn. Meanwhile, he must be a Master. Exercise control.

Control.

He opened the door and studied the second-floor hallway beyond the girl's room. Deserted. A chandelier was aglow at the far end, at the head of the stairs, in front of the entrance to the master bedroom, producing too much light for his comfort if he had not had his sunglasses. He still needed to squint.

He must butcher neither the child nor the mother until he had both of them in the museum of the dead, where he had killed all the others who were part of his collection. He knew now why he had been drawn to Lindsey and Regina. Mother and daughter. Bitch and mini-bitch. To regain his place in Hell, he was expected to commit the same act that had won him damnation in the first place: the murder of a mother and her daughter. As his own mother and sister were not available to be killed again, Lindsey and Regina had been selected.

Standing in the open doorway, he listened to the house. It was silent.

He knew the artist was not the girl's birth mother. Earlier, when the Harrisons were in the dining room and he slipped into the house from the garage, he'd had time to poke around in Regina's room. He'd found mementoes with the orphanage name on them, for the most part cheaply printed drama programs handed out at holiday plays in which the girl had held minor roles. Nevertheless, he had been drawn to her and Lindsey, and his own master apparently judged them to be suitable sacrifices.

The house was so still that he would have to move as quietly as a cat. He could manage that.

He glanced back at the girl on the bed, able to see her better in the darkness than he could see most of the details of the too-bright hallway. She was still unconscious, one of her own scarves wadded in her mouth and another tied around her head to keep the gag in place. Strong lengths of cord, which he had untied from around storage boxes in the garage attic, tightly bound her wrists and ankles.

Control.

Leaving Regina's door open behind him, he eased along the hallway, staying close to the wall, where the plywood sub-flooring under the thick carpet was least likely to creak.

He knew the layout. He had cautiously explored the second floor while the Harrisons had been finishing dinner.

Beside the girl's room was a guest bedroom. It was dark now. He crept on toward Lindsey's studio.

Because the main hallway chandelier was directly ahead of him, his shadow fell in his wake, which was fortunate. Otherwise, if the woman happened to be looking toward the hall, she would have been warned of his approach.

He inched to the studio door and stopped.

Standing with his back flat to the wall, eyes straight ahead, he could see between the balusters under the handrail of the open staircase, to the foyer below. As far as he could tell, no lights were on downstairs.

He wondered where the husband had gone. The tall doors to the master bedroom were open, but no lights were on in there. He could hear small noises coming from within the woman's studio, so he figured she was at work. If the husband was with her, surely they would have exchanged a few words, at least, during the time Vassago had been making his way along the hall.

He hoped the husband had gone out on an errand. He had no particular need to kill the man. And any confrontation would be dangerous.

From his jacket pocket, he withdrew the supple leather sap, filled with lead shot, that he had appropriated last week from Morton Redlow, the detective. It was an extremely effective-looking blackjack. It felt good in his hand. In the pearl-gray Honda, two blocks away, a handgun was tucked under the driver's seat, and Vassago almost wished he had brought it. He had taken it from the antique dealer, Robert Loffman, in Laguna Beach a couple of hours before dawn that morning.

But he didn't want to shoot the woman and the girl. Even if he just wounded and disabled them, they might bleed to death before he got them back to his hideaway and down into the museum of death, to the altar where his offerings were arranged. And if he used a gun to remove the husband, he could risk only one shot, maybe two. Too much gunfire was bound to be heard by neighbors and the source located. In that quiet community, once gunfire was identified, cops would be crawling over the place in two minutes.

The sap was better. He hefted it in his right hand, getting the feel of it.

With great care, he leaned across the doorjamb. Tilted his head. Peeked into the studio.

She sat on the stool, her back to the door. He recognized her even from behind. His heart galloped almost as fast as when the girl had struggled and passed out in his arms. Lindsey was at the drawing board, charcoal pencil in her right hand. Busy, busy, busy. Pencil making a soft snaky hiss as it worked against the paper.

* * *

No matter how determined she was to keep her attention firmly on the problem of the blank sheet of drawing paper, Lindsey looked up repeatedly at the window. Her creative block crumbled only when she surrendered and began to *draw* the window. The uncurtained frame. Darkness beyond the glass. Her face like the countenance of a ghost engaged in a haunting. When she added the spider web in the upper right-hand corner, the concept jelled, and suddenly she became excited. She thought she might title it 'The Web of Life and Death,' and use a surreal series of symbolic items to knit the theme into every corner of the canvas. Not canvas, Masonite. In fact, just paper now, only a sketch, but worth pursuing.

She repositioned the drawing tablet on the board, setting it higher. Now she could just raise her eyes slightly from the page to look over the top of the board at the window, and didn't have to keep raising and lowering her head.

More elements than just her face, the window, and the web would be required to give the painting depth and interest. As she worked she considered and rejected a score of additional images.

Then an image appeared almost magically in the glass above her own reflection: the face that Hatch had described from nightmares. Pale. A shock of dark hair. The sunglasses.

For an instant she thought it was a supernatural event, an apparition in the glass. Even as her breath caught in her throat, however, she realized that she was seeing a reflection like her own and that the killer in Hatch's dreams was in their house, leaning around the doorway to look at her. She repressed an impulse to scream. As soon as he realized she had seen him, she would lose what little advantage she had, and he would be all over her, slashing at her, pounding on her, finishing her off before Hatch even got upstairs. Instead, she sighed loudly and shook her head as if displeased with what she was getting down on the drawing paper.

Hatch might already be dead.

She slowly put down her charcoal pencil, letting her fingers rest on it as if she might decide to pick it up again and go on.

If Hatch wasn't dead, how else could this bastard have gotten to the second floor? No. She couldn't think about Hatch being dead, or she would be dead herself, and then Regina. Dear God, Regina.

She reached toward the top drawer of the supply cabinet at her side, and a shiver went through her as she touched the cold chrome handle.

Reflecting the door behind her, the window showed the killer not just leaning around the jamb now, but stepping boldly into the open doorway. He paused arrogantly to stare at her, evidently relishing the moment. He was unnaturally quiet. If she had not seen his image in the glass, she would have had no awareness whatsoever of his presence.

She pulled open the drawer, felt the gun under her hand.

Behind her, he crossed the threshold.

She drew the pistol out of the drawer and swung around on her stool in one motion, bringing the heavy weapon up, clasping it in both hands, pointing it at him. She would not have been entirely surprised if he had not been there, and if her first impression of him only as an apparition in the windowpane had turned out to be correct. But he was there, all right, one step inside the door when she drew down on him with the Browning.

She said, 'Don't move, you son of a bitch.'

Whether he thought he saw weakness in her or whether he just didn't give a damn if she shot him or not, he backed out of the doorway and into the hall even as she swung toward him and told him not to move.

'Stop, damn it!'

He was gone. Lindsey would have shot him without hesitation, without moral compunction, but he moved so incredibly fast, like a cat springing for safety, that all she would have gotten was a piece of the doorjamb.

Shouting for Hatch, she was off the high stool and leaping for the door even as the last of the killer – a black shoe, his left foot – vanished out of the door frame. But she brought herself up short, realizing he might not have gone anywhere, might be waiting just to the side of the door, expecting her to come through in a panic, then step in behind her and pound her across the back of the head or push her into the stair railing and over and out and down onto the foyer floor. Regina. She couldn't delay. He might be going after Regina. A hesitation of only a second, then she crashed through her fear and through the open door, all this time shouting Hatch's name.

Looking to her right as she came into the hall, she saw the guy going for Regina's door, also open, at the far end. The room was dark beyond when there ought to have been lights, Regina studying. She didn't have time to stop and aim. Almost squeezed the trigger. Wanted to pump out bullets in the hope that one of them would nail the bastard. But Regina's room was so dark, and the girl could be anywhere. Lindsey was afraid that she would miss the killer and blow away the girl, bullets flying through the open doorway. So she held her fire and went after the guy, screaming Regina's name now instead of Hatch's.

He disappeared into the girl's room and threw the door shut behind him, a hell of a slam that shook the house. Lindsey hit that barrier a second later, bounced off it. Locked. She heard Hatch shouting her name – thank God, he was alive, he was alive – but she didn't stop or turn around to see where he was. She stepped back and kicked the door hard, then kicked it again. It was only a privacy latch, flimsy, it ought to pop open easily, but didn't.

She was going to kick it again, but the killer spoke to her through the door. His voice was raised but not a shout, menacing but cool, no panic in it, no fear, just businesslike and a little loud, terrifyingly smooth and calm: 'Get away from the door, or I'll kill the little bitch.'

*   *   *

Just before Lindsey began to shout his name, Hatch was sitting at the desk in the den, lights off, holding *Arts American* in both hands. A vision hit him with an electric sound, the crackle of a current jumping an arc, as if the magazine were a live power cable that he had gripped in his bare hands.

He saw Lindsey from behind, sitting on the high stool in her office, at the drawing board, working on a sketch. Then she was not Lindsey any more. Suddenly she was another woman, taller, also seen from behind but not on the stool, in an armchair in a different room in a strange house. She was knitting. A bright skein of yarn slowly unraveled from a retaining bowl on the small table beside her chair. Hatch thought of her as 'mother,' though she was nothing whatsoever like his mother. He looked down at his right hand, in which he held a knife, immense, already wet with blood. He approached the chair. She was unaware of him. As Hatch, he wanted to cry out and warn her. But as the user of the knife, through whose eyes he was seeing everything, he wanted only to savage her, tear the life out of her, and thereby complete the task that would free him. He stepped to the back of her armchair. She hadn't heard him yet. He raised the knife high. He struck. She screamed. He struck. She tried to get out of the chair. He moved around her, and from his point of view it was like a swooping shot in a movie meant to convey flight, the smooth glide of a bird or bat. He pushed her back into the chair, struck. She raised her hands to protect herself. He struck. He struck. And now, as if it was all a loop of film, he was behind her again, standing in the doorway, except she wasn't 'mother' any more, she was Lindsey again, sitting at the drawing board in her upstairs studio, reaching to the top drawer of her supply cabinet and pulling it open. His gaze rose from her to the window. He saw himself – pale face, dark hair, sunglasses – and knew she had seen him. She spun around on the stool, a pistol coming up, the muzzle aimed straight at his chest—

'Hatch!'

His name, echoing through the house, shattered the link. He shot up from the desk chair, shuddering, and the magazine fell out of his hands.

'Hatch!'

Reaching out in the darkness, he unerringly found the handgrip of the Browning, and raced out of the den. As he crossed the foyer and climbed the stairs two at a time, looking up as he went, trying to see what was happening, he heard Lindsey stop shouting his name and start screaming 'Regina!' Not the girl, Jesus, please, not the girl. Reaching the top of the stairs, he thought for an instant that the slamming door was a shot. But the sound was too distinct to be mistaken for gunfire, and as he looked back the hall he saw Lindsey bounce off the door to Regina's room with another crash. As he ran to join her, she kicked the door, kicked again, and then she stumbled back from it as he reached her.

'Lemme try,' he said, pushing past her.

'No! He said back off or he'll kill her.'

For a couple of seconds, Hatch stared at the door, literally shaking with frustration. Then he took hold of the knob, tried to turn it slowly. But it was locked, so he put the muzzle of the pistol against the base of the knob plate.

'Hatch,' Lindsey said plaintively, 'he'll kill her.'

He thought of the young blonde taking two bullets in the chest, flying backward out of the car onto the freeway, tumbling, tumbling along the pavement into the fog. And the mother suffering the massive blade of the butcher knife as she dropped her knitting and struggled desperately for her life.

He said, 'He'll kill her anyway, turn your face away,' and he pulled the trigger.

Wood and thin metal dissolved into splinters. He grabbed the brass knob, it came off in his hand, and he threw it aside. When he shoved on the door, it creaked inward an inch but no farther. The cheap lock had disintegrated. But the shank on which the knob had been seated was still bristling from the wood, and something must have been wedged under the knob on the inside. He pushed on the shank with the palm of his hand, but that didn't provide enough force to move it; whatever was wedged against the other side – most likely the girl's desk chair – was exerting upward pressure, thereby holding the shank in place.

Hatch gripped the Browning by its barrel and used the butt as a hammer. Cursing, he pounded the shank, driving it inch by inch back through the door.

Just as the shank flew free and clattered to the floor inside, a vivid series of images flooded through Hatch's mind, temporarily washing away the upstairs hall. They were all from the killer's eyes: a weird angle, looking up at the side of a house, this house, the wall outside Regina's bedroom. The open window. Below the sill, a tangle of trumpet-vine runners. A hornlike flower in his face. Latticework under his hands, splinters digging into his skin. Clutching with one hand, searching with the other for a new place to grip, one foot dangling in space, a weight bearing down hard over his shoulder. Then a creaking, a splitting sound. A sudden sense of perilous looseness in the geometric web to which he clung—

Hatch was snapped back to reality by a brief, loud noise from beyond the door: clattering and splintering wood, nails popping loose with tortured screeches, scraping, a crash.

Then a new wave of psychic images and sensations flushed through him. Falling. Backward and out into the night. Not far, hitting the ground, a brief flash of pain. Rolling once on the grass. Beside him, a small huddled form, lying still. Scuttling to it, seeing the face. Regina. Eyes closed. A scarf tied across her mouth—

'Regina!' Lindsey cried.

When reality clicked into place once again, Hatch was already slamming his shoulder against the bedroom door. The brace on the other side fell away. The door shuddered open. He went inside, slapping the wall with one hand until he found the light switch. In the sudden glare, he stepped over the fallen desk chair and swung the Browning right, then left. The room was deserted, which he already knew from his vision.

At the open window he looked out at the collapsed trellis and tangled vines on the lawn below. There was no sign of the man in sunglasses or of Regina.

'Shit!' Hatch hurried back across the room, grabbing Lindsey, turning her around, pushing her through the door, into the hall, toward the head of the stairs. 'You take the front, I'll take the back, he's got her, stop him, go, go.' She didn't resist, picked up at once on what he was saying, and flew down the steps with him at her heels. 'Shoot him, bring him down, aim for the legs, can't worry about hitting Regina, he's getting away!'

In the foyer Lindsey reached the front door even as Hatch was coming off the bottom step and turning toward the short hallway. He dashed into the family room, then into the kitchen, peering out the back windows of the house as he ran past them. The lawn and patios were well lighted, but he didn't see anyone out there.

He tore open the door between the kitchen and the garage, stepped through, switched on the lights. He raced across the three stalls, behind the cars, to the exterior door at the far end even before the last of the fluorescent tubes had stopped flickering and come all the way on.

He disengaged the dead-bolt lock, stepped out into the narrow side yard, and glanced to his right. No killer. No Regina. The front of the house lay in that direction, the street, more houses facing theirs from the other side. That was part of the territory Lindsey already was covering.

His heart knocked so hard, it seemed to drive each breath out of his lungs before he could get it all the way in.

She's only ten, only ten.

He turned left and ran along the side of the house, around the corner of the garage, into the backyard, where the fallen trellis and trumpet vines lay in a heap.

So small, a little thing. God, please.

Afraid of stepping on a nail and disabling himself, he skirted the debris and searched frantically along the perimeter of the property, plunging recklessly into the shrubbery, probing behind the tall eugenias.

No one was in the backyard.

He reached the side of the property farthest from the garage, almost slipped and fell as he skidded around the corner, but kept his balance. He thrust the Browning out in front of him with both hands, covering the walkway between the house and the fence. No one there, either.

He'd heard nothing from out front, certainly no gunfire, which meant Lindsey must be having no better luck than he was. If the killer had not gone that way, the only other thing he could have done was scale the fence on one side or another, escaping into someone else's property.

Turning away from the front of the house, Hatch surveyed the seven-foot-high fence that encircled the backyard, separating it from the abutting yards of the houses to the east, west, and south. Developers and realtors called it a fence in southern California, although it was actually a wall, concrete blocks reinforced with steel and covered with stucco, capped with bricks, painted to match the houses. Most neighborhoods had them, guarantors of privacy at swimming pools or barbecues. Good fences make good neighbors, make strangers for neighbors – and make it damn easy for an intruder to scramble over a single barrier and vanish from one part of the maze into another.

Hatch was on an emotional wire-walk across a chasm of despair, his balance sustained only by the hope that the killer couldn't move fast with Regina in his arms or over his shoulder. He looked east, west, south, frozen by indecision.

Finally he started toward the back wall, which was on their southern flank. He halted, gasping and bending forward, when the mysterious connection between him and the man in sunglasses was re-established.

Again Hatch saw through the other man's eyes, and in spite of the sunglasses the night seemed more like late twilight. He was in a car, behind the steering wheel, leaning across the console to adjust the unconscious girl in the passenger seat as if she were a mannequin. Her wrists were lashed together in her lap, and she was held in place by the safety harness. After arranging her auburn hair to cover the scarf that crossed the back of her head, he pushed her against the door, so she slumped with her face turned away from the side window. People in passing cars would not be able to see the gag in her mouth. She appeared to be sleeping. Indeed she was so pale and still, he suddenly wondered if she was dead. No point in taking her to his hideaway if she was already dead. Might as well open the door and push her out, dump the little bitch right there. He put his hand against her cheek. Her skin was wonderfully smooth but seemed cool. Pressing his fingertips to her throat, he detected her heartbeat in a carotid artery, thumping strongly, so strongly. She was so *alive*, even more vital than she had seemed in the vision with the butterfly flitting around her head. He had never before made an acquisition of such value, and he was grateful to all the powers of Hell for giving her to him. He thrilled at the prospect of reaching deep within and clasping that strong young heart as it twitched and thudded into final stillness, all the while staring into her beautiful gray eyes to watch life pass out of her and death enter —

Hatch's cry of rage, anguish, and terror broke the psychic connection. He was in his backyard again, holding his right hand up in front of his face, staring at it in horror, as if Regina's blood already stained his trembling fingers.

He turned away from the back fence, and sprinted along the east side of the house, toward the front.

But for his own hard breathing, all was quiet. Evidently some of the neighbors weren't home. Others hadn't heard anything, or at least not enough to bring them outside.

The serenity of the community made him want to scream with frustration. Even as his own world was falling apart, however, he realized the appearance of normality was exactly that – merely an *appearance*, not a reality. God knew what might be happening behind the walls of some of those houses, horrors equal to the one that had overcome him and Lindsey and Regina, perpetrated not by an intruder but by one member of a family upon another. The human species possessed a knack for creating monsters, and the beasts themselves often had a talent for hiding away behind convincing masks of sanity.

When Hatch reached the front lawn, Lindsey was nowhere to be seen. He hurried to the walkway, through the open door – and discovered her in the den, where she was standing beside the desk, making a phone call.

'You find her?' she asked.

'No. What're you doing?'

'Calling the police.'

Taking the receiver out of her hand, dropping it onto the phone, he said, 'By the time they get there, listen to our story, and start to *do* something, he'll be gone, he'll have Regina so far away they'll never find her – until they stumble across her body someday.'

'But we need help—'

Snatching the shotgun off the desk and pushing it into her hands, he said, 'We're going to follow the bastard. He's got her in a car. A Honda, I think.'

298

'You have a license number?'

'No.'

'Did you see if—'

'I didn't actually *see* anything,' he said, jerking open the desk drawer, plucking out the box of 12-gauge ammunition, handing that to her as well, desperately aware of the seconds ticking away. 'I'm connecting with him, it flickers in and out, but I think the link is good enough, strong enough.' He pulled his ring of keys from the desk lock, in which he had left them dangling when he had taken the magazine from the drawer. 'We can stay on his ass if we don't let him get too far ahead of us.' Hurrying into the foyer, he said, 'But we have to *move*.'

'Hatch, wait!'

He stopped and swiveled to face her as she followed him out of the den.

She said, 'You go, follow them if you think you can, and I'll stay here to talk to the cops, get them started—'

Shaking his head, he said, 'No. I need you to drive. These ... these visions are like being punched, I sort of black out, I'm disoriented while it's happening. There's no way I won't run the car right off the damn road. Put the shotgun and the shells in the Mitsubishi.' Climbing the stairs two at a time, he shouted back to her: 'And get flashlights.'

'Why?'

'I don't know, but we'll need them.'

He was lying. He had been somewhat surprised to hear himself ask for flashlights, but he knew his subconscious was driving him at the moment, and he had a hunch why flashlights were going to be essential. In his nightmares over the past couple of months, he had often moved through cavernous rooms and a maze of concrete corridors that were somehow revealed in spite of having no windows or artificial lighting. One tunnel in particular, sloping down into perfect blackness, into something unknown, filled him with such dread that his heart swelled and pounded as if it would burst. *That* was why they needed flashlights – because they were going where he had previously been only in dreams or in visions, into the heart of the nightmare.

He was all the way upstairs and entering Regina's room before he realized that he didn't know why he had gone there. Stopping just inside the threshold, he looked down at the broken doorknob and the overturned desk chair, then at the closet where clothes had fallen off the hangers and were lying in a pile, then at the open window where the night breeze had begun to stir the draperies.

Something . . . something important. Right here, right now, in this room, something he needed.

But what?

He switched the Browning to his left hand, wiped the damp palm of his right hand against his jeans. By now the son of a bitch in the sunglasses had started the car and was on his way out of the neighborhood with Regina, probably on Crown Valley Parkway already. Every second counted.

Although he was beginning to wonder if he had flown upstairs in a panic rather than because there was anything he really needed, Hatch decided to trust the compulsion a little further. He went to the corner desk and let his gaze travel over the books, pencils, and a notebook The bookcase next to the desk. One of Lindsey's paintings on the wall beside it.

Come on, come on. Something he needed . . . needed as badly as the flashlights, as badly as the shotgun and the box of shells. Something.

He turned, saw the crucifix, and went straight for it. He scrambled onto Regina's bed and wrenched the cross from the wall behind it.

Off the bed and on the floor again, heading out of the room and along the hall toward the stairs, he gripped the icon tightly, fisted his right hand around it. He realized he was holding it as if it were not an object of religious symbolism and veneration but a weapon, a hatchet or cleaver.

By the time he got to the garage, the big sectional door was rolling up. Lindsey had started the car.

When Hatch got in the passenger's side, Lindsey looked at the crucifix. 'What's that for?'

'We'll need it.'

Backing out of the garage, she said, 'Need it for what?'

'I don't know.'

As the car rolled into the street, she looked at Hatch curiously. 'A crucifix?'

'I don't know, but maybe it'll be useful. When I linked with him he was . . . he felt thankful to all the powers of Hell, that's how it went through his mind, thankful to all the powers of Hell for giving Regina to him.' He pointed left. 'That way.'

Fear had aged Lindsey a few years in the past ten minutes. Now the lines in her face grew deeper still as she threw the car in gear and turned left. 'Hatch, what are we dealing with here, one of those Satanists, those crazies, guys in these cults you read about in the paper, when they catch one of them, they find severed heads in the refrigerator, bones buried under the front porch?'

'Yeah, maybe, something like that.' At the intersection he said, 'Left here. Maybe something like that . . . but worse, I think.'

'We can't handle this, Hatch.'

'The hell we can't,' he said sharply. 'There's no time for anybody else to handle it. If we don't, Regina's dead.'

They came to an intersection with Crown Valley Parkway, which was a wide four- to six-lane boulevard with a garden strip and trees planted down the center. The hour was not yet late, and the parkway was busy, though not crowded.

'Which way?' Lindsey asked.

Hatch put his Browning on the floor. He did not let go of the crucifix. He held it in both hands. He looked left and right, left and right, waiting for a feeling, a sign, something. The headlights of passing cars washed over them but brought no revelations.

'Hatch?' Lindsey said worriedly.

Left and right, left and right. Nothing. Jesus.

Hatch thought about Regina. Auburn hair. Gray eyes. Her right hand curled and twisted like a claw, a gift from God. No, not from God. Not this time. Can't blame them all on God. She might have been right: a gift from her parents, drug-users' legacy.

A car pulled up behind them, waiting to get out onto the main street.

The way she walked, determined to minimize the limp. The way she never concealed her deformed hand, neither ashamed nor proud of it, just accepting. Going to be a writer. Intelligent pigs from outer space.

The driver waiting behind them blew his horn.

'Hatch?'

Regina, so small under the weight of the world, yet always standing straight, her head never bowed. Made a deal with God. In return for something precious to her, a promise to eat beans. And Hatch knew what the precious thing was, though she had never said it, knew it was a family, a chance to escape the orphanage.

301

The other driver blew his horn again.

Lindsey was shaking. She started to cry.

A chance. Just a chance. All the girl wanted. Not to be alone any more. A chance to sleep in a bed painted with flowers. A chance to love, be loved, grow up. The small curled hand. The small sweet smile. *Goodnight . . . Dad.*

The driver behind them blew his horn insistently.

'Right,' Hatch said abruptly. 'Go right.'

With a sob of relief, Lindsey turned right onto the parkway. She drove faster than she usually did, changing lanes as traffic required, crossing the south-county flatlands toward the distant foothills and the night-shrouded mountains in the east.

At first Hatch was not sure that he had done more than guess at what direction to take. But soon conviction came to him. The boulevard led east between endless tracts of houses that speckled the hills with lights as if they were thousands of memorial flames on the tiers of immense votive-candle racks, and with each mile he sensed more strongly that he and Lindsey were following in the wake of the beast.

Because he had agreed there would be no more secrets between them, because he thought she should know – and could handle – a full understanding of the extremity of Regina's circumstances, Hatch said, 'What he wants to do is hold her beating heart in his bare hand for its last few beats, feel the life go out of it.'

'Oh God.'

'She's still alive. She has a chance. There's hope.'

He believed what he said was true, had to believe it or go mad. But he was troubled by the memory of having said those same things so often in the weeks before cancer had finally finished with Jimmy.

Part Three

DOWN AMONG
THE DEAD

Death is no fearsome mystery.
He is well known to thee and me.
He hath no secrets he can keep
to trouble any good man's sleep.

Turn not thy face from Death away.
Care not he takes our breath away.
Fear him not, he's not thy master,
rushing at thee faster, faster.
Not thy master but servant to
the Maker of thee, what or Who
created death, created thee
– and is the only mystery.

— The Book of Counted Sorrows

SEVEN

·1·

Jonas Nyebern and Kari Dovell sat in armchairs before the big windows in the darkened living room of his house on Spyglass Hill, looking at the millions of lights that glimmered across Orange and Los Angeles counties. The night was relatively clear, and they could see as far as Long Beach Harbor to the north. Civilization sprawled like a luminescent fungus, devouring all.

A bottle of Robert Mondavi chenin blanc was in an ice bucket on the floor between their chairs. It was their second bottle. They had not eaten dinner yet. He was talking too much.

They had been seeing each other socially once or twice a week for more than a month. They had not gone to bed together, and he didn't think they ever would. She was still desirable, with that odd combination of grace and awkwardness that sometimes reminded him of an exotic long-legged crane, even if the side of her that was a serious and dedicated physician could never quite let the woman in her have full rein. However, he doubted she even expected physical intimacy. In any case, he didn't believe he was capable of it. He was a haunted man; too many ghosts waited to bedevil him if happiness came within his reach. What each of them got from the relationship was a friendly ear, patience, and genuine sympathy without maudlin excess.

That evening he talked about Jeremy, which was not a subject conducive to romance even if there had been any prospect of it. Mostly he worried over the signs of Jeremy's congenital madness that he'd failed to realize – or admit – *were* signs.

Even as a child Jeremy had been unusually quiet, invariably preferring solitude to anyone's company. That was explained away as simple shyness. From the earliest age he seemed to have no

305

interest in toys, which was written off to his indisputably high intelligence and a too-serious nature. But now all those untouched model airplanes and games and balls and elaborate Erector sets were disquieting indications that his interior fantasy life had been richer than any entertainment that could be provided by Tonka, Mattel, or Lionel.

'He was never able to receive a hug without stiffening a little,' Jonas remembered. 'When he returned a kiss for a kiss, he always planted his lips on the air instead of your cheek.'

'Lots of kids have difficulty being demonstrative,' Kari insisted. She lifted the wine bottle from the ice, leaned out, and refilled the glass he held. 'It would seem like just another aspect of his shyness. Shyness and self-effacement aren't faults, and you couldn't be expected to see them that way.'

'But it wasn't self-effacement,' he said miserably. 'It was an inability to feel, to care.'

'You can't keep beating yourself up like this, Jonas.'

'What if Marion and Stephanie weren't even the first?'

'They must have been.'

'But what if they weren't?'

'A teenage boy might be a killer, but he's not going to have the sophistication to get away with murder for any length of time.'

'What if he's killed someone since he slipped away from the rehab hospital?'

'He's probably been victimized himself, Jonas.'

'No. He's not the victim type.'

'He's probably dead.'

'He's out there somewhere. Because of me.'

Jonas stared at the vast panorama of lights. Civilization lay in all its glimmering wonder, all its blazing glory, all its bright terror.

★ ★ ★

As they approached the San Diego Freeway, Interstate 405, Hatch said, 'South. He's gone south.'

Lindsey flipped on the turn signal and caught the entrance ramp just in time.

At first she had glanced at Hatch whenever she could take her eyes off the road, expecting him to tell her what he was seeing or receiving from the man they were trailing. But after a while she

306

focused on the highway whether she needed to or not, because he was sharing nothing with her. She suspected his silence simply meant he was seeing very little, that the link between him and the killer was either weak or flickering on and off. She didn't press him to include her, because she was afraid that if she distracted him, the bond might be broken altogether – and Regina lost.

Hatch continued to hold the crucifix. Even from the corner of her eyes, Lindsey could see how the fingertips of his left hand ceaselessly traced the contours of the cast-metal figure suffering upon the faux dogwood cross. His gaze seemed to be turned inward, as if he were virtually unaware of the night and the car in which he traveled.

Lindsey realized that her life had become as surreal as any of her paintings. Supernatural experiences were juxtaposed with the familiar mundane world. Disparate elements filled the composition: crucifixes and guns, psychic visions and flashlights.

In her paintings, she used surrealism to elucidate a theme, provide insight. In real life, each intrusion of the surreal only further confused and mystified her.

Hatch shuddered and leaned forward as far as the safety harness would allow, as if he had seen something fantastic and frightening cross the highway, though she knew he was not actually looking at the blacktop ahead. He slumped back into his seat. 'He's taken the Ortega Highway exit. East. The same exit's coming up for us in a couple of miles. East on the Ortega Highway.'

* * *

Sometimes the headlights of oncoming cars forced him to squint in spite of the protection provided by his heavily tinted glasses.

As he drove, Vassago periodically glanced at the unconscious girl in the seat beside him, facing him. Her chin rested on her breast. Though her head was tipped down and auburn hair hung over one side of her face, he could see her lips pulled back by the scarf that held in the gag, the tilt of her pixie nose, all of one closed eyelid and most of the other – such long lashes – and part of her smooth brow. His imagination played with all the possible ways he might disfigure her to produce the most effective offering.

She was perfect for his purposes. With her beauty compromised by her leg and deformed hand, she was already a symbol of God's

307

fallibility. A trophy, indeed, for his collection.

He was disappointed that he had failed to get the mother, but he had not given up hope of acquiring her. He was toying with the idea of not killing the child tonight. If he kept her alive for only a few days, he might have an opportunity to make another bid for Lindsey. If he had them together, able to work on them at the same time, he could present their corpses as a mocking version of Michelangelo's *Pietal*, or dismember them and stitch them together in a highly imaginative obscene collage.

He was waiting for guidance, another vision, before deciding what to do.

As he took the Ortega Highway off-ramp and turned east, he recalled how Lindsey, at the drawing board in her studio, had reminded him of his mother at her knitting on the afternoon when he had killed her. Having disposed of his sister and mother with the same knife in the same hour, he had known in his heart that he had paved the way to Hell, had been so convinced that he had taken the final step and impaled himself.

A privately published book had described for him that route to damnation. Titled *The Hidden*, it was the work of a condemned murderer named Thomas Nicene who had killed his own mother and a brother, and then committed suicide. His carefully planned descent into the Pit had been foiled by a paramedic team with too much dedication and a little luck. Nicene was revived, healed, imprisoned, put on trial, convicted of murder, and sentenced to death. Rule-playing society had made it clear that the power of death, even the right to choose one's own, was not ever to be given to an individual.

While waiting execution, Thomas Nicene had committed to paper the visions of Hell that he had experienced during the time that he had been on the edge of this life, before the paramedics denied him eternity. His writings had been smuggled out of prison to fellow believers who could print and distribute them. Nicene's book was filled with powerful, convincing images of darkness and cold, not the heat of classic hells, but visions of a kingdom of vast spaces, chilling emptiness. Peering through Death's door and the door of Hell beyond, Thomas had seen titanic powers at work on mysterious structures. Demons of colossal size and strength strode through night mists across lightless continents on unknown missions, each clothed in black with a flowing cape and upon its

308

head a shining black helmet with a flared rim. He had seen dark seas crashing on black shores under starless and moonless skies that gave the feeling of a subterranean world. Enormous ships, windowless and mysterious, were driven through the tenebrous waves by powerful engines that produced a noise like the anguished screams of multitudes.

When he had read Nicene's words, Jeremy had known they were truer than any ever inked upon a page, and he had determined to follow the great man's example. Marion and Stephanie became his tickets to the exotic and enormously attractive netherworld where he belonged. He had punched those tickets with a butcher knife and delivered himself to that dark kingdom, encountering precisely what Nicene promised. He had never imagined that his own escape from the hateful world of the living would be undone not by paramedics but by his own father.

He would soon earn repatriation to the damned.

Glancing at the girl again, Vassago remembered how she had felt when she shuddered and collapsed limply in his fierce embrace. A shiver of delicious anticipation coursed through him.

He had considered killing his father to learn if that act would win him back his citizenship in Hades. But he was wary of his old man. Jonas Nyebern was a life-giver and seemed to shine with an inner light that Vassago found forbidding. His earliest memories of his father were wrapped up in images of Christ and angels and the Holy Mother and miracles, scenes from the paintings that Jonas collected and with which their home had always been decorated. And only two years ago, his father had resurrected him in the manner of Jesus raising cold Lazarus. Consequently, he thought of Jonas not merely as the enemy but as a figure of power, an embodiment of those bright forces that were opposed to the will of Hell. His father was no doubt protected, untouchable, living in the loathsome grace of that *other* deity.

His hopes, then, were pinned on the woman and the girl. One acquisition made, the other pending.

He drove east past endless tracts of houses that had sprung up in the six years since Fantasy World had been abandoned, and he was grateful that the spawning multitudes of life-loving hypocrites had not pressed to the very perimeter of his special hideaway, which still lay miles beyond the last of the new communities. As the peopled hills passed by, as the land grew steadily less hospitable though still inhabited, Vassago drove more slowly than he would have done any other night.

He was waiting for a vision that would tell him if he should kill the child upon arrival at the park or wait until the mother was his, as well.

Turning his head to look at her once more, he discovered she was watching him. Her eyes shone with the reflected light from the instrument panel. He could see that her fear was great.

'Poor baby,' he said. 'Don't be afraid. Okay? Don't be afraid. We're just going to an amusement park, that's all. You know, like Disneyland, like Magic Mountain?'

If he was unable to acquire the mother, perhaps he should look for another child about the same size as Regina, a particularly pretty one with four strong, healthy limbs. He could then remake this girl with the arm, hand, and leg of the other, as if to say that he, a mere twenty-year-old expatriate of Hell, could do a better job than the Creator. That would make a fine addition to his collection, a singular work of art.

He listened to the contained thunder of the engine. The hum of the tires on the pavement. The soft whistle of wind at the windows.

Waiting for an epiphany. Waiting for guidance. Waiting to be told what he should do. Waiting, waiting, a vision to behold.

★ ★ ★

Even before they reached the Ortega Highway off-ramp, Hatch received a flurry of images stranger than anything he had seen before. None lasted longer than a few seconds, as if he were watching a film with no narrative structure. Dark seas crashing on black shores under starless and moonless skies. Enormous ships, windowless and mysterious, driven through the tenebrous waves by powerful engines that produced a noise like the anguished screams of multitudes. Colossal demonic figures, a hundred feet tall, striding alien landscapes, black capes flowing behind them, heads encased in black helmets as shiny as glass. Titanic, half-glimpsed machines at work on monumental structures of such odd design that purpose and function could not even be guessed.

Sometimes Hatch saw that hideous landscape in chillingly vivid detail, but sometimes he saw only descriptions of it in words on the printed pages of a book. If it existed, it must be on some far world, for it was not of this earth. But he was never sure if he was receiving pictures of a real place or one that was merely imagined. At times it seemed as vividly depicted as any street in Laguna but at other times seemed tissue-paper thin.

★ ★ ★

Jonas returned to the living room with the box of items he had saved from Jeremy's room, and put it down beside his armchair. He withdrew from the box a small, shoddily printed volume titled *The Hidden* and gave it to Kari, who examined it as if he had handed her an object encrusted with filth.

'You're right to wrinkle your nose at it,' he said, picking up his glass of wine and moving to the large window. 'It's nonsense. Sick and twisted, but nonsense. The author was a convicted killer who claimed to have seen Hell. His description isn't like anything in Dante, let me tell you. Oh, it possesses a certain romance, undeniable power. In fact, if you were a psychotic young man with delusions of grandeur and a bent for violence, with the unnaturally high testosterone levels that usually accompany a mental condition like that, then the Hell he describes would be your ultimate wet-dream of power. You would swoon over it. You might not be able to get it out of your mind. You might *long* for it, do anything to be a part of it, achieve damnation.'

Kari put the book down and wiped her fingertips on the sleeve of her blouse. 'This author, Thomas Nicene – you said he killed his mother.'

'Yes. Mother and brother. Set the example.' Jonas knew he had already drunk too much. He took another long sip of his wine anyway. Turning from the night view, he said, 'And you know what makes it all so absurd, pathetically absurd? If you read that damn book, which I did afterward, trying to understand, and if you're not psychotic and disposed to believe it, you'll see right away that Nicene isn't reporting what he saw in Hell. He's taking his inspiration from a source as stupidly obvious as it is stupidly ridiculous. Kari, his Hell is nothing more than the Evil Empire in the *Star Wars* movies, somewhat changed, expanded upon, filmed through the lens of religious myth, but still *Star Wars*.' A bitter laugh escaped him. He chased it with more wine. 'His demons are

311

nothing more than hundred-foot-tall versions of Darth Vader, for God's sake. Read his description of Satan and then go look at whichever film Jabba the Hut was a part of. Old Jabba the Hut is a ringer for Satan, if you believe this lunatic.' One more glass of chenin blanc, one more glass. 'Marion and Stephanie died – ' A sip. Too long a sip. Half the glass gone. ' – died so Jeremy could get into Hell and have great, dark antiheroic adventures in a fucking Darth Vader costume.'

He had offended or unsettled her, probably both. That had not been his intention, and he regretted it. He wasn't sure what his intention had been. Maybe just to unburden himself. He had never done so before, and he didn't know why he'd chosen to do so tonight – except that Morton Redlow's disappearance had scared him more than anything since the day he had found the bodies of his wife and daughter.

Instead of pouring more wine for herself, Kari rose from her armchair. 'I think we should get something to eat.'

'Not hungry,' he said, and heard the slur of the inebriate in his voice. 'Well, maybe we should have something.'

'We could go out somewhere,' she said, taking the wine glass from his hand and putting it on the nearest end table. Her face was quite lovely in the ambient light that came through the view windows, the golden radiance from the web of cities below. 'Or call for pizza.'

'How about steaks? I've got some filets in the freezer.'

'That'll take too long.'

'Sure won't. Just thaw 'em out in the microwave, throw 'em on the grill. There's a big Gaggenau grill in the kitchen.'

'Well, if that's what you'd like.'

He met her eyes. Her gaze was as clear, penetrating and forthright as ever, but Jonas saw a greater tenderness in her eyes than before. He supposed it was the same concern she had for her young patients, part of what made her a first-rate pediatrician. Maybe that tenderness had always been there for him, too, and he had just not seen it until now. Or perhaps this was the first time she realized how desperately he needed nurturing.

'Thank you, Kari.'

'For what?'

'For being you,' he said. He put his arm around her shoulders as he walked her to the kitchen.

312

Mixed with the visions of gargantuan machines and dark seas and colossal demonic figures, Hatch received an array of images of other types. Choiring angels. The Holy Mother in prayer. Christ with the Apostles at the Last Supper, Christ in Gethsemane, Christ in agony upon the cross, Christ ascending.

He recognized them as paintings Jonas Nyebern might have collected at one time or another. They were different periods and styles from those he had seen in the physician's office, but in the same spirit. A connection was made, a braiding of wires in his subconscious, but he didn't understand what it meant yet.

And more visions: the Ortega Highway. Glimpses of the night-scapes unrolling on both sides of an eastward-bound car. Instruments on a dashboard. Oncoming headlights that sometimes made him squint. And suddenly Regina. Regina in the backsplash of yellow light from that same instrument panel. Eyes closed. Head tipped forward. Something wadded in her mouth and held in place by a scarf.

She opens her eyes.

Looking into Regina's terrified eyes, Hatch broke from the visions like an underwater swimmer breaking for air. 'She's alive!'

He looked at Lindsey, who shifted her gaze from the highway to him. 'But you never said she wasn't.'

Until then he did not realize how little faith he'd had in the girl's continued existence.

Before he could take heart from the sight of her gray eyes gleaming in the yellow dashboard light of the killer's car, Hatch was hit by new clairvoyant visions that pummeled him as hard as a series of blows from real fists:

Contorted figures loomed out of murky shadows. Human forms in bizarre positions. He saw a woman as withered and dry as tumbleweed, another in a repugnant state of putrefaction, a mummified face of indeterminate sex, a bloated green-black hand raised in horrid supplication. The collection. His collection. He saw Regina's face again, eyes open, revealed in the dashboard lights. So many ways to disfigure, to mutilate, to mock God's work. Regina. *Poor baby. Don't be afraid. Okay? Don't be afraid. We're only going to an amusement park. You know, like Disneyland, like Magic Mountain?* How nicely she will fit in my collection.

313

Corpses as performance art, held in place by wires, rebar, blocks of wood. He saw frozen screams, silent forever. Skeletal jaws held open in eternal cries for mercy. The precious collection. Regina, sweet baby, pretty baby, such an exquisite acquisition.

Hatch came out of his trance, clawing wildly at his safety harness, for it felt like binding wires, ropes and cords. He tore at the straps as a panicked victim of premature burial might rip at his enwrapping shrouds. He realized that he was shouting, too, and sucking in breath as if in fear of suffocation, letting it out at once in great explosive exhalations. He heard Lindsey saying his name, understood that he was terrifying her, but could not cease thrashing or crying out for long seconds, until he had found the release on the safety harness and cast it off.

With that, he was fully back in the Mitsubishi, contact with the madman broken for the moment, the horror of the collection diminished though not forgotten, not in the least forgotten. He turned to Lindsey, remembering her fortitude in the icy waters of that mountain river the night that she had saved him. She would need all of that strength and more tonight.

'Fantasy World,' he said urgently, 'where they had the fire years ago, abandoned now, that's where he's going. Jesus Christ, Lindsey, drive like you've never driven in your life, put the pedal to the floor, the son of a bitch, the crazy rotten son of a bitch is taking her down among the dead!'

And they were flying. Though she could have no idea what he meant, they were suddenly flying eastward faster than was safe on that highway, through the last clusters of closely spaced lights, out of civilization into ever darker realms.

* * *

While Kari searched the refrigerator in the kitchen for the makings of a salad, Jonas went to the garage to liberate a couple of steaks from the chest-style freezer. The garage vents brought in the coolish night air, which he found refreshing. He stood for a moment just inside the door from the house, taking slow deep breaths to clear his head a little.

He had no appetite for anything except perhaps more wine, but he did not want Kari to see him drunk. Besides, though he had no surgery scheduled for the following day, he never knew what

314

emergency might require the skills of the resuscitation team, and he felt a responsibility to those potential patients.

In his darkest hours, he sometimes considered leaving the field of resuscitation medicine to concentrate on cardiovascular surgery. When he saw a reanimated patient return to a useful life of work and family and service, he knew a reward sweeter than most other men could ever know. But in the moment of crisis, when the candidate for resuscitation lay on the table, Jonas rarely knew anything about him, which meant he might sometimes bring evil back into the world once the world had shed it. That was more than a moral dilemma to him; it was a crushing weight upon his conscience. Thus far, being a religious man – though with his share of doubts – he had trusted in God to guide him. He had decided that God had given him his brain and his skills to use, and it was not his place to out-guess God and withhold his services from any patient.

Jeremy, of course, was an unsettling new factor in the equation. If he had brought Jeremy back, and if Jeremy had killed innocent people . . . It did not bear thinking about.

The cool air no longer seemed refreshing. It seeped into the hollows of his spine.

Okay, dinner. Two steaks. Filet mignon. Lightly grilled, with a little Worcestershire sauce. Salads with no dressing but a squirt of lemon and a sprinkle of black pepper. Maybe he *did* have an appetite. He didn't eat much red meat; it was a rare treat. He was a heart surgeon, after all, and saw firsthand the gruesome effects of a high-fat diet.

He went to the freezer in the corner. He pushed the latch-release and put up the lid.

Within lay Morton Redlow, late of the Redlow Detective Agency, pale and gray as if carved from marble but not yet obscured by a layer of frost. A smear of blood had frozen into a brittle crust on his face, and there was a terrible vacancy where his nose had been. His eyes were open. Forever.

Jonas did not recoil. As a surgeon, he was equally familiar with the horrors and wonders of biology, and he was not easily repulsed. Something in him withered when he saw Redlow. Something in him died. His heart turned as cold as that of the detective before him. In some fundamental way, he knew that he was finished as a man. He didn't trust God any more. Not any more.

315

What God? But he was not nauseated or forced to turn away in disgust.

He saw the folded note clutched in Redlow's stiff right hand. The dead man let go of it easily, for his fingers had contracted during the freezing process, shrinking away from the paper around which the killer had pressed them.

Numbly, he unfolded the letter and immediately recognized his son's neat penmanship. The post-coma aphasia had been faked. His retardation was an immensely clever ruse.

The note said, *Dear Daddy: For a proper burial, they'll need to know where to find his nose. Look up his back end. He stuck it in my business, so I stuck it in his. If he'd had any manners, I would have treated him better. I'm sorry, sir, if this behavior distresses you.*

★ ★ ★

Lindsey drove with utmost urgency, pushing the Mitsubishi to its limits, finding every planning flaw in a highway not always designed for speed. There was little traffic as they moved deeper into the east, which stacked the odds in their favor when once she crossed the center line in the middle of a too-tight turn.

Having snapped on his safety harness again, Hatch used the car phone to get Jonas Nyebern's office number from information, then to call the number itself, which was answered at once by a physician's-service operator. She took his message, which baffled her. Although the operator seemed sincere in her promise to pass it on to the doctor, Hatch was not confident that his definition of 'immediately' and hers were materially the same.

He saw all the connections so clearly now, but he knew he could not have seen them sooner. Jonas's question in the office on Monday took on a new significance: Did Hatch, he had asked, believe that evil was only the result of the acts of men, or did he think that evil was a real force, a presence that walked the world? The story Jonas had told of losing wife and daughter to a homicidal, psychopathic son, and the son himself to suicide, connected now to the vision of the woman knitting. The father's collections. And the son's. The Satanic aspects to the visions were what one might expect from a bad son in mindless rebellion against a father to whom religion was a center post of life. And finally – he and Jeremy Nyebern shared one obvious link, miraculous resurrection at the hands of the same man.

'But how does that explain anything?' Lindsey demanded, when he told her only a little more than he had told the physician's-service operator.

'I don't know.'

He couldn't think about anything except what he had seen in those last visions, less than half of which he understood. The part he *had* comprehended, the nature of Jeremy's collection, filled him with fear for Regina.

Without having seen the collection as Hatch had seen it, Lindsey was fixated, instead, on the mystery of the link, which was somewhat explained – yet not explained at all – by learning the identity of the killer in sunglasses. 'What about the visions? How do they fit the damned composition?' she insisted, trying to make sense of the supernatural in perhaps not too different a way from that in which she made sense of the world by reducing it to ordered images on Masonite.

'I don't know,' he said.

'The link that's letting you follow him—'

'I don't know.'

She took a turn too wide. The car went off the pavement, onto the gravel shoulder. The back end slid, gravel spraying out from beneath the tires and rattling against the undercarriage. The guardrail flashed close, too close, and the car was shaken by the hard bang-bang-bang of sheet metal taking a beating. She seemed to bring it back under control by a sheer effort of will, biting her lower lip so hard it appeared as if she would draw blood.

Although Hatch was aware of Lindsey and the car and the reckless pace they were keeping along that sometimes dangerously curved highway, he could not turn his mind from the outrage he had seen in the vision. The longer he thought about Regina being added to that grisly collection, the more his fear was augmented by anger. It was the hot, uncontainable anger he had seen so often in his father, but directed now against something deserving of hatred, against a target worthy of such seething rage.

* * *

As he approached the entrance road to the abandoned park, Vassago glanced away from the now lonely highway, to the girl who was bound and gagged in the other seat. Even in that poor light he could see that she had been straining at her bonds. Her wrists were chafed and beginning to bleed. Little Regina had hopes of breaking free, striking out or escaping, though her situation was so clearly hopeless. Such vitality. She thrilled him.

The child was so special that he might not need the mother at all, if he could think of a way to place her in his collection that would result in a piece of art with all the power of the various mother–daughter tableaux that he had already conceived.

He had been unconcerned with speed. Now, after he turned off the highway onto the park's long approach road, he accelerated, eager to return to the museum of the dead with the hope that the atmosphere there would inspire him.

Years ago, the four-lane entrance had been bordered by lush flowers, shrubbery, and groupings of palms. The trees and larger shrubs had been dug up, potted, and hauled away ages ago by agents of the creditors. The flowers had died and turned to dust when the landscape watering system had been shut off.

Southern California was a desert, transformed by the hand of man, and when the hand of man moved on, the desert reclaimed its rightful territory. So much for the genius of humanity, God's imperfect creatures. The pavement had cracked and hoved from years of inattention, and in places it had begun to vanish under drifts of sandy soil. His headlights revealed tumbleweed and scraps of other desert brush, already brown hardly six weeks after the end of the rainy season, chased westward by a night wind that came out of the parched hills.

When he reached the tollbooths he slowed down. They stretched across all four lanes. They had been left standing as a barrier to easy exploration of the shuttered park, linked and closed off by chains so heavy that simple bolt cutters could not sever them. Now the bays, once overseen by attendants, were filled with tangled brush that the wind had put there and trash deposited by vandals. He pulled around the booths, bouncing over a low curb and traveling on the sun-hardened soil of the planting beds where lush tropical landscaping would once have blocked the way, then back to the pavement when he had bypassed the barrier.

At the end of the entrance road, he switched off his headlights. He didn't need them, and he was at last beyond the notice of any highway patrolmen who might pull him over for driving without lights. His eyes immediately felt more comfortable, and now if his

318

pursuers drew too close, they would not be able to follow him by sight alone.

He angled across the immense and eerily empty parking lot. He was heading toward a service road at the southwest corner of the inner fence that circumscribed the grounds of the park proper.

As the Honda jolted over the pot-holed blacktop, Vassago ran-sacked his imagination, which was a busy abattoir of psychotic industry, seeking solutions for the artistic problems presented by the child. He conceived and rejected concept after concept. The image must stir him. Excite him. If it was really art, he would know it; he would be moved.

As Vassago lovingly envisioned tortures for Regina, he became aware of that other strange presence in the night and its singular rage. Suddenly he was plunged into another psychic vision, a flurry of familiar elements, with one crucial new addition: He got a glimpse of Lindsey behind the wheel of a car . . . a car phone in a man's trembling hand . . . and then the object that instantly resolved his artistic dilemma . . . a crucifix. The nailed and tor-tured body of Christ in its famous posture of noble self-sacrifice.

He blinked away that image, glanced at the petrified girl in the car with him, blinked her away as well, and in his imagination saw the two combined – girl and cruciform. He would use Regina to mock the Crucifixion. Yes, lovely, perfect. But not raised upon a cross of dogwood. Instead, she must be executed upon the seg-mented belly of the Serpent, under the bosom of the thirty-foot Lucifer in the deepest regions of the funhouse, crucified and her sacred heart revealed, as backdrop to the rest of his collection. Such a cruel and stunning use of her negated the need to include her mother, for in such a pose she would alone be his crowning achievement.

*　*　*

Hatch was frantically trying to contact the Orange County Sher-iff's Department on the cellular car phone, which was having transmission problems, when he felt the intrusion of another mind. He 'saw' images of Regina disfigured in a multitude of ways, and he began to shake with rage. Then he was struck by a vision of a crucifixion; it was so powerful, vivid, and monstrous that it almost rendered him unconscious as effectively as a skullcracking blow from a hard-swung hammer.

He urged Lindsey to drive faster, without explaining what he had seen. He couldn't speak of it.

The terror was amplified by Hatch's perfect understanding of the statement Jeremy intended to make by the perpetration of the outrage. Was God in error to have made His Only Begotten Child a man? Should Christ have been a woman? Were not women those who had suffered the most and therefore served as the greatest symbol of self-sacrifice, grace, and transcendence? God had granted women a special sensitivity, a talent for understanding and tenderness, for caring and nurturing – then had dumped them into a world of savage violence in which their singular qualities made them easy targets for the cruel and depraved.

Horror enough existed in that truth, but a greater horror, for Hatch, lay in the discovery that anyone as insane as Jeremy Nyebern could have such a complex insight. If a homicidal sociopath could perceive such a truth and grasp its theological implications, then creation itself must be an asylum. For surely, if the universe were a rational place, no madman would be able to understand any portion of it.

Lindsey reached the approach road to Fantasy World and took the turn so fast and sharp that the Mitsubishi slid sideways and felt, for a moment, as if it would roll. But it remained upright. She pulled hard on the wheel, brought it around, tramped on the accelerator.

Not Regina. No way was Jeremy going to be permitted to realize his decadent vision upon that lamb of innocence. Hatch was prepared to die to prevent it.

Fear and fury flooded him in equal torrents. The plastic casing of the cellular-phone handset creaked in his right fist as though the pressure of his grip would crack it as easily as if it had been an eggshell.

Tollbooths appeared ahead. Lindsey braked indecisively, then seemed to notice the tire tracks through the drifting, sandy earth at the same time Hatch saw them. She whipped the car to the right, and it bounced over the concrete border of what had once been a flower bed.

He had to rein in his rage, not succumb to it as his father had always done, for if he didn't remain in control of himself, Regina was as good as dead. He tried to place the emergency 911 call again. Tried to hold fast to his reason. He must not descend to the level of the walking filth through whose eyes he had seen the bound wrists and frightened eyes of his child.

* * *

The surge of rage pouring back across the telepathic wire excited Vassago, pumped up his own hatred, and convinced him that he must not wait until both the woman and the child were within his grasp. Even the prospect of the single crucifixion brought him such a richness of loathing and revulsion that he knew his artistic concept was of sufficient power. Once realized through the flesh of the gray-eyed girl, his art would reopen the doors of Hell to him.

He had to stop the Honda at the entrance to the service road, which appeared to be blocked by a padlocked gate. He had broken the massive padlock long ago. It only hung through the hasp with the appearance of effectiveness. He got out of the car, opened the gate, drove through, got out again and closed it.

Behind the wheel once more, he decided not to leave the Honda in the underground garage or go to the museum of the dead through the catacombs. No time. God's slow but persistent paladins were closing in on him. He had so much to do, so much, in so few precious minutes. It wasn't fair. He needed time. Every artist needed *time*. To save a few minutes, he was going to have to drive along the wide pedestrian walkways, between the rotting and empty pavilions, and park in front of the funhouse, take the girl across the dry lagoon and in by way of the gondola doors, through the tunnel with the chain-drive track still in the concrete floor and down into Hell by that more direct route.

* * *

While Hatch was on the phone with the sheriff's department, Lindsey drove into the parking lot. The tall lamp poles shed no light. Vistas of empty blacktop faded away in every direction. Straight ahead a few hundred yards stood the once glittery but now dark and decaying castle through which the paying customers had entered Fantasy World. She saw no sign of Jeremy Nyebern's car, and not enough dust on the acres of unprotected, windswept

321

pavement to track him by his tire prints.

She drove as close to the castle as she could get, halted by a long row of ticket booths and crowd-control stanchions of poured concrete. They looked like massive barricades erected on a heavily defended beach to prevent enemy tanks from being put ashore.

When Hatch slammed down the handset, Lindsey was not sure what to make of his end of the conversation, which had alternated between pleading and angry insistence. She didn't know whether the cops were coming or not, but her sense of urgency was so great, she didn't want to take time to ask him about it. She just wanted to move, move. She threw the car into park the moment it braked to a full stop, didn't even bother to switch off the engine or the headlights. She liked the headlights, a little something against the cloying night. She flung open her door, ready to go in on foot. But he shook his head, no, and picked up his Browning from the floor at his feet.

'What?' she demanded.

'He went in by car somehow, somewhere. I think I'll find the creep quicker if we stay on his trail, go in the way he went in, let myself open to this bond between us. Besides, the place is so damned huge, we'll get around it faster in a car.'

She got behind the wheel again, popped the Mitsubishi into gear, and said, '*Where?*'

He hesitated only a second, perhaps a fraction of a second, but it seemed that any number of small helpless girls could have been slaughtered in that interlude before he said, 'Left, go left, along the fence.'

·2·

Vassago parked the car by the lagoon, cut the engine, got out, and went around to the girl's side. Opening her door, he said, 'Here we are, angel. An amusement park, just like I promised you. Isn't it fun? Aren't you amused?'

He swung her around on her seat to bring her legs out of the car. He took his switchblade from his jacket pocket, snapped the well-honed knife out of the handle, and showed it to her.

Even with the thinnest crescent moon, and although her eyes were not as sensitive as his, she saw the blade. He saw her see

322

it, and he was thrilled by the quickening of terror in her face and eyes.

'I'm going to free your legs so you can walk,' he told her, turning the blade slowly, slowly, so a quicksilver glimmer trickled liquidly along the cutting edge. 'If you're stupid enough to kick me, if you think you can catch my head maybe and knock me silly long enough to get away, then *you're* silly, angel. It won't work, and then I'll have to cut you to teach you a lesson. Do you hear me, precious? Do you understand?'

She emitted a muffled sound through the wadded scarf in her mouth, and the tone of it was an acknowledgement of his power.

'Good,' he said. 'Good girl. So wise. You'll make a fine Jesus, won't you? A really fine little Jesus.'

He cut the cords binding her ankles, then helped her out of the car. She was unsteady, probably because her muscles had cramped during the trip, but he did not intend to let her dawdle. Seizing her by one arm, leaving her wrists bound in front of her and the gag in place, he pulled her around the front of the car to the retaining wall of the funhouse lagoon.

★ ★ ★

The retaining wall was two feet high on the outside, twice that on the inside where the water once had been. He helped Regina over it, onto the dry concrete floor of the broad lagoon. She hated to let him touch her, even though he still wore gloves, because she could feel his coldness through the gloves, or thought she could, his coldness and damp skin, which made her want to scream. She knew already that she couldn't scream, not with the gag filling her mouth. If she tried to scream she only choked on it and had trouble breathing, so she had to let him help her over the wall. Even when he didn't touch her bare hand with his gloved one, even when he gripped her arm and there was also her sweater between them, the contact made her belly quiver so badly that she thought she was going to vomit, but she fought that urge because, with the gag in her mouth, she would choke to death on her own regurgitation.

Through ten years of adversity, Regina had developed lots of tricks to get her through bad times. There was the think-of-something-worse trick, where she endured by imagining what more terrible circumstances might befall her than those in which she actually found herself. Like thinking of eating dead mice dipped in chocolate when she felt sorry for herself about having to eat lime Jell-O with peaches. Like thinking about being blind on top of her other disabilities. After the awful shock of being rejected during her first trial adoption with the Dotterfields, she had often spent hours with her eyes closed to show herself what she *might* have suffered if her eyes had been as faulty as her right arm. But the think-of-something-worse trick wasn't working now because she couldn't think of anything worse than being where she was, with this stranger dressed all in black and wearing sunglasses at night, calling her 'baby' and 'precious.' None of her other tricks were working, either.

As he pulled her impatiently across the lagoon, she dragged her right leg as if she could not move fast. She needed to slow him down to gain time to think, to find some new trick.

But she was just a kid, and tricks didn't come that easy, not even to a smart kid like her, not even to a kid who had spent ten years devising so many clever tricks to make everyone think that she could take care of herself, that she was tough, that she would never cry. But her trick bag was finally empty, and she was more afraid than she had ever been.

He dragged her past big boats like the gondolas in Venice of which she had seen pictures, but these had dragon prows from Viking ships. With the stranger pulling impatiently on her arm, she limped past a fearful snarling serpent's head bigger than she was.

Dead leaves and moldering papers had blown down into the empty pool. In the nocturnal breeze, which occasionally gusted heartily, that trash eddied around them with the hiss-splash of a ghost sea.

'Come on, precious one,' he said in his honey-smooth but unkind voice, 'I want you to walk to your Golgotha just as He did. Don't you think that's fitting? Is that so much to ask? Hmmm? I'm not also insisting that you carry your own cross, am I? What do you say, precious, will you *move your ass?*'

She was scared, with no fine tricks left to hide the fact, no tricks left to hold back her tears, either. She began to shake and cry, and her right leg grew weak for real, so she could hardly remain standing let alone move as fast as he demanded.

324

In the past, she would have turned to God at a moment like this, would have talked to Him, talked and talked, because no one had talked to God more often or more bluntly than she had done from the time she was just little. But she had been talking to God in the car, and she had not heard Him listening. Over the years, all their conversations had been one-sided, yes, but she had always heard Him listening, at least, a hint of His great slow steady breathing. But now she knew He couldn't be listening because if He was there, hearing how desperate she was, He would not have failed to answer her this time. He was gone, and she didn't know where, and she was alone as she had never been.

When she was so overcome by tears and weakness that she could not walk at all, the stranger scooped her up. He was very strong. She was unable to resist, but she didn't hold onto him, either. She just curled her arms against her chest, made small fists of her hands, and pulled away within herself.

'Let me carry my little Jesus,' he said, 'my sweet little lamb, it will be my privilege to carry you.' There was no warmth in his voice in spite of the way he was talking. Only hatred and scorn. She knew that tone, had heard it before. No matter how hard you tried to fit in and be everybody's friend, some kids hated you if you were too different, and in their voices you heard this same thing, and shrank from it.

He carried her through the open, broken, rotting doors into a darkness that made her feel so small.

* * *

Lindsey didn't even bother getting out of the car to see if the gate could be opened. When Hatch pointed the way, she jammed the accelerator to the floor. The car bucked, shot forward. They crashed onto the grounds of the park, demolishing the gate and sustaining more damage to their already battered car, including one shattered headlight.

At Hatch's direction, she followed a service loop around half the park. On the left was a high fence covered with the gnarled and bristling remnants of a vine that once might have concealed the chainlink entirely but had died when the irrigation system had been shut off. On the right were the backs of rides that had been too permanently constructed to be dismantled easily. There were also buildings fronted by fantastic facades held up by angled supports that could be seen from behind.

Leaving the service road, they drove between two structures and onto what had once been a winding promenade along which crowds had moved throughout the park. The largest Ferris wheel she had ever seen, savaged by wind and sun and years of neglect, rose in the night like the bones of a leviathan picked clean by unknown carrion-eaters.

A car was parked beside what appeared to be a drained pool in front of an immense structure.

'The funhouse,' Hatch said, for he had seen it before through other eyes.

It had a roof with multiple peaks like a three-ring circus tent, and disintegrating stucco walls. She could view only one narrow aspect of the structure at a time, as the headlight swept across it, but she did not like any part of what she saw. She was not by nature a superstitious person – although she was fast becoming one in response to recent experience – but she sensed an aura of death around the funhouse as surely as she could have felt cold air rising off a block of ice.

She parked behind the other car. A Honda. Its occupants had departed in such a hurry that both front doors were open, and the interior lights were on.

Snatching up her Browning and a flashlight, she got out of the Mitsubishi and ran to the Honda, looked inside. No sign of Regina.

She had discovered there was a point at which fear could grow no greater. Every nerve was raw. The brain could not process more input, so it merely sustained the peak of terror once achieved. Each new shock, each new terrible thought did not add to the burden of fear because the brain just dumped old data to make way for the new. She could hardly remember anything of what had happened at the house, or the surreal drive to the park; most of it was gone for now, only a few scraps of memory remaining, leaving her focused on the immediate moment.

On the ground at her feet, visible in the spill of light from the open car door and then in her flashlight beam, was a four-foot length of sturdy cord. She picked it up and saw that it had once been tied in a loop and later cut at the knot.

Hatch took the cord out of her hand. 'It was around Regina's ankles. He wanted her to walk.'

326

'Where are they now?'

He pointed with his flashlight across the drained lagoon, past the three large gray canted gondolas with prodigious mastheads, to a pair of wooden doors in the base of the funhouse. One sagged on broken hinges, and the other was open wide. The flashlight was a four-battery model, just strong enough to cast some dim light on those far doors but not to penetrate the terrible darkness beyond.

Lindsey took off around the car and scrambled over the lagoon wall. Though Hatch called out, 'Lindsey, wait,' she could not delay another moment – and how could he? – with the thought of Regina in the hands of Nyebern's resurrected, psychotic son.

As Lindsey crossed the lagoon, fear for Regina still far outweighed any concern she might have for her own safety. However, realizing that she, herself, must survive if the girl were to have any chance at all, she swept the flashlight beam side to side, side to side, wary of an attack from behind one of the huge gondolas.

Old leaves and paper trash danced in the wind, for the most part waltzing across the floor of the dry lagoon, but sometimes spinning up in columns and churning to a faster beat. Nothing else moved.

Hatch caught up with her by the time she reached the funhouse entrance. He had delayed only to use the cord she had found to bind his flashlight to the back of the crucifix. Now he could carry both in one hand, pointing the head of Christ at anything upon which he directed the light. That left his right hand free for the Browning 9mm. He had left the Mossberg behind. If he had tied the flashlight to the 12-gauge, he could have brought both the handgun and the shotgun. Evidently he felt that the crucifix was a better weapon than the Mossberg.

She didn't know why he had taken the icon from the wall of Regina's room. She didn't think he knew, either. They were wading hip deep in the big muddy river of the unknown, and in addition to the cross, she would have welcomed a necklace of garlic, a vial of holy water, a few silver bullets, and anything else that might have helped.

As an artist, she had always known that the world of the five senses, solid and secure, was not the *whole* of existence, and she had incorporated that understanding into her work. Now she was merely incorporating it into the rest of her life, surprised that she had not done so a long time ago.

With both flashlights carving through the darkness in front of them, they entered the funhouse.

*　*　*

All of Regina's tricks for coping were not exhausted, after all. She invented one more.

She found a room deep inside her mind, where she could go and close the door and be safe, a place only she knew about, in which she could never be found. It was a pretty room with peach-colored walls, soft lighting, and a bed covered with painted flowers. Once she had entered, the door could only be opened again from her side. There were no windows. Once she was in that most secret of all retreats, it didn't matter what was done to the other her, the physical Regina in the hateful world outside. The *real* Regina was safe in her hideaway, beyond fear and pain, beyond tears and doubt and sadness. She could hear nothing beyond the room, most especially not the wickedly soft voice of the man in black. She could see nothing beyond the room, only the peach walls and her painted bed and soft light, never darkness. Nothing beyond the room could really touch her, certainly not his pale quick hands which had recently shed their gloves.

Most important, the only smell in her sanctuary was the scent of roses like those painted on the bed, a clean sweet fragrance. Never the stench of dead things. Never the awful choking odor of decomposition that could bring a sour gushing into the back of your throat and nearly strangle you when your mouth was full of crushed, saliva-damp scarf. Nothing like that, no, never, not in her secret room, her blessed room, her deep and sacred, safe and solitary haven.

*　*　*

Something had happened to the girl. The singular vitality that had made her so appealing was gone.

When he put her on the floor of Hell, with her back against the base of the towering Lucifer, he thought she'd passed out. But that wasn't it. For one thing, when he crouched in front of her and put his hand against her chest, he felt her heart leaping like a rabbit whose hindquarters were already in the jaws of the fox. No one could possibly be unconscious with a thundering heartbeat like that.

Besides, her eyes were open. They were staring blindly, as if she could find nothing upon which to fix her gaze. Of course, she could not see him in the dark as he could see her, couldn't see anything else for that matter, but that wasn't the reason she was staring through him. When he flicked the eyelash over her right eye with his fingertip, she did not flinch, did not even blink. Tears were drying on her cheeks, but no new tears welled up.

Catatonic. The little bitch had blanked out on him, closed her mind down, become a vegetable. That didn't suit his purposes at all. The value of the offering was in the vitality of the subject. Art was about energy, vibrancy, pain, and terror. What statement could he make with his little gray-eyed Christ if she could not experience and express her agony?

He was so angry with her, just so spitting angry, that he didn't want to play with her any more. Keeping one hand on her chest, above her rabbity heart, he took his switchblade from his jacket pocket and popped it open.

Control.

He would have opened her then, and had the intense pleasure of feeling her heart go still in his grip, except that he was a Master of the Game who knew the meaning and value of control. He could deny himself such transitory thrills in the pursuit of more meaningful and enduring rewards. He hesitated only a moment before putting the knife away.

He was better than that.

His lapse surprised him.

Perhaps she would come out of her trance by the time he was ready to incorporate her into his collection. If not, then he felt sure that the first driven nail would bring her to her senses and transform her into the radiant work of art that he knew she had the potential to be.

He turned from her to the tools that were piled at the point where the arc of his collection currently ended. He possessed hammers and screwdrivers, wrenches and pliers, saws and a miter box, a battery-powered drill with an array of bits, screws and nails, rope and wire, brackets of all kinds, and everything else a handyman might need, all of it purchased at Sears when he had realized that properly arranging and displaying each piece in his collection would require the construction of some clever supports and, in a couple of cases, thematic backdrops. His chosen medium was not as easy to work with as oil paints or watercolors or clay or sculptor's granite, for gravity tended to quickly distort each effect that he achieved.

He knew he was short on time, that on his heels were those who did not understand his art and would make the amusement park impossible for him by morning. But that would not matter if he made one more addition to the collection that rounded it out and earned him the approbation he sought.

Haste, then.

The first thing to do, before hauling the girl to her feet and bracing her in a standing position, was to see if the material that composed the segmented, reptilian belly and chest of the funhouse Lucifer would take a nail. It seemed to be a hard rubber, perhaps soft plastic. Depending on the thickness, brittleness, and resiliency of the material, a nail would either drive into it as smoothly as into wood, bounce off, or bend. If the fake devil's hide proved too resistant, he'd have to use the battery-powered drill instead of the hammer, two-inch screws instead of nails, but it shouldn't detract from the artistic integrity of the piece to lend a modern touch to the reenactment of this ancient ritual.

He hefted the hammer. He placed the nail. The first blow drove it a quarter of the way into Lucifer's abdomen. The second blow slammed it halfway home.

So nails would work just fine.

He looked down at the girl, who still sat on the floor with her back against the base of the statue. She had not reacted to either of the hammer blows.

He was disappointed but not yet despairing.

Before lifting her into place, he quickly collected everything he would need. A couple of two-by-fours to serve as braces until the acquisition was firmly fixed in place. Two nails. Plus one longer and more wickedly pointed number that could fairly be called a spike. The hammer, of course. Hurry. Smaller nails, barely more than tacks, a score of which could be placed just-so in her brow to represent the crown of thorns. The switchblade, with which to re-create the spear wound attributed to the taunting Centurion. Anything else? Think. Quickly now. He had no vinegar or sponge to soak it in, therefore could not offer that traditional drink to the dying lips, but he didn't think the absence of that detail would in

330

any way detract from the composition.

He was ready.

* * *

Hatch and Lindsey were deep in the gondola tunnel, proceeding as fast as they dared, but slowed by the need to shine flashlights into the deepest reaches of each niche and room-size display area that opened off the flanking walls. The moving beams caused black shadows to fly and dance off concrete stalactites and stalagmites and other manmade rock formations, but all of those dangerous spaces were empty.

Two solid thuds, like hammer blows, echoed to them from farther in the funhouse, one immediately after the other. Then silence.

'He's ahead of us somewhere,' Lindsey whispered, 'not real close. We can move faster.'

Hatch agreed.

They proceeded along the tunnel without scanning all the deep recesses, which once had held clockwork monsters. Along the way, the bond between Hatch and Jeremy Nyebern was established again. He sensed the madman's excitement, an obscene and palpitating need. He received, as well, disconnected images: nails, a spike, a hammer, two lengths of two-by-four, a scattering of tacks, the slender steel blade of a knife popping out of its spring-loaded handle . . .

His anger escalating with his fear, determined not to let the disorienting visions impede his advance, he reached the end of the horizontal tunnel and stumbled a few steps down the incline before he realized that the angle of the floor had changed radically under his feet.

The first of the odor hit him. Drifting upward on a natural draft. He gagged, heard Lindsey do the same, then tightened his throat and swallowed hard.

He knew what lay below. At least some of it. Glimpses of the collection had been among the visions that had pounded him when he had been in the car on the highway. If he didn't get an iron grip on himself and stifle his repulsion now, he would never make it all the way into the depths of this hellhole, and he had to go there in order to save Regina.

Apparently Lindsey understood, for she found the will to

331

repress her retching, and she followed him down the steep slope.

★ ★ ★

The first thing to attract Vassago's attention was the glow of light high up toward one end of the cavern, far back in the tunnel that led to the spillway. The rapid rate at which the light grew brighter convinced him that he would not have time to add the girl to his collection before the intruders were upon him.

He knew who they were. He had seen them in visions as they evidently had seen him. Lindsey and her husband had followed him all the way from Laguna Niguel. He was just beginning to recognize that more forces were at work in this affair than had appeared to be the case at first.

He considered letting them descend the spillway into Hell, slipping behind them, killing the man, disabling the woman, and then proceeding with a *dual* crucifixion. But there was something about the husband that unsettled him. He couldn't put his finger on it.

But he realized now that, in spite of his bravado, he had been avoiding a confrontation with the husband. In their house earlier in the night, when the element of surprise had still been his, he should have circled behind the husband and disposed of him first, before going after either Regina or Lindsey. Had he done so, he might have been able to acquire both woman and child at that time. By now he might have been happily engrossed in their mutilation.

Far above, the pearly glow of light had resolved into a pair of flashlight beams at the brink of the spillway. After a brief hesitation, they started down. Because he had put his sunglasses in his shirt pocket, Vassago was forced to squint at the slashing swords of light.

As before, he decided not to move against the man, choosing instead to retreat with the child. This time, however, he wondered at his prudence.

A Master of the Game, he thought, must exhibit iron control and choose the right moments to prove his power and superiority.

True. But this time the thought struck him as spineless justification for avoiding confrontation.

Nonsense. He was afraid of nothing in this world.

The flashlights were still a considerable distance away, focused

332

on the floor of the spillway, not yet to the midpoint of the long incline. He could hear their footsteps, which grew louder and developed an echo as the pair advanced into the huge chamber.

He seized the catatonic girl, lifted her as if she weighed no more than a pillow, slung her over his shoulder, and moved soundlessly across the floor of Hell toward those rock formations where he knew a door to a service room was hidden.

*   *   *

'Oh, my God.'

'Don't look,' he told Lindsey as he swept the beam of his flashlight across the macabre collection. 'Don't look, Jesus, cover my back, make sure he's not coming around on us.'

Gratefully, she did as he said, turning away from the array of posed cadavers in various stages of decomposition. She was certain that her sleep, even if she lived to be a hundred, would be haunted every night by those forms and faces. But who was she kidding – she would never make a hundred. She was beginning to think she wouldn't even make it through the night.

The very idea of breathing *that* air, reeking and impure, through her mouth was almost enough to make her violently ill. She did it anyway because it minimized the stink.

The darkness was so deep. The flashlight seemed barely able to penetrate. It was like syrup, flowing back into the brief channel that the beam stirred through it.

She could hear Hatch moving along the collection of bodies, and she knew what he had to be doing – taking a quick look at each of them, just to be sure that Jeremy Nyebern was not posed among them, one living monstrosity among those consumed by rot, waiting to spring at them the moment they passed him.

Where was Regina?

Ceaselessly, Lindsey swept her flashlight back and forth, back and forth, in a wide arc, never giving the murderous bastard a chance to sneak up on her before she brought the beam around again. But, oh, he was fast. She had seen how fast. Flying down the hallway into Regina's room, slamming the door behind him, fast as if he'd flown, had wings, bat wings. And agile. Down the trumpet-vine trellis with the girl over his shoulder, unfazed by the fall, up and off into the night with her.

333

Where was Regina?

She heard Hatch moving away, and she knew where he was going, not just following the line of bodies but circling the towering figure of Satan, to be sure Jeremy Nyebern wasn't on the other side of it. He was just doing what he had to do. She knew that, but she didn't like it anyway, not one little bit, because now she was alone with all of those dead people behind her. Some of them were withered and would make papery sounds if somehow they became animated and edged toward her, while others were in more horrendous stages of decomposition and sure to reveal their approach with thick, wet sounds . . . And what crazy thoughts were these? They were all *dead*. Nothing to fear from them. The dead stayed dead. Except they didn't always, did they? No, not in her own personal experience, they didn't. But she kept sweeping her light back and forth, back and forth, resisting the urge to turn around and shine it on the festering cadavers behind her. She knew she should mourn them rather than fear them, be angry for the abuse and loss of dignity that they had suffered, but she only had room at the moment for fear. And now she heard Hatch coming closer, around the other side of the statue, completing his circumnavigation, thank God. But in the next breath, horribly metallic as it passed through her mouth, she wondered if it was Hatch or one of the bodies moving. Or Jeremy. She swung around, looking past the row of corpses rather than at them, and her light showed her that it was, indeed, Hatch coming back.

WHERE WAS REGINA?

As if in answer, a distinctive creak sliced through the heavy air. Doors the world over made that identical sound when their hinges were corroded and unoiled.

She and Hatch swung their flashlights in the same direction. The overlapping terminuses of their beams showed they had both judged the origin of the sound to have come from a rock formation along the far shore of what would have been, with water, a lake larger than the lagoon outside.

She was moving before she realized it. Hatch whispered her name in an urgent tone that meant *move aside, let me, I'll go first.* But she could no more have held back than she could have turned coward and retreated up the spillway. Her Regina had been among the dead, perhaps spared the direct sight of them because of her strange keeper's aversion to light, but among them nevertheless and surely aware of them. Lindsey could not *bear* the thought of that innocent child held in this slaughterhouse one minute longer. Lindsey's own safety didn't matter, only Regina's.

As she reached the rocks and plunged in among them, stabbing here with her light, then there, then over there, shadows leaping, she heard the wail of distant sirens. Sheriff's men. Hatch's phone call had been taken seriously. But Regina was in the hands of Death. If the girl was still alive, she would not last as long as it would take the cops to find the funhouse and get down to the lair of Lucifer. So Lindsey pressed deeper into the rocks, the Browning in one hand, flashlight in the other, turning corners recklessly, taking chances, with Hatch close behind her.

She came upon the door abruptly. Metal, streaked with rust, operated by a push-bar rather than a knob. Ajar.

She shoved it open and went through without even the finesse that she should have learned from a lifetime of police movies and television shows. She exploded across the threshold as might a mother lion in pursuit of the predator that had dared to drag off her cub. Stupid, she knew that it was stupid, that she could get herself killed, but mother lions in a fever of matriarchal aggression were not notably creatures of reason. She was operating on instinct now, and instinct told her that they had the bastard on the run, had to keep him running to prevent him from dealing with the girl as he wanted, and should press him harder and harder until they had him in a corner.

Beyond the door in the rocks, behind the walls of Hell, was a twenty-foot-wide area that had once been crowded with machinery. It was now littered with the bolts and steel plates on which those machines had been mounted. Elaborate scaffolding, festooned with spider webs, rose forty or fifty feet; it provided access to other doors and crawlspaces and panels through which the complex lighting and effects equipment – cold-steam generators, lasers – had been serviced. That stuff was gone now, stripped out and carted away.

How long did he need to cut the girl open, seize her beating heart, and take his satisfaction from her death? One minute? Two? Perhaps no more than that. To keep her safe, they had to breathe down his goddamned neck.

Lindsey swept her flashlight beam across that spider-infested conglomeration of steel pipes and elbow joints and tread plates.

She quickly decided their quarry had not ascended to any hiding place above.

Hatch was at her side and slightly behind her, staying close. They were breathing hard, not because they had exerted themselves, but because their chests were tight with fear, constricting their lungs.

Turning left, Lindsey moved straight toward a dark opening in the concrete-block wall on the far side of that twenty-foot-wide chamber. She was drawn to it because it appeared to have been boarded over at one time, not solidly but with enough planks to prevent anyone entering the forbidden space beyond without effort. Some of the nails still prickled the block walls on both sides of the opening, but all of the planks had been torn away and shoved to one side on the floor.

Although Hatch whispered her name, warning her to hold back, she stepped straight to the brink of that room, shone her light into it, and discovered it was not a room at all but an elevator shaft. The doors, cab, cables, and mechanism had been salvaged, leaving a hole in the building as sure as an extracted tooth left a hole in the jaw.

She pointed her light up. The shaft rose three stories, having once conveyed mechanics and other repairmen to the top of the funhouse. She swung the beam slowly down the concrete wall from above, noticing the iron rungs of the service ladder.

Hatch stepped in beside her as the light found its way to the bottom of the shaft, just two floors below, where it revealed some litter, a Styrofoam ice chest, several empty root beer cans, and a plastic garbage bag nearly full of trash, all arranged around a stained and battered mattress.

On the mattress, huddled in a corner of the shaft, was Jeremy Nyebern. Regina was in his lap, held against his chest, so she could shield him against gunfire. He was holding a pistol, and he squeezed off two shots even as Lindsey spotted him down there.

The first slug missed both her and Hatch, but the second round tore through her shoulder. She was knocked against the door frame. On the rebound, she bent forward involuntarily, lost her balance, and fell into the shaft, following her flashlight, which she had already dropped.

Going down, she didn't believe it was happening. Even when she hit bottom, landing on her left side, the whole thing seemed unreal, maybe because she was still too numb from the impact of the bullet to feel the damage it had done, and maybe because she fell mostly on the mattress, at the far end of it from Nyebern, knocking out what wind the slug had left in her but breaking no bones.

Her flashlight had also landed on the mattress, unharmed. It lit one gray wall.

As if in a dream, and though unable to get her breath quite yet, Lindsey brought her right hand slowly around to point her gun at him. But she had no gun. The Browning had spun from her grip in the fall.

During Lindsey's drop, Nyebern must have tracked her with his own weapon, for she was looking into it. The barrel was impossibly long, measuring exactly one eternity from firing chamber to muzzle.

Beyond the gun she saw Regina's face, which was as slack as her gray eyes were empty, and beyond that beloved countenance was the hateful one, pale as milk. His eyes, unshielded by glasses, were fierce and strange. She could see them even though the glow of the flashlight forced him to squint. Meeting his gaze she felt that she was face to face with something alien that was only passing as human, and not well.

Oh, wow, surreal, she thought, and knew that she was on the verge of passing out.

She hoped to faint before he squeezed the trigger. Though it didn't matter, really. She was so close to the gun that she wouldn't live to hear the shot that blew her face off.

* * *

Hatch's horror, as he watched Lindsey fall into the shaft, was exceeded by his surprise at what he did next.

When he saw Jeremy track her with the pistol until she hit the mattress, the muzzle three feet from her face, Hatch tossed his own Browning away, onto the pile of planks that once boarded off the shaft. He figured he wouldn't be able to get off a clear shot with Regina in the way. And he knew that no gun would properly dispatch the thing that Jeremy had become. He had no time to wonder at *that* curious thought, for as soon as he pitched away the Browning, he shifted the crucifix-flashlight from his left hand to his right, and leaped into the elevator shaft without any expectation that he was about to do so.

After that, everything got weird.

It seemed to him that he didn't crash down the shaft as he should have done, but glided in slow motion, as if he were only slightly heavier than air, taking as much as half a minute to reach bottom.

Perhaps his sense of time had merely been distorted by the profundity of his terror.

Jeremy saw him coming, shifted the pistol from Lindsey to Hatch, and fired all eight remaining rounds. Hatch was certain that he was hit at least three or four times, though he sustained no wounds. It seemed impossible that the killer could miss so often in such a confined space.

Perhaps the sloppy marksmanship was attributable to the gunman's panic and to the fact that Hatch was a moving target.

While he was still floating down like dandelion fluff, he experienced a reconnection of the peculiar bond between him and Nyebern, and for a moment he saw himself descending from the young killer's point of view. What he glimpsed, however, was not only himself but the image of someone – or something – superimposed over him, as if he shared his body with another entity. He thought he saw white wings folded close against his sides. Under his own face was that of a stranger – the visage of a warrior if ever there had been one, yet not a face that frightened him.

Perhaps by then Nyebern was hallucinating, and what Hatch was receiving from him was not actually what he saw but only what he imagined that he saw. Perhaps.

Then Hatch was gazing down from his own eyes again, still in that slow glide, and he was sure that he saw something superimposed over Jeremy Nyebern, too, a form and face that were part reptilian and part insectile.

Perhaps it was a trick of light, the confusion of shadows and conflicting flashlight beams.

He could not explain away their final exchange, however, and he dwelt upon it often in the days that followed.

'Who are you?' Nyebern asked as Hatch landed catlike in spite of a thirty-foot descent.

'Uriel,' Hatch replied, though that was not a name that he had heard before.

338

'I am Vassago,' Nyebern said.

'I know,' Hatch said, though he was hearing that name for the first time, as well.

'Only you can send me back.'

'And when you are sent back by such as me,' Hatch said, wondering where the words came from, 'it is not as a prince. You'll be a slave below, just like the heartless and stupid boy with whom you hitched a ride.'

Nyebern was afraid. It was the first time he had shown any capacity for fear. 'And I thought *I* was the spider.'

With strength, agility, and economy of motion that Hatch had not known he possessed, he grabbed Regina's belt in his left hand, pulled her away from Jeremy Nyebern, set her aside out of harm's way, and brought the crucifix down like a club upon the madman's head. The lens of the attached flashlight shattered, and the casing burst open, spilling batteries. He chopped the crucifix hard against the killer's skull a second time, and with the third blow he sent Nyebern to a grave that had been twice earned.

The anger Hatch felt was righteous anger. When he dropped the crucifix, when it was all over, he felt no guilt or shame. He was nothing at all like his father.

He had a strange awareness of a power leaving him, a presence he had not realized was there. He sensed a mission accomplished, balance restored. All things were now in their rightful places.

Regina was unresponsive when he spoke to her. Physically she seemed unharmed. Hatch was not worried about her, for somehow he knew that none of them would suffer unduly for having been caught up in . . . whatever they had been caught up in.

Lindsey was unconscious and bleeding. He examined her wound and felt it was not too serious.

Voices rose two floors above. They were calling his name. The authorities had arrived. Late as always. Well, not always. Sometimes . . . one of them was there just when you needed him.

·3·

The apocryphal story of the three blind men examining the elephant is widely known. The first blind man feels only the elephant's trunk and thereafter confidently describes the beast as a great snakelike creature, similar to a python. The second blind

339

man feels only the elephant's ears and announces that it is a bird that can soar to great heights. The third blind man examines only the elephant's fringe-tipped, fly-chasing tail and 'sees' an animal that is curiously like a bottle brush.

So it is with any experience that human beings share. Each participant perceives it in a different way and takes from it a different lesson than do his or her compatriots.

* * *

In the years following the events at the abandoned amusement park, Jonas Nyebern lost interest in resuscitation medicine. Other men took over his work and did it well.

He sold at auction every piece of religious art in the two collections that he had not yet completed, and he put the money in savings instruments that would return the highest possible rate of interest.

Though he continued to practice cardiovascular surgery for a while, he no longer found any satisfaction in it. Eventually he retired young and looked for a new career in which to finish out the last decades of his life.

He stopped attending Mass. He no longer believed that evil was a force in itself, a real presence that walked the world. He had learned that humanity itself was a source of evil sufficient to explain everything that was wrong with the world. Obversely, he decided humanity was its own – and only – salvation.

He became a veterinarian. Every patient seemed deserving.

He never married again.

He was neither happy nor unhappy, and that suited him fine.

* * *

Regina remained within her inner room for a couple of days, and when she came out she was never quite the same. But then no one ever is quite the same for any length of time. Change is the only constant. It's called growing up.

She addressed them as Dad and Mom, because she wanted to, and because she meant it. Day by day, she gave them as much happiness as they gave her.

She never set off a chainreaction of destruction among their

340

antiques. She never embarrassed them by getting inappropriately sentimental, bursting into tears, and thereby activating the old snot faucet; she unfailingly produced tears and snot only when they were called for. She never mortified them by accidentally flipping an entire plate of food into the air at a restaurant and over the head of the President of the United States at the next table. She never accidentally set the house on fire, never farted in polite company, and never scared the bejesus out of smaller neighborhood children with her leg brace and curious right hand. Better still, she stopped worrying about doing all those things (and more), and in time she did not even recall the tremendous energies that she once had wasted upon such unlikely concerns.

She kept writing. She got better at it. When she was just fourteen, she won a national writing competition for teenagers. The prize was a rather nice watch and a check for five hundred dollars. She used some of the money for a subscription to *Publishers Weekly* and a complete set of the novels of William Makepeace Thackeray. She no longer had an interest in writing about intelligent pigs from outer space, largely because she was learning that more curious characters could be found all around her, many of them native Californians.

She no longer talked to God. It seemed childish to chatter at Him. Besides, she no longer needed His constant attention. For a while she had thought He had gone away or had never existed, but she had decided that was foolish. She was aware of Him all the time, winking at her from the flowers, serenading her in the song of a bird, smiling at her from the furry face of a kitten, touching her with a soft summer breeze. She found a line in a book that she thought was apt, from Dave Tyson Gentry: 'True friendship comes when silence between two people is comfortable.' Well, who was your best friend, if not God, and what did you really need to say to Him or He to you when you both already knew the most – and only – important thing, which was that you would always be there for each other.

* * *

Lindsey came through the events of those days less changed than she had expected. Her paintings improved somewhat, but not tremendously. She had never been dissatisfied with her work in the first place. She loved Hatch no less than ever, and could not possibly have loved him more.

One thing that made her cringe, which never had before, was hearing anyone say, 'The worst is behind us now.' She knew that the worst was never behind us. The worst came at the end. It *was* the end, the very fact of it. Nothing could be worse than that. But she had learned to live with the understanding that the worst was never behind her – and still find joy in the day at hand.

As for God – she didn't dwell on the issue. She raised Regina in the Catholic Church, attending Mass with her each week, for that was part of the promise she had made St Thomas's when they had arranged the adoption. But she didn't do it solely out of duty. She figured that the Church was good for Regina – and that Regina might be good for the Church, too. Any institution that counted Regina a member was going to discover itself changed by her at least as much as she was changed – and to its everlasting benefit. She had once said that prayers were never answered, that the living lived only to die, but she had progressed beyond that attitude. She would wait and see.

* * *

Hatch continued to deal successfully in antiques. Day by day his life went pretty much as he hoped it would. As before, he was an easy-going guy. He never got angry. But the difference was that he had no anger left in him to repress. The mellowness was genuine now.

From time to time, when the patterns of life seemed to have a grand meaning that just barely eluded him, and when he was therefore in a philosophical mood, he would go to his den and take two items from the locked drawer.

One was the heat-browned issue of *Arts American*.

The other was a slip of paper he had brought back from the library one day, after doing a bit of research. Two names were written on it, with an identifying line after each. 'Vassago – according to mythology, one of the nine crown princes of Hell.' Below that was the name he had once claimed was his own: 'Uriel – according to mythology, one of the archangels serving as a personal attendant to God.'

He stared at these things and considered them carefully, and always he reached no firm conclusions. Though he did decide, if you had to be dead for eighty minutes and come back with no memory of the Other Side, maybe it was because eighty minutes of that knowledge was more than just a glimpse of a tunnel with a light at the end, and therefore more than you could be expected to handle.

And if you had to bring something back with you from Beyond, and carry it within you until it had concluded its assignment on this side of the veil, an archangel wasn't too shabby.

The Vision

This book is for
Claire M. Smith
with love and gratitude

MONDAY,
DECEMBER 21

ONE

'Gloves of Blood.'

The woman raised her hands and stared at them, stared *through* them.

Her voice was soft but tense. 'Blood on his hands.' Her own hands were clean and pale.

Her husband leaned forward from the back seat of the patrol car. 'Mary?'

She didn't respond.

'Mary, can you hear me?'

'Yes.'

'Whose blood do you see?'

'I'm not sure.'

'The victim's blood?'

'No. In fact . . . it's his own.'

'The killer's?'

'Yes.'

'He has his own blood on his hands?'

'That's right,' she said.

'He's hurt himself?'

'But not badly.'

'How?'

'I don't know.'

'Try to get inside of him.'

'I am already.'

'Get deeper.'

'I'm not a mind reader.'

'I know that, darling. But you're the next best thing.'

The perspiration on Mary Bergen's face was like the ceramic glaze on the plaster countenance of an altar saint. Her smooth skin gleamed in the green light from the instrument panel. Her dark eyes also shone, but they were unfocused, blank.

Suddenly she leaned forward and shuddered.

In the driver's seat Chief of Police Harley Barnes shifted uneasily. He flexed his big hands on the steering wheel.

'He's sucking the wound,' she said. 'Sucking his own blood.'

After thirty years of police work, Barnes didn't expect to be surprised or frightened. Now, in a single evening, he had been surprised more than once and had felt his heartbeat accelerate with fear.

The tree-shrouded streets were as familiar to him as the contours of his own face. However, tonight, cloaked in a rainstorm, they seemed menacing. The tyres hissed on the slick roadway. The windshield wipers thumped, an eerie metronome.

The woman beside Barnes was distraught, but her appearance was less disturbing than the changes she had wrought inside the patrol car. The humid air became clearer when she entered her trance. He was certain he was not imagining that. The ordinary sounds of the storm and the car were overlaid with the soft humming of ghost frequencies. He sensed an indescribable power radiating from her. He was a practical man, not at all superstitious. But he could not deny what he felt so strongly.

She bent as far towards the dashboard as her seat belt would allow. She hugged herself and groaned as if she were having labour pains.

Max Bergen reached out from the rear seat, touched her.

She murmured and relaxed slightly.

His hand looked enormous on her slender shoulder. He was tall, angular, hard-muscled, hard-faced, forty years old, ten years older than his wife. His eyes were his most arresting feature; they were grey, cold, humourless.

Chief Barnes had never seen him smile. Clearly, Bergen harboured powerful and complex feelings for Mary, but he gave no indication that he felt anything but contempt for the rest of the world.

The woman said, 'Turn at the next corner.'

Barnes braked gently. 'Left or right?'

'Right,' she said.

Well-kept, thirty-year-old stucco houses and bungalows, most of them California-Spanish in style, lay on both sides of the street. Yellow lights glowed vaguely behind drapes that had been drawn against the chill of the damp December night. The road was much darker than the one they had left. Sodium vapour lamps stood only at the corners, and purple-black, rain-pooled shadows filled the long blocks between them.

After he made the turn, Barnes drove no faster than ten miles an hour. From the woman's attitude, he gathered that the chase would end nearby.

Mary sat up straight. Her voice was louder and clearer than it had been since she began to use her strange talent, her clairvoyance. 'I get an impression . . . of a . . . a fence. Yes . . . I see it now . . . he's cut his hand . . . on a fence.'

Max stroked her hair. 'And it's not a serious wound?'

'No . . . just a cut . . . his thumb . . . deep . . . but not disabling.' She raised one thin hand, forgot what she meant to do with it, let it flutter back into her lap.

'But if he's bleeding from a deep cut, won't he give up tonight?' Max asked.

'No,' she said.

'You're sure?'

'He'll go on.'

'The bastard's killed five woman so far,' Barnes said. 'Some of them fought like hell, scratched him and cut him and even tore out his hair. He doesn't give up easily.'

Ignoring the policeman, Max soothed his wife, caressed her face with one hand and prompted her with another question. 'What kind of fence do you see?'

'Chain-link,' she said. 'Sharp and unfinished at the top.'

'Is is high?'

'Five feet.'

'What does it surround?'

'A yard.'

'Storage yard?'

'No. Behind a house.'

'Can you see the house?'

'Yes.'

'What's it like?'

'It's a two-story.'

'Stucco?'

'Yes.'

'What about the roof?'

351

'Spanish tile.'

'Any unique features?'

'I can't quite see . . .'

'A verandah?'

'No.'

'A courtyard maybe?'

'No. But I see . . . a winding tile walkway.'

'Front or back?'

'Out front of the house.'

'Any trees?'

'Matched magnolias . . . on either side of the walk.'

'Anything else?'

'A few small palms . . . farther back.'

Harley Barnes squinted through the rain-dappled windshield. He was searching for a pair of magnolias.

Initially he had been sceptical. In fact, he'd been certain the Bergens were frauds. He played his role in the charade because the *mayor* was a believer. The mayor brought them to town and insisted the police cooperate with them.

Barnes had read about psychic detectives, of course, and most especially about that famous Dutch clairvoyant, Peter Hurkos. But using ESP to track down a psychopathic killer, to catch him in the act? He didn't put much faith in that.

Or do I? he wondered. This woman was so lovely, charming, earnest, so convincing that perhaps she'd made a believer of him. If she hasn't, he thought, why am I looking for magnolia trees?

She made a sound like an animal caught in a sawtoothed trap for a long time. Not a screech of agony, but a nearly inaudible mewl.

When an animal made that noise, it meant, 'This still hurts, but I'm resigned to it now.'

Many years ago, as a boy in Minnesota, Barnes had hunted and trapped. It was that same pitiful, stifled moan of the wounded prey that caused him to give up his sport.

Until tonight, he had never heard precisely the same sound issue from a human being. Apparently, as she used her talent to zero in on the killer, she suffered from contact with his deranged mind.

Barnes shivered.

'Mary,' her husband said. 'What's the matter?'

352

'I see him . . . at the back door of the house. His hand on the door . . . and blood . . . his blood on a white door frame. He's talking to himself.'

'What's he saying?'

'I don't . . .'

'Mary?'

'He's saying filthy things about the woman.'

'The woman in the house – the one he's after tonight?'

'Yes.'

'He knows her?'

'No. She's a stranger . . . random target. But he's been . . . watching her . . . watching her for several days . . . knows her habits and routines.'

With those last few words she slumped against the door. She took several deep breaths. She was forced to relax periodically to regroup her energies if she were to maintain the physic thread. For some clairvoyants, Barnes knew, the visions came without strain, virtually without effort; but apparently not for this one.

Phantom voices whispered and crackled, came and went in staccato bursts on the police radio.

The wind carried fine sheets of rain across the roadway.

The wettest rainy season in years, Barnes thought. Twenty years ago it would have seemed normal. But California had steadily become a drought state. This much rain was unnatural now. Like everything else that's happening tonight, he thought.

Waiting for Mary to speak, he slowed to less than five miles an hour.

Matched magnolia trees flanking a winding tile walk . . .

He found it taxing to see what lay in the headlights directly in front of him, and extremely difficult to discern the landscaping on either side. They might already have passed the magnolias.

Brief as it was, Mary Bergen's hesitation elicited Dan Goldman's first words in more than an hour. 'We haven't much time left, Mrs Bergen.'

Goldman was a reliable young officer, the chief's most trusted subordinate. He was sitting beside Max Bergen, behind Barnes, his eyes fixed on the woman.

Goldman believed in psychic powers. He was impressionable. And as Barnes could see in the rearview mirror, the events of the evening had left a haunted look on his broad, plain face.

'We don't have much time,' Goldman said again. 'If this madman's already at the woman's back door—'

Abruptly, Mary turned to him. Her voice was freighted with
concern. 'Don't get out of this car tonight – not until the man
is caught.'

'What do you mean?' Goldman asked.

'If you try to help capture him, you'll be hurt.'

'He'll kill me?'

She shuddered convulsively. New beads of sweat popped out at
her hairline.

Barnes felt perspiration trickle down his face, too.

She said to Goldman, 'He'll stab you . . . with the same knife
he's used on all the women . . . hurt you badly . . . but not kill
you.' Closing her eyes, speaking between clenched teeth, she said,
'*Stay in the car!*'

'Harley?' Goldman asked worriedly.

'It'll be all right,' Barnes assured him.

'You'd better listen to her,' Max told Goldman. 'Don't leave
the car.'

'If I need you,' Barnes told Goldman, 'you'll come with me.
No one will be hurt.' He was concerned that the woman was
undermining his authority. He glanced at her. 'We need a number
for the house you've described, a street address.'

'Don't press,' her husband said sharply. With everyone but
Mary he had a voice like two rough steel bars scraped against
each other. 'It won't do any good whatsoever to press her. It'll
only interfere.'

'It's okay, Max,' she said.

'But I've told them before,' he said.

She faced front once more. 'I see . . . the rear door of the house.
It's open.'

'Where's the man, the killer?' Max asked.

'He's standing in a dark room . . . small . . . the laundry
room . . . that's what it is . . . the laundry room behind the
kitchen.'

'What's he doing?'

'He's opening another door . . . to the kitchen . . . no one in
there . . . a dim light on over the gas range . . . a few dirty dishes
on the table . . . he's standing . . . just standing there and
listening . . . left hand in a fist to stop the thumb from

354

bleeding . . . listening . . . Benny Goodman music on a stereo in the living room . . .' Touching Barnes' arm, a new and urgent tone in her voice, she said, 'Just two blocks from here. On the right. The second house . . . no, the third from the corner.'

'You're positive?'

'For God's sake, *hurry*!'

Am I about to make a fool of myself? Barnes wondered. If I take her seriously and she's wrong, I'll be the punch line of bad jokes for the rest of my career.

Nevertheless, he switched on the siren and tramped the accelerator to the floor. The tyres spun on the roadway. With a squeal of rubber, the car surged forward.

Breathlessly she said, 'I still see . . . he's crossing the kitchen . . . moving slowly . . .'

If she's faking all this, Barnes thought, she's a hell of a good actress.

The Ford raced along the poorly lit street. Rain snapped against the windshield. They swept through a four-way stop, then towards another.

'Listening . . . listening between steps . . . cautious . . . nervous . . . taking the knife out of his overcoat pocket . . . smiling at the sharp edge of the blade . . . such a big knife . . .'

In the block she had specified they fishtailed to a stop at the kerb in front of the third house on the right: a pair of matched magnolias, a winding walk, a two-storey stucco with lights on downstairs.

'Goddamn,' Goldman said, more reverently than not. 'It fits her description perfectly.'

TWO

Barnes got out of the car as the siren moaned into silence.

The revolving red emergency lights cast frenetic shadows on the wet pavement. Another black-and-white had pulled in behind the first, adding its beacons to the cascade of bloody colour.

Several men had already climbed out of the second car. Two uniformed officers, Malone and Gonzales, hurried towards Barnes. Mayor Henderson, round and shiny in his black vinyl rain slicker, looked like a balloon bouncing along the street. Close behind him was whip-thin little Harry Oberlander, Henderson's most vocal critic on the city council.

The last man was Alan Tanner, Mary Tanner Bergen's brother. Ordinarily, he would have been in the first car with his sister; but he and Max had argued earlier and were keeping away from each other.

'Malone, Gonzales . . . split up,' Barnes said. 'Flank the house. Go around it and meet at the rear door. I'll take the front. Now move it!'

'What about me?' Goldman asked.

Barnes sighed. 'You better stay here.'

Goldman was relieved.

Taking the .357 Magnum from his holster, Barnes hurried up the tile walk. The name 'Harrington' was printed on the mailbox. As he rang the doorbell, the rain suddenly lost most of its power. The downpour became a drizzle.

Alerted by the sirens, she had watched his approach from the window. She answered the door at once.

'Mrs Harrington?'

'*Miss* Harrington. After the divorce, I took my maiden name.'

She was a petite blonde in her early forties. She had a lush figure, but she wasn't carrying any excess weight.

Apparently, her primary occupation was taking good care of herself. Although she wore jeans and a T-shirt and didn't appear to be going out for the evening, her hair looked as if it had been styled minutes ago; her false eyelashes and makeup were perfectly applied; and her nails were freshly painted the colour of orange sherbet.

'Are you alone?' Barnes asked.

Lasciviously, she said, 'Why do you ask?'

'This is police business, Miss Harrington.'

'What a shame.' She had a drink in one hand. He knew it wasn't her first of the night.

'Are you alone?' he asked again.

'I live by myself.'

'Is everything all right?'

'I don't like living by myself.'

'That's not what I meant. Are you all right? Is there any trouble here?'

She looked at the revolver that he held at his side. 'Should there be?'

Exasperated with her and with having to talk above the loud swing music that boomed behind her, he said, 'Maybe. We think your life's in danger.'

She laughed.

'I know it sounds melodramatic, but—'

'Who's after me?'

'The newspapers call him "The Slasher." '

She frowned, then instantly dropped the expression as if she had remembered that frowning caused wrinkles. 'You're kidding.'

'We have reason to believe you're his target tonight.'

'What reason?'

'A clairvoyant.'

'A what?'

Malone entered the living room behind her and switched off the stereo.

She turned, surprised.

Malone said, 'We found something, Chief.'

Barnes stepped into the house, uninvited. 'Yeah?'

'The back door was open.'

'Did you leave it open?' Barnes asked the woman.

'On a night like this?'

'Was it locked?'

'I don't know.'

'There's blood on the door frame,' Malone said. 'More of it on the door between the laundry room and the kitchen.'

'But he's gone?'

'Must have run when he heard the sirens.'

Sweating, aware of his too-rapid heartbeat, wondering how to fit clairvoyance and the other psychic phenomena into his previously uncomplicated view of life, Barnes followed the younger officer through the kitchen and laundry room. The woman stayed close beside him, asking questions that he didn't bother answering.

Hector Gonzales was waiting at the back door.

'There's an alleyway behind that chain-link fence,' Barnes told him. 'Get back there and search for our man, two blocks in each direction.'

The woman said, 'I'm bewildered.'

So am I, Barnes thought.

To Malone he said, 'Beat the shrubs around both sides of the house. And check out that line of bushes near the fence.'

'Right.'

'And both of you, keep your guns drawn.'

*　*　*

Waiting by the squad cars in front of the house, Harry Oberlander was baiting the mayor. He shook his head as if the very sight of Henderson amazed him. 'What a mayor you are,' he said with heavy sarcasm. 'Hiring a witch to do police work.'

Henderson responded like a weary giant spotting yet one more tiny challenger with delusions of grandeur. 'She's not a witch.'

'Don't you know there's no such thing as a witch?'

'Like I said, Councilman, she's not a witch.'

'She's a fake.'

'A clairvoyant.'

'Clairvoyant, shmairvoyant.'

'So clever with language.'

'It's just a fancier name for a witch.'

Dan Goldman watched Oberlander, as weary of the argument as the mayor was. There are no worse enemies, he thought, than two men who used to be best friends. He would have to separate them if Harry became dissatisfied with words and started to throw a few fast but largely ineffective punches at the mayor's well-padded belly. It had happened before.

'You know why I sold you my half of the furniture business?' Oberlander asked Henderson.

'You sold out because you didn't have any vision,' Henderson said smugly.

'Vision, smision. I sold out because I knew a superstitious fool like you would run it into the ground sooner or later.'

'The store's more profitable now than ever before,' Henderson said.

'Luck! Blind luck!'

Fortunately, before the first punch could be thrown, Harley Barnes came to the front door of the house and shouted, 'It's all right. Come on.'

'Now we'll see who's the fool,' Henderson said. 'They must have caught him.' He ran across the sidewalk and the slippery wet lawn with that unexpected grace peculiar to certain very fat men.

Oberlander scurried after him, an angry mouse snapping at the heels of a behemoth.

Suppressing a laugh, Goldman followed.

*   *   *

Alan Tanner sat behind the steering wheel in order to be in the front seat with his sister. When he saw Harley Barnes at the door of the house, he said, 'Did they get the killer, Mary?'

'I don't know,' she said. Her voice was hollow; she sounded drained.

'Wouldn't there have been a shot?'

'I don't know.'

'There would have been *some* commotion.'

'I guess so.'

From the rear seat Max said urgently, 'Mary, is it safe for Goldman?'

She sighed and shook her head and pressed her fingertips to her eyes. 'I really can't say. I've lost the thread. I don't see anything else.'

Max rolled down his window. The damp air carried his voice well. 'Hey, Goldman!'

The officer was halfway across the lawn. He stopped and looked back.

'Maybe you'd better stay here,' Max said.

'Harley wants me,' Goldman said.

'Remember what my wife told you.'

'It's all right,' Goldman said. 'Nothing's going to happen. They caught him.'

'Are you sure of that?' Max asked.

But Goldman had already turned and was headed for the house again.

Alan said, 'Mary?'

'Hmmmm?'

'Are you feeling well?'

'Well enough.'

'You don't sound good.'

'Just tired.'

'He presses you much too hard,' Alan told her solicitously. He didn't even glance back at Max. He spoke as if he and his sister were alone in the car. 'He doesn't realise how fragile you are.'

'I'm okay,' she said.

Alan wouldn't quit. 'He doesn't know how to prompt you, how to help you refine the visions. He doesn't have any finesse. He always presses too hard.'

You creepy little bastard, Max thought, staring hard at his brother-in-law.

For Mary's sake, he said nothing. She was easily upset when the two men in her life argued. She preferred to pretend that they were charmed by each other. And while she never entirely took Alan's side, she always blamed Max when the argument became particularly bitter.

To get his mind off Alan, he studied the house. A shaft of light thrust through the open door, silhouetted some of the dense lumps of shrubbery. 'Maybe we should lock the car doors,' he said.

Mary turned sideways in her seat and stared at him. 'Lock the doors?'

'For protection.'

'I don't understand.'

360

'For protection from what?' Alan asked.

'The cops are all up at the house, and none of us has a weapon.'

'You think we'll need one?'

'It's a possibility.'

'Are *you* getting psychic now?' Alan asked.

Max forced himself to smile. 'Nothing psychic about it, I'm afraid. Just good sense.' He locked his and Mary's doors, and when he saw that Alan wouldn't cooperate, he latched both doors on the driver's side.

'Feel safe now?' Alan asked.

Max watched the house.

★　★　★

Barnes, Henderson, and Oberlander crowded into the laundry room to examine the smears of blood that the killer had left behind.

Miss Harrington squeezed in beside the chief, determined not to miss any of the excitement. She appeared to be delighted to have been the madman's choice.

Dan Goldman preferred to remain in the kitchen. As Barnes explained how these few pieces of physical evidence matched the clairvoyant's visions, the mayor would begin to gloat. Harry Oberlander would be embarrassed, then outraged. The nasty bickering would quickly escalate into a loud and vicious exchange. Goldman had had enough of that.

Besides, the big kitchen deserved an appreciative inspection. It had been designed and furnished by someone who enjoyed cooking and who could afford the best.

Miss Harrington? Goldman wondered. She didn't seem to be a woman who would welcome the opportunity to pass several hours in front of a stove. No doubt, the cook had been her ex-husband.

Quite a lot of money had been spent to create a professional kitchen with a country home atmosphere. The floor was of Mexican tile with brown grouting. There were oak cabinets with porcelain hardware, white ceramic counter tops, two standard ovens and a microwave oven, two large refrigerator-freezers, two double sinks, an island cooking surface, a built-in appliance centre, and a dozen other machines, tools, and gadgets.

Goldman liked to cook, but he had to make do with a battered

361

gas range and the cheapest pots, pans, and utensils on the market.

His envious appraisal of the kitchen was interrupted when, from the corner of his eye, he saw a door opening beside and somewhat behind him, no more than a yard away. It had been ajar when he'd entered the room, but he hadn't thought anything of it. Now he turned and saw a man in a raincoat stepping out of a pantry that was lined with canned goods. The stranger's left hand was bloody, the thumb tucked into a tight fist.

She was right, Goldman thought. *Christ!*

In his raised right hand the killer held a butcher knife by its thick wooden handle.

Time ceased to have meaning for Goldman. Each second extended itself a hundredfold. Each moment expanded like a soap bubble, encapsulated him, separated him from the rest of the world where clocks maintained their proper pace.

In the distance Henderson and Oberlander were arguing again. It didn't seem possible that they were only one room away. They sounded extremely odd, as if they had been recorded at seventy-eight revolutions per minute and were being played back at forty-five.

The stranger stepped forward. Light slithered along the well-honed edge of the blade.

As if moving against incredible resistance, Goldman reached for the revolver at his hip.

The knife ripped into his chest. High and to the left. Too deep to contemplate.

Curiously he felt no pain, but the front of his shirt was suddenly soaked with blood.

Mary Bergen, he thought. How could you know. What are you?

He unsnapped his holster.

Too slow. Too damned slow!

Although he didn't realise that the blade had been wrenched loose from him, he watched with horror as the knife arched down again. The stranger jerked the weapon free, and Goldman collapsed against the wall, framed by a spray of his own blood.

There was still no pain, but his strength was draining out of him as if there was a tap in his ankle.

Can't fall down, he told himself. Don't dare fall down. Wouldn't have a chance.

But the killer was finished. He turned and ran towards the dining room.

Clutching his wounds with his weakening left hand, Goldman staggered after the man. By the time he reached the archway and leaned against it to catch his breath, the killer was nearly to the living room. Goldman had the gun out of his holster, but he found it too heavy to lift. To get Harley's attention, he fired into the floor. With that explosion time resumed its normal flow and pain finally smashed through his chest, and suddenly he found it difficult to breathe and his knees buckled and he went down.

★ ★ ★

Alan interrupted himself in the middle of a sentence. 'What was that?'

'A shot,' Max said.

Mary said, 'Something's happened to Goldman. I know it as sure as I'm sitting here.'

Someone rushed out of the house. His raincoat flapped and billowed like a cape.

'That's *him*,' Mary said.

When he saw the squad cars, the man stopped. Confused, he looked left and right, didn't seem to trust either route, and turned back towards the house.

Harley Barnes appeared at the open door. Even from where he sat, even through the dirty window and the shadows and the thin rain, Max could see the oversized revolver in the cop's hand. Obscenely, fire licked from the muzzle.

The madman spun as if in an inept ballet, then fell, rolled along the walk. Surprisingly, he scrambled to his feet and headed for the street again. He hadn't been hit. If he'd taken a bullet from the .357 Magnum, he would have stayed down.

Max was certain of that. He knew a great deal about firearms. He owned an extensive collection of guns.

Barnes fired again.

'Dammit!' Max said furiously. 'Small town cops. Over-armed and undertrained. If that ass misses his man, he'll kill one of us!'

The third shot took the killer in the back as he reached the sidewalk.

Max could tell two things about the bullet. Because it didn't exit from the killer's chest and pierce the car window, it had been insufficiently packed with powder. It was designed for use on crowded streets; it had just enough punch to stop a guilty man

363

without passing through him and harming others. Secondly, considering how it had lifted the man off his feet, the bullet was surely hollow-nosed.

After an instant of graceless flight, the killer slammed hard into the police cruiser. For a moment he clung to Mary's door. He slid down until he was peering at her. 'Mary Bergen . . .' His voice was hoarse. He clawed at the window. 'Mary Bergen.' Blood spouted from his mouth and painted the glass.

Mary screamed.

The corpse dropped to the sidewalk.

THREE

The ambulance carrying Dan Goldman turned the corner as fast as it could without flipping on its side.

Max hoped the siren was fading more rapidly than the young patrolman's life.

On the sidewalk the dead man lay on his back. He stared at the sky and waited patiently for the coroner.

'She's upset about the killer knowing her name,' Alan said.

'He saw her picture in her newspaper column,' Max said. 'Somehow he heard she was coming to town to find him.'

'But only the mayor and the city council knew. And the cops.'

'Somehow this guy heard. He knew she was in town and he recognised her. There's nothing supernatural about it. Is that what she thinks?'

'I know there's a simple explanation, and you know it. Deep down, she knows it, too. But considering what she's seen in her life, she can't help wondering. Now, I've talked to Barnes. He can spare a man and a car for us. We should get Mary back to the hotel so she can lie down.'

'We will,' Max said, 'when everything's settled with the mayor.'

'That could be hours.'

'Half an hour at most,' Max said. 'Now, if that's all you wanted to talk to me about—'

'She's dead tired.'

'Aren't we all? She'll be okay.'

'The loving husband.'

'Go to hell.'

They were standing behind the first squad car. Mary still sat inside with her eyes closed and her hands folded in her lap. The rain had stopped. The air was moist and fragrant.

Glancing nervously at the people who had come out of their

homes to gather around the pathetic scene, Alan said, 'There'll be reporters here any minute. I don't think she should have to put up with a lot of reporters tonight.'

Max knew what his brother-in-law wanted. Tomorrow Alan began a two-week vacation. Before leaving he hoped to have a final conversation with his sister, just the two of them, one last uninterrupted hour in which to convince her that she had married a man who was terribly wrong for her.

His fists were the only tools Max had to prevent this domestic sedition. He was six inches taller and forty pounds heavier than Alan. He had shoulders and biceps designed for dock work, and the outsized hands of a basketball star. However, he knew that split lips and broken teeth and a cracked jaw would silence Alan Tanner only temporarily. Short of killing him, there was no way to put an end to his meddling.

Anyway, Max no longer tried to solve his problems with his fists. He had promised Mary and himself that his violent days were gone forever.

Other than strength and the will to use it, Alan had all the weapons in this intensely personal war. Not the least of them was his appearance. He had black hair and blue eyes, like Mary. He was handsome, while Max was so rough-hewn that he barely avoided ugliness. Alan's powerfully sensuous features, highlighted by a look of boyish innocence, could affect even a sister.

Especially a sister.

Alan's voice was as sweet and persuasive as an actor's. He was able to create moods and build drama with his voice. He employed it subtly to gain Mary's sympathy and to cause her to look upon her new husband with mild, unconscious, but insidious pleasure.

Max knew his mind was better than average, but he also knew that Alan was his intellectual superior. It wasn't the voice alone that won arguments. There was wit behind those mellifluous tones.

And charm?

Whenever Alan needed it, charm oozed from him.

I'd like to roll him up tight like an empty tube of toothpaste, Max thought. Squeeze all the charm out of him and see if there's any truth behind it.

Most important of all, Alan and Mary had shared thirty years;

366

he was thirty-three and, as an older brother, was welded to her by blood, common experience, more than a little tragedy, and three decades of day-to-day life.

As the crowd grew around him, Max watched yet another police car approach. He said, 'You're right. She shouldn't be here any longer than necessary.'

'Of course not.'

'I'll take her to the hotel right away.'

'You?' Alan asked, surprised. 'You have to stay here.'

'Why?'

'You know why.'

'Tell me anyway.'

Grudgingly, Alan said, 'You're better at this than I am.'

'Better at what?' Max asked.

'You know why you need to hear it? Because it's all you've got going for you. It's the only thing you can use to hold her.'

'Better at what?'

'So insecure.'

'Better at what?'

'You're better at getting the money. Does that satisfy you?'

Mary made a good living as the author of a syndicated newspaper column about psychic phenomena. She had also earned a lot of money with three best-selling books about her career, and she could have survived quite well on her speaking fees alone if she'd wanted.

Although she travelled extensively, aiding authorities with investigations of violent homicides whenever they asked her to do so, she didn't profit from any of that. She didn't charge for her visions. Once she helped a famous actress locate a hundred-thousand-dollar diamond necklace that was lost, and she took no fee. She never required more than expenses – airline tickets, car rentals, meals, and lodging – from those whom she assisted; and she refused even that much if she thought she'd been of little or no service.

When Max first came into her life, the collection of expense money was her brother's duty. But Alan had no talent or taste for quibbling with mayors, councilmen, and bureaucrats. As often as not, when Mary had done her work and the guilty man had been found, the local politicians who had summoned her tried to get rid of her without paying what they owed. Alan seldom pressured them. As a result, tens of thousands of dollars in expenses were lost each year; and although Mary earned considerable sums, she was slowly going broke.

Within two months following the wedding Max straightened out Mary's financial affairs. He renegotiated her contract with the lecture bureau and doubled her speaking fee. When her contract with the newspaper syndicate came due to renewal, he made a far more advantageous deal than she had thought possible. And he never failed to get a cheque for expenses.

'Well?' Alan said.

'All right. You take her back to the hotel. But remember what you said. I'm better at getting the money. And I always will be.'

'Of course. You have a nose for it,' Alan said. His smile had no warmth. 'You sniffed out Mary's money pretty damned fast, didn't you?'

'Go,' Max said.

'Too much truth in that for you?'

'Get out of here before you find yourself looking up your own ass for the rest of your life.'

Alan blinked.

Max didn't.

Alan walked over to Harley Barnes.

Gradually Max became aware of a number of people in the crowd who were staring at him. He stared back at them, one at a time. Each grew self-conscious and turned away – but each looked at him again as soon as he moved his gaze.

None of them was close enough to have heard the argument. He realised that they were staring because his face was contorted by rage, because his shoulders were drawn up like those of a stalking panther, because his huge hands were in tight fists at his sides. He tried to relax, to let his shoulders fall. And he put his hands in the pockets of his raincoat so that no one could see he was too infuriated to uncurl them.

FOUR

The hotel room had four ugly lamps with garishly patterned shades, but only one of them was on.

In a black vinyl armchair that stood on a swivel base, Alan folded his hands around a glass of Scotch that he wasn't drinking. The light fell over him from the left, carving his face with sharp shadows.

Mary was sitting up in bed, on top of the covers, well out of the light. She wished Max would get back so they could go out for a late supper and a couple of drinks. She was hungry and tired and emotionally exhausted.

'Still have a headache?' Alan asked.

'The aspirin helped.'

'You're drawn . . . so pale.'

'There's nothing wrong that eight hours of sleep won't cure.'

'I worry about you,' he said.

She smiled affectionately. 'You've always worried about me, dear. Even when we were children.'

'I care about you very much.'

'I know that.'

'You're my sister. I love you.'

'I know, but—'

'He presses you too hard.'

'Not this again, Alan.'

'He does.'

'I wish you and Max could get along.'

'So do I. But we never will.'

'But *why*?'

'Because I know what he is.'

'And what's that?'

'For one thing, he's so different from you,' Alan said. 'He's not

369

as sensitive as you are. He's not as kind.' He seemed to be pleading with her. 'You're gentle and he's—'

'He can be gentle, too.'

'Can he?'

'With me he can. He's sweet.'

'You're entitled to your opinion.'

'Oh, thank you very much,' she said sarcastically. Anger flared briefly in her but was quickly extinguished. She couldn't stay angry with Alan for more than a minute. Even a minute was stretching it.

'Mary, I don't want to argue with you.'

'Then don't.'

'We never had cross words, not in thirty years . . . until he came into the picture.'

'I'm not up to this tonight.'

'You're not up to anything because he presses you too hard and too fast when he's guiding you through your visions.'

'He does it well.'

'Not as well as I did it.'

'At first he was too insistent,' she admitted. 'Too anxious. But not anymore.'

Alan put down his Scotch, got up, turned his back on her. He went to the window. Moody silence enveloped him.

She closed her eyes and wished Max would get back.

After a minute Alan walked away from the window. He stood at the foot of the bed, staring down at her. 'I'm afraid to go away on vacation.'

Without opening her eyes, she said, 'Afraid of what?'

'I don't want to leave you alone.'

'I won't be alone. I'll be with Max.'

'That's what I mean – alone with Max.'

'Alan, for Christ's sake!'

'I mean it.'

She opened her eyes, sat up straighter. 'You're being silly. Ridiculous. I won't listen to any more of this.'

'If I didn't care what happens to you, I could walk out right now. Whether you want to hear it or nor, I'm going to say what I think is true about him.'

She sighed.

'He's an opportunist,' Alan said.

'So what?'

'He likes money.'

'So do I. So do you.'

'He likes it too much.'

She smiled indulgently. 'I'm not sure you can ever like it too much, dear.'

'Don't you understand?'

'Enlighten me.'

Alan hesitated. There was sadness in his beautiful eyes. 'Max likes *other people's* money too much.'

She stared at him, surprised. 'Look . . . if you're saying he married me for my money—'

'That's precisely what I'm saying.'

'Then it's *you* who's pressing me too hard.' There was steel in her voice now.

He changed his tone with her, spoke softly. 'All I'm trying to do is make you face facts. I don't—'

She raised herself up, away from the headboard. 'Am I so ugly that no one would want me if I were poor?'

'You're beautiful. You know that.'

She wasn't satisfied. 'Then am I some mindless little twit who bores men to death?'

'Don't shout,' Alan said. 'Calm down. Please.' He seemed genuinely grieved that he had hurt her. But he didn't change the subject. 'Plenty of men would give everything they own to marry you. And for all the right reasons. Why you ever picked Max—'

'He was the first decent prospect, the first full-fledged man who asked.'

'That's not true. I know of four others who asked.'

'The first two were spineless wonders,' she said. 'The third one was about as gentle and considerate in bed as a bull is in the ring. The other one was virtually impotent. Max wasn't any of that. He was different, interesting, exciting.'

'You didn't marry him because he was exciting, or because he was intelligent or mysterious or romantic. You married him because he was big, strong, and gruff. A perfect father image.'

'Since when have you practised psychiatry?'

She knew Alan didn't want to pick at her like this. He continued only because he felt she needed to hear it. He was being a conscientious big brother. Even though he was misguided, his

371

intentions were admirable. If she hadn't been certain of that, she would have asked him to leave.

'I don't have to be a psychiatrist to know that you need to lean on someone. You always have. From the day you realised what your clairvoyance was, what it meant, you've been frightened of it, unable to deal with it yourself. You leaned on me for a while. But I wasn't tall enough or broad-shouldered enough to fill the role for long.'

'Alan, for the first time in my life I have the urge to slap your face.'

He came around and sat down on the edge of the bed. He took her left hand in both of his. 'Mary, he was a newspaper hack, a washed-up reporter who hadn't covered a major story in ten years. You knew him just six weeks before you were married.'

'That's all the longer I *needed* to know him.' She relaxed, squeezed Alan's hand. 'It's working out fine, dear. You should be happy for me.'

'You've only been married four months.'

'Long enough to like him even better than I did when he proposed.'

'He's a dangerous man. You know his past.'

'A few fights in barrooms . . . and he doesn't go to barrooms anymore.'

'It's not as innocent as that. He nearly killed some people in those brawls.'

'When they've had too much to drink and are feeling mean, some men will go after the biggest man in the room. Max was a natural target. He didn't start any of those fights.'

'So he says.'

'No one ever pressed charges.'

'Maybe they were afraid to.'

'He's changed. What he needed was someone who loved him, someone he could feel responsible for. He needed me.'

Alan nodded forlornly. 'Want a drink?'

'I'll wait for Max.'

He drank his Scotch in three swallows. 'You're absolutely sure about him?'

'About Max? Positive.'

He went to the window again, studied the night sky for a moment. 'I don't think I'll be returning to work with you after my vacation.'

She got up, went to him, took hold of his shoulder and turned him around. 'Say again?'

'I'm a fifth wheel now.'

'Nonsense. You take care of so much of my business—'

'That's nothing a secretary couldn't handle,' Alan said. 'Before Max, I was vital. I was your guide through the visions. But there's nothing important for me to do anymore. And I don't need this constant friction with Max.'

'But what will you do?'

'I'm not sure. I think I'll start by taking two months vacation instead of two weeks. I can afford it. You've been very generous to me and—'

'Not generous. You earned your share, Alan—'

'I've got enough money put away to keep me for years. Maybe I'll go back to the university . . . finish that degree in political science.'

'Will you move out of the house in Bel Air?'

'That would be best. I can find an apartment.'

'Will you live with Jennifer?'

'She dropped me,' he said.

'What?'

'For another guy.'

'I didn't know.'

'I didn't want to talk about it.'

'I'm sorry.'

'Don't be. She wasn't my type.'

'You two seemed happy.'

'We were . . . briefly.'

'What went wrong?'

'Everything.'

'You won't move far away, will you?'

'Probably just to Westwood.'

'Oh, then we'll practically be neighbours.'

'That's right.'

'We'll have lunch once a week.'

'All right,' he said.

'And dinner occasionally.'

'Without Max?' he asked.

'Just you and me.'

'Sounds lovely.'

A childlike tear rolled out of the corner of her eye.

'No need for that,' he said, wiping it away.

'I'll miss you.'

'A brother and sister can't live in the same house forever. It's unnatural.'

The sound of a key in the lock made them turn to the door.

Max came in and stripped off his raincoat.

Mary went to him, kissed him on the cheek.

Putting an arm around her, refusing to acknowledge Alan, Max asked, 'Feeling better?'

'Just tired,' she said.

'Everything went smoothly in spite of Oberlander,' Max said. 'I got the cheque for expenses.'

'You always do,' she said proudly.

During that exchange Alan went to the door and opened it. 'I'll be going.'

Only minutes ago she had hoped he would leave before Max returned in order to avoid one of those tiresome quarrels. Now she felt that Alan was drifting out of her life, and she was unwilling to let go of him so soon or so easily. 'Can't you stay for another drink?'

He looked at Max and shook his head. 'I don't think that would be wise.'

Max said nothing. He didn't move, smile, or even blink. His arm at Mary's waist was like a stone bannister against which she rested.

She said, 'We haven't talked about what happened tonight. There's so much to be discussed.'

'Later,' Alan said.

'You're still going to spend your vacation driving up the coast?'

'Yeah. I'll spend some time in San Francisco. I know a girl there who's invited me for Christmas. Maybe after that I'll head for Seattle.'

'You'll call me?'

'Sure.'

'When?'

'A week or so.'

'Christmas Day?'

'All right.'

'I'll miss you, Alan.'

'Watch out for yourself.'

374

'I'll watch out for her,' Max said.

Alan ignored him. To Mary he said, 'Be careful, will you? And remember what I said.'

He went out, closing the door behind him, leaving her alone with Max.

* * *

The small downtown tavern was dimly lit, quite busy as late evening approached, but cosy in spite of the crowd. Max and Mary sat in a corner booth, and the bartender made two perfect vodka martinis. Later they ate roast beef sandwiches and split a bottle of red wine.

When she had finished half of her large sandwich, she pushed the rest aside, poured a third glass of wine for herself, and said, ' I wonder if Dan Goldman's hospital bills will be covered.'

'The town carries a comprehensive insurance policy on its cops,' Max said. 'Goldman got hurt in the line of duty, so he won't be stuck for a penny of it.'

'How can you be so sure?'

'I knew you'd want me to be.'

'I don't understand.'

'I knew you'd wonder about Goldman's hospital bills, so I asked the mayor.'

'Even if the bills are covered,' she said, 'I guess he'll lose some pay while he's off work.'

'No,' Max said. 'I asked about that, too.'

She was surprised. 'What are you – a mind reader?'

'I just know you too well. You're the softest touch there ever was.'

'I am not. I just think we should do something nice for him.'

Max put down his sandwich. 'We can buy him either a new electric range or maybe a microwave oven.'

She blinked. 'What?'

'I asked some of Goldman's buddies what he needs. Seems he's a serious amateur chef, but his kitchen leaves a lot to be desired.'

She smiled. 'We'll get him the range *and* the oven, and the best set of pots and pans—'

'Hold on a minute,' Max said. 'He's got an apartment kitchen, not a restaurant. Besides, why do you think you owe him *anything*?'

Staring into her wine, she said, 'If I hadn't come to town, he wouldn't have been hurt.'

'Mary Bergen, the female Atlas, carrying the world on her shoulders.' He reached across the table and took her hand. 'Do you remember the first conversation we ever had?'

'How could I forget? I thought you were weird.'

The night they'd met he had been uncharacteristically shy. They'd been guests at the same party. He'd seemed at ease and self-confident with everyone but her. His approach had been so self-conscious and awkward that she felt sorry for him. He had begun with one of those analyse-yourself party games.

She smiled, remembering. 'You asked me what machine I would choose to be if I could be any machine in the world. Weird.'

'The last woman who answered that question said she'd be a Rolls-Royce and go to all the best places. But you said you'd be some piece of medical equipment that saves lives.'

'Was that a good answer?'

'At the time,' Max said, 'it sounded phony. But now I know what you are, and I realise you were serious.'

'And what am I?'

'The kind of person who always asks for whom the bell tolls – and always cries buckets at even slightly sad movies.'

She sipped her wine. 'I played the game right back at you that night, asked you what machine you'd be. Remember?'

Max nodded. He pushed his unfinished sandwich aside, picked up his wine. 'I said I'd be a computer dating service so I could hook you up with me.'

She laughed girlishly. 'I liked it then, and I like it now. It was a surprise finding a romantic under that big tough exterior.'

Max leaned across the table, spoke softly. 'Know what machine I'd be tonight?' He pointed to the colourfully lighted juke box at the far end of the bar. 'I'd be that music machine. And no matter what buttons people pushed, I'd play love songs for you.'

'Oh, Max, that's positively saccharine.'

'But you like it.'

'I love it. After all, I'm the lady who cries buckets at even slightly sad movies.'

FIVE

The nightmare woke her, but the dream continued. For a minute after she rose up in fear from her pillows, colourful snatches of the nightmare swam in the air before her. Ethereal snapshots. Blood. Shattered bodies. Broken skulls. They were more vivid than any visions she'd ever known.

The shadows of the hotel room settled over her once more. When she grew accustomed enough to the darkness to see the outlines of the furniture, she got up.

The room was a carousel. She reached out for a brass pole that wasn't there, for something to steady her.

When she regained her balance, she went into the bathroom. She didn't close the door because she worried she might wake Max. For the same reason, she didn't use the main light. Instead, she turned on the much dimmer, orange-filtered heat lamp.

In that light her mirror image disturbed her; dark rings around the eyes, skin slack and damp. She was used to a reflection that was the envy of most women: silky black hair, blue eyes, fine features, a flawless complexion. Now the person looking back at her seemed a stranger, an alien.

She felt personally threatened by what she had seen. The dead bodies in the nightmare were the first parts of a chain in which she might be the final link.

She drew a glass of cold water, drank it, then another. The tumbler rattled against her teeth. She had to use both hands to hold it.

Each time she shut her eyes, she saw the same remnant of the nightmare. A dark-haired girl with one blue eye gazing sightlessly at the ceiling. The other eye swollen in a macabre wink. Face torn, bruised, misshapen.

Worst of all, Mary felt that if the blood were swabbed from that

377

face, and if its smashed features were restored, she would know it at once.

She put the glass down, leaned against the sink.

Who? she thought. Who was that girl?

The distorted face would not resolve itself.

As if she craved more fear than the dream had given her, she remembered the psychopath who had died that same night: his twisted features; his marble-chip teeth; his hands pressed to the squad car windows; his whispery voice, cool as cellar air when he spoke her name.

He had been an omen, a warning to her.

But an omen of what?

There might be nothing mysterious about his knowing her name. He could have heard she was in town, even though that information was limited to a select few. He might have recognized her from the photograph that accompanied her column, although the picture was not a good one and was six years old. That was Alan's explanation.

Although she had no good reason to disagree with Alan, she knew that his explanation was inadequate.

Maybe the madman had known her because he'd had his first (and necessarily last) telepathic experience in the instant that death seized him.

Or perhaps there was a meaning to the incident that couldn't be defined in rational terms. When she recalled the madman's demonic face, one thought circled through her mind: *He's a messenger from Hell, a messenger from Hell* . . . She didn't know what that meant. But she didn't dismiss the thought simply because it had a supernatural ring to it.

Through her extensive travels, through her many conversations with clairvoyants like Peter Hurkos and Gerard Croiset, through her conversations and correspondence with other psychically gifted people, she had come to think anything was possible. She'd been in homes where poltergeists were active, where dishes and paintings and bric-a-brac and heavy furniture sailed through the air and exploded against the walls when no one had touched them or been near them. She hadn't decided whether she'd seen ghosts at work or, instead, the unconscious telekinetic powers of someone in the house; but she did know that *something* was there. She had seen Ted Serios create his famous psychic photographs, which *Time* and *Popular Photography* and many other national publications had tried unsuccessfully to debunk. He projected his thoughts onto unexposed film, and he did so under the intense scrutiny of sceptical scientists. She had seen an Indian mystic – a fakir but not a faker – do the impossible. He planted a seed in a pot of earth, covered it with a light muslin sheet, then went into a deep trance. Within five hours, while Mary watched, the seed germinated, the plant grew, and fruit appeared – several tiny mangoes. As a result of two decades of contact with the extraordinary in life, she scoffed at nothing. Until someone proved beyond doubt that all psychic and supernatural phenomena were pieces of a hoax (which no one ever would), she would put as much faith in the unnatural, supernatural, and suprarational as she did in what more dogmatic people believed to be the one, true, natural, and only world.

     . . . messenger from Hell.

Although she was half convinced that life existed after death, she didn't believe that it was accurately described by the Judeo-Christian myths. She didn't accept the reality of Heaven and Hell. That was too simplistic. Yet, if she didn't believe, why this unshakeable certainty that the madman was a satanic omen? Why phrase the premonition in religious terms?

She shuddered. She was cold to her bones.

She returned to the bedroom but left on the bathroom light. She was uneasy in the dark. She put on her robe.

Max snored peacefully. She stroked his cheek with her fingertips.

He was instantly awake. 'What's the matter?'

'I'm scared. I need to talk. I can't stand to be alone.'

He closed his hand around her wrist. 'I'm here.'

'I saw something awful . . . horrible.' She shuddered again.

He sat up, switched on the lamp, looked around the room.

'Visions,' she said.

Still holding her wrist, he pulled her down to the bed.

'They started when I was asleep,' she said, 'and went on after I woke up.'

'Started when you were sleeping? That's never happened before, has it?'

'Never.'

'So maybe it was a dream. '

'I know the difference.'

He let go of her wrist, pushed his hair back from his forehead. 'A vision of what?'

'Dead people.'

'An accident?'

'Murder. Beaten and stabbed.'

'Where?'

'Quite a distance from here.'

'Name of the town?'

'It's south of us.'

'That's all you've got?'

'I think it's in Orange County. Maybe Santa Ana. Or Newport Beach. Laguna Beach. Anaheim. Someplace like that.'

'How many dead?'

'A lot. Four or five women. All in one place. And . . .'

'And what?'

'They're the first of many.'

'You sense that?'

'Yes.'

'Sense it psychically?'

'Yes.'

'The first of how many?'

'I don't know.'

'You saw the killer?'

'No.'

'Pick up anything about him?'

'No.'

'Not even the colour of his hair?'

'Nothing, Max.'

'Have these killings taken place yet?'

'I don't think so. But I can't be sure. I was so surprised by the visions that I didn't make any attempt to hold on to them. I didn't pursue them like I should have.'

He got out of bed and slipped into his own robe. She stood up, moved against him. 'You're shivering,' he said.

She wanted to be loved and sheltered. 'It was horrible.'

'They always are.'

'This was worse than usual.'

'Well, it's over.'

'No. Maybe it is over or shortly will be for those women. But

380

not for us. We're going to get tangled up in this one. Oh, God, so many bodies, so much blood. And I think I knew one of the dead girls.'

'Who was she?' he asked, holding her still closer.

'The face I saw was so badly disfigured. I couldn't tell who she was, but she seemed familiar.'

'It had to be a dream,' he said reassuringly. 'The visions don't come to you out of the blue. You've always had to concentrate, focus your attention in order to pick them up. Like when you start tracking a killer, you have to handle something that belonged to his victim before you can receive images of him.'

He was telling her what she already knew, soothing her in the manner of a father explaining to his still frightened young daughter that the ghosts she had seen in the dark bedroom were only the draught-stirred curtains she could now see with the lights on.

Actually it didn't matter to her what he said. Just hearing him speak and feeling him close, Mary grew calm.

'Even when you're searching for a lost ring or necklace or brooch,' Max said, 'you have to see the box or drawer where it was kept. So what you saw tonight *had* to be a dream because you didn't seek it.'

'I feel better.'

'Good.'

'But not because I believe it was a dream. I know it was a vision. Those women were real. They're either dead by now or they soon will be.' She thought of the brutally beaten faces and she said, 'God help them.'

'Mary—'

'It was *real*,' she insisted, letting go of his hand and sitting on the mattress. 'And it's going to involve us.'

'You mean the police will ask for your help?'

'More than that. It's going to affect us . . . intimately. It's the start of something that'll change our lives.'

'How can you know that?'

'The same way I know everything else about it. I sense it psychically.'

'Whether or not it's going to change our life,' he said, 'is there any way we can help those women?'

'We know so little. If we called the police, we couldn't tell them anything worthwhile.'

'And since we don't know what town it will happen in, which police department would we call? Can you pick up the vision again?'

'No use trying. It's gone.'

'Maybe it'll return spontaneously, just the way it came the first time.'

'Maybe.' The possibility chilled her. 'I hope not. As it is, I've got too many nasty visions in my life. I don't want them to start flashing on me when I'm not prepared, when I'm not *asking* for them. If that became a regular thing, I'd end up in a madhouse.'

'If there isn't anything we can do about what you saw,' Max said, 'then we have to forget about it for tonight. You need a drink.'

'I had some water.'

'Would *I* ever suggest water? I meant something with more bite.'

She smiled. 'At this hour of the morning?'

'It's not morning. We went to bed early, remember. And we've been asleep only half an hour or so.'

She looked at the travel clock. Eleven-ten. 'I thought I'd been conked out for hours.'

'Minutes,' he said. 'Vodka and tonic?'

'Scotch, if you're having it.'

He went to the small breakfast table by the window. The liquor bottles, glasses, and ice were there. In spite of his size, he was not awkward. He moved like a wild animal – fluidly, silently. Even the preparation of drinks was a study in grace when Max did it.

If everyone were like him, Mary thought, the word 'clumsy' wouldn't exist.

He sat beside her on the edge of the bed. 'Will you be able to get back to sleep?'

'I doubt it.'

'Drink up.'

She sipped the Scotch. It burned her throat.

'What are you worrying about?' he asked.

'Nothing.'

'You're worrying about the vision.'

'Not at all.'

'Look, worry accomplishes nothing,' he said. 'And whatever you do, don't think about a blue giraffe standing in the centre of a giant custard pie.'

She stared at him incredulous.

Grinning, he said, 'What are you worrying about now?'

'What else? A blue giraffe in a custard pie.'

'See? I stopped you from worrying about the vision.'

She laughed. He had such a stern, forbidding face that his humour always came as a surprise.

'Speaking of blue,' he said, 'you look perfect in that robe.'

'I've worn it before.'

'And every time you wear it you're breathtaking. Perfect.'

She kissed him. She explored his lips with her tongue, then teasingly drew back.

'You look perfect in it, but you'd look even better out of it.' He put his drink beside her on the nightstand and untied the sash that was knotted at her waist, opened the long blue robe.

A pleasant tremor passed through her. The cool air caressed her bare skin. She felt soft, vulnerable; she needed him.

With his heavy hands, now light as wings, he traced lazy circles on her breasts, cupped them, pressed them together, gently massaged them. He got to his knees before her, nuzzled her cleavage and kissed her nipples.

She took his head in her hands, pushed her fingers through his lush, shining hair.

Alan was wrong about him.

'My lovely Max,' she said.

He moved his lips down her taut belly as she lay back, kissed her thighs, delicately licked the warm centre of her. He slipped his hands under her buttocks, lifted slightly.

After many minutes during which her murmurs rose and fell, rose and fell again like the enigmatic susurration of the sea, he raised his head and said, 'I love you.'

'Then love me.'

He took off his robe and joined her on the bed.

★ ★ ★

Agreeably exhausted, they separated at midnight, but the spell was not broken. Still enchanted, eyes closed, she drifted. In some ways she was more intensely aware of her body than she had been during intercourse.

Within minutes, however, memories of the vision returned to

383

her: bloodied and crumpled faces. With her eyes closed, the backs of her lids were like twin projection screens on which she saw nothing but carnage.

She opened her eyes and the dark room appeared to crawl with strange shapes. Although she didn't want to disturb Max, she couldn't keep herself from tossing and turning.

Eventually he switched on the light. 'You need a sedative.' He swung his legs out of bed.

'I'll get it,' she said.

'Stay put.'

A minute later he came back from the bathroom with a glass of water and one of the capsules that she too frequently required.

'Maybe I shouldn't take it on top of liquor,' she said.

'You drank only half of your Scotch.'

'I had vodka before that.'

'The vodka's through your system by now.'

She took the sedative. It stuck in her throat. She choked it down with another swallow of water.

In bed again, he held her hand. He was still holding it when the chemically induced sleep finally began to creep over her.

As consciousness spun away from her like a child's ball rolling down a hillside, she thought about how wrong Alan was about Max, how terribly and completely wrong.

TUESDAY,
DECEMBER 22

SIX

'Anaheim police.'

'Are you a police officer, Miss?'

'I'm the receptionist.'

'Could I speak to an officer?'

'What's the nature of your complaint?'

'Oh, no complaint. I think you people do a wonderful job.'

'I meant, are you reporting a crime?'

'I'm not sure. A very strange thing happened here.'

'What is your name?'

'Alice. Alice Barnable.'

'Your address?'

'Peregrine Apartments on Euclid Avenue. I'm in apartment B.'

'I'll connect you with someone.'

'Sergeant Erdman speaking.'

'Are you really a sergeant?'

'Who's this?'

'Mrs Alice Barnable.'

'What can I do for you?'

'Are you really a sergeant? You sound too young.'

'I've been a policeman for twenty years. If you—'

'I'm seventy-eight, but I'm not senile.'

'I didn't say you were.'

'So many people treat us senior citizens as if we're children.'

'I don't, Mrs Barnable. My mother's seventy-five, and she's sharper than I am.'

'So you better believe what I've got to tell you.'

'And what's that?'

'Four nurses share an apartment above mine, and I know they're in some sort of bad trouble. I called up there, but no one answers the phone.'

'How do you know they're in trouble?'

'There's a puddle of blood in my spare bathroom.'

'Whose blood? I'm afraid I don't follow you.'

'You see, the water pipes that serve the apartment above mine are exposed, and they run up one corner of my spare bath. Now, I don't want you to think I live in a cheap place. The pipes are painted white, hardly noticeable. The building's old but elegant in its way. It's not cheap. It's quaint. My Charlie left me enough to let me live very comfortably.'

'I'm sure he did, Mrs Barnable. What about the blood?'

'Those pipes run through a hole in the ceiling. The hole's a tiny bit bigger than it needs to be. Just a quarter of an inch of space all the way around the pipe. During the night, blood dripped out of that hole. The pipes are streaked with it, and there's a large sticky spot on my floor.'

'You're sure it's blood? It might be rusty water or—'

'Now you're treating me as if I'm a child, Sergeant Erdman.'

'Sorry.'

'I know blood when I see it. And what I wondered – I wondered if maybe your people should take a look upstairs.'

★ ★ ★

Patrolmen Stambaugh and Pollini found the door to the apartment ajar. It was spotted with fingerprints that were cast in dried blood.

'Think he's still in there?' Stambaugh asked.

'Never can tell. Back me up.'

Pollini went in with his gun drawn and Stambaugh followed.

The living room was inexpensively but pleasantly furnished with wicker and rattan. On the white walls were colourful framed prints of palm trees and native villages and bare-breasted, nut-brown girls in striped sarongs.

The first body was in the kitchen. A young woman in black and green pyjamas. On the floor. On her back. Long yellow hair streaked with clotted red bands spread around her like a fan. She had been stabbed – and kicked in the face more than once.

'Christ,' Stambaugh said.

'Something, huh?'

'Don't you feel sick?'

388

'Seen it before.'

Pollini pointed to several items on the counter by the sink – a paper plate, two slices of bread, a jar of mustard, a tomato, a package of cheese.

'Important?' Stambaugh asked.

'She woke up during the night. Maybe she was an insomniac. She was making a snack when he came in. Doesn't look like she put up a fight. He either surprised her, or she knew and trusted him.'

'Should we be talking like this?'

'Why not?'

Stambaugh gestured toward the rooms that they hadn't yet investigated.

'The killer? He's long gone.'

Stambaugh greatly admired his partner. He was eight years younger than Pollini. He'd been a cop only six months, while the older man had been on the force for seven years. In his view, Pollini had everything that a great lawman required – intelligence, courage, and street wisdom.

Most important of all, Pollini was able to do his job without letting it touch him. He didn't flinch at the sight of shattered bodies, not even when he encountered the most pathetic victim of all – the battered child. Pollini was nothing less than a rock.

Although he tried to imitate his mentor, Stambaugh usually got sick to his stomach in the midst of too much spilled blood.

'Come on,' Pollini said.

He led Stambaugh back through the hall to the spare bath, where the harsh light glared on blood-splashed porcelain and on the hideously stained white vanity top.

'There was a struggle this time,' Stambaugh said.

'But not much of one. It was over in seconds.'

Another young woman, wearing only panties, was curled foetally in a corner of the bathroom. She had been stabbed repeatedly in the breasts and stomach, back and buttocks. There were between fifty and a hundred wounds.

Her blood had pooled around the pipes that came up from Alice Barnable's first-floor apartment.

'Funny,' Pollini said.

'*Funny?*' Stambaugh had never seen such slaughter. He could not comprehend the violent mind behind it.

'Funny that he didn't rape either of them.'

'Is that what he should have done?'

'His kind does, ninety per cent of the time.'

Across the hall the spare bedroom contained two unmade beds but no bodies.

In the master suite they found a nude redhead on the bed nearest the door. Her throat had been cut.

'No struggle at all,' Pollini said. 'He caught her while she was sleeping. Doesn't look like he raped this one either.'

Stambaugh nodded. He was unable to speak.

Both women in the master bedroom appeared to be Catholics, who were, if not devout, at least attentive to their faith. A number of religious objects were scattered on the floor.

A damaged crucifix lay beside the redhead's nightstand. The wooden cross had been broken into four pieces. The aluminium image of Christ was bent at the waist, so that its crown of thorns touched its bare feet; and its head was twisted around so that Christ was looking over his shoulder.

'This wasn't just broken in a scuffle,' Pollini said, stooping over the remains of the icon. 'The killer pulled this off the wall and spent a good bit of time demolishing it.'

Two small religious statues had been on the redhead's dresser. These were also broken. Some of the pieces had been ground into chalky dust; there were a few white heel prints on the carpet.

'He sure has something against Catholics,' Pollini said. 'Or against religion in general.'

Stambaugh reluctantly followed him to the last bed.

The fourth dead woman had been stabbed repeatedly and strangled with a rosary.

In life she had been beautiful. Even now, naked and cold, her hair matted with blood, nose broken, one eye swollen shut, face dark with bruises, there were still traces of beauty. Alive, her blue eyes would have been as clear as mountain lakes. Washed and combed, her hair would have been thick, lustrous. She had long shapely legs, a narrow waist, a flat belly and lovely breasts.

I've seen women like her, Stambaugh thought sadly. She would have walked with her shoulders back, with evident pride in herself, with joy apparent in every step.

'She was a nurse,' Pollini said.

Stambaugh looked at the uniform and cap that were on a

390

chair near the bed. His legs felt weak.

'What's the matter?' Pollini said.

Stambaugh hesitated, cleared his throat. 'Well, my sister's a nurse.'

'This isn't your sister, is it?'

'No. But she's about my sister's age.'

'You know her? She work with your sister?'

'Never saw her before,' Stambaugh said.

'Then what's wrong?'

'This girl might have been my sister.'

'You cracking up on me?'

'I'm okay. I'm fine.'

'You'll get used to this stuff.'

Stambaugh said nothing.

'This one was raped,' Pollini said.

Stambaugh swallowed hard. He was dizzy.

'See that?' Pollini asked.

'What?'

'On the pubic hair. It's semen.'

'Oh.'

'I wonder if he had her before or after.'

'Before or after what?'

'Before or after he killed her.'

Stambaugh hurried into the master bath, dropped to his knees before the toilet, and threw up.

When his stomach spasms passed, he knew that in the past ten minutes he had learned something important about himself. In spite of what he'd thought this morning, he *never* wanted to be like Ted Pollini.

SEVEN

Max came back to the room at eleven-thirty, just as she finished dressing. He kissed her lightly on the mouth. He smelled of soap, shaving lotion, and the cherry-scented pipe tobacco that he favoured.

'Out for a walk?' Mary asked.

'When did you wake up?'

'Only an hour ago.'

'I was up at eight-thirty.'

'I slept *ten* hours. When I finally managed to throw myself out of bed, I felt dopey. I shouldn't have taken the sedative on top of liquor.'

'You needed it.'

'I didn't need to feel the way I felt this morning.'

'You look wonderful now.'

'Where have you been?'

'At the coffee shop downstairs. Had some toast and orange juice. Read the papers.'

'Anything that's connected with what I saw last night?'

'The local paper has a nice story. You and Barnes catching The Slasher. They say Goldman is already off the critical list.'

'That's not what I meant. The dead women in the vision. What about them?'

'Nothing in the papers.'

'There will be this afternoon.'

A worried look crossed his face. He put a hand on her shoulder. 'You've got to relax once in a while. You've got to let your head clear out now and then. Don't run after this one, Mary. Forget about it. Please. For me?'

'I can't forget,' she said unhappily. She wished desperately that she could.

Before leaving town, they stopped at an appliance store, chose and paid for an electric range and microwave oven for Dan Goldman.

Later they got off the freeway at Ventura to have lunch at a restaurant they knew. They ordered salads, manicotti, and a bottle of Cabernet Sauvignon by Robert Mondavi.

From their table they had a view of the ocean. The slate-grey water looked like a mirror reflecting the turbulent sky. The surf was high and fast. A few gulls swooped along the shoreline.

'It'll be good to get home,' Max said. 'We should be in Bel Air before two o'clock.'

'The way you drive, we'll be there long before.'

'We can go over to Beverly Hills for a few hours of Christmas shopping.'

'Since we're going to get home in time, I'd rather see my analyst. I've got a four-thirty appointment. I've been missing too many of them lately. I'll do my shopping tomorrow. Besides, I haven't given any thought to Christmas gifts. I don't have any idea what to get you.'

'I can see your problem,' he said. 'I *am* the man who has everything.'

'Oh, are you?'

'Naturally. I have you.'

'That's corny.'

'But I mean it.'

'You make me blush.'

'That's never been difficult.'

She put her right hand to her cheek. 'I can feel it. I wish I could control it.'

'I'm glad you can't,' he said. 'It's charming. It's a sign of your innocence.'

'Me? Innocent?'

'As a baby,' he said.

'Remember me in bed last night?'

'How could I forget?'

'Was that innocence?'

'That was heaven.'

'So there.'

'But you're still blushing.'

'Oh, drink your wine and shut up.'

'Still blushing,' he said.

'I'm flushed from the wine.'

'Still blushing.'

'Damn you,' she said affectionately.

'*Still* blushing.'

She laughed.

Beyond the window thick curdled clouds continued to roll in from the ocean.

Over the spumoni and coffee Mary asked, 'What do you think of adoption?'

He shook his head in mock despair. 'We're too old to find parents now. Who would want kids as big as us?'

'Be serious,' she said.

He stared at her for a long moment, then put down his spoon without eating the spumoni on it. 'You really mean you and me . . . adopting a child?'

She was encouraged by the wonder in his voice. 'We've talked about having a family,' she said. 'And since I'll never be able to have a baby of my own . . .'

'But maybe you will.'

'No, no,' she said. 'The doctor made that very clear to me.'

'Doctors have been known to be mistaken.'

'Not this time,' she said, almost too softly to be heard. 'There's too much wrong . . . inside of me. I'll never have a baby, Max. Never.'

'Adoption . . .' Max thought about it while he sipped his coffee. Gradually he began to grin. 'Yeah. It would be nice. A cute little baby girl.'

'I was thinking about a little boy.'

'Well, sure as hell this is one thing we can't compromise on.'

'We can,' she said quickly. 'We'll adopt a girl *and* a boy.'

'You've thought of everything, haven't you?'

'Oh, Max, you really do like the idea. I can tell. We could talk to an adoption agency this week. And if—'

'Hold on,' he said, his smile fading. 'We've been married only four months. We should take our time, get to know each other and ourselves better than we do. Then we'll be *ready* for children.'

She didn't hide her disappointment. 'How long will that take?'

'It'll take as long as it takes. Six months . . . a year.'

'Look, I know you. You know me. We love each other and we like each other. We've got intelligence, common sense, and loads of money. What else do we need to be good parents?'

'We need to be at peace with ourselves, in ourselves,' he said.

'You don't fight anymore. You're at peace with yourself.'

'I'm only halfway there,' he said. 'And you've got things to face, too.'

Defiantly, although she knew the answer, she said, 'Like what?'

'You've got to face up to what happened twenty-four years ago, remember what you've refused to remember . . . every detail of the beating you took . . . everything about what that man did to you when you were six years old. Until you come to terms with that, you'll continue to have the nightmares. You'll never know real peace of mind until those memories are confronted and exorcised.'

She tossed her head, throwing her long hair over her shoulders. 'I don't have to face what happened then to be a good parent now.'

'I think you do,' he said.

'But Max, there are so many kids without homes, without hope or a future. Right now we could give two of them—'

He squeezed her hand. 'You're playing Atlas again. Mary, I understand you. There's more love in you than in anyone I've ever known. You want to share it; that's the meaning of you. And I promised you'll have the opportunity. But adoption is a big step. We'll take it only when we're ready.'

She couldn't get angry. She smiled and said, 'I'll wear you down. I promise.'

He sighed. 'You probably will.'

★ ★ ★

Mary didn't like to drive fast. When she was nine years old her father died in an accident. She'd been in the car when it happened. To her, the automobile was a treacherous machine.

As a passenger, she endured high speeds only when Max was at the wheel. With him in command, she was able to relax and even to feel exhilarated as the scenery whipped past her window. Max was her guardian. He watched over her and protected her. It was inconceivable that anything bad could happen to her when she was with him.

395

He took great pleasure in handling the Mercedes at speeds that tested his skills and his ability to avoid police detection. He enjoyed the car as much as he did his gun collection; and when he drove, he was as single-minded as when he made love. On a long, uncrowded straight stretch of freeway, with all his attention rivetted to the car beneath him, and on the blurred tarmac that succumbed to him, he rarely had patience for conversation. He looked like a bird of prey, flint-eyed, silent, hunched over the steering wheel.

When he drove like that, Mary could see the recklessness, the taste for excitement and violence that had got him into dozens of fights. Oddly, she wasn't frightened by that aspect of him; instead, she found him more attractive than ever.

They rocketed towards Los Angeles at ninety miles an hour.

* * *

The eighteen-room English Tudor house in Bel Air looked cool and elegant in the shade of thirty-foot trees. The two-acre estate had cost her virtually every dollar that she had earned from her first two best-sellers, but she had never regretted the cost.

When they parked in the circular drive, Emmet Churchill came out to greet them. He had grey hair and a neat moustache. He was sixty years old, but his face was unlined. A life in service had been remarkably agreeable to both Emmet and his wife. 'Good trip, Mr Bergen?'

'Fine,' Max said. 'Had it up to one-twenty for a few miles, and Mary didn't scream once.'

'I would have,' Emmet said.

Mary had expected to find another Mercedes in the driveway. 'Isn't Alan home?'

'He stopped by for fresh clothes,' Emmet said. 'But he was anxious to be off on vacation.'

She was disappointed. She'd hoped for another chance to convince him that he and Max *could* get along if they tried. 'How's Anna?' she asked Emmet.

'Couldn't be better. When you called this morning to say that you'd be home, she started planning dinner right away. She's in the kitchen now.'

'As soon as Max freshens up, he'll be going to Beverly Hills to do some shopping,' Mary told Emmet. 'You'll want to get our

396

luggage out of the Mercedes before he leaves.'

'Right away.'

She started toward the front door. 'And would you get my car out of the garage? I've got a four-thirty appointment with Dr Cauvel. I want—'

The man coming at her, relentless, power in the blow, a knife deep in her stomach, blade twisting, flesh tearing, blood erupting, pain erupting, blackness flowing, flowing . . .

* * *

She regained consciousness as Max put her down on the bed in the second-floor master suite. She clung to him. She couldn't stop shaking.

'Are you all right?'

'Hold me,' she said.

He did. 'Easy. Easy now.'

She could feel the strong, unhurried beat of his heart. After a while she said, 'I'm thirsty.'

'Is that all? Aren't you hurt? Should I call a doctor?'

'Just get me some water.'

'You passed out.'

'I'm fine now.'

When he came back from the bathroom with the water, he helped her sit up. He held the glass, tilted it as she drank, nursed her as if she were a sick child. When she was finished, he said, 'What happened?'

Leaning against the headboard, she said, 'Another vision that I didn't ask for. Only . . . it's different from anything that's come before.'

She must have gone pale, for he said, 'Calm down. It's over.'

He looked good. Marvellous. So big and reliable.

She did calm down somewhat, merely because he told her she should.

'I didn't just *see* the damned thing, Max. I *felt* it. A knife. I felt a knife going into me, ripping me apart . . .'

She put one hand on her belly. There was no wound. No bruise. The flesh wasn't even tender.

'Let's get this straight,' he said. 'You saw yourself being stabbed to death?'

'No.'

397

'What *did* you see?'

She got up, waved him away as he moved to support her. She want to the window and looked out at the forty-foot pool behind the main house, at the lush grounds and at the Churchills' little house at the far end of the property. Ordinarily she would have been calmed further by this evidence of prosperity; but now it had no effect on her. 'I saw another woman. Not me. But I felt her pain as if it were mine.'

'That's never happened before.'

'It did this time.'

'Have you ever heard of another clairvoyant having the same experience? Hurkos? Croiset? Dykshoorn?'

'No.' She turned from the window. 'What's it mean? What's going to happen to me.'

'Nothing will happen to you.' Convinced that she wasn't ill, he began the gentle interrogation that could guide her through a vision in progress or through the memory of a vision that had passed. 'Has this thing you just saw happened yet?'

'No.'

'This woman who will be stabbed . . . was she one of those you saw in the nightmare last evening?'

'No. A new one.'

'Did you see her face clearly?'

'I did. But only briefly.'

Mary sat in a wing-back chair by the window. Her hands, against the brown crushed-velvet upholstery, were pale, almost translucent. She felt lighter than air, as if her existence were tenuous, as if she were fading away.

'What did this woman look like?' Max asked.

'Pretty.'

He paced before her. 'Colour of hair?'

'Brunette.'

'Eyes?'

'Green or blue.'

'Young?'

'Yes. About my age.'

'Did you sense her name?'

'No. But I think I've seen her before.'

'You thought the same of one of them last night.'

She nodded.

398

'What gives you the idea you know her?'

'I can't say. It's just an impression.'

'Was the scene of this crime the same as in last night's vision?'

'No. This woman will be murdered . . . in a beauty parlour.'

'At a hairdresser's?'

'Yes. The beautician is a man.'

'What will happen to him?'

'He'll be killed, too.'

'Any other victims?'

'A third. Another woman.'

She had sensed a great deal in the few seconds that the psychic images had coruscated through her mind. However, with each datum came the brutal recollection of that knife she had shared mystically with the dying woman.

'What's the name of the beauty shop?' Max asked.

'I don't know.'

'Where's it located?'

'Not far from here.'

'In Orange County again?'

'Yes.'

'Which town?'

'I don't know.'

He sighed, sat down in the armchair opposite hers. 'Is the killer the same as the one you saw last night?'

'No doubt about it.'

'So he's a repeater, a psychopath, a mass murderer. He's going to kill four or five people in one place and three in another.'

'That may only be the start,' she said softly.

'What does he look like?'

'I still don't know.'

'Is he a big man or small?'

'I don't know.'

'What's his name?'

'I wish I knew.'

'Is he young or old?'

'I don't even know that.'

The room was stuffy. The air was stale, almost rank. She got up and opened the window.

'If you can't get an image of him,' Max said, 'how can you tell it's the same killer in both visions.'

'I just *can*, that's all.'

She sat down, face to the window.

She felt hollow, light. She could imagine being carried off by the breeze, slight as it was. The unbidden visions had sucked a lot of energy from her. She wouldn't be able to endure many more of them. Certainly not a life full of them.

Pretty soon, she thought, I won't need a tornado like Dorothy did. Just a puff of air will carry *me* off to Oz.

'What can we do to keep him from killing?' Max asked.

'Nothing.'

'Then let's put him out of our minds for now.'

She scowled. 'Know when I feel worst? You know when I feel so awful I hardly want to live?'

He waited.

Her hands were in her lap, her fingers at war with one another. 'It's when I know something horrible will happen – but I don't know enough to stop it from happening. If I must have this power, why wasn't I given it without strings attached? Why can't I turn it on and off like a television set? Why does it sometimes get all cloudy for me when I need it the most? Am I supposed to be tormented? Is it a nasty joke? A lot of people are going to die because I can't see clearly. Dammit, dammit, dammit!' She jumped up, strode to the television. She turned the set on, off, on, off, on, off, with nearly enough force to break the switch.

'You can't feel responsible for what you see in your visions,' he said.

'But I do.'

'You've got to change.'

'I won't. I can't.'

He stood up, went to her, took her hand from the television controls. 'Why don't you freshen up? We'll do some shopping.'

'Not me,' she said. 'I have an appointment with Dr Cauvel.'

'That's two and a half hours from now.'

'I'm not up to shopping,' she said. 'You go. I'll make the rounds tomorrow.'

'I can't leave you here alone.'

'I won't be alone. Anna and Emmet are here.'

'You shouldn't drive.'

'Why not?'

400

'What if you have another attack while you're behind the wheel?'

'Oh. Then Emmet can drive me.'

'What'll you do until you see the analyst?'

'Write a column,' she said.

'We sent a packet to the syndicate last week. We're already twenty columns ahead of schedule.'

Although she didn't feel well, she managed a light tone. 'We're twenty ahead because you wrote fifteen of them. It's time I did my share. Being twenty-one ahead won't hurt.'

'There's some material on my desk about that woman in North Carolina who can predict the sex of unborn babies just by touching the mother. They're studying her at Duke University.'

'Then that's what I'll write about.'

'Well, if you're positive . . .'

'I am. Now scoot over to Gucci, Giorgio's, The French Corner, Juel Park, Courrèges, Van Cleef and Arpels – and buy me beautiful things for Christmas.'

Trying to keep from smiling, he said, 'But I already have something picked out at Woolworth's.'

'Oh,' she said, playing along with him, 'then you won't mind that I'm only getting you a gift certificate for some McDonald's hamburgers.'

He pretended to be disappointed. 'Well, I might stop at Gucci and Edwards Lowell for a few things that'll go with the Woolworth's piece.'

She grinned. 'You do that. Then maybe I'll let you sleep in here tonight instead of on the couch.'

He laughed and kissed her.

'Mmmm,' she said. 'Again.'

She knew that she was loved, and that knowledge compensated somewhat for the horror of the past few days.

EIGHT

The focal point of Dr Cauvel's office was a collection of hundreds of glass dogs that were displayed on glass and chrome shelves to one side of his desk. No member of the menagerie was larger than Mary's hand, and most were a great deal smaller than that. There were blue dogs, brown dogs, red dogs, clear dogs, milky white dogs, black dogs, orange and yellow and purple and green dogs, transparent and opaque, striped and polka-dotted, hand-blown and solid glass dogs. Some of them were lying down, some sitting, standing, pointing, running. There were basset hounds, greyhounds, Airedales, German shepherds, Pekingese, terriers, Saint Bernards, and a dozen other breeds. A bitch with a litter of fragile glass puppies stood near a comic scene of dogs playing tiny glass instruments, flutes and drums and bugles for beagles. Several curious figures shone darkly in the silent zoo: snarling hellhounds, demons with dog faces and forked tongues.

Glass was also the focal point of the doctor himself. He wore thick spectacles that made his eyes appear abnormally large. He was short, athletic looking, and compulsively neat about himself. The spectacles were never smudged; he polished them continually.

Mary and the doctor sat across from each other at a folding table in the middle of the room.

The psychiatrist shuffled a deck of playing cards. He dealt ten of them face-down in a single row.

She picked up a six-inch loop of wire that he had provided and held it over the cards. She moved it back and forth. Twice it dipped towards the table as if invisible fingers were tugging it out of her hands. After less than a minute of dowsing, she put down the loop and indicated two of the ten cards. 'These are the highest values in the batch.'

'What are they?' Cauvel asked.

'One might be an ace.'

'Of which suit?'

'I don't know.'

He turned them over. An ace of clubs. A queen of hearts. She relaxed.

He revealed the other cards. The highest value was a jack.

'Incredible,' he said. 'This is one of the most difficult tests we've tried. But out of ten attempts, you've been ninety per cent accurate. Ever think of going to Las Vegas?'

'To break the bank at the twenty-one tables?'

'Why not?' he asked.

'The only way I'd have a chance is if they spread out the cards and let me use a wire loop on them before they dealt.'

Like all his movements and expressions, his smile was economical. 'Not likely.'

For the past two years her Tuesday and Friday appointments had begun at four-thirty and ended at six o'clock. On these days she was Cauvel's final patient. During the first three quarters of an hour she participated in some experiments in extra-sensory perception for a series of articles he intended to publish in a professional journal. He devoted the second forty-five minutes to treating her in his capacity as a psychiatrist. In return for her cooperation he waived his fee.

She could afford to pay for treatment. She permitted the current arrangements because the experiments interested her.

'Brandy?' he asked.

'Please.'

He poured Remy Martin for both of them.

They moved from the card table to a pair of armchairs that faced each other across a small round cocktail table.

Cauvel used no standard technique with his patients. His style was very much his own. She liked his quiet, friendly approach.

'Where would you like to begin?' he asked.

'I don't know.'

'Take your time.'

'I don't want to begin at all.'

'You always say that, and you always begin.'

'Not today. I'd just like to sit here.'

He nodded, sipped his brandy.

'Why am I always so difficult for you?' she asked.

'I can't answer that. *You* can.'

'Why don't I want to talk to you?'

'Oh, you do want to talk. Otherwise you wouldn't be here.'

Frowning, she said, 'Help me start.'

'What were you thinking about on your way here?'

'That's no place to start.'

'Try it.'

'Well . . . I was thinking about what I am.'

'And what's that?'

'A clairvoyant.'

'What about it?'

'Why me? Why not someone else?'

'The top researchers in this field believe we all have the same paranormal talents.'

'Maybe,' she said. 'But most people don't have it to the extent that I do.'

'We just don't recognize our potential,' he said. 'Only a handful of people have found a way to use their ESP.'

'So why did *I* find a way?'

'Haven't all of the best clairvoyants suffered head injuries at some time prior to the discovery of their psychic powers?'

'Peter Hurkos did,' she said. 'And a number of others. But not all of us.'

'Did you?'

'Suffer a head injury? No.'

'Yes, you did.'

She sipped her brandy. 'What a wonderful taste.'

'You were injured when you were six years old. You've mentioned it a few times, but you've never wanted to pursue it.'

'And I don't want to pursue it now.'

'You should,' Cauvel said. 'Your reluctance to discuss it is proof that—'

'You're talking too much today.' Her voice was hard, too loud. 'I pay you to listen.'

'You don't pay me at all.' As always, he spoke gently.

'I could walk out of here right now.'

He took off his glasses and polished them with his handkerchief.

'Without me,' she said sharply, disliking his studied calm, 'you wouldn't have the data to write those articles that make you a big man among the other shrinks.'

'The articles aren't that important. If you want so much to walk out, do it. Shall we terminate our arrangement?'

She sagged back into her chair. 'Sorry.' She seldom raised her voice. It wasn't like her to shout at him. She was blushing.

'No need to apologize,' he said. 'But don't you see that this experience twenty-four years ago might be the root of your problem? It could be the underlying cause of your insomnia, of your periodic deep depressions, of your anxiety attacks.'

She felt weak. She closed her eyes. 'You want me to pursue it.'

'That would be a good idea.'

'Help me start.'

'You were six years old.'

'Six . . .'

'Your father had money then.'

'Quite a lot of it.'

'You lived on a small estate.'

'Twenty acres,' she said. 'Most of it landscaped. There was a full-time . . . a full-time . . .'

'Gardener.'

'Gardener,' she said. She wasn't blushing anymore. Her cheeks were cold. Her hands were icy.

'What was his name?'

'I don't remember.'

'Of course you do.'

'Berton Mitchell.'

'Did you like him?'

'At first I did.'

'You said once that he teased you.'

'In a fun way. And he had a special name for me.'

'What did he call you?'

'Contrary. As if that were my real name.'

'*Were* you contrary?'

'Not the least bit. He was teasing. He got it from the nursery rhyme. "Mary, Mary, quite contrary" . . .'

'When did you stop liking Berton Mitchell?'

She wanted to be home with Max. She could almost feel his arms around her.

'When did you stop liking him, Mary?'

'That day in August.'

'What happened?'

'You know.'

'Yes, I do know.'

'Well then.'

'But we never seem to get further into this thing unless we start from the top each time.'

'I don't *want* to get further into it.'

But he was relentless. 'What happened that day in August when you were six years old?'

'Have you got any new glass dogs recently?'

'What did Berton Mitchell do that day in August?'

'He tried to rape me.'

* * *

Six P.M. Early winter night. The air was cool and fresh.

He left the car at the coffee shop and walked north along the highway, his back to the traffic.

He had a knife in one pocket, a revolver in the other. He kept his hands on both weapons.

His shoes crunched in the gravel.

The wind from the passing cars buffeted him, messed his hair, pasted his overcoat to his legs.

The beauty shop, Hair Today, occupied a small detached building on Main Street, just north of the Santa Ana city limits. With its imitation thatched roof, leaded windows, plaster and exposed-beam exterior, the place resembled a cottage in the English countryside – except for the floodlights shining on the front of it, and except for the pink and green paint job.

The block was strictly commercial. Service stations, fast-food restaurants, real estate offices, dozens of small businesses, all of them nestled in neon and palm trees and jade-plant hedges, flourished like ugly flowers in the money-scented Orange County air. South of Hair Today was the sales lot of an imported automobile dealership. Row after row of sleek machines huddled in the night. Only the windshields and chrome gleamed malevolently under mercury-vapour lights. North, beyond the beauty shop, lay a three-screen motion picture theatre, and beyond that a shopping centre.

A dirty white Cadillac and a shiny Triumph stood on the macadam parking area in front of Hair Today.

He crossed the lot, walked between the cars, opened the cottage door, and went inside.

The narrow front room was a lounge where women marked time until their appointments. The carpet was purple and plush, the chairs bright yellow, the drapes white. There were end tables, ashtrays, and stacks of magazines, but at this late hour there were no customers waiting.

At the rear of the room was a purple and white counter. A cash register rested on it, and a woman with bleached blonde hair sat on a stool behind it.

Behind the woman a curtained archway led to the working part of the shop. The sound of a hand-held dryer penetrated the curtain like the buzz of angry bees.

'We're closed,' the bleached blonde said.

He went to the counter.

'Are you looking for someone?' she said.

He took the revolver out of his pocket. It felt good in his hand. It felt like justice.

She stared at the gun, then into his eyes. She licked her lips. 'What do you want?'

He didn't speak.

She said, 'Now wait.'

He pulled the trigger. The sound was masked somewhat by the noisy dryer.

She fell off the stool and didn't get up.

The hair dryer shut off. From the back room someone said, 'Tina?'

He walked around the dead woman, parted the curtains and stepped through them.

Of the four salon chairs, three were empty. The last customer of the day sat in the fourth chair. She was young and pretty, with an impossibly creamy complexion. Her hair was straight and wet.

The hairdresser was a burly man, bald, with a bristling black moustache. He wore a purple uniform shirt with his first name, Kyle, embroidered in yellow on the breast pocket.

The woman drew a deep breath, but she couldn't find the courage to scream.

'Who are you?' Kyle asked.

He shot Kyle twice.

★ ★ ★

407

'My father wasn't at home that day,' Mary said.

'And your mother?'

'She was up at the main house. Drunk as usual.'

'And your brother?'

'Alan was in his room, working on his model airplanes.'

'The gardener, Berton Mitchell?'

'His wife and son were away for the week. Mitchell . . . got me into this place, enticed me into it.'

'Where was this?'

'Down at the far end of the estate, a little cottage with a green shingle roof. He often told me that elves lived with his family.'

An awesome force pressed against her from all sides. She felt as if she was enfolded by leather wings, muscular wings that were draining the heat from her, squeezing the life out of her.

'Go on,' Cauvel said.

Relentlessly the warmth dropped out of her like mercury falling in a thermometer. She was a cold, hollow reed of glass, brittle, breakable. 'More brandy?'

'When you've finished telling me,' Cauvel said.

'I need help with this.'

'I'm here to help you, Mary.'

'If I tell, he'll hurt me.'

'Who? Mitchell? You don't believe that. You know he's dead. He was found guilty of child molestation, of assault with intent to kill. He hung himself in his cell. I'm the only one here, and I won't let anyone hurt you.'

'I was alone with him.'

'You're speaking so softly I can't hear you.'

'I was alone with him,' she said again. 'He . . . touched . . . me . . . exposed himself.'

'Were you frightened?'

'Yes.'

The pressure was intense, unbearable, and getting worse.

Cauvel didn't speak, and she said, 'I was frightened because he wanted me . . . to do things.'

'What things?'

The air was foul. Although only she and the doctor were in the room, she felt that some creature had its lips to hers and was forcing its rank breath into her lungs.

'I need brandy,' she said.

'What you need is to tell me all of this, to remember every last detail, to get it out in the open once and for all. What things did he want you to do?'

'Help me. You've got to guide me.'

'He wanted to have intercourse, didn't he?'

'I'm not sure.'

Her hands were numb. She could feel cords biting into them. But there were no cords.

'Oral intercourse?' Cauvel asked.

'But not only that.'

Her ankles were sore. She could feel cords that were not there. She moved her feet. They were leaden.

'What else did he want to do?' Cauvel asked.

'I don't recall.'

'You can remember if you want to.'

'No. Honestly, I can't. I can't.'

'What else did he want you to do?'

The embrace of the imaginary wings was so tight that she had difficulty breathing. She could hear them beating the air – *wicka-wicka-wicka* . . .

She stood up, walked away from the chair.

The wings held her.

'What else did he want you to do?' Cauvel asked.

'Something awful, unspeakable.'

'A sex act of some sort?'

Wicka-wicka-wicka . . .

'Not just sex. More than that,' she said.

'What was it?'

'Dirty. Filthy.'

'In what way?'

'Eyes watching me.'

'Mitchell's eyes?'

'Not his.'

'Who then?'

'I can't remember.'

'You can.'

Wicka-wicka . . .

'Wings,' she said.

'Rings? You're speaking too softly again.'

'Wings,' she said. 'Wings.'

409

'What do you mean?'

She was shaking, vibrating. She was afraid her legs would fail her. She returned to the armchair. 'Wings. I can hear them flapping. I can *feel* them.'

'You mean Mitchell kept a bird in the house?'

'I don't know.'

'A parrot perhaps?'

'I couldn't say.'

'Work at remembering it, Mary. Don't let go of this thought. You've never mentioned wings before. It's important.'

'They were everywhere.'

'The wings?'

'All over me. Little wings.'

'Think. What did he do to you?'

She was silent a long while. The pressure began to ease a bit. The sound of wings faded.

'Mary?'

Finally she said, 'That's all. I can't recall anything else.'

'There is a way to unlock those memories,' he said.

'Hypnosis,' she replied.

'It works.'

'I'm afraid to remember.'

'You should be afraid *not* to remember.'

'If I remember, I'll die.'

'That's ridiculous, and you know it.'

She pushed her hair back from her face. For his benefit, she forced a smile. 'I don't hear the wings now. I can't feel them. We don't need to talk about wings anymore.'

'Of course we do.'

'I *won't* talk about wings, dammit!' She shook her head violently. She was surprised and frightened by her own vehemence. 'Not today anyway.'

'All right,' Cauvel said. 'I'll accept that. That's not the same thing as saying you don't *need* to talk.' He began to polish his glasses once more. 'Let's go back to what you remember. Berton Mitchell beat you.'

'I suppose he did.'

'You were found in his place?'

'In his living room.'

'And you were badly beaten?'

'Yes.'

'And later you told them he did it.'

'But I can't remember it happening. I recall the pain, terrible pain. But only for an instant.'

'You could have lost consciousness with the first blow.'

'That's what everyone said. He must have kept hitting me after I passed out. I couldn't have stood up to him for long. I was just a little girl.'

'He used a knife, too?'

'I was cut all over.'

'How long were you in the hospital?'

'More than two weeks.'

'How many stitches for the wounds?'

'More than a hundred altogether.'

* * *

The beauty shop smelled of shampoo, cream rinse, and cologne. He could also smell the woman's sweat.

The floor was littered with hair. It swirled around them as he moved onto her and into her.

She refused to respond to him. She neither welcomed him nor struggled against him. She lay still. Her eyes were like the eyes of the dead.

He didn't hate her for that. In the long run he'd never cared for passion in his women. For the first few months a new lover's aggression and delight in sex was tolerable. He could be tender for a short time. But always, after a few months, he needed to see fear in them. That was what brought him to climax. The more they feared him, the better he liked them.

As he lay on her, he could feel this woman's heart thumping wildly, accelerated by terror. That excited him, and he began to move faster within her.

* * *

'You took a number of Mitchell's blows on your head,' Cauvel said.

'My face was black and blue. My father called me his little patchwork doll.'

411

'Did you suffer a concussion?'

'I see where all of this is leading,' she said. 'But no. No concussion. Absolutely not.'

'When did your visions begin?'

'Later the same year.'

'A few minutes ago you asked me why you'd been singled out to be a clairvoyant. Well, there's nothing mysterious about it really. As in the case of Peter Hurkis, your psychic talent came after a serious head injury.'

'Not serious enough.'

He stopped polishing his spectacles, put them on, and studied her with huge, magnified eyes. 'Is it possible that a severe psychological shock could trigger psychic abilities in the same way that certain head injuries seem to do?'

She shrugged.

'If you didn't acquire your power as a result of a physical trauma, then maybe you acquired it because of a *psychological* trauma. Do you suppose that's possible?'

'It could be,' she said.

'Either way,' he said, thrusting a bony finger at her, as if repeatedly tapping a window between them, 'either way, your clairvoyance probably goes back to Berton Mitchell, to what he did to you that you can't remember.'

'Maybe.'

'And your insomnia goes back to Berton Mitchell. Your periodic depressions go back to him. What he did to you is the underlying cause of your anxiety attacks. I tell you, Mary, the sooner you face up to this the better. If you ever let me use hypnosis to regress and guide you through the memories, then you'll never need my help again.'

'I'll always need your help.'

He scowled. His deeply tanned face was scored by lines like sabre slashes. An ambitious portrait painter would have wanted to catch him with that expression, for it made him look fierce, yet fair and reliable. It was that expression that drew her to him at a party three years ago; and his distant but paternal manner caused her to seek his advice when her dependency on sleeping pills became absolute.

'If you'll always need my help,' he said, 'then I'm not helping you at all. As a psychiatrist, I must make you find all the strength you need inside yourself.'

She went to the bar and picked up the decanter of brandy. 'You said I could have another if I kept talking for a while.'

'I never break a promise.' He joined her at the bar. 'The day's nearly over. I'll have another, too.'

As she poured for them, she said, 'You're wrong about Mitchell.'

'In what sense?'

'I don't think all of my problems date back to him. Some of them started the day my father died.'

'I've heard you expound on that theory before.'

'I was in the car with him when he was killed. I was in the back seat and he was driving. I saw him die. His blood sprayed all over me. I was only nine. And the years after he died weren't easy. In three years my mother lost all the money my father left us. We went from rich to poor between my ninth and twelfth birthdays. I think an experience like that would leave some scars, don't you?'

'It has,' he said. He picked up his brandy glass. 'But it's not responsible for the *worst* scars.'

'How do you know?'

'You're able to talk about it.'

'So?'

'But you aren't able to talk about what happened with Berton Mitchell.'

* * *

When he finished with the woman, he stood, pulled up his pants, zipped his fly. He hadn't even taken off his coat.

He stepped back from her, looked at her.

Given the opportunity, she made no effort to cover herself. Her skirt was bunched around her hips. Her blouse was unbuttoned; one plump breast was visible. Her hands were fisted. Her fingernails had gouged her palms, and ribbons of blood were on her hands. Terrorized, reduced to little more than a cowering animal, she represented his ideal woman.

He took the knife out of his coat pocket.

He expected her to scream and scramble away from him, but as he moved in for the kill, she lay as if she were dead already. She was past fear now, past feeling anything.

Kneeling beside her, he placed the point of the blade at her throat. The flesh dimpled around it, but she didn't blink.

413

He raised the blade high, held it in her line of sight, over her breasts.

No response.

He was disappointed. When time and circumstance allowed, he preferred to kill slowly. To get any thrill from that game, he required a lively woman for prey.

Angry with her for spoiling the moment, he rammed the knife down.

★ ★ ★

Mary Bergen gasped.

The razor edge ripping her skin, opening muscle, opening the reservoir of blood, opening the dark place where pain was stored . . .

She leaned into the corner formed by the wall and the side of the antique oak bar. She was only half aware that she knocked over an unopened bottle of Scotch.

'What's the matter?' Cauvel asked.

'It hurts.'

He touched her shoulder. 'Are you sick? Can I help?'

'Not sick. The vision. I feel it.'

The knife again, thrust deep . . .

She put both hands to her stomach, trying to contain the eruption of pain. 'I won't faint this time. I won't!'

'A vision of what?' Cauvel asked worriedly.

'The beauty shop. The same one I saw a few hours ago. Only it's happening now. The slaughter . . . God almighty . . . happening somewhere, happening right this minute.' She put her hands to her face, but the images would not be shut out. 'Oh, God. Sweet God. Help me.'

'What do you see?'

'A dead man on the floor.'

'The floor of the beauty shop?'

'He's bald . . . moustache . . . purple shirt.'

'What is it you're feeling?'

The knife . . .

She was sweating. Crying.

'Mary? *Mary?*'

'I feel . . . the woman . . . being stabbed.'

'What woman? There's a woman?'

414

'Mustn't black out.'

She started to sag, and he held her by both shoulders.

She saw the knife gouging flesh again, but she felt no pain this time. The woman in the vision was dead; therefore, there was no more pain to share.

'Have to see his face, have to get his name,' she said.

The killer standing up from the body, standing in a cape, no, a long coat, an overcoat . . .

'Can't lose the thread. Mustn't lose the vision. Have to hold it, have to find where he is, who he is, *what* he is, stop him from doing these awful things.'

The killer standing, standing with the butcher knife in one hand, standing in shadow, his face in shadow but turning now, turning very slowly and deliberately, turning so that she'll be able to see his face, turning as if he is looking for her—

'He knows I'm with him,' she said.

'Who knows?'

'He knows I'm watching.'

She didn't understand how that could be true. Yet the killer knew about her. She was certain of that, and she was scared.

Suddenly half a dozen glass dogs leaped from the display shelves, flew through the air, and smashed with a great deal of force into the wall beside Mary.

She screamed.

Cauvel turned to see who had thrown them. 'What the hell?'

As if they had come to life and had acquired wings, a dozen glass dogs swept off the top shelf. They spun, glittering like fragments of an exploded prism, to the high centre of the room. They bounced off the ceiling, struck one another with the musical rattle of Chinese wind chimes.

Then they streaked towards Mary.

She raised her arms, covered her face.

The miniatures battered her harder than she had expected. They stung like bees.

'Stop them!' she said, not certain to whom she was speaking.

A hellhound with pointy horns struck the doctor in the forehead between the eyes and drew blood.

Cauvel turned away from the shelves, moved against her, tried to shield her with his body.

Another ten or fifteen dogs bulleted around the room. Two of

415

them smashed through a stained glass panel in the bar. Others burst to pieces on the wall around Mary, icing her hair with chunks and slivers of coloured glass.

'It's trying to kill me!' She was struggling unsuccessfully to avoid hysteria.

Cauvel pressed her into the corner.

More glass dogs whistled across the room, swooped over the psychiatrist's desk, scattered a sheaf of onionskin papers. The figurines clattered against the venetian blinds without shattering, rose up again, zigzagged crazily from one end of the chamber to the other, then pelted Cauvel's shoulders and back, rained fragments over Mary's bowed head.

Yet another squadron of dogs took flight. They danced in the air, swarmed ominously, fluttered against Mary, flew away, came back with greater determination, struck her with incredible force, stung, bruised, hung over her like locusts.

As suddenly as the macabre assault began, it ended. Almost a hundred glass miniatures remained on the display shelves, but they did not move.

Mary and Cauvel huddled together, not trusting the calm, waiting for another attack.

Silence prevailed.

Eventually he let go of her and stepped back.

She was unable to control the tremors that broke like waves within her.

'Are you all right?' he asked, oblivious to the blood on his own face.

'I wasn't meant to see him,' she said.

Cauvel was dazed. He stared, uncomprehendingly.

'His face,' she said. 'I wasn't meant to see it.'

'What are you talking about?'

'When I tried to see the killer in the vision,' she said, 'I was stopped. What stopped me?'

Cauvel gazed at the shards of glass on all sides of them. He began to pick splinters of glass from the shoulders and sleeves of his suit jacket. 'Did you do this? Did you make the dogs fly?'

'Me?'

'Who else?'

'Oh, no. How could I?'

'Someone did.'

416

'Some*thing*.'

He stared at her.

'It was a . . . spirit,' she said.

'I don't believe in life after death.'

'I wasn't sure about that myself. Until now.'

'So we're haunted?'

'What else?'

'Many possibilities.' He looked concerned about her.

'I'm not crazy,' she said.

'Did I say you were?'

'We've seen a poltergeist in action.'

'I don't believe in them either,' he said.

'I do. I've seen them work before. I was never sure if they were spirits or not. But now I am.'

'Mary—'

'A poltergeist. It came to stop me from seeing the killer's face.'

Behind them the display shelves toppled and struck the floor with a thunderous crash.

NINE

Max was not at home.

Without him Mary felt that the house was a mausoleum. Her footsteps on the hardwood floor seemed louder than usual, the echoes full of sinister voices.

'He called earlier,' Anna Churchill said, as she wiped her hands on her apron. 'He asked me to delay dinner half an hour.'

'Why?'

'He said to tell you he wouldn't be back until eight o'clock because Woolworth's is open late for Christmas shopping.'

She knew that Max had meant to make her laugh with that message, but she couldn't even smile. The only thing that would lift her spirits was the sight of him. She didn't want to be alone.

As she went through the parlour on her way to the mahogany staircase, she felt dwarfed by the heavy European furniture. With the memory of the poltergeist fresh in her mind, she expected each piece of furniture to come to life, and she didn't know how she would survive if the chairs and sofas and corner cabinets began to rush at her with murderous intent.

The furniture did not move.

Upstairs, in her bathroom, she took a bottle of valium from the medicine cabinet. She had been able to conceal her nervousness when she was with Emmet and Anna; but now her hands shook so badly that she needed almost a minute to get the safety cap off the container. She poured a glass of cold water, swallowed one of the capsules. One didn't seem like much. She felt she could use two. Maybe three. 'God, no,' she said, and she quickly replaced the cap before temptation got the better of good judgement.

As she was leaving the bathroom, the empty water glass fell to the floor, shattered. Startled, she whirled around. She was sure she hadn't set the tumbler on the edge of the sink. It had not fallen: something had knocked it off.

'Max, please come home,' she said softly.

★ ★ ★

She waited for him in the second-floor den, his favourite room, a room crammed full of guns and books. Antique rifles expertly restored and mounted in wall display boxes. Matched sets of Hemingway, Stevenson, Poe, Shaw, Fitzgerald, Dickens. A pair of 1872 No. 3 Colt Derringers in a silk-lined, brass-bound carrying case. Novels by John D. Macdonald, Clavell, Bellow, Woolrich, Levin, Vidal; volumes of nonfiction by Gay Talese, Colin Wilson, Hellman, Toland, Shirer. Shotguns, rifles, revolvers, automatic pistols. Raymond Chandler, Dashiell Hammett, Ross MacDonald, Mary McCarthy, James M. Cain, Jessamyn West.

Guns and books were an odd combination, Mary thought. However, next to her, they were the two things that Max liked most.

She tried to read a current bestseller that she had been meaning to begin for weeks, but her mind wandered. She put the book aside, went to Max's desk, sat down. She took a pen and a writing tablet from the centre drawer.

For a while she stared at the blank page. Finally she wrote:

> *Page 1*
> *Questions:*
> *Why am I having these visions when I don't*
> *seek them out?*
> *Why, suddenly, for the first time, am I able*
> *to feel the pain that the victims in the*
> *visions feel?*
> *Why hasn't any other clairvoyant ever felt*
> *his visions?*
> *How could the killer in the beauty shop*
> *possibly know I was watching?*
> *Why would a poltergeist attempt to keep me*
> *from seeing this killer's face?*
> *What does all this mean?*

Ever since she was a child, through major and minor crises, she

419

had felt that it helped to write down her problems. When they were before her, summarized in a few words, somehow more concrete in ink than in reality, they usually ceased to appear insoluble.

After she finished composing the list, she read each question carefully, first silently and then aloud.

On the next page of the tablet she wrote: *Answers.*

She thought for a few minutes. Then: *I don't have any answers.*

'Dammit!' she said.

She threw the pen across the room.

* * *

'Harley Barnes speaking.'

'Chief Barnes, this is Mary Bergen.'

'Why, hello. Are you still in town?'

'No. I'm calling from Bel Air.'

'What can I do for you?'

'I'm writing a column about what happened last night, and I had some questions. The man we caught last night . . . what was his name?'

'Can't you get it with your clairvoyance?'

'I'm afraid not. I can't see everything I want.'

'Name's Richard Lingard.'

'A resident of your town, or an outsider?'

'Born and raised here. I knew his dad and mom. He owned a pharmacy.'

'His age?'

'Early thirties, thereabouts.'

'Is he . . . was he married?'

'Divorced years ago. No children, thank God.'

'Are you sure . . .'

'Sure there aren't children? Oh, yes. Positive.'

'No. I meant . . . is he . . . really dead?'

'Dead? Of course he's dead. Didn't you see him?'

'I just thought . . . Have you found anything unusual about him?'

'Unusual? In what way?'

'Did his neighbours think he was odd in any way?'

'They liked him. Everyone liked him.'

420

'Was anything strange found in his home?'

'Nothing. He lived like anyone else. It's frightening how ordinary he was. If Dick Lingard could turn out to be a psychopathic killer, then who can you trust?'

'No one.'

'Mrs Bergen . . .' Barnes hesitated. 'Did you take the knife?'

'What knife?'

'Lingard's knife.'

'You can't find it?'

'It vanished from the scene.'

'Vanished? Does that happen often?'

'Never before to me.'

'I don't have it.'

'Perhaps your brother picked it up.'

'Alan wouldn't do that.'

'Or your husband?'

'We've worked with the police many times, Chief. We know enough not to make souvenirs out of the evidence.'

'We've searched Miss Harrington's place from top to bottom. The knife isn't there.'

'Maybe Lingard dropped it on the front lawn.'

'We've gone over every inch of that, too.'

'He might have dropped it in the gutter when he collapsed against your squad car.'

'Or on the sidewalk. We didn't search for the knife immediately, like we should have done, and there was a large crowd of spectators. Maybe one of them picked it up. We'll ask around. I imagine we'll come across the thing. At least we don't need it for any trial. Death solved that problem. There's no way a smart attorney can get Richard Lingard out on the streets again.'

★   ★   ★

At seven-thirty the all-news radio station in Los Angeles carried a story about four young nurses who had been found beaten and stabbed to death in their Anaheim apartment.

Beverly Pulchaski.

Susan Haven.

Linda Proctor.

Marie Sanzini.

421

Mary didn't recognize even one of them.

Perplexed, she sat back from the edge of her chair. She recalled the battered face in last night's vision: the black-haired, blue-eyed woman. She was *certain* she knew that face.

* * *

8.00 P.M.

She met Max at the front door. When he came inside and closed the door, he put his arms around her. His clothes were cold, crisp with the night air, but the warmth of his body pressed through the fabric.

'Six hours of shopping,' she said, 'and no packages?'

'I left them to be gift-wrapped. I'll pick them up tomorrow.'

Grinning, she said, 'I didn't know Woolworths did gift-wrapping.'

He kissed her cheek. 'Missed you.'

She leaned back in his arms. 'Hey, where's your overcoat? You'll catch the flu.'

'It got splashed with mud,' he said. 'I dropped it off at the dry cleaner's.'

'How'd it get muddy?'

'I had a flat tyre.'

'A Mercedes *wouldn't*.'

'Ours did. The spot where I had to change it was muddy. I got splashed by a passing car.'

'Did you get his licence number? If you did, I'll—'

'Unfortunately I didn't,' Max said. 'At the time it happened I thought, "If I could get the bastard's number, Mary would find out who he is and thrash him within an inch of his life." '

'Nobody hurts my Max and gets away with it.'

'I also cut my finger changing the tyre,' he said, holding up his right hand. The cuff of the shirt sleeve was soaked with blood, and one finger was bound in a bloody handkerchief. 'There's a sharp metal edge on the jack,' he said.

She took hold of his wrist. 'So much blood! Let's see the cut.'

'It's nothing.' He pulled his hand away before she could remove the handkerchief. 'It's stopped bleeding.'

'Maybe it needs stitches.'

'It needs pressure, that's all. It's a deep cut, but the area's too

422

small to take stitches. And the sight will ruin your dinner.'

'Let me look. I'm a big girl now. Besides, it has to be properly cleaned and bandaged.'

'I'll take care of that,' he said. 'You go ahead to the table. I'll join you in a few minutes.'

'You can't handle it yourself.'

'Of course I can. I wasn't always married, you know. I lived alone for years.' He kissed her forehead. 'Let's not upset Mrs Churchill. If we don't get to the table soon, she'll be in tears.'

With his good hand he pushed Mary towards the dining room.

'If you bleed to death,' she said, 'I'll never forgive you.'

Laughing, he hurried to the stairs and climbed the steps two at a time to the second floor.

★ ★ ★

Dinner was to Mary's taste, hearty yet not heavy. They had onion soup, salad, châteaubriand with beкarnaise sauce, and strips of zucchini marinated in oil and garlic, then broiled briefly.

Over coffee in the library, drifting on a pool of serenity formed by a second valium taken just before Max arrived for dinner, she told him about her day: Cauvel, the pain-filled vision, the poltergeists that had kept her from probing the vision for the name and face of the killer. They discussed the radio report of the dead nurses in Anaheim, which he had also heard, and last of all she told him about her conversation with Harley Barnes.

'You're emphasizing the missing knife,' Max said. 'Isn't Barnes' explanation credible enough? A spectator *could* have taken it.'

'Could have – but didn't.'

'Then who did?'

She was sitting beside him on the sofa. She kicked off her shoes, drew one leg under her, delaying until she could summon the right words. This was a delicate situation. If Max was unable to believe what she had to tell him, he would think her at least *slightly* mad.

'These visions are totally different from any I've ever known,' she said at last. 'Which means the killer, the source of the psychic emanations, is different from any killer I've ever tracked before. He isn't an ordinary man. I've been trying to find a theory that will make sense of what's happened to me since last night, and

423

when I talked with Barnes I found the key. The missing knife is the key. Don't you see? Richard Lingard has the knife.'

'Lingard? He's dead. Barnes shot him. Lingard couldn't have taken his knife anywhere but to a drawer in the morgue.'

'He could have taken it wherever he wanted. Barnes killed Lingard's body. Lingard's spirit took the knife.'

Max was amazed. 'I don't believe in ghosts. And even if spirits *do* exist, they don't have substance, at least not as we think of it. So how could Lingard's spirit, a thing of no substance, carry off a very substantial knife?'

'A spirit has no substance, but it does have *power*,' she said emphatically. 'Two months ago, when you helped me cover that story in Connecticut, you saw a poltergeist in action.'

'What of it?'

'Well, a poltergeist has no apparent substance, yet it tosses around solid objects, doesn't it?'

Reluctantly he said, 'Yes. But I don't believe a poltergeist is the spirit of a dead person.'

'What else could it be?' Before he responded she said, 'Lingard's spirit carried away the butcher knife. I *know* it.'

He drank his coffee in three long swallows. 'Suppose that's true. Where's his spirit now?'

'In possession of someone living.'

'*What?*'

'As soon as Lingard's body died, his spirit slipped out of it and into someone else.'

Max got up, walked to the bookshelves. He looked at Mary with eyes that studied, weighed, and judged. 'In every session with Cauvel, you've come closer to remembering what Berton Mitchell did to you.'

'So you think that because I'm on the verge of knowing, I might be seeking escape from the truth, escape in madness.'

'*Can* you face up to what he did?'

'I've lived with it for years, even if I have suppressed it.'

'Living with it and accepting it are two different things.'

'If you think I'm a candidate for a padded room, you don't know me,' she said, irritated in spite of the valium.

'I don't think that. But demonic possession?'

'Not demonic. I'm talking about something less grand than that. This is the possession of a living person by the spirit of someone dead.'

424

His square, almost ugly face was creased with worry. He spread his arms, his hands palms up, a supplicant bear. 'And who is this living person?'

'The man who killed those nurses in Anaheim. He's possessed by Lingard, and that's why the psychic emanations he puts out are so different.'

Max returned to the sofa. 'I can't accept it.'

'That doesn't mean I'm wrong.'

'The poltergeist phenomena in Cauvel's office . . . You think—'

'That was Lingard,' she said.

'There's a problem with that theory,' he said.

She raised her eyebrows.

'How could Lingard's spirit be in two places at once?' he asked. 'How could Lingard be in possession of a man who he's forcing to commit murder – and at the same time be throwing glass dogs around Cauvel's office?'

'I don't know. Who's to say what a ghost can do?'

* * *

At ten o'clock, Max came to the master bedroom. He had gone downstairs to the library for a novel and had returned carrying a thick volume – not the book he'd been after. 'I talked to Dr Cauvel just now,' he said.

Mary was sitting up in bed. She used a flap of the dust jacket to mark her place in the book she was reading. 'What did the good doctor have to say?'

'He thinks *you* are the poltergeist.'

'Me?'

'He says you were under stress—'

'Aren't we all?'

'Especially you.'

'Was I?'

'Because you remembered about Berton Mitchell.'

'I've remembered about him before.'

'This time you recalled more than ever. Cauvel says you were under great psychological stress in his office, and that *you* caused the glass dogs to fly about.'

She smiled. 'A man your size looks just too cute in pyjamas.'

'Mary—'

'Especially yellow pyjamas. You should wear just a robe.'

425

'You're avoiding this.' He came to the foot of the bed. 'What about the glass dogs?'

'Cauvel just wants me to pay for them,' she said airily.

'He didn't mention money.'

'That's what he was angling for.'

'He's not the type,' Max said.

'I'll pay half the value of the dogs.'

Exasperated, Max said, 'Mary, that's not necessary.'

'I know,' she said lightly. 'I didn't break them.'

'I mean, Cauvel isn't asking to be paid. You're trying to avoid the main issue.'

'Okay, okay. So *how* did I cause glass dogs to fly about?'

'Unconsciously. Cauvel says—'

'Psychiatrists always blame the unconscious.'

'Who's to say they're wrong?'

'They're stupid.'

'Mary—'

'And you're stupid for believing Cauvel.'

She didn't want to argue, but she couldn't control herself. She was frightened by the direction the conversation was taking, although she didn't know why she should be. She was terrified of some knowledge that lay within her, but she couldn't understand what that might be.

Standing like a preacher, holding his book as if it were a Bible, Max said, 'Will you listen?'

She shook her head to indicate she found him too irritating to bear. 'If I'm responsible for his figurines getting busted up, am I also to blame for the bad weather in the East, for the war in Africa, for inflation, for poverty, for the recent crop failures?'

'Sarcasm.'

'You encourage it.'

The tranquilliser was doing her no good whatever. She was tense. Trembling. Like a shallow-water, feathery sea anemone quivering in the subtle currents that preceded a storm, she was nervously aware of unseen forces that could destroy her.

Suddenly she felt threatened by Max.

That doesn't make sense, she thought. Max isn't any danger to me. He's trying to help me find the truth, that's all.

Dizzy, confused, on the verge of anomie, she leaned back against her pillows.

426

Max opened his book and read in a quiet but urgent voice: ' *"Telekinesis* is the ability to move objects or to cause changes within objects solely by the force of the mind. The phenomenon has most often and most reliably been reported in times of crisis or in severe stress situations. For example, automobiles have been levitated from injured people, debris from the dying in fire-swept or collapsed buildings." '

'I *know* what telekinesis is,' she said.

Max ignored her, kept reading: ' "Telekinesis is often mistaken for the work of poltergeists, which are playful and occasionally malevolent spirits. The existence of poltergeists as astral beings is debatable and certainly unproven. It should be noted that in most houses where poltergeists have appeared, there resides an adolescent with serious identity problems, *or some other person under severe nervous strain.* A good argument could be made that the phenomena often attributed to poltergeists are usually the product of unconscious telekinesis." '

'This is ridiculous,' she said. 'Why should I pitch those dogs around just when I was about to see the killer's face in the vision?'

'You really didn't want to see his face, so your subconscious threw those figurines to distract you from the vision.'

'That's absurd! I *wanted* to see it. I want to stop this man before he kills again.'

Max's hard grey eyes were like knives, dissecting her. 'Are you sure you want to stop him?'

'What kind of question is that?'

He sighed. 'Do you know what I think? I think you've sensed, through your clairvoyance, that this psychopath will kill you if you pursue him. You've seen a possible future, and you're trying like hell to avoid it.'

Surprised, she said, 'Nothing of the sort.'

'The pain you felt—'

'Was the pain of the victims. It wasn't a foreshadowing of my own death.'

'Maybe you haven't foreseen the danger consciously,' Max said. 'But subconsciously, perhaps, you've seen yourself as a victim if you pursue this case. That would explain why you're trying to mislead yourself with poltergeists and with talk about possession.'

'I'm not going to die,' she said sharply. 'I'm not hiding from anything like that.'

427

'Why are you afraid to even consider it?'

'I'm not afraid.'

'I think you are.'

'I'm not a coward. And I'm not a liar.'

'Mary, I'm trying to help you.'

'Then believe me!'

He looked at her quizzically. 'You don't have to shout.'

'You never hear me unless I shout!'

'Mary, why do you want to argue?'

I don't, she thought. Stop me. Hold me.

'*You* started this,' she said.

'I only asked you to consider an alternative to this business about possession. You're overreacting.'

I know, she thought. I know I am. And I don't know why. I don't want to hurt you. I need you.

But all she said was, 'Listening to you, I'd think I was never right about anything. I'm always overreacting or mistaken or misled or confused. You treat me as if I'm a child.'

'You're treating *yourself* with condescension.'

'Just a silly little child.'

Hug me, kiss me, love me, she thought. Please make me stop this. I don't want to argue. I'm scared.

He started towards the bedroom door. 'This isn't the time to talk. You're not in the mood for constructive criticism.'

'Because I'm behaving like a child?'

'Yes.'

'Sometimes you fucking piss me off.'

He stopped, turned back to her. 'That's like a child,' he said calmly. 'Like a child who's trying to shock a grownup with a lot of dirty words.'

She opened her book to the page she had marked and, refusing to acknowledge him, she pretended to read.

* * *

She would rather have suffered disabling pain than even temporary estrangement from Max. When they argued, which was rarely, she felt miserable. The two or three hours of silence that invariably followed a disagreement, and which were usually her fault, were unbearable.

She spent the remainder of the evening in bed with a copy of

428

The Occult by Colin Wilson. As she began each page, she could not remember what had been on the page before it.

Max stayed on his side of the bed, reading a novel and smoking his pipe. He might as well have been a thousand miles away.

The eleven o'clock television news, which she switched on by remote control, headlined a grisly story about slaughter in a Santa Ana beauty salon. There was film of the blood-smeared shop and interviews with police officials who had nothing to say.

'You see?' Mary said. 'I was right about the nurses. I was right about the beauty salon. And, by God, I'm right about Richard Lingard, too.'

Even as she spoke, she regretted the words, and especially her tone of voice.

He looked at her but said nothing.

She looked away, down at her book. She hadn't meant to revive the argument. Quite the opposite. She wanted to get him talking once more. She wanted to hear his voice.

Although she often started arguments, she had never been able to initiate the conclusion of one. Psychologically, she wasn't capable of making the first gesture for peace. She left that move to the men. Always. She knew that wasn't fair, but she could not change.

She supposed that this inadequacy dated back to her father's violent death. He had left her so suddenly that she still sometimes felt abandoned. All of her adult life she had worried about men walking out on her before *she* was prepared to end the relationship.

And of course she wasn't ever going to be ready to end her marriage; that was for keeps. Therefore, whenever she and Max argued, whenever she had reason to worry about his leaving, she forced him to pick up the olive branch. It was a test which he could pass only if he would sacrifice more pride than she; and when he had done that, he would have proved that he loved her and that he would never leave her as her father had done.

The death of her father *was* more important than whatever Berton Mitchell had done to her.

Why couldn't Dr Cauvel see that?

＊　＊　＊

In the dark bedroom, when it became evident that neither of them could sleep, Max touched her. His hands affected her in the same way that the rapidly vibrating tines of a tuning fork would affect fine crystal. She trembled uncontrollably and shattered. She broke against him, weeping.

He didn't speak. Words no longer mattered.

He held her for a few minutes, and then he began to stroke her. He slid one hand over her silk pyjamas, along her flank, across her buttocks. Slow, warm movement. And then he popped open two buttons on her blouse, slipped his hand inside, felt her warm breast, his fingers lingering on her nipple only for an instant. She put her open mouth to his neck, against the hard muscle. His strong pulse was transmitted to her through her tender lips. He undressed her and then himself. The bandage on his hand brushed her bare thigh.

'Your finger,' she said.

'It'll be fine.'

'The cut might come open,' she said. 'It might start to bleed again.'

'Sshhh,' he said.

He was not in the mood to be patient, and although she hadn't said a word, he sensed she was equally anxious. He rose above her in the lightless air, as if taking flight, then settled over her. Although she had expected nothing more than the special joy of closeness, she climaxed within a minute. Not intensely. A gentle rush of pleasure. However, when she came a second time, moments before he finished far down inside of her, she cried out with delight.

For a while she lay at his side, holding his hand. Finally she said, 'Don't ever leave me. Stay with me as long as I live.'

'As long as you live,' Max promised.

* * *

At five-thirty on Wednesday morning, in the middle of a nightmare vision of the killer's next crime, Mary was catapulted from sleep by the sound of gunfire. A single shot, ear-splitting, too close. Even as the *boom* was bouncing off the bedroom walls, she sat up, threw off the blanket and sheet, swung her legs out of bed. 'Max! What's wrong? Max!'

Beside her, he switched on the lamp, jumped up from the bed. He stood, swaying, blinking.

430

The sudden light hurt her eyes. Although she was squinting, she could see there was no intruder in the room.

Max reached for the loaded handgun that he kept on the nightstand. It was not there.

'Where's the pistol?' he asked.

'I didn't touch it,' she said.

Then, as her eyes adjusted to the light, she saw the gun. It was floating in the air near the foot of the bed, floating five feet above the floor, as if it were suspended from wires, except that there were no wires. The barrel was pointed at her.

The poltergeist.

'Jesus!' Max said.

Although no visible finger pulled the trigger, a second shot exploded. The bullet tore into the headboard inches from Mary's face.

She panicked. Gasping, whimpering, she ran across the room, hunched as if she were crippled. The gun traversed to the left, covering her. She came to a corner, stopped. Trapped. She realised she should have gone in the opposite direction, where she could have at least locked herself in the bathroom.

The third shot smashed into the floor beside her feet. Bits of a throw rug and splinters of wood sprayed up.

'Max!'

He grabbed at the gun, but it slid away from him, rose and fell and swung from side to side, bobbled and weaved, forced him into a clumsy ballet.

She looked for something to hide behind.

There was nothing.

The fourth shot passed over her head, piercing a framed, glass-covered watercolour of Newport Beach harbour.

Max connected with the pistol, clutched it. The barrel twisted in his hands until it was pointed at his chest. Sweating, cursing, he struggled to pull the weapon from a pair of hands that he couldn't see. Surprisingly, after a few seconds, the unseen contestant surrendered, and Max staggered backwards with the prize.

She stood with her back to the wall, hands to her face. She couldn't take her eyes from the barrel of the gun.

'It's safe now,' Max said. 'It's over.' He started toward her.

'For God's sake, unload it!' she said, pointing at the gun in his hand.

431

He stopped, stared at the pistol, and then took the magazine out of the handgrip.

'All of the bullets should be taken from the clip,' she said.

'I doubt that's necessary if I—'

'*Do it!*'

His big hands were shaking as he took the bullets from the magazine. He placed all the pieces on the bed: pistol, empty magazine, unspent ammunition. For a minute he studied the items, as she did, waiting for one of them to rise off the blanket.

Nothing moved.

'What was it? he asked.

'Poltergeist.'

'Whatever it was – is it still here?'

She closed her eyes, tried to relax, tried to *feel*. After a while she said, 'No. It's gone.'

WEDNESDAY, DECEMBER 23

TEN

Percy Osterman, THE Orange County sheriff, opened the door for Max and Mary, motioned for them to go ahead of him.

The room was grey. The paint was grey, the floor tile grey, the windowsills grey with dust. A set of grey metal storage shelves was bolted to one wall, and the wall opposite the shelves contained a lot of built-in file drawers with burnished steel fronts. The few pieces of furniture were fashioned of tubular steel and grey vinyl. The screens over the ceiling lights were grey, and the fuzzy fluorescent illumination transformed the scene into a chiaroscuro print.

The only spots of brightness in the room were the well scrubbed porcelain sinks and the slanted autopsy table, which was fiercely white with polished, gleaming stainless steel fixtures.

The sheriff was all hard lines and sharp angles. He was nearly as tall as Max, but forty pounds lighter and far less muscular. Yet he did not appear wasted or weak. His hands were large, bony, almost fleshless, the fingers like talons. His shoulders sloped forwards. His neck was thin with a prominent Adam's apple. In his pinched, sun-browned face, his eyes were quick, nervous, a curious pale shade of amber.

Osterman's frown was ominous, his smile easy and kind. He was not smiling when he opened one of the six large drawers and pulled the shroud from the face of the corpse.

Mary stepped away from Max, moved closer to the dead man.

'Kyle Nolan,' Osterman said. 'Owned the beauty shop. Worked there as a hair stylist.'

Nolan was short, broad-shouldered, barrel-chested. Bald. A bushy moustache. Shave off the moustache, Mary thought, and he'd look like that actor, Edward Asner.

She put one hand on the drawer and waited for a rush of

435

psychic impressions. Although she didn't understand how or why, she knew that, for a time after passing away, the dead maintained a bubble of energy around them, an invisible capsule that contained memories, vivid scenes of their lives and especially of their last minutes. Ordinarily, contact with the victim of a murder, or with the victim's belongings, would generate a torrent of clairvoyant images, sometimes clear as reality and sometimes hopelessly blurry and meaningless, most of them dealing with the moment of death and with the identity of the killer.

In this case, for the first time in her experience, she sensed absolutely nothing. Not even a shapeless flurry of movement or colour.

She touched the dead man's cold face.

Still nothing.

Osterman closed the drawer, opened the one next to it. As he folded back the shroud, he said, 'Tina Nolan. Kyle's wife.'

Tina was an attractive but hard-faced woman with brittle, bleached hair that her husband should have found professionally embarrassing. Although they had been closed hours ago by the coroner, her eyes had come open again. She stared at Mary as if she were trying to impart some dreadfully important news; but in the end she provided nothing more than poor Kyle had done.

The woman in the third drawer was in her late twenties. She had once been beautiful.

'Rochelle Drake,' Percy Osterman said. 'Nolan's last customer for the day.'

'Rochelle Drake?' Max said. He came closer, peered into the drawer. 'Don't I know that name?'

'Recognize her?' Sheriff Osterman asked.

Max shook his head. 'No. But . . . Mary? Does that name mean anything to you?'

'No,' she said.

'When you foresaw these killings, you said you thought you knew one of the victims.'

'I was wrong,' she said. 'These people are strangers.'

'That's odd,' Max said. 'I'd swear . . . well, I don't know *what* I'd swear . . . except this one's name . . . Rochelle Drake . . . it's familiar.'

Mary was not paying much attention to him, for she perceived a familiar electricity in the air, a stirring of psychic forces. The

436

Drake woman was going to provide what the other bodies should have offered but didn't. Mary opened her mind to the psychic emanations, made herself as receptive as she could, and put her hand on the dead woman's forehead.

Wicka-wicka-wicka!

Wings.

Startled, Mary pulled her hand away from the corpse as if she had been bitten.

She felt wings, leathery wings, shuddering like the membranes of drums.

This isn't possible, she thought frantically. The wings have something to do with Berton Mitchell. Not with this dead woman. Not with the man who killed her. The wings have to do with the past, not the present. Berton Mitchell couldn't be involved in this. He hung himself in a gaol cell nearly twenty-four years ago.

But now she could smell the wings as well as feel them, smell the wings and the creatures behind them – a dank, musty, musky odour that nauseated her.

What if the man who murdered Rochelle Drake and the others was not possessed by the spirit of Richard Lingard? What if, instead, he was possessed by the soul of another psychopath, by the spirit of Berton Mitchell? Wasn't it conceivable that Lingard himself had been possessed by Berton Mitchell? And when Barnes shot Lingard, perhaps Mitchell's spirit moved on to another host. Perhaps she had unknowingly crossed the path of an old nemesis. Perhaps she would spend the remainder of her life in pursuit of Berton Mitchell. Perhaps she would be compelled to follow him from one host to another until he finally found the opportunity to kill her.

No. That was madness. She was thinking like a lunatic.

Max asked, 'Is something wrong?'

Wings brushed her face, her neck, shoulders and breasts and belly, fluttered against her ankles and up her calves and then against her inner thighs.

She was determined not to succumb to fear. But she was also half convinced that if she didn't stop thinking about the wings, they would carry her off into everlasting darkness. A ridiculous notion. Nevertheless, she turned away from the morgue drawer.

'Are you receiving something?' Max asked.

'Not now,' she lied.

'But you were?'

'For an instant.'

'What did you see?' he asked.

'Nothing important. Just meaningless movement.'

'Can you pick it up again?' Max asked.

'No.'

She mustn't pursue it. If she did, she would see what lay behind those wings. She must never see what lay behind those wings.

Osterman closed the drawer.

Mary sighed with relief.

★ ★ ★

Sheriff Osterman went with them to the far corner of the municipal parking lot, where they'd left their car.

The December sky was like the morgue – shades of grey. The fast-moving clouds were reflected in the polished hood of the Mercedes.

Shivering, Mary put her hands in her coat pockets and hunched her shoulders against the wind.

'Heard good things about you,' Osterman told Mary in his peculiarly economical way of speaking. 'Often thought about working with you. Pleased when you called this morning. Hoped you'd come up with a lead.'

'I hoped so, too,' she said.

'Foresaw these murders, did you?'

'Yes,' she said.

'Those nurses in Anaheim, too?'

'That's right.'

'Same killer, you think?'

'Yes,' she said.

Osterman nodded. 'We think so, too. Have some evidence of it.'

'What sort of evidence?' Max asked.

'When he killed the nurses,' Osterman said, each word sharp and quick, 'he busted up some stuff. Religious things. Two crucifixes. Statuette of the Virgin Mary. Even strangled one girl with a rosary. Found something similar in this beauty shop case.'

'What?' Mary asked.

'Pretty ugly bit of business. Maybe you don't want to hear it.'

'I'm used to hearing and seeing ugly things,' she said.

He regarded her for a moment, amber eyes hooded. 'Guess

that's true.' He leaned against the Mercedes. 'This woman in the beauty shop. Rochelle Drake. She wore a necklace. A gold cross. He raped her, killed her. Tore the cross off her neck. Pushed it up . . . inside of her.'

Mary felt ill. She hugged herself.

'Then he's a psychopath with some sort of religious hangup,' Max said.

'Appears so,' Osterman said. He looked at Mary and asked, 'So where do you go from here?'

'Down to the shore,' she said.

'King's Point,' Max said.

'Why there?'

She hesitated, glanced at Max. 'That's where the next murders will take place.'

Osterman did not seem surprised. 'Had another vision, did you?'

'Early this morning,' she said.

'When will it happen?'

'Tomorrow night,' she said.

'Christmas Eve?'

'Yes.'

'Where in King's Point?'

'On the harbour,' she said.

'Pretty good-sized harbour.'

'It'll be near the shops and restaurants.'

'How many will he kill?' Osterman asked.

'I'm not sure.'

She was so *cold*, colder than could be accounted for by the California winter day and the wind, cold in the pit of her stomach, cold in her heart. She was wearing a stylish but thinly lined calfskin coat from North Beach Leather. She wished she'd chosen her heaviest fur.

'Maybe I'll be able to stop him before he kills anyone else,' she said.

'You feel a responsibility to stop him?' Osterman asked.

'I won't have peace of mind until I do.'

'Wouldn't want this talent you've got.'

'I never asked for it,' she said.

A truck rumbled by in the street. Osterman waited for the noise to die down.

'King's Point used to be in my jurisdiction,' he said. 'Two years

439

ago they voted in their own police force. Now I can't poke my nose in unless they ask. Or unless a case that starts in the county ends up on their doorstep.'

'I wish I could be working with you,' Mary said.

'You'll be working with a jackass,' Osterman said.

'Excuse me?'

'Chief of police at King's Point. Name's Patmore. John Patmore. A jackass. He gives you trouble, tell him to call me. He kind of respects me, but he's still a jackass.'

'We'll use your name if we have to,' Mary said. 'But we aren't entirely without influence down there. We know the owner of the *King's Point Press.*'

Osterman smiled. 'Lou Pasternak?'

'You know him?'

'Damned good newspaperman.'

'Yes, he is.'

'Quite a character, too.'

'A little bit of one,' she agreed.

The sheriff offered his hand to Mary, then to Max. 'Hope you two do my job for me this time.'

'Thanks for your help,' Max said.

'Don't hesitate to ask for more if you need it. It's been my pleasure.'

As Mary got into the Mercedes, a gust of wind sang in the power lines overhead.

* * *

They reached King's Point at two-thirty in the afternoon. The first glimpse of it, as they topped a rise in the road, was from high above the harbour.

The sky was low. Thick grey clouds scudded inland. A mile offshore the ocean was shrouded in mist; and closer to the beach formidable waves churned beneath half a dozen scuba-suited surfers, fell frothily onto the sand, and exploded into spray against the stone breakwaters on both sides of the harbour entrance.

The town was on the Pacific Coast Highway, a few miles south of Laguna Beach, in a perpetually smogless pocket of sunshine and money. The sun was in hiding today, but the money was everywhere evident. Houses on the verdant hillsides were priced from $75,000 to $500,000, nearly all of them with well manicured decorative gardens and ocean views. Waterfront homes with docks were not as expensive as those in Newport Beach, but real estate brokers had no time for would-be customers who flinched at a base price of a quarter of a million dollars. In the flat land between harbour and hills the houses were cheaper – there were some apartment buildings, too – but even they were expensive by most standards.

The travel guides said that King's Point was 'charming' and 'quaint' and 'picturesque,' and for once they were telling the truth. The lawns were lush and green; the many small parks were filled with palms of all varieties, oleander, jade plants, magnolia trees, schefflera, dracaena, olive trees, and seasonal flowers. The houses were well cared for, freshly painted every year or two as protection against the corrosive sea air. Businessmen were required to forgo the most offensive neon signs, and were forbidden by law to paint their stores in anything but soft natural tones.

The residents of King's Point appeared to think that with the proper local ordinances they could keep out everything that made the rest of the world a less desirable place to live. And they *did* keep out much that was tasteless, cheap, and gaudy.

But they can't keep out everything they don't want, Mary thought. A killer has come in from outside. He's walking among them now. They can't use local ordinances to keep out death.

From spring through early autumn the population of King's Point was sixty per cent higher than in the winter. During these vacation months the hotels were booked weeks in advance, the restaurants raised their prices except for locals who were recognized, the shops hired extra help, and the white beaches were crowded. Now, two days before Christmas, the town was quiet. When Max turned off the main highway onto a city street, they encountered very little traffic.

King's Point Police Headquarters was a single-storey brick building of absolutely no architectural period, style, charm, integrity, or responsibility. It looked like an oversized, flat-roofed storage shed with windows. Even three blocks from the harbour, in the flats below the hills, in a limbo between the highest-value real estate parcels – waterfront and view – it was no credit to its neighbourhood.

Inside, the public reception room was depressingly

institutional: brown tile floor, muddy green walls, washed-out green ceiling, strictly utilitarian furniture. Tax money had purchased three desks, six-drawer filing cabinets, IBM typewriters, a copier, a small refrigerator, a United States flag, a glass-fronted case full of riot guns and pistols, a dispatcher's corner with radio – and a civilian secretary (Mrs Vidette Yancy, according to the name plate on her desk) who was in her fifties, a woman with tightly curled white hair, pale skin, bright red lipstick, and an enormous bosom.

'I'd like to see Chief Patmore,' Mary said.

Mrs Yancy took a minute to correct a word she had just typed. 'Him?' she said at last. 'He's out.'

'When will he be back?'

'The chief? Tomorrow morning.'

'Could you give us his home address?' Max asked, leaning against the Formica counter that separated the foyer from the work area.

'His home address?' Mrs Yancy said. 'Surely. I can give you that. But he isn't at home.'

'Where is he?' Mary asked impatiently.

'Where is he? Why, he's up in Santa Barbara. He won't be back until ten tomorrow morning.'

Mary turned to Max. 'Maybe we should talk to a deputy.'

'Deputy?' Mrs Yancy said. 'There are five officers under the chief. Of course, only two of them are on duty right now.'

'If this guy's like we've heard,' Max said, 'it won't do any good to talk to subordinates. He'll expect to be dealt with directly.'

'Time's running out,' Mary said.

'Don't we have until seven o'clock tomorrow evening?' Max asked.

'If my vision's accurate, we do.'

'Then if we see Patmore early tomorrow, that'll be soon enough.'

'The officers on duty are out on patrol right now,' Mrs Yancy said. 'Did you want to report a crime?'

'Not exactly,' Mary said.

'Not exactly? Well, I have the forms right here, you know.' She opened a desk drawer, began to rummage through it. 'I can take down the information and have an officer get back to you.'

'Never mind,' Max said. 'We'll be in tomorrow at ten o'clock.'

* * *

442

At the bay end of the harbour, valuable shoreline was occupied by commercial enterprises – yacht clubs, yacht sales offices, dry docks, restaurants, and shops. Each of these businesses was as clean and attractive and well maintained as the many expensive homes that lined both sides of the harbour channel.

The Laughing Dolphin was a restaurant and cocktail lounge that fronted on the harbour. On the second level a narrow open-air deck was suspended over the water. In good weather patrons could get pleasantly drunk while the sun warmed their faces. This afternoon the deck was deserted. Max and Mary had it to themselves.

Holding a mug of coffee laced with brandy, Mary leaned against the wooden railing.

If you stepped out of the brisk sea breezes, the day was only chilly; but the wind from the ocean was downright cold. It nipped at her face and brought a healthy colour to her cheeks.

When she looked up and to her right, she could see the Spanish Court, the hotel where she and Max had reserved a room. It stood on the north hill, high above the harbour. It was majestic, all white plaster and natural woods and red tile.

Closer to hand, eight dinghies were sailing in formation, snaking back and forth across the smooth slate-coloured water. Against a backdrop of sixty-, eighty-, and hundred-foot sailing ships and motor yachts, the small vessels were lovely and amusing. Even today, without the sun upon them, their sails were dazzlingly white. Their graceful progress was a definition of serenity.

'Study the boats, the houses, the entire harbour,' Max said. 'Maybe something you see will trigger the vision.'

'I don't think so,' she said. 'It was knocked out of my mind forever when I woke up and found I was being shot at.'

'You've got to try.'

'Do I?'

'Isn't that why you wanted to come?'

'If I don't go after this killer,' she said, 'he'll eventually come after me.'

The wind gusted suddenly, flapped Mary's leather coat against her legs, rattled the large plate-glass windows of the cocktail lounge behind them.

She sipped her coffee. Tentacles of steam writhed across her face and dissolved in the wintry air.

Max said, 'Maybe it'll help if you tell me again how it's going to

443

happen.' When she didn't answer, he coaxed her. 'Tomorrow night at seven o'clock. Not too far from where we're standing right now.'

'Within a couple of blocks,' she said.

'You said he'll come with a butcher knife.'

'Lingard's knife.'

'Some knife, anyway.'

'Lingard's,' she insisted.

'You said he'll stab two people.'

'Yes, two.'

'Kill them?'

'Maybe one of them.'

'But not the other.'

'At least one will live. Maybe both.'

'Who are these people he'll stab?'

'I don't know their names,' she said.

'What do they look like?'

'I couldn't see their faces.'

'Young women, like in Anaheim?'

'I really don't know.'

'What about the high-powered rifle?'

'I saw it in the vision.'

'He's got a butcher knife and a gun?'

'After he's stabbed those two people,' she said, 'he'll take the rifle up into a tower. He intends to shoot everyone.'

'Everyone?'

'A lot of people, as many as he can.'

At the far end of the harbour, a dozen sea gulls kited in from the ocean, riding very high on the wind, white feathers silhouetted dramatically against the stormy sky.

'How many will he kill?' Max asked.

'The vision ended before I could see.'

'Which tower will he use?'

'I don't know.'

'Look around,' Max said. 'Look at each one of them. Try to sense which it will be.'

To her right, three hundred yards farther around the bend of the harbour's bay end and five hundred yards from the Laughing Dolphin, the Roman Catholic Church of the Holy Trinity lay one block from the waterfront. She had been inside it once. It was a

444

brooding Gothic structure, an impressive fortress of weathered granite and darkly beautiful stained glass windows. The hundred-foot bell tower, which had a low-walled open deck directly beneath its peaked roof, was the highest point within two blocks of the harbour.

The sound of sea gulls distracted her for a moment. Above the formation of sailboats that were playing follow the leader, still soaring inland, the gulls began to squeal with excitement. Their sharp voices were like fingernails scraped across a blackboard.

She tried not the hear the birds, concentrated on Trinity. She received nothing. No images. No psychic vibrations. Not the vaguest premonition that the killer would strike out at King's Point from Trinity's bell tower.

St Luke's Lutheran Church was between Mary and the Church of the Holy Trinity. It was two hundred yards north and half a block from the harbour. It was a Spanish-style building with mass-ive carved oak doors, and a bell tower slightly more than half as high as the one at the Catholic church.

Nothing from St Luke's either.

Just the ghostly wind and the cries of agitated sea gulls.

The third tower was to her left, two hundred yards away, at the edge of the water. It was only four storeys high, part of Kimball's Games and Snacks, a clapboard and cedar-shingled pavilion that housed an amusement arcade. In the summer camera-laden tour-ists climbed to the top and took photographs of the harbour. Now the place was closed for the season, quiet, empty.

'Will it be Kimball's tower?' Max asked.

'I don't know,' she said. 'It could be any of them.'

'You've got to try harder,' he said.

She closed her eyes and concentrated.

Screeching angrily, a gull swooped down, flashed past their faces with only eight or ten inches to spare.

Mary jumped back in surprise, dropped her coffee mug.

'You okay?' Max asked.

'Startled. That's all.'

'Did it touch you?'

'No.'

'They don't dive that close unless you trespass on their nesting grounds. But there's nowhere around here they'd lay eggs. Besides, it's not the time of year for that.'

445

The dozen gulls that had entered the harbour a few minutes ago were circling overhead. They weren't taking advantage of the wind currents as gulls usually do; there was nothing lazy or graceful about their flight. Instead, they twisted and fluttered and soared and dived and darted frantically among one another within a tightly defined sphere of air. They seemed tortured. It was surprising that they didn't collide. Screeching at one another, they performed an unnatural, frenzied dance in midair.

'What's upset them?' Max wondered.

'Me,' she said.

'You? What did you do?'

She was trembling. 'I tried to use my clairvoyance to see which tower the killer will use.'

'So?'

'The gulls are here to stop me from doing that.'

Astounded, he said, 'Mary, that makes no sense. Trained gulls?'

'Not trained. Controlled.'

'Controlled by whom? Who sent them?'

She stared at the birds.

'Who?' he asked again. 'Lingard's ghost?'

'Maybe,' she said.

He touched her shoulder. 'Mary—'

'You saw the poltergeist that was after me, dammit!'

In a let's-calm-down-and-be-reasonable tone of voice that drove her mad, he said, 'Whatever causes poltergeist phenomena can lift and hurl inanimate objects – but not living animals.'

'Listen,' she said, 'you don't know everything. You don't know—' She looked away from him, looked up.

'What's wrong?' he asked.

'The birds.'

The gulls still capered maniacally overhead, but they were silent. Perfectly silent.

'Strange,' Max said.

'I'm going inside,' she said.

She almost reached the mullioned door that connected the deck to the second-floor cocktail lounge when a sea gull struck her from behind, between the shoulders, like a hammer blow. She stumbled and instinctively put one arm across her face. The wings beat at her neck. Battered the back of her head. Thundered in her ears. These weren't like the wings that she associated with Berton

446

Mitchell. Those wings had been leathery, membranous. These were feathered. But that didn't make the sea gulls any less frightening. She thought of the bird's wickedly sharp, hooked beak, thought of it pecking out her eyes, and she screamed.

Max shouted something that she couldn't hear.

She started to reach for the bird, realised it might tear her fingers, jerked her hand back.

Max knocked the gull away from her. It flopped on the deck, temporarily stunned.

Max opened the door, pushed her inside, went in after her, and pulled the door shut.

The bartender had seen the attack, and he was hurrying around the end of the counter, wiping his hands on a towel.

A heavyset, red-haired man at the bar swivelled around on his stool to see what was happening.

In one of the black vinyl booths by the windows a young couple – a pretty blonde in a green dress and a dark, intense man – looked up from their drinks.

Before the bartender had taken three steps, a sea gull struck the mullioned door behind Max. Two small panes broke inward. Glass tinkled musically on the floor.

The cocktail waitress dropped her tray and ran towards the stairs that led down to the restaurant foyer.

With a sound like a shotgun blast, another gull slammed into one of the five-foot by six-foot windows that overlooked the harbour. The glass cracked but held. The injured bird toppled backwards to the deck outside, leaving a smear of blackish blood to mark the collision.

'They'll kill me.'

'No,' Max said.

'That's what they want!'

He held her protectively, but for the first time since she had known him, his arms didn't seem big enough, his chest broad enough, his body strong enough to guarantee her safety.

A sea gull caromed off the window beside the young couple's table. The glass cracked in a jagged, lightning-bolt pattern. The pretty blonde shrieked and scrambled out of the booth.

An instant after her companion prudently followed her, another gull rammed the same window and shattered it. Large shards of glass collapsed onto the dark pine table, bounced up in many

447

smaller pieces, and showered over the vinyl where the couple had been sitting.

The decapitated gull landed in the centre of the table; and its bloody head plopped into the woman's martini.

Two more gulls flew in through the broken window.

'Don't let them!' Mary shouted hysterically. 'Don't let them, don't, don't, oh don't, *please* don't!'

The young couple went to their knees, taking shelter behind and half beneath a table.

Max pushed Mary into the nearest corner. He shielded her as best he could with his body. One of the birds sailed straight at him. He threw up one arm to ward it off. The creature squealed in anger, shied away, circled through the room.

The other gull attempted to land on one of the round tables in the middle of the lounge. Its wings knocked over a centre-piece – a copper and stained-glass lantern with a candle inside – and the candle set fire to the tablecloth.

The bartender used his damp towel to extinguish the flame.

The gull swooped from the table to the shelves of liquor behind the bar. Two, three, four, half a dozen, eight bottles crashed to the floor. On his stool, a few feet from the crazed gull, the red-haired man was too bewildered to be frightened. He watched the bird with fascination as it flapped and kicked and sent more bottles to the floor. The fragrance of whisky blossomed through the room.

The first gull flew at Max again. It came in above him, fluttered wildly in the corner, then with malign intelligence dropped behind his back, onto Mary's head.

Its feet tangled in her hair.

'*God, no! No!*'

She grabbed at the bird, not caring about its beak, not caring if it pecked her fingers. It was unclean. She had to get it off her. Max reached for it, too. Then it rose from her, up and away once more, circling into the room. In a second, however, it darted back and thumped into the wall beside her head. It dropped to the floor at her feet and twitched spasmodically.

Gasping for breath, her hands to her face and fingers spread, she backed away from it.

'It's terror-stricken,' Max said.

'Kill it!' She hardly recognized her own voice; it was altered by fear and hatred.

He hesitated. 'I don't think it's dangerous anymore.'

'Kill it before it flies up!'

He kicked the bird into the corner, raised his foot, and with evident reluctance stepped on its head.

Gagging, Mary turned away.

The other gull flew away from the bar and left the room through the broken window.

Everything was quiet, still.

At last the intense, dark-skinned young man stood up, helped the blonde to her feet.

The heavyset, red-haired man at the bar tossed down his drink in one gulp.

'Christ, what a mess!' the bartender said. 'What happened? Did anyone ever see gulls act like that before?'

Max touched her cheek. 'Are you okay?'

She leaned on him and wept.

ELEVEN

6:30

Lights speckled the night-time King's Point hills like orange flame gleaming from within a jack-o'-lantern with a thousand eyes. To the west the ocean and sky melted into a single black shroud.

Max parked at the kerb, switched off the headlights. He leaned over and kissed Mary. 'You look lovely tonight.'

She smiled. Surprisingly, in spite of what had happened to her today, she felt lovely, feminine, buoyant. 'That makes six times you've told me.'

'Seven's a lucky number. You look lovely tonight.' He kissed her again. 'Do you feel better? Are you relaxed?'

'The man who invented valium should be made a saint.'

'*You* should be made a saint,' he said. 'Now don't move. I'm feeling terribly chivalrous. I'll come around and open your door.'

The wind from the sea was no stronger than it had been during the day, although with nightfall it grew colder and seemed also to grow noisier. It shook badly fitted shutters until they clattered. It worried loosely hinged garage doors, made them groan and creak. It scraped tree branches against the side of the house, tipped over empty trash barrels, stirred brittle feathered-end palm fronds together in a chorus of snakelike hissing, and rolled a few discarded soda cans along the streets.

Sheltered from the worst of the wind by dense shrubs, pine trees and date palms, the small single-storey house at 440 Ocean Hill Lane looked warm and cosy. Soft light radiated from the leaded windows. A carriage lamp glowed beside the front door.

Lou Pasternak – owner, publisher, and editor of the twice-a-week *King's Point Press* – answered the bell and hustled them inside. While they told each other how well they looked and how

450

happy they were to see each other again, Pasternak kissed Mary on the cheek, shook hands with Max, and hung their coats in the closet.

Being in Lou's presence was, she thought, as relaxing as taking a tranquilliser. Except for Max and her own brother, Mary liked Lou more than any other man she'd ever met. He was intelligent, kind, too generous. He was also the worst cynic she had ever met, but the cynicism was tempered by humility and a marvellous sense of humour.

She worried about him because he drank too much. But he knew he did, and he was able to talk about his drinking dispassionately. He argued that if you understood how screwed up the world was, if you saw how like a paradise it *could* be, if you understood that what could be never *would* be because most people were hopeless jackasses – well, then you needed a crutch to get through life with your sanity intact. For some people, he said, it was money or drugs or any of a hundred other things. His crutch was Scotch. And damned good bourbon.

'My mother,' Mary sometimes said to him, 'led a miserable life as an alcoholic.'

'Your mother,' Lou always responded, 'sounds like an alcoholic who didn't know how to hold her liquor. There's nothing worse than a sloppy drunk – unless it's a self-pitying drunk.'

His drinking didn't appear to interfere with the full life he led. He had built and still operated an extremely successful business. His editorials and reportage had won several national awards. At forty-five, although he had never been married, he had more women friends than any man Mary knew. At the moment he lived alone, but that would not last.

Although she had seen him consume Herculean quantities of liquor, she had never seen him drunk. He did not stagger, slur his speech, become maudlin or loud or obnoxious. He not only could hold his liquor, but he thrived on it.

'I don't drink to escape my responsibilities,' he had once told her. 'I drink to escape the consequences of other people's inability to meet *their* responsibilities.'

'Alcohol killed my mother,' she warned him. 'I don't want to see you die.'

'We all die, my dear. It's just as good to drop of a rotted liver as it is to be felled by cancer or a stroke. Actually, I think it's better.'

451

She loved him as much as she loved Max, though in different ways.

He was a stocky man, a full foot shorter than Max's six four, even slightly shorter than Mary. He was solidly constructed. His neck, shoulders, arms, and chest were thick with muscle, powerful. He was wearing a white shirt; the sleeves were rolled up; and his forearms were matted with hair.

His face was in stark contrast to his body. He had the fine features of an inbred aristocrat. He combed his brown hair straight back from his face. His brow was high; his lively brown eyes were deeply set and sensitive; his nose was narrow, the nostrils delicate; and his mouth was almost prim. He wore wire-rimmed spectacles that made him look as if he was a college professor.

'Bourbon and ice,' he said, picking up a tall glass from the slate-topped foyer table. 'My third since I got home from work. In case the wind blows down the power lines later on, I intend to be so lit up that I can do my bedtime reading by my own light.'

Although there were armchairs and a comfortable sofa, the living room was primarily furnished with books, magazines, record albums, and paintings. Stacks of books stood beside and behind the couch; books filled the space under the coffee table; recent issues of magazines overflowed a rack meant to hold a hundred of them. The one wall that was free of records and books was covered with original oils, pastels, and watercolours by local painters. Dozens of pieces in every imaginable style had been squeezed so close that their beauty overlapped; they intruded upon one another; but Lou's taste was so good that even under these circumstances the eye was caught and held by each work at some point during a long evening. One of the armchairs was more tattered and lumpy than the other. That was where Lou sat, reading half a dozen books each week, drinking too much, and listening to opera, Benny Goodman, or Bach.

It was the friendliest room Mary had ever seen.

Lou brought their drinks. He put Bach, interrupted by Eugene Ormandy, on the stereo at low volume. 'Now let's hear the whole story. Since you called this morning, I've been half crazy wondering what this is about. You were so mysterious.'

Interrupted frequently by Lou's questions, digressing into discussions of poltergeists, Mary told him everything. She began

452

with the tracking down of Richard Lingard and ended with the sea gull attack at the Laughing Dolphin.

When she finished, the house was abnormally quiet. A grandfather clock ticked solemnly in the dining room.

Thinking about what she had said, Lou poured himself more bourbon. When he returned to his armchair, he said, 'So tomorrow night at seven o'clock this killer will stab two people, perhaps killing one of them. Then he'll climb a tower and start to shoot.'

'You believe me?' she asked.

'Of course. I've followed your work for years, haven't I?'

'You believe about Lingard's spirit?'

'If you say I should, why wouldn't I?'

She glanced at Max.

'Will this man have anyone to shoot at tomorrow night?' Max asked. 'Won't just about everyone be at home with their families on Christmas Eve?'

'Oh,' Lou said, 'he'll have plenty of targets around the harbour. There'll be Christmas Eve parties on dozens of boats. People on the decks. People on the docks. People everywhere.'

'I don't think we can stop the stabbings from taking place,' Mary said. 'But maybe we can keep him from shooting anyone. Policemen can be stationed in all three towers.'

'One problem,' Lou said.

'What's that?'

'John Patmore.'

'Your chief of police.'

'Unfortunately, he is. It's not going to be easy to convince him that he should heed your visions.'

'If he thinks there's even the slightest chance I might be right,' Mary said, 'why shouldn't he cooperate? After all, his job is to protect the people of King's Point.'

Lou smiled crookedly. 'My dear, you should know by now that many cops don't see their jobs quite the same way as taxpayers do. Some cops think that all they're required to do is wear fancy fascist uniforms, ride around in flashy patrol cars, collect envelopes of graft money, and retire at the public expense after twenty or thirty years of "service".'

'You're too cynical,' she said.

'Percy Osterman told us Patmore's difficult,' Max added.

'Difficult? He's stupid,' Lou said. 'Ignorant beyond description.

453

The only reason you can't accuse him of being scatterbrained is because he doesn't have any brains to scatter. I'm sure he's never heard the word "clairvoyant." And when we are finally able to make him understand what it means, he won't believe it. If something's not within his personal experience, he doesn't accept its existence. I'm positive he'd argue against the reality of Europe simply because he's never been there.'

'He can call some police chiefs I've worked with,' Mary said. 'They'll convince him I'm genuine.'

'If he's never met them, he won't believe a word they say. I tell you, Mary, if ignorance is really bliss, then he's the happiest man in the world.'

'Sheriff Osterman said we could tell Patmore to call him for an endorsement,' Max said.

Lou nodded. 'That might help. Patmore's impressed with Osterman. And I'll go with you to see him if you'd like. But I've got to warn you that I won't help your cause very much. Patmore hates me.'

'I can't imagine why,' Max said. 'Except, you probably talk like this about him to his face.'

Grinning, Lou said, 'I've never been able to hide my true feelings, and that's a fact. You've met Mrs Yancy, his flunky?'

'She was the only one in the office this afternoon,' Max said.

'Isn't she a gem?'

'Is she?'

'A miracle worker,' Lou said. 'It's a miracle when she works.'

'She *didn't* seem too efficient,' Mary said.

Lou said, 'She's a steady worker – and if she gets any steadier, she'll be motionless.'

Mary laughed, sipped her dry sherry.

'Now, getting back to those sea gulls,' Lou said. 'Do—'

'No more about the gulls,' Mary said. 'No more about any of that. Tomorrow's soon enough. Tonight I want to forget about clairvoyance and talk about something else. Anything else.'

★ ★ ★

Dinner was filet mignon, salad, baked potatoes, and cold asparagus spears.

As Max was opening the bottle of red wine they'd brought as a gift, Lou noticed the bandage. 'Max, what happened to your finger?'

'Oh . . . I cut it changing a tyre.'

'Stitches?'

'It wasn't that serious.'

'He should have seen a doctor,' Mary said. 'He wouldn't even let me look at it. There was so much blood – blood all over his shirt.'

'I thought you might have been in a fight again,' Lou said.

'I don't go to bars any more,' Max said. 'I don't fight these days.'

Lou looked at Mary, raised an eyebrow.

'It's true,' she said.

'You worked two years for me,' Lou said. 'In all that time you never went more than a month or six weeks without getting in a bad fight. You went to the worst bars along the coast – biker bars and worse, to all the places where you were most likely to wind up in trouble. Sometimes I wondered if you went drinking more for the fighting than for the liquor.'

'Maybe I did,' Max said, frowning. 'I had problems. What I needed was someone who needed me. Now I've got Mary, and I don't fight.'

Although he had promised not to talk about clairvoyance any more that night, Lou found himself unable to drop the subject during dinner. 'Do you think the killer knows you're in town?'

'I don't know,' Mary said.

'If he's possessed by a spirit, and if the same spirit possessed those gulls, then surely he knows.'

'I guess he does.'

'Won't he play it safe until after you leave town?'

'Maybe he will,' she said. 'But I doubt it.'

'He wants to get caught?'

'Or he wants to catch me.'

'What do you mean by that?'

'I don't know.'

'If—'

'Can we change the subject?'

★ ★ ★

455

After she had finished eating, Mary excused herself from the table and went to the bathroom at the far end of the house.

When he was alone with Max, Lou asked, 'What about this notion of hers?'

'That Lingard's come back from the dead?'

'Do you put any stock in that?'

'You're the student of the occult,' Max said. 'You're the one with hundreds of books on the subject. Besides, you've known her longer than I have. You're the one who introduced us. What do you think?'

'I've got an open mind,' Lou said. 'I gather you don't.'

'Her analyst says *she* threw those glass dogs.'

'Unconscious telekinesis?' Lou asked.

'That's right.'

'Has she ever shown telekinetic ability before?'

'No,' Max said.

'What about the revolver?'

'I think she was controlling that, too.'

'Shooting at herself?'

'Yes,' Max said.

'And she was guiding the sea gulls?'

'Yes.'

'Controlling living animals . . . that's not telekinesis.'

'It's telepathy of a sort,' Max said.

Lou refilled his wine glass. 'That's rare.'

'It has to be telepathy. I can't believe those sea gulls were guided by a dead man's spirit.'

'Why would she want to kill herself?'

'She doesn't,' Max said.

'Well, if *she* is the poltergeist behind these phenomena, if *she* levitated that revolver, then it seems to me that she was trying to kill herself.'

'If she was suicidal,' Max said, 'she wouldn't have missed. But she *did* miss with the glass dogs, with the revolver, and with the gulls.'

'Then what's she doing?' Lou asked. 'Why is she playing the part of a poltergeist?'

Max frowned. 'I have a theory. I think there's something special about this case, something unusual. She's foreseen something about it that she refuses to face up to. Something devastating.

456

Something that would completely unhinge her if she thought about it for long. So she pushed it out of her mind. Of course, she could only push it out of her *conscious* mind. The subconscious never forgets. Now, every time she attempts to pursue a vision that's connected to this case, her subconscious uses the poltergeist phenomena to distract her.'

'Because her subconscious knows it will be harmful for her to pursue this man.'

'That's right.'

An icy tremor passed through Lou Pasternak. 'What could she have foreseen?'

'Maybe this psychopath will kill her,' Max said.

The thought of Mary dead hit Lou with surprising force. He had known her for more than a decade, had liked her from the moment he met her, and had grown to like her more each year. Liked her? Only that? No. He loved her, too. In a fatherly way. She was so gentle, good-natured. So vulnerable. But until this moment he had not realised how deeply he had come to love her. Mary dead and gone? He felt sick, feverish.

Max watched him with steady grey eyes that revealed nothing of his own emotions. He appeared unaffected, unmoved by the prospect of his wife's death.

He's had more time to consider it than I have, Lou thought. He's had time to become accustomed to the idea of Mary dead. He cares as much as I do, but his feelings have settled from the surface into darker, more affecting regions.

'Or maybe the psychopath will kill me,' Max said.

'The two of you should give up on this one,' Lou said. 'Go home right now. Stay out of it.'

'But if she *did* foresee something of that sort,' Max said, 'won't it happen regardless of what we do to avoid it?'

'I don't believe in predestination.'

'Neither do I. Yet . . . what she foresees always seems to happen. So if we don't go after this killer, will he come after us?'

'Damn you,' Lou said. 'You've made me stone cold sober.' He drank his wine, poured more.

'There's something else,' Max said. 'When she was six years old, a man apparently sexually molested her.'

'Berton Mitchell,' Lou said.

'How much has she told you about it?'

'Not much. The general outlines of it. I gather she can't remember most of it.'

'Did she tell you what happened to Mitchell?'

'He was found guilty,' Lou said. 'He hung himself in his prison cell, didn't he?'

'Do you know that for a fact?'

'She told me.'

'But do you know it for a fact?'

Lou was puzzled. 'Why would she lie?'

'I'm not saying she lied. But what if no one ever told her the truth?'

'I don't follow you.'

'Suppose,' Max said, 'that Berton Mitchell was never sentenced to a prison term. Suppose he had a good attorney who got him off scot-free though he was guilty. It happens. If you were the father of a six-year-old who'd been molested and horribly traumatized, would you want to tell her that her assailant had walked away unpunished? Wouldn't you worry that she might suffer even more serious psychological damage if she knew that the monster who had abused her was on the streets, free to try for her again? If Berton Mitchell was acquitted, Mary's father might have decided the best thing was for her to believe that Mitchell was dead.'

'Surely she would have discovered the truth when she got older,' Lou said.

'Not necessarily. Not if she didn't want to discover it.'

'Alan would have told her.'

'Maybe Alan never knew the truth either,' Max said. 'He was only nine at the time. Their father would have lied to both of them. And if—'

Lou held up one hand for silence. 'Let's say you're right. Let's say Berton Mitchell was acquitted. What's that have to do with this case?'

Max picked up his fork and poked at the rumpled pile of potato skin on his plate. 'I told you I think Mary's foreseen something that terrifies her.'

'That she'll be killed. Or you will.'

'Perhaps that's it. But maybe she's also seen that the killer we're after is . . . Berton Mitchell.'

'He'd be sixty years old if he was alive!'

'Is there some law that says all psychopathic killers have to be young?' Max asked.

458

* * *

In the bathroom Mary washed her hands, picked up the towel, looked into the mirror above the washbasin – and did not see her own face. Instead, she saw the face of a total stranger – a young woman with pale yellow hair and even paler skin and wide-set blue eyes, her features distorted by terror.

The mirror had become a window on another dimension, for it did not reflect anything in the bathroom. The blonde woman's face was disembodied, floating in misty shadows. Above and to the right of her, the only other object in the void beyond the mirror was a golden crucifix.

Mary dropped the towel, backed away from the sink until she bumped into the wall.

In the mirror a man's hand, also disembodied, appeared in the foreground of the surrealistic collage of psychic images. It was gripping a butcher knife.

Mary had never received a clairvoyant vision in this fashion. For a moment she didn't know what to expect. She didn't know what she should do; she was afraid both to move and to stay still.

The disembodied hand raised the knife. The blonde's face receded like a ball flying away, whirling and spinning and tumbling through endless space. The hand and the butcher knife receded too, in pursuit of her.

Concentrate, Mary told herself. For God's sake, don't let the vision get away from you. Hold on to it at all costs. Hold it and expand upon it. Develop it until it provides the name of the man whose hand holds the knife.

The crucifix swelled until it filled the mirror. Then, in perfect, eerie silence, the icon exploded into a dozen jagged pieces and was gone.

Concentrate . . .

The woman's face reappeared. And the knife loomed large in the mirror. The blade gave off a fierce light of its own, as if it were made of neon tubing.

'Who are you?' Mary asked aloud. 'You with the knife. Who in the hell are you?'

Suddenly the hand was no longer disembodied. The woman's face vanished, and the shoulder and the back of a man's head entered the scene, cloaked in shadow. The killer started to turn slowly, turned through laces of wan light and shifting shadows,

459

turned so he would be facing out from the mirror, turned as if he knew Mary was now behind him, turned slowly and silently, turned as if in response to her request for his name . . .

Worried that she might lose the vision an instant before she had her answer, as had happened to her in Dr Cauvel's office the day before, Mary said, 'Who? Who are you? I demand to know!'

To her right, six feet away, the latch on the bathroom window opened with a sharp *click!*

Startled, Mary looked away from the image in the mirror.

The window slid up.

The wind threw aside the flimsy brown and black curtains and rushed into the room, making banshee noises as it came.

The night beyond the window was dark, far darker than she had ever seen.

Over the howling of the wind came another sound: *Wicka-wicka-wicka!*

Wings. Leathery wings. Just beyond the window.

Wicka-wicka-wicka!

Perhaps it was a coincidental sound. The curtain rod vibrating in its fixtures? A branch or shrub rustling rhythmically against the side of the house?

Whatever the cause of it, she was certain she was not merely imagining the sound this time; nor was she receiving it as part of her psychic impressions. Some creature was actually close at hand, beyond that open window, some unimaginably bizarre creature with wings.

No. Insanity.

Well, go look, she told herself. Go see what it is that has these wings. See if it's anything at all. End this forever.

She couldn't move.

Wicka-wicka-wicka!

Max, help me, she said. But the words formed without sound.

To her left, beside the sink, the door of the medicine cabinet was wrenched open by invisible hands. Thrown shut. Wrenched open. Thrown shut. The next time it came open, it stayed that way. All of the contents of the cabinet – bottles of Anacin, aspirin, cold tablets, iodine, cough syrup, laxatives; tubes of toothpaste, skin cream, shampoo; boxes of throat lozenges, Band-Aids, gauze pads – leaped from the shelves to the floor.

The shower curtain was flung back by an invisible hand, and

460

the shower rod sagged and bent as if someone quite heavy was hanging from it. The rod tore out of the wall and fell into the tub.

The commode seat began to bash itself up and down, faster and faster, making an incredible din.

She took one step towards the bathroom door.

It swung open as if urging her to leave – then a second later went shut with a crash like a thunderclap. It opened and closed itself repeatedly, almost in time with the clatter of the commode seat.

She put her back to the wall once more, afraid to move.

'Mary!'

Max and Lou were on the other side of the door, briefly visible as it swung open. They were staring, amazed.

The door closed with even greater power than it had before, flew open, shut, open, shut.

Max tried to come in as the door opened again, but it slammed in his face. The next time it opened he grabbed the doorknob and forced his way inside.

The door stopped moving.

The wind at the window decreased to a slight draught.

There were no wings beating now.

Stillness.

Silence.

Mary looked at the mirror above the washbasin and saw that, while the images in it had changed, it was still not an ordinary mirror and did not reflect the room in front of it. The pale blonde, the crucifix, and the man with the butcher knife were gone. The mirror was black – except for the very bottom of it, where blood appeared to seep through the glass and over the frame, where it dripped into the room, as if the world on the other side was nothing but a lake of gore with a surface that reached slightly above the lower edge of the mirror. The blood splashed on the faucets that were directly below the mirror, splattered the white porcelain sink.

Confused, Max said, 'What the devil is this? What's happening here?' He looked from the mirror to Mary. 'Are you hurt? Have you cut yourself!'

'No,' she said. And only then did she realise that *he* saw the blood, too.

461

Max touched the rim of the mirror. Impossibly, incredibly, the blood came off on his fingers.

Lou squeezed into the small bathroom to have a better look.

Gradually the blood – on the mirror, faucets, porcelain, and on Max's finger – became less vivid, less brilliantly red, less substantial, faded until it was gone, as if it had never been.

* * *

Mary sat on the living room sofa and accepted a glass of brandy from Lou. When she brushed her hair back from her forehead, it felt greasy and cold. There was no colour in her face. Her hands were clammy. The brandy burned her throat and brought a welcome warmth.

Standing in front of her, Max said, 'What you saw in that mirror before we came after you – does that mean someone will die tonight?'

'Yes,' Mary said. 'The girl I saw. She'll die. She'll be stabbed before morning.'

'What's her name?'

'I didn't see it.'

'Where does she live?'

'Here in King's Point. But I didn't sense any address for her.'

'Does she live on the hills, in the flats, or around the harbour?'

'It could be any place,' Mary said.

'What does she look like?'

'She's got very light yellow hair, almost white. Kinky hair, worn long. Pale skin. Big blue eyes. She's young, in her twenties, very cute. Delicate. No, a better word . . . ethereal.'

Max turned to Lou as the newspaperman finished a double shot of Wild Turkey. The way he tossed it back, he might as well have been drinking milk or cyanide. 'This is your town, Lou. Do you know anyone who fits that description?'

'We've got ten thousand permanent residents,' Lou said. 'I don't know all of them. I don't *want* to know all of them. Nine tenths of them are hopeless jackasses, dullards, and bores. Besides, a lot of pretty young blondes are drawn to the Southern California beach life. Sun, sand, sea, sensitivity sessions, sex, and syphilis. In this town there must be at least two hundred tender, achingly ethereal blondes who could be the one Mary saw.'

462

Unconsciously Max had picked up a copy of *The Nation* and had rolled it into a tight tube. He slapped it into the palm of his left hand. 'If we don't locate the girl, she'll be killed tonight.'

Mary's fear had metamorphosed into a depression like an endless plain of ashes; but beneath the ashes were scattered glowing coals of anger. She was not angry with Max or Lou or with herself, but with fate. Even as the anger built, she knew it was a luxury, that it had no effect or meaning; for the only weapon anyone had against fate was resignation.

'You forget what it means when I foresee something,' she told Max. 'It doesn't matter if we find this girl and warn her. Nothing matters. She'll die anyway. *I've seen it!* I can't see the names of the winning horses in tomorrow's races. I can't see what stocks will rise in price and which will fall next week. All I can see is people dying.' She stood up. 'Jesus, but I'm sick of the way I have to live. I'm sick of seeing violence and being unable to prevent it. I'm sick of seeing innocent people in trouble and being unable to help them. I'm tired of a life filled with corpses and violated women and battered children and blood and knives and guns.'

'I know,' Max said gently. 'I know.'

She went to the bar and jerked the stopper from the bottle of brandy. 'I don't want to be a funnel for other people's misery! I want to be a mechanism for the destruction of that misery, for the amelioration of that misery, for the prevention of it.' She poured herself a brandy. 'If I'm going to have the all-seeing eye of a god, then dammit, I should have the power of a god, too. I should be able to reach out with that power right this minute and find the man we're after. I should be able to squeeze his heart in a vice of power until it bursts. But I'm not a god. I'm not even a complete mechanism. I'm like half a radio set. I can receive, but I can't transmit. I can be affected, but I can't cause an effect.' She drank the brandy as quickly and smoothly as Lou might have done. 'I hate it. Hate it. Why do *I* have to have this power? Why *me*?'

* * *

Later, at the front door, Lou said, 'I wish you'd stay here tonight.'

'We've seen your guest room,' Max said. 'Magazines and books, but no furniture. We appreciate your intellect and the size of your library, but we don't relish sleeping on stacks of old paperbacks.'

'I could use the living room sofa tonight,' Lou said. 'You two could sleep in my room.'

Mary kissed him on the cheek. 'You're a darling man. But we'll be fine. Really we will. At least until tomorrow night.'

THURSDAY,
DECEMBER 24

TWELVE

At one o'clock in the morning, rain slashed inland from the sea. It made the bare earth slick, flattened the dry grass, bounced off the macadam roadway.

He parked the Mercedes at the end of the paved lane, switched off the engine. Darkness wrapped the car. There was so little light that he could not even see his own hands on the steering wheel. The only sound was the incessant drumming of the rain on the hood and roof.

He decided to wait until the storm passed. The rainy season had come to Southern California; however, sudden cloudbursts like this one seldom lasted long.

The butcher knife was on the seat beside him. He felt for it, picked it up. He could barely see it in the poor light; but he was thrilled by the feel of it as much as by the sight of the well-honed blade. He pressed one finger to the cutting edge, not firmly enough to draw his own blood but hard enough to feel the energy of death lying inert but ready within the tempered steel.

At one-ten the rain slowed to a drizzle. Five minutes after that, it stopped altogether. He opened the car door and got out.

The air was clean and cool. The wind had died down.

Three quarters of a mile to his left and below him, the night around the harbour was strung with lights like Christmas decorations.

The only nearby light came from one of three cottages that stood two hundred yards to the west. These houses were lined up along the cliff, facing seaward, presenting their back doors to the dead-end macadam road. The northernmost cottage, which belonged to Erika Larsson, was seventy yards from its neighbour and stood in a cluster of trees; lights shone from many of its windows.

467

As he had expected, Erika was awake. Probably working. One of her sombre watercolours. Or a disquieting oil painting full of brooding faces rendered in blues and deep greens. She did most of her painting in the calm, early morning hours and went to bed at dawn.

He walked around the back of the Mercedes and opened the trunk. It was littered with guns – an Italian shotgun, two rifles, and seven handguns – and boxes of ammunition. He chose a .45 Auto Colt, a custom-made collector's piece, all the metalwork heavily engraved with wild animals fleeing from the muzzle back towards the handgrips. It was already loaded. All of the guns were loaded. He put the Colt in his jacket pocket and closed the trunk.

Holding the knife at his side, he walked down the dirt lane towards the lighted house. The night was so unrelievedly dark that he occasionally stumbled over the driveway ruts. His shoes squished in the mud.

* * *

Mary murmured in her sleep.

In her dream she was with her father. He looked as he had when she was nine years old; and she was a child again. They were sitting on a velvety green lawn. The sun was high; it came straight down on top of them; and they cast no shadows.

'If I help people with my ESP, maybe they'll love me. I want people to love me, Daddy.'

'Well, Sweetcakes, I love you.'

'But you'll leave me.'

'Leave my little girl? Nonsense.'

'You'll die in the car. Die and leave me.'

'You mustn't say things like that.'

'But—'

'If I did die, you'd still have your mother.'

'She's left me already. Left me for her whisky.'

'No, no. Your mother still loves you.'

'She loves whisky. She forgets my name.'

'Your brother loves you.'

'No, he doesn't.'

'Mary, what a terrible thing to say!'

'I don't blame Alan for not loving me. All his pets die because of me.'

468

'That's not your fault.'

'You know it is. But even if Alan loves me, he'll leave me someday. Then I'll be alone.'

'Someday you'll meet a man who'll marry you and love you.'

'Maybe he'll love me for a little while. But then he'll leave, won't he? Like everyone leaves. I need protection against being left alone. I'm scared of being alone. I need lots of people who love me. If lots and lots of people love me, they won't all be able to go away at the same time.'

'Look at the time! I've got to be going.'

'Daddy, you can't leave me.'

'I don't have any choice.'

'I found Elmo this morning.'

'Alan's cat?'

'I found him all bloody.'

'Found him where?'

'At the playhouse.'

'Not another dead animal?'

'Someone cut him to pieces.'

'Does Alan know?'

'Not yet. Daddy, he'll cry.'

'Jesus, the poor kid.'

'He'll be awful mad at me.'

'Mary . . . you didn't . . .'

'No! Daddy, I wouldn't do something like that.'

'After what happened last week . . .'

'It wasn't me! It wasn't!'

'Okay, then it was the Mitchell boy again.'

'I wish Mrs Mitchell would move out of town.'

'Berton Mitchell's boy cut up Elmo. Alan won't be mad at you.'

'But it's because I had his daddy sent away that he's coming here and killing all of Alan's pets.'

'Alan understands. He doesn't hold you responsible.'

'Alan's still mad because I threw his turtles in the creek last week.'

'You haven't explained why you did that.'

'Something told me to.'

'You deserved your punishment, you know. They were Alan's turtles, not yours.'

'Something told me to.'

'Who told you to?'

'Something. Something.'

469

'Mary, you're a strange child at times.'

'Stay here, and I'll be good.'

'Got to go.'

'I'll be alone if you go.'

'Got to go.'

'I'll be alone with the wings.'

'Good-bye.'

'Daddy, the wings!'

Whimpering, weighted down in sleep by the sedative she'd taken, Mary turned over, unaware that she was alone in bed.

★ ★ ★

He pushed up the unlocked bedroom window and slipped inside without making a sound.

Towards the front of the cottage a stereo was playing one of Joan Baez's most soulful albums.

He crossed the bedroom and went down the narrow hall to the living room. Erika Larsson was sitting on a high wooden stool with her back to him. She was at a large easel, working on an oil painting.

The girl's black cat, Samantha, was curled up on an easy chair. It raised its head and stared at him with yellow eyes as he came out of the hallway.

There was a pleasant odour in the air. She had made herself some popcorn not long ago.

He was only ten feet from her when she sensed him and turned. 'You,' she said.

She was as beautiful as he remembered her. Thick, kinky blonde hair. Pale, almost translucent skin. Huge blue eyes. She was wearing jeans and a T-shirt, and her dark nipples were prominent against the thin white material.

She got up from the stool. 'What are you doing here?'

He didn't answer.

The black cat knew something was terribly wrong. It jumped down from the chair and ran into the kitchen.

He took another step towards Erika.

She edged around the easel. 'Get out of here.'

He knocked over the easel.

'What do you want?' she asked.

He held up the knife.

'No. Oh, no.'

She backed up against the windows that looked out on the Pacific Ocean.

She held her hands in front of her, as if she would push him away when he tried to close the last few feet between them.

'Mary will know,' Erika said.

He said nothing.

'Mary will see who did it,' she said.

He reached for her.

'She'll turn you over to the cops. Mary will know!'

* * *

Near dawn.

The black cat named Samantha came out of the kitchen cabinet in which she had hidden and fallen asleep. She yawned and stretched. Then she stood for a minute with her head held high, listening

The cottage was quiet. The wind soughed softly across the roof.

At last, Samantha padded into the living room. The Christmas tree had been knocked on its side. Ornaments were strewn across the floor; and many of them had been stamped to slivers and dust. Samantha sniffed at a broken glass angel, pushed at its head with one paw. She tasted a crushed candy cane and investigated a broken crucifix that had once hung on the living room wall above the hall door. She nosed around a discarded pair of jeans and a rumpled white T-shirt.

Finally, warily, Samantha circled the body of Erika Larsson and tasted the blood as she had tasted the candy cane.

THIRTEEN

Like scarecrows flapping on an empty snow-covered field, nightmares had studded her sleep. Most of them were based upon the worst moments of her childhood. This morning filthy rags of those dreams hung around her and made her uneasy, nervous.

Ordinarily, after she showered and before she dressed, she half dried her hair with a towel, then applied one hundred vigorous brush strokes. Now, curiously disturbed by her nakedness, she counted the twenty-eighth stroke and knew that she couldn't wait through seventy-two more before putting on her clothes.

She usually enjoyed performing this and other morning rituals in the nude. She admitted to being an exhibitionist. (See me, see my lovely breasts and ass and legs, see how unmarked, see how very pretty, like me, love me, love me.) But she was motivated by more than exhibitionism. She felt that by beginning the day unclothed, she acquired a sense of lightness and freedom that stayed with her through the afternoon. Dr Cauvel said that perhaps by starting each day naked, she was trying to prove to herself that her nightly dreams had left no sign on her, that Berton Mitchell had left no sign on her, but she couldn't see the logic in that bit of analysis.

Sometimes Max would sit in perfect silence and watch as she brushed her hair and exercised in the nude. He could make her blush by referring to his voyeurism as 'reading beautiful poetry.'

But now Max was in the shower. There was no one in the motel room to read her poetry. Yet she felt that someone was staring at her.

Shivering, she put on a brassiere and panties.

When she opened the closet to get slacks and a blouse, she saw Max's muddy shoes and mud-streaked, blood-stained jacket. As she was examining the dark reddish blots on the jacket, Max came

472

out of the bathroom. He was drying his hair with a towel, and another towel was wrapped around his waist.

'Did you hurt yourself?' she asked.

'All I did was take a shower.'

She didn't smile. She held up the soiled jacket.

'Oh,' he said. 'The cut on my finger came open.'

'How did that happen?'

'The bandage tore loose when I tripped and fell.'

'Fell? When was this?'

'Last night,' he said. 'After you took your sedative you went right to sleep, but I couldn't keep my eyes closed. I went for a walk. I was three blocks from the hotel when it started to rain. It was a regular cloudburst. Surprised the hell out of me. I started to run back. Took a short cut through the vacant lot next door, tripped on a stone and fell. Pretty stupid of me. The bandage came off my finger and the cut popped open.'

She winced. Looking down at the jacket in her hands, she said, 'You bled a lot.'

'Like a stuck pig.' He held up his hand. The injured finger was swathed in clean gauze and adhesive tape. 'It still aches.'

He tossed aside the towel with which he'd been drying his hair, took the jacket from her, turned it over in his hands. 'I don't think any dry cleaner is going to make this look like new.' He took the jacket to the wastebasket and threw it away.

'You should have awakened me when you came in last night,' Mary said.

'You were a mile under.'

'You should have tried.'

'What for? It wasn't anything serious. I applied pressure for fifteen minutes, until the bleeding completely stopped. Then I put on a new bandage. Nothing to worry about.'

'You should see a doctor.'

He shook his head. 'No need.'

'Well, it's apparently not healing.'

'Give it time. It had just begun to heal when I fell and pulled it open,' he said. 'I'll be more careful.'

'The next time you change bandages,' she said, 'I want to see the cut. If it isn't healing, you'll go to a doctor even if I have to drag you there.'

He came to her and put his hands on her slender shoulders.

473

'Yes, Mother.' He had a charming smile which he reserved almost exclusively for her.

She sighed and leaned against his chest, where she could hear the slow, steady beat of his heart. 'I worry about you.'

'I know,' he said.

'Because I love you.'

'I know.'

'Because I'd die if I lost you.'

He unhooked her brassiere.

'But we don't have time,' she said.

'We'll skip breakfast.'

She moved her hands over him. He was solid, powerful. His size and strength had tremendous impact on her. She felt drugged and excited at the same time. Her eyes grew heavy, her legs weak; yet, in her breasts and belly and thighs, she felt an extraordinary heat and tension. The texture of his skin, the steeliness of his muscle and sinew and bone mesmerized her.

He stripped her, then took off the towel he had been wearing around his waist. He kissed her throat. She felt weightless. His hands slid down her back and cupped her buttocks.

'You could hold me so tight,' she said, 'squeeze me so tight that you'd cut off my breath. You're strong enough to break my neck.'

'I don't want to break your neck,' he murmured.

'But you could. So easily.'

He took her earlobe between his lips.

'If you . . . broke my neck . . . I don't think . . . I'd care.'

He moved one hand between them and touched the moist centre of her.

'You'd be so gentle,' she said dreamily. 'Even as you broke me, you'd be gentle. There wouldn't be pain. You wouldn't allow pain.'

He took her to the bed.

As he entered her, as the piston of lovemaking grew slick with her clear oils, she thought about being crushed to death in his arms, and she thought how odd it was for her to consider such a thing, and how much stranger still to consider it without fear and something very like desire, a melancholy longing, a curiously pleasant anticipation, not a death wish but a sweet resignation, and she knew that Dr Cauvel would say this was a sign of her sickness, that now she was prepared to surrender even her ultimate responsibility (the fundamental responsibility for her own life, for deciding whether or not she was worthy of life), and he would say that she needed to rely more on herself and less on Max, but she didn't care, didn't care at all; she just felt the power, Max's power, and began to call his name, dug her fingers into his unyielding muscle and surrendered willingly.

* * *

'Roger Fullet speaking.'

'Your name fits. Fullet, you're full of it.'

'Lou? Is that you? Lou Pasternak?'

'I called and asked for Roger Fullet, the reporter, and was promptly told it's now Roger Fullet, the editor.'

'It happened a month ago.'

'The *Los Angeles Times* is degenerating swiftly.'

'They finally recognized brilliance.'

'Oh? You mean after just promoting you they're giving your job to someone else?'

'Very funny.'

'Thank you.'

'You're a funny man.'

'Thank you.'

'Plastic surgery might help.'

'Watch it, Fullet. You're no match for me.'

'Sorry. Lost my head.'

'It wouldn't be the first time.'

'Hey, Lou, I've got an office with this job that's almost as large as your whole shop.'

'They gave you an office so they could lock you in it and keep you out from under foot.'

'I dine with the brass.'

'Because they don't trust you with the silver.'

'Christ, it's good to hear your voice.'

'How are Peggy and the kids?'

'Fine. Wonderful. Everyone's healthy.'

'Give them my love and wish them a merry Christmas for me.'

'I will. You'll have to come visit for a weekend soon. You know we haven't seen each other in six months? We live so close, only an hour or so apart, Lou, why don't we get together more often?'

'Maybe subconsciously we loathe each other.'

'Nobody could possibly loathe me. I'm just a big Hershey Bar. My daughter says so.'

'Well, Mr Hershey Bar, I wonder if you could do me a favour.'

'Name it, Lou.'

'I'd like you to go back through the *Times'* morgue and get me all available background on a crime that interests me.'

'What sort of crime?'

'Child molestation.'

'Ugly.'

'Also assault with intent to kill.'

'Where did it happen?'

'Somewhere in West Los Angeles. A pretty good neighbourhood. The girl lived on a twenty-acre estate that's probably since been subdivided.'

'When was this?'

'Twenty-four, maybe twenty-five years ago.'

'Who was the victim?'

'This gets touchy.'

'How so?'

'Roger, she's a dear friend.'

'I see.'

'She's also a celebrity of sorts, very much in the public eye.'

'I'm intrigued.'

'I don't intend to write about this. And I don't want anyone else writing about it.'

'If it's twenty-five years old, it's dead material for a newspaper.'

'I know that. But someone might be able to use it in a magazine piece. It would hurt her badly if it were all dredged up again.'

'If you aren't writing about it, why do you need to know?'

'She's in trouble. Bad trouble. I want to help her.'

'Why can't you get the details of this thing from her?'

'She was only six years old when it happened.'

'My God.'

'She can't possibly remember it all – or remember it correctly.'

'And what happened back then has some connection with the bad trouble she's in now?'

'I think it might.'

'Okay. I won't send someone else to do the work. There'd be a leak if I did. I'll go down to the morgue and pick through the files myself.'

476

'Thanks, Roger.'

'And I'll go as your friend, not as a reporter.'

'That's good enough for me.'

'What's the victim's name?'

'Mary Bergen. No, wait . . . back then it was Mary Tanner.'

'The clairvoyant?'

'That's right.'

'We carry her column.'

'So do I.'

'Who was the assailant?'

'Berton Mitchell. B-E-R-T-O-N. M-I-T-C-H-E-L-L. He was the caretaker for the Tanner estate.'

'I'll get the full background. Is there something about it that specially interests you?'

'I want to know if Mitchell ever stood trial. If he had his day in court, I want to know whether he was acquitted and set free, or found guilty.'

'You said he was the assailant.'

'That doesn't mean he was found guilty. You know what a good attorney can accomplish.'

'Anything else?'

'Most of all, if Mitchell *was* found guilty, I want to know if he committed suicide.'

'Is that what you've been told?'

'Yes. But I don't know if it's true.'

'Lou, if he's still alive, and if he's not in prison, I doubt I could find him through our files.'

'I'm not asking you to find him. If Mitchell's alive, then I think I know where he is.'

'I'll get back to you this afternoon.'

'I'll be at the office.'

When he concluded his conversation with Roger Fullet, Lou placed a long-distance telephone call to the home of Dr Oliver Railsbeck, an old friend who worked at Stanford University. They talked for fifteen minutes.

An nine-thirty, after he had learned what he could from Ollie Railsbeck, Lou walked down the hall to the guest bath. He had cleaned up the mess the previous night; the broken glass and spilled cough syrup were gone. He stood in the centre of the small room and studied the mirror above the washbasin. There was no reflection but his own.

He touched the glass and the mirror frame, touched the faucets and the porcelain sink. The night before, all of these things had been splashed with blood that Mary had conjured up and briefly sustained with her psychic power. Thick wet blood that was real . . . yet not real. Blood that had substance, colour, and texture (if only for a few seconds), but which was not of this world.

He wondered whose pain and suffering it had represented. It could be the symbolic blood of the blonde whose death Mary had predicted. Or perhaps it was Mary's blood that had vanished from Max's fingertips.

An omen of her death?

'God help her,' Lou said aloud.

478

FOURTEEN

Mary sat on an uncomfortable metal chair, her purse on her lap, her hands on the purse.

Max was on a chair at her left side. He knew she didn't like long conversations with policemen, and that the dreary, cold, atmosphere of police stations unnerved her. Several times during the past quarter hour he had reached out and touched her. Nothing obvious. Little pats and squeezes of affection and reassurance. As always, his presence buoyed her.

To her right Lou had turned another chair around so that he could sit with his arms crossed on the back of it.

The room smelled of stale cigar smoke. The overhead lights were too bright. The only decorations on the walls were photographs of the late J. Edgar Hoover, Chief Patmore's idol, and a military calendar that had a different battle scene for each month.

John Patmore, senior officer of the King's Point police force, hunched over his cluttered desk and spoke earnestly into the telephone to Percy Osterman. Apparently the sheriff was doling out a considerable amount of flattery in order to persuade Patmore to cooperate with Mary. A smile that was almost a smirk played at the corners of Patmore's weak mouth.

He was a surprisingly bland-looking man. Late forties. Round face. Mostly bald. Brown eyes. Plain features. Average height and average build.

She worried that they hadn't made a strong case in their plea for Patmore's assistance. Lou had advised her not to discuss the more bizarre aspects of her story. She had said nothing about flying glass dogs, deadly sea gulls, or bathroom mirrors brimmed with blood. All of that, Lou insisted, would confuse Patmore. After Lou explained the nature of Mary's psychic powers, she had told the policeman only that the mass murders of the last few days

479

were the work of one man, that he had killed a young woman in King's Point last night (although the body had not yet been found), and that at seven o'clock this evening he would open fire with a high-powered rifle from one of the three towers that overlooked the harbour.

At last, Patmore said good-bye to Percy Osterman and put down the receiver. He leaned back in his chair. For almost a minute he stared off into space. He was smiling.

'Don't let the chief upset you. He doesn't *mean* to be insulting,' Lou said to Max and Mary. 'Every once in a while he stops to think and forgets to start again.'

Ignoring the newsman, Patmore turned to Mary. 'I don't like this – a lunatic killer in my town.'

She said, 'If we—'

Taking a cigar from the centre drawer of his desk, Patmore said, 'Not one bit do I like it. I run a very tight little town as chief of police.'

'We can—'

'In each of those towers,' Patmore said, 'because Percy Osterman vouched for you, although I still have my doubts about this psychic stuff, at six o'clock, one hour ahead of schedule if you're right, I'll have the men.'

Not certain that she had properly interpreted that convoluted sentence, Mary said, 'Then you'll put men in the towers tonight?'

Patmore blinked. He had started to wet the end of his cigar. He took it out of his mouth. 'Now, didn't I just say that?'

'You'll have to excuse the chief,' Lou said. 'He thinks that "syntax" is the money the church collects from sinners.'

Much to Mary's relief, the policeman studiously ignored Lou. He said, 'Let's have the details again; your vision from start to finish.'

She sighed and relaxed slightly.

She thought: this particular horror is drawing to an end.

Then: Is it? Or is it only just beginning?

'Are you feeling well?' Max asked.

'Yes,' she lied.

★ ★ ★

On the sidewalk in front of police headquarters, Max turned

480

to Lou and said, 'Well, that was a lot easier than you said it would be.'

Lou shrugged. 'I'm surprised. Ordinarily it takes a surgical procedure to get a new idea into his head.'

'Evidently,' Mary said, 'he's even more impressed by Percy Osterman than you thought.'

Lou said, 'That's definitely a part of it. But I guess it's also self-preservation. He knows that if he called you a charlatan and threw you out of his office, and then the killer *did* strike from one of those towers, I'd call for his resignation on the front page of my newspaper twice every week until he was out of a job.'

Max suggested they leave the cars parked and walk two blocks to the harbour. 'We can have drinks and lunch at The Sea Locker while we watch the boats.'

She walked between Max and Lou, and gradually her spirits lifted. The breeze scoured Patmore's cigar smoke from her; it sluiced away some of her tension and anxiety as well.

The weather had improved. Although the sky was still overcast, and although rain was forecast for tomorrow, this was one of those widely advertised Southern California winter days. The temperature had risen to seventy degrees. The air was so clean and fresh that it almost wasn't there. This was the kind of day that made all of the transplanted Easterners happy they had moved.

A block from the harbour they came to a pet shop where two spaniel pups peered out from a window cage.

'Oh, aren't they cute!' Mary said. She slipped from between Max and Lou, went to the window.

The puppies stood with their front paws on the glass and tried to sniff the hand she offered them. Their tails whipped frantically back and forth.

'Never cared for dogs,' Lou said. 'They're too dependent.'

'They're sweet,' she said.

'I don't like cats either.'

Max said, 'Why not?'

'They're too *in*dependent.'

'Lou, you're trying too hard,' Max said.

Smiling, the newsman said, 'Well, in some quarters I'm known as a bitter curmudgeon. I've got to uphold my reputation, don't I?'

Mary spoke to the dogs through the window, and they wiggled and barked ecstatically.

'I know how much you love animals,' Max said. 'I thought about getting you a dog for Christmas. Maybe I should have done it.'

'Oh, no,' she said, still playing with the puppies. 'It would have died.'

Lou looked at her curiously. 'What an odd thing to say.'

Memories of mutilated cats and dogs and rabbits and other small creatures flickered in disgusting colours behind her eyes.

She turned away from the spaniels. 'Alan had a great many animals when he was a boy. I had a few myself. But all of them were tortured and killed.'

'Tortured and killed?' Lou asked. 'What in the name of God are you talking about?'

'Berton Mitchell's boy did it,' Mary said. 'He thought I'd falsely accused his father. So he kept sneaking onto the estate and slaughtering our pets. One by one. Year after year. Until we finally stopped keeping animals.'

With a tenderness that touched her, Max said, 'So the nightmares didn't end when Mitchell hanged himself in that prison cell.'

His grey eyes, so often flat and expressionless, were filled with sympathy and love.

Lou said, 'I didn't know that Berton Mitchell had a family.'

Mary nodded. 'A wife and son. Of course, they moved off the estate after . . . after what happened. But they never left the city. They were always nearby.'

She glanced at the spaniels, but they no longer appealed to her. When she looked at them now, she couldn't see anything but Alan's dogs; dead dogs with broken legs and dozens of knife wounds, gutted dogs, beheaded dogs, dogs with their eyes punched out.

Lou said, 'This Mitchell boy—'

'No more about this,' she said shakily. 'Let's go to The Sea Locker. I can use a drink.'

★ ★ ★

The men's room at the restaurant reeked of pine-scented disinfectant.

As they washed their hands at the twin sinks (Max being careful

482

to keep his bandaged finger dry), Lou said, 'Did I ever mention my friend, Ollie Railsbeck?'

'I don't recall the name,' Max said.

'He's in charge of a relatively new research effort at Stanford University. They're investigating all kinds of paranormal things – clairvoyance, precognition, psychometry, telepathy, telekinesis, astral projection, *everything*.'

'I think I *do* remember the name,' Max said. He turned off the water and jerked a paper towel from the dispenser. 'I think they've asked Mary to cooperate in some experiments, but she hasn't found the time yet.'

Pulling a towel from the dispenser on the wall, Lou said, 'Ever since we learned that the Russians are spending almost a billion dollars a year on research to find military applications for psychic phenomena, the Pentagon's been willing to part with a few bucks to fund general studies in the field. Ollie's department and the one that Dr Rhine started years ago at Duke University are the best programmes of their sort in the country.'

'Mary's done some work at Duke.'

'This morning I called Ollie Railsbeck and asked his opinion about what happened at the house last night, about the blood that came out of the mirror.'

'What did he say?'

'He called it "ectoplasm." '

'I'm familiar with that word,' Max said. He threw away his paper towel and turned towards the men's room door.

'Wait,' Lou said. 'I didn't want to bring this up in front of Mary.' Max leaned against the wall. 'Go ahead.'

'According to Ollie, that kind of experience isn't as unique as I thought it was. He says similar things occur at séances.'

Max raised his eyebrows. 'Your friend's spending our tax dollars to study séances? Those phony sessions the gypsies run, that dark room-and-candles bit where people who want to talk to dead relatives get bilked out of their money?'

'There are some highly respectable mediums who take their work seriously, who don't want money or notoriety, and who conduct some of the damnedest, scariest séances.'

'They talk to ghosts?'

'Maybe. They think they do. They talk to *something* that seems to talk back. Anyway, Ollie says that every now and then the form

483

of a spirit or an object will appear above the séance table or over the medium's head while she's in a trance.'

'And it's not done with slide projectors focused on a plastic sheet or anything like that?'

'These apparitions have been seen and studied by researchers in a controlled laboratory environment,' Lou said. 'Sometimes blood will drip out of thin air. Or what appear to be tears. Whatever the nature of the manifestation, it has substance, just as if it's real.'

'But only for a short time. Last night the blood that came out of that mirror faded quickly.'

'Right. It usually lasts seconds. Sometimes a full minute. Ollie knows of a case where a child's face floated above the medium for twenty minutes, but that's rare. Temporarily solid apparitions like these are supposedly composed of ectoplasm, a supernatural material that, the mediums say, is able to pass between the dimensions of life and death.'

Max said, 'This friend of yours believes in ghosts?'

'No. He says most of the genuinely talented mediums have highly developed psychic abilities. They score well on card tests for telepathy. Most of them have well documented records of accurate predictions. Ollie thinks that somehow, by the use of a psychic ability we don't understand, they unconsciously create the ectoplasm.'

'He doesn't believe it's material from another world?'

'No. And especially not from the afterlife.'

Max thought about that for a moment. He said, 'Then in Railsbeck's view ectoplasm is sort of the realised flesh of a psychic's subconscious thoughts.'

'Exactly,' Lou said.

'So Railsbeck supports what I've been saying.'

'That's why I wanted to tell you when we were alone,' Lou said. 'I didn't want to upset Mary.'

'There's no supernatural, demonic force operating here.'

Lou sighed and shook his head. 'I'm not absolutely convinced of that. You're probably right. But I'm keeping an open mind. However, you *are* convinced, and Ollie sides with you, so I'll keep my mouth shut.'

Max made a fist of one hand and pounded it into the other. The sound was sharp; it startled Lou, and it echoed off the tile

484

walls. '*Mary* created the blood that came out of the mirror, like she caused the poltergeist, but she doesn't realise it and refuses to believe it. She's seen something terrible, Lou. To keep from facing it, she's used psychic powers she never knew she had in order to construct a façade of "supernatural" events to mislead herself. She's seen something she's had to force out of her mind, something she's buried in her subconscious. She's using poltergeists and other supernatural bunk to distract herself from the thing she most fears about this case.'

Tense and depressed, Lou said, 'We can't help her because we don't know what she's hiding from herself.'

Max was grim. 'We'll know at seven o'clock tonight.' He looked at his watch. 'A little more than seven hours to go.'

★ ★ ★

The grey water looked cold and oily. It rolled against the docks; and the prows of boats cleaved it like knives slicing dark gelatine.

They had a window table at The Sea Locker. Initially, while Max and Lou talked politics, Mary sat in silence and studied the sky for sea gulls. But there were no birds today, and gradually she shifted her attention to the traffic on the harbour and to the conversation.

Although there were no gulls to worry her, she wasn't able to relax. She ate too little and drank too much; there were jokes about her trying to drink Lou under the table; but the whisky didn't steady her hands.

At two o'clock, after Lou had gone to his office and they had returned to the motel, she stretched out on the bed, on her side, intending to take a nap. She would need to be rested and alert for the manhunt tonight.

She closed her eyes and tried to switch off her mind. The wine she had drunk at lunch was some help. She felt she was drifting in lazy circles on a rubber raft in a gigantic swimming pool. She began some light meditation, repeating the word 'one' to herself until it filled her and pushed out all other thoughts.

At the borderland of sleep she heard onrushing wings: *wicka-wicka-wicka!*

She opened her eyes.

Nothing there.

485

Imagination.

Max was behind her in an armchair, reading the *King's Point Press*. If there had been any unusual sound, he would have spoken.

She closed her eyes and began thinking the word 'one' again.

Wicka-wicka-wicka!

She opened her eyes. Still nothing.

She knew the wings had something to do with Berton Mitchell. And they were also part of the case she was working on now. The killer she was stalking was somehow connected to Berton Mitchell. Impossible. Unthinkable. But . . .

She felt tormented. All she wanted was some peace. All she wanted was to be left alone. All she wanted was to *get through this case!*

She squeezed her eyes shut and tried to stop the tears, but they spilled down her cheeks anyway.

She was frightened. She wanted Max. She wanted him to get up and come to her. She started to roll towards him, was about to say his name, and then she thought: *No, by God! Be strong for once.*

Sooner or later she would have to learn to handle some of her own problems. She was increasingly aware of the fragility of life. She could feel her mortality – and not merely her own but Max's and Lou's and Alan's too – feel it as surely as if it were fragments of ice melting through her fingers. Someday Max might be gone, and how would she survive if she couldn't deal with adversity on her own?

She would have to face up to what had happened twenty-four years ago. She would have to think, force herself back in time, find the meaning of the wings. She wouldn't be able to uncover the connection between Berton Mitchell and this killer until she remembered all about the wings and what had happened in the caretaker's cottage.

She waited until the tears had dried, then got up from the bed.

'Something wrong?' Max asked.

'Can't sleep.'

'Do you want to talk?'

'Go ahead and read the paper. I just want to think.'

She picked up the spiral-bound notebook and pen that were on the nightstand. She went to the small desk and sat down.

She would do what she always did when she had a problem that no one could solve for her: she would write about it. She would

486

write dozens of questions, one on every sixth or seventh line, and search for answers to put on the lines between them. That process always relaxed her. Of course, she sought more than relaxation. She wanted answers. Sometimes she got them.

However, after all these years, she could no longer delude herself. Knowing the solution and being able to act on it were two very different things. She had the wit but not the strength. Although she had performed this ritual with notebook and pen hundreds of times, she had never got from it what she most expected: she had yet to reach an important decision entirely on her own; she had yet to handle a serious problem without someone's help.

This time would be different. It *had* to be different. She sensed that if she failed to find a new strength within herself, she wouldn't survive much longer.

She opened the notebook which she had purchased the day before but had not yet used, and she saw writing on the first ruled page.

Mary! Run for your life!

It was written in ballpoint pen. The words appeared to have been put down in haste. And although it was definitely her own handwriting, she had no memory whatsoever of having scribbled it.

★ ★ ★

Roger Fullet called at four o'clock and gave Lou a detailed synopsis of the Berton Mitchell story as it had been reported by the *Los Angeles Times* '. . . and after only twenty minutes of deliberation, the jury found him guilty of all charges. His lawyer immediately filed an appeal based on technicalities, but Mitchell must have realised there wasn't any chance of a new trial. His sentences on all counts were to be served consecutively and amounted to a minimum of twenty-five years.'

'And he hanged himself?' Lou asked.

'Just like you've been told. He did it the day after the sentencing, before he was transferred from the county gaol to prison.'

'You mentioned his family.'

'The wife and one son.'

'What was the son's name?'

'Barry. Barry Mitchell.'

'How old was he when this happened?'

'I didn't make a note of it. But I seem to remember he was sixteen.'

'Was there anything more on him in your files?' Lou asked.

'He visited his father in gaol every day. He was convinced Mitchell was innocent like he claimed.'

'Anything else?'

'These days the press would badger the hell out of the wife and son. America's gotten more ghoulish in the past couple of decades. Every day newspaper readers have a greater interest in peeking into personal tragedies than they had the day before. But twenty-four years ago Americans still had some sense of privacy and propriety. The wife and son were left alone. There's nothing more in our files.'

Lou drummed a pencil on the top of his desk. 'I wonder what happened to the son.'

'Can't help you, I'm afraid.'

'You've done more than enough. Thanks, Roger.'

After they exchanged another round of holiday greetings, Lou hung up.

As he put down his receiver, his secretary came in to wish him a merry Christmas before going home. The office was quiet after she had gone.

He hadn't turned on any lights when he came back from lunch. Now, as the early darkness gradually descended, he sat alone in lengthening shadows, staring; thinking.

What was it that Mary feared?

What was so special about this case?

One pet theory had been demolished by what Roger Fullet had told him. The psychopathic killer loose in King's Point was not Berton Mitchell.

The son? Barry Mitchell? He would be forty, Max's age. Not much older than his father had been when he attacked Mary. Madness sometimes ran in families, didn't it? Like father, like son. Maybe it would be Barry Mitchell who would climb those tower stairs at seven o'clock tonight.

As the muddy evening light replaced the afternoon, the office grew chilly. Finally, for warmth, Lou got up and poured a double shot of bourbon.

* * *

Determined not to run to Max with the five-word warning in the front of her notebook, Mary wrote down fifty-four questions and half as many answers, seeking understanding and solutions in the only way she knew. As yet she had discovered nothing new about the tortures and outrages that had transpired in that cottage twenty-four years earlier, not the slightest clue to the meaning of the wings, but she was not ready to quit.

Although it interrupted her train of thought and made her increasingly nervous, she repeatedly turned back to the first page and read the two short sentences: *Mary! Run for your life!* She tried to convince herself that it was someone else's work, that some stranger had sneaked into the motel room and had written the warning while she and Max were out. Perhaps the killer had done it. But she knew that wasn't true. It made no sense. Besides, she recognized the penmanship. She must have got out of bed in the middle of the night without disturbing Max and, while still sound asleep, scrawled an urgent message to herself. Asleep, she had foreseen great danger. But what knowledge had she possessed in sleep that eluded her now that she was awake?

Getting out of the armchair behind her, Max said, 'Do you want to freshen up?'

She turned. 'What?'

'It's five-thirty. We're to meet Lou at six. I thought you'd want to freshen up.'

'Oh, sure.' She closed the notebook. She stood.

'Are you okay?' he asked.

'Yes.'

He stared at her, concerned.

'No,' she said. 'I'm not.'

He came to her, kissed her cheek.

'I'm scared,' she said.

'So am I,' he said.

'What's going to happen to me?'

'Nothing bad,' he said.

'I don't know.'

489

'I *do* know,' he said. 'Stay close to me tonight, until they catch the bastard.'

She asked, 'What if they don't catch him?'

'You said they would.'

'No. I just said he'd be in one of the towers.'

'If they're waiting for him, they'll catch him,' Max said soothingly.

'Maybe.'

FIFTEEN

6:00 P.M.

Officer Lyle Winterman parked the squad car out of sight in an alleyway and walked two blocks to St Luke's Lutheran Church. Even with a streetlight every hundred feet Harbour Avenue seemed dark.

Winterman kept his right hand on the holstered revolver at his hip. The flap of the holster was unsnapped. His palm was on the gun butt. He expected someone to leap out at him. After Patmore's talk at the station, the deputy was jumpy as hell.

Reverend Richard Erdman was waiting in the nave of the church. They shook hands and went to the door that opened on the bell tower stairs.

'What's all this about?' Erdman asked.

'We're working on a tip,' Winterman said.

'A tip about what?'

'Chief Patmore would rather I didn't say.'

'Is there going to be violence?'

'There might be.'

'I don't want violence in my church.'

'Neither do I, Reverend.'

'This is God's house. It will remain a place of peace.'

'I hope so. Just the same, you'd better go back to the rectory and lock your doors.'

'I have a Christmas Eve service to prepare for.'

'That doesn't start until later, does it?'

'Eleven,' Erdman said. 'But I begin preparing at ten.'

'I'll be gone long before that,' Winterman said.

The officer unhooked a flashlight that was clipped to his belt and switched it on. He directed its beam to the tower stairs, hesitated, then began to climb.

Erdman shut the door behind him.

* * *

6:05 P.M.

Officer Rudy Holtzman wasn't supposed to be working on Christmas Eve. It was his night off. All the way up the tower stairs he cursed John Patmore.

Psychics, premonitions, fortunetellers, extra-sensory perception – it was all bullshit. The chief was making a fool of himself. Nothing new about that, of course. But a clairvoyant? Too much.

Holtzman reached the top of the tower at Kimball's Games and Snacks. Under him the deserted building was quiet.

He switched off his flashlight and looked out at the harbour for a moment. On a half dozen boats, parties had already got underway.

'Damn!' Holtzman said.

He sat down with his back to the waist-high wall around the observation deck. He put his revolver on the floor beside him.

He half hoped that some bastard with a rifle *did* try to come up those stairs. Maybe he would feel better if he could shoot someone.

* * *

6:10 P.M.

A well lighted eighty-foot yacht cruised around the bay end of the harbour and started down the north channel towards the sea. Waves from its wake slapped rhythmically against the sea wall.

The wind from the ocean carried a vague odour of decay.

John Patmore and his assistant – a young, overweight officer name Rollins – used a corner of The Laughing Dolphin Restaurant's parking lot as a command post for the operation. From there they had a view of all three towers.

The Mercedes was parked beside the patrol car. Mary leaned against the fender. Max was at her left side, Lou at her right.

She was hoping for another vision. She still had time to foresee which tower the killer would try to use, time to help the police consolidate their efforts, perhaps even time enough to prevent the slaughter to come. Thus far, however, she had received no new images.

She was shivering uncontrollably, but not because of the cool night air.

At six-fifteen, Officer Teagarten, who was assigned to the Roman Catholic Church of the Holy Trinity, called Patmore on the walkie-talkie to say religious services were in progress. Furthermore, the Knights of Columbus were having a party in the church basement that would last until confessions began prior to midnight Mass. It was Teagarten's opinion that no killer, not even a psychopath, would attempt to use Trinity's bell tower if he had to walk through so many witnesses to get there. Teagarten wanted to go home.

'You,' Patmore said over the walkie-talkie, 'until I've told you different, stay right the hell where you are.'

Officer Rollins divided his attention among the three towers, studying them through binoculars.

Patmore ignored Mary. He hadn't bothered to say hello when she arrived, and he still refused even to look at her.

'If this doesn't work out,' Lou said, 'the chief will swear he never met you.'

* * *

6:30 P.M.

A dozen boat parties were in progress all along the harbour. Within an hour there would be a dozen more. Laughter, the squeals of young women, and music from several stereos drifted across the water.

Most of the craft, from the smallest sailboats to the largest motor yachts, were decorated for the season. Strings of coloured lights wound around the deck railings and encircled the ports. A few of the biggest yachts, able to tap the power in their huge engines and banks of batteries, were swathed in layers of light, as if weighed down beneath scores of incandescent Hawaiian leis. There were boats with green lights arranged to form Christmas trees on their masts, boats that used golden lights to transform their masts into gigantic crosses, boats carrying life-size statues of Santa Claus, boats with cardboard and Styrofoam reindeer capering across cabin roofs, boats draped with paper chrysanthemums, evergreen boughs, holly, and fresh flowers. The ships blazed against the night.

In his own way Lou Pasternak was proud of King's Point. He

493

could deliver an hour-long monologue dissecting its many faults, but he never failed to point out that it was, if nothing else, the loveliest beach town in California.

Pretty as it was, however, the harbour could not distract him for more than a few minutes tonight. He finally turned to Mary and said, 'Can we talk about Barry Mitchell?'

She jerked as if he'd pinched her.

'Mary?' he said.

'You startled me.'

'I'm sorry.'

'What about Barry Mitchell?' she asked.

'He was about . . . ten years older than you?'

'About that, I think.'

'Do you recall what he looked like?'

'He was tall, a big boy.'

'What colour was his hair?'

'Dark,' she said. 'Brown, I suppose.'

'His eyes?'

'I don't remember.'

'You said he killed Alan's pets.'

'And the few I had as well.'

'Was he caught at it?'

'Alan saw him killing a squirrel we owned.'

'Was he apprehended in the act?'

'No. He was too big for Alan.'

'Were charges ever brought?'

'We had no proof,' she said.

'You had Alan's testimony.'

'The word of one boy against another.'

'So you stopped keeping pets,' Lou said.

'Yes.'

Max put his arm around Mary's shoulders.

'Nothing was done to Barry Mitchell?' Lou asked.

'My father's attorney had a talk with his mother.'

'What did he accomplish?'

'Nothing. Barry Mitchell denied killing them.'

Max asked, 'Why all these questions, Lou?'

Lou hesitated, then decided there was no reason to keep his suspicions a secret. 'You've told me there's something very unusual about the killer we're after tonight. Max has told me the

494

same thing. The two of you disagree as to *what* is unusual about him. But suppose . . . what if the man we're tracking is Berton Mitchell's son?'

She shook her head. 'No.'

'Why not?' Lou asked.

'He's dead,' she said.

Lou stared in surprise.

'You mean Barry Mitchell's dead?' Max asked.

'His mother, too,' Mary said.

'What?'

'His mother died, too. The same night.'

Lou asked, 'When did this happen?'

'I was eleven at the time.'

'Nineteen years ago.'

'That's about right.'

'They died together?'

'Yeah.'

'How?'

'They were killed by an intruder.'

'A burglar?' Lou asked.

'I suppose so. I don't remember.'

'You don't know the killer's name?'

'Is that important?'

'Did they ever catch anyone?'

'I don't know,' she said.

'Who told you about this?' Lou asked.

'Alan.'

'Are you certain he knew what he was talking about?'

'Oh, yes,' she said. 'I think he might have showed me a newspaper clipping about it.'

Lou sagged against the Mercedes, disappointed that yet another theory had been demolished.

But if the wife and son had been murdered just five years after Berton Mitchell committed suicide, why hadn't Roger Fullet found that information in the *Los Angeles Times'* files on the case?

Something exceedingly strange was happening. He was not a theatrical man given to bursts of melodrama. Nonetheless, he swore he could *feel* evil in the air that night.

A woman's laughter bounced across the rippled water, high and shrill.

* * *

7:00 P.M.

Mary squeezed Max's hand and waited tersely. Any minute the walkie-talkie would crackle with a report from one of the deputies. Any second there would be news of a man sneaking up the stairs in one of those towers; and when it came, the chase would begin in earnest.'

7:03.

Mary repeatedly glanced at her watch in the back glow of the police cruiser's headlights. She shifted restlessly from one foot to the other.

7:04.

For the first time in more than an hour, Chief Patmore looked at her, met her eyes. He wasn't happy.

7:06.

She was beginning to feel that she had been outmanoeuvred, outwitted. For the first time in her career she had encountered an adversary who was a match for her. She was tracking a man against whom all her psychic abilities provided no advantage.

7:09.

She was numb with fear. 'Something's wrong,' she said.

'What is it?' Max asked.

'The killer's not coming.'

Lou said, 'But you *saw* him do it.'

'And what you see always happens,' Max said.

'Not this time,' she said. 'This one's different. He knows I'm after him. He knows the cops are watching the towers.'

Lou said, 'If Patmore's men have been too obvious—'

'No,' she said. 'It's just that the killer's able to anticipate me. He isn't coming.'

Lou said, 'Don't tell Patmore. We've got to wait a little while. We can't give up yet.'

* * *

When there was no sign of a suspect at any of the towers by 7:30, John Patmore began to stride back and forth in front of his patrol car, scowling. As the minutes passed, he paced faster.

At 7:45, he picked up the walkie-talkie from the hood of the

496

car; for fifteen minutes he talked without pause to Winterman, Holtzman and Teagarten. Twice he lost control and shouted at them.

Finally he put down the walkie-talkie and came to Mary.

'The man isn't coming,' she said.

'Was he *ever* really expected?' Patmore asked.

'Yes, of course.' She was miserable. She felt she'd hurt Lou by using his influence and then failing to deliver what she promised.

'What made him change his mind?' Patmore asked.

'He knows we're waiting for him,' Max said.

'Yeah? Who told him?'

'No one,' Mary said. 'He senses it.'

'Senses it? How?'

'He must . . . he probably . . .'

'Yeah?'

She sighed. 'I don't know.'

'In my office,' Patmore said angrily, 'you knew so much this morning. Everything you knew. Now you don't know anything all of a goddamned sudden. Obviously you also don't know that if I want, I can get nasty about someone coming to my office, this false crime report, a thing like that, wasting my time and the time of my men only to have some laughs, all for some sort of a lark!'

'Don't have a stroke,' Lou said. 'And don't try to give Mary a stroke.'

Patmore turned away from her, faced Lou. 'You'd share the blame if I pursued this.'

'You don't have anything to pursue,' Lou said patiently. 'You know perfectly well that we didn't file a crime report – let alone one that was false. We simply came to your office to tell you that we had good reason to believe a crime would be committed.'

Patmore glared at him. 'You set me up.'

'John, that is ridiculous.'

'And Percy Osterman helped you. Why? Hell, no. You don't have to tell me. I see it, why he did. When people here voted, and Percy was against it from the start, for their own police, he was upset. He doesn't care for me much, does he? He never showed it, but he sure mustn't.'

Lou said. 'You're all wrong. Be reasonable, John. There's no conspiracy against you. Mary's sincere. Percy was sincere. We all are. We—'

497

'You want to make me look like a fool.' Patmore wagged his finger in Lou's face. 'You damned well better not print in your paper anything about this, about me falling for this psychic crap, because I'll sue you if you do for libel. I'll sue you for everything you've got.' There was an uncharacteristic fire in his usually dull brown eyes.

Mary took hold of Lou's arm. 'I'm wrung out, Lou. I don't want trouble for you or me.'

'Yeah,' Max said. 'Let's drop it. Let's go.'

Exasperated with the policeman, Lou said, 'John, I'm not going to write about you. I haven't any desire to make you look like a fool in the *Press*. You've got to realise there's a psychopathic killer loose in this town and—'

Still seething, Patmore said, 'You've written about me before.'

Lou was getting angry. 'I've always written tame "loyal opposition" articles when I've disagreed with you. I've never been unfair to you. In fact, I think I've been too tolerant. It's not my style to do a hatchet job. God knows, if I'd wanted to make you look like an idiot, I could have done it.'

Mary squeezed Lou's arm, tugged at him.

Patmore said, 'You're a crummy reporter with a stinking two-bit newspaper, and you're lousy drunk to boot.'

For an instant she thought Lou was going to hit him. But he only stared hard at Patmore and said, 'A drunk can always go on the wagon and sober up. But a stupid man who has a bottom-of-the-bucket IQ has to live with what he has forever.'

'Shit,' Patmore said. He walked back to the front of the squad car, picked up the walkie-talkie, and called Winterman, Holtzman and Teagarten out of the towers.

'I'm sorry,' Mary said to Lou. 'I'm so sorry.'

'It's not your fault he's an idiot.'

Max opened the car door. 'Come on. Let's get out of here.'

★ ★ ★

When they were settled in Lou Pasternak's book-strewn living room once more, Max asked, 'What now?'

'We wait,' Mary said.

'For what?' Lou asked.

Wearily, she said, 'We wait for him to start killing people again.'

FRIDAY,
DECEMBER 25

SIXTEEN

The motel room was dark.

She was lying on her side. She turned onto her back.

She felt claustrophobic, as if the ceiling had begun to descend upon her.

'Can't shut off your mind?' Max asked.

'I thought you were asleep.'

'I've been waiting for you to doze off first.'

'You were so quiet,' she said.

'Trying not to disturb you.'

'What time is it?'

'Three o'clock.'

'Go to sleep, darling. I'll be fine.'

'I can't sleep if I know you're worried.'

'I keep thinking I hear someone trying the door.'

'No one's been at the door. I'd have heard it.'

'And I keep thinking someone's at the window.'

'Not that either. It's nerves.'

'Screaming mimis,' she said.

'Maybe you should take a sedative.'

'I had a sleeping pill two hours ago.'

'So take another.'

'What is he, Max?'

'Who?'

'The killer.'

'Just a man.'

'No.'

'Yes, Mary. Yes. Just a man.'

Darkness pulsed around her.

'He's something more,' she said.

'Take another sleeping pill.'

501

'I guess I should. But I was beginning to cut down. I was beginning to break the habit.'

'After this case you can go cold turkey. But right now the pills aren't an indulgence. You've got good reason to need them.'

'Will you get one for me?'

He fetched a glass of water and the sedative, waited while she took it, switched off the light and returned to bed.

'Move close,' she said.

Her back was against his chest. Her buttocks against his groin. Two spoons in a drawer.

Several minutes passed in warm silence.

At last she said, 'I'm getting sleepy.'

'Good.' He stroked her hair.

Still later: 'Max?'

'Hmmm?'

'Maybe he can't help being bad and doing awful things. Maybe he was born bad. Maybe evil isn't *always learned*. Maybe parents and environment aren't *always* to blame for an evil child. Sometimes maybe it's in the genes.'

'Will you hush?'

'Max, am I going to die?'

'Eventually. We all do.'

'But soon? Will I die soon?'

'Not soon. I'm here.'

'Hold me.'

'I'm holding you.'

'I want to be strong.'

'You are strong.'

'I am?'

'You just don't realise it.'

In ten minutes she was asleep.

He continued to stroke her hair.

He listened to her breathing.

He didn't want her to die. He hoped she didn't *have* to die. He wished with all of his heart and mind that she would give up on this case. Let the killing be done. She shouldn't feel responsible. Just let the killing be done. Did society feel responsible? No. Did the police feel responsible? They sometimes did their jobs, occasionally made an effort to find the killer, but they had as much contempt for victim as for victimizer; and none of them lost

502

sleep over it. So let the killing be done. Forget it, Mary. Maybe she thought she was something special. Was that it? Unconsciously she might think that because of her psychic powers she couldn't die. Well, she could. Like all the rest of the tender, sweet young girls who thought they, too, would live forever. She would be as vulnerable, as soft against the knife as all the others had been. So she should stop. Go away from this. If she forced the issue, if she pursued the case, she might have to die. She was standing in front of a juggernaut. She was in the path of a force she didn't understand, a force that drew its greatest strength from the past, from an event that was twenty-four years old.

In the darkness, holding her as she slept, he wept at the thought of life without her.

★ ★ ★

Although sunrise was not far away, his flashlight was the only relief from inky blackness. His footsteps were the only sounds in the deserted arcade. He crossed the large main room. In summer it was filled with pinball machines and electronic games. Now the floor was bare, the main room empty. He entered the stairwell above which hung a large sign: THIS WAY TO OBSERVATION DECK.

The enclosed stairwell of the tower of Kimball's Games and Snacks was narrow, cold, and dirty. It had not yet been repainted for the next season. His flashlight played off yellow-white walls that bore a thousand stains: children's handprints, streaks of spilled soft drinks, names and messages scrawled in pencil and felt-tip markers.

The wooden steps creaked.

When he reached the walled platform at the top of the winding stairs, he switched off the flashlight. He doubted anyone would be watching at this hour; however, he didn't want to risk drawing attention to himself.

Dawn was nothing but a thin, lustrous purple line on the eastern horizon, as if a razor had been drawn lightly across the skin of the night.

He stared out at the harbour.

He waited.

In a few minutes, from the corner of his eye, he caught movement in the air. He heard the flutter of wings.

Something roosted in the crossbeams of the peaked roof, rustled for a moment, then was silent.

He stared into the crouching shadows above and trembled with pleasure.

Tonight, he thought. Tonight, the blood again.

He could feel death all around him, a thick and tangible current in the air.

To the east, the wound in the sky grew wider, deeper. Morning oozed into the world.

He yawned and wiped the back of one hand across his mouth. He would have to get back to the hotel soon, get some rest. He hadn't slept much in the past few days.

Three times within the next ten minutes, the sound of wings came again. On each occasion there was a temporary commotion in the rafters, and each time silence swiftly returned.

Eventually anaemic light filtered through congealed masses of storm clouds and gradually painted the harbour, hills, and houses of King's Point.

He was filled with a deep sense of loss. With light came depression. He functioned best in the blackest hours. Always had. But recently that was increasingly true. He felt at home in the night.

Overhead the highest rafters remained shrouded in shadows. The inside of the roof – a hollow, inverted funnel – was fifteen feet high; and even at noon darkness clung to its upper regions.

Dim as it was, morning had arrived; and now his flashlight wouldn't be noticed by anyone below. He switched it on and pointed it up into the hollow roof.

This was what he had come to see: bats. A dozen bats or more. Clinging to the wooden rafters. Wings folded tightly around them. Some with eyes shut. Some with open eyes that gleamed iridescently in the beam of light.

The sight exhilarated him.

Tonight, the blood again.

* * *

At nine o'clock that morning Lou called Roger Fullet. 'I'm sorry to have to bother you on Christmas.'

'You're never a bother. Besides, you just saved me from a tedious little chore. The electric train went off the track and all the cars came uncoupled. If I talk to you for a few minutes, I'll get back to the layout after junior's got everything put back together.'

'I've learned something very interesting about this Berton Mitchell case.'

'Such as?'

'Apparently, Mitchell's wife and son were murdered.'

'My God, when?'

'Five years after what he did to Mary.'

'You've got to be wrong.'

'Did you check to see if there were separate morgue files for the wife and son?'

'No. But even if there are, everything of importance should be duplicated in the Berton Mitchell file.'

'Doesn't the *Times* make mistakes?'

'We're loathe to admit it. But occasionally things don't get done right. Who killed the Mitchells?'

'Mary doesn't know.'

'Nineteen years ago?'

'That's what she says.'

'It happened here in LA?'

'I gather it did. Do me a favour?'

'I'm not working today, Lou.'

'The *Times* doesn't shut down altogether on holidays. There are people working. Can't you call in and have someone check this out for me?'

'It's that important?'

'A matter of life and death.'

'What do you want to know?'

'Everything about the murders . . . if they took place.'

'I'll call you back.'

'How long will it take?'

'Maybe two hours.'

Roger called back in an hour and a half. 'There was a separate file on the murders of the wife and son. The story wasn't cross-filed as it should have been.'

'It's nice to know even you big city slickers can be wrong.'

'This is really a sick one, Lou.'

'Tell me about it.'

'After Berton Mitchell committed suicide, Virginia Mitchell

505

and her son, Barry Francis Mitchell, rented a small house on the west side of Los Angeles. Judging from the address, I'd say it couldn't have been more than a mile from the Tanner estate. Nineteen years ago, on October 31, Halloween, at two o'clock in the morning, someone used gasoline to start a fire that nearly burned the place to the ground with the mother and son inside.'

'Fire. That's the death I fear most.'

'This has ruined my appetite for Christmas dinner.'

'I'm sorry, Roger. I had to know.'

'That's not the worst of it. Although the bodies were badly burned, the medical examiner was later able to deduce that mother and son were stabbed to death in their sleep before the blaze started.'

'Stabbed . . .'

'Virginia had been stabbed so often in the throat that she'd been pretty much decapitated.'

'Sweet Jesus.'

'The son, Barry . . . was stabbed in the throat and chest. Then . . .'

'Then what?'

'His genitals were cut off.'

'There goes my dinner, too.'

'Before the fire burned out, that place must have looked like a slaughterhouse. What kind of man could do all of that, Lou? What kind of maniac would be so gruesomely thorough?'

'Did they ever solve the case?'

'Never arrested anyone.'

'Did they at least have suspects?'

'Three of them.'

'What were their names?'

'I didn't bother jotting them down. Each of them had an alibi, and each alibi eventually checked out.'

'So their killer might still be alive and loose. Were the police sure of the bodies?'

'Sure of them in what sense?'

'Identities.'

'I guess they weren't burned beyond recognition. Besides, the house was occupied by Virginia and her son.'

'The woman's body was probably Virginia's. But isn't it conceivable that the dead man they found was her lover and not her son?'

'They were killed in different bedrooms. Lovers would have been found together. And if Barry was alive, he'd have come forward.'

'Not if he was the killer.'

'*What*?'

'It's not impossible.'

'Nothing's impossible, but—'

'Barry would have been twenty-one when the house burned that night. Maybe almost twenty-two. Roger, isn't that a bit old for a boy to be living with his mother?'

'Hell, no. Lou, we didn't all rush out to grab our piece of the action at sixteen, like you did. I lived with my folks until I was twenty-three. Why are you so anxious to believe Barry's alive?'

'It would make things easier to understand down here.'

'You're too good a newsman to try to reshape facts to fit some preconceived notion.'

'Yeah. You're right. I've run into another stone wall.'

'What's the story with this Mary Bergen? What are you involved in?'

'I'm afraid it's going to be very messy. I don't want to talk about it yet.'

'And maybe I don't want to hear about it either.'

'Go play with your train.'

'Somehow I'm no longer in the mood for play. Take care of yourself, Lou. Be careful. Be damned careful. And . . . Merry Christmas.'

SEVENTEEN

They sat in Lou's living room, listening to music – and waiting for something to happen. Mary couldn't imagine a grimmer Christmas. She and Max weren't even able to exchange gifts. The things he had got her were at the stores where he'd left them to be wrapped, and as she'd become preoccupied with this case, she'd had no opportunity to go shopping for him.

Her spirits lifted when Alan called at three o'clock to say he was in San Francisco at his friend's house. He'd tried the number in Bel Air, and the housekeeper had told him to call Lou. He was worried, but she understated the gravity of her situation and calmed him. No sense ruining *his* Christmas, too. When Alan finally hung up, her spirits sank again; she missed him so much.

Because no one had eaten breakfast or lunch, Lou served an early dinner at five o'clock. Chicken Kiev on a bed of rice. Cylinders of grilled zucchini filled with spinach paté. Tomatoes stuffed with hot cheese, bread crumbs, and peppers. There were baked apples for dessert.

No one was hungry. They picked at their food. Mary didn't even taste her wine. By six o'clock they were finished.

Over coffee, Mary said, 'Lou, do you have a Ouija board?'

He put down his cup. 'I have one, but I haven't used it in years.'

'Do you know where it is?'

'The spare bedroom closet, I think.'

'Would you get it while Max and I clear the table?'

'Sure. What are we going to do with it?'

'I'm tired of waiting for the killer to make the next move,' she said. 'We're going to try to force the issue.'

'I'm all for that. But how?'

Max said, 'Sometimes, when Mary can't recall the fine details of a vision, she can prod her memory with a Ouija board. She

508

doesn't get answers from the spirit world, mind you. The things she wants to know are things she's forgotten. They're buried in her subconscious. Not always, but often enough to make it worthwhile when nothing else works, the Ouija board provides her with a pipeline to her subconscious.'

Lou nodded with understanding. 'The answers the board gives actually come from Mary.'

'Right,' Max said.

'But I don't consciously guide the trivet,' she said. 'I let it go where it wants to go.'

'Where your subconscious wants it to go,' Max said. 'You *do* influence the trivet with your fingers, but in a way that you're not aware of.'

'I suppose,' she said.

Lou put a few more drops of cream in his coffee and said, 'So the Ouija board acts like a lens.'

'Exactly,' she said. 'It focuses my attention, my memory, and my psychic abilities.'

Lou drank his coffee in three long swallows and stood up. 'It sure sounds interesting. Anything's better than sitting around waiting for the axe to fall. I'll be right back.' He hurried out of the dining room and down the hall towards the spare bedroom.

Max and Mary stacked the dishes and silverware in the kitchen sink. She finished wiping off the glossy pine dining table just as Lou returned.

'One Ouija board, as requested,' he said.

Mary went into the living room to fetch her notebook from the sofa where she'd left it with her purse.

Lou said, 'Got to clean out that spare bedroom closet one of these days. The board was literally buried in crap.'

'Literally?' Max was amused.

'Well, it was under at least a hundred issues of *The New York Review of Books*.'

'Ouch,' Max said. 'You set me up for that one.'

Lou took a note pad and pencil from the kitchen counter and sat down at the table. He was prepared to record each letter that the Ouija board gave them.

Mary opened the board on one corner of the table. She placed the felt-footed trivet on it.

Max sat down, laced his fingers, and cracked his knuckles.

509

She opened her spiral-bound notebook to a page filled with her handwriting.

'What's that?' Lou asked.

'Questions I want to ask it,' Mary said.

She pulled up her chair and sat down at a ninety-degree angle to Max. She put the tips of her fingertips on one side of the plastic triangle. Max put his fingertips on another side of it; his hands were nearly too large for the game.

'Start easy,' Max told her.

She was tense, and that was not good. The trivet wouldn't move an inch if her touch was too heavy. She took several deep breaths. She tried to make her arms limp. She wanted her fingers to feel independent of her – loose, soft, like rags.

Max wasn't as nervous as she was. He didn't appear to need any preparation.

Finally, when she had achieved a relatively relaxed state of mind and body, she stared at the board in front of her and said, 'Are you ready to give us answers?'

The indicator didn't move.

'Are you ready to give us answers?'

Nothing.

'Are you ready to give us answers?'

Under their fingers, as if it were suddenly imbued with a life energy of its own, the indicator glided to that part of the board marked YES:

'Good,' she said. 'We are in pursuit of a man who has killed at least eight people in the last few days. Is he still here in King's Point?'

The indicator swept around the board, returned to YES.

She asked, 'Is King's Point this man's hometown?'

NO.

'Where does he come from?'

ALL OUR YESTERDAYS.

'Make sense to anyone?' Lou asked.

Refining the question, trying to be more specific, Mary asked, 'Where does the killer *live*?'

Letter by letter: BEAUTIFUL.

'Beautiful?' Lou asked. 'Is that in answer to your question, Mary?'

'A town named Beautiful?' she asked.

510

The trivet didn't move.

'Where does the killer live?' she asked again.

The trivet picked out seventeen letters.

Lou wrote them down as they were given, and when the indicator ceased to move, he said, 'It says, "THE AIR IS BEAUTIFUL." What's that supposed to mean?'

The air at Mary's back seemed suddenly colder, as if an icy breath had been expelled against the nape of her neck. The answers the Ouija board gave were less direct and more perplexing than usual. Supposedly the Ouija messages came from her, from deep in her subconscious mind. Ordinarily she believed that was true. But not now. Tonight she felt another presence, an unseen presence looming over her.

'We're getting sidetracked,' Max said impatiently. He looked at the trivet. 'Where is the killer staying in King's Point?'

The indicator slid back and forth, then quickly moved from one letter to another.

Lou copied them down, but the word was so simple that Mary didn't need to ask what had been recorded: HOTEL.

'Which hotel?' Max asked.

The indicator didn't move.

'Which hotel?'

Again, it spelled HOTEL.

Lou said, 'Try something else.'

Mary said, 'The man we're after has killed women with a knife. Where did he get that knife?'

'That's not important,' Max said.

The trivet moved: LINGARD.

'*You* made it spell that,' Max said.

'I don't believe I did.'

'Then why did you ask it such a question? We don't really have to know where the knife came from.'

'I wanted to see what it would say.'

Max studied her with piercing grey eyes.

She looked away from him, consulted her notebook and addressed the board again. 'Did I ever know a girl by the name of Beverly Pulchaski?'

SHE IS DEAD.

'Did I ever know her?'

SHE IS DEAD.

511

'Did I know a girl named Susan Haven?'
SHE IS DEAD.
Cold breath on the neck again.
She shuddered.
'Did I ever know Linda Proctor?'
SHE IS DEAD.
'Did I know Marie Sanzini?'
SHE IS DEAD.
Mary sighed. The muscles in her arms and shoulders flexed repeatedly, involuntarily. It was a struggle to stay sufficiently relaxed to allow the Ouija indicator to function. Already she was weary.

Lou said, 'Who were those women?'

She said, 'The nurses who were murdered in Anaheim. When I first foresaw their deaths, I had the notion that I knew or at least had met one of them. But if I ever did, I can't remember where or when it was.'

'Probably because you don't *want* to remember,' Max said.

'Why wouldn't I?'

'Because maybe if you remembered, we'd know who the killer was. And maybe you don't want to know that.'

'Don't be absurd, Max. I want to know very much.'

'Even if the killer's connected somehow to Berton Mitchell and the wings? Even if, by finding the killer, you're forced to remember what you've spent your life forgetting?'

She stared at him and licked her lips. 'I'm feeling something right now that I never thought I'd feel.'

'What's that?'

'I'm scared of you, Max.'

There was an unearthly quiet in the house. The three of them seemed suspended in time.

Max spoke softly, but his voice filled the room. 'You're scared of me because you think I'm going to force you to face up to what happened twenty-four years ago.'

'Is that all it is?'

'What else?'

'I don't know,' she said.

Max asked the board another question, but he did not take his wintry grey eyes from her. 'Did Mary know Rochelle Drake?'

SHE IS DEAD.

512

'I know she's dead,' Max said irritably, still watching Mary, suffocating her with his attention, pinning her with his gaze. 'But did Mary ever know her?'

DEAD.

'Who's Rochelle Drake?' Lou asked.

Mary took the opportunity to look away from Max. Her mouth was dry. Her heart was beating much too fast.

To Lou, Max said, 'Rochelle Drake was the girl who was killed in that Santa Ana beauty salon a few days ago. I swear I've heard the name before. Haven't you?'

'Can't say I have,' Lou said.

'Well, I'm positive I heard the name before Percy Osterman used it in the morgue. I don't think I ever met the girl. But I heard the name. I can't imagine where.'

Mary said, 'Well, I *don't* remember her. I would have recognized her at the morgue if I'd ever seen her before.'

Suddenly, beneath their hands, the trivet began to move in wide, aimless circles.

'What the hell?' Max said, surprised.

Lou said, 'No one asked it a question.'

Mary allowed her hands to float freely with the indicator as it moved less erratically and with increasing purpose. Her thoughts were too muddled at the moment, and she was too frightened to have the wit to decipher the chain of letters as it grew. Finally the trivet stopped. She took her hands from it at once; they ached with the strain of forced relaxation.

Lou said, 'It's a name.' He held up the note pad for them to see. P-A-T-R-I-C-I-A-S-P-O-O-N-E-R.

Patricia Spooner? Mary thought. She stared at the name in disbelief.

She felt as if a snake of ice lay at the centre of her, its crystalline tongue flicking rapidly, its sinuous body radiating cold like the coils of a freezer.

'Who's Patricia Spooner?' Max asked.

'Means nothing to me,' Lou said.

'I . . . knew her,' Mary said stiffly.

'When?' Max asked.

'Eleven . . . twelve years ago.'

'You never mentioned her.'

'She was a good friend at UCLA.'

513

'A college friend?'

'Yes. A very pretty girl.'

'Why does her name come up now?'

'I don't have any idea.'

'It came from your subconscious.'

'No. I'm not controlling the trivet.'

'Nonsense,' Max said.

'There's someone . . . something here with us.'

'Maybe the board just gave us the name of the next victim,' Lou said, to avert a quarrel. 'Have you kept in touch with this Patricia Spooner? Maybe we should call her and see if she's okay.'

Max said, 'Should we call Patricia Spooner? Mary?'

'She's dead,' Mary said.

Lou said, 'Oh, my God. Then the man we're after's already killed her?'

She had difficulty speaking. 'Patty . . . Patty's been . . . dead . . . dead almost . . . eleven years.'

Although the room was not warm, Lou was perspiring. He wiped his aristocratic face with his broad, thick-fingered, big-knuckled hand. He looked as pale as she felt. 'How? Mary, how did Patty Spooner die?'

Mary shivered and closed her eyes. She opened them at once because the memories behind them were too ugly, too brutal. 'She was . . . murdered.'

The dead, Mary thought, don't stay dead. Not forever. Not even for long. They rise up from their graves. The ground doesn't hold them. Remorse doesn't hold them. Neither grief nor acceptance, neither fear nor forgetfulness holds them. Nothing holds them. They come back. Berton Mitchell. Barry Mitchell. Virginia Mitchell. My mother. My father. And now Patty Spooner. Oh, God, don't let them come back. I've been haunted by the dead most of my life. I've had enough!

'Murdered,' Lou said quietly, almost as if in shock.

Mary said, 'There was a church. Patty and I sometimes went to Mass together. I was a practising Catholic then. It was a lovely church. It had a very large, hand-carved wooden altar that was made in Poland and shipped over here in the early nineteen hundreds. The church was open all the time, night and day. Patty liked to go and sit in the front pew when no one else was there. Late at night. Her mother had died of a heart condition a few years before. She was always lighting candles for her mother. Patty was very devout. She . . . she died there.'

'In the church?' Lou asked.

Max was watching her intently. He put a hand on her shoulder; vibrations, more emotional than physical, neither good nor bad but powerful, exploded through her from the point of contact.

Max said, 'Who killed her?'

'They never found him.'

Lou leaned across the table. His eyebrows were drawn together, his face pinched. 'She was your good friend. Didn't you use your psychic talent to see the killer's face, his name?'

'I tried,' Mary said faintly. 'I got a few things. Bits and pieces of images. But it was one of those cases when my power didn't help much. She was strangled with a priest's white silk stole. I got terrible emanations from it. Wicked, evil vibrations. No clear pictures. Just formless images. The church was filled with them. Like . . . invisible clouds of evil. The killer had damaged the altar . . . urinated on it.'

Lou got up so abruptly that he knocked over his chair, but he didn't appear to notice it. He stood with one hand on his head as if attempting to force back an unsettling idea. 'It's madness. *What are we up against?* Is it possible that the man we're trying to find here in King's Point is the same man who killed your friend?'

'His style is the same, isn't it?' Max said.

'So damned brutal,' Lou said. 'And with the religious angle. The roots of these recent killings might go back at least eleven years. Perhaps a lot further than that.'

Mary saw what he meant, though curiously, until this moment, she had never seen a connection between Patty's death and any other.

Sensing the effect Lou's revelation had upon her, Max squeezed her shoulder reassuringly. Sometimes he didn't seem to know his own strength; his grip was slightly painful.

Agitated as she had never seen him, moving quickly and jerkily, Lou went into the kitchen and got a twelve-ounce tumbler from the cabinet beside the refrigerator. He picked up a bottle of Wild Turkey that was on the counter by the sink, and he poured about four ounces for himself. Glass in hand, he came back and stood in the dining room archway. 'It gets more complicated all the time. How many other people has this man killed that we don't even know about? Over the years, how many other unsolved murders was he responsible for?' Lou swallowed some bourbon. 'This creature, whoever and whatever he is – and I'm increasingly disposed to think of him as a *thing* – has been prowling about, raping, killing, completely unchecked, unhindered for at least eleven years. It scares the hell out of me.'

A peal of thunder punctuated his last few words. It reverberated in the window seat. The Christmas night rainstorm was on the way, as forecast.

Max glanced at the plastic trivet. 'Let's ask the board how many victims there have been.'

She almost objected. My arms ache, she almost said. Too tired for more of that. Exhausted. Drained.

But she knew that fear was the real reason she didn't want to begin questioning the Ouija board again. She was afraid of what it might tell them.

If she surrendered to her fear so easily, she would never learn to rely on herself. And although she found the possibility disturbing, she had an ever-growing feeling that soon she would find herself in greater danger, against which Max could not or would not offer her protection.

She put her hands on the trivet, and so did Max.

Lou put his overturned chair on its feet. He sat down and picked up his pencil.

She spoke to the Ouija board. 'Are you prepared to answer more questions?'

YES.

Thunder rumbled over King's Point. The bulbs in the hanging lamp above the table flickered, nearly went out, then glowed brightly again.

'The man who killed Rochelle Drake has murdered other people, too. How many has he killed?'

35.

Lou said, 'My God! He's a regular Jack the Ripper.'

'Jack the Ripper didn't kill that many,' Max said. 'The board's wrong. It has to be. Ask it again, Mary.'

Her voice wavered as she repeated the question.

35.

The hanging lamp flickered and went out.

'Power failure,' Lou said.

Mary said, 'I don't want to sit in the dark.'

516

'If it lasts more than a minute,' Lou said, 'I'll go get candles from the hall closet.'

An incredible barrage of lightning pulsed outside the windows. The sharp bursts of blue-white light created a series of choppy, stroboscopic images: Lou reaching in a half dozen seemingly disconnected movements for his glass of bourbon; Max turning his head towards her as if he were a character on a motion picture screen, with the film slipping and stuttering in the projector.

Then the lightning passed; the darkness was complete; the thunder receded to a distant growl. Rain should have followed that display, but it didn't; the sky held back the deluge.

Less than a minute after the lights went out, they fluttered dimly and came back on full strength.

She sighed with relief.

Max was eager to continue the questioning. 'Ask the board when this man will strike again.'

Mary repeated the question.

TONIGHT.

'What time tonight?'

7.30.

Lou said, 'Little more than an hour from now.'

'Where will he strike?' Mary asked the Ouija board.

THE HARBOUR PARADE.

'You know what it means,' Lou said to Max. He was grim. 'For thirty years,' he told Mary, 'there's been a Christmas night parade of lighted boats on the harbour. Never heard of it?'

'Now that you mention it, yes.'

'All those decorated boats you saw last night will be part of it. Plus some that don't use our harbour as home port. Maybe a hundred and fifty or more.'

'They have parades like this at Long Beach and Newport Beach in the week before Christmas,' Max told Mary. 'But the King's Point shindig is more spectacular than any of the others.'

Lou said, 'There's pretty damned good prize money for the best decorated boats, thanks to a trust fund set up by one of our richer sailors who loved the parade. It's quite a sight. Most of the harbour restaurants open for it. They only serve a limited menu, but they're sold out a week or two in advance.'

Mary looked at the Ouija board and asked, 'Is the killer after anyone special in the boat parade?'

YES.

517

'Who?'

HE HAS A RIFLE.

'Who will he shoot?'

HE WANTS TO KILL THE QUEEN.

'The queen?' Mary asked.

'The queen of the parade,' Lou said. 'She'll make an easy target. She stands on the rear deck of the biggest boat in the lineup, usually midway in the procession. She's in the centre of a spotlight. Literally.'

'And,' Max said, 'she makes two complete circuits of the harbour along with the other boats. So if he isn't satisfied with the target he's got on the first circuit, he can wait to see if she presents herself any better the second time around.'

Although it had not been asked another question, the plastic trivet moved beneath their fingers, slid through a new series of letters.

KIMBALL'S GAMES AND SNACKS.

'Will he use the tower there?'

YES. KIMBALL'S TOWER.

'One hour to stop him,' Max said.

Lou stood up. 'I'll call the police.'

'Patmore?' Mary asked dubiously.

'He's the man with the authority.'

She said, 'But will he listen to you after the false alarm last night?'

'He's got to listen!'

Thunder again. And wind.

Mary took her hands from the trivet and hugged herself. She was still cold. 'But what if Patmore *does* agree to put a stakeout on the tower?'

'That's what we want, isn't it?'

'Don't you see?' she said. 'Won't tonight be a repeat of last night? Last night the killer knew that we were waiting for him. Why won't he know this time, too?'

Lou hesitated, surprised by the question, worried, indecisive. Finally he picked up the tumbler and drank the last of his bourbon. 'Maybe he will anticipate us. Maybe we don't have a chance against him. If the Ouija board's right, if he's really killed thirty-five people and never been caught, then he's damned clever. Probably too clever for us. But we've got to try, don't we? We can't just

518

sit here and talk about the weather and the latest books and the newest Paris fashions while he goes on killing!'

'You're right,' Max said.

Lou put down his empty glass and went to use the telephone in the entrance foyer.

Mary began to exercise her cramped hands. She closed them into fists, opened them, closed them.

'You look exhausted,' Max said.

'I am.'

'We'll get to bed early.'

'If we get to bed at all.'

'We will. Nothing's going to happen to us.'

'I've got awful feelings,' she said.

'You've had a vision?'

'No. Just feelings.'

'Then forget it.'

'Tonight will be bloody.'

'Don't worry,' he said soothingly.

She thought of Patty Spooner.

Rochelle Drake in the morgue drawer.

That feeling again: something behind her, chilly breath on the nape of her neck.

'I don't want to die,' she said.

Max said, 'You aren't going to. Not tonight.'

'You sound so sure of that.'

'I am. I won't let you die.'

'Are you strong enough to stop it from happening, Max? Are you stronger than destiny?'

Lightning ripped open the sky again: the reflection of light from its blade shone through the windows; and for an instant it turned Max's eyes into icy blanks.

★ ★ ★

'King's Point Police.'

'Missing persons, please.'

'I can help you, sir.'

'No. I want to talk to someone in the missing persons' bureau. Didn't you hear me?'

'We don't have a separate department for missing persons' reports.'

519

'You don't?'

'We're a small police force. Can I help you?'

'What's your name?'

'Ms Newhart.'

'I'm Ralph Larsson. Let me talk to a policeman.'

'We've only got two on duty tonight.'

'One of them will be enough for me.'

'They're both in cruisers right now.'

'Dammit, my daughter's missing!'

'How old is your daughter, sir?'

'Twenty-six. She was—'

'How long has she been missing?'

'Look, Ms Newhart, I'm in San Francisco. I live in San Francisco, and my daughter lives in King's Point. I just talked to her a week ago. She was fine then. But now that I think she may no longer be fine, I can't just jump in my car and drive several hundred miles to look in on her. This could be an emergency. She was supposed to call me on Christmas Eve, but she never did.'

'Maybe she went to a party or something.'

'I thought for sure she'd call sometime today, but she hasn't. I've tried calling her, but there's no answer. Now, dammit, it's not like her to do something like this! It's not like her to forget her family on Christmas.'

'Have you tried calling her friends? They might know something.'

'I don't know Erika's friends.'

'Maybe her neighbours—'

'She hasn't got neighbours. She—'

'Everyone has neighbours.'

'She lives in one of those three cottages on the South Bluff, at the end of the paved road. She's the only one who lives there year 'round.'

'You know what? I'll bet your daughter's trying to call you right now. Why don't you hang up and see? If she doesn't call tonight, then ring us back tomorrow.'

'Are you serious?'

'Well, we can't do anything anyway.'

'What do you mean?'

'It is a policy of this department, and of most police depart-

520

ments, not to enter a missing person's case if the report involves an adult who's been gone less than forty-eight hours.'

'She has to be missing more than two days before you're interested?'

'That's our policy.'

'Well, how do I know she didn't disappear the day after she last called me, six days ago?'

'You said she was supposed to call last night.'

'And didn't.'

'So officially, she's only been missing since last night.'

'Jesus!'

'I'm sorry. That's policy.'

'If my daughter was ten years old instead of a twenty-six—'

'That's different. Children are different. But your daughter isn't a child.'

'So your officers can't become involved until tomorrow night?'

'That's right. But, sir, I'm certain your daughter will call you long before then.'

'Ms Newhart, my name is Ralph Larsson. I told you once before, but I want you to remember it. Ralph Larsson. I'm an attorney. A very successful attorney. I was also the governor's college roommate. Now, Ms Newhart, if your officers don't take a drive out to my daughter's house to check on her right away, tonight, within the next half an hour, and if later we should discover that something happened to my daughter between this moment and tomorrow night, I will come down there to King's Point and find a reputable cooperating attorney. I will devote the next few years of my life to breaking you and your idiotic superiors. I will sue your fucking goddamned police department, and I will sue your chief for his stupid arbitrary policies. And by God, Ms Newhart, I will also sue you for every nickel you now have or ever hope to earn. And even if I don't win the case, Ms Newhart, you will go broke paying for your own lawyers. Do you read me clearly?'

* * *

Lou Pasternak was angry. Furious. The chief of police had hung up on him *twice*! The third time, his wife answered the phone and said he wasn't at home.

521

'A demitasse would fit Patmore's head like a sombrero!'

'I gather,' Max said, 'that he wouldn't put a stakeout on Kimball's tower?'

Lou snatched his empty glass from the table, went into the kitchen, and picked up the bottle of Wild Turkey. 'If the bastard had a little more sense, he'd be a half-wit.'

From the dining room Mary asked, 'Shouldn't we call the sheriff?'

'Remember, Percy Osterman can't step into King's Point police business unless Patmore asks him to.'

'But when a man's killed people all over the country, isn't there an exception? Something called "hot pursuit"?'

Lou said, 'If a guy robs a bank that's in the county's jurisdiction, hops into a car, and flees into a city with its own cops, the sheriff's men can chase and arrest him. *That's* hot pursuit. This isn't.'

Max said, 'Maybe Osterman can persuade Patmore to cooperate again.'

'Not a chance. Not after last night.' Lou returned to the table with a fresh glass of bourbon.

'So what now?' Max asked.

Mary said, 'We'll have to stop him ourselves. We'll have to go down to the tower.'

Lou stared at her in amazement. 'Are you serious?'

'It's absolutely out of the question,' Max said.

She said, 'What would you prefer to do? We can't just sit here and talk about the weather and the latest books and the newest Paris fashions while he goes on killing.'

Lou recognized his own words, and he had no effective argument against them.

'If we just sit here,' she said, 'he'll kill the queen of the boat parade. And most likely a lot of other people, too.'

'The rain might force the queen and her court inside, off the open deck,' Max said. 'Then she wouldn't be a target.'

'It isn't raining,' Mary said.

'It'll start soon.'

'Do you want to bet their lives on that?' she said. 'Lou, we have to stop this man. We haven't any choice.'

'I don't want him to kill again,' Max said. 'But he isn't our responsibility.'

'If not ours, whose?' she asked.

522

Lou saw an uncommon determination in her lovely face. Unshakeable resolve in those big blue eyes. He suspected that neither he nor Max could change her mind about this. Might as well argue with a post. He could see that. But he was frightened for her. And as her friend, he felt he should at least try to make her reconsider. 'Mary, we're no match for this man.'

'Why not?' she asked. 'Isn't it just one of him against the three of us?'

'But he's a killer,' Max said.

'And we're not killers,' she said.

'Exactly.'

'Knowing what he's done,' she said, 'and what he'd do to you if he had the chance, couldn't you shoot him if he came at you with a gun?'

Max said, 'Of course, in self-defence—'

'That's just what this is,' she said. 'Self-defence.'

'But this psychopath will have a rifle,' Lou said. 'And probably a knife. What would we have? Our hands?'

'There's a pistol in the dashboard of the Mercedes,' Mary said. 'Max is licensed to carry it.'

He looked at Max and raised his eyebrows. 'You're allowed to carry a concealed weapon?'

Getting up from his chair, heading towards the kitchen, Max said, 'Yeah.'

'How'd you manage to wrangle the permit? They usually reserve those for people in businesses where they've got to carry around diamonds or a lot of cash.'

In the kitchen Max poured himself a double shot of Wild Turkey. 'We worked on a couple of cases with the LA County sheriff's office. The sheriff saw what dangerous situations Mary can find herself in. He knew I collected guns. He knew I was a marksman, and he figured I wasn't the type to get excited and accidentally blow someone apart.' Max drank his bourbon neat and quick: a nervous thirst that briefly exposed the tension that lay beneath his studied composure. 'So the sheriff got me the permit.' He rinsed out his glass under the kitchen faucet, came back to the dining room, and stood over Mary. 'But I'm not going to load that pistol and go out hunting someone to shoot.'

'You wouldn't be hunting just anyone,' she said. 'You'd be hunting a man who has—'

'Forget it,' Max said. 'I won't do it.'

'Let's talk about it,' she said.

'No use. It's decided.'

Lou saw a spark of anger in her eyes. Max's resistance would do nothing but harden her resolve.

She said, 'Okay, Max. Stay here. I'll take the gun and go by myself.'

'Mary, for God's sake, you don't know how to handle a pistol!'

She stared up at him without blinking and said, 'You take off the safeties and jack a bullet into the chamber, point, pull the trigger – and the son of a bitch falls down.'

Lou knew how stubborn Max could be sometimes. He saw the set of the man's jaw, the drawing up of his shoulders, and he wanted to warn him off. Max was accustomed to playing father-lover to her, accustomed to saying what would be done and what wouldn't. But tonight she wasn't the easygoing Mary they both knew. Even now changes were occurring in her. Conflicting emotions played across her face, but the primary expression was always determination. She was going to make her own decision, and she wasn't going to heed anyone's advice. He had never seen such strength in her before, such purpose. It was exciting, attractive. He sat mute, wanting to advise Max against an authoritarian approach but unable to interfere.

'This is absurd,' Max said. 'Mary, I won't let you have the pistol.'

'Then I'll go without it.'

He glared down at her. 'You aren't going anywhere.'

She stood up, faced him. She met his eyes and held them, as if to prove, through the directness of her gaze, the depth of her commitment. She spoke with quiet intensity and with a foreboding tone that chilled Lou to the bone. 'I'm up against something so big, so evil that I can only guess at the dimensions like a blind child feeling an elephant's leg. These past few days have been a living hell for me, Max.'

'I know. And—'

'You can't know. No one can know.'

'If you—'

'Don't interrupt,' she said. 'I want you to understand. So you've just got to listen. Max, I'm afraid to go to sleep, and I'm afraid to wake up in the morning. I'm afraid to open every door I come to, afraid to turn around. I'm afraid of the dark. I'm afraid of what might happen – and of what might *not* happen. Dammit, I'm even afraid to go to the bathroom alone! I cannot live like this. I refuse to live like this. There's something about this case that makes it different from all others, something that's working inside of me like acid, eating me alive. This case touched my life like nothing else I've worked on, but I don't know why. Max, I sense, I feel, I *know* that if I don't pursue this man with every ounce of energy I have and in every way I know how, then he'll come after me.'

The trivet on the Ouija board moved, but Lou was the only one to see it. It slid to the spot marked EYES, as if in agreement with Mary's prediction.

'If I don't take the initiative,' she said, 'I'll lose what little advantage I might now have. I can't walk away. If I try to run, I won't get far. I'll die.'

Max said, 'And if you pursue this man, if you insist on going down to that tower tonight, then you'll probably die sooner.'

'I might,' she said. 'But if I do, at least I'll have taken responsibility for my own life and death. All my life, I've been scared of everything, and I've let someone else deal with my bogeymen for me. Not anymore. Because this time no one else *can* help me. The answer is inside of me, and if I don't find it soon, I'm finished. It's past time I stopped hiding behind strong men. I've got to take chances. When I risk something and fail, I've got to suffer the consequences like anybody else. If I'm always pampered, cuddled, and cushioned from shock, then my successes in life are meaningless. I've decided that no one – not Alan, not you, Max, and especially not that part of me that's still a dependent six-year-old – *no one* is going to stop me from living a full life.'

They stood in silence for a while.

The grandfather clock chimed the quarter hour.

Lou said, 'Forty-five minutes until he takes a shot at the queen of the boat parade.'

Mary said, 'Well, Max?'

Finally he nodded. 'We better get moving.'

★ ★ ★

Blood. Blood like ribbons tangled in her hair. Blood spotting her punctured breasts. Blood on her hands, her arms, her belly, her

525

thighs. Blood on the sofa and chair. Blood on the draperies, on the wall. Bloody little footprints of a cat all across the light tan carpet.

Trying to hold down the taste of vomit, Officer Rudy Holtzman stepped carefully around the mutilated body of Erika Larsson, went into the dark kitchen, and turned on the lights. He used the wall phone to dial headquarters.

When the night girl, Wendy Newhart, answered, Holtzman said, 'I'm out here at the Larsson place.' His voice was strained and hoarse; it cracked on a couple of words. He cleared his throat. 'The lights were on when I got here. Nobody answered the bell, but the door was ajar. She's dead.'

'Oh, my *God!* Well, I'm not going to tell her father. That's out of the question. Someone else will have to tell him.'

'Better get Charlie over here with the other squad car,' Holtzman said. 'Call the medical examiner right away. And Patmore, of course. Tell Charlie to move his ass; I don't like being here alone.'

Wendy Newhart asked, 'When was she killed?'

'How should I know? The medical examiner will know.'

'I mean, did it just happen before you got there? Within the past half hour?'

'What's it matter?' Holtzman asked.

'Rudy, tell me! Did it just happen?'

'The blood's mostly caked and dry. I can't pinpoint the time of death, but it must surely have been a good many hours ago.'

'Thank the Lord for small miracles,' she said.

'What?'

She had hung up.

Holtzman put down the receiver and turned to see a black cat standing in the doorway between the kitchen and the front room, no more than five feet from him. Its fuzzy white muzzle had been tinted red-brown with blood. Holtzman took one step, kicked out at the cat, missed.

It squealed and ran.

★ ★ ★

They arrived at the harbour at five minutes past seven.

Max parked the Mercedes in a corner of the lot that, in season, served both a restaurant called Italian Villa and Kimball's Arcade. Tonight the restaurant's side of the lot was nearly full, while the other side was nearly empty.

526

The three of them got out of the car.

Lou drew up his shoulders against the cold. As the storm air had moved in from the Pacific, the temperature had dropped rapidly from a one o'clock high of seventy degrees to a current low of forty-four. The wind had increased, too; it whipped in from the harbour, lashed King's Point, made the night seem even cooler than it was.

Lou said, 'I still think I should go with Max, and you should stay here, where it's safe.'

'It's not safe anywhere for me,' Mary said.

'At least if you stayed here in the car—'

She waved one hand impatiently, interrupted him. 'We've got two weapons we can use against this man we're after: one is Max's handiness with guns, and the other is my psychic talent. The two of us shouldn't split up.'

The sea wind lifted her long hair, made it flap like a banner behind her.

Max put one hand on Lou's shoulder. 'I don't want her in the thick of the action any more than you do. But maybe she's right. She's probably not in any greater danger there than here. Besides, neither of us is going to change her mind.'

'I feel so useless,' Lou said.

'We need someone here in the car,' Max said. 'You're our early warning system.'

'We're wasting time,' Mary said.

Lou nodded glumly. He kissed her cheek and told Max to take good care of her.

They hurried into the wind, across the parking lot towards the huge, deserted barnlike building that housed the array of souvenir stands, trinket stores, amusements, and coffee shops known collectively as Kimball's Games and Snacks.

He got behind the wheel of the Mercedes and closed the door. Through the windshield he could barely see Max and Mary as they drew further away and blended into the darkness around the clapboard and cedar-shingled pavilion.

A fierce gust of wind rocked the car. Forks of lightning stabbed through the sky, but still there was no rain.

Lou settled back, resigned to his role as a sentinel. If the killer didn't anticipate Mary tonight, as he had last night, he would probably approach Kimball's openly, brazenly. If Lou spotted a man moving towards the building, he would switch on the

Mercedes' ignition and alert Max with two short blasts of the horn. The pavilion and tower stood only sixty yards farther along the boardwalk that connected seven or eight businesses on this section of the harbour. The sound of the horn would travel that far undiminished, but it wasn't likely the killer would recognize it as a signal. Even if Mary was able to foresee the exact time and direction of the man's approach, the horn would be a welcome confirmation of her vision.

Of course, the psychopath might have anticipated them again and already be at the pavilion.

Lou shifted uneasily behind the wheel.

He thought of Patty Spooner, strangled to death with a priest's stole. He thought of Barry Mitchell, hideously mutilated.

He looked left and right, peered into the rearview mirror. No one. He squinted at the deep shadows along the side of the pavilion. All was still.

★ ★ ★

The black cat crouched on the top of a seven-foot-high set of bookshelves, no more than eight or ten inches from the ceiling in the front room of the cottage. Its forepaws hung over the edge of the shelf; it was motionless, staring down at Rudy Holtzman with suspicion and contempt.

Filthy damned thing. He hated cats. Always had. And it gave him the creeps just to think about this one eagerly lapping up the murdered woman's blood.

It made a deep, throaty sound, as if daring him to approach it.

He didn't want to wait with the cat and the corpse, not even for the few minutes Charlie would need to get here in the other cruiser. He walked down the short hallway to inspect the part of the house he'd not yet seen.

In the bedroom he found an open window, where the wind played havoc with a pair of flimsy curtains and an oilcloth blind that was drawn down only halfway. The recent storms had soaked and badly stained the carpet.

Holtzman was suddenly excited. He studied the room, recreating in his mind those first few seconds when the sanctity of the house had been violated. He knew that more than rain had come in through that window. He was certain that he'd found the killer's entrance. And as his glance travelled over the floor, he could hardly believe what he saw. It was one of those lucky breaks you seldom get in police work. Apparently the pistol had fallen unnoticed from a coat pocket as the killer climbed through the window.

Holtzman knelt on the damp carpet to get a closer look at the weapon. He was careful not to spoil any fingerprints that might be on it. If this killer was the same man who had slaughtered those nurses and the people in that beauty salon – and the style sure seemed the same to Holtzman – then the Anaheim and Santa Ana police already had more than enough good prints. So far prints had been of no use in cracking the case because the killer evidently had never had his taken by any police organization in the country. Nevertheless, because he prided himself on being more professional than anyone with whom he worked, Holtzman didn't grasp the pistol and smear the evidence. He took a ball-point pen from his shirt pocket, slipped it through the trigger guard, lifted the gun off the floor, and held it in front of his eyes.

It was an unusual piece – a .45 Auto Colt. But nothing off the shelf. Something special. A collector's item. The metal was engraved with delicate leaves and vines. There were also a number of animals – rabbits, deer, pheasants, foxes – etched in positions of flight beginning at the forward sight on the barrel, all of them incredibly detailed, beautifully rendered, all racing towards the butt.

He saw what appeared to be printing on the steel, where it met the wooden handgrip. The bedroom light was poor. The letters were tiny, between a quarter and a half inch high, inscribed with a spidery flourish of the engraver's tool. Holtzman couldn't read them.

He stood up and, carrying the Colt on the pen, went to the nearest lamp.

By W. Thorben
Seattle 1975

A collector's piece like this one often passed through the hands of many owners who purchased and resold it at gun shows without bothering to register it with authorities. Nevertheless, with the engraver's name (and providing the gun had not been stolen from a collection), they should be able to find the man who had commissioned it from Thorben. From him they had a chance of tracing it to the man who'd dropped it while coming through the window.

Still manipulating the weapon with his ball-point pen, Holtzman looked at the opposite side. Again, where the steel met the wooden handgrip, there was writing. Not the same words. He squinted. He read it. Then read it again. 'Well, I'll be damned.'

A siren rose in the distance and grew rapidly nearer.

Holtzman went down the hall to the side of the house that faced the dead-end macadam road. He stood in the open doorway he'd first found ajar.

Another police car, emergency beacons blazing, roared up the long hill from town. Patmore's station wagon wasn't far behind it.

Beneath the hall light Holtzman held up the Colt and read the second legend again.

commissioned by
Max Bergen

EIGHTEEN

The darkness around the pavilion was lumpy, velvety, and deep. It offered dozens of hiding places.

Mary carried the flashlight, hooding it with one hand. Every time she made a sudden move in response to imagined noises, shadows danced.

She stayed close to Max as they circled the building, looking for a place where the killer might have got inside. Last night the police had entered with a key provided by the owners. That was a convenience denied both them and their quarry. The killer would have to break something to get in and reach the tower; he would have to leave a trail.

She was impatient. Twice she urged Max to hurry.

Already the parade of lighted boats had begun its first circuit of the harbour, entering from the staging area at sea, still far down the channel but approaching fast. By seven-thirty the queen of the parade might well have begun her first pass of the tower.

On the west side of the pavilion, which faced the harbour and was flanked with a railed boardwalk, they found a shattered pane of glass in one of the mullioned windows that looked in on the lightless, deserted coffee shop.

'Did the killer do this?' Max asked.

She directed the flashlight at the ground, and in the soft glow of its backwash, she studied the damaged window. With the fingertips of her left hand she traced the wooden ribs that framed the missing pane. The night was already chilly, but the air got suddenly colder as she concentrated on the psychic impressions that the window held for her.

Wicka-wicka-wicka!

She shuddered, squeezed the flashlight as hard as she could, gritted her teeth but refused to panic.

'Something?' Max asked.

'Yes. He did this.'

'Is he inside now?'

'No. He was here . . . late yesterday . . . after the police left . . . I can see . . . many hours after the police left . . . early this morning . . . at dawn . . . up in the tower.' She took her hand from the window, and an invisible connection snapped. 'But he hasn't returned yet tonight.'

'You're positive about that?'

'Absolutely.'

'But he'll be here any minute?'

'Yes. So hurry.'

Wicka-wicka-wicka!

Ignore it, she told herself. It's not real. Max doesn't hear it, does he? Only you hear it. Psychic impressions. Nothing is really overhead. No wings. No danger. No wings at all.

'We don't want to make this any more of a spectacle than we have to,' Max said. 'Some of these restaurants farther around the harbour might have a pretty good view of us. Better shut off the flashlight.'

She did as he said.

The night closed around her.

Max put one hand through the missing pane, reached up, and fumbled for the latch on the vertical, metal centre post. 'Do you realise this is breaking and entering?'

'I suppose it is,' she said.

'Doesn't that bother you?'

'Max, will you *hurry*?'

He swung the tall halves of the window outward without making a sound.

She climbed onto the sill, which was only three feet above the boardwalk, stepped down into the coffee shop. She glanced around the room, but she couldn't see anything.

Max looked both ways along the boardwalk, then followed her, closed and latched the window.

'It's even darker in here than it was out there,' she said. 'We'll be tripping over something every other step if I don't use the flash.'

'Just be sure you don't point it at a window,' he said. 'Keep it hooded.'

She switched on the light, shielding half the lens with her left hand.

The restaurant contained approximately thirty tables, all of them bolted to the floor. Apparently because the chairs couldn't be bolted down as well, they had been removed and put in storage until Kimball's reopened in the spring.

The only public entrance to the coffee shop – a pair of many-paned glass doors that matched the big mullioned windows – was from inside the pavilion, of which this restaurant was but one small part. The killer had smashed the lock. When Max pushed open the doors, they moved stiffly and grated on their unlubricated hinges.

He stood still for a moment, listening to the settling sounds of the building. Finally he said, 'You're really sure he's not here already?'

'Positive.'

Although the psychic impressions were not always complete, they'd never deceived her. She hoped her talent hadn't failed this time; because if it had, if the killer *was* already here and waiting, she was as good as dead.

From the coffee shop they entered a corridor that curved out of sight in both directions. It was lined with small gift shops: Silly T-Shirts, The Ceramic Factory, The House of Glass Miniatures, and a dozen more, all empty and dark.

Max and Mary turned left and quickly discovered that the long corridor was a semicircle leading, at both ends, into the cavernous main hall of the arcade. That huge room was bare now, but in season it would be filled with a variety of pinball machines, shuffleboard bowling, shooting galleries, electronic games, and carnival booths where you could get your fortune told or where a boy could spend ten dollars in quarters to win a three-dollar toy animal for his best girl.

They walked to the centre of the room. Their footsteps echoed hollowly from wall to wall and from curve to curve of the high domed ceiling.

Mary stopped and pointed the flashlight where Lou had said to look. She saw an archway at the rear of the room, steps beyond it. Above the arch was a sign: THIS WAY TO OBSERVATION DECK.

Screams, the sound of wings, a body hurtling off the bottom steps and through the archway, wings, a body writhing on the wooden arcade floor, wings, strangled cries for help . . .

She swayed under the impact of the psychic images.

'What's the matter?' Max asked.

533

'I see . . .' She tried to hold on to the vision, but it rapidly faded and would not be coaxed to return. 'Someone's going to die tonight at the foot of those stairs.'

'One of us?'

'I don't know.'

'The killer?'

'I hope.'

'It'll be him,' Max said. 'Not us. We'll live. We've got to. I know it.'

Not as certain as he was, reluctant to think about it for fear her courage would vanish, she asked, 'Where should we wait for him?'

'I'll wait at the bottom of the steps. You'll wait at the top of the tower.'

'At the top of . . . oh, no!'

'Oh, yes.'

'I'm staying with you,' she said.

'Look, if Lou uses the car horn to warn us, we probably won't hear it in here. But you'd be certain to hear it if you were in the tower—'

'Forget it.'

'—on the open deck.'

'Max, I'm staying here.'

'No, dammit!'

She took a step back from him.

His face was dark with anger. '*I'm* the one who's an expert with guns. If it comes down to a shooting match, you'll be in my way. If I have to move fast, I don't want to have to stop and worry whether you're in the line of fire.'

'I'm not a hopeless idiot,' she said. 'I can stay out of your way.'

He glared at her and said nothing.

She said, 'But what if I have a vision while I'm up there, something important? How will I let you know what's going to happen?'

'I'll be here at the bottom of the steps – not more than sixty feet from you. You can reach me quickly if it's necessary.'

'I don't know . . .'

'I'll put it more bluntly,' Max said. 'Either do what I say and go to the observation deck, or so help me God, I'm going to take a punch at you, lightly as I can, but hard enough to knock you out. Then I'll carry you back to the Mercedes and call this whole thing off.'

'You wouldn't.'

'Wouldn't I?'

She knew he wasn't making idle threats.

'I'll do it because I love you,' he said. 'I don't want you to get killed.'

'And I don't want *you* killed,' she said.

'Good. Then you'll listen to me. We've both got a better chance of living through this if you're not here to distract me when and if the shooting starts.'

She was filled with conflicting emotions. 'Will you kill him?'

'If he forces me to.'

'Don't hesitate to do it,' she said. 'Don't give him a chance. He's too clever. Shoot him the second you see him.'

'The police might have something to say about that.'

'To hell with the police.'

'Mary, *are* you going upstairs? There's not much time. Do we stay or do I carry you out of here? It's entirely your decision, but you've got to make your mind up fast.'

Partly because she saw a glimmer of truth in his argument, but mainly because she had no choice, she said, 'All right.'

They walked quickly to the archway. At the foot of the stairs he put his hands on her shoulders, and she raised her face to him. They kissed.

'When you get to the top,' he said, 'don't stand around looking at the sights. Even at night someone on the ground might be able to see you. If the killer spots you, he might back off. You say we'll have to have a showdown with him sooner or later. So we may as well do what we can to end it tonight.'

'Who gets the flashlight?' she asked.

'You keep it. '

She was relieved, but she said, 'You'll be in the dark down here . . . with him.'

'If I switched on a flashlight when I heard him coming,' Max said, 'I'd only be making a target of myself. Besides, if he isn't aware I'm waiting for him, he's not going to enter a pitch-black building and try to navigate through it without a flash. I'll be able to see him by his own light.'

She kissed him again, turned away, and climbed the eight flights of stairs alone.

At the top she doused the flashlight and stood for a moment in the fierce wind, looking out at the parade of lighted boats on the harbour. Then she heeded Max's advice and sat down with her back to the waist-high wall that bordered the deck.

Darkness. Some light. Not much.

Alone now. All alone.

No. Not alone. Where did a thought like that come from? Max was nearby.

The wind raced through the belfry, moaned like a human voice.

She huddled in her leather coat and wished for a sweater.

It would rain soon. She could smell it in the air.

She pushed the read-out button on her digital wrist-watch, and lighted numerals glowed blood-red in the dark.

The eyes.

She suddenly remembered the luminous, reddish eyes that she had seen in Berton Mitchell's cottage. She could not conjure up a face to go with them. Just the eyes . . . and the sound of wings . . . and the feel of wings all over her . . . and still the eyes, wild, inhuman.

She remembered something else, too; remembered it with a jolt – a small voice at the back of her mind, whispery, but intense: '*I'm a demon and a vampire. I like the taste of blood.*'

Someone had spoken those very words to her in Mitchell's cottage twenty-four years ago.

Who? Berton Mitchell himself? Who else could it have been?

Although she tried to use her psychic talent to transform the vivid memory into a clairvoyant vision, she was not able to bring much light to the gloomy, penumbral images that swam and pulsed malignantly. The mysterious face of the creature that spoke to her remained just out of sight.

But the inner voice grew louder. Somehow it swelled and thundered and overwhelmed her, yet remained a whisper. The harsh words came faster, even faster, and she was shaken by them. '*I'm a demon and a vampire. I like the taste of blood. I'm a demon and a vampire, I like the taste of blood, I'm a demon and a vampire—*'

'Stop it!' she said.

She put her hands to her ears and willed the voice from her mind. Gradually it faded. When it was gone, she slumped forward, dizzy.

'I'll be all right,' she said softly, urgently. 'It'll be all right. No one will die. It'll be all right. Tonight it ends. It'll be fine after tonight.'

Slowly the realities of the night impressed themselves upon her once more: wind, cold, darkness.

Distracted by the memory of those luminous eyes, she hadn't noticed the time when she pressed the button on her watch. She pressed it again.

7:24.

Six minutes to go.

* * *

Heavy ebony clouds, vaguely phosphorescent at their bearded edges, sailed soundlessly towards the east. The sky was silent for long minutes, a muffling blanket tented over the earth; but now it crashed and flared again.

The wind lifted a scrap of paper from the pavement, pasted it to the windshield of the Mercedes for a few seconds, then tore it away.

Lou shifted uneasily, leaned into the steering wheel, squinted at the purple-black shadows that flanked the pavilion. The longer he stared, the more the darkness seemed to shimmer as if it were alive. He kept seeing movement where there was none; his eyes played a hundred tricks on him. He didn't have the proper temperament for a sentinel. He had no patience.

He looked at his watch.

7:29.

Someone rapped three times, hard, on the window to his left, inches from his head.

He jerked around.

A familiar face peered in at him, smiled.

Confused and somewhat embarrassed by the terror that must have been visible on his face, Lou said, 'Hey! You startled me.' He felt for the latch, opened the door, and got out of the car. 'What are you doing here?'

Too late, he saw the butcher knife.

* * *

Lights were on in most of the downstairs rooms at 440 Ocean Hill Lane, but when Rudy Holtzman rang the bell, no one answered.

Patmore tried the door and found it wasn't locked. He pushed

537

it open. Wind rushed past him and swept a stack of unopened mail off the small table in the foyer.

Patmore couldn't see anyone in the entranceway or in the living room beyond. He leaned through the door and shouted, 'Pasternak! You in there?'

No one answered.

'Maybe he's dead,' Holtzman said.

Because he was wearing civilian clothes, Patmore took a silvery badge from the pocket of his overcoat and pinned it to his lapel. He drew his service revolver from the outer coat pocket, and holding it with the barrel pointed at the ceiling, he stepped into the house.

Behind him, Holtzman cleared his throat and said, 'We don't have a warrant.'

Patmore stopped, looked back at him, and said, 'Rudy, your ass, get it in here.'

★ ★ ★

Syrupy darkness. A coppery odour. Barbed wire twisting inside him.

His tongue hurt. He'd bitten it. A coppery taste.

He was lying on his stomach. On the macadam parking lot. Near the Mercedes. His arms flung out in supplication. Head to one side. Ear against the ground as if listening for the approach of an enemy.

He opened his eyes but just barely. A pair of shoes were in front of his face. Inches from him. Gucci loafers. They turned and walked away. Towards the pavilion. In seconds they were out of sight, but he could still hear footsteps.

He tried to raise his head. Couldn't.

He tried to remember how many times he'd been stabbed in the stomach. Three, maybe four times. Could have been worse. But it was surely bad enough. He was dying. He had no strength at all; and now even his weakness was draining out of him.

I'm such an idiot, he thought bitterly. How could I have been so careless? A damned fool. The closest I'll ever come to a brainstorm is a light drizzle.

Should have known who the killer was. Should have known the moment the Ouija board said the target was the queen of the boat parade. She was one of his old girl friends. Seemed to get along

538

with a woman for only a few months. So now he was going to kill one of his old girl friends. Probably had killed others. Why? No matter why. Should have known.

He felt as if thousands of insects were crawling inside of him, stinging and biting his guts.

He closed his eyes and thought, I don't want to die, I *won't*!

Then: You fool. Do you think you have a choice?

A coppery odour. Syrupy darkness.

It didn't look bad.

Inviting, actually.

He floated in the inviting darkness. He sank down and down, away from the pain, away from everything.

* * *

Curious, John Patmore paged through the spiralbound notebook that lay open beside the Ouija board on the dining room table. The ruled pages were filled with neat, feminine handwriting that he supposed belonged to Mary Bergen.

Mostly she had recorded questions and answers that appeared to be connected with the case she claimed to be investigating. In the middle of the notebook, however, there was a page that contained only five hastily scrawled words: *Mary! Run for your life!*

The same message was repeated in the centre of the following page. And then on a third.

Under the third warning there were more questions and answers:

> *When did I write these warnings?*
> *Don't know.*
> *What do I mean by them?*
> *Don't know.*
> *Who am I afraid of?*
> *Don't know, don't know, don't know!*
> *Am I going crazy?*
> *Maybe.*
> *Where can I run to?*
> *Nowhere.*

Strange.

It made him nervous.

There was a note pad at the other side of the Ouija board. Patmore began leafing through it.

A-L-L-O-U-R-Y-E-S-T-E-R-D-A-Y-S
ALL OUR YESTERDAYS.
B-E-A-U-T-I-F-U-L
BEAUTIFUL
T-H-E-A-I-R-I-S-B-E-A-U-T-I-F-U-L
THE AIR IS BEAUTIFUL

He glanced at the Ouija board, at the trivet, then down at the note pad again. He remembered working a board with his mother when he was a boy. He began to read every other line of the transcript.

When he finished, he thought of Erika Larsson and realised she matched the description of the girl whose death Mary Bergen had predicted. Reluctantly, he admitted to himself that perhaps the clairvoyant was not a fake after all. 'Holtzman!'

Rudy Holtzman returned from the far end of the house. 'No one's here.'

'Max Bergen intends to kill the queen of the boat parade.'

Blinking in surprise, Holtzman said, '*What?* Jenny Canning?'

'Apparently Mary Bergen doesn't realise her husband's the man she's after.' Patmore looked at his watch. 'We might be too late.' He ran through the cluttered living room, out the front door.

★ ★ ★

Marie Sanzini.

Unbidden, the name came to Mary.

Marie Sanzini.

Marie Sanzini was one of the nurses killed in Anaheim – and suddenly the name was familiar. Mary knew it, but she didn't know where she'd heard it before. Marie. Marie Sanzini. It teased her.

She closed her eyes, tried to see the woman's face, but it eluded her.

She thumbed the button on her watch.

540

7:33.

No signal from Lou.

Was tonight just another wild-goose chase?

* * *

Standing in absolute darkness, Max began to feel that he was closed inside a coffin. Then he heard the coffee shop doors grating noisily on their hinges, and his claustrophobia was replaced by an even more elemental fear. Quietly, he stepped out of the archway into the arcade, the gun in his right hand.

A hundred feet away a man with a flashlight came out of the curved corridor that served the restaurant and gift shops. He kept the beam pointed at the floor ahead of him; behind it he, too, was in darkness.

Mustn't have come across the parking lot, Max thought. Lou hadn't blown the car horn. Must have sneaked between two buildings farther north along the harbour, and then down the boardwalk.

Max intended to wait until they were only fifty feet apart before ordering the killer to stop. Fifty feet would give him safety, room to manoeuvre. And if he's fifty feet from the corridor, Max thought, I'll have time to pull off a few good shots if the bastard tries to dodge out of sight.

Seventy feet now.

Sixty.

Fifty.

The killer spoke first, a hoarse, whispered: '*Max?*'

Shocked at being called by name, Max took one step into the darkness and asked, 'Who's there?'

The man kept walking, hidden behind the light.

Forty feet.

'Who's there?' Max demanded.

Again, a forced whisper. '*It's me. Lou.*'

Thirty feet.

Max lowered his gun. 'Lou? For God's sake, it's only a few minutes past seven-thirty. We can't quit yet.'

Lou said, still whispering. '*Trouble.*'

Twenty feet.

'What trouble?' Max asked. 'What do you mean?'

541

Ten feet.

Suddenly Max knew it wasn't Lou Pasternak.

The killer jerked the flashlight up, in the direction of Max's voice. temporarily blinding him.

Although for an instant he could see nothing, Max raised the gun and pulled the trigger. Once. Twice. The shots crashed like cannon fire in the huge, high-ceilinged room.

Simultaneous with the explosion, perhaps even a fraction of a second prior to it, the flashlight spun up and up, out to the right.

I hit him! Max thought.

Even before he completed the thought, the knife ripped into him, rammed out of the darkness and into him, felt like the blade of a shovel, enormous, devastating, so devastating that he dropped the gun, feeling pain like nothing he'd ever known, and he realised that the killer had pitched the flashlight aside as a diversion, hadn't really been hit at all, and the knife was withdrawn from him, and then shoved hard into him again, deep into his stomach, and he thought of Mary and his love for Mary and about how he was letting her down, and he grappled with the killer's head in the dark, got handfuls of short hair, but the bandage came off his finger and the cut was wrenched open again and he felt that pain separate from all the others, and he cursed the sharp edge on the car's jack, and the flashlight hit the floor ten feet away, spun around, cast lunatic shadows, and the knife ripped loose from him again, and he reached for the hand that held it, but he missed, and the blade got him a third time, explosive pain, and he staggered back, the man all over him, the blade plunging again, high this time, into his chest, and he realised that the only way he could hope to survive now was to play dead, so he fell, fell hard, and the man stumbled over him, and he heard the man's rapid breathing, and he lay very still, and the man went for the flashlight and came back and looked down at him, stood over him, kicked him in the ribs, and he wanted to cry out but didn't, didn't move and didn't breathe, even though he was screaming inside for breath, so the man turned away and went towards the arch, and then there were footsteps on the tower stairs, and, hearing them, he felt like such a useless ass, outsmarted, and he knew he wasn't going to be able to recover his gun and climb those stairs and rescue Mary because stuff like that was for the movies, pain was pulverizing him, he was leaking all over the floor, dripping like a squeezed fruit, but he

542

told himself he had to try to help her and that he wasn't going to die, wasn't going to die, wasn't going to die, even though that was exactly what he seemed to be doing.

⋆ ⋆ ⋆

She stood up when the shots were fired. She went to the head of the tower stairs, and within a minute she heard footsteps.

'Max?'

No answer.

'Max?'

Just footsteps coming up.

She backed away from the stairs, across the observation deck, until her buttocks encountered the low wall.

Wicka-wicka-wicka!

Marie Sanzini.

She saw Marie's face, and she knew it.

Rochelle Drake. She knew Rochelle, too.

Erika Larsson. That was the name of the fuzzy-haired blonde – the delicate, ethereal woman who had been in the vision in the mirror at Lou's place.

Mary had known them all along, but she had forced the knowledge into her subconscious. If she cared to pursue it, the answer was there now, waiting. But she still didn't want to face the truth. *Couldn't* face it.

She reminded herself of her announced determination to find her own strength, her own solutions to the problems of life. Defeated already? But she couldn't shame herself; right now, she would accept perpetual weakness and dependence and continued ignorance of the past for a chance to get out of here.

From the stairwell: the slow ascent of footsteps.

'No,' she said desperately. She pressed back against the low wall, eyes fixed on the entrance to the stairs. 'I don't want to know.' Her voice was high, tremulous. 'Oh, God. No. Please!'

Lightning slashed the sky, sharp and bright. Thunder cracked. At last the storm broke: scattered pellets of rain testing the earth; then a sudden downpour; stinging, eroding sheets of water slanting in from the ocean.

The wind drove the rain under the overhang of the belfry roof. Fat droplets pummelled the back of her leather coat, soaking her

543

long black hair. But she didn't care if she got wet. The only thing that worried her now was the past, for it kept coming back to her against her will:

The living room of Berton Mitchell's cottage. Windows with paper blinds drawn almost to the sills. Lacy curtains. The only light, grey light, filtering in from a cloudy afternoon. Shadowy corners. Pale yellow walls. A dark brown davenport with a pair of matching, over-stuffed chairs. Pine floor, rag-twist rugs.

A six-year-old girl lying on the floor. Long dark hair tied into two ponytails with orange ribbons. Beige dress with Kelly-green piping and buttons. Me. The little girl is me. On my back. Dazed. Confused. The side of my face hurts real bad. And the back of my head. What did he do to me? My legs are spread. I can't move them. Each of my ankles is tied securely to a different foot of a bulky armchair. My arms are stretched out behind me. My wrists are tied to the feet of another chair. Can't move. Try to raise my head to look around. Can't.

Maybe Mrs Mitchell will come untie me. No. She's gone away. Visiting relatives with Barry. Mr Mitchell is off someplace trimming hedges.

Scared. So scared.

Footsteps . . . Just him. Nothing frightening. Just him. But what's he want? What's he doing?

He kneels beside me. He has a pillow in his hands . . . big feather pillow . . . he shoves it . . . in my face . . . presses down on it. This isn't a good game . . . not good at all. This is wrong . . . scary. No light . . . no air . . . I scream . . . but the pillow muffles my voice. Try to breathe . . . can't draw in anything but linen. I thrash in my bonds. Daddy, help me! And then he pulls the pillow away. He's giggling. I gulp air and start to cry. He rams the pillow into my face again. I twist my head, can't get out from under. I bite and chew the pillow. Spinning. Dizzy. Weightless. Dying. Hollering in my mind for Daddy, thinking oh-so-hard of him, knowing he can't hear me. And then the pillow is taken away again; cool, delicious air rushes over my face, into my hot lungs. And the pillow is jammed onto me again. And in the final moment before I faint it's removed. Repeatedly reprieved on the verge of suffocation, I reach the thin red line between sanity and madness. And he's giggling as he tortures me. But finally he lifts the pillow and tosses it aside, finished with the game.

But there are worse games to come:

544

He takes my head in both hands . . . his fingers like iron claws. The ache at the back of my skull is getting infinitely worse . . . unbearable. He forces my head to one side . . . descends upon me . . . breathes across my face . . . hissing like a snake . . . moves towards my exposed neck . . . lips on my neck now . . . he takes a pinch of my skin between his teeth, bites hard, bites it off, swallows. I cry out at the sharp little pain . . . struggle . . . the cords bind. He puts his mouth to the tiny wound in my neck . . . sucks . . . draws blood. And when he finally raises his head and lets go of me . . . and I turn . . . I see him grinning, blood smeared around his mouth and streaks of blood on his teeth.

He is only nine years old, three years older than me, but his face is carved with a very adult hatred.

Weeping, choking, I say, 'What are you doing?'

He leans even closer, inches from my face. His breath is fetid, corrupted by my own blood.

'I am a demon and a vampire,' Alan says. There is a childish tone of make-believe in his voice. Yet he is also serious. 'I like the taste of blood.'

Mary said, 'Ahhhh,' as if she had opened an enormous heavy door after many hours of strenuous effort.

And a flashlight beam swung back and forth at the head of the tower stairs.

And Alan walked onto the observation deck.

And he centred the light on her, but not in her eyes.

And they stared at each other.

And finally he grinned and said, 'Hello, Sis.'

I am still spread-eagled on the floor.

Alan returns . . . wearing gloves . . . carrying a wooden box with a wire lid. He reaches through a spring trap in the lid . . . clutches something, withdraws it . . . a small dark creature, its head thrust out of the top of his fist . . . eyes luminous . . . a bat . . . a brown bat . . . one of those he found in the attic of the manor house. It doesn't appear to be scared of him . . . seems almost tame, not wild at all.

He isn't allowed to keep the bats as pets. They're dirty. Daddy told him to get rid of them

He changes his grip on the beast, which flutters but is more docile than not . . . holds it with both hands . . . but lets the wings free. Wicka-wicka-wicka! He holds the bat above my head . . . six or eight inches from me . . . then slowly lowers it until the luminous eyes are staring directly into my eyes . . . until I beg to be released . . . beg him to take the bat away, put it in the box . . . until the membranous wings lightly brush me . . . until the wings strike my face with increasing force, with leathery flapping sounds. Wicka-wicka-wicka!

When peals of thunder tolled over the harbour, Mary felt as if they were waves of some tangible substance passing through her; for deep within she shook sympathetically with each crash.

The past and present were two bottomless caverns of terror between which and above which she walked on a fine thread of self-control. She needed all of her attention and will-power to maintain her equilibrium as the memories swooped over her; she wasn't even able to speak to Alan; she couldn't find the strength to form words.

Without switching it off, Alan put his flashlight on the belfry floor, snug against the wall, where the rain hadn't dampened the boards. A rifle was slung from his left shoulder; he slipped the strap off his arm and put the gun down, too.

He still held the butcher knife.

He picked up the flashlight and pointed it towards the ceiling, into the hollow, cone-shaped roof. 'Look, Mary. Look up. Go ahead. You should see this. Look!'

She looked – and tried to draw back from the sight. She was already pressed against the low wall; there was nowhere to run.

'They're not all here at the moment,' Alan said. 'Some have gone hunting, of course. But most of them stayed in tonight. They sensed the coming rain. See them, Mary? See the bats?'

I am only six years old, and I am tied up, on the floor, my legs spread. Alan holds the bat with both hands. He moves it between my legs, under my dress. It squeals. I am sobbing, gasping for breath, pleading with him. Alan pushes my dress up immodestly. He's sweating. His face is pale. His lips quiver. He doesn't look like a nine-year-old boy; he is truly demonic.

The tips of the bat's wings tickle my bare thighs.

Tickle . . . then scratch painfully.

Although I am much too young to understand the more mysterious functions of my body, too young to imagine what pleasure and pain it will one day give me, I am engulfed by primal fear, overwhelmed by terror at the thought of the bat shoved against the exposed centre of me. I find this much harder to bear than having the creature on my face,

*and I squirm and kick uselessly at Alan, and the wings beat in the
cramped space between my spread legs, and then I felt what I most
dread, for Alan has forced the bat against me, and the thing writhes
and nips and claws and screeches shrilly against me, and Alan is trying
to ram it inside of me, and I scream at the thought, spit, cry, and the
bat is screeching, too, so Alan has great difficulty merely holding on to
the thing, but he forces it against me with all of his strength, and
suddenly a pain, a monstrous pain, shoots up through me—*

The memories were physical as well as mental agony. She had
refused to face them for twenty-four years; and in that time they
had acquired incredible power. They struck her as if they were a
man's fists. She ached. She resisted the urge to vomit. Her legs
were weak. She wept.

Alan put the flashlight on the floor again and shifted the knife
from his left to his right hand.

Richard Lingard's knife.

Max had been right about that: no ghost had picked it up. She
had refused to confront the truth, had been incapable of dealing
with it; therefore, she'd convinced herself that the missing knife
could be explained only as the work of supernatural forces.

'I killed Max,' Alan said.

She knew that must be true, but she didn't want to consider it.
The tears for that, the shattering grief would have to come later –
if she lived long enough to grieve.

The observation deck was fifteen feet across. Less than three
yards of wet pine flooring separated her from him.

He spoke softly, not much louder than the monotonous hiss of
the rain. 'I'm glad you came. It's time I finished what I started
twenty-four years ago.'

When asked where the killer was from, the Ouija board had
said, THE AIR IS BEAUTIFUL. That wasn't a literal translation of 'Bel
Air,' but it was close enough.

Why hadn't she seen that?

She hadn't wanted to see it.

At their feet the beam of the flashlight was diffused and cast
back by the glossy paint on the deck wall, highlighting his chin and
cheeks and nose. Because the rising light created odd shadows on
his face, he was not handsome now; instead, he resembled one of
the fright masks worn by a witch doctor in some savage ceremony.

He held the knife in front of him, but he didn't come any closer.

'I *knew* you'd come tonight. We're so close, Mary. As close as two people can ever be. We share blood, but more than that, we share pain. I've dealt it out, and you've endured it. Pain binds us. Pain makes a far stronger cement than love does. Love is an abstract human concept, meaningless, nonexistent. But pain is real. I knew we were so close that I could communicate with you at a distance, without words. I knew I could make you come after me. Each day since Monday night I've meditated, put myself in a light trance. When my mind was clear, when I was relaxed, I tried to send thoughts to you, images of murders I intended to commit. I wanted to trigger your clairvoyant vision. And it worked, didn't it?'

He was a raving lunatic – and yet he had such a calm demeanour, spoke in such measured tones.

'Didn't it work, Mary?'

'Yes.'

He was pleased. 'I kept a watch on Lou's house, and when you showed up there, I knew you were after me.'

An especially fierce gust of wind buffeted her, drove deafening blasts of torrential rain against the hollow roof.

He took one step towards her.

'Stop right there!' she said frantically.

He obeyed her. He hadn't decided suddenly to be merciful. And certainly he wasn't afraid of her. He stopped because he was willing, even eager, to see her cower before him and to kill her slowly.

If she played along with him, she would gain minutes of life, might even find a way to escape. 'If you wanted to kill me, you could have done it Monday night at the motel, before Max returned.'

'That was too easy. By making you pursue me, I had more fun.'

'Fun? Killing is fun?'

'There's nothing like it.'

'You're insane.'

'No,' he said serenely. 'I'm just a hunter. And everybody else is a game animal. I was born to kill. It's my purpose. I've no doubts about that. I've been killing all my life. It started with the bugs.'

She remembered: she was about four years old and Alan was seven; there was a praying mantis in a big glass jar; and Alan

548

unscrewed the lid, squirted lighter fluid on the mantis, dropped a match into the jar. For years he had gathered insects for the sole purpose of torturing them to death with chemicals, razor blades, pins, and fire.

She said, '*You* were the one who killed our cats and dogs.'

'And all the other pets.'

'Barry Mitchell had nothing to do with that.'

He shrugged. 'I got tired of the damned bugs.'

He took a step towards her.

'Stop!'

He stopped, grinned.

That morning she had suggested to Max that evil was not always acquired, not always learned by example. Most educated people were convinced that, without exception, the motivations behind the antisocial acts of violent people had their roots in poverty, broken homes, childhood traumas, parental neglect or parental ineptitude. Sociologists insisted criminals were spawned primarily by social systems founded on injustice. Most psychologists appeared secure in the belief that any neurosis or psychosis could be explained in terms of Freudian or Jungian theory. But was it possible that some people were rotten from the start, hopelessly corrupt before environment had an opportunity to affect them? Was that a reactionary, medieval thought? She'd read a great deal about the XYY-man, the genetically ordained criminal type that had inspired so much scientific research over the past few years. Some people might be born less civilized than most – for chemical or genetic reasons that no one fully understood.

That was a dangerous theory. It could be misinterpreted. Every racist group would point to every hated minority as evidence of genetic inferiority. In fact, if there *were* people who were born to do evil, they were evenly distributed among all races, religions, sexes, and nationalities.

Born evil . . .

A bad seed . . .

She looked at Alan and knew that's what he was: a very special creature, both more and less than human.

A bat darted in from the rain, swooped into the hollow roof with a leathery flutter of wings that made her gasp and cringe.

Wicka-wicka-wicka!

'I wanted to meet you here at Kimball's,' Alan said, 'because

549

neither of the other towers had bats in them. I thought they'd help you remember what happened twenty-four years ago.'

—and Alan takes the bat from between her legs, and it is dead, its neck is broken, soaked with her blood as well as its own, and she hurts so bad, and Alan tosses the dead bat into the box from which he got it, and he turns back to her, and she is unable to scream anymore, unable to resist, drained of strength and will, and he begins to pound her with his fists, blows landing on her stomach and chest and neck and face, a flurry of small fists driving her down into darkness . . . and when she comes to a short while later, he is standing over her with a knife he's got from the Mitchells' kitchen, and he brings it down, into her arm, then her side, the knife, Oh, God, the knife!

★ ★ ★

Clean thrusts. In and right out again. Clean, quick thrusts. No ripping. No tearing. No long, ugly gashes.

Max explored the dimensions of the bleeding holes with his hands and figured there wasn't any danger of his intestines sliding out of him through an enormous jagged rent in his flesh.

He supposed he should be thankful for that.

He was losing a lot of blood. His clothes were gluey, his hands sticky, the floor stained with a warm and spreading puddle. But in the dark it probably felt like a lot more than it really was. It felt like *quarts*!

After resting only a few seconds, before the sound of footsteps ascending the tower stairs faded away, he got up on his hands and knees.

The four punctures in his chest and stomach throbbed wildly, incessantly. He choked on the pain. He felt as if a knife still protruded from each wound.

There was no special agony when he drew his breath. Neither of his lungs had been damaged.

Another small blessing.

He crawled to the left, then to the right, dripping on the floor, groping in the perfect blackness for the gun he had dropped. He found it sooner than he'd expected.

He located the nearest wall, pressed one hand against it to steady himself, and got to his feet in spite of the pain that slammed through him like an endless series of electric shocks.

He couldn't possibly climb the tower stairs. He was barely able to walk on level ground; the steep stairs would kill him. And if by some miracle he *did* reach the observation deck, he would make so much noise in the ascent that the killer would be waiting for him; he'd be blown away the instant he achieved the top step.

The only thing he could do was go for help. Back to the parking lot. To the Mercedes. Fast as he could move. Let Lou know what had happened.

Aware that every second wasted might count against Mary, he pushed away from the wall. He staggered into the vast, dark room. Although he was dizzy and slightly disoriented, he thought he knew which way to go to find the corridor that served the coffee shop; but in any event, he could do nothing but trust his instinct. Each step caused new bubbles of pain to burst in his guts. He felt as if he were walking miles, and he wondered if he were going in circles.

Just as despair began to grip him, he stumbled around a corner into a corridor that was less dark than the main hall of the arcade. Vague greyish light, the next thing to non-existent, shimmered farther down the hall: light from the harbour boat parade, light shining through the coffee shop's exterior windows, bouncing around, then leaking thinly through the mullioned doors.

He walked down the corridor with his right hand on his stomach, as if trying to squeeze shut his wounds. He went through the coffee shop doors, between the tables, and fell to his knees at the window that looked out on the boardwalk and harbour. It was closed, and he didn't think he had the strength to lift it.

Love is strength, he told himself. Find strength in your love for Mary. What would you have or be without her? Nothing.

Outside, lightning ripped open the sky again. The reflections of light from its electric blade shone through the window; and for an instant it seemed to turn to ice the rain that streamed down the glass.

★ ★ ★

In the cold rain Chief John Patmore stooped beside Lou Pasternak and turned him onto his back, used the flashlight to study his face and then his blood-sodden clothes. 'Bergen got to him. He's been stabbed.'

Holtzman said, 'Is he dead?'

The chief felt for a pulse in one of the cool, limp wrists. 'I think he is. But you'd better call an ambulance anyway. There might be others.'

Holtzman ran back to the patrol car.

* * *

Only seven or eight feet of rain-slicked planks separated her from Alan.

She had to keep him talking. The moment he lost interest in the conversation, he'd use the butcher knife. Besides, even if she were going to die, there were things she still had to know.

'So Berton Mitchell never touched me,' she said.

'Not even once.'

'I sent an innocent man to prison.'

Alan nodded, smiled, as if she'd merely told him that he was wearing a pretty shirt.

'I caused him to commit suicide,' she said.

'Wish I could have seen him swinging.'

'I disgraced his family.'

Alan laughed.

'Why would I do that?' she asked. 'Why would I tell them that he attacked me when it was actually you?'

Alan said, 'You were in the intensive care unit at the hospital for four days. When the crisis passed and you no longer needed the support machines, they transferred you to a private room.'

'I remember.'

'Father and I virtually lived there for two weeks. Even Mother crawled out of her bottle to visit every couple of days. I played the concerned big brother, oh-so-attentive for a nine-year-old boy.'

'The nurses thought you were cute,' she said.

'There were lots of times when I was alone with you in that hospital room. Sometimes just for minutes, sometimes for as much as an hour.'

Another bat flew in from the storm and settled in the rafters overhead.

Alan said, 'Your lips and gums were so badly swollen and full of stitches that you couldn't talk for eight days – but you could *listen*. You were conscious most of the time. And when I was alone with you, I told you over and over again what I would do to you if you

552

dared to expose me. I told you I'd come after you with the bats again . . . let them tear you apart.' He was leering at her. 'I told you I'd force you to eat the bats alive, that I'd make you bite off their heads and swallow if you told on me. I warned you that you'd better put all the blame on Berton Mitchell – or else.'

She was shaking. She had to get control of herself, had to be prepared to move fast if she was given an opportunity to escape. However, the tremors continued, no matter how hard she tried to still them.

Alan said, 'Then a funny thing happened. You told them it was Mitchell who did it to you – but you *believed* it. I'd achieved more than I thought. I'd gotten way down in you, way down where it counts, and I'd worked a little magic. You actually came to believe it *was* Berton Mitchell. You couldn't accept the truth, couldn't tolerate living in the same house with me after what I'd done to you, so you convinced yourself that I hadn't done anything at all, that I was your friend and that the bogeyman was someone else.'

'Why?' she asked weakly. 'Why did you hurt me?'

'I meant to kill you. I thought you were dead when I left the cottage.'

'Why did you want to kill me?'

'It was fun.'

'That's all? Just because it was "fun"?'

'I hated you,' he said.

'What had I done?'

'Nothing.'

'Then why did you hate me?'

'I hate everyone.'

Lightning.

A gust of wind.

'You killed Mitchell's family.'

'Seemed like a good idea, wiping out an entire family.'

'Why? Was that "fun", too?'

'You should have seen the house burn.'

'God Almighty, you were only fourteen then.'

'That's old enough to kill,' he said. 'Don't forget, I tried to kill you five years before that. And when I thought you were dead . . . when I pulled the knife out of you for the last time . . . oh, Mary, you can't know how that felt! So natural. Like it wasn't my first

553

kill at all. Like I'd stabbed people to death a thousand times before. And I was only nine!'

He stepped closer.

His shoes squished on the wet floor.

Desperately she said, 'You killed Patty Spooner, too. Didn't you, Alan?'

'She was a bitch.'

'No. She was sweet.'

'A rotten bitch.'

'Why did you defile the altar?'

The question clearly intrigued him. 'Killing Patty in that church . . . was so different . . . so special. I knew that night that I truly *was* a demon and a vampire. I realised I was meant to destroy anything holy, anything good.'

'You killed Marie Sanzini.'

'And her three roommates.'

'At one time, you loved Marie.'

'No. I only dated her.'

'Why would you want to kill her?'

'Why not?' he asked.

'You murdered Rochelle Drake.'

'Don't tell me I loved her, too.'

'You once said you did.'

'I lied. I love no one.'

'Why did you kill the beautician and his wife?'

'They were in my way.'

A ship's horn blared across the water.

'You murdered Erika Larsson . . . and now you're going to kill the queen of the Christmas boat parade.'

He glanced at the lighted vessels cruising slowly through the winter rain. 'The storm will have driven her off the deck. I'll have to take her some other time.'

'But what is she to you?'

'Don't you know who's queen? Jenny Canning.'

'Ah, not her. She's good. So gentle. She mustn't die.'

'She's just the most recent of my bitches. She's game like all the others.' He was getting weary; he looked at the blade in his hand and licked his lips.

'Your women always leave you,' Mary said.

'Or I leave them.'

554

'Why can't you hold one?'

'Sex,' he said. 'Tenderness is a bore. They all want me to be tender. I can only manage it for a few weeks or months.'

'What do you mean?'

'I like sex rough,' he said, his voice almost a growl. 'The rougher the better. After a while, when the novelty of a new body . . . a new girl . . . wears off, then the only way I can come is when I hurt them. And that turns them off . . . that and the other thing.'

'What other thing?' she asked.

'They won't let me drink their blood.'

She stared, shocked.

He said, 'Now and then I like to have sex . . . and drink their blood.'

'You cut them?'

'No, no. Menstrual blood.'

Shocked, she closed her eyes.

Heard him move.

Opened her eyes!

He took two quick steps and was less than the length of the knife from her.

*   *   *

Max rolled from the yard-high windowsill onto the boardwalk, and the short fall seemed like twenty miles. In his mind, at least, he tumbled over and over. For a long moment after he fell, floating in a sea of pain, he considered the appealing, beckoning emptiness that welled up inside him. Then he thought about Mary and about transforming love into physical strength. Somehow he smothered the pain and clambered to his feet.

The pistol was still in his left hand. It felt impossibly heavy. He tried to drop it, but he wasn't able to let go. His paralytic fingers were hooked tightly, immovably around the butt.

He swayed and looked at the line of decorated boats gliding through the rain and thought how pretty they were – and suddenly realised that he wasn't here to watch the parade. Silently cursing himself, he lumbered along the boardwalk. Each shaky step he took was an adventure ten times greater than the one before it; and each yard of ground he covered was a triumph.

On all sides of him, the night pumped in and out, in and out like the muscles of a heart.

He turned the corner of the pavilion and saw that no more than a hundred feet away two men were coming behind flashlights.

Lou and who else?

He tried to shout.

He had no voice.

★ ★ ★

Alan's eyes seemed to have light *behind* them. They were blue eyes like hers, but a peculiar and piercing blue. Eyes like the blade of the knife in his hand – sharp, cold, deadly.

'How many people have you killed?'

He didn't answer.

He raised his left hand. He put his icy fingertips against her temple, felt the pulse thumping there. He slid his fingers down, traced the delicate line of her jaw, then raised them and touched her lips.

Trembling, she said, 'You've killed more than thirty-five, haven't you?'

'How'd you know that?'

'If you killed so many over the years,' she said, 'why didn't I go after you before this?'

'You were asked to work on some of the murders I committed,' Alan said, 'but you refused. I advised you to turn down all of those cases, and you listened to me. I think you suspected the truth, but you hid it from yourself.'

'You tried to murder me when I was six years old. So why have you waited twenty-four years to try again?'

'Oh, I originally intended to get you a few months after you were released from the hospital. I figured I'd have to wait that long to allay suspicions. But then I was going to knock you off in a carefully planned accident.'

His fingertips gently stroked her brows.

He said, 'I thought of throwing you down a long flight of stairs and then saying you tripped and fell. But I finally settled on drowning you in the swimming pool.'

'Why didn't you?'

'By the time I could safely go after you again, you'd begun to exhibit psychic powers. You fascinated me. I wanted to see what would happen to you next.'

She said, 'If Max is dead, I'll need your help again. I'll need you to guide me through the visions.'

He laughed. 'Darling, I'm not naïve.'

'Do you think I'd turn you in to the police? I haven't told them about you for twenty-four years. Why would I now?'

'Then, you didn't know,' he said. 'But now you do.'

He put his hand on her breast.

She flinched.

'My lovely little sister,' he said.

'Don't.'

★ ★ ★

Carrying a flashlight in his left hand and a revolver in his right, his shoulders drawn up in an unsuccessful attempt to keep the cold rain off the back of his neck, Rudy Holtzman accompanied the chief along the side of the pavilion.

Patmore stopped suddenly.

'What's the matter?' Holtzman asked nervously. He was very keyed up.

'There's a man ahead.'

Holtzman raised his flashlight.

A man was approaching them, no more than fifty feet away.

'It's Bergen,' Patmore said.

Bergen was staggering like a drunk.

'He's got a gun!' Patmore said.

Remembering Erika Larsson's viciously mutilated body, remembering the blood splashed everywhere inside her house, remembering Lou Pasternak on the macadam parking lot, Holtzman raised his service revolver and fired.

Max Bergen was flung backwards by the impact of the bullet.

★ ★ ★

Alan pressed against her. He put his left hand around her throat.

She told herself to resist, to fight back. She was strong, not weak. A weak person would have sought escape in madness twenty-four years ago. But she was strong; she had hung on to her

557

sanity and had developed psychic abilities as a way to keep herself alive. She should be able to find the will to fight him now.

He held the blade to her cheek as if branding her, the point below her right eye.

'I wonder,' he said, 'if you were blind, could you still see your clairvoyant visions?'

She snapped. Abruptly, violently, her fear vanished in an explosion of anger and hatred far more intense than any emotion she'd ever known. Twenty-four years of hidden, festering hatred went off like a bomb in her subconscious. She despised him. Loathed him. He wasn't fit to live. Never had been. Never would be. All she wanted was a chance to hurt him as badly as he had hurt her. She didn't even care any longer whether she lived or died. She wanted only to get him down, tie him down, torture him, hurt him, cut him, choke him, beat him, see him cry. She wanted most of all to put the bats on him, to rub them in his face, make them claw and bite, force them into his mouth while they were squirming and still alive—

Overhead two dozen bats began to scream in the darkness: a shrill chorus of tiny voices.

Startled, Alan looked up.

A single bat swept down, hooked its claws into Alan's coat collar. It fluttered wildly at his neck.

She couldn't believe what she had done.

Alan let go of her, reached behind him, grabbed the animal. He struggled with it, finally tore it loose and pitched it away from him.

His hand was bleeding.

In the past few days, every time she'd had a vision in which the killer's face began to be revealed as Alan's, she had chased away the truth by distracting herself with poltergeists. She had been responsible for the glass dogs careening around Dr Cauvel's office; the pistol floating in air; the sea gulls at The Laughing Dolphin Restaurant; inanimate objects flying this way and that in Lou's bathroom. Max had been right.

Now she would use the bats.

Another one flew down and clung to Alan's face.

He screamed. Ripped it away. Dropped the knife.

Blood streamed from his forehead into his eyes.

Chittering, beating the air furiously with their wings, three

558

more bats attacked him. One tangled in his hair. The other two fixed themselves to his throat.

'Kill him,' she said.

Flailing at himself, Alan turned away from her. He weaved across the platform towards the stairs.

Every bat in the rafters descended upon him. They tore at his head and face and neck, clawed his hands, bit his fingers and hung on and wouldn't be shaken loose. When he screamed, one of them got into his mouth.

He stumbled down the tower stairs, bouncing from wall to wall.

She picked up the flashlight and followed him.

The bats stayed with Alan. If anything, their cries grew louder, angrier.

Five steps down he fell, rolled to the next landing, got up, went on, plucked a bat from his nose, tried to shield his eyes with one arm, fell again, couldn't keep from screaming, had to bite another bat that crawled from his chin into his mouth, had to spit out part of it, gagged, choked, stumbled, leaped from the final flight of stairs into the dark arcade and collapsed.

She walked out of the archway and stood over him.

He was very still.

One by one the bats rose from the body, circled, and flew back up the stairwell to the belfry.

AFTER . . .

At noon the December sun fell straight down on the cemetery, leaving virtually no shadows on the grass. There was a chill in the air that didn't come from the sea wind; it radiated from the tombstones and the silent mourners and, most of all, from the plain dark casket suspended above the open grave.

As the winch motor began to purr and the coffin lowered out of sight, Mary turned away. She walked between the small granite and marble monuments towards the open wrought-iron gate, walked by herself, unassisted, alone, because that was what she wanted.

She sat for a while behind the wheel of the Mercedes and stared down the hills to the sea. She was waiting for her hands to stop shaking.

Yesterday, she had buried Alan; and in spite of what he had been and done, she had grieved for him. But this final ceremony was far sadder than yesterday's. She felt as if a piece of her own flesh had been torn from her.

She needed to cry and wash some of the pain from her system, but she choked the sobs before they could start and squeezed back the tears. She had one more duty to perform before she could allow herself to break down.

She started the Mercedes and drove away from the cemetery.

★   ★   ★

Sunlight streamed through the venetian blinds and banded the private hospital room with shadow and light.

Max was sitting up in bed, one shoulder heavily bandaged, one arm in a sling. He was drawn, sallow, sunken-eyed; but he had a gentle smile for Mary when she came through the door.

She kissed him and sat in the chair beside his bed. They held hands in silence for perhaps a minute; then she began to tell him about Lou's funeral. When she had nothing more to say, she leaned away from her chair, rested her forehead on the edge of the mattress and finally began to weep. He murmured soothingly, massaged her neck, stroked her hair. She broke down completely. She cried out loud for Lou, but for herself as well; his death left a hole in her life. However, her despair couldn't last forever; eventually, gradually, her sobbing subsided.

For a while they listened to classical music on the radio, neither of them able to speak.

Later, over dinner in the hospital room, her eyes grew heavy, and she couldn't stifle her yawns. 'Sorry. I didn't get much sleep.'

'Nightmares?' Max asked, concerned.

'No. In fact, I had lovely dreams – the first pleasant dreams I've ever had in my life. I woke up about four-thirty in the morning, exhilarated, full of energy. I even went for a nice long walk.'

'You? A walk? Alone at night?'

She smiled. 'I don't mind being alone as much as I used to,' she said. 'And I'm not afraid of the dark anymore.'